Perfect Fit

Linda Wells

To

Tania and Catherine
Bill and Rick
And all who supported me while creating
this story

Chapter 1

"**I** wonder if anyone will notice if I leave early." Darcy mused to himself as he picked up his wine glass and took a healthy swallow. He looked wearily at the packed dance floor. Bodies were moving, gyrating to the loud music from the live band. People shouted to be heard and the colored lights flashed incessantly. He sat alone at the huge round table amongst a sea of similar tables. All were littered with uneaten wedding cake and countless empty glasses. He glanced around the room. The only other seated people seemed to have white hair and alarming wrinkles. At twenty-seven, Darcy felt as old as his great-uncle Morris sleeping in the corner.

The rustle of silk drew his attention and his hands were gripped. "Come on William, dance with the bride!" He was faced with his beaming cousin.

"Anne, you should be dancing with your husband." Darcy resisted her insistent pulling.

"Oh, *come on!*" She yanked him to his feet and dragged him to the floor. Reluctantly he followed and attempted to move with some semblance of rhythm. "You never appreciated your dance lessons!" She shouted and grabbed his hips, trying to make them sway.

"Ballroom dance is at least dignified." He muttered as he looked down at his rooted feet. The song blessedly ended and Darcy sighed with relief. "All right Anne, now, may I wish you and Greg every happiness and take my leave?"

"*No!*" She whined. "You must stay! Please?"

"The party will not be hurt by my departure." Darcy assured her and he could see her looking around the room, obviously searching for someone to pair him with. He squeezed her hand to gain her attention and shook his head.

Anne hugged him and spoke in his ear, "Someday I hope that I will dance at your wedding, William."

He smiled slightly and kissed her cheek. "Take care." Turning, he ran straight into a small young woman with brunette hair, held in place with sparkling combs. He grunted. "Look where you are going!"

"Excuse me, but *you* are the one that spun around!" She glared up at him then took a step. "Great." She sighed and looked down as she stumbled. "My heel is broken." She looked back at him accusingly.

Darcy swallowed hard and stared at her flashing eyes. "Um, may I help you to a chair?"

"*Now* you are a gentleman." Elizabeth muttered under her breath and took his offered arm. They made their way slowly through the crowd, and she looked up at the man she had been watching all evening. He was intriguing enough from a distance, but up close she saw how handsome he was, not in a chiseled movie-star way, but he was very tall, solid, fascinating . . . She bit her lip and took the chair he drew out for her. "Thank you." He took the seat beside her and stared as she slipped off the damaged shoe. She noticed his eyes stayed glued to her ankle. "You don't have to stay; it looked like you were leaving."

"I . . . it seems that your heel is irreparable. There is a . . . shoe store in the lobby; may I buy you a new pair?" He lifted his eyes and spoke quietly. She had to strain to hear him over the sound of the party.

"It isn't necessary. I have a room in this hotel; I'll just run upstairs and change." She met his gaze and saw him biting his lip, and could see him thinking rapidly.

"But . . . these are obviously new." He turned the damaged shoe over, and could see no scuff marks on the sole. "Manolo Blahnik, that's some designer, isn't it?"

She rolled her eyes as she took the shoe back. "Some designer, yes." Her face could not hide her disappointment as she looked at the heel hanging sadly.

He jumped at her expression. "See? You obviously bought these especially for tonight. Please let me make this up to you."

"Perhaps I have so many pairs of shoes that losing this one doesn't matter to me?" She lifted her chin. "Obviously you were not impressed with them, you in your Armani suit."

He looked down at his finely tailored black suit and back to her. "Is that what this is?"

"Oh come on, don't tell me you don't know what you are wearing? Open up the jacket, look at the label." She reached forward and unbuttoned it for him. He pulled it away from his body, allowing the spicy musky scent of his cologne to be released in a pleasant waft into the air. Elizabeth blinked and gathered her senses. "There, Armani. I knew it. Surely you must have seen that when you bought it?"

"I . . . I don't really go shopping, I have someone who does that for me." He looked up and saw her blush. "I guess that I don't really pay much attention to things like that, but then, I am a guy. Designers and things are more for the ladies, aren't they?"

"I suppose so, I wouldn't know, I'm mostly a JC Penney's and Macy's girl." She gathered up her shoes and started to stand.

"So those shoes *were* something very special." He persisted.

"I don't have a personal shopper and an unlimited bank account. I saved for seven months to buy these and . . . why am I even bothering talking to you? Goodbye Mr. Armani." She huffed and started to walk away in her bare feet, then stopped when she felt his hand on her arm and looked up in surprise.

"Look, I'm not trying to insult your . . . ability to purchase shoes; I just wanted to . . . replace what I obviously broke. You are correct; I was about to leave here, so why not accompany you to the shoe store on my way out? Do you have a purse here somewhere? Can we get it and I'll escort you?"

"Why do you care?" She stopped dead and put her hands on her hips. "I am nothing to you."

"Fine, look, I tried." He took a card from his breast pocket and wrote his room number on it. "Here, have the shoes charged to this room. Forgive me for . . . trying to make things right." He handed it to her and walked away.

She read the card, "William," and closed her eyes. "He wanted to know me, and I didn't give him a chance, you *have* to stop this, Elizabeth!" She looked at his retreating back and caught up to him. "Wait here." Darcy stopped and watched as she disappeared for a few moments then returned clutching a small beaded bag and carrying the shoes. "I'm sorry, I . . . I'm touchy about some things." Looping her hand in his arm, they started walking.

"What things?" He looked down at her and a small smile appeared. "You are very short."

She looked at him askance. "You have a talent for pointing out the obvious, I see." The shoes were shaken in front of his face. "Stilettos are not worn for comfort, you know."

"I thought they were worn to attract a man's eye." His smile grew. Elizabeth watched how his face transformed with the gesture, and saw a little twinkle appear. It was very becoming.

"They are also employed to add height to the . . . diminutive." His warm laugh was a revelation and she could not help but smile and laugh with him. They exited the ballroom, but not without attracting the attention of several members of the crowd.

Richard Fitzwilliam broke away from his date and craned his neck, his cousin hadn't been with a woman in years, and here he had picked one up at Anne's wedding! He followed them down the hallway, hid behind a potted palm, and looked towards the elevators. To his surprise he saw the couple wander into a shoe store. He felt a touch on his shoulder and turned to see his mother standing by his side with a stern expression on her face. "Leave him alone, Richard."

"I just wanted to . . ."

"He's a grown man; now get back to the party." She turned and watched him heading back.

"You just don't know how to have fun, Mom." He called back to her.

Arlene Fitzwilliam looked back at the shoe store and saw through the glass as her nephew kneeled before the unknown young woman and slipped a shoe on her foot, and how he looked up to her with a wide smile. The girl was obviously laughing. Nodding with satisfaction she returned to the wedding, maybe Cinderella had been found.

Inside of the store a clerk bustled up. "May I help you?" He looked over the well-dressed man appreciatively and down at the girl in the chair.

"The lady's shoe was damaged; do you have something similar here to replace it?" Darcy handed him the broken shoe and the man's eyes lit up.

"Ah, no Manolo Blahniks, but I do have some beautiful Jimmy Choos, if the lady would be interested, size?"

"Oh, five, I think." She looked away and the clerk grinned.

"Ladies never admit their shoe size; it is like admitting their age." He took a look at the damaged shoe and smiled at her with a wink and walked away. Darcy looked after him sternly, and was no happier when the man seated himself before her and began touching her ankles and feet. His jaw was set and he watched every move. Elizabeth suppressed a smile and noted with pleasure how this man she had met less than an hour before was feeling possessive of her toes. The clerk moved away and Darcy held out his hand instantly to help her up.

"Oh these are beautiful!" She walked to the mirror and admired them, doing a little twirl, and again seeing Darcy's appreciative gaze in the reflection. "How much are they?"

"Seven hundred."

Her face fell. "Oh, oh no, I can't accept them, they are far more than what I paid for the others." She started to slip them off and Darcy stopped her.

"What did you pay for the damaged pair?"

"Five hundred, but that was on sale." She smiled. "I was very pleased with myself for the find!"

He chuckled, and kept a grip on her hand. "What was the savings?"

"Two hundred." She said.

"Then this is a logical exchange, don't you think?" He smiled and turned to the clerk. "Please

"Oh, really please, you can not . . ."

"No arguing, please, this makes me happy." He turned to the desk and signed a slip while Elizabeth stared down at her new purchase in awe. "Perhaps the others may be repaired?" He looked back at the clerk enquiringly.

"Oh yes, there is a cobbler just down the street, I can have the concierge take care of it for you." He took the other shoes and Elizabeth startled.

"But I will be checking out in the morning!" She protested. "I can surely find someone closer to home."

"And where might that be?" Darcy said softly.

"The Upper West Side." She looked down but did not miss his smile.

"You live in the city?" He could not hide the delight in his voice, and turned to the clerk. "If you have her address, couldn't the shoes be sent on to her home?"

"Of course, sir." Darcy nodded and watched closely as she wrote it down and gave it to the clerk, memorizing it.

"So Elizabeth Bennet; shall we?" He held out his arm and she laughed.

"You were spying!"

"I was; I was hoping that you might deign to tell me your name, but now that I know it, I will use it freely. My name is William Darcy." He gave her hand a squeeze. "I suppose that you want to return to the party now."

"No, I . . . I really should have left ages ago." He raised his brows and she sighed.

He had a growing suspicion and decided to test it. "Are you a friend of Anne or Greg?"

"Neither, really . . . I am the wedding coordinator's sister. My sister Jane was hired to plan everything. I help out on the really big affairs, and I sort of got to know Anne in the process, and she . . . well she said that when we finished our duties, she would be happy if we got to enjoy the party a little." Elizabeth blushed at Darcy's stare.

"You crashed my cousin's wedding?"

"Well, we *were* asked, in a way!" She huffed.

"In a way, indeed." He shook his head. "I could never have done something like that, go to a party where I knew nobody and had as much fun as you did."

"How do you know I was having fun?"

"I . . . I was watching you." He blushed and looked away, then sent her a sideways look. "I think that I saw you maybe looking my way, once or twice?"

It was Elizabeth's turn to blush. "Yes."

They were standing in the lobby, and it was full of people. There were six ballrooms and every one of them was busy that night. Darcy scanned the area for a nonexistent quiet place to talk. "Maybe, would you like to go and . . . get some coffee somewhere?"

"I don't know about you, but if I drink coffee at this time of night, I might as well forget about sleeping until noon the next day." She laughed.

"Well that probably eliminates the idea of a drink, too." He stared down at where her hand remained on his arm. "I really don't want this to end." Their eyes met. "I mean, I am not suggesting anything more than talking, but . . . would you object to coming to my room? There is a nice seating area, and I . . . I really would like to know you better, and well, frankly, it is so hard to talk with all of these people around. I am not asking or expecting or . . ." She squeezed his arm, and he stopped.

"Okay." He relaxed. "Could I meet you there? If I'm going to be talking half the night, I'd like to do it wearing something comfortable." She grinned and looked down at her dress and back up to him with dancing eyes. "Perhaps a running suit?"

His brow lifted as they moved to the elevators. "Do you plan on exercising?"

"Only if I have to escape you." She teased and he pursed his lips. "I want to be comfortable, that's all. What is your room number?"

He shook his head. "I will not have you wandering the halls alone this late at night. I'll wait outside of your door."

"You don't believe I'll come!" Her eyes grew wide and her hands landed on her hips.

Instantly his hand guided hers back onto his arm. "No, I . . . I just want to be sure that you arrive safely." The sincerity of his look was reassuring in a way she had never experienced before. The door opened and as promised, he escorted her to her room and leaned against the wall. "Take your time."

She disappeared inside and stood in the dark room for a several moments, closing her eyes and breathing. "What on earth are you doing?" Elizabeth murmured. "You know what he wants! It was quite prominently displayed; even the shoe clerk couldn't take his eyes off that impressive package!" She switched on the bathroom light and spoke to herself in the mirror. "He said that he just wants to talk. Admit it Lizzy, you were staring at him all night, and wanted to approach him, and here you are going to his room." She slipped off the dress and took down her hair, then washed the makeup from her face. Brushing her teeth she stopped and stared. "You can always get up and leave, he seems more shy than anything, he certainly had nobody at the party." She rinsed and applied a much softer version of her makeup, then went out to find her new velour jogging suit and walking shoes. Leaving her hair loose, she finished in the bathroom and took one last look at herself. "Come on, take a chance for once." Half expecting him to be gone she opened the door to see him immediately straighten. His eyes lit up at her appearance.

"You look wonderful!" He declared and took her hand to place back on his arm. "Do you have your key?"

"Yes, lead on!" Darcy grinned and led her to the elevator, almost tripping as he walked. "You know, you'll do much better if you take your eyes off of me."

"No, I prefer this view. I like your hair down like this, it is lovely." He touched the curls and sighed happily. Elizabeth laughed. Darcy pushed the button for the top floor.

"Penthouse?" He nodded. "Why am I surprised?"

"I'd prefer a lower floor, I'm terrified of fire." He said softly and his face clouded. Elizabeth tilted her head but his expression had become as stone. The doors opened and they approached one of the few rooms in the hallway. He slipped in the card key, opening the door and stepping back. "Please."

"Oh my, you definitely are not paying the same rate I am for the room!" She heard his chuckle again and turned to see his eyes twinkling. "Well; let's be honest about it. I have no fireplace, no sunken living room, no fabulous view . . ." Walking in she smiled. "I suppose that the minibar is included?"

"I imagine that it is. Go ahead and raid it while I change, okay?" He strode into the bedroom and closed the door. Elizabeth did as he bid and opened the well-stocked cabinet, and pulled out a number of treats. He did not take half as long as she to change, and was soon back, casually dressed in running pants and a long-sleeved t-shirt that did nothing to hide the obviously well-toned body beneath. "Did you find anything worthwhile?" He stood behind her and peered over her shoulder into the open cabinet. Darcy's goal was to be close to her and he drank in the scent of her hair, consciously attempting to control his strong desire to slip his arms around her waist and draw her back to rest against his chest.

Elizabeth was not immune to the proximity of his warm body and felt an involuntary thrill travel up her spine, and shuddered with the sound of the low seductive tones of his voice in her ear. She could catch the hint of peppermint on his breath, and realized that he too was being prepared, just in case . . . "Oh, yes, how about some ginger ale?"

"Well, it's not quite champagne, but I suppose we have had enough of that tonight." He took two cans and poured them out into glasses and she sat down on one end of the sofa, removed her shoes, and swung her legs up. Darcy read the signal; she was not going to let him get too close. He pushed a button and the fireplace burst into life, and took a seat opposite her, stretching out his legs alongside hers, his sock-covered toes reaching her hips. "Now, Elizabeth Bennet, party crasher, tell me everything about yourself." He smiled and folded his arms.

"What would you like to know?" She assumed a similar stance and leaned her head on the back of the sofa.

"Well, Upper West Side; that is not cheap real estate . . . so why can't you afford these shoes that have so captured your desire?"

"Rent control, my dear Watson." She laughed. "My family has owned our building since, oh my, since before World War I. Every apartment was once filled with Bennets, but now we have tenants in most of them. My sister Jane and I each have our own places there and my parents have another. My other sisters are in school. Obviously we don't have to pay anything formally, but our income helps dad with the taxes and upkeep." She smiled at his nodding head. "Not too difficult to imagine, is it?"

"No, not at all, my family has owned our home here for, well, just as long, probably longer. I have our family estate in the Hamptons, as well."

"Where do your parents live? Here or out there?"

"They died about five years ago. There was a gas leak in a building down the block from our home and the fire spread very rapidly through the old buildings. They were built before proper fire codes were in place, and well, they did not escape in time. I was in school, and my little sister was away visiting a friend that night, thank God, or I would have lost her, too." Darcy's face expressed his pain and his eyes filled with tears. He swallowed hard and looked down. Suddenly he felt arms wrapping around his shoulders and he buried his face in Elizabeth's hair. "I am sorry; I didn't mean to . . . I'm sorry." Her embrace tightened, and they held onto each other and listened to the fire crackling in the background. She heard him finally take a breath and she drew away to wipe his eyes with her hand.

"Better?" He nodded. Elizabeth kissed his cheek, and remained perched on the edge of the sofa.

Darcy took her hands in his. "Thank you, I don't speak of it very often."

"Perhaps you should, then it won't be so painful." She caressed his hair from his forehead and he watched as her eyes followed her hand's movement. "Shall I return to my seat?"

"Do you have to?" Darcy said softly. He sat up and she stood, then settled beside him, leaning against his chest. He draped one arm around her shoulders and took her hand with the other, studying her unadorned fingers. "So, what do you with your time, not earning rent money?" He tried to laugh, and instead squeezed her fingers.

"I write." She looked back and was pleased to see him look surprised. "Mysteries."

"Really?" His eyes lit up. "Do you have a pen name? I love to read, well, anything, but I was very partial to mysteries at one time."

"I am Beverley Croft." His brow creased. "I am sure that you have not run across me, I write for . . . well, teen-age girls." She laughed at his rolling eyes. "It is a very good niche market!"

"I'm sure that it is. I know that my sister was fond of Nancy Drew." His lips pursed and Elizabeth noted that the tears on his long lashes were gone. "I imagine your stories are a bit more . . . challenging."

"Why do you think that?" Elizabeth laughed.

"Because I have noticed over the long hours of our acquaintance that you are not at all shy to voice your opinion, undoubtedly your characters are the same. How many books have your written?"

"Six." His eyes grew wide. "I write two a year, and I started in college."

"So that would make you . . ."

"I am twenty-two as of last week."

"I am sorry that I missed your birthday party." He whispered and kissed her cheek. Elizabeth drew in a sharp breath but did not move away. He could feel her heart beating rapidly where she nestled against his chest, and it only inspired his to match the increased pace.

"I suppose that the shoes are my belated gift?" She laughed nervously.

"Hmm. No, I would like to do far better." He rested his cheek on her head.

Elizabeth squeezed her eyes shut and attempted to clamp down on the shivers that were traveling over her. "Wh . . . what do you do with your time? Surely you must have some occupation?"

"Ironically, I am in the paper business. Perhaps some of our trees have been made into your books." He looked down to see her smile, and could feel her relax. "It's several things really, the forestry is separate from the paper industry, and that is entirely separate from the actual landownership." He brushed his lips over her hair. "My family owns vast tracts of land all over the country, just as thousands of other families do as an investment tool, and we all contract with foresters to actually manage the planting and harvesting. It's pretty complicated and unusual being both the landowner and the manufacturer, and it's important to keep all of that separate. The landownership is what we pass down generation to generation, and we work with many groups to help maintain the wildlife. We want to be good stewards of our natural resources, and of course that benefits the company as well. It's interesting how it has all grown over the years."

"Your family has done well, then. Isn't it a conflict of interest to be both the landowner and the manufacturer?"

He smiled, her mind had seized on the problem that he was facing and he watched as she thought. She was listening to him, and he deeply appreciated it. "Yes, that is why I am actually considering selling our land's timber to another company, thus eliminating the conflict." Darcy's hands lowered to wrap around her waist and rest over hers.

A distinct and unfamiliar ache started in the pit of her stomach. "Sooo, I am twenty-two, and that would make you . . ."

"Twenty-seven." He breathed in her ear, allowing his lips to barely touch the skin.

"I suppose it is silly to ask at this point, but well, you don't seem to have a girlfriend or wife . . ." Her fingers played over his ring-free hands, and he instantly entwined his fingers with hers. "So, why did you find it necessary to stay in this magnificent penthouse suite when you have a perfectly good home not so far away? For me it is an adventure and a little vacation. For you, well, you can't claim a little holiday from home away from the kids . . . Can you?" She looked up at him.

"I have no girlfriend, no wife, no ex-wife, and no children, Elizabeth." He met her questioning eyes. "I did not know what to expect tonight, how long the party would last, and I did not see any point in keeping my driver waiting for hours when I could just take a room for the night here."

"There are an abundance of cabs in New York, I've noticed."

Darcy chuckled. "So there are, but I was anticipating my cousins making me far drunker than I became. I thought it would be nice to just stumble onto an elevator instead of trying to figure a tip."

"Do you often drink to excess?" She questioned worriedly.

"No, but you have not met my cousin Richard or his elder brother John." He kissed her ear this time. "Have you a boyfriend, husband, ex-husband or whatever?"

"No." She sighed, and melted into his arms.

"Would you like one?"

Elizabeth's breath caught, her heart was pounding in her ears. "Wh . . . which one would that be?"

"You choose." Darcy touched her chin, tipping it up to his face, and looked into her eyes. "I want to know you, very much. Will you let me?"

Elizabeth licked her lips and Darcy's eyes followed her tongue's path. "Why? Why me? You could have anyone, couldn't you?"

"Obviously I do not want just anyone." He ran his tongue over his lips and Elizabeth stared at his mouth. "I have been alone for years, Elizabeth."

"Yes."

"Yes to what?" Darcy's mouth hovered over hers.

"I want to know you, too." She whispered.

"May I kiss you?" His lips brushed over her cheek and back to linger over her mouth.

"Please."

Chapter 2

*E*lizabeth blinked her eyes open and became aware of the warm hard body pressed to her back, and the leg nestled between hers. Lifting the sheet that covered her, she sighed with relief. She was dressed in her t-shirt and running pants, but she also noticed the enormous masculine hand that was curled possessively around her waist. She followed the hand up to a bare arm and turned her head to see William's peaceful sleeping face, nuzzled against her shoulder. *What happened?*

She carefully extricated herself from him and froze when he murmured a sleepy protest. Freed from his embrace, she escaped the bed and watched as he grabbed hold of her warm pillow, and saw a contented smile appear just before his face buried in it. His body was mostly uncovered, and she could see that he was dressed only in his boxers. His clothes were neatly folded on the dresser and her jacket, purse, and shoes were beside them. *What should I do? I just can't leave can I? I don't think that anything happened, and if he was going to try anything he would have already . . . wouldn't he?* Elizabeth stood and studied him, just as she had all during the reception. What she really wanted was to return to his embrace. He began to stir, and startled, she picked up her things and hurried to the bedroom on the opposite side of the suite. After looking at herself in the mirror, she decided to shower, then dressed again in her clothes from the night before. She was just exiting the bathroom when she spotted William, now dressed in his jogging pants and t-shirt. His hair was damp and he was seated on a chair outside of the bedroom door, looking down at his clasped hands. His head snapped up and he stood. "I thought you had gone, but I heard the shower." He looked worried. "Did I do anything to upset you?"

"No . . . no, I woke and was confused, I don't remember how I came to be in your bed." She bit her lip and looked down. "The last thing I remember is . . . kissing you."

"Elizabeth." Darcy stepped up to her and bent his head to see her eyes. "Nothing else happened between us. I wanted it to, very, very much, but we have only just met, and well, I could see how sleepy you were. We just lay on the couch and talked and . . . kissed . . . and held each other until you fell asleep. I carried you into the room, and took off your top, and . . . joined you. I . . . I did kiss you goodnight." He added shyly. "I couldn't stop myself."

Elizabeth's tension eased and she smiled. "I doubt that I would have protested if I had been awake to receive it. You have a very talented mouth." She lightly traced his lips with her index finger and he grabbed her hand to kiss the tips.

"Provocative statements like that will do nothing to cool my desire, Miss Bennet." He wrapped his arms around her, and kissed her smile. "I can see that you will be an unending temptation."

"Is that a problem?" She laughed as his eyes grew dark, and her boldness dissipated. "I see that it is. Well perhaps I should go now." Elizabeth wiggled but could not escape his vise-like embrace. "Um, what are your intentions, Mr. Darcy?"

"There are so many, I can't even begin to enumerate them." He smiled and then laughed at her widening eyes. "I guess that we should begin by discussing our new . . . friendship?" He tilted his head. "I'm not sure what to call it? Can I call you my girlfriend after one evening together?"

She raised her brow and considered him. "I guess that would be moving too fast, so friend works for now."

He shook his head. "I hope that we progress very rapidly." Still not letting go, he gently kissed her, and loved how she leaned into him. "What were your plans for the day?"

"I am supposed to meet my sister for the brunch they have here on Sunday mornings, then check out and go home." Unable to resist, she kissed him back. "And you?" Darcy's eyes were closed and he was just letting her lips have their way with his face and mouth. "William."

"mmmmmm." Her laughter finally coaxed his eyes open and he blinked at her slowly. "I am supposed to meet the family for brunch . . . let's stay here." He ran his hands down her back, and allowed them to settle on her hips. "We have so much to talk about."

"I think that talking is the last thing on your mind." She smiled and caressed her hands down his arms. "Hello?" Elizabeth gave him a little pinch.

"Ow!" Darcy blinked out of his pleasant haze, and sighed. "All right, why don't you and your sister join my family for brunch? Then you could meet everyone."

"Oh, I don't know about that, I mean, well how would you introduce me? I would be the girl you picked up at the wedding reception, hardly an auspicious beginning. I want these people to like me, not think of me as a . . . one night stand." She bit her lip and looked down; Darcy began to recognize the habit.

"Elizabeth." He lifted her chin. "My family will be delighted to see me with any woman. They have been hoping to see me happy for years. And, I am certain that our departure together was noted by any number of them last night."

"Oh no!"

"Oh yes." He smiled. "And it is definitely not a habit of mine."

"But *they* don't know that!" She fretted. "I should probably just wait and meet them, I don't know, at church or something."

Darcy started laughing. "Oh yes, shall you come in wearing your vestal virgin white?" He raised his brows at her glaring eyes. "You do know that I find your angry expressions to be very enticing, don't you?" Elizabeth immediately closed her eyes. "Look, my aunts probably already know your sister, they were all involved in the wedding preparations, so if she is sitting in the same restaurant, they would probably greet her anyway. I will introduce you as her sister and my . . . friend, and we will go from there. Be warned though, you will be undergoing a very close scrutiny."

"Why? Because you picked me up!" She declared.

"No, because you are a woman and . . . I haven't been very active in the dating department lately." He looked down and back up at her. "It really has been years since . . ." He sighed and closed his eyes.

"William." Elizabeth squeezed his hands. "Did you have a bad relationship, and it just threw you off?"

"No, yes . . . I don't know. I did have a very bad breakup in college, but well, I told you last night that I have an MBA and a law degree, and finished with both by the time I was twenty-two." She nodded. "I started at Harvard when I was sixteen, so obviously dating college girls was out because they didn't want a nerd, a young one at that. Then when I was older, I was working so hard on the double majors that I didn't have time for girls, but when I finally did get close to graduation, I met a girl . . . and since she was my first girlfriend I didn't know how to handle the whole relationship, you know, the right things to say, I was just so inexperienced, I guess. But then my parents died, and I turned to her for help, to get me through it, and all that mattered to her was that I had inherited all of this money and the homes and the business . . . it was all she could talk about, and was pushing me constantly to get married. It . . . it really soured my opinion of her, so I got up my courage one day and broke up. It was hard because . . ."

"It's easier to just stay in something bad then to start over again." Elizabeth nodded and brushed his hair back from his forehead.

"You understand?" He met her gaze with awe. "You did this, too?"

"Not quite the same, but yes, I had a boyfriend of longstanding in college, and I realized one day after his mother called me, begging me to save him from failing out, that I didn't want to be with a man who couldn't take responsibility for his life. Every time something went wrong it was the professor's fault, or the employer, or the bank, or whatever. It was never him for not studying or not showing up on time, or not filing the paperwork. I just got tired of being the patient supportive partner who only got yelled at when I did well. I didn't leave him until I graduated, but the day I did, I never spoke to him again, even when he showed up at my door and pounded on it, screaming at me. It . . . it turned me off of dating anyone. That was two years ago. You are the only man I have . . . touched since then." She bit her lip and looked down again.

Darcy rested his hand on her shoulder and her head came up. "You are the only woman I have touched for a very long time, years. I was overwhelmed after I took over my father's business, and dealt with it by becoming self-destructive, drinking, women . . . My uncle took me aside one day and told me that whatever demon I was fighting, it was taking down the company that my family had spent countless generations building, and that I had better stop it fast before the board of directors voted me out. It was a sobering confrontation, but it certainly pointed out my youth and inexperience, and gave those who were angry with my taking over the presidency as a birthright fuel for their calls to remove me. I have done nothing but care for the well-being of the company and its employees since then, and my sister, to the best of my ability."

"So here we are today." Elizabeth said softly. "Both eager to find the right partner."

"I am ready for the relationship of my lifetime." Darcy gripped her hands and spoke with intensity. "Look, I know that this is ridiculously soon to be saying these things . . . I fully realize that we have only known each other less than a day; and I am behaving in a way that I can not recognize, let alone explain, but I want you to know that I am drawn to you as I have never been before to any other person. I can not describe it. I watched you for hours last night, and did not have the courage to approach. When I turned and walked into you, I looked into your eyes and I saw . . . happiness, despite your affront." He smiled slightly and touched her face. "I am unwilling to let this possibility go, not now, not after spending last night talking with you."

"This is so overwhelming, I don't know if . . ." She whispered and stared into the depths of his searching blue eyes. "I do understand." He smiled as he realized that she really did. Elizabeth laughed nervously. "You aren't suggesting something outlandish like a sudden trip to Las Vegas or something?"

Darcy laughed and hugged her. "No, I appreciate that we need to know each other well before we consider that particular trip; I just don't want you to doubt my desire." He smiled down at her relieved expression. "So, shall we start by having you meet my family, and me meeting your sister?"

"Well, I'm game if you are." She took a deep breath and pulled out of his arms. "I need to go to my room and change into something suitable for a restaurant, and I have no doubt that my sister has probably called the police by now since I didn't sleep in my room, so I'll have to talk to her . . ."

"Your cell phone didn't ring."

"What cell phone?" Elizabeth laughed. "I just don't get the need to be constantly in contact with everyone. Who exactly do I need to be talking to twenty-four hours a day?" She smiled at William's surprise. "Oh so you are glued to your blackberry, aren't you? Well, I have a phone, but it is never on."

"How am I supposed to call you? I am the one you need to talk to twenty-four hours a day!" He announced.

"You have taken possession of my hours pretty quickly!"

"Come on Elizabeth, let me turn you on." Her eyes widened, and he added, "Turn your phone on." Darcy smiled and drew her back to whisper in her ear. "I want to wish you goodnight whether I am there or not."

"Oh I'm going to like this friend business!" Elizabeth laughed and withdrew enough to lean over and grab a pad of hotel stationary and a pen. She wrote down her address, home and cell numbers, and her email address. She handed him the pen and he did the same for her, adding work numbers.

He handed the pen back. "Give me your sister's number, too."

"Why?"

"Because she is likely to keep her phone on, and if I can't locate you, I bet that she can. Now, give me her number." He insisted and she rolled her eyes and added Jane's information to her list.

"Are you happy?"

He kissed her cheek and carefully placed the precious paper in his pocket. "Yes, I really am."

"WHERE HAVE YOU BEEN?" Jane Bennet spotted Elizabeth walking off of the elevator. "I have been knocking on this door for an hour! I thought that you just got tired and went to bed, but I called and called, you really have to start turning that phone on, Lizzy!"

"I didn't have it with me, so it wouldn't have mattered." Elizabeth smiled and opened the door.

"Are you telling me that you are just returning to your room . . . *now*?" Jane closed the door and grabbed her sister's face. "Are you okay? What happened? Did someone slip something in your drink?"

"Jane, obviously I came here and changed clothes last night . . . I just didn't sleep here, that's all." Elizabeth ducked away from her and went into the bathroom to put on her makeup, sighing in relief that she didn't look too frightening for William without it.

Jane stood in the doorway with her arms folded. "Where were you?"

"I had a date with a friend." Elizabeth said. "You'll meet him at breakfast."

"I will, will I? And what's this friend's name?" Jane was tapping her foot and Elizabeth laughed.

"William. William Darcy, and . . . I think that he might just be the guy for me." She looked back to the mirror and caught her sister's gaping expression. "I know Jane, I never talk about this stuff, but we spent the night together and . . ."

"Did he use a condom?" She demanded.

"We did NOT have sex!" Elizabeth turned and glared. "Really, I thought that you knew me better than that!"

"You were drinking last night Lizzy, and I know it only takes you one glass of wine to loosen up."

"I had cranberry juice and ginger ale. Just because YOU decided to drink . . ."

"I was stone sober."

"Fine, whatever, I met William, we got to talking, he asked me up to his suite, and we fell asleep on the couch. End of story." She finished her face and began packing up her things.

"And I'll be meeting him at breakfast?" Jane watched her frenzied movements suspiciously.

"Yes, he is meeting his family at brunch and wants to introduce me to them. You know some of them already, he thinks. His cousin is Anne de Bourgh, I mean Rothschild."

"Wait a minute, William Darcy, Anne's cousin? The man that her mother wanted her to marry?" Jane's eyes grew wide.

"Anne's mother wanted her to marry her first cousin? That's sick! And illegal! What is her problem?" Elizabeth bustled past her and pulled out a dress from the closet to wear to brunch and began packing everything else in her suitcase.

Jane sank wearily onto the bed. "I have no idea. I think she's a little over-medicated, or maybe not enough, I never decided. I was just happy when they cut the cake and my work was finished on that wedding. Now you tell me that I have to deal with her again? I hope that your Mr. Darcy doesn't take after his mother's side of the family."

"He is very well-adjusted, I assure you." Elizabeth put on the dress and searched around, finding her new shoes under the bed where she had hidden them.

"Where did you get *those*?" Jane's eyes focused on them immediately.

"William bought them for me last night." Elizabeth smiled dreamily and Jane became alarmed.

"WHAT?"

"It's not how it sounds! He stepped on me and broke the Manolo Blahniks and offered to replace them with a new pair, we got them in the store downstairs, and just started talking. I know what you are thinking so stop it. I'm not mercenary and he's not a playboy." Zipping up her bag, she looked around the room for any forgotten items. "Okay, I'm ready, let's go meet the family!"

"I don't know what to say, Lizzy." Jane looked her over as if she was an alien. "I am at a complete loss."

"Well, just stand and be stunningly beautiful and distract them all from looking at me and I'll be fine. I can't wait for you to meet him!" She turned around as Jane followed her out of the door. "Oh, William gets shy pretty quickly, so don't be put off by it."

"You got picked up at a wedding. I can't believe it." Jane shook her head and closed the door behind her.

"I did not get picked up, I was rescued." Elizabeth corrected. "And I gave him my cell phone number." She reached into her purse for the phone and dramatically turned it on. Immediately it rang, and she looked at Jane in surprise. "Hello?" Giggling, she whispered, "We're just getting on the elevator." She ended the call and bit her lip.

"Welcome to the twenty-first century, Lizzy."

THE ELEVATOR DOOR opened and Darcy moved forward with a smile. "Hi!"

"Wow!" Jane exclaimed and looked him up and down.

Elizabeth took his arm and smiled up at him. "William, this is my sister Jane. Jane, this is my . . ."

"Go ahead, say it. You know that you want to." Darcy bent down and spoke softly.

". . . friend." Darcy groaned, and Elizabeth smirked. "William Darcy."

"I missed something here." Jane looked between the two.

"Me too." Darcy whispered.

"Not yet." Elizabeth whispered back.

"When?"

"Can we at least make it to twenty-four hours first?"

He shook his head slowly and did not break eye contact. "Too long."

"Hi, I'm still here!" Jane called out.

"Sorry, Jane." Elizabeth blushed and looked away from William's intense gaze.

The spell was broken and he turned to Jane and held out his hand. "I am delighted to meet you. My cousin's wedding was wonderful. You did a great job."

She studied the suddenly very formal man. "Thanks, it was nearly a year of work, and it was definitely a challenge." They began walking towards the restaurant, and Jane kept her eye on the way the couple just seemed to lean into each other.

Elizabeth glanced back and nodded to William. "She doesn't like your Aunt Catherine."

"Lizzy!"

"Neither do I and I haven't even met her yet. What's this about her wanting you to marry Anne?"

"So she tortured someone besides me with that declaration." The weariness in his expression was obvious.

"We were debating if adjusting the dosage on her meds might help." Elizabeth hugged his arm and gave him a smile.

Darcy relaxed and chuckled. "No, no drugs just . . . I can't explain her." He offered his other arm to Jane and they entered the restaurant. Scanning the room, he spotted his family. "There they are, shall we ladies?" He smiled softly and gave Elizabeth's cheek a kiss.

Elizabeth's gaze was fixed on the table. "So, how surprised will they be to see you with . . .?"

"Darcy! Good Lord, you hit the jackpot!" Richard jumped up and the heads of the others swiveled to take in the extraordinary sight. The trio stopped.

"Everyone, um, some of you may know Jane Bennet, she planned the wedding, and this is her sister Elizabeth who is my . . ." Elizabeth's eyes met his. "Very good friend." He smiled and raised her hand to his lips, "My very good friend." Elizabeth blushed. "Ladies, this is my cousin Richard Fitzwilliam, his mother Arlene, my uncle David, and my cousin John, and this is my sister Georgiana."

Elizabeth smiled. "I am pleased to meet you all. William invited us to join you for brunch, but I see there is no room at your table, so Jane and I will just find a different place to sit."

"Nonsense!" David's voice boomed. He signaled a waitress. "We can fit two more places here can't we?"

Magically two chairs were added and everyone squeezed together. Jane found herself between the Fitzwilliam brothers, and Elizabeth was seated between William and his sister.

"I saw you dancing last night. Do you know Anne?" Georgiana asked quietly.

"Only a little. She invited Jane and me to enjoy the evening when our work was finished. I was here to help my sister." She smiled. "Your brother tells me that you attend Julliard."

"I did, but I have taken the last semester off. Maybe I'll go back in the fall." She looked down at her folded hands and became quiet. Elizabeth looked to William who watched his sister with concern, then met Elizabeth's questioning eyes.

"I'm sorry; I meant to say that Georgiana hoped to return to Julliard. Just like you and me, she began her post-secondary education at the age of sixteen."

"You went to college when you were sixteen?" Georgiana looked at Elizabeth.

"Yes, I finished my bachelor's degree by the time I was twenty. I majored in English, and now I'm a writer."

"Did you get a master's?"

"No, I was needed at home, and I had a fairly successful career by then, so further education was not necessary. If I had decided to teach it would be different, but I wanted to be a novelist."

She felt Darcy's hand creep onto her leg and take hers. Turning her head he leaned to her ear. "I will have to explain my sister to you, but she has said more to you just now then she has to me in a week." He smiled. "Thank you." Elizabeth did not know what to say and glanced across at Jane, who was valiantly fending off the attentions of the Fitzwilliam brothers, Richard noticed her and pounced.

"So Elizabeth, I saw you purchasing some new shoes last night?" Richard grinned. "I believe that your salesman enjoyed his position at your feet." He shot Darcy a look and then back to Elizabeth. "I hope that the transaction proved satisfactory?"

"Is your cousin always this witty?" Elizabeth asked William.

"No, his jokes usually land with a thud."

"I believe that I told him last night to leave this alone." Arlene sent a pointed glare at her youngest son.

"You did Mom, but it is a new day, and it seems that this young woman will be a regular visitor to our cousin's home." His smiling eyes took on a speculative look. "Are you often in the habit of picking up billionaires at weddings?"

"Billionaire?" Elizabeth looked at William. "Is he kidding? I thought you owned a paper business."

"I do." His face was flushed and his shoulders drooped, and he became silent. He had hoped to keep that aspect of his life as private as possible for as long as he could.

"I seem to have blown your cover Darcy, I'm sorry." Richard read his cousin's disappointed face and realized too late what he had hoped to accomplish. "Elizabeth, I was just joking, he is a pauper."

She squeezed the hand that still covered hers, and he weakly responded. "Did I tell you that the guy I was dating in college had a trust fund that he would get when he reaches twenty-five, worth millions? That was why he never felt the need to apply himself to anything. If I had just stuck it out, I could have been married to him by now."

Darcy met her eyes. "You don't care about money, just character." She nodded and felt his hand grip hers hard. "Thank you. I want to be liked for myself, that's why I didn't tell you . . . everything."

"There was no reason to; we barely know each other, don't we?" She smiled and remembered the rest of the family. They were all staring at the couple. She looked expressively at Jane.

"Oh, that was Bill Collins; I can't tell you how relieved we all were when that relationship ended. We all thought he was a jerk, well except Mom, of course." She smiled

"Of course." Elizabeth rolled her eyes.

"Your mother liked the idea?" David laughed. "Sounds like my sister!"

"Where is Aunt Catherine, by the way?" John asked.

"She went home, as soon as Anne and Greg headed upstairs, she left. We have to pick up her luggage and drop it off for her, lucky us."

A waiter came over and took their orders and the party stood to walk over to the buffet. Darcy stayed by Elizabeth, watching as she made her selections, and noting her likes and dislikes. She felt his presence and cast him a quizzical look. "You are paying close attention to me."

Darcy smiled. "I'm learning."

"That seems to be something you enjoy doing." She smiled and picked up her omelet from the chef. "I like that."

Elizabeth turned to Georgiana, who was just behind her. "So what do you study when you're in school? Music or dance, or are you an actress?"

"Oh." Georgiana startled from her silence. "I . . . I play piano. I hoped to join an orchestra or maybe get into being a session musician in a recording company, I never wanted to have a solo career, I'd be happier being in the background."

"That sounds great, it's all the little pieces that make up the whole, and your contribution would be an important part." Elizabeth smiled and led the Darcys back. They began to eat and the table became quiet. Darcy could not move his gaze from her and Jane was watching as Elizabeth kept sending him little glances and rolling her eyes at his attention. He just smiled every time she looked at him.

John leaned over to Jane. "Well, what do you think?"

"About what?" Jane raised her brow.

"Look, my cousin hasn't so much as glanced at a girl in forever, is your sister going to hurt him?"

"What kind of a question is that?" Jane glared at him. "I could, no; I should ask the same thing of you about your cousin!"

"Hey, you're in the wedding business. How many of these things do you plan and see a divorce in the papers a year or two later? Don't they all look like them in the beginning?" He gestured across the table.

"So that means that nobody should even try? How many times have you been married, or are you one of those men who don't want to leave home and Mama?" John flushed, and Jane nodded. "Grow up and maybe you'll find someone worthwhile someday." Jane looked at her sister and her new friend. "I happen to believe in love at first sight."

Richard leaned over. "So, are you seeing anyone?"

"No, and I'm not looking." She smiled and Richard sighed.

David and Arlene were watching the couple closely as well, and kept sending looks to each other, and delighted in what they observed. The meal ended and Arlene approached Elizabeth. "It is good to see my nephew with a . . . friend, as you call it. I hope that this is the beginning of something good for both of you."

"Thank you, Mrs. Fitzwilliam. I hope so, too." Elizabeth looked back to where William was hugging his sister. "I think that he is fascinating."

"Well, by the way he looks at you, I'd say he thinks the same." David took her hand and gave it a squeeze. "I'm sure that we'll be seeing you again." He called over to the siblings. "Come along Georgiana, we need to check out and return home." He shook Darcy's hand, and leaned close to him to speak softly. "I like her Son, but take your time and be sure."

"I will, and thanks. Thanks for keeping Georgie, too. She's better off with Aunt Arlene." He cast a worried glance at his silent sister.

"I don't know, I think this . . . friend of yours might be a good influence." He raised his brows and saw how Elizabeth had approached Georgiana to say goodbye. "She certainly got her to talk."

The family parted and Jane and Elizabeth stood in the lobby with William. Jane felt distinctly unneeded and held out her hand. "Give me your key, I'll collect the luggage and check us out."

"Thanks, Jane." Elizabeth gave her the card and she was left looking up at William.

He took her hand, "Come up to the room and I'll get my things." They rode up to the penthouse again, and she saw his bags sitting by the door.

"You are ready to go." She looked up in surprise. "I thought that you needed to . . ."

Suddenly his arms came around her and she was drawn hard against his chest. Darcy's mouth stroked over hers and they sank into each other. With one hand in her hair and the other firmly holding her bottom, his lips and tongue tasted and tantalized her. He groaned. "I have wanted to do this all morning."

"I . . . I was thinking about it, too." She stared into his eyes and grabbed his face, pulling it down to reach his mouth and kiss him hungrily.

Darcy groaned again. "I saw a box of condoms in the bathroom."

"Really? They supply everything here." Elizabeth ran her hands down his back.

"Yes, what do you think?" He drew back and licked his lips. Elizabeth was about to answer when her phone began ringing in her purse. It broke the heady mood, and she stared at the bag in confusion. Darcy tried to calm his breathing and handed it to her.

"Hello?" Elizabeth asked shakily. He stood before her and held her waist. She closed her eyes against his gaze. "Yes Jane, I'm coming." She peeked up to see him smile contritely and nod.

Darcy gently touched her face. "You're right, not yet."

Chapter 3

*D*arcy climbed out of the car and entered his home, the feel of Elizabeth's soft lips on his still very much on his mind. His housekeeper broke into his musings as another servant disappeared with his bags. "Mr. Darcy, this was delivered an hour ago."

"Thank you, Mrs. Reynolds." He walked into his office with the FedEx package and opened it while noticing the neat piles of papers his secretary had sent over, waiting for his attention. *Gone one day and already there is a week's worth of work here, I thought that I took care of everything before I left.* He sank into his chair and pulled the report out of the package, and removed the attached letter. Darcy sighed and began to read, but was stopped almost immediately by the ringing phone.

"Darcy."

"So have you read it?" The voice of his best friend Charles Bingley filled his ear.

"I just walked in the door, Charles. Give me a chance . . . why don't you tell me the situation and save me the time?"

"The wildfires have really hit the timber hard. We've lost a lot, and it's going to take a huge effort to clean this out and replant. I think that you need to see it all for yourself; a picture just doesn't do it justice. Can I expect you in the morning? I'll meet you at the airport."

Charles listened and heard nothing. "Hello? Darcy? Are you still there?"

"I'm here."

"Oh, I thought my cell died. It's pretty remote out here; service is pretty much at the whim of the gods." He laughed and heard nothing again. "Darcy?"

"I'm here."

"Okay, what's wrong? I mean besides seeing Pemberley's profits literally go up in smoke?"

"Do you really need me there?"

Charles stared at his phone as if he could somehow see his friend's face; then raised it back to his ear. "Well, yes . . . is it Georgiana? Is something wrong?"

"No, she's okay, still not talking." He paused and closed his eyes. "I have a date tomorrow night." It was his turn to wait in silence. "Charles?"

"A date, I heard that right? With a woman?"

"No, with a dog. Of course with a woman!" Darcy said tersely.

"I'm sorry, but you and dating seem to be . . . I don't know, like having a root canal, something to be avoided at all costs. How did this happen? Do I know her?"

"No, I met her at Anne's wedding. I just dropped her and her sister off at their building; they live on West 87th Street, near the park."

Charles whistled. "That's prime real estate, of course you have your own private park . . . Hey, you're in walking distance!"

"I know Charles, look; I really don't want to break this date, if this is just some arm-waving tour . . ."

"No Darcy, I'm sorry but I'm afraid that your physical presence is important. The loggers need to see you, and the local politicians need to be assured that Pemberley isn't going to pull out of the area."

He sighed. "They should know better than that. The foresters will replant . . . I *have* to cut the connection between Pemberley and our land, this situation just makes it clearer."

"Well until you just become another forestry family, you have to make an appearance. Everything is image Darcy, and you're the face they want to see, even if you won't provide a sound bite. You are personally affected by this and that makes you particularly wanted."

"All right, I'll be there. Let me call Patricia and make the arrangements . . . then I'll call Elizabeth." He sounded dejected.

Charles really felt for him, he knew how lonely he was. "Is that her name?"

"Yes." He said quietly.

"I can't wait to hear all about her. It's about time." He tried to sound upbeat.

"Yes, and I'm leaving her, before we've even had a chance to begin." Darcy hung up and reluctantly began making the necessary calls.

"DID YOU HAVE a good time at the wedding, Lizzy?" Tom Bennet asked.

She smiled and took a seat in his library. "I did, Jane didn't really need me, but it was interesting to see just how much can be spent on things nobody ever notices. I hope for a very simple wedding someday."

"You'll have to actually date someone first." His lips twitched.

"Ha ha, Dad, well I'll have you know that I met a man at the wedding and he's taking me out tomorrow night. So there!" Her eyes danced with triumph.

He sat up in surprise. "Really? What's his name?"

"William Darcy, he owns a paper company."

Tom furrowed his brow. "Executive type? Uptight, overworked, hmm, you could be just the thing to relax such a busy man." He eyed her blushing face. "I'm on the mark?"

"He could certainly use some liveliness, definitely needs dance lessons, but I think there is a lot of fun lurking under his polished exterior. He's like me, in school at sixteen and never really got to enjoy his teenage years, and luckless in love." She said the last dramatically and grinned.

"If we had to do it over Lizzy, I would have kept you in high school with your peers." He looked at her apologetically.

"I would have been bored to tears, and you know it, Dad. It was for the best." She gave his hand a squeeze.

"Hey!" Jane walked into the room. "Good idea giving William my number. He tried your place and your cell, then gave up and called me. He needs to talk to you soon, he sounded really upset."

"What happened?" Elizabeth stood up to go to her apartment.

"He didn't say, but he was thrilled not to get voicemail." She pulled her phone out of her pocket. "It's not heavy Lizzy, just take it with you." She watched her go and laughed.

"So Lizzy has a boyfriend? Do you like him?" Tom watched his eldest child closely; she was good at hiding her true opinions.

She shook her head and became thoughtful. "He's an enigma. He ranges from shy to powerful to playful in the blink of an eye, and seems very intense regardless of the underlying emotion. He has a nice family if you don't count my client's mother. Don't tell mom, but he's rich."

"That isn't surprising; Lizzy said he's the president of a paper company."

Jane's head wagged slowly. "No, beyond that . . . I mean he's RICH." Her gaze met his pointedly.

His eyes narrowed. "What does he want with my Lizzy?" His gaze turned to the piles of tabloids his wife bought, full of headlines about super-rich men and their bad behavior. Tom wondered if Elizabeth had just found one, her first boyfriend had certainly been a dud.

Jane shrugged. "Maybe he wants what every couple who hires me wants, to be happy."

"You do need to take off those rose-colored glasses, Jane." Tom laughed and smiled.

"Nope, I like the view from the sunny side just fine, thanks!" She kissed him and returned to her apartment.

Elizabeth took a seat on her wide windowsill and nervously listened to William's phone ring. "Hello? Elizabeth?" His soft rich voice filled her ear.

She immediately relaxed and smiled. "Hi! Jane said that you called, is something wrong?"

"Yes, you don't carry your phone." He complained.

"*That's* why you called?" She laughed. "It's hard to break a habit, I'll do better."

"It's okay, I just . . ." He sighed. "I'm sorry, but I have to break our date. I have to go out of town this afternoon. I'm not sure when I'll be back."

"Oh."

"Elizabeth?" He said worriedly.

A feeling of overwhelming disappointment swept over her. "I guess that you got home and thought . . ."

He interrupted. "No Elizabeth, I have no second thoughts about . . . us . . . not at all. This is not a coward's ploy to get out of seeing you. I really have to go. Look, turn on CNN right now."

She stood and turned on the TV. "Okay, it's on."

"Those wildfires are on some of my property, and I have to make an appearance as both a landowner and the company president. A lot of the company's assets are burning, and if the fires are not controlled soon, this may affect paper prices for awhile. . . stock up now for your next book." He tried to make light of it, but listened anxiously, hoping that she believed him.

Embarrassed by jumping to conclusions she kicked herself, this was a different man from Collins. "Oh William, I'm sorry for doubting you. Of course you must go. I understand. I'll still be here when you return."

"Do you promise?" He asked seriously.

She could hear his worry. "Yes, I'll be right where you left me. We'll just get started when you return. Besides, I have a busy week ahead, so we probably wouldn't see much of each other anyway."

He breathed a very audible sigh of relief, and she heard the smile in his voice. "Thank you, I needed to hear that, I was afraid that you would be angry. What will be occupying your time?"

"Oh, I have a meeting with my editor Charlotte Lucas, and then another with the girl who maintains my website, who is actually Charlotte's sister Maria. Then I will be going to a few bookstores for personal appearances in New Jersey, and I have a school to visit too, but luckily that's in the city. The real travel begins when the book is published and I do a sort of book tour through more stores and schools, and there are the big conferences in Chicago, and here, and one in Vegas. But before that it's just dealing with all of the red ink from my editor and all of the people who get preview copies to criticize." She laughed softly. "You definitely need a thick skin and a good speaking voice for this career."

"I thought that you wrote books."

"I do."

"But you have to travel?" He was confused.

"Well, I want them to sell, after all this is my income. Travel really is not a big part of it; it's just around the time that a new book is published. I'd say that most of my time is spent here." She listened and just heard his quiet breathing. "You have to travel for work too, don't you?"

Darcy closed his eyes, "Yes, in fact . . . I have to go, my driver is here and I have to get to Teterboro for the flight. Do me a favor and please keep your phone handy. I will try to call you in the evenings, and I'd hate to bother Jane again."

Elizabeth laughed. "I will. Take care."

"You too." He said softly.

"Are you going to hang up?" Elizabeth asked after a moment of silence.

"You first."

She sighed and smiled. "On the count of three. One, two, three . . . Bye Will." She whispered.

"Bye Lizzy." He listened until he was sure she was gone then hung up.

"IT'S HIM!" Elizabeth jumped up and shouted to her empty apartment. She stood in front of the television, trying to hear William beneath the voice-over from the reporter and studied him. He was dressed in jeans and hiking boots, a dark blue jacket was open over his shirt. He looked like he belonged as opposed to the Senator and Congressman who were walking over the burned-out area in their suits and shiny shoes. She noticed a handsome young man at William's elbow with chaotic blonde hair and a laptop tablet in his hands, taking notes rapidly as the men talked. The story was over too soon, but at least she had seen him.

"He looks so tired." She turned the sound back down and noted the time, expecting the report to be repeated in a half hour. It had been a week, and William had only managed one brief phone call to her when he landed, and attempted one every other night, but each was always ended suddenly by the bad connection. His location in the wilds of Montana was not conducive to cell service. Either the mountains or the damaged microwave towers made communication difficult.

A garbage truck rumbling down the street served as a reminder to the lateness of the hour. She reluctantly decided to go to sleep and climbed into bed, the television becoming her nightlight. The soft trilling of her phone woke her from the doze she had found and she looked around in confusion, then realizing what the sound was became fully awake, and grabbed it. "William?"

There was a pause then a very quiet, "Thank you."

"What did I do?" Elizabeth laughed and settled back in bed, rearranging the covers over her legs.

"The anticipation in your voice . . . hearing my name spoken so hopefully, is gratifying in a way I can't possibly explain."

"You're beaming, I can hear it."

"I am. How are you, Elizabeth? I am sorry to be so long in calling you, and to be doing it so late."

"I just lay down. I saw you on the news, you looked tired."

"I am . . . You're in bed?"

"Oh, so we are going to the important subject, are we?" She giggled. "Yes, I'm in bed."

"What are you wearing?" Darcy kicked off his shoes and lay back on the pillows.

"Guess."

"I'd rather imagine. I can't stop thinking of how it feels to kiss you. We should be experts by now." She heard the regret in his tone, and felt a thrill run over her.

"Do you think so? Well, I have been doing some dreaming of my own." She teased, and traced the pattern of the flowers on her bedspread, imagining she was touching him.

"And?" He grinned and pictured her face.

"Oh things that I'd like to try . . . I was wondering what you would do if . . ." She paused

"*Tell me!*" He whispered urgently.

"Well, I had a very nice view of your bottom when you were asleep in your underwear, and I wondered what it would be like to take a nibble."

Darcy moaned. "What else of mine would you like to nibble?"

"I think there are any number of tasty places." She giggled and heard another low moan.

"I miss you so much."

"But we have only spent sixteen hours together!"

"So you don't miss me?" He whined.

"I do." She sighed. "Where are you?"

"I'm in Seattle, we have an office here. I flew in about four hours ago and had a dinner meeting. Since I'm in the vicinity, I'll take care of some chores that I was going to do next month, it saves me the trip then, although I really need to get home. I shouldn't have left Georgie so long, and then . . . there's you." Elizabeth was biting her lip. "You're blushing, and looking in a corner."

"How do you know?" Her cheeks grew brighter.

"You're chewing your lip, aren't you?" He smiled; he could see it so clearly.

"You do pay attention." She tried to get a grip on herself.

Darcy enjoyed the effect he had on her. "We haven't had a chance to talk a great deal during my earlier calls. Did you take care of your business?"

"Business? Oh, my meetings? Yes, nothing exciting, just prodding about when I'll be finished, and looking at ideas for updating my website content." Elizabeth sighed. "It's pretty routine now."

His ears perked up. "It sounds as if you are dissatisfied. How were the personal appearances? Were you mobbed by fans?"

"Mobbed?" Elizabeth laughed. "There weren't lines circling the block, but there was a steady stream for the hour that I was at each location. I enjoyed meeting the fans, it's really the feedback from those appearances and the comments on the website that make me want to continue. I've learned not to look at the reviews online, you just hope for more good ones than bad."

Darcy was unsure what he heard in her voice, but his perception that something was bothering her remained. "I can't imagine being on display like that."

"You just were, to millions, I just had perhaps a hundred teenage girls."

"No, what you go through is far more painful than my experience. I was in front of maybe twenty people and a camera crew, and nobody records me because I tend to clam up in uncomfortable situations. No good sound bites as Charles would say."

"Is he the blonde guy who was following you and taking notes?"

"Yes, he is my . . . you know I really don't have a good definition for him. He keeps me aware of all of the balls I have in the air and tells me which one is about to fall." He smiled to hear her laugh. "He's also my very good friend, and I would be lost without him."

"I'm glad that you have someone to rely on." Elizabeth said quietly, remembering that William had described her that same way to his family.

"I am, too." He said softly, and hoped she thought of his words of introduction.

Elizabeth's memory of the restaurant triggered another. "Can you tell me about your sister? I know that something is terribly wrong for her to drop out of school."

She heard a long sigh. "Only the family knows this."

"You don't have to . . ."

"She was lured by an internet predator. She started talking online with a man who claimed he was a seventeen-year-old boy, and he talked her into flying down to Orlando and going to the theme parks with him. She thought it sounded like fun, she has never really had a boyfriend . . . well, she was met at the airport by a twenty-eight-year-old man who took her to a hotel room . . ." Elizabeth heard his voice crack.

"Will, you don't have to say anything else; I think that I know what happened."

"The FBI tracked her down pretty fast." Darcy wiped the tears from his face. "The man was not a stranger; he was . . . my father's godson, George Wickham. Georgie didn't know him, not really, he would come for parties and things sometimes when my parents were alive, he was always jealous of me. My parents were really great and his split up. My dad helped to send him to school when his stopped making alimony payments. He just let this jealousy of us fester and, well, I don't know how he got into contact with Georgiana at school, but we think that his goal was to take pictures and sell them, or rather threaten to and blackmail me. I refused to give him a job at Pemberley, I knew his poor work habits already, and I wouldn't loan him some money last year, so that is probably what set him off." He sighed. "This was all three months ago. She wouldn't come home with me, she was so embarrassed or ashamed, I don't know, but she is probably better off with my aunt and uncle. They are a better example of parenthood then living with her workaholic brother." He said the last with obvious bitterness.

"You are not blaming yourself for this, are you?"

"If I was more attentive . . ."

"Will, this was a man with a jealous grudge; he would have found a way to hurt your family. You and I both went away to school at that same age, I know how terribly alone I felt, being so young and not fitting in. At that age two years makes a big difference. The five years between you and me is not a big deal now because we're adults, but when you're sixteen . . . I imagine that she felt very isolated, but didn't want to disappoint you or herself by admitting that she didn't belong there. You and I survived, maybe because we have similar personalities, but your sister is not you."

"So it was my fault for putting her in school too early."

"No, it was her fault for doing what she undoubtedly knew was wrong; and just being sixteen and easily manipulated. I'm not trying to put the blame on anyone Will; I'm just seeing how it could have happened. Have you talked to her about it at all?"

"She really hasn't spoken to anyone, except you." He was quiet for a moment. "Why is that?"

"I'm a stranger; I wasn't going to judge her because I knew nothing about it. If she finds out that I do know, she may not want to talk to me either, or maybe she'll be looking to see if I accept her, and seeing that I do, she might feel better about herself. Have you taken her to a psychologist?"

"She started almost immediately; we have to prepare her to testify." He mused. "I talked to her and my aunt and uncle a couple of times since I left." He added quickly. "They were very brief, just like my calls to you, I . . ."

"I'm not your wife, Will."

"But you are my girlfriend." He said quietly.

"I am?" Elizabeth blushed and played with the buttons on her pajamas.

"I hoped for it from the moment you first glared at me on the dance floor. I was determined to win your heart." He smiled at the memory.

Elizabeth could hear the lightness in his voice and laughed. "Well then, I suggest that you get yourself home and start to work on that."

"Do I have a great deal of work to do?" He imagined her dancing eyes.

"I'll let you know when I see you."

"I'll be home tomorrow night. I'll come by your place on the way back from the airport and you can elaborate." He listened and heard her sigh. "It is almost one o'clock there, you should get to sleep."

"I wish I was there with you." She whispered.

"Maybe tomorrow you could . . . no, too soon." He stopped himself; he felt that he had pushed her too hard in the hotel, especially after he thought of Georgiana.

"Sleep over at your house?" She suggested after he was quiet for too long. It was so easy to be bold over the phone.

"Yes, but let's have that first date, then we can . . . get serious about this boyfriend business."

"Who's my boyfriend?" She teased.

"I am." He growled.

"William?"

"Yes?"

"Goodnight, I can't wait to see you."

"Goodnight Elizabeth, I feel the same way." Darcy heard the phone hang up and put his back in the cradle. Lacing his fingers beneath his head, he stared up at the ceiling and smiled, imagining her face as they talked and imagining how that conversation would have been if she was curled next to him in bed. It felt good, and he couldn't wait to spend countless sleepless nights conducting a great deal of pillow talk with Elizabeth, whether she was there or not.

"DO YOU WANT me to go with you?" Charles asked. "I mean, you are a nervous wreck, Darcy. You are torturing that newspaper." He looked down at the abused paper. Darcy had been steadily folding the crossword into smaller and smaller squares and opening it back up to start over again.

Darcy looked at the paper then at his ink-stained hands and put it down. "I'm fine, I'm just . . . I don't want to blow this, you know?" He looked out at the unmoving traffic. "We should have flown in."

"Then you would be sitting in traffic in Manhattan. Relax, we'll be at my building soon and then you'll be on your way." He smiled and tilted his head. "So, what's your game plan?"

"Do I need one?" He looked at him worriedly.

"Well I guess you could just rely on sweeping her off of her feet with your stunning reappearance, but do you have any ideas for, I don't know, dinner, maybe a date? One that you won't break this time?"

"YOU made me break the last one, I'll remind you." Darcy sighed. "I talked to Patricia, she reserved me tickets for everything all over town, I have a concert, a show, a Yankee game, dinner . . . whatever she wants, all of them if she wants . . . I work too much. That's part of the problem with Georgiana, I think. She felt neglected and wanted attention; she just didn't count on the consequences of doing something so foolish."

"When is the court date, she has to testify doesn't she?" Charles watched his friend beating himself up once again.

"I'm not sure what the schedule is. It's a felony, I think. He didn't physically transport her over state lines but it's something about using the internet to do the luring and then holding her hostage . . . I studied business law not criminal. I'm hoping that he takes a deal, and spares us of it, but I'm betting that he won't. He'll want to see our names splashed over the tabloids."

"Nobody really knows who you are; you're just another rich guy in the crowd of New York. You'll make the local papers, but I don't see you being exposed by the national press, you keep way too low of a profile."

"It's not me, it's the sensational aspect. *Billionaire's Sister Lured by Predator*, I can see the headlines now. The talking heads would want us on their shows, saying *If it can happen to a girl who had everything it can happen to you!*" He shook his head in disgust. "I'm sorry; this is going to be pretty rough for awhile. I've already talked to Elizabeth about it.

"Good!" Charles smiled. "You need that."

"But what a lousy way to start off our relationship, I don't want to be dwelling on Georgiana, this should be a happy experience, that is what I need." He looked down, feeling guilty for being happy when his sister was suffering.

"If she is willing to hear you out Darcy, be grateful for it, that's an important quality in whoever you marry." He looked at Darcy's tilted head and became defensive. "What?"

"*You* are talking about qualities in a wife? *You*; the man of a million girlfriends?" He smiled and saw Charles roll his eyes. "What happened to you?"

He shrugged. "I'm getting old."

"You are twenty-five!" Darcy laughed.

"Look, I'm just tired of partying, I want to settle down. I'm dreading hearing what new girl Caroline has lined up for me to date. Why she thinks that my love life will help hers is beyond me. And why she thinks that I'm going to set something up with you . . ." He laughed at Darcy's stare. "Don't worry; I know that you think she is Satan's spawn."

Darcy's eyes lit up. "Well, not quite that bad, but no I don't want to date her. She should just settle down with some nice guy and live on Long Island like your parents did."

"Nope, I've got this great job and she thinks she can skim off of me. She thinks that I didn't work to get this position, she thinks it's all because of our friendship."

"But we didn't meet until you got the job." Darcy shook his head. "Well, as long as she doesn't have my number, I could care less what she fantasizes about."

The car pulled up to an apartment building. Darcy stared up at the seemingly endless floors. "Are you sure you want to live up so high?"

"Seeing those burned-out houses really got to you this week." Charles gripped his shoulder. "I like it up in the clouds. Go kiss Elizabeth." He smiled and climbed out, then ducked his head back in the doorway. "Maybe I can meet this sister of hers? A double date?" He laughed and closed the door. Soon the car was weaving through traffic, and pulled up in front of Elizabeth's building.

She was sitting on the stoop, reading a book. Darcy opened the door and walked up to her, and stood looking down at her bent head. "Hi."

Elizabeth startled and looked up. "William!" She stood and beamed at him. "I didn't hear you pull up!" She glanced at the black car at the curb. "This is a good story; I guess that I don't hear anything when I'm reading." She saw his warm smile and twinkling eyes and blushed. "I'm babbling." The step she was standing on gave them some assistance with their height differences, and she looked almost evenly into his eyes. "Hi."

Darcy slipped his arms around her waist and pulled her close. "So, I think that we have some time to make up." He leaned forward and kissed her softly. They both sighed and Elizabeth's arms wrapped around his neck. "I have never anticipated a kiss so much in my life." He licked his lips and searched out hers again. Their tongues touched and he gently probed her mouth. She tilted her head and began suckling his upper lip, slowly sliding her tongue over his open mouth and felt him shudder. His hips pressed against her, and he held her back firmly, trying to get as close as possible. Their kisses moved from their mouths to their faces, and each took possession of an ear lobe. "Oh Lizzy." One hand traveled up to her hair and she sighed.

"Get a room!" Someone called from a passing car.

"What a good idea." Elizabeth whispered. "Come on, let's go upstairs."

"I don't trust my self-control." He withdrew and caressed her cheek with the back of his fingers.

"Do you trust mine?" She smiled. "We can't be afraid to be alone. I think that we are capable of exchanging kisses without slipping into a frenzy of disrobing." Slipping her hands inside of his suit jacket she ran them over his chest. "That is unless you want to."

"You are temptation incarnate." He stared into her eyes then lowered his gaze to travel down to her pursed lips then lower to rest upon her cleavage. Elizabeth slipped a hand underneath his chin and lifted his head to kiss him. "Come on."

Taking his hand she determinedly started to lead him up the steps. He began to follow in a haze of desire when he blinked and turned back to his car. The driver was standing next to it. "I'll come back in an hour sir; I'll just drop off your luggage at the house." Darcy nodded and turned back to see Elizabeth's dancing eyes.

"Maybe I won't be finished with you in an hour."

"Oh, I hope not!" Laughing, she opened the door and they walked up the steps. "This is my parent's place . . ." She pointed at the first door on the landing. They arrived at the second floor. "The door at the end is Jane's and this one," they stopped by the first door, "is mine." She opened it and they stepped into the bright space. Darcy looked around and smiled, it was a very relaxed atmosphere, comfortable furniture, a lot of plants, it felt instantly like home.

"I really like this." He looked at the prints of paintings she had hanging about the walls, and noticed with satisfaction that he owned one of them, and looked forward to showing her the original. He explored the rooms, walking over to look at family pictures and knickknacks, then turned to see her standing with her arms folded. "Don't mind me; I'm just getting to know you." He grinned and wandered into the kitchen and saw an obvious fondness for earthenware and a display of handmade bowls in many colors on a shelf. The cookware was not cheap, he recognized the manufacturer. "You enjoy cooking."

"Yes, I'm pretty good at it. Maybe I can make you dinner sometime?"

"I would love that." Darcy smiled. "My life is restaurants or my chef at home; I can't remember ever making something for myself, unless you count the ramen noodles I'd cook at school."

Elizabeth laughed. "I remember making macaroni and cheese in a coffee pot. We weren't allowed microwaves but I could hide the pot in my closet." Darcy smiled and kissed her cheek, then took her hand and led the way as he kept looking around. They came to a door and he paused. "Your bedroom?" She nodded and he bit his lip and opened it. "Ah." There was a huge bed, a dresser, and a chair that could easily accommodate two. "This room is designed for relaxation." He turned and took both of her hands in his. "I want to know what is like to sleep in this bed with you someday."

"I'd love to have you find out." She reached up to touch his face and he leaned down to embrace her head with his hands. His first kiss was tender, and he watched as her eyes closed. Slowly he drew her closer and held her tightly to him, and they stood kissing, swaying together, and discovering the pleasure of touching each other.

"I know that it's too soon, but I don't want to stop." He murmured as his lips caressed her ear. "It is in your hands, Elizabeth." Darcy's breath was ragged and his hands caressed down over her breasts. Every moment that she did not withdraw, he became bolder. He saw that her eyes were still closed and he lifted her chin. "Please look at me, Lizzy. Do you want this? All you have to do is tell me no. I want this to be your decision."

Her eyes fluttered open. "I've never felt like this before."

Darcy caressed her cheek and his brow creased as he looked at her. "What do you feel?"

She looked at him in confused wonder. "I . . ." A sudden screech renting the air made them jump apart.

"LIZZY!" Fran Bennet stood in the bedroom doorway, her face the picture of shock. Quickly Elizabeth spun and Darcy stood in horror, moving behind Elizabeth and hiding the evidence of his very apparent desire.

"Mom! What are you doing here? The door was locked!" She glanced back at William, his face was bright red and he was obviously mortified.

"I . . ." Fran stopped, unable to come up with an explanation for her snooping. Instead she tried to distract her daughter. "What are you doing with a man in your bedroom?" She stared at Darcy. "Who is he? Is he attacking you? Should I call the police?"

"Mom, stop it. This is William Darcy, he's my boyfriend." Elizabeth glared at her and took William's hand and squeezed.

"I am?" He smiled widely.

"Yes you are!" She shared her glare with him and turned back to her mother. "Now, I'm a grown woman and this is my home, and we need to establish some new rules. Don't assume that I'm not home and come waltzing in here. Whatever you want can wait until you see me. Just because Dad has the master key doesn't mean that you can use it anytime you want!"

"I don't like your tone, young woman!" Mrs. Bennet snapped.

"And I don't like your unending invasion of my privacy!" Elizabeth snapped back. She turned to see William watching the exchange and flushed. "I'm sorry William, you shouldn't be seeing this, it has been a long time coming."

"I gathered that." He put his hands on her shoulders. "Maybe I should go home."

"No sir, you are going to stay right here in this building and meet my father. We're going to get this over with right now. Everyone can have a good look at you so there will be no compelling reason to burst in here unannounced again." She was furious, and Darcy watched her in fascination. Elizabeth took his hand and pulled him out of the apartment, and headed for the stairs. Jane came out and leaned on her door to watch the show. Darcy noticed her as they started down.

"Hi Jane."

"Meeting the folks, are you?" She laughed and followed them down, and was nearly knocked over by her mother rushing from Elizabeth's apartment.

"No wonder Mary, Kitty and Lydia left here as soon as they could!" Elizabeth muttered as they moved along.

"Who are they?" William asked.

"My sisters. Mary is at Princeton Theological Seminary, Kitty is at Penn State, and Lydia is at a boarding school in Vermont." She grimaced, "She's the difficult one, the youngest and therefore the most indulged." They reached her parent's apartment and she stopped to look up at him. "Are you sure that you still want to . . . have a relationship with me? The door to freedom is right there if you want to escape now." She looked up at him worriedly.

Darcy smiled and put his hands on her shoulders and drew her to him for a tight hug. "I can think of nothing better than to be your calm port in the storm of your chaotic family." He drew away and kissed her. "I was afraid that you were just too perfect and that I would be the only one with unending baggage, but it looks like we'll be rescuing each other." Elizabeth relaxed and laughed. He smiled. "Let's go meet your Dad."

"Not quite the afternoon we had planned, is it?"

"Who planned? I had no preconceived notions, and sure, my body is in shock, but it will just make our first time together, whenever that happens, so much sweeter." He bent to her ear. "And we'll definitely have to continue our interrupted conversation, I think that you were about to say something very important." His hand found hers and their fingers entwined. "Am I correct?"

"I'm not sure." She bit her lip and blushed, looking away from him.

"I am." He smiled and touched her mouth. "Your poor abused lip confirms it."

Jane and Mrs. Bennet arrived and Elizabeth's ire returned. She opened the door to her parent's apartment. "Dad?" She called and Tom came out of his library, newspaper and reading glasses in hand. He looked over the scene and raised one brow.

"What's all this?"

"Dad, I would like you to meet my boyfriend, William Darcy. He lives on Riverside Drive, has no romantic encumbrances, is gainfully employed, and I like him very much. I will be spending time with him, hopefully frequently, and that will include inviting him to visit my apartment. Please respect our privacy."

Mr. Bennet had folded his arms during her speech and turned to regard Darcy speculatively. "I gather by this display that some family member," He looked pointedly at Fran, "has invaded your privacy?" Tilting his head he took in the tall, almost regal-looking young man. Darcy was standing behind Elizabeth, and had assumed a stance that was clearly protective. His face was unreadable, but he seemed to understand that Elizabeth was very serious, and was supporting her.

"If I do not answer a knock, there is no reason to come in, unless a water pipe has burst or the gas has gone off." She felt William's hand on her shoulder and looked up to him.

"Mr. Bennet, I am pleased to meet you." Darcy held out his hand and gave Tom a firm handshake. "I hope to become better acquainted with your family, but particularly with Elizabeth. I have not dated anyone in a very long time, and I believe that the wait was worth it to have met her."

"I understand that you are doing well in your chosen profession?" Tom said carefully, and glanced at his wife.

"I am successful, yes." Darcy caught the look and understood to not say anything too revealing.

"I am also aware," He nodded to the tabloids on the table, "of the habits of successful men. I hope that you will not treat my daughter in a similar fashion?"

Darcy glanced at the headline, seeing the story of an unexpected pregnancy between a millionaire athlete and a hotel concierge, and flushed. "As I said sir, I have been waiting for the right girl."

Elizabeth felt his embarrassment, "Just as I have been waiting for the right man." She turned to look at her father. "Now, you have met and given him your fatherly warning to behave himself and not hurt me, can we now behave as adults, or must we continue to stare at each other warily?"

She saw a small smirk appear on her father's lips and then felt William's chest move against her back. He was chuckling quietly. Jane clapped her hands and laughed out loud and Fran looked between them all in confusion. Tom stepped forward and held out his hand to Darcy, "Very well then Mr. Darcy, let's see what comes of this."

Darcy shook his hand and nodded. "I anticipate success, sir."

Chapter 4

" *T*his is impossible." Darcy hung up in frustration.
　　　Charles knocked and entered his office. "What's the problem?"

"Who has a phone without text messaging anymore? My girlfriend, that's who!" He ran his hand through his hair. "I can't find her!"

"Darcy calm down. She's not Georgiana." He was instantly the recipient of a furious glare. "I'm sorry, that was uncalled for I know, but she is *not* missing. Doesn't she have a job?"

Darcy closed his eyes. "She's a writer . . . she writes from eight to noon and edits in the afternoon, except for the occasions when she travels." He glanced at the clock, it was almost twelve. "I imagine that she doesn't like to be disturbed when she is concentrating and leaves the phone off."

"So call her in a half-hour and see if you're right." Charles shook his head and looked at him pointedly. "You need to come to grips with this, it's only a week and you're insane. I don't know this girl, but I can bet that she is not going to be a fan of you being so controlling."

Darcy thought of Elizabeth's reaction to her mother the afternoon before and knew that he didn't want to be the object of her fury. "It's been twelve days." He sighed, "You're right, I know. I'm used to being in control here. I'm just a failure outside of this building. But I'm not trying to control her; I just need to speak to her. I don't know how to do this dating business. Maybe that's why I took so long to . . . no, I was waiting for the right one." He looked up at his smiling friend. "Just ignore me."

Charles saw that it was safe and sat down. "I can tell that you are going to be useless today. Have you settled on a plan for tonight?"

"Yes, we're going to dinner then maybe I'll show her the house." He glanced up and closed his eyes against the smirk that greeted him. "Enough Charles, let's get to work and occupy my mind." They stood and walked towards the conference room.

"If you need any advice for tonight . . ." Charles laughed at the renewed glare. They entered the room and greeted the others, the frivolity was gone and they became all business.

ELIZABETH STRETCHED her arms over her head and relaxed. She hit the save button then printed out the morning's efforts. Charlotte would be pleased; the new book was perhaps two chapters from completion. *Then maybe I can be free.* The career that had begun as a release for her troubles was not satisfying her as it once had. She was ready to try something new . . . there was a kernel of an idea prodding her imagination; maybe a change was in order. The new chapter finished printing and she closed her computer-weary eyes for a moment, and then checked her email. There was one from an address she vaguely recognized . . . "William!" She clicked on it and eagerly read.

I am attempting to remain calm and reasonable and assume that the explanation for why I can't reach you is because you are writing. Please email me and confirm that you're alive. I'm in a meeting, but I'll see it.

I'll pick you up at six; the restaurant is quiet and intimate, and recommended highly by my romantic secretary. I can't wait to see you.

Will

Elizabeth laughed and switched her phone on, then walked out to look at the answering machine. She pushed the message button; all she heard was a long groan. She laughed again and picked up her ancient cell phone, and found the message there. Another groan. Returning to her computer, she bit her lip and started typing.

Darcy heard the soft beep and glanced down to see that a new email had arrived. He noted the time and tried to resist looking, and failed. Charles caught his eye and he ignored the raised brows.

Hi Will!

I'm breathing, but I can't say the same for the unlucky bad guy in my story, so sad, but nobody will really miss him. I loved your messages, so little said but the sentiment was clear.

I have my dress picked out for dinner; I hope that it's okay for the mysterious destination you have chosen. I'm counting the hours, and I will definitely be ready and waiting for you!

Lizzy

A slow smile spread over Darcy's face and he looked up to see the eyes of the room upon him. Instantly his somber mask reappeared and his attention returned to the meeting. Later when he returned to his office he discovered that his notebook was covered with the same word, over and over . . . *Lizzy.*

"HOW'S IT GOING?" Richard leaned on the countertop in his parent's kitchen and watched Georgiana reading a cookbook. She did not speak. "Come on, you have to talk sometime, I haven't heard a word out of you since Anne's wedding, and that was all for Elizabeth Bennet." Still nothing. "Maybe you would like to talk to her again?" Finally Georgiana's eyes fixed on him. "Should I take you home? I think that your brother might know how to contact her."

"I can't go home." Georgiana whispered.

"Why not?" Richard took a seat next to her, anxious to finally hear her open up.

"William must hate me." Her eyes filled with tears.

"I can't believe he thinks that, he loves you. I know that he is very worried, and even more hurt that you wouldn't let him bring you home." Richard took her hand.

"I know, he has said so many . . . wonderful things to me, but I can't go back there. I have disappointed him so much." She looked up and swallowed. "I have disappointed myself. Why did I go away? I could have turned around at any time and just gone back. But there was a man with my name on a piece of cardboard and I blindly climbed into a car with him and willingly . . . stayed with him."

"What happened there?" Richard asked gently. "Sweetie, you will have to tell someday. He will go to trial and they need your testimony to convict him."

"But I let him . . ."

"Georgiana, he is nearly twice your age. You are a minor, no matter how much of an adult you think you are. Going to college doesn't change that fact."

"I never should have gone."

"Did you want to leave school? Didn't you like it there? Darcy thought maybe you started too young, but Julliard would not have accepted you if you didn't have the talent. It was your decision to apply." Arlene Fitzwilliam had heard their voices and came to lean on the kitchen door and listen.

"No, I wanted to go to school. I guess that living away from home was harder than I expected. But William did it; he went to Harvard at sixteen! I could just get in a cab and be home in a few minutes, but when he went, he was so far away! And I just want to play the piano, he has two advanced degrees! I am such a disappointment to him! Mom and Dad would have been so ashamed of me if I had dropped out, and now I have! I can't face him, I can't!" She burst into tears and Richard looked up and saw his mother. He shook his head helplessly, not knowing what to do.

"Call William, he needs to come here."

Arlene sat down and held Georgiana's hand and Richard left the room. David looked up from his newspaper. "Did I hear Georgiana?"

"Yes, she's talking, but God knows what to say to her. Mom told me to get Darcy here." David nodded and watched him make the call.

Darcy had just arrived at Elizabeth's apartment. Tom saw him approach the door and opened it for him. "So, where are you two going this evening?"

"I have reservations at a small restaurant recommended by my secretary . . ." His sentence was interrupted by the sound of heels clicking down the hallway and the appearance of shapely legs descending the stairs.

"Hi!" Elizabeth arrived and Darcy took her hand and squeezed it.

"Hi." He said softly. "You look beautiful." His eyes traveled over her and took in everything from head to toe, and noted the reappearance of her repaired shoes.

Elizabeth blushed under his scrutiny and brushed his suit jacket. "You look gorgeous." She laughed at his embarrassed smile and turned to her father. "I'll see you tomorrow, Dad."

"Staying out late?" He watched as Darcy held the door for her.

"I don't know," She looked up to William. "What is the plan?"

"For once in my life, I don't really have one." He grinned and looked back at Tom. "Goodnight, sir." They entered the car and the driver closed the door behind them. Darcy drew her into his arms. "Now, let's have a proper hello."

"If you mess up my makeup . . ." Elizabeth warned with a smile.

"We'll just have to go home and repair it." He bent to kiss her upturned face when his phone began to ring. "That's my uncle."

"How do you know?" Elizabeth watched him pull the phone out of his pocket.

"I know the ring." He answered. "Hello?"

Richard started speaking rapidly. "Darcy, Georgiana's talking . . . I think that she's ready to tell us what happened."

Darcy sat up straight and asked urgently, "What has she said?"

"Enough to tell us that she thinks you never want her home again."

Darcy closed his eyes in frustration. "Let me take Elizabeth home, and I'll be there."

Surprised, Richard asked, "She's with you? Bring her along, she might help."

"I don't know, wait." Darcy put his hand over the phone and looked at her.

"What is wrong?" Elizabeth touched his face and searched his eyes.

"My sister is starting to talk about what happened, and they want me to come . . . . our evening . . . I'm sorry, Elizabeth."

"I understand." She felt as disappointed as he did, but wanted so much to stay with him when he clearly needed support. "Maybe I can help? I'll be happy to talk to her if she wants me to."

Darcy felt his heart soar. "You would do that?"

"Of course." She took his free hand and gripped it.

He kissed her. "Thank you, I feel so alone and don't know what to do."

"Neither do I, but I if you want, I'll try."

Darcy put the phone back to his ear. "We're on our way. Elizabeth wants to come."

"Great! We'll see you soon."

"Frank." Darcy addressed his driver.

"Yes sir, to the Fitzwilliam's apartment." He moved the car into another lane.

Darcy put the phone away and took Elizabeth's hand and kissed it. "Thank you so much. I'm sorry; we just seem destined to never have this first date."

"Well this *is* our first date, just an unconventional one." She leaned against him and he studied their entwined fingers. They rode on in silence, unwittingly sharing the same thoughts. Darcy looked down and their eyes met. Elizabeth touched his cheek and their mouths joined in a slow, tender kiss. Darcy rested his forehead on hers. "What are you thinking?"

"I'm wondering if we'll be holding each other like this . . ."

"Years from now?" He said softly, and opened his eyes to look into hers again.

"Maybe we should talk about that after our fiftieth date." She smiled.

"Maybe, but it won't be far from my mind until we do." He looked at her seriously.

Elizabeth drew a sharp breath when a memory intruded and became cautious. "We have a great deal of talking to do."

He jumped on the subject. "Will you let me buy you a new phone?"

Elizabeth eyed him warily, she had been with a controlling man before, and she swore it wouldn't happen again, the little bubble of happiness she had just felt burst. "Why are you so worried about my whereabouts?"

Darcy did not notice that her expression had changed; he only saw an opportunity to press his point. "I need to know that I can find you."

"Why am I to be at your beck and call?" She sat up and moved away from him.

He did not understand her reaction at all. "Look, I'm very busy. I can't be playing phone tag when I need to contact you. It's as simple as that!"

Elizabeth bristled. "Well maybe I don't want to be a slave to your whims! You will have to accept that during a certain block of time, I am unavailable."

"That is absolutely ridiculous! Anything could happen during those hours and I would be left with no option but to hope that your parents or Jane were home, or to drop everything and go to your apartment!"

She stared at him incredulously. "Because I wouldn't answer the phone?"

"Because I would not know where you are! It is even more important if you leave town!" He met her stare with one just as disbelieving. Why couldn't she see his point?

The car had stopped in front of an apartment building. Darcy noted the location. "Look, we're here, we'll discuss this later."

"No, I think that I'll go home." She opened the door and stepped out before Frank could exit.

"Elizabeth!" Darcy struggled to unlatch the seatbelt and slid across to the door, following her onto the curb. She was glancing around, searching for a way to leave. "What are you doing?" He towered over her.

Not at all intimidated, she stared up at him. "I have no desire to be under the thumb of another man who is going to tell me how to think or act or if I can speak to another person, or . . . follow me or use me for his own desires or demand that I be accountable for every movement of my day. I thought you were different, but I guess that I am great at finding the wrong man. Goodbye William, I am sorry but I can't go through this torture again."

She turned and hurried away. Darcy was stunned and he watched with increasing disbelief as she ran off. "But I am not doing any of those things!" He said to himself, and ran after her. "Elizabeth!" Grabbing her arm to stop her, she turned to face him; her cheeks were covered in tears. "Elizabeth, you don't understand."

Spotting a cab pulling up to the curb, she cried, "No, I understand all too well." The passengers exited and she climbed in, and in a moment it was gone. Darcy watched it pull into the sea of yellow cabs and quickly lost track of it.

"What just happened?" He ran his hand through his hair. "I am not what she described; I am not anything like that, am I?" Desperately he thought over the conversation. "Good God, I've lost her and I don't know how!" He swallowed hard as the emotion began to well up in his chest. "How can she accuse me of . . . controlling her?" He closed his eyes and heard Charles's voice from that morning, warning him. "But I never had a chance to explain myself, to tell her why . . . and now I wonder if I ever will."

Everything in him screamed to go after her, but he knew that he needed to go to his sister. "What am I going to be to her now? Elizabeth was going to help me, and now I'm . . . I don't know what to do." He turned back towards the car. Frank averted his eyes. "I'll call you when it's over." He said dully.

"Yes, sir." Frank got in the car and drove away. Darcy remained outside, staring at a fountain in the small plaza in front of the building. He did not want to go in alone. The sound of his phone ringing finally made him blink back out of the numb haze he was feeling and mechanically, he dipped his hand into his pocket and answered without seeing who it was.

"Darcy."

"I'm sorry."

"Elizabeth?" He said hopefully.

"I have to keep reminding myself that you are not Collins."

He rubbed his face in relief and dismay. "What did this man do to you?"

"Too many things, too many to talk about now, but the most pertinent one is that he made me very wary of anything that resembles arrogance." She sighed. "I overreacted to your wish to keep me easily accessible."

"I did not mean it to sound that way. I . . . Charles said something to me today when I was talking about you . . . that I seem to have a possessive attitude about you, and that you would probably not appreciate it. I suppose that is true, I do, and I do not regret it, but the reason that I want to always know where you are, or at least be able to somehow contact you is . . . after losing my parents and nearly losing Georgiana, and after these years of being alone, I am so grateful for finding you." He sighed. "The FBI found Georgiana through the GPS chip in her phone, if she didn't have that . . . it could have been so much worse. I'm not suggesting that you will be kidnapped or something but, you just can't understand how good it is to know that there is someone in the world who I can call or send a little message to, and hear back, and know that she is there for me, not the President of Pemberley, but me." His hand again passed through his hair as he struggled to explain himself. "I will forever be possessive and worried if I can not find the people I care about. I know that this is a jumble of thoughts, but I'm not thinking very clearly right now. Your running has me stunned." He realized that he was pacing back and forth before the fountain and came to a halt, staring down at his shoes.

"I am so sorry for my reaction, Will. I misinterpreted your motivation entirely. I have been so happy to know you, and although we have barely begun, I admit that I have allowed my imagination to be rather free with hopes. It was just the demand in your voice, the delivery of your pronouncement, which reminded me so much of a man who made my life hell. I did what my instincts told me to do; I got up and ran without giving you a chance to explain."

"I am not noted for my skills in oration." He relaxed a little with her explanation. "I am also accused of behaving arrogantly in my business relationships, but in those situations it is admired as strength and determination, outside of the office though, such behavior it seems would not be looked upon with favor, as you have clearly pointed out to me this evening."

"The same behavior in a woman would be seen as bitchy." Elizabeth said with a lift in her voice. Darcy's lips twitched and she heard a slight laugh, and added softly, "You seem to have become attached to me fast."

He nodded. "Yes, do you mind?"

"No, I am feeling the same way I think, and it frightens me, maybe that has something to do with my flight as well."

"I wish that you were here. I wish that I could find a way to reassure you." He watched the water flowing over the fountain then stared back down at his shoes.

"Turn around."

Confused, he slowly spun to see Elizabeth facing him. "You came back." He kept talking into the phone while staring at her only steps away.

"I never really left. The cab dropped me off a block away and I walked back. I overreacted . . . I believed the worst because I'm afraid of being hurt again." She looked up and saw his intense gaze. "I want so much to believe that you are different."

"I won't hurt you, Lizzy." He stepped closer and touched her hair.

She closed her phone and fell into his arms. He held her firmly to his chest and kissed her forehead, and drew a shaking breath. His eyes were squeezed shut. "So, we had our first fight."

"I didn't like it." Elizabeth whispered.

"I didn't either." He looked down and they kissed. "If we didn't have to go see my sister, I believe that I would be coaxing you to my house for make-up sex." He smiled and laughed to see her wide eyes. "Well I've heard that it is to be expected behavior in all good relationships to seal the reunion."

She leaned back and examined him carefully. "So I have to sleep with you tonight?"

Darcy pulled her back and murmured into her ear. "Who said anything of sleep?"

"William!"

He kept his mouth close to her ear. "I think that I am falling for you." Her sharp intake of breath and squeeze around his waist reassured him that he was not alone in the feeling. "Come on; let's go see what my sister has to say. I believe that your help will be much appreciated." Darcy rested his forehead on hers. "That is if you still wish to come."

"Of course I want to come, this is family." She smiled and his face lit up. They kissed and holding hands, walked into the building. Darcy greeted the doorman who recognized him and waved them on to the elevators. "I have never been in such a posh building." She looked around at all of the amenities. "I wonder, is there a ladies' room in the lobby? I have a feeling that I am a bit unkempt from our . . . emotional interlude." Her eyes danced.

"I imagine that I am as well." He smiled and leaned into the hand that was rearranging his hair. They each stepped into the restrooms, taking a moment to stare into the mirrors and talk to their reflections. Darcy washed his hands then rested his palms on the sink, leaning forward to speak.

"You are not falling, you're gone." He studied the fool in the mirror and closed his eyes. "Don't blow this, Darcy."

"Well Lizzy, you can stop lying to yourself now." Elizabeth shook her brush at herself. "This isn't flirtation. This is serious." She nodded and straightened. "This man is not playing around. He really wants you!" Putting her things back in her bag, she took one last look at the wide nervous eyes of her twin. "It's okay to care for him, and it's okay to let him care for you."

She stepped out into the lobby and Darcy turned from where he had been standing vigil nearby. He scanned her face; something was different in her expression. "Are you all right?"

Smiling, she stepped up to his side. "Yes." Entwining her fingers with his, she stood on her toes to kiss him. "Yes, Will." He smiled, whatever had changed, it was decidedly in his favor.

Darcy kissed her hand and they boarded the elevator. Elizabeth watched the floors fly by. "They are way up there, aren't they?" She observed. "Not conducive to your housing needs."

"No, I'll stick with my little house." He smiled.

"I was tempted to look at your little house while you were away, but I decided to leave that for you to show me someday." She noted his surprise. "Did you think I would rush right over to Riverside Drive?"

"Well, a mercenary woman would have, but not you." He kissed her cheek. "No, not you." The door opened and they continued to hold hands as they made their way down the corridor. They came to a door and he rang the bell.

"Darcy, where were you? That took forever!" Richard stepped back and let them in. "Elizabeth, it is wonderful to see you again!" He kissed both of her cheeks and closed the door, she looked at William but he seemed unaffected by it.

"We had a little detour, sorry for the delay, how is she?" Darcy shook his uncle's hand and nodded to John, who had recently arrived.

"She has clammed up again. There was that burst of conversation, but well, she essentially said that you were wonderful but that she could not return to your home, she had disgraced the family." Darcy blew out a long breath and looked at Elizabeth.

David came forward and kissed her cheeks as his son had, which surprised her again. "I am so happy to see you escorting Darcy; he needs a good woman beside him."

Elizabeth laughed. "You give me far too much credit, I may be his worst nightmare, you know!"

The men laughed and John slapped Darcy's back. "Well, I think that statement only confirms that he's caught a good one." He stepped up and kissed her as well. "So, do you think that you might convince our cousin to speak? God knows we've tried for months."

"Where is she?" Darcy stepped up to Elizabeth and placed his hand on the small of her back, eliciting glances between Richard and his father.

"In the kitchen, have at it, Darcy." John waved them on.

"I have much experience in speaking to troubled girls. I was the one who was in charge of my sister Lydia." Elizabeth confided as they moved towards the kitchen.

"Is she the reason you had to come home and not continue your education?"

"Yes, I was the only family member she would listen to. If I hadn't come home, she would not be in Vermont, but either run away or maybe in prison for prostitution. She was a wild child, and my parents were not very effective in controlling her. She is doing much better now in a very structured environment." Elizabeth smiled at his wide eyes. "I told you we have much to talk about."

"It seems we will never be in want of challenging subjects." He looked at her closely and realized that her experiences gave her a sense of maturity that other young women her age might not achieve for many more years. Pushing open the swinging kitchen door, they walked in to see Georgiana seated on a stool by the large kitchen island. Arlene was nearby. "Georgie, Aunt Arlene, you both remember Elizabeth, don't you?"

Arlene stood up and took her hand. "I am so happy to see you again, my dear." She smiled and patted Darcy's cheek. "Very happy." Glancing at Georgiana, she walked out of the room, closing the door behind her.

Darcy immediately began, "Georgie, I hear that you have expressed . . . concern that I might not welcome you back home. You must know that I would love to have you come home. I am not ashamed of you, and I know that Mom and Dad would not feel anything but love and concern for you." He tried to see into her downcast eyes and looked at Elizabeth helplessly.

She took a stool beside the girl. "Which recipe has captured your imagination?" Georgiana startled and looked up to the smiling woman beside her.

After a few moments of hesitation she spoke. "This one, for a kind of frittata, it has fried potatoes on the bottom and eggs on top, and lots of cheese." She pointed at a colorful picture.

"Mmm, so I see that you are drawn to the healthy recipes." Elizabeth laughed and noted Georgiana's small smile. "Well, do you think that your aunt has the ingredients? William and I missed dinner, and I'll be honest with you, I'm starving. Why don't we give this a try?"

"I . . . I have never cooked anything in my life!" Georgiana stared at her.

"Well it's time that you learned, don't you think?" Elizabeth looked at William. "Why don't you go out and visit with your family and we'll get to work?"

"Um, okay, if you want . . ." He watched as Elizabeth rooted around in some drawers and found an apron, then went to stand in front of the open refrigerator, ignoring him entirely.

"Find us some potatoes Georgiana, I think six will do." She began poking around and Georgiana jumped off of the stool and started searching. Darcy stared and closed his open mouth, then silently left the room.

"What's going on?" David looked at him and then heard a crash that was undoubtedly cookware, and the sound of loud girlish giggling.

"They're cooking dinner." Darcy said in wonder, and sank into a chair, staring at the closed door. "Georgiana picked out a recipe, and Elizabeth told her they were going to make it since we had missed our reservations." He looked back at his family. "I was dismissed."

Richard laughed. "Wow!"

"That's a smart girl you've got there, Son." David shook his head and stood up to walk over to the bar. He poured out a glass of wine and brought it to him.

"Do you think that she'll talk to Elizabeth?" John looked at his mother.

"Well, at least they'll be friends, and if not tonight, maybe the next time they meet she'll say something. I can only be impressed with her ease. Tell us about her, William."

"She has four sisters." He swung his head at the sound of a wail.

Elizabeth's head poked out of the door. "Do you have any bandages?"

"What happened?" Darcy stood.

"Nothing life-threatening." She smiled and he relaxed. Arlene returned with a box. "Thank you!"

Soon the smell of eggs and potatoes filled the apartment, and the sound of giggling was gone. In fact, it was very quiet. Darcy was pacing the room, constantly sending looks to the closed door until he could stand it no longer, and went to press his ear to the wood. The pressure of his head moved the well-balanced door and he peeked inside to see Georgiana resting in Elizabeth's arms, crying, and clearly whispering to her. Elizabeth glanced up to see his anxious face and smiled over Georgiana's head, nodded and mouthed, "Come in."

Cautiously he entered. Elizabeth pulled back and wiped Georgiana's eyes. "I think that dinner is ready. Why don't you get some plates, and we can feed your brother our creation."

"William." Georgiana noticed him and blushed.

"Are you okay?" He stepped forward and touched her shoulder. She fell into his open arms and he hugged her tight. "It's okay, sweetie, I love you."

"I love you, too." She looked up to his worried face. "May I come home?"

"Of course!" His eyes closed and he hugged her again.

"Just for a little while. The summer session starts at the beginning of July, and I can make up some of the time I lost last semester, then I won't be so far behind when I go back to school in the fall." She smiled shyly. "Do you think you might be able to take some time off while I'm home?"

"I haven't taken time off for years; I believe that I probably have some vacation coming to me." He smiled and relaxed. "What would you like to do?"

"Let's go to the Hamptons. Elizabeth has to see the house." She turned and smiled at her. "You'll love it there!"

"Oh, well, that sounds wonderful, but I don't want to be in the way. You and William should be together." She wanted the reunion between the siblings but didn't count on being brought along for the trip.

"You want Elizabeth with us, don't you?" Georgiana spun back to face him. Darcy was reading Elizabeth's expression, and trying to understand what it said.

"I would love to have both of my ladies with me, but I can't demand that Elizabeth come with us. I can only say that she would be deeply missed if she did not. However, this is really only our first date, and since your summer session won't begin until July, I suggest that we leave that trip for the middle of June, and Elizabeth and I can spend the next six weeks or so . . . adding to our date count." He smiled and saw that he had done the right thing.

"Thank you, I agree that we need to get to know each other better, but by the time you plan to go, I . . . I think that I would love to come." She met his eyes and breathed a sigh of relief. No, William Darcy was *not* Bill Collins, not at all.

The three of them got to work, setting out plates and silverware, and served themselves their little feast. Arlene was the next to open the kitchen door after hearing the sound of their laughter. "Well, it seems that a party is happening and we were not invited."

"Oh, I'm sorry, Mrs. Fitzwilliam." Elizabeth jumped up and grabbed a plate, filled it, and handed her a fork. "Please join us." She took her seat again and Arlene stood in surprise with the plate in her hand then saw William's twinkling eyes and Georgiana's smile. She took a stool and sat down.

"I should not even smell this concoction let alone eat it." They laughed as she took a small bite and groaned in pleasure. The rest of the men entered and were soon served; standing about with plates in hand and relaxing in a way the household had not felt in months.

Darcy took Elizabeth's hand and leaned over to her. "What happened?"

"She told me everything." Elizabeth whispered. "I'll tell you when we're alone, okay?"

He nodded and saw with relief how his sister had found a smile. "Thank you, for whatever you did."

"She was ready to talk, I'm just used to girls her age, and she found me easier to speak to than your aunt or the psychologist." She glanced around and kissed his cheek.

Darcy smiled in delight. "So will you really come with us?"

"If I won't be in the way." She looked at him shyly.

Slowly, he shook his head. "No, I think that I would be very happy to trip over you." He touched the dimples that appeared as she laughed. "After all, it's how we met."

Chapter 5

"So? How was the big date?" Charles bounded into Darcy's office the moment he arrived. Darcy held up his hand and shot him a glance that clearly told him to be quiet. Laying down his briefcase, Charles closed the door and took a seat across from the desk and listened to the conversation.

"That's quite a difference in possibilities; can't we just lock him away forever?" Darcy spoke into the phone. He closed his eyes and nodded. "Very well, I'll bring Georgiana to our attorney's office to make the statement at ten. Thank you." He hung up and rubbed his face, then looked up at his friend. "Good morning."

"Well, I was expecting you to have a distinct after-glow this morning, but clearly that is not the case. Did something happen with Georgiana?"

"We wound up having our first fight in front of my uncle's building. We were summoned there because Georgiana was ready to talk." Darcy leaned back in his chair and rested his hands on the arms. "You were right by the way, Elizabeth does *not* respond well to controlling boyfriends. That is a subject we have only begun to explore, but I am increasingly concerned about what that man did to her." Glancing out the window at the beautiful day, he licked his lips and drew a deep breath. "Anyway, we survived that bump intact and went up to the apartment. Elizabeth was . . . magnificent. I am so fortunate to have met her. Georgiana told her everything, and will be coming back home this afternoon. We spent most of the evening with the family, and then it was too late to show Elizabeth the house so I took her home. I went up to her apartment, and . . . she told me what happened to Georgiana. I just got off the phone with the prosecutor. He wants her to make a sworn statement this morning and send it down to Florida."

"From your response, I take it that you are not pleased with the repercussions Wickham will face." Charles leaned forward and watched his friend carefully.

Darcy shot him a look and laughed hollowly. "No, it seems that there will be two options, either he will be charged with a second degree felony, which is a maximum of fifteen years and a $10,000 fine, or a misdemeanor, which would mean a year and a $1000 fine. The only thing that is good about those possibilities . . . well, it means that he didn't hurt her as badly as he could have." He hung his head and looked down at his twisting hands. "Georgiana said that he did talk about sex in the chats and emails, but he never hurt her or threatened her. She claims that she willingly participated. A camera and video equipment were found in the room, but she was located before he was able to implement that part of the plan."

"Did she say why she didn't walk away when she realized the man meeting her was not a seventeen-year old boy?"

Still looking down, Darcy spoke to his hands. "She said that he had a ready explanation for that, and he convinced her that he was afraid she would reject him if he told her how much older he was, and that he knew that he was in love with her, and wanted so much to meet her." He swallowed down the bile rising in his throat. "I remember him as being utterly charming, I can't disbelieve her statement that she felt almost obligated to stay with him and reassure him that she was his friend. They spent the next two days wandering around the parks, and little by little he would ingratiate himself with her. First buying little gifts; and holding her hand, then . . . kissing her on the rides. By the time they got back to the hotel room, she . . . didn't say no." He blinked and wiped his eyes. "And once he got started, he was very . . . happy to repeat the act. She thought they were in love, and was completely taken by surprise when the FBI arrived. It was only when she was in the hospital being examined that it hit her what she had done. Then the guilt set in and she stopped talking." He sighed and looked up at Charles' face. "That's the gist of it."

"Darcy, I'm sorry . . ."

He interrupted and spoke quickly. "There's nothing to be done. I hope that we don't have to go to trial, but maybe he will get what he deserves. Since this is his first offense, and she is sixteen, I have a feeling he'll get off with the lighter sentence." He shook his head and glanced at the clock. "Frank is going to pick her up and meet me here, then we'll be gone for the rest of the morning, I doubt that I'll be back this afternoon."

"Okay, I'll work on the contracts for the Darcy properties. So besides the fight and the confession, things went well with Elizabeth?" He lifted his brow and smiled.

A small smile appeared on Darcy's face. "Yes, very well. She's great." He looked up and his smile grew. "Just wonderful. Georgiana suggested that we go out to Pemberley for a few weeks before she goes back to Julliard for the summer session, and asked Elizabeth to come with us. She said yes." Charles raised his hands in the air for a silent cheer, and Darcy laughed. "She agreed to let me buy her a new phone, too!"

"Wow, you *are* charming!" He laughed. "So when do you go?"

"Not until mid-June, so I have plenty of time to get things in order because I do *not* want to be disturbed." He looked at his right-hand man pointedly.

"Got it." Charles stood and opened the door. "I'll look at what's looming and see what absolutely requires your input. I know this is rough for you, but there has to be some relief to finally have it all move forward." Darcy nodded and he left the room.

He glanced at the clock; it was not quite eight yet. He picked up the phone and selected a number. "Hi Will!" The happy voice greeted him, and instantly he smiled and relaxed.

"Hi Lizzy, I thought I'd try to catch you before you disappeared into the oblivion."

Elizabeth rolled her eyes. "Yes Will, I get the point." She heard his chuckle. "Anything exciting to report?"

"I'll take Georgiana to make her statement this morning as planned, and then I thought that I'd take the afternoon off."

"Good idea, you two need some time alone." Elizabeth nodded.

"Um, if she wants, maybe we could swing by your place and take you to the house for lunch?" He bit his lip and listened.

"Oh, well sure if I wouldn't be in the way, I'd love to see this humble abode of yours." She laughed at the sound of his snort. "I just don't want to be an impediment to your reestablishing your relationship with her."

"I appreciate that, Lizzy, I do, but well, you probably haven't noticed but I'm a rather awkward speaker . . ."

"Oh no, I haven't noticed at all." She giggled.

"Ahem, and Georgiana is pretty much the same, so it is very likely that the two of us would be dancing around each other and smiling but not really saying anything, if you know what I mean."

"So a catalyst to conversation in the form of me is needed?" She smiled at the vision of his blushing face.

"Um, well, yes." He twisted his neck and pulled awkwardly on his collar. "Okay?"

"I'd be happy to be your go-between. So, sometime after noon?"

"I'll call you when we're on our way, which means that you might just have to leave your phone *on* today." He jabbed and relaxed.

"Yes, dear." She said with a sigh, then added gently, "Thank you for caring about me."

"You're welcome." Darcy drew a long breath and looked up, seeing a shadow outside his office door. "Charles is here."

"Did he give you much grief over our date? That's what best friends are for, and from your description, I think that he would not hesitate." Elizabeth laughed hearing him groan.

"Well, fortunately I was on the phone with our lawyer when he came in so it wasn't as bad as it could be, but he'll interrogate me as soon as he finds an opening." Darcy could not hide the smile in his voice. "I won't tell him anything of course, but . . . it sure is wonderful having something to keep secret."

"I know what you mean." She said softly.

Hearing a knock, Darcy cleared his throat. "Um, I have to get something done this morning before I leave. I'll call you later on."

"Okay, good luck, and . . . I can't wait to see you, Will." Elizabeth bit her lip and listened, hearing his soft intake of breath.

"I feel the same way. Bye."

"Bye." Elizabeth listened and still hearing him breathing; giggled and hung up first.

"HAVE YOU MET THIS GUY?" Jane asked. She was in her office awaiting the arrival of a new bride-to-be.

"No, but I did see Charles with William on the news. He's pretty hot." Elizabeth laughed as she heard Jane's sigh. "Come on, you were impressed with Will, and he's gorgeous, don't you think?"

"Yes, he is." Jane thought of the last William in Elizabeth's life. "How far along have you two gone?"

"Jane, I'm not going to discuss my sex life with you."

"So you don't have one to discuss yet, I take it. That's good Lizzy, go slow."

"I am not going to over-analyze this, it will happen when it does." She bit her lip and stared out the window. "This feels so different . . ."

"That's because this is man who cares about you." Jane said gently. "And you care about him."

"I just thought I cared about Collins, didn't I?"

"No, you felt like you had to because he was your first. I don't know how you got it into your head that you had to stay with him, as if you were obligated to just because you slept with him."

"He said that we would get married, I thought that settled it, and I ignored everything else. I guess that I thought I could save him from his bad habits." She sighed and thought of Georgiana. "Young and stupid."

"And now?" Jane smiled.

"Cautious but optimistic." Elizabeth laughed. "Well, more than optimistic!" She looked out of the window. "Oh, they're here, I have to go!"

"Take a look at that house very carefully; I want a full report tonight!" Jane hung up and shook her head. Elizabeth had been through the wringer with her last relationship, and she hoped this one would be everything that she deserved.

Darcy met her at the building's entry, and before she could exit, he slipped inside. "Hi." His hands slid around her waist and he stole a kiss. "I needed that." He felt her embrace and let the tension of the morning go.

"How was it?"

"Worse for me than for Georgiana, I think. She seemed relieved to finally tell the story. Besides, she just had to write it all out, but since I had to sit and listen to it being read back, I . . . well, it was hard. She said that talking to you was harder than today since it was her first time really confronting it all, but that you made it so easy, as if you understood." Darcy moved his face from where he had hidden it in her hair and looked at her. "You really did understand, didn't you?" Elizabeth nodded. Darcy kissed her nose. "I thought so."

"Let's go." She whispered.

He took her hand and they left the building to climb into the car. "We stopped and got you something, Elizabeth." Georgiana shook a bag.

"What is it?" She looked between the two, and Darcy grabbed the bag and hid it.

"Later." He smiled and sent a look to his sister. "After we eat." The car easily traveled the ten blocks to Riverside Drive, and slowing, Darcy pointed to a white marble mansion with a green copper roof, and built in the French Renaissance style. "We're home."

"This is yours?" Elizabeth stared at him. "I've walked and ridden past here a million times and always wondered . . . I remember there was something about this place in the news not too many years ago?"

They pulled into a driveway at the back of the house and got out. Darcy took her hand while Georgiana ran ahead to hug the housekeeper. "Yes, after the fire the historical commission was very concerned that I would choose not to repair the damage, and sell the lot for development." He pointed up to the back corner of the house. "See where the roof is new? The copper hasn't aged to green yet? That is the part that was damaged, some debris from the building next door fell through and the smoke poured into the house, which is what took my parents." He shook off the memory and continued. "It was built by the man who designed Carnegie Hall in 1909, and is the only free-standing single-family mansion left in

Manhattan." They looked up in silence. "I could not even consider abandoning this place; the historical people had nothing to fear."

Elizabeth touched his shoulder and drew his eyes back down from the roof. "And to think we grew up so close together."

"Yes, if I didn't have my own private park to play in, I might have ventured over your way more often, and I might have tripped over you sooner." He smiled and kissed her. "I took riding lessons in Central Park. Have you ever done that?"

"Yes, actually I enjoy it very much." They held hands and entered through the back door.

"Perhaps on our trip to Pemberley we can ride sometime."

"Pemberley?"

"That's the name of our estate in the Hamptons, and the name of our ancestral estate in England. I'll have to show you that place sometime, too." Elizabeth bit her lip and he touched it. "I want to show you everything."

"Mr. Darcy, lunch will be ready in a half-hour." An older woman announced and looked curiously at Elizabeth, and noted that her hand was tightly clutched by Darcy.

"Thank you Mrs. Reynolds. This is Elizabeth Bennet." He smiled happily and looked back at his housekeeper. "I'm giving her the tour." Mrs. Reynolds studied him then moved her gaze to Elizabeth. She could not remember the last time she saw him so elated.

"I suppose that I'll find you in the library when it's time to eat." She smiled at him with a nod of approval. "It is good to meet you Miss Bennet."

"I'm happy to meet you as well." She watched the lady bustle off and looked to him. Darcy was watching the woman go and had a very pleased smile on his face. "What's this about the library?"

He laughed. "When in doubt, look for me there. So maybe we should start elsewhere, or we will never see the rest of the place. I guess that Georgiana went to her room." He looked around, just realizing that she was gone. "Well, shall we?"

They walked around the magnificent home. There were countless beautiful rooms, evidence of behavior from a bygone age, a large ballroom, eight bedrooms, and fireplaces in every conceivable place. He watched as she explored, noting all of the little pauses and expressions that appeared on her face as she took in the details. They did not visit his bedroom. Darcy instead took her into his private office and she drank in the atmosphere of the library. "You spend a great deal of time in here, don't you?"

"Yes, I do, but I think that I need to make a change to that habit." She turned from a painting of a large house situated before a lake, and tilted her head. "I buried myself in work for several reasons, one to prove myself to all of the employees of Pemberley and well, everything else that I'm in charge of, and two, to not go back into that cycle of self-destruction I was caught in. I think that I am safe in both of those areas now." He stepped up and looked down into her eyes, gently wrapping a long curl of her hair around his finger. "I'm ready to leave the past behind." Leaning down, he kissed her lips, then drew her back against his chest, turning her to face the painting. Elizabeth's heart was pounding, and she molded herself against him, holding the hands that gripped her waist. "That is the original Pemberley. It is in Derbyshire, England."

"Does anyone still live there?" She asked softly. Darcy's lips touched her cheek, then moved to her ear. "It is available for visits by tourists, but we still own it as our estate. I try to visit there at least once a year. I was planning a trip for August." His mouth wandered down her neck and he felt the sharp breath she took. "You are trembling."

Elizabeth's eyes closed. "I feel so . . ."

"Please tell me. Are you afraid?"

"No . . . I . . . I've never felt anything like this before."

"Like what?" Again his lips caressed her neck and she felt the soft tickle of his nose brushing her skin. His hands remained in place but he pressed her body back against him.

"I feel . . . like . . . sparks are running all over me." Elizabeth bent her head back and he gladly accepted her invitation to caress her more. Now his hands slipped out from under hers, and one began to lightly caress her breasts. "ohhhhh." His other hand touched her hip, then up over her stomach, and back down, slowly touching her, and gradually moving lower.

"What do you feel now?" He whispered.

"I feel . . . I feel oh, I don't know!" Elizabeth turned in his arms and looked up to him. "Kiss me."

Without a word they embraced, kissing passionately. Darcy's hands rested on her bottom, lifting her up to press himself hard against her. A jolt of pleasure shot through Elizabeth with the sensation and she moaned into his stroking mouth. Darcy dragged his lips to kiss her face, her neck, now down to her shoulders, his hand moving between them to touch her breasts. Again she moaned with his touch, and moved her hands to run over his body.

Darcy groaned, feeling her hand on his hip. "Yes." Her hand moved between them and she felt the rock hard arousal beneath her fingers. "Oh yes." He moaned and moved against her hand, rocking his hips as she explored his length and began stroking on her own. Darcy's hand lowered to the hem of her dress, and slowly slid it up her thigh. He felt nothing at all beneath and then came across the tiny threads of her thong. Elizabeth shuddered with the feel of his warm hand on her skin. "Do you like this, Lizzy? Do you want me to stop?" He panted.

"You would stop if I asked?" She looked up to his eyes for the truth.

He sensed her withdrawing. "Yes, of course." Darcy lowered her dress and moved his hands up to hold her cheeks. "What did he do to you?" He demanded. "Why have you never felt . . . You have never felt anything before have you? You submitted to him, is that what happened? Lizzy? You never loved him, did you?" He searched her face for an answer, and only saw her retreating further away. Mrs. Reynolds' knock and announcement of lunch ended the discussion. He closed his eyes and drew her back to kiss her forehead and felt her relax again into his arms, he did not know what to do, but he was determined to not make her feel the need to run away again. "Come on, Lizzy, it's time to employ your brilliant skills with conversation."

Elizabeth was screaming at herself to stop being frightened and accept his touch. She pushed the memories that kept intruding away; and looked up to him.

He looked worried, not angry, so she smiled. "I am sure that you would do just fine without me, but I am glad that you want me here." He nodded and smiled, clearly relieved. "Let's go."

GEORGIANA SAT at the small table in the breakfast room and watched her brother sending little smiles to Elizabeth. She rarely saw him so relaxed. The William she knew was always concentrating on his work, and although he was ready to talk to her or do things with her at any time, he was also obviously very busy, and she often shied away from approaching for fear of disturbing him. She liked this happier man, and she knew that the change was entirely due to the woman sitting across from her. "Elizabeth, William told me a little more about your writing. I'm sorry but I have not read your books yet."

"Well, they are really written for your age group. I would love to hear your opinion of them; you could tell me where I'm going wrong. I suppose that I am rapidly growing too old to write for my audience." She laughed. "It was easier when I was in school or when my sisters were still at home, I could watch and learn that way, now it's just me and, well, you can see that I am technologically impaired." Elizabeth laughed and noticed that the siblings exchanged a quick conspiratorial smile.

"I would love to read them, I'll order them all as soon as we're finished eating." She glanced at William then back at Elizabeth. "I was wondering, your writing, you can do that anywhere can't you? It doesn't matter where you live, I mean. You have a very flexible and portable career."

"Yes, that is very true." Elizabeth tilted her head, wondering what the point of this was. Darcy had an inkling, but wanted to see where she went with it.

"I was just thinking that someday if you married, your career would be easy to continue, no matter what your husband did. He could have his job and no matter where it took him or the time he spent away, you would still be able to do yours, and even go with him if he had to travel." She looked at William and away again.

Darcy smiled and saw with pleasure Elizabeth's blushing face. "Yes, that is a very astute observation Georgiana. Elizabeth's choice of career would be unaffected by her choice of husband, whoever that fortunate man may be someday."

"I'm glad that you both think so." She said quietly.

Georgiana looked at her worriedly then back at her brother. Darcy was watching Elizabeth. "I hope that I didn't embarrass you. I just thought you might not have noticed . . . that." She looked between them again and stood up. "I think that I'll go order those books now."

Darcy watched her flee the room and then back at Elizabeth. "She meant well."

"I know." Elizabeth looked up at him. "It's okay."

"She really likes you; she mentioned this morning how much she wished she had a sister." Darcy reached out and touched her hand. "I'm afraid that I haven't been much of a playmate for a little sister, besides my work, there is the age gap. She was a bit of a surprise baby for my parents. A wonderful surprise, but a surprise nonetheless. In some ways we both grew up as only children."

"It seems that she is hoping to expand the family." Elizabeth said softly.

Darcy nodded slowly. "It seems that she has determined just how to do that."

"William, I think that it isn't the time to have this conversation, we're not ready for this yet." Elizabeth moved her hand from the table, and onto her lap.

Darcy studied her and leaned back in his chair. "No Elizabeth, this is exactly the time for this conversation. I'm getting so many conflicting signals from you. Sometimes you are encouraging, sometimes frightened, sometimes you seem as if you are dying to leap into my arms and have me carry you off to my bed, and sometimes I feel as if . . . I'm trying to dance with a partner who doesn't want to learn the steps." She looked up at him and he smiled a little. "I guess that we are moving fast in some ways, but I don't know. I can't deny that I am very physically attracted to you and I can't wait to make love to you." He shrugged. "It is the truth, and I will not deny it, I felt that when I first saw you. But, I also know that you, Elizabeth, feel exactly the same thing. Your responses give you away even if your better judgment does not." He leaned forward and touched her face. "But as much as I dearly want to hold you in my arms, I want even more to earn your love, and all that it entails, friendship, respect, partnership, everything. I think that I have made it fairly clear to you, but I'll say it straight out. I hope that someday not long from now, I will be able to ask you an important question. That is my goal; that is why I am . . . courting you. I don't want to look for anyone else ever again." He watched her watching him. "What are your thoughts?"

"I suppose that I keep telling you that we have a lot to talk about, and I should be happy that you want to take this head on. I can see why you are so successful in your work." She closed her eyes then looked back to meet his intense and steady gaze. His face held no expression, and she realized that it was an effort to hold back his emotion. "William . . . like you, it would be a lie to deny that I am very physically attracted to you, and was when I watched you all evening at your cousin's wedding. I kept wondering about the lonely man sitting at the table, and I tried to work up my courage to approach you. I was actually standing behind you on the dance floor because I was so driven to be by your side." Darcy's eyes widened. "You are also correct that I send out conflicting signals. I know that I do, and it frustrates me as it does you. I left a man who treated me terribly and afterwards spent the better part of a year following me around until he found some other girl to occupy his attention. It made me wary, and what I thought was love was just . . . I don't know, but it wasn't love. Your assessment is true, I submitted to him and felt nothing in return, and since he was my first, I didn't know any better. He never made any effort to bring anything to the relationship. I stayed. I thought that I was smarter than that, but I wasn't. I allowed him to control me." She looked up and he took her hand. "I feel things with you, physically, emotionally, that I have never experienced before, and I believe that, no, I *know* that your goals are the same as mine." A warm smile appeared on his face, and Elizabeth's eyes filled with tears. "I'm just so afraid of being hurt again. You won't do that to me, will you?"

Darcy stood and pulled her up into his arms. They embraced and he stroked her back while she cried. "No honey, I won't." He kissed her forehead as she let out the long-repressed emotion. "My parents met and were married within three months, they just knew it from the start, they had found their partner and I guess that I look to them as my example. I am a man who sees what he wants and sees no reason to wait, but if that is what you need to be sure of me, that is what I'll do. I hope that you are my future, Elizabeth."

Her muffled voice rose from his chest. "I hope that you are mine." He breathed a sigh of relief, and kissed her damp cheek when she lifted her head to speak. "Let's see how the next six weeks goes, and if we take the little vacation to Pemberley, well, that will be a good test of how much we can really tolerate each other on a twenty-four hour basis, and then after that we can . . . talk again."

"I can live with that." He kissed her again. "I'll just have to be extraordinarily charming, won't I?"

"You already are." She laughed softly.

"You are the first person who has recognized that!" He laughed. "Well, other than Charles, he was impressed with my skills in attracting your admiration."

"Is he picking up tips?" She wiped her eyes with the back of her hand, then accepted his handkerchief.

"No, Charles is quite experienced . . . now don't read that the wrong way, he's just exceptionally friendly and women love him. But he has told me that he's ready to settle down." He laughed at Elizabeth's narrowed eyes. "You are thinking he is not such a good friend for me?"

"Mmm, actually no, I was thinking he is not such a good friend for Jane." She saw his surprise. "Well, I thought that he must be a good man or he wouldn't be your friend. After all, I'm bound to meet him sometime aren't I? And you will see more of Jane . . ."

"So it is inevitable that my best friend and your sister will be thrown together someday. That does not mean we have to play matchmakers." His fingers ran through her hair and Darcy smiled. "I think we should concentrate on us alone for awhile."

"Hmm, that's true." She smiled and caressed his cheek. "I am so comfortable with you."

His eyes glowed to hear her confession and he immediately encouraged her. "I feel the same way, as if we have known each other for years."

"Would I fit into your world? Would I be accepted?" She watched closely as he considered the question, it was certainly not an unreasonable one.

"I don't see why you wouldn't Lizzy. You are a successful, intelligent, kind and fascinating woman. And so beautiful." Elizabeth looked down and he smiled at her blush. "I can't see any reason why you wouldn't be accepted, in fact, you would be far more liked than I have ever been." His head tilted and his lips twitched, "That is if you decide to accept the position if it is offered someday." He grinned and she laughed.

"Well, I suppose we should continue the interviewing process." Elizabeth gasped with his crushing hug.

"Oh honey, the job is yours for the taking." They kissed and a huge smile appeared as a brilliant thought occurred to him. "But, in the meantime my Lizzy, it seems that we have some work to do. You and I are going to banish your misgivings, and both of our pasts, and together learn how to feel everything." He fixed her with a determined stare and smiled into her wide eyes. "I am sure that both of us will enjoy the education." He laughed to see the growing smile and hugged her, feeling the joy of knowing that she cared for him. "Please keep in mind that I am very rusty, so it may take several attempts to relearn the ropes, but in the end, I think we will both be satisfied." Again he smiled at her. "That is if you want to try."

Elizabeth felt years of regret dropping away from her as she smiled up to his warm eyes. "I do want to try, very much. You seem quite determined."

"I am!" He laughed. "So, will you let me express my feelings for you? We'll just take it a step at a time, and I hope that by the time we go away together, we will be ready for . . . anything."

"I hope so, too." Elizabeth hugged him and rested against the solid wall of his chest, listening to his heart beating in her ear. "I can't wait."

"WELL IT IS certainly good to have you home again, Miss Darcy." Mrs. Reynolds said. She was in Georgiana's bedroom helping to unpack the many suitcases that arrived with her. "Your brother was sick with worry these past few months." She glanced at the girl and returned to her work.

"That's what everyone told me. He always put on a happy face when he visited, and never spoke of anything upsetting when he called. I guess that I thought he was getting on fine without me, and happy to have me out of the house since I was so stupid."

"You know better than that, Miss Darcy!" The older woman scolded.

"No, you're right, I do. I guess that the truth was that I was afraid to come home. William is wonderful, but sometimes he, well, he's hard to talk to and I thought that it was better to not be here and, well, tiptoe around each other."

"I believe in having it out, and being done with it." She shook out a dress and put it on a hanger. "He's been different lately. He has a smile on his face and a spring in his step. That young woman he brought home with him is the reason behind it, I suppose." She shot Georgiana a look and saw her smile. "Do you like Miss Bennet?"

"Very much, if it wasn't for her, I wouldn't be here now." Georgiana sat on her bed and pulled Mrs. Reynolds down beside her. "I think that William is going to propose to her someday." She whispered excitedly.

"Oh, how wonderful! He needs a good woman by his side!" She hugged the girl who was as good as a daughter to her. "Now, what can we do to encourage him?"

"Well, I'm in here, aren't I?" Georgiana smiled. "I said some things about marriage and then saw how much they wanted to talk to each other. I think that when we all go out to Pemberley, I'll look for chances to go off on my own. I bet that by the time we return, they'll be engaged!"

"You can visit with your friends. I'm sure that many families are there for the summer." Mrs. Reynolds nodded her head. "I wish that I could come with you, but I don't think Maggie would be too happy with me butting in on her territory." She smiled thinking of the Pemberley housekeeper. "But you and I have a few weeks before they go, let's work out some ideas for their time here and when they are at Pemberley."

Georgiana giggled. "You mean romantic dinners and things?"

"Well, if you can't help along two lovers at that house on the beach, where can you?" Mrs. Reynolds beamed. "I've been hoping to see that boy happy for years. He does care for her doesn't he?"

"Oh, he looks at her with the biggest puppy dog eyes you've ever seen!" Georgiana whispered. "And she is just as silly." She smiled and held Mrs. Reynolds' hand. "I think that my psychologist would call this healthy therapy."

"Where are they now?"

"William and I bought her a new phone on the way home today; I think that he is teaching her how to use it."

ELIZABETH BIT her lip and concentrated. She swore under her breath, attempted to erase her mistake, groaned and tried again. Finally she pushed another button and gave a cry of triumph as she saw her message disappear.

Across the room, Darcy sat and observed with an amused smile on his face. He heard a soft beep from the phone in his hand. Elizabeth watched him with bright, sparkling eyes and he laughed.

"Well, did it work?" She asked eagerly.

Darcy touched the message and his eyes opened wide. "Elizabeth!" She giggled. With a much-practiced hand he quickly tapped out his reply, and looked up to her with a glint in his eye.

Elizabeth's new phone beeped and once again her lip was caught in her teeth. She deliberately searched and found his message. "William!" She looked up to him in surprise.

He stood and moved over to sit by her side. "Well what sort of a response did you expect after that highly suggestive message?" He took the phone out of her hands and set it down on a table. "Come here." He kissed her once, then again softly. Elizabeth's hand stole up into his hair as his arms encircled her, and slowly their lips caressed. Her eyes closed and she thought of nothing but the feel of their tongues gently warring with each other and was hardly aware of how he pressed her down onto the sofa. Darcy lay on his side, slightly on top of her, and gradually moved his kisses from her mouth to her throat, his free hand leaving a trail of sensation down her bare arm as he dragged his fingertips lightly up and down. Elizabeth's breathing became erratic, and her hand stroked down over his broad back. His kisses found their way back up to her lips and the movement of their hands ceased as they concentrated on the joining of their mouths. Darcy drew away to look down at her half-closed eyes and whispered, "How do you feel?"

"Ohhh, sooo good." She smiled and he laughed, and brushed the hair from her eyes.

"I am sooo happy to hear that. We're going to enjoy this education, I think." Elizabeth laughed and they kissed, then embraced and sighed. The sound of Georgiana's approach was clear; the rest of this lesson would have to wait.

She entered the library to find them leaning together. "Oh, am I interrupting?"

"Yes." "No." Darcy and Elizabeth exchanged glances and he fended off her gently slapping hand. He laughed and looked at his sister. "Of course not, come in."

"Did you figure it out? It's really not that hard." Georgiana picked up the phone that was lying on the table and started running through the features.

"There's a camera and the internet and music, and even games!" She held it up to show them. "William said that he wanted to be able to contact you when you're writing. I can't imagine forcing myself to sit and come up with something brilliant for four hours a day."

"Sometimes it feels like that, but most of the time I just write something that I dreamed about the night before." She smiled at her.

"So you dream about bloody knives and evil plot twists?" Darcy kissed her cheek and hugged her. "You definitely need some new inspiration."

"Hmm, well I want to finish this story so that I can try something new. I was thinking of a romance."

"Ohhhhhhh." Georgiana breathed.

"I'm not sure about this." Darcy raised his brow. "Based on whose experience?"

"Oh, I've been dreaming of this one for ages, it just feels real now." Their gazes met and he smiled.

"I'm very happy to have helped you, then." His smile faded and he squeezed her hand. "I'm afraid that I'll be very busy for the remainder of the week, we'll just have to use your new phone to stay in touch. For me to go away unexpectedly like I did last week, and then today's absence, well, I'll have to do some serious work to make it all up."

"Will we still have our date on Thursday?" She tried to hide her disappointment.

"Definitely, but I'll really have to stick to the work schedule for the rest of the time. I'm sorry; I don't like it any more than you do, but once I'm caught up, I'll try keep regular hours, and my weekends free. I think that I need to start thinking about delegating some responsibilities to others. I don't want my life to be spent in an office or airplane; I have much better uses for my time now."

Elizabeth smiled to see the unmasked feelings in his eyes. "That seems to be an excellent idea, Will." His happiness with her approval was very clear, but with Georgiana present, their response was tempered. She squeezed his hand and changed the subject. "I've never asked; what does the Fitzwilliam side of the family do? Are they involved in your business?"

"Not really. They all own land as well, but my uncle is a retired congressman, and works as a consultant to political candidates now. My aunt is, well, a socialite." Georgiana rolled her eyes, and he laughed. "My cousin John has a budding political career and will probably run for his father's old seat someday, and then Richard is ex-military, a West Point grad, and actually heads a firm that provides security to high-profile people in New York." He watched her digesting the information. "As you have seen our homes, you know that we are all well-off, and Georgiana has a very significant trust fund that will become hers when she reaches twenty-five."

"I just have to make sure that whoever marries me isn't hoping for a piece of it." Georgiana said quietly. "Aunt Arlene impressed that on me over the last few months. She said that money was part of George Wickham's motivation."

"Well he didn't want to marry it, he wanted to extort it." Darcy said bitterly. Elizabeth touched his hand and he relaxed. "Anyway, it's old money, but we were raised to respect it, earn our own, and put it all to good use."

"Such as?"

"We have a foundation that is fully endowed. I hope that someday Georgiana will take it over for the family." He smiled. "It's called the Pemberley - Matlock Foundation, named for our families' ancestral homes. Matlock was the Fitzwilliam family estate in England."

"And what is the purpose of the foundation?"

"Well, my father started it in honor of my cousin Anne when she was a baby." He smiled at Elizabeth's raised brows. "She has epilepsy, and thankfully the proper medication was finally found for her, but for all of the years that her seizures were uncontrolled, she suffered. It was not the physical problems alone; it was the ignorance of the populace. People really have a lot of misconceptions about seizures. Our foundation raises money for awareness and to help out the families who have trouble with affording the medications, research into new treatments, and also to run a summer camp for kids to just get away from it all. There's no reason why they can't have a normal life just like everyone else. My Aunt Catherine never accepted that her daughter could have such a problem and denied it for years. She couldn't believe that anyone would ever marry her either, that's how she came up with her harebrained idea that I would." He shook his head. "Anne and I just learned to ignore her. The man she married, Greg Rothschild, is really great, and I'm very happy for them."

He smiled at Georgiana. "We have an annual fundraising ball every autumn. Anne has taken over the planning duties since my mom died, but our intention is that someday Georgiana will be able to resume mom's place, or at least be Anne's partner in crime." She giggled. "This year I think you should come to the ball."

"Oh William!" Georgiana sat up.

"You'll be seventeen by then; it can be a sort of coming out for you. We will show the world what a beautiful young woman you are, and it will give you a taste for what I hope will be your affair to help run in the years ahead. What do you think?" He tilted his head and watched a myriad of emotions pass over her face. This was an enormous signal to her that he truly felt she had not disgraced the family.

"I think that Aunt Arlene would have to help me get ready for this." She said cautiously.

"I sincerely doubt that you would be able to escape her." He laughed and added, "Or Aunt Catherine's assistance either. Luckily Anne will probably step in to repair whatever those ladies choose for you."

Georgiana groaned. "Oh, I hope so! Maybe Elizabeth will help me, too." She looked at her eagerly.

"Oh, I, well, I . . ." Elizabeth blushed and twisted her hands; this would be a foray into an unknown world. Darcy wrapped his arms around her.

"I could not possibly attend without you by my side. Perhaps you might even coax me to dance." He kissed her soundly.

She relaxed and smiled. "Perhaps we can take some dance lessons together."

"I can dance!"

"All evidence to the contrary. The one time I saw you at your cousin's wedding you resembled a towering redwood, not a swaying pine." She laughed to see his affront.

Georgiana joined in. "Elizabeth is right, you know. You can't dance."

"I prefer ballroom to . . . gyrating." He blushed.

"Ohhh. So I will take the slow dances with you and circulate for the others." She raised her brow and he looked at her sharply. "No? You aren't willing to share?"

Looking between the two, Georgiana realized that her presence was not needed. "Um, I think I'll go practice." She got up and looked back to where they were still embraced and staring intently at each other, and with a giggle headed for her piano.

"Lizzy. I know your opinions about men's behavior, so I won't voice what I'm thinking about sharing you with anyone, which saves you the trouble of becoming angry."

"However Will, you should know that had I been told that I was the object of your strong opinion on this particular subject, my feelings would be of great pleasure, not anger." She lifted her chin and smiled.

"Is that so?" He smiled back. "Well, I will keep that in mind for the future."

"You do that." Their lips met for a passionate exchange. Darcy withdrew and Elizabeth attempted to gather her wits. He did not miss the flare of desire in her eyes.

He stood and took her hands in his. "Would you like to see our garden?"

"Yes, I can't get over the fact that you have a private yard." She followed his tug and stood by his side. "It's just something that you don't think about in this city."

"Well, it helps when your family claims the lot a hundred years earlier." He laughed and they walked outside. Through an open window they could hear Georgiana playing scales. "She is going to be at it for a while, I think. She's limbering her fingers."

"I didn't notice, was there a piano at the Fitzwilliam's home?"

"They rented an upright for her to use while she was staying there. I'm sure that she is pleased to be home with her grand piano again." He smiled and they moved away into the lush garden.

"It's surprisingly quiet here." She looked around at the flower beds and peeked into an archway formed by a trellis. "This will be full of roses in a few weeks, won't it?"

"Yes, yellow, my mom's favorites." They wandered inside and Elizabeth gasped. "Oh, it's almost like a room." She looked up to examine the pergola extending from the roof of a potting shed. Heavy vines of wisteria climbed over it and sheltered them from the warm sunshine. All around them were hedges giving them complete privacy. Comfortable furniture, chairs, a swing, and a chaise were arranged together, waiting for a group of friends to come and enjoy some wine and conversation. "Oh Will, I love this place!" She beamed up at him and he led her to the chaise.

They sat down and he smiled. "It feels so good to share this with you. I wondered if I would ever find someone to show this to."

"Do you come here often?" Elizabeth leaned forward and kissed him.

Darcy scooted so that he was laying back and drew her to lie beside him. "I come out here when I want peace from my responsibilities." His lips touched hers then drifted up to her ear. "I would dream of you."

"Me?" Elizabeth closed her eyes as she relaxed against him and felt his strength, even in the gentle touch of his slowly drifting fingers.

"I imagined finding a woman to share my life with." Their eyes met and then their lips. "Tell me what you are feeling, honey." His mouth traced down her neck, and settled on her shoulder, slowly nibbling, then back up below her ear. "Do you want me to stop?"

"No, please don't stop." She whispered.

He spoke softly. "Do you realize that this is the first time we have managed to be alone and kiss without interruption?"

"Do you want to continue?"

"Yes, but . . . there's no hurry, is there?" He kissed her gently and felt her melt into his arms. *Trust, we are building trust.* Darcy's eyes closed and he rested his cheek in her hair.

"Tell me about Pemberley."

"Which one?" He smiled.

"Whichever one you love the most, I just want to listen to you."

"Really?" Darcy's eyes opened to find Elizabeth smiling. She kissed him then settled back down into his arms.

"Really."

Chapter 6

"William, are you busy?" Georgiana stood in the library doorway Wednesday evening. She knew it was a stupid question. He had been buried in work from the moment he returned from escorting Elizabeth home on Monday. The unexpected travel had left him wading through a mountain of neglected demands. His days at the office were followed by late nights in the library, and his face bore the focused intense expression of a very busy and important man. This was the mood she was accustomed to seeing.

Darcy stared at her for a moment, then set his pen down. "Come in." He watched her perch on the edge of the chair across from his desk. As predicted, neither one knew what to say. Finally he spoke. "What can I do for you?"

"I really like Elizabeth." She looked up from her folded hands and saw that his attention was all hers. "I was wondering; are you going to marry her?"

His eyes widened and a small smile lifted his lips. "You did hint rather baldly that she would fit in well with my life, but I have not proposed, if that is your question. We really have only known each other a very short time, and need to spend a lot more time dating, which we will be doing tomorrow night."

"But . . . will you propose someday?" She pressed and recognized his face losing all expression as he controlled his response, and spoke quickly. "I like. . . I like how you are when she is with you, and I think that you are happier, too."

"I am happy with Elizabeth, very happy, and I do hope for a future with her." He took a deep breath. "I hope that what I am doing will be sufficient to convince her that it is a good idea." He let down his guard and smiled at her. "Thank you for your vote in her favor, I was fairly sure that you would like her."

"I do, William."

He nodded, and decided that a change of subject was necessary. "It is good to hear the sound of the piano in the house again."

"Oh, it is wonderful to play; I'm so out of practice. The neighbors complained in the apartment building if I played for more than an hour or so. I guess that the soundproofing isn't too good, or maybe I'm just spoiled living in a house." She smiled. "I can't wait to go to Pemberley and play the piano there, it's my favorite."

"It was Mom's favorite, too. You definitely inherited your musical talent from her; Dad couldn't play anything if his life depended on it." He smiled and she laughed. "I'm glad that you stopped in Georgie, but I need to get back to work."

"I understand." She stood up then walked over to kiss his cheek. "See how much better you feel when you smile?"

Darcy looked up at her, and noticed that his little sister was no longer a little girl. "I feel better knowing that you want to be here again. That makes me smile. It was very lonely here without you."

Georgiana sat on the edge of his desk. "But I've been gone since school started, were you lonely then?"

"That was different, I missed you, but I knew that you were where you were supposed to be. These months with you in your self-imposed exile were painful because I didn't know how to make things better, and I didn't know if you would ever come and . . . bother me while I'm working again." She laughed and he pushed her off the papers she was wrinkling.

"I'll be back in school again soon, but since I won't be a freshman I can live here again. I think that this year you would have been pretty happy to send me on my way." Her head tilted and he smiled. "I'm looking forward to our date next week. Are you sure that you have time to go out?"

"Well, I am making the time by working now. Elizabeth will be out of town, and besides, you and I really need to work on our communication. Maybe if that had been better, you would have been able to tell me your worries about school and wouldn't have been so susceptible to Wickham's plans."

Georgina looked down at her hands and nodded. "I know; you've taken care of me since mom and dad died, I was wrong to not realize that I can come to you with anything. You're just always so busy."

"I'm never too busy to talk to you." He gave her hand a squeeze and smiled. "Believe me."

"I do." A soft beep came from his phone and he looked at the screen quickly, then up at Georgiana. She laughed and walked out of the room. "I'll see you tomorrow."

"OH THIS IS so exciting!" Elizabeth stared up at the poster of the grinning green ogre. "I know this is ridiculous, but here I am living in this incredible city and I can't remember the last time I attended a performance on Broadway. And a musical! With a guy!" She giggled and squeezed William's hand. "You are doing this willingly, aren't you?"

Darcy was having a hard time holding in his laughter at her enthusiasm. "Of course this is being done willingly. If ever there was a musical that a man could tolerate, it's one with an ogre and a talking donkey!" He watched her as she took in the crowd, her bright eyes examining everyone around her. "So *Shrek* was a good choice? You wouldn't have preferred some Shakespearian experience?"

"I would have loved that, too. I have dragged Jane to the performances in the park for years." Elizabeth looked up at him and grinned. "She hated it, well she claims that she did, but I know she liked looking at the actors in their tights." She giggled. "I would pay her back by going to all of the bridal shows with her. I swear she must have a hundred Barbie dolls dressed up in gowns inspired by those visits. Maybe she should have been a dress designer." Elizabeth mused as the line advanced, then looked up to see William smiling down at her. "What?"

"Nothing." He kissed her cheek.

"You like my nonsense don't you?" She tilted her head.

"Very much, you are extraordinarily entertaining." He laughed at her pursed lips. "And I meant that in a nice way."

"Hmm."

"Darcy!" A man's voice called, and he looked up and scanned the crowd. "Well, this is a nice surprise. It is good to see you again, Elizabeth!" Richard grinned and he bent to kiss her lips. He straightened to encounter his cousin's glare and raised his brow.

"I'm pleased to see you again, Richard. Are you here on a date?" Elizabeth recovered from her surprise and looked between the two as William's grip on her hand tightened.

"No, no, I just escorted a client inside. I usually leave this duty to the staff, but they insisted on me for tonight. What can I say, I'm irreplaceable." He shrugged. "So now I have what, three hours to kill before I have to escort them back?"

"Don't you stay inside the whole time?" She asked.

"I don't divulge my operational methods." He gave her a wink. "So, you managed to get my cousin out of the house for something besides a business meeting. Well done, Elizabeth!" He grinned at Darcy. "You look haggard."

"It has been a busy week; this is our first time together since Monday." He looked at Richard pointedly.

"Ah, and I am cramping your style." He leaned down to Elizabeth and said conspiratorially. "Take pity on him, and ignore his inept skills, he'll get it right sometime."

"I'm not sure what skills you refer to, but his conversation is fascinating, his manners are impeccable, and everything else he has displayed is unsurpassable. Perhaps you are the one who should take lessons from him, although it would be a faint copy at best." She turned to smile at William and was met by his fiery eyes.

Darcy stared at her as he spoke, and did not even glance at Richard. "You heard the lady; your assessment is as poor as your opening lines, now go away."

Richard shot glances between the two. "I would be hurt if I didn't know that I deserved that." He chuckled and slapped Darcy's back. "I'll see you later. Go have fun in the dark." He kissed Elizabeth, who turned so he touched her cheek, and chuckled as he sauntered away.

The line moved forward as the doors opened. Darcy showed the tickets and they headed up to the mezzanine. "Thank you for your wonderful defense. What did I do to deserve that?"

"Well, I was just speaking the truth!" They settled into their seats and she leaned into him. "You really are wonderful, you know."

Darcy flushed and looked down. "Thanks."

"You're welcome."

"I didn't like him kissing you."

"He's done it before, your whole family did. I was very surprised at the time, kissing just isn't something that my family does."

He shook his head and studied the program twisting in his hands. "That was your cheeks, this was your lips. He did it on purpose to see if I cared and to see what you would do."

"Well I wanted to slap him, but I thought that would draw too much attention. I was just ready for it the second time. You clearly did care." Elizabeth snuck her hand into his. "I think that I would have strangled any woman who I saw do that to you."

"*That* definitely would have attracted some attention." He smiled and peeked back over to her. "Thanks." The house lights came down and the audience cheered with the beginning of the show. Darcy took the opportunity to pull her close for a kiss. He could just make out her smile in the dark. "Maybe after dinner we can continue to improve your opinion of my skills."

"Oh there, you see, you are brilliant." She kissed him again and turned to watch the stage. Darcy looked down at her hand in his and relaxed, he was exactly where he wanted to be.

"WELL, IT LOOKS good so far."

"Give it to me straight Charlotte, it's crap." Elizabeth sighed and flipped through the colorful manuscript. "It's a wonder that Lucas Lit is willing to keep me on if I make so many errors."

"It's not as bad as it looks." Charlotte laughed. "You've been through this six times before, you know the drill."

"Yes, and I thought that I knew enough to be able to avoid some of your comments . . . Oh good heavens, I used a character name from my last book in this one!" Elizabeth sighed again. "You have a good eye."

"That's what I'm paid to have." Charlotte watched her staring blankly at the moving pages. "Okay, spill, what's the problem?"

"Nothing."

Charlotte folded her arms and looked at her sternly. "Elizabeth, you are one of our most successful authors. If something is on your mind, I need to know."

"You are not helping me with this, Charlotte." Elizabeth bit her lip. "Look, I know that Lucas is small, and that a few books in your stable selling in the top 10,000 on Amazon is, well, keeping you afloat . . ."

"What is it?" She said urgently.

"I'm tired." Elizabeth looked up to meet Charlotte's concerned expression. "I've been cranking out manuscripts for nearly eight years, since I was in high school. That wasn't so bad, but when I got published . . . I've been pushing so hard, and I'm burned out."

"You are very popular with your following, and part of that is because they can depend on something fresh regularly."

"But two a year, it's too much. I . . . I realize why I was able to do it now."

"Collins." Charlotte said perceptively. "You worked on the books so hard in school to shield yourself from him when you were together, and then to recover from it when he was gone. It was your self-styled and unconscious therapy. I haven't missed the fact that either someone in each book is killed who resembles him, or that he's the murderer." She looked over Elizabeth's deeply blushing face and nearly bleeding lip. "You've met someone."

"Maybe." She said evasively.

"And you think that if you are happy with him you won't need to bury yourself in the fantasy world of your imagination?"

"You are too smart for your own good, Charlotte." Elizabeth looked up and reached for the box of tissues on her desk. "It's just . . . it's something that I have been thinking about while trying to write this last one. It's feeling forced, not flowing like it used to, and I'm really ready to try something else."

"I'm really sorry to hear that, Lizzy." She spoke quietly. "You do have a contract with us . . ."

"It only runs to the publication of this coming book. I read it all through last night. I would not be violating any promise that I made. I kind of had this in mind when I signed it last year, that's why there is no mention of promotion in it. But now, I'm surer than ever that my gut is right." Charlotte's mouth dropped open and Elizabeth leaned forward. "Maybe I just need some time off."

"You are only twenty-two, what would you do with the rest of your life if you didn't have your writing career? Your royalties now are significant, but without fresh stories, your popularity would gradually wane and you would be replaced by some new author. You can't tell me that you are hoping to marry some rich guy and never work again, even if you did he could roll over one day and say that he's tired of you and demand a divorce."

"Charlotte, please . . . I'm not thinking of that. Maybe a different genre, I'm just . . ."

"Okay, enough, I've pushed enough." Charlotte sighed and smiled. "I'm having a hard time being the friend when it's my family's company that would be hurt . . . no I'm sorry, I'm loading you with more guilt. I hope that this guy is worth it."

Elizabeth shook her head, "It's not about a guy, it's about me. I'm ready for a change; I just don't know what it is." She laughed. "Do you have any openings for evil editors? Maybe I am qualified to torture authors now?"

Charlotte lifted her cup of coffee in a toast. "Great payback, Lizzy. Come on, let me buy you lunch."

"No, I . . . I think that I need to walk." She stood up and placed the bloody manuscript in her bag. "I'll talk to you soon." She gave her friend a hug. "Take care."

"You too." Charlotte watched her go; she knew that expression, Elizabeth was going to be doing some serious thinking.

DARCY BLEW OUT the breath he had been holding when his trainer gave him a poke. "Sorry, I was lost in thought."

"You're going to lose those dumbbells on your feet if you don't concentrate on what you're doing." He threw him a towel. "I think that you've had enough of me. Why don't you finish off on the bike and call it a day. Maybe you can pedal off whatever is eating you." The young man smiled and walked off to meet another client in the exclusive health club. Darcy wiped his face and hands then walked over to climb on the bike. He stared blankly at the TV monitor then out of the window at the scene of people hurrying down the crowded sidewalks. He felt rudderless. Elizabeth had left for the American Librarian Association convention in Chicago a few days earlier. Between his work and her commitments for this new book, their time together had been limited, and neither one was happy about it.

"This is so hard." He spoke and a woman at the next bike looked over and smiled invitingly at him.

"It's not so bad, it's a good workout."

"Oh, I . . . I was talking to myself." He looked back down and closed his eyes, pedaling faster as if he could put distance between himself and the disappointed woman. He heard her bike quiet and noticed that she had left, and slowed back down. *She didn't want to go. That was clear; you have to take heart from that.* He murmured to his reflection in the plate glass window. *And you definitely didn't want her to go. But how can I tell her to stop doing . . . what she must enjoy?* He looked down and watched the sweat dripping off of his forehead. *You can't and you know it, but that's just it, I don't think she does enjoy it anymore. I keep feeling like she is hoping I'll say something. What can I say? I don't want her to think that I'm demanding that she give up her career for me. Is that what I want? Is it selfish to want her to be with me all of the time?*

Darcy looked at the reflection again. *Yes, it is, but damn it, that's what I want!* A man had taken over the empty bike and looked over at Darcy and received a scowl. He looked away, and Darcy pedaled on. *Arrogant, you are being arrogant, and she hates that. Think! What does she want?* A cheer went up in the background and he saw a group of women surrounding another holding a newborn. His pedaling slowed. *Is motherhood what she wants? We haven't even talked about our feelings for children; we should cover that topic shouldn't we?* That brought to mind Georgiana's pronouncement of Elizabeth's writing career being conducive to his. *Well, it would be if she . . . no Darcy, you can not dictate her career, why don't you concentrate on yours? How can you make your life more manageable?*

He kept pedaling and worked out in his mind a vast redistribution of responsibility. He had felt a need to take complete control of everything when he replaced his father because he wanted to prove to everyone that he was competent. Now he was rapidly burning out, and had only snippets of precious time with Elizabeth. "When she is here, that is." He said softly. Darcy decided that when he returned to the office he would call in all of his managers and pull out the organizational charts that the company followed under his father. His memory of dinner with his parents every night was very strong. *Maybe if I show Elizabeth what I am doing to change for her . . . she might ask me how I can help her, too.* The realization finally hit him. *She is just as burned out as I am.* His pedaling slowed. *What can I do to help her?*

"Excuse me, are you Fitzwilliam Darcy?"

Darcy was pulled out of his thoughts to stare at the small thin man at the bike by his side. *Who the hell are you?* Nobody called him Fitzwilliam, as only family knew that name. "I am William Darcy."

He smiled widely. "I thought so; you were pointed out to me. I am Bill Collins."

He offered a sweaty hand and Darcy stared at it and back up at him. *Bill Collins, this couldn't possibly be . . .* Looking him over with a critical eye, Darcy spoke. "You say that I was pointed out to you?"

"Yes! I have taken an apartment in the same building as your aunt, Catherine de Bourgh, she speaks of you often. She is on the condo board and I heard that if her opinion was won it would be smooth sailing to be allowed in." He smiled with satisfaction. "She was very impressed with my verbal skills, I am quite adept with my flattery of the ladies. It always gets me what I want. I am sure that you know what I mean." He smiled at him knowingly. "Yes, it is quite effective; it has won me many ladies' favor over the years."

Darcy stared at him. *This is the man that abused Elizabeth? How? How did my fiery Elizabeth ever consider this man? Or was it the experience of surviving him that made her into the obstinate, fascinating woman she is today?* He had to know. "Where did you learn these skills? Surely you were not born with them."

Collins preened with the attention of the powerful man. "Ah, well I admit to having a natural charm. However there was a girl I met in college, she was only sixteen and well, extraordinarily beautiful. She was nervous and I . . . offered my assistance, as an older student. She was grateful for it, very grateful." He leered. "She expressed it quite often."

Darcy could not bear to imagine the years that Elizabeth spent with this man, let alone imagining him touching her, but forced himself to continue. "How did you manage to keep her happy once she was not so nervous?"

"Oh well, by that time she thought that she loved me, and I presented enough of a sad case that she wanted to fix me." Collins laughed, obviously pleased with his conquest.

Somehow Darcy managed to hide his disgust and growing rage, obviously this bastard was dying to tell his story, and as much as he hated hearing it, Darcy had to know what happened. "Did she ever express a desire to meet someone else?"

"I never gave her the opportunity; I changed my major and took all of the same classes so we were always together. We worked at the student union, and she stayed at my apartment. We were never apart. I controlled everything." He smiled with satisfaction. "It was perfect."

"And yet you didn't stay together?" Darcy's hands gripped the bike handles hard.

Collins scowled. "No, she graduated and went home. That ended it."

Thank God. Darcy glanced around the crowded gym. There was no visible sign, but his anger was even greater than what he felt for Wickham. Georgiana's experience had been horrific, but it lasted only days, Elizabeth suffered for years, and now his relationship with her was affected by it at every turn. *I want to kill him! What can I do? How can I pay him back for what he has done to her?* Throwing him through the window would unfortunately be noticed. He considered beating him in the locker room where there were no security cameras . . . *No, there are other ways to get to him. Maybe Richard knew somebody . . . No, I am not violent man, no matter how angry I am. There must be something I can do . . . But first I must know more.* He realized that the way to this man's secrets was flattery, and assumed a tone of calm indifference. "So you have done well for yourself if you have taken an apartment in my aunt's building."

"I inherited five million dollars; my father hit the lottery just before he died." Collins preened. "I am moving in the highest society now, and am happy to be your equal. I hope that you will introduce me around to your friends."

Darcy's calm snapped and he stood up and snarled, bending to press his face close to Collins. "Do not dare to compare yourself with me! You use flattery to influence old women and control to abuse young girls. Those are the behaviors of a weak man, a poor man, and one with no conscience. You want my introduction? I'll give it to you." He straightened and spoke in his loudest voice. "Ladies and Gentleman, may I have your attention, please?" All eyes turned his way, and the sounds of the machines died away. Darcy gestured to Collins. "This man, Bill Collins, has asked me for an introduction. He is in possession of five million dollars and has recently used his considerable skills in manipulation to convince my aunt to approve his admittance into her building. He honed his skills by taking the innocence of a sixteen-year-old girl and controlling her every movement for four years. This man wishes for admittance into your society, I leave it to you to decide if you want him in your midst. I will gladly introduce his name to everyone I know." Darcy stared down at the gaping red-faced man. "I know that he will never be welcomed by my family." Lowering his voice he said softly, "I will speak to my aunt about you." Darcy picked up his towel and strode away, the eyes of the gym followed him then centered on Collins, all with expressions of disgust. He cringed under the examination, but was afraid to run to the locker room and encounter Darcy again. He sat on the bike and began pedaling, and watched the reflection of eyes observing him as people resumed their workouts.

Darcy walked into the locker room, *Five million dollars is nothing in New York, not when a one-bedroom apartment could run over a million. I won't have to ruin you, you'll do that on your own soon enough, but I guarantee I'll be watching you do it.*

Several people came up to him and he quietly confirmed the worthlessness of the man. Darcy's word was gold; Collins' name would be passed amongst the gossips before the day was out. He paused at his locker and took out the picture of Elizabeth he kept in his wallet. *Innocent, unaware, idealistic Elizabeth caught in the hands of a manipulator learning his craft. Now I understand. He is just another form of Wickham.* Darcy smiled grimly and headed for the showers. When he left the club, he walked past the window with the line of bikes and stopped to stare directly into Collins' eyes. The man seemed to grow smaller as he flinched and ran away. "I want you here with me all of the time Lizzy, but not like that. I am not like that."

"HEY! DREAM GIRL!" Jane leaned outside of her door.

Elizabeth smiled and put her hands above her head like a ballerina and performed a little twirl. "How's that?"

"Lovely." Jane laughed. "Come on inside, we haven't talked in ages." She stood back as Elizabeth entered her apartment, tossed her purse on a table, and flopped onto the couch. "Do you want anything to drink?"

"Mmm. No, we had the most delicious wine; I don't want to lose the flavor of it." She smiled and closed her eyes.

"I'm betting that it's the taste of someone's kisses that you don't want to lose." She sat cross-legged opposite Elizabeth and laughed to see her blush. Jane reached out and took her hand. "So, have you decided, will you go to Pemberley with him?"

Elizabeth sat up. "Yes. I feel so good when I'm with him, and we just seem so . . . well-matched."

"You sound like that romance novel you're trying to write." Jane laughed at her grimace. "I know; you'll show me when you're ready. But it's been over a month since he asked you to go."

"Five weeks, and we've known each other nearly seven." Elizabeth corrected. "I'm sorry that I haven't been much of a sister to you lately. Between William and the book promotion, I just haven't had time. I've missed you."

"Save that for your neglected father, I know that you haven't missed me one little bit."

"No, I haven't." Elizabeth giggled. "Oh Jane, he's . . . he's so caring and serious, and has a wicked sense of humor. He loves to argue with me. Did I tell you how we fought over equal pay for equal work between men and women? There he was, astonished that I would take a position that the women executives in his company should be paid every bit as much as the men. He was staunchly declaring that it was the man who supports the family and should therefore have the higher income, and I brought up the example of all of the single mothers and what about single unmarried women, and what did marriage have to do with it in the first place . . . oh, and just as I was about to storm away from him I caught that little glimmer in his eye. He was baiting me!" She said in an incredulous voice, as if it had happened only that night instead of weeks ago. "He said that he just loves to see me defending my stance and purposely made ridiculous declarations just . . . for the pleasure of my reaction!"

"What was your revenge?" Jane wrapped her arms around her knees and smiled.

"I denied him any affection until he begged me for forgiveness." She said with satisfaction.

"Mmm, I can just imagine how much you both enjoyed that making-up session." Jane smiled. "How did you two even get on that subject in the first place? I like much less weighty conversations with my dates."

"Yes, I know, Jane. All is sunny in your world." Jane kicked her. "We were discussing our thoughts on children." She looked down. "We haven't . . . yet."

"No sex yet?" Jane stared at her. "Oh Lizzy, this poor man must be blue! If you are having such vigorous arguments, plus the way you wander in here every time you see him, I have no doubt that you are exploring nearly every other aspect of the experience. Is he pressuring you?"

"No. I know that he wants to, he told me outright over a month ago, and it's pretty clear at other times like when he has to hide behind furniture and well, you saw him when mom had dinner for us, he had to go and stand by the window for a little while . . ."

"He was hiding a hard-on?" Jane grinned.

"Oh he really is so patient, but he promised that he wouldn't press me, and he is a man of his word." She bit her lip. "It's one of the things that has convinced me of my feelings."

"And what are they, Lizzy?"

"I think that I love him." She whispered. "I haven't said it to him yet, but when we go away, and the right opportunity comes along, I will." She looked up at Jane. "Is it too soon?"

"No. You have spent so much time together, how you managed to do it with his workload and both of your travel is amazing. I've really enjoyed seeing you two. I've gotten to know him better, and I think that he is an exceptional man, and not because he's rich, but because of who he is. He's far too intense for me. But your description of his best friend is intriguing, much more my type!" Elizabeth laughed. "I guess that what I'm trying to say is that he is very much in love with you, and will do anything to make you feel safe and comfortable with him. He fell for you very fast, and is just waiting for you to let yourself love him. That is my favorite thing about him; he is willing to wait forever for you if you asked him. I can't think of any man I know who would do that."

"We both got tested for STDs, and I started taking birth control." Elizabeth said softly.

"I wasn't talking about waiting for sex, Lizzy."

"I know." She played with the tassel on the throw pillow she was clutching. "He wants all of me."

"So are you ready for that commitment?"

Elizabeth was saved from answering by the ringing of her phone. She grabbed her purse and answered. "Hi Will!"

"Hi honey, where are you? I tried your apartment, did you go out again?"

"I never actually made it inside, Jane kidnapped me." She smiled and stood up. "Let me get over there and change, then I'll call you back, okay?"

"Hurry." He whispered.

"Oh, like you'll waste away in fifteen minutes." She blushed and looked away from Jane's rolling eyes. Elizabeth grabbed her things, gave Jane a wave and walked back out into the hallway.

"Let me know what you decide, Lizzy." Jane called after her as she shut the door.

"Decide? What are you doing?" Darcy asked.

"It's none of your business." She juggled her phone and purse to dig out her keys. "Okay, I'm inside, just give me a few minutes and I'll call."

"Okay. I miss you already."

"You are silly." She grinned and ended the call, then raced into the bedroom to tear off her things.

Darcy sighed and got up from his position lying on his bed and looked out the window, watching some boats traveling down the Hudson. It was getting harder and harder to say goodbye and watch Elizabeth disappear up the steps after they spent their evening together. It didn't matter what they did, attending the theater or going to dinner, watching a movie or taking the glorious walks in the park, whatever it was, he felt so happy when she was by his side, and almost desperately alone when she was gone. "Maybe when I know that she wants to be with me forever, I won't feel so scared that each goodbye will be the last." He leaned against the window and looked out at the buildings across the river. Darcy thought of the day two weeks earlier, when Georgiana had been miserable with a cold. She must have called Elizabeth, and she had come to comfort her. He had arrived home to see Elizabeth standing in the hallway, dripping wet after being splashed by a bus as she walked the ten blocks to the house. They had laughed over her sorry appearance, and he gladly aided her in toweling off her hair, and even offered to lend her some clothes, which she declined in favor of Georgiana's. Oh, how he wished she had worn his instead!

The phone rang and he dove onto the bed. "Lizzy?"

"Hi! See that wasn't too long, was it?"

"It was interminable." He growled.

"What am I going to do with you?"

"Do you really want me to answer that?"

"Hmm, probably not." She giggled. "Why did you call?"

"Can't I miss you and need to hear your voice?" He whined. "Or are you tired of me? Maybe I should just go on a long business trip and see if you miss me then."

"Or you could just turn off your phone." She suggested, "Or better yet, I'll return to turning off mine. You're the only one who calls me anyway. That sounds like a fine plan. Well, good night, Will." Elizabeth said cheerily.

"Elizabeth Regina Bennet!"

"Yes, Fitzwilliam Andrew Darcy?" She said coyly.

"Don't you dare hang up on me!"

"I'm not afraid of you."

There was a long pause and Darcy's voice was very quiet. "You don't know how good it makes me feel to hear you say that."

"You don't know how good it feels to be able . . . I miss you too, Will." Elizabeth took a shaky breath and wiped her eyes. "Did you speak to Charles?"

Darcy blinked and swallowed hard. "Yes, go ahead and tell Jane we're on for Thursday. Georgiana is so glad that her not coming is allowing us to be matchmakers, and before you say anything, yes I remember saying that this is precisely what we would not do." He chuckled.

She recovered her composure and laughed. "All right, I won't point that out; anyway, I can't picture you as a yenta. But then again I can't picture Georgiana enjoying a baseball game either, so I guess that asking her was a mistake to begin with. I heard that the weather this week will be ideal, so it should be great. Good seats? Outside? Not some rich guy box?"

"Whatever you want, it's yours, Lizzy." He said softly.

Elizabeth was quiet for a few moments, realizing that a lot more than baseball was being discussed. "Thank you." She murmured.

"You're welcome, honey. I guess that I should let you get to sleep." Darcy desperately wished that he could be there saying those words in person.

"You have the early day; I just have to wander into my living room." Elizabeth wished that she was there to wake him up.

"Well, I . . . I'll call you when I find out the details . . . and about picking you up."

"Okay. Good night."

"Good night." He stayed on the line and listened, hearing her sigh of regret, and smiled as she hung up first. "I love you, Elizabeth."

"DO YOU THINK either of them will ever blink?" Elizabeth whispered into William's ear. They were standing inside of Yankee Stadium, and had just introduced Jane to Charles.

"I've never seen anything like it." Darcy gave Charles a shove. "Hey! Wake up!"

Charles came back to life and turned beet red, all the way up to the roots of his hair. "Damn it, Darcy!" He glared at him and recognized that Jane was just as embarrassed. "Um, I'm . . . I'm happy to meet you, Jane." He held out his hand and she reached to shake it, but Charles lifted it to his lips. Jane laughed nervously.

"What was that?" Darcy grinned and laughed.

Elizabeth took Jane's arm and peered into her eyes. "I think that we need to visit the ladies' room. We'll be right back." She smiled at William and cast a quizzical look at Charles. His eyes followed them as they disappeared.

"Breathe Charles."

"She is an angel!" He sighed, then looked up at Darcy. "You were a big help, laughing at me!"

"When have you ever needed help with a girl?" Darcy leaned against a wall and crossed his arms. "So cupid has struck? I don't feel so bad now about Elizabeth."

"When did you feel bad about her?" Charles took a position by his side and regained his senses. "You've been in love with her since that first night." He jumped and faced him. "Hey, so you have no business telling me anything!"

"Relax; I'm just enjoying the show." Darcy saw some women looking their way, and instantly he scowled. One of them whispered something to the other and they walked away, obviously disappointed. He looked back at Charles, who was staring intently at the exit to the ladies' room. "I felt bad because I was afraid that we were, well I was, rushing it. But now, it just feels right."

"I'm numb." Charles murmured. Darcy laughed. "Distract me; tell me something unrelated to Jane."

"I hear that Collins is moving out of my aunt's building." Darcy said with satisfaction. "That didn't take long."

"What happened? I guess that your aunt had something to do with it."

"I gave her a call, and told her about her new neighbor's confessions. She looked into his application for the apartment more carefully; apparently he had been rather creative with his references. She got Richard to do a background check on him through his contacts with the police, and the building's management did some more research into his credit. He was in bankruptcy when he got the trust fund and had been evicted from his last two apartments for non-payment. They kicked him out for lying on the application and he agreed to leave immediately if he could get the security deposit back." Darcy nodded with satisfaction. "It seems that he also went to Atlantic City to try and add to his fortune, luckily his skill with cards is poorer than his skills with flattery."

"He lost all of it? What was it, three weeks ago that you saw him?" Charles laughed. "What a jerk!"

Darcy just smiled. "I don't know if it's all gone, but I would like to see him find a job with the degree in English that he got through Elizabeth's work. Somehow I have a feeling he's going to wind up flipping burgers. I'll be watching him."

"Will you tell her about it?" Charles watched his friend and grinned.

He shrugged. "Maybe someday, we have more important things to discuss." He smiled at Charles and seeing his friend straighten, noticed the sisters' return.

"Ready?" He offered his hand to Elizabeth and she grinned up at him.

"Absolutely! So where are we sitting?"

Darcy led the way and they were soon in their places behind home plate. Elizabeth looked around at the incredible seats and laughed. "Nope, no rich guy box in the sky, just rich guy seats outside." She smiled and sat beside him. "You do realize that we'll be on television all night?" Darcy's eyes widened. "You didn't think of that, did you?" She giggled as he groaned.

"How am I supposed to take advantage of you? Your father is probably watching us!" He smiled and sighed. "Well, I'll hold your hand and steal a kiss whenever the batter is finished."

"I think that is a brilliant plan." She glanced over to where Charles and Jane were sitting, he was excitedly talking and she was patiently listening. "She is dumbstruck over him."

"He is too."

"He is talking a mile a minute!" Elizabeth pointed out.

Darcy leaned around to look, then moved back to her. "He does that when he's nervous." Studying her face he moved in to kiss her. "I can't tell you how much I've missed you this week. Sometimes I think that our calls and messages just make it worse. It is so much work to be allowed to play. I have had little bits of time with you but . . . this is what I want." He looked down at their entwined fingers. "I can't wait for Saturday."

Elizabeth blushed and kissed him. "I've never been out to the Hamptons, how long does it take?"

"With traffic, it could be three hours. Do you want to fly?" Darcy smiled at her widening eyes.

"Fly?"

"Yes, I have a helicopter at my disposal."

"Oh."

"I'm overwhelming you, aren't I? I don't mean to, it's just my life." He touched her lip. "You're going to draw blood if you keep that up." Elizabeth immediately stopped biting and sent him a glare. "I thought it would be nice not to waste time in a car, but if that is what you prefer, we'll do it."

"No, as you said, this is your life, and I want to see exactly what that entails, so . . ." She drew a breath. "Let's fly!"

"Great! I'll have Patricia make the arrangements and let you know the details tomorrow." He glanced at Charles and Jane. "Do you think that your sister would want to come? Charles is a regular guest there."

"Oh, I'm sure that she would, but the weekend, well Saturdays are kind of busy for her, especially in the summer months. It's actually pretty amazing that she agreed to this evening out. She doesn't date much during wedding season, or at all, actually. She trusted my assessment of how handsome Charles was."

"Do you think he's handsome?" Darcy sat up and looked at his friend with a critical eye then back at her.

She saw where he had looked and smiled. "You're jealous!"

"I am not, I just . . . you said he was handsome." He looked down and pursed his lips.

"He is." She tilted her head and watched him stroking her hand, and took pity on him. "Will, whose hand am I holding?"

"Mine." He smiled. "Ignore me."

"That is impossible." Elizabeth laughed.

TOM KNOCKED on Elizabeth's apartment door. He could hear frenzied activity within, but nobody answered. After several more attempts, he decided to risk his daughter's ire, and used his key to let himself in, standing in awe of the incredible mess that was before him. The room was littered with clothes, shopping bags, and several open suitcases.

Elizabeth flew past. "Hi Dad."

He shifted an outfit laid over the sofa and took a seat. "Did your closet explode or did you just go on a spending spree?"

She stopped and looked around. "A little of both, I think."

"So you are really going away with him?"

Glancing at him, she picked up two swimsuits, and held them for inspection. "Yes Dad, I am. Please do not try to talk me out of it."

"I wouldn't think of it, Lizzy. I am not the one to advise you on love. After all, the only reason your mother and I are not long-divorced is because she would get half of this building in the settlement. I'm not selling my family's legacy to appease her greed." He spoke bitterly and saw Elizabeth closing her eyes. "I'm sorry, you've heard this before. I should stop repeating myself."

"I would appreciate it." She said wearily. "What exactly are you worried about?"

He sat forward. "You barely know him. I rushed into marriage; I don't want you to do the same."

Her brow lifted. "I've known him nearly two months and besides, you got mom pregnant and Grandpa Gardiner threatened to shoot you if you didn't get married."

Falling back against the sofa he eyed her. "You know, this speech is far more effective when I am the only one talking."

Elizabeth shrugged. "I know the details far too well, and I'm still not going to take sides." She set down the dress she was folding. "Now I know that you do love her, so let's just get to the point. Do you like William? Has he done anything that made you think he's not sincere?"

"I have hardly seen him. He darts in here or you go running out to him." Tom was not happy with the absence of his favorite daughter from his life.

"Well I *have* seen him, and I do not doubt him at all." She looked at him pointedly.

His gaze matched hers, and spoke seriously. "Are you sure, Lizzy? Everything will change between you after this trip. You have been down this road before."

"So I should never trust another man?" She stopped and her hands dropped to her hips. "Look, I almost ruined everything by allowing my past experience to cloud this one. William is NOT the same man as Bill Collins."

"All right." He laced his fingers and watched her return to her packing. "I looked him up online." Elizabeth rolled her eyes. "Do you know how wealthy he is?"

"Yes, and I don't care."

"He is going to change you, Lizzy." He looked worried.

"He already has." She kissed his cheek and closed one suitcase.

"Do you love him?"

Elizabeth stopped and said softly, "The first man to hear that declaration will not be you."

Tom smiled, then said carefully, "And have you heard that declaration yet from him?" Her silence satisfied him. Neither one was throwing those three words around carelessly. He stood and placed his hands on her shoulders. "Have a wonderful time."

She looked at him in surprise. "Really?"

Nodding, he kissed her forehead, and embraced her. "I've never seen you so happy. Your grandmother always said to look at your past as it gives you pleasure, do you remember that?" She nodded. "Well, I think that you would be better served by looking at your future, it is far brighter."

"Thank you, Dad."

Chapter 7

"**T**here it is!!" Georgiana called. She grabbed Elizabeth's arm and pulled her over to look out of the window. Below was a beautiful home, perched near the ocean. A sweeping green lawn led to the private walkway down to the beach.

The helicopter set down and Darcy helped Elizabeth to remove the seatbelt while watching her expression. She was valiantly trying to appear nonplussed but was failing spectacularly. He could not help but be delighted with the wonder in her eyes. The door was opened and they stepped out, Elizabeth bending far lower than necessary, and he gripped her hand tightly. "Welcome to Pemberley." He smiled and kissed her hand. He nodded to the waiting man who was there to collect the luggage and they walked on towards the house. "What do you think?"

"I don't know what to think." She looked up at him. "This is like some featured house on those real estate shows that play on Sunday mornings, but without the bad music." Elizabeth smiled and he shook his head and laughed. "I would be lying if I said I was unimpressed with this, but without you here, it's just a big house with a great view." Darcy beamed. "It's just lovely. When was it built?"

"The original house was built in 1920, but the structure was completely renovated a few years ago to reinforce it for any weather conditions. All of the interior rooms were redone as well, the redecoration was the last thing that was completed before my parents died, but they never saw it." He felt her hand squeeze his and he smiled. "After their funerals, this is where I stayed for a few months while our house in town was made habitable again. Georgiana stayed with our aunt and uncle because she was in school. I was just beginning to learn the ropes of the company then, but I couldn't stand being in a hotel room. I needed to feel my dad around me, so I came here." He looked at her shyly. "Pretty silly, don't you think, as if seeing his things could make it easier?"

"Did it help?"

He stopped and watched as Georgiana went inside. Turning to survey the view, he looked out over the water. "No, I was utterly overwhelmed. I dealt with it poorly, and didn't appreciate that so many people would be courting my attention. For a young man who had just suffered a spectacular breakup, the loss of his parents, and the burdens of the business, and was suddenly being inundated by people wanting things, particularly money, I . . . I fell into the trap of thinking that they wanted me. Well, I attempted to deal with my losses by accepting their attention. I partied and drank, and was unwise with my choices."

"Your choices in women." She said softly.

"Yes." He took her into his arms and rested his head on hers. "Young and stupid, isn't that the phrase you used for yourself and Georgiana? Do you think it can be applied to me as well?"

"I can't change my past any more than you can change yours, Will. But we both have learned from it, and we have made a fresh beginning haven't we?" She looked up to see him smile.

"I guess that I was asking you for forgiveness, and it wasn't necessary." Darcy kissed her. "Thank you."

"I . . . I care very much for you, Will." Elizabeth whispered. His embrace tightened, it was the closest she had come to speaking her feelings to him.

"I care deeply for you, Lizzy." He felt her arms squeeze him and looked back down to kiss her. "Come on; let's see which room you want." She looked at him in surprise. "Unless . . . I didn't want to push you, I know that we discussed our . . . educating each other, and I would love it if you wanted to stay with me."

She could not possibly miss his hopeful tone. "I really want to." Darcy's face lit up with a brilliant smile, and she laughed. "I guess that was a big decision to make."

"I'm happy that it was in my favor." He kissed her and with lightness in his step, pulled her forward to the house.

It was too early to eat, and not quite warm enough yet to swim, so Darcy gave her a tour. Elizabeth laughed to see another library, and loved the sunroom. They wandered into the kitchen and Darcy introduced her to the chef, who was the same man he employed in town, and she met Miss Maggie, the ancient housekeeper who had been there since his father was a young man, and Maria, the home's real housekeeper. When they left the kitchen and found their way outside to a terrace, he looked at her askance. "What's bothering you?"

"Oh, nothing." She bit her lip and rested her hands on the railing.

"Lizzy, you haven't said a thing since we left the kitchen." He leaned his elbows on the railing and looked back at her.

"I guess that I . . . I was hoping to cook for you, I haven't had the opportunity since the evening at the Fitzwilliam's apartment." She smiled and shrugged. "Sort of a little way to thank you for your hospitality."

"Just agreeing to be here is all the thanks I needed." He smiled and pushed back the hair that was blowing around her face. "Perhaps we can give Jerry a few nights off. I want you to enjoy yourself here. You are the guest of honor, after all."

"I just thought it would be fun to go shopping and gather the ingredients together, and well, hang out in the kitchen, and talk and . . ."

"Feed each other?" He said softly and raised his brows. "I've never done any of those things before."

"We'd have to get something for Georgiana to do if that is the case . . . I think that it could get out of hand pretty quickly." She met his expression with raised brows of her own.

"I think that we'll have to return here after she is back in school, don't you agree?" Darcy's hands landed on her shoulders and drawing her forward, felt her tremble. His eyes grew dark and he bent to claim her lips. Their breathing soon became labored as his mouth followed the familiar path to her throat. "When will this day be over?" He moaned and held her to him, kissing below her ear, and heard the reward of her gasp. "Tell me what you are feeling." He said hoarsely.

"I can't breathe." She gasped again. His lips found hers and caressed them slowly as she melted into him to meet his motion, stroke for stroke. Darcy's hands traveled over her, and they were lost in the sensation.

The insistent ringing of a bell filtered through to Elizabeth and she withdrew a little. Darcy was not so easily stopped, and continued searching for her mouth. She took his face in her hands and caressed his cheeks. Finally he moved away to stare at her with unmasked desire. The bell rang again and he blinked and focused. Her expression completely matched his. Taking a slow deep breath, he touched her swollen lips. "I think that lunch is ready."

"Oh, good." She whispered, but continued to run her hands over his broad shoulders.

"I suppose that we should go." He looked down at the obvious bulge in his shorts then back up to her. Elizabeth lowered a hand to fondle him. Darcy's eyes closed, and he leaned his head onto hers.

"Hey! Let's eat!" Georgiana called. "You guys have all day to hug!" She returned to the house as Darcy's head flew up, and he stared into Elizabeth's wide eyes.

She started to laugh, and covered her mouth while he tried to regain control. "It's lucky that your back was to her." Elizabeth giggled.

"Go ahead Lizzy, laugh, I'm in pain." He took some deep breaths and stood awkwardly. "Why don't you head inside; I'll join you in a minute."

"Are you sure?" Elizabeth looked at him worriedly. "Is there anything I can do?"

"YES! There IS something you can do, but not here and now." He laughed in frustration. "I'm sorry; please go ahead, I'll be along." He gritted his teeth.

"I'm sorry, if it makes you feel any better, I'm having trouble standing upright." She touched his cheek and he looked at her with interest. "That's a good thing, don't you think?"

"That is a very good thing." He grinned and kissed her, then determinedly turned her around and swatted her behind. "Now go before I do something I won't regret."

Elizabeth laughed and made her way back into the house. She turned to look at him and saw that he had disappeared. Biting her lip, she felt a sense of satisfaction come over her, and entered the dining room with a wide smile. "Mmm. This looks wonderful!" Taking a seat she looked at Georgiana. "Do you like living here more than in town?"

"Sometimes, it depends on the season. Winter is pretty wicked by the ocean." She looked around. "Where's William?"

"He needed to look after something, he'll be along soon." She smiled and began to dig into her salad. A few minutes later he appeared, looking far more relaxed. Elizabeth had a difficult time controlling her laughter.

"Is something striking your fancy, Elizabeth?" He said with some annoyance.

"I was just thinking that you are right to employ a chef here. There must be so many more interesting things to occupy one's time when visiting this beautiful place." Her eyes were dancing and his lips lifted in a little smile. "I look forward to discovering them with you."

He chuckled and took her hand. "I can't wait to discover them myself."

"Well, I want to go take a walk on the beach. I have some thinking to do." Georgiana announced and was pleased to see how her brother's eyes lit up and he stared at Elizabeth. She had worked out her plans to make herself scarce frequently. "I thought that maybe after dinner we could go into town for some ice cream, then I was going to go to bed early. Tomorrow I'll see if any of my friends are around, if that's okay with you?"

"Oh, that sounds great, Georgie, just great!" Darcy said quickly. "I'll be happy to drive you wherever you need to go."

"My bike is here, I can use the exercise." She shrugged. "Why take time away from Elizabeth shuttling me around?"

"It would not be a problem, Georgiana; this is your vacation, too." Elizabeth squeezed William's knee when he stared at her expressively.

"Well, exactly, it's my vacation, and I have spent enough time shut away indoors, I think that some time alone outside would be good for me. My psychologist gave me some homework to do over the course of our trip, and I want to come back and really have something to say to her for once."

"I can't tell you how pleased I am to hear this Georgiana." Darcy smiled. "May I ask what has brought on this feeling of . . ." He searched for the word and looked to Elizabeth.

"Empowerment?" She suggested.

"I . . . I guess finally speaking about what happened released the guilt I was feeling. Being welcomed back home . . . yes, I know that I was always welcome . . . but I didn't really let myself believe that until I actually walked in the door . . . and watching you two."

"Us?" Elizabeth and Darcy exchanged glances. "What did we do?" Darcy asked.

"Oh come on, there's nothing more romantic than watching a man pine for his girlfriend." She giggled and Darcy flushed red. "Elizabeth, he was at the office working late every day this week, except for the night you went to the ball game. He would come home and spend time with me over dinner, then go to his library. I know that he was miserable and watched the clock, waiting until the appointed time when he would call you . . . but I would walk by and see how he would be constantly checking for messages and how excited he was when one appeared. And then the day of your date, he was just silly getting ready for it!" Elizabeth was watching him look everywhere but at her. "I guess that seeing a man in love just reassured me that someday I will find a guy who really loves me, too." Darcy's chin shot up when she said love and he looked at Elizabeth to see her reaction.

Her gaze did not waver from his eyes. "You are so right Georgiana; there is nothing more attractive than a man who is in love, especially to the woman who loves him."

"Lizzy."

Georgiana's eyes opened wide as she realized this was a very important moment. She picked up her salad and hurried from the room and into the kitchen, leaving them alone.

"Did I hear you . . . you said that you love me?" His voice had a strain in it.

"Yes, I do." She kissed the hand that was gripping hers tightly, and caressed it along her cheek. "I love you, Will."

He was on his feet and pulled her out of the chair in a moment. "Lizzy, I love you!" The strength of his embracing arms stole her breath, and he gave her absolutely no opportunity to revive before his mouth crushed hers in an ecstatic series of kisses. Elizabeth finally managed to push him back, and laughed to see the uncontained elation that was radiating from him. "I can't tell you how good it feels to say that to your face! I love you, I love you, I love you!!" Each cry was punctuated with another kiss.

She threw her arms around his neck. "I love you so much, Will!" He kissed her again and she delighted in his happiness. Elizabeth ran her fingers down his cheek, encountering dimples and lips that eagerly nibbled her hand. "Who have you been declaring your love to, if not me?"

His brow creased for a moment then cleared, and his face took on a decidedly pink flush. "Oh, I . . . um, talk to you . . . well, the imaginary you . . . in bed at night." He glanced down then back up and saw her smile. "I hope that those conversations won't be so one-sided anymore."

She slowly shook her head. "No, I think that both of us will actually have real partners to enjoy our late-night talks with from now on."

"You do that, too?" He beamed with incredulous amusement. "Then I'm not insane!"

She laughed and hugged him, "No sweetheart, and if you were, then we are certainly perfect for each other."

Darcy closed his eyes and nestled his face into her hair, his embrace had not relaxed at all, he never wanted to let go. "I was hoping so much that you would let me say how I feel, but I was waiting for you. I wanted you to say it without feeling obligated to answer my declaration. I'm so happy, honey." He lifted his head and saw that her eyes were bright with tears.

"You're crying, too." Elizabeth wiped his face.

"Will you marry me?"

She gasped and covered her mouth, and he gathered her hands into his clasp. "I know that you wanted to see how this trip went, and how we got along and well, Elizabeth, I told you weeks ago that I don't want to look anywhere else, how could I find anyone to compare with you? You located my smile and my laugh, you care for me and not at all about what I have, we can talk about anything and I miss you deeply when you are away. If it makes you feel better, we'll have a long engagement, but please say yes. Please, Lizzy." His begging ended and he held his breath.

Elizabeth's eyes wandered over his face, she brushed back his hair, she followed the line of his jaw with her fingers, and then she met his penetrating gaze. "I lost my smile years ago. I forgot how to feel happy, and went through my days in a sort of numb haze, not allowing anyone except my family to get close to me. I pushed everyone and everything else away." She touched his cheek and he leaned into her palm. "The first spark of life returned to me when we met, and my hope was born on that sofa in the penthouse the first time you held me. I knew then that I had found my place. I just had to . . . get used to the idea." She smiled and saw his eyes crinkle. "Thank you for your patience with me, even though I predict that on our golden wedding anniversary, we'll look back at these past weeks as just a blink of the eye in our marriage."

"Does that mean yes?" He whispered.

"Yes Will, I want to marry you." She smiled and he held her to him, the desperately clutching embrace was replaced by one of utmost care. They settled into each other as Darcy's lips brushed down her face, seeking her mouth. "Will . . ." She whispered against his gentle strokes.

"Yes?"

"Could we go upstairs?"

Darcy drew away and looked into her eyes. "Upstairs? And what do you want to do . . . upstairs?" His breathing had taken on a decided hitch.

Her hands moved up his chest and around his shoulders. "You have been patient long enough, and I don't want to wait a moment longer. Please make love to me."

"Nothing would make me happier." He leaned down to kiss her, then taking her hand in his he took a steadying breath. "Come with me." She smiled and looked down at their clasped hands as they walked out of the dining room and up the stairs. Elizabeth glanced up at him, his eyes were fixed straight ahead, and he was obviously working hard to remain calm. They reached the bedroom and she entered first, pausing by the bed and turning when she heard him close the door and turn the lock. Darcy approached her, and lifted his hand to touch her hair. "I have dreamed of this."

"So have I." Elizabeth embraced him and his arms came around to hold her. She felt his lips slowly caress down from her hair to her cheeks and finally find her mouth. They stood and swayed as their arms locked around each other, the only movement was their kisses, their tongues and lips tasting and exploring, while their hearts pounded harder and their bodies begged for them to continue. Darcy's hands began to move, one down her back to caress and cup her bottom, and the other up to her hair to support her head. His kisses became deeper and demanding, taking on a fervor he had not displayed before. Elizabeth clung to him and matched his strokes, and gasped as he lifted her to press against his groin. Now his hands moved to the bottom of her shirt, and he lifted it up, dragging his lips from hers long enough to pull it over her head and cast it down to the floor. He looked down to see the lace of her bra and moaned. "Beautiful." Next his hands worked the clasp of her shorts and with a moment of struggle, they were down at her ankles where she stepped from them along with her shoes. Darcy stepped back and held her hands in his. "So beautiful."

"Will you undress, too?" Elizabeth asked and touched his shirt. He bit his lip and watched her work the buttons loose, then helped her to slip it from his shoulders. She ran her hands over his expansive chest, touching the dark hair and feeling the muscle. "You are beautiful, Will." Their eyes locked and he kissed her hungrily. Elizabeth's hands fell to his waist and she quickly had his shorts and underwear slipped over his hips and onto the floor. Her neck was under the assault of his mouth, and he bit her the moment she touched his erection. His head rested on her shoulder and he groaned.

"Oh baby, I have wanted that for so long." He looked down to see her small hands caressing over him, then up to see her eyes, wide with wonder, and touched her face. "What is wrong?"

Elizabeth bit her lip. "I . . . it's so . . . big." She laughed nervously and he smiled, then chuckled, then clasped her to him.

"I can only take that as a compliment, Lizzy." He pulled away and held her face in his hands. "I love you."

Laughing, she kissed him. "I love you."

"Can we remove this now?" He reached around to unhook her bra and she slipped off her panties. "Ohhhhh honey." Scooping her up in his arms, she squealed. Darcy laughed and lay her down on the bed, climbing next to her to lay by her side. Happily he caressed his hand over her breasts, watching them move with his touch, exploring the hard tight nipples with his fingers, feeling and kneading them with absolute fascination.

"Are they okay?"

Giving her an incredulous look he saw the worry in her eyes. "Perfect, absolutely perfect, all of you." He leaned down to kiss her lips then her breasts while stroking his hand down her stomach to touch between her legs. "You do want this." He said softly, feeling the warmth and the wetness under his fingers. "Are you ready, honey?"

"Yes." She watched as he moved to hover over her. They kissed, and slowly joined. The warmth, the tightness, the woman he deeply loved all drove him to move, far faster than he intended. He could not help himself. Darcy was lost deep in the sensation of finally loving the woman he had been longing for and in moments found himself gasping in release. When he caught his breath and opened his eyes, he looked at Elizabeth, and nearly broke down in tears. He lifted up from her, and sat on the edge of the bed with his head in his hands.

"It's okay, Will." Elizabeth reached out and stroked his back.

"No, Lizzy. It is NOT okay!" He closed his eyes. "I have been anticipating our making love nearly from my first sight of you. I thought about it every time we talked, every time I called, every time we saw each other, and woke up with you in my dreams. I wanted to make this so special Lizzy, especially after knowing how you have been denied the pleasure you so deserved." He sighed and shook his head. "Instead I behave like an overexcited teenager."

"You said yourself that you were rusty and that we would need to work at it." She came and leaned on his back, and wrapped her arms around him.

Darcy's hands dropped to cover hers. "I said I was rusty, I didn't anticipate being a creaking gate at an abandoned cemetery." Elizabeth's giggle made him look up. "What is so funny? I find nothing funny at all in this."

"I'm sorry, but the imagery is just delicious, may I use that in my next book?" Elizabeth sat up on her knees and began kissing his neck. "Come on Will; don't tell me that you are a man who gives up after one try? I think that all of this anticipating simply made it impossible to hold back. I didn't feel what you did, but I certainly felt more than I ever have before."

"You did?" He asked softly.

"Yes, I did."

Darcy turned and hugged her. "I wanted it to be so perfect, honey."

"I know, and for me it was. For the first time I was being loved, not used." Elizabeth kissed him and he played with her hair. "Now, it is still very early in the afternoon, I suggest that we put on our bathing suits and go enjoy this beautiful day. Then tonight when we are alone and there is no rush, we can just . . . take our time and you can teach me how to feel."

"I hardly know how to teach you, it's not like I was taken somewhere for an education on the subject." He relaxed and smiled.

"Then we will home school ourselves."

Kissing her tenderly, he traced his fingers down her neck to cup and admire her breasts. "You don't want to start trying now?"

"Mmmm. No." She laughed and Darcy pushed her down onto the bed and landed on top of her. His nose touched hers and he smiled.

"NO?" She shook her head vigorously. "I think that isn't a good decision, and I'm sorely disappointed in your lapse of judgment."

"Is that so?" Elizabeth gasped when his mouth began devouring her throat. "Ohhhhhh!"

"What? What was that? Did you say that you wanted more?" He spoke into her ear and his hands claimed her breasts, rubbing and caressing them. "I believe that your body wants more." His mouth descended to suckle her, and his hands stroked over the curves of her waist. Elizabeth whimpered. Darcy looked up to make sure that she was enjoying herself, and grinned to see her lip between her teeth. Glancing back down, he saw that he was ready for her. "It seems that my body wants more, too." He took her hand to let her feel how hard he was. Elizabeth immediately began stroking him. "Oh, baby, no, let's do that from the inside."

"Well, what are you waiting for?" She gasped.

He laughed and kissed her. "THAT is what I was waiting for." Already slick from their first attempt, he slid into her easily. Both moaned and closed their eyes as they joined, and then opened them to meet the smiles of their partner. "I love you." Darcy began moving and lifted her legs to wrap around his waist. "Don't think of anything, just feel." He said hoarsely, and continued the steady motion.

"Kiss me." Instantly his mouth encompassed hers and she drew him down to her. "Harder." His thrusts became deeper, as did her kisses. "Ohhhhhhhh," She tore her mouth away from his and gasped. "Ohhhhh, Will!" He pushed back up above her and her hands clutched at his driving hips. Suddenly, he felt her clasp, deep inside of her glorious body.

"YES!!" He roared and let go, falling back down to kiss her ecstatically. He gasped for air and rolled onto his side, bringing her with him. "Yes, oh Lizzy, you felt it, I know that you did!"

"Oh, my . . . oh, when can we do this again?" She swallowed and panted, holding his face in her hands while he grinned in triumph. They both started to laugh and hugged each other. "I love you, Will."

Darcy kissed her and buried his face in her hair, gradually his breathing calmed. "I love you, Lizzy. Are you happy?"

"I can't possibly describe what I'm feeling." Elizabeth caught her breath and rubbed her face on the thatch of hair on his chest. "I'm so happy that you didn't listen to my sensible advice."

"I just couldn't leave here without trying again. It was just too important." He kissed her forehead and she looked up. "You can't have a marriage without this; it is what will bind us together more than anything."

"I understand that now." Elizabeth pushed the hair from his brow. "It was an act to be tolerated before, and now . . . it is one to be anticipated."

"And explored." He grinned.

"Oh my." Elizabeth laughed.

He rolled over onto his stomach and rested his head on the pillow of her breasts. "Of the countless times I imagined our first time together, this just wasn't what I thought it would be."

She stroked the dark hair on his head and smiled. "It wasn't my vision either, but then I'm glad that we were both surprised, since I could only hope that your ideas matched mine."

"Maybe they did. What did you dream about?" He looked up at her sparkling eyes. "I'll go first. I imagined you wearing a pair of red stilettos . . ."

"Oh Good Lord." She moaned. "What is it about men and heels?" Elizabeth laughed as he picked up her legs and began nibbling her calves. "Stop! That tickles!"

"I love your legs." His lips traveled down to her ankles and then to her feet. "And your toes." He kissed his way back up to her thighs and lay back down on top of her. "Tell me your dream." His mouth hovered over hers. "What did you hope for?"

Elizabeth's hands ran down his back, and up to embrace his neck. "This."

"What do you mean?" His kiss was tender and soft, his hands caressed her gently, and when he joined with her again, she moaned. "Tell me honey, did you dream of us slowly making love?"

"Oh yes." She searched out his mouth. "Make it last, Will, please."

Gone was the urgent need for instant gratification that his body demanded the first time, and gone was the determination to succeed that he demanded of his behavior the second time. This time they made love as true partners, both working slowly and steadily to ultimately reach the heights of their heart's expression. Darcy cuddled her limp body to his, kissing her cheek and whispering in her ear, "This is what I hoped for, too." He felt her smile.

"I had a feeling that you did." They lay together and listened to the sound of the ocean, and relaxed into a position that they would assume for decades to come, and dozed.

Eventually Darcy's stomach rumbled and Elizabeth rubbed it. "I wonder if our lunches are still available."

"Well, let's go find out, then we can take a walk and I'll show you the grounds." He sat up and stood, offering her his hand. Elizabeth stood and gasped. He looked at her with alarm. "Did I hurt you?"

"No, I . . . I remember this. It is like being a virgin again, and the morning after." She laughed. A slow smile came over Darcy's face. "What are you thinking?"

He shrugged. "I'm your first."

"Male pride." Elizabeth touched his groin.

"Watch it Lizzy, I might just have to prove how proud I am again." She giggled and he watched her walk away to the bathroom, and admired her nude body from an angle he had only imagined before. The door closed and sighing happily; he went to put on his trunks and a shirt. In the mirror he saw a face that he did not know. "Look at you. Proud of yourself, aren't you? Definitely satisfied." He startled when he heard the sound of singing from the bathroom. He had never heard Elizabeth's voice before and sank down to lean on the dresser and listen. Darcy was utterly enchanted, he had no idea what she was singing, it sounded like a waltz. Glancing again at the mirror he saw that the proud cock of before was now replaced by the happy besotted fool. "Wow, what this girl can do to me."

The door opened and Elizabeth appeared, dressed in a yellow bikini and wrapped in a matching sarong. "What do you think?" She spun around and laughed at his admiring gaze. "I take it that you approve?"

"Beautiful. What were you singing? It sounded familiar."

She bit her lip, and he touched her mouth. "It was the *Cinderella Waltz*."

Bowing gallantly he looked up and smiled. "Cinderella, eh? What fairy tale melody is next?"

"Hmm, maybe the theme song from *Shrek*?" Elizabeth giggled and he disappeared into the bathroom.

From behind the door she heard his deep voice singing, "All that glitters is gold, only shooting stars break the mold[i]." He reappeared a few moments later with a silly grin.

Elizabeth laughed. "That wasn't exactly what I had in mind." He raised his brow and she sang, "There's no more mystery. It is finally clear to me. You're the home my heart searched for so long. It is you I have loved all along.[ii]"

"You sentimental girl." He hugged her. "Come on honey; let me show you our home."

AFTER FINALLY FINISHING their lunch, they strolled out onto the lawn. Darcy squeezed her hand and pointed. "We own about three acres, which is really a large lot for this location, and also speaks to how long the Darcys have had a presence here. This is not the first home on this site." He stopped and smiled. "I can't tell you how many times I have been approached to sell a piece of the land, and I have only owned it for five years."

"This wouldn't be the same with another enormous home next door." She smiled. "I suppose it would go where that building is over there." She pointed to a structure built to copy the style of the house. "What is that?"

"A stable." He smiled at her wide eyes.

"You have your own horses!"

"Just two, they are boarded elsewhere most of the time but I had them brought out for our visit. How long has it been since you last rode?" They started moving again and Elizabeth twisted and just caught sight of a horse's swishing tail around the corner of the building.

"Oh, it has been at least a year. I will certainly feel the lack of practice the next time I try." She rubbed William's rear and he laughed.

"Maybe tomorrow we can test that presumption?"

"I'd like that." He kissed her hand then looked at it. "You, my love, need a ring."

She raised her brow and held up her hand for inspection. "Hmm. So I do."

"Well, I thought of presenting you with one of our heirloom rings, but well, I have been party to enough complaining by the newly engaged ladies in the office to know that the smart groom lets the bride choose her ring."

"Oh I am SO impressed with you!" Elizabeth laughed and gave him a hug.

He grinned and looked at her sideways. "Well, Anne's husband made the mistake of choosing something and they returned to Tiffany's the next day."

"Yes, I heard that story." Elizabeth giggled. "Poor man!"

"She made it up to him, I'm sure." He kissed her when she rolled her eyes. "What would you like? You can have anything."

"Oh, something simple. No ten-carat monstrosity. I will be wearing this ring everyday for the rest of my life, after all." He stopped walking and she turned to look up at him. "Will?"

"I . . . That just hit me, you want to be with me for the rest of your life." He shook his head and drew her to his chest. "Why? I'm nothing special."

"Neither am I, but you want to spend the rest of your days with me." Elizabeth stroked his brow, and he lowered his mouth to tenderly kiss her. "I want you because you make me happy and feel good about myself, you challenge me and you need me. I love too many things to list here and now, but it all adds up to wanting to spend my days with you." She kissed him, then squeezed his rear. "And you have a delicious butt!"

Darcy started laughing. "And here I was about to cry with your sweet words." He rubbed his hands over her. "I could repeat exactly the same sentiments to you, including the bottom reference, although it's your eyes that won me. I feel so much the same. You have given me so much to anticipate, that I can't wait to begin." He drew a deep breath. "So, when would you like to marry? I said that I won't complain about a long engagement, it is entirely in your hands."

"But you don't want a long engagement." Elizabeth caressed his face and smiled. "It is as clear as day that you would gladly load me onto your jet and fly me off to Vegas this moment."

"Yes." He admitted.

"Well, I have no desire for a huge affair."

"Good."

Elizabeth laughed. "I thought you would like that after watching your lack of enthusiasm for Anne's wedding. Do you have any obligation to invite clients or business acquaintances, or even have scores of friends whose weddings you have attended and must recompense with invitations to yours?"

"My friends would completely understand me having a small private wedding. They are my friends for a reason." He looked at her pointedly then added softly. "Which is, of course, why I have so few."

"You have me." He hugged her tight. "I propose August, and a small gathering of family here. Could we hire a local magistrate to perform a ceremony here on the lawn? Maybe set up a tent and have a catered picnic or something?"

Darcy's eyes lit up. "That *would* be simple! You wouldn't want a formal dinner or . . . I don't know, all of the frills and things that your sister creates?"

"Definitely not." She said emphatically. "I see no need for bags of Jordan almonds, or peacocks, or engraved glasses or whatever the latest trend is. I want a simple gown, you in a comfortable suit, and a happy, relaxed atmosphere. Notice that I am not asking that we marry while skydiving and then attempting to consummate in mid-air."

"Well thank God for that!" Darcy chuckled. "No ceremony on a roller coaster either?"

"I'm afraid not." They hugged, and Elizabeth searched his eyes. "Is that really acceptable to you? I know that Jane will insist on helping, but she can do simple weddings, too."

"That sounds perfect. Will you mother approve?" Darcy stopped walking when Elizabeth came to a halt. "Lizzy? What's wrong?"

"I forgot about Mom. Oh she is going to be just horrible! She's going to want to see your house, you know, and that means she'll finally figure out how rich you are. And then she'll broadcast to the world our engagement, and want to be involved in everything . . . oh and she will want to pick out my dress!" Elizabeth wailed then clutched his arm. "Fire up the jet, let's elope!"

"Fine with me! Let's go!" His arms wrapped around her. "How bad can she be?"

"Bad."

"We'll get through it, or rather you will mostly since she's your mom. Why August, by the way?"

"All of my sisters will be home. They are all attending summer sessions or about to at their schools, but they all have breaks in August."

He nodded. "I was already planning my trip to Pemberley, the real one, for August. Perhaps we could start our honeymoon there then travel somewhere else in Europe. Is there anywhere you would like to go?"

"I haven't been anywhere." Elizabeth looked down. "I don't even have a passport."

"Well, I think that is something we have to remedy today. I heard that the delays in getting them processed are terrible. Let's go inside and see if we can start the application online." He took her hand and they moved back towards the house. "I wonder if Georgiana is returned, I want to tell her our news." He smiled. "She will be thrilled."

"I hope so." Elizabeth was still quiet.

"What's wrong?" He touched her cheek.

"I just suddenly felt the difference between us. If just a passport makes me feel inadequate, what will the people you know do to me?" She looked out and saw the roof of his neighbor's mansion just over the trees. "I suppose everyone around here is like you."

"It is a very wealthy neighborhood, yes." He said softly. "But I am sure that you will fit right in."

"I don't know how to play tennis." She said as they passed the court.

"I'll teach you."

"Okay."

They entered the house through the kitchen door. Darcy was worried about her continued silence and startled with the sound of an acerbic voice. "Well?" Miss Maggie crackled.

Elizabeth looked at her then to William. He was smiling at her. "I had hoped to tell Georgiana first, but I suppose that you won't leave me alone until I tell you."

"You know that!" She cackled. "So are you marrying the girl?" Elizabeth felt sharp eyes examining her.

"Yes ma'am." Darcy grinned and leaned to kiss Elizabeth's cheek.

"You treat her like your daddy did your mama, and you'll be just fine." The old woman peered at Elizabeth. "Do you love my boy?" Darcy's hand squeezed hers hard.

"Yes, very much, Miss Maggie."

She nodded then pointed an imperious finger to the door. "I'm sure that you have something to do, I want to speak to your young lady."

"Miss Maggie . . ." He began and met her steely eye. "Yes, ma'am." He leaned in to Elizabeth. "She is very protective, but means no harm. I'll just go look up the passport information." He kissed her cheek again and was gone before Elizabeth could respond. She turned and stood before the old woman and studied her. William had told her that Maggie was at Pemberley still purely as a ceremonial position and actually lived at a retirement village, only coming to the house when the family was in residence.

"Sit down, my dear." Her bony, knotted hand took Elizabeth's small soft one in her grasp. "My boy loves you."

"Yes, I know, and I love him."

"He is very, very rich, just like his daddy and his family before him, but riches didn't make any one of them happy. Now these rich men get it in their heads sometimes that they know everything, and nobody can tell them boo, but your job is to take his big head and knock it down to size from time to time." Elizabeth's mouth opened and she began to smile. "Now, my Will was always a very sweet shy boy, but sometimes I thought he was just too smart a man for his own good, but you look like you're a smart girl. He needs a girl who will fight him back. Don't let him get too easy, send him back to school every once in a while."

"So I should keep him guessing?"

"That's it!" The woman crowed. "You are smart!" Elizabeth laughed.

Maggie leaned forward and spoke quietly, and grasped her hand as tight as her arthritis allowed. "But what he really needs is you to love him. Do you know what I mean? Not what you two do in that bed upstairs. You are going to be the only person he can come to when he needs to not be the big rich businessman. That's what his mama did for his daddy, and my boy is the picture of his dad."

Elizabeth smiled and knew that she would be very fond of this protector of her William. She very gently squeezed her hand. "Yes, I know exactly what you mean. I promise you, Miss Maggie, I will take very good care of him."

Maggie began to cry and Elizabeth held her. "I have been waiting for him to be happy, he's been so lonely. I made a promise to his parents at their funeral that I wouldn't rest until I talked to the girl he brought home."

Tearing up, Elizabeth whispered, "Do you think that Mr. and Mrs. Darcy would like me?"

"Well, my little Georgie told me all about you, and she is so happy that I know he found a good one." She pulled out of the embrace and wiped her eyes.

"So you already liked me?"

"You made my boy smile, dear. I liked you from the very start." She patted Elizabeth's cheek. "What am I to call you?"

"Call me Lizzy, that's what my family calls me." Maggie nodded and Elizabeth kissed her cheek. "Thank you, Miss Maggie, I like you, too."

CHARLES HEARD his phone ring and stopped his jogging. He collapsed onto a park bench and pulled it out of his pocket. "Darcy! What are you doing calling me? Trouble in paradise already?" He laughed with his friend's groan, and could picture his face.

Darcy sat at his desk and shook his head. "I called to tell you my news."

"News?"

"Elizabeth and I are engaged." He said with obvious elation and pride.

"Damn, you didn't waste any time at all! What happened to this waiting period of getting to know each other better for two weeks?"

"Obviously that changed." Darcy said icily.

"I'm sorry Darcy, congratulations, it's wonderful news! She is an incredible girl." Bingley smiled. "What are your plans, or have you even discussed them yet?"

"We want to marry in August when all of her sisters are home from their various schools. I was already planning to be away in England for a few weeks. When you go in on Monday, look at the September calendar and see if there is anything that I absolutely have to attend, particularly the first half of the month. I'd like to try for four weeks for the honeymoon."

Bingley whistled. "I can't imagine you not working for so long; hell I can't imagine the trip you're on now! I'll see what's going on. Should I call you or just send an email?"

"Email, I still don't want to be disturbed." Darcy relaxed, that was handled. "I'm going to take her ring shopping tomorrow."

"Where?"

"There's a Tiffany's in East Hampton."

"Oh that's right, I forgot." Bingley grinned. "How much is that going to cost?"

"She wants something simple, and I don't care." Darcy smiled. "I can't believe this is happening."

"I am very happy for you, it's about time." Charles said sincerely.

"Yeah."

"Does her sister know?"

"No, she hasn't told anyone, we haven't even told Georgiana yet." He laughed. "Poor Elizabeth is undergoing an interrogation by Maggie right now. I hope that she doesn't pack up and leave when it's over."

"Maggie is something else. How old is she?"

"Ninety-five, last April."

"Must be all of the sea air."

"Well, she swears like a sailor if you get her riled up." Darcy laughed, then paused. "Why did you ask about Jane knowing?"

"Oh, um, well, I have a date with her tomorrow. Sunday seems to be her free day between weddings." Bingley played with the hem on his shorts, and heard silence. "Darcy?"

"What's going on there?"

Charles sat up. "Nothing, I like her, and I think that she likes me, and I . . . I just, oh leave me alone, Darcy."

He chuckled. "Maybe we'll be brothers someday, and how convenient, your bride can plan your own wedding!"

"Enough!" Bingley turned red. "Hey . . . when is the court date for Wickham? Won't it be about that time? Will that screw up your honeymoon plans?"

Darcy groaned. "I didn't think about that. Okay, when you go in Monday, ask Patricia to send me the prosecutor's number, and I'll call to see if anything has been set." He sighed heavily. "I hope that with Georgiana's statement in hand, he or at least his lawyer; will see the benefit of taking a plea."

"You know, if news of your engagement is out, he might think this is a good opportunity to embarrass you by *not* taking a plea. What does he care? He's going to prison regardless, and he's a vindictive SOB."

"Vegas is sounding better and better." Darcy muttered.

"What was that?"

"Never mind. Look, you take care of those things for me and I'll let you know what's going on as soon as I can. Thanks. Sorry for interrupting your run."

"How did you know I was jogging?"

"I hear the park in the background, and other than girl watching, that's the only time you go there." Darcy smiled at Bingley's curse. "Look I had better go and rescue Lizzy. I'll be in touch."

"Okay, kiss the bride for me."

"No, the only kisses she gets are from me." Darcy growled and Bingley laughed. He hung up and went back to his passport search. He downloaded the forms and printed them out. It looked like it could not be handled until they returned to the city. Approaching the kitchen, he heard Maggie's unmistakable cackle and Elizabeth's warm laugh and relaxed, she was accepted. He pushed open the door and found that Georgiana had joined the group.

Elizabeth beamed at him. "Hi!"

"Hi, I guess your talk went well?" He smiled and stood behind her. "What's this?"

"Oh, I thought that Elizabeth would like to see some of your baby pictures." Georgiana smiled. "I like this one best." She pointed to the photo of a very serious looking boy glaring at a butterfly. Darcy blushed.

"Is this really necessary?" He said quietly.

"Show him the one that Miss Maggie liked!" Elizabeth giggled. Georgiana flipped the pages and the picture was of a slightly younger boy, viewed from the back, naked and running through a sprinkler. "I think that is my favorite, too!" Darcy reached forward and closed the album to the combined protests of the ladies.

"That is quite enough." His face was still red, and Elizabeth stood up and wrapped her arms around him.

"I think that you were a beautiful baby, and I can't wait to see our own someday." She kissed him softly and he sighed. Elizabeth whispered in his ear. "It seems that you have always had a delicious bottom!" Her hand dipped to rub him and he laughed.

"I can't win here, can I?" Darcy tipped his head. "I will have to look at *your* baby pictures when we return.

"Oh no, I don't think so!"

"All's fair in love and war, besides, we need to find a copy of your birth certificate for the passport, so that will certainly put your mother in mind for reminiscing about you!" He pursed his lips and held back his laugh.

"I take back anything nice that I said about your rear!" Elizabeth huffed and sat down.

Darcy laughed and sat beside her. "So Georgiana, I guess that you know our news?

"Yes, and I'm so happy for you!" She beamed at them both. "You'll marry in August?"

"That is the current plan." He said softly and Elizabeth turned her head and looked at him carefully.

"Is that plan subject to change?"

"Possibly." He glanced at Georgiana and shook his head.

"Oh, well, I'm sure that you will inform me when you do know." Elizabeth wondered what could possibly have changed in the last half hour and her face reflected her concern.

"I should know sometime Monday, at least I hope to. However, there is always the Vegas idea." He leaned over and kissed her. "Don't worry honey, I'm all yours."

Chapter 8

*D*arcy looked over to Elizabeth and took her hand to give it a squeeze. "Are you excited?"

"I am nervous, I think." She smiled at him. His head had turned to pay attention to the road.

"What's to be afraid of? It's a jewelry store."

"It's Tiffany's."

"So a coat of aqua blue paint makes it so different?" He laughed and glanced over to see her blush. "I guess it's the aura of the place."

"I've only peeked in the windows; I've never actually gone in. Kind of like Audrey Hepburn." She smiled.

"Shall I sing *Moon River*[iii] for you?" He said seductively and caught her eye.

"You do have a devastating voice."

"Hmm." Darcy kissed her hand and looked forward, then bit his lip and softly sang, "Two drifters, off to see the world, there's such a lot of world to see, we're after the same rainbow's end, waitin' 'round the bend, my huckleberry friend, moon river, and me." He kissed her hand again and peeked over to see her smile.

"How did you know that?"

"Oh, my mom insisted on music with dinner every night, so she would have a stack of records ready to play, I had no choice but to learn the words to every romantic song of her youth. Her taste was pretty eclectic, we had everything from show tunes to solo artists. I learned them all, whether I liked them or not." He laughed. "Dad and I would frequently roll our eyes at each other, but he wouldn't ever tell her she couldn't listen to her *pretty music*, as she called it." Darcy glanced over to see her blink slowly.

"You can sing to me any time." Elizabeth whispered dreamily.

"Lizzy, please think of something else; or I'm going to have to pull over and make love to you in the back seat." She looked over to see that his face was set. He was staring ahead with great focus, and gripping the steering wheel hard. "Please save those expressions for when we're alone."

"We are alone, Will." She ran her hand down from his shoulder to his elbow.

He shot her a look. "I'm serious."

Elizabeth laughed. "Okay, I'll stop. No more torture, but Will, I can't promise to never look at you with desire in my eyes."

"Just not when I'm driving." He looked at her meaningfully and slid his hand beneath her skirt to rest between her parted legs. "You're so warm." Still looking forward, he caressed her and listened to her soft moan. "Oh honey, I want you." Elizabeth's head was back against the seat and her eyes were closed. "Just wait until we get home."

Elizabeth looked at him languidly as they drove into the little town and parked. They stared at each other for a few moments, and he forced his body to move. She got out before he could open the door for her and smiled at his disappointment. "Sorry." They entwined their fingers and began walking down the sidewalk. She took in the names of the expensive stores, then looked over the well-dressed people visiting them, and noticed the curious attention that they were attracting. He noticed her silence and saw her lip caught in her teeth.

"Lizzy?"

She looked up and shook her head. "Nothing." They arrived at the jewelers and Darcy held the door for her. Elizabeth stepped into the silent store and just breathed in the atmosphere. She wore very little jewelry, but recognized quality when she saw it. Shaking off her nerves she lifted her chin. "Well, let's see if they have anything worthwhile."

He laughed and a woman approached. "Good afternoon, is there anything special I can show you today?" She glanced at their joined hands, seeing no ring on Elizabeth's finger.

"We are here to purchase my fiancée her engagement ring." Darcy said proudly.

"Well, we will certainly be sure to find the perfect piece. Come over this way." She led them to two chairs and a case full of diamond rings. "Do you have anything in particular in mind?" Her gaze was on Elizabeth who was looking down through the glass with wide eyes.

"Oh, I want a platinum setting, a solitaire, emerald cut." She said very definitely. Darcy grinned.

"I'm really glad that I didn't buy you something beforehand."

"What would you have chosen?" Elizabeth laughed.

"Hmm, I don't know. I'll scan the rings and point one out to you."

The woman took out several trays. "Now we can obviously design a setting for you, and put in any stone, so you are not limited to what we have here. What you see are our classic Tiffany designs. Do you have any preference for carat size?" This time her gaze was on Darcy; the one who would be paying.

He met her eye. "There is no limit."

The woman's eyes brightened. "I see that you have excellent taste, sir."

"Yes, but he doesn't have to wear it, and I do. I want something manageable." Elizabeth smiled and saw the disappointment register in the woman's face. The vision of her ring was so clear that she quickly had the choice narrowed down to four. She looked up to see him watching her closely. "I just don't know."

"Well, I think that the only way you can tell is to put one on your finger and see if you like it." He looked over the selection and chose the one he preferred, then taking her hand, slipped it onto her ring finger and looked into her eyes. "With this ring, I thee wed."

"Oh." She didn't even look down. "That one, definitely."

"Are you sure? Maybe you should look at it." He said softly.

"You chose it, I gave you the right direction, but you chose it. This is the one I want." Elizabeth leaned towards him and they kissed, then finally she looked down to view her ring. "I love it."

"Then it is yours." He smiled and kissed the ring. Looking to the clerk he said, "I suppose that we should purchase our wedding bands while we are here."

"Of course, sir, do you like platinum as well?"

"Yes, I do."

She put away all of the other rings then returned with new trays. "Now, we have some lovely bands with diamonds . . ."

"No, I just want a simple plain ring." Elizabeth declared.

"So do I."

"And I would like to have an engraving added to his." She smiled and her eyes sparkled at him.

He tilted his head and raised his brow. "I would like the same."

The clerk handed each of them pens and sheets of paper, where they jotted down their words. They handed them back to her. First she read Elizabeth's and smiled, then looked at the other. She laughed. "Well, you too are well-matched, I would say." She walked away to write up the order and Elizabeth poked him.

"What does yours say?"

"Tell me yours." Her head wagged slowly, as he leaned to her. "Then you'll just have to wait for our wedding day, won't you?"

MONDAY MORNING, Darcy wandered down to the library to wait for Elizabeth while she dressed, and looked up from the newspaper he was reading at the sound of her clearing throat. "You look great!"

She looked down at the outfit. "Well, it's not quite what the ladies in East Hampton would choose, but I guess it will do."

"I knew you were feeling insecure there for some reason. I'll be honest with you; I saw absolutely no difference between your clothes and anyone else there." He smiled and saw her shaking head. "What?"

"So says the man who has no idea what he wears."

"Honey I could care less about clothes, well, except maybe your shoes." He laughed with her groan.

"So you say that you saw nothing but me."

"And apparently I was not enough of a distraction for you, if you are so concerned with the opinions of everyone else." He pouted.

Elizabeth saw his blue eyes twinkling and went over to kiss him. "Did it occur to you that I was looking around to purposely distract myself from your handsome presence?" He chuckled. "Do I have time to check my email? You looked as if you were engrossed in that article."

"Sure, go ahead."

Elizabeth sat at his desk and quickly accessed her account. She read the messages of congratulations from each sister and laughed over Jane's. Darcy smiled and stood up behind her, gently caressing her back, and reading Jane's reaction to the news.

Elizabeth then clicked on Charlotte's message and felt a tight grip on her shoulder. She looked up, his face was unreadable. She bit her lip. "It looks like I'll be leaving as soon as we get back."

"Yes." He let go and went to stand by the window. *I will not say anything; this is her career. I am not Collins.*

Tension radiated from him, and she tried to relieve it. "I'm not looking forward to it. It's just because the new book is coming out. I know it seems that I'm away all of the time lately, but usually it's not like this. Most of the time I'm home."

She saw him staring out of the window. "It was exciting at one time, but now . . . it has become a necessary evil."

"Then why go?" He said quietly.

"It's just part of what's required of me, Will. You should understand about honoring these things." She tried to laugh, "You'll probably be so swamped with work that you won't even notice my absence." He made no response. "Will?"

"Yeah. Vegas, huh? That should be fun for you."

Elizabeth watched his stiff posture and spoke slowly. "I'll see some friends, other authors, and maybe a show one night, but I'm not going to party, it's business."

"And you have to tour the bookstores, too?" He said softly.

"Just a few and maybe a school or two. Charlotte packages it all up in just a couple of days. I've made it clear to her that I don't want to be away for long."

He nodded and turned from the window. "Well, let's go walk."

"Will . . ."

"Lizzy if you don't want me to say something that will make you angry, please let's just go." He took her hand and they walked out of the house. Darcy's mind was full of thoughts and his grip on Elizabeth's hand was tight.

She finally stopped walking and he was jolted back to awareness when he suddenly could not move forward. "Please do not treat me this way. Talk to me if something bothers you. It is apparent that you are not happy about this trip." He was wrong, she was not angry, she was hurt.

"Come here." Darcy drew her into his arms and kissed her. "I have thought of this so much, having a life with you, and here I am shutting you out already. I'm sorry, I am just so afraid of doing something that would make you want to call everything off. Looking back to how we met, our first night together, I can't believe that you didn't run away from me as fast as you could."

"Why would I have done that?" Elizabeth's hand gently stroked up and down his arm.

"I think that I was acting too possessively, and I think that if I hadn't had to go away so quickly, you might have become frightened of my . . . neediness."

"It did frighten me, until I understood it. The wait was worth it though, don't you think?"

"Yes, of course." He rested his forehead on hers. "I told you that I am working on plans to rearrange the power structure of all of my interests, spreading it all around, so that things can be accomplished without my intimate involvement, I'm still in charge of it all, but the burden is shared." Elizabeth nodded. "I did that in anticipation of us marrying. I did that so we could have a life together. I will still have to travel, but not as often, and I will still have occasional periods where my work is going to take up a lot of time, but I think that the way we are working things out, I will be home far more often than you would probably wish." He smiled with her laugh. "I realize that I was trying to do too much, and I want to nip this before I become completely burned out and therefore useless to my employees, and most of all, to you." He drew a deep breath. "That is what I am doing for us." His gaze bore into hers. "Now, what can we do for you?"

"Me?" Elizabeth was surprised.

"I have been loath to speak about this because I am trying so hard to not be like the man in your past." Elizabeth's eyes closed. "I have come to grips with the fact that you are a popular writer and people will want to meet you at book signings occasionally. I admit that I am an enormous hypocrite when I say that I hate you having to travel when I have to do it myself, but sweetheart; it is clear as day that you are unhappy with your career. I don't know exactly what the problem is, but I wonder if you are tired of it and . . . as my wife, you would be able to do such wonderful things with your talents, the need to work for an income is no longer going to be an issue."

"These things that I could do would keep me nearby?" She said softly.

"I am not trying to control you." He sighed. "I knew that I shouldn't speak of this. I knew it would come out wrong."

"Will, I am not accusing you of anything. I *am* tired of what I'm doing, and the driving force behind my writing is no longer present. If it doesn't flow easily then it will show in the work. I have considered several options, from stopping all together, to only producing something once a year or maybe once every eighteen months, or doing something entirely new. I know that you are thinking of our best interests, and yes, I know that you hate my being away, as infrequently as it would be if I change my schedule. You are not trying to control me, I appreciate that. What is your idea?"

"Really?"

"I trust you."

"Honey, those words are just as sweet as hearing you say that you love me." He hugged her. "Thank you."

They stood and held each other quietly until they both relaxed. "Okay, so we're past the uncomfortable part, now tell me your brilliant plan." Elizabeth smiled. "Realize, however, that I will feel free to reject it."

He laughed. "How could you possibly reject my brilliance?" They kissed and entwining their fingers started walking again. "I thought of a scholarship program for young writers, like you were in high school. I bet that there are great numbers of budding novelists out there who can't afford school. Perhaps you could devise some sort of paper that they would have to write, describing why they are deserving and have them send a sample of their work."

"Maybe we could even offer to publish the top ten papers or stories? There would probably have to be a size limit to the story, I could talk to Charlotte about it and hire Lucas Lit as the publisher."

"Sure, maybe even do a series of scholarships, ones based on income, age, or creativity. There are any number of ways to go with it." He smiled and saw her lost deep in thought. "You really like it?"

Elizabeth smiled up at him. "Oh yes, I do. I think that I might need a small staff . . ."

"It is yours." He grinned. "Anything you want. We can set up the foundation with our lawyers, figure out a budget and set the scholarship amounts. Once we determine that we can move whatever funds will be needed to keep it going for, I don't know, at least ten years? And then decide if we want to continue it after that."

"Will I need to do any fundraising?" She asked worriedly. "I'm good with people but I don't know about getting them to pry open their wallets."

Darcy stopped and hugged her. "No, this is our money alone. It's just a thought, and you might find that you want to write again at some point. This would give you a focus on something new, but still in the area that you love."

"And I won't have to become a socialite like your aunt."

"Oh no, please don't do that!" He closed his eyes. "I apologize, I shouldn't have been afraid to talk to you about this."

"Well, I'm sorry if I gave you the impression that you couldn't." She caressed his cheek and he looked down at her with a smile. "So, I'll go to Vegas next week, you'll catch up on all that you have missed, and when I get back we'll plan the wedding."

He grinned. "And get married."

"And honeymoon." She whispered.

"Then what? A baby?" He tilted his head and laughed at her gasp. "I knew you would look at me like that." Elizabeth pinched his rear and they started walking again. "Watch it Lizzy, you're going to want me to care for your sore bottom after we go riding."

"Hmm, I think that can go two ways." She laughed at his raised brows. "You seem fond of my nibbling."

"What do you say about skipping the riding and just go roll in the hay?" His hand caressed over her back and downwards.

"Can't we do both?"

Darcy brought her hand up to his lips and gave her a kiss. "I would be happy to oblige." Elizabeth laughed and they took the walkway down to the beach. Further along they could see their neighbor's children playing in the surf, and a few umbrellas dotting the sand. He looked down at their entwined fingers and watched the sunlight sparkling on her ring.

"I fell in love with your eyes first." Elizabeth said quietly. He looked up and she brushed the hair blowing across his forehead, then caressed his face. "All of you is in your eyes, you know."

He swallowed and looked back down at the sand. "I . . . I think the same of you."

"You said that you have very few friends, now the man I know is warm and kind. I have never seen you with anyone except your family and Charles so I have to wonder, what happens when you are away from your comfortable places?"

"Do you really want to know?" He glanced over at her and saw her nod. "I become painfully shy, which is interpreted as rudeness. People approach me if they want something, but for the most part just stay away, and that has worked out very well since I really didn't want to talk to them anyway."

"Because you didn't know what to say?"

"I guess. I tried to figure it out once and read that people who are considered . . . intelligent, often lack in social skills. I took a lot of abuse for it in school; kids don't like ones who are different." He shrugged. "I don't know, maybe you didn't face the same bullying, you're very intelligent, but seem to get along with everybody."

"I wasn't always that way. I was a lot more like Jane when I was younger, you know, all is bright and beautiful," she laughed then spoke softly. "I was more reserved, and I did face my fair share of bullying." She saw the understanding in his eyes. "I've changed to be willing to question and provoke people, and to really want to know them before I . . . open up."

"Because of Collins." He said softly.

"Yes, perhaps that's the one favor he did for me." Elizabeth looked ahead and she felt his hand grip hers.

"I met him."

She looked over quickly. "You met him?"

"I was at the gym when you were in Chicago, and he introduced himself to me. It was all I could do not to kill him then and there. He wanted my friendship; instead I embarrassed him before the crowd and made sure that his name was ruined amongst our society. He had used false information to get an apartment in my aunt's building. She was angry with how he manipulated her and saw that he was thrown out. I understand that he has lost a great deal of his inheritance gambling. The last report I heard had him working at a pizza shop and living with his mother, and going out on weekends to feed his gambling obsession."

Elizabeth stared at him in disbelief. "I . . . I don't know what to say. You . . . removed the chance of him ever meeting me again."

"Well, I admit that I certainly wanted to make sure that he was not welcomed in the circles we will inhabit, but I think that most of the ruin was done by his own hands, and I have been keeping an eye on him to be sure he was away from you." His lips lifted slightly. "I met him just at the moment I realized we both were burning out from our careers and was trying to figure ways for us to be together."

"Did he know . . . about us?"

"No, he knew me through Aunt Catherine, but . . . he did detail what he did to you, as a sort of triumphant example of his worth. That's when I . . . behaved atypically." He bit his lip and looked back down at their clasped hands.

"Will." He met her eyes. "You avenged me." He nodded and looked down again. "How can I ever thank you? I can't begin to tell you how grateful I am to know that I will never run the risk of meeting him again. It has been plaguing my mind. I knew his plans to live in the city when his trust fund came in. I was so worried that he would come back for me. And now, he never will."

Darcy stopped and turned to pull her into his arms. "I only care about us, honey. Can we put him away forever now?" He smiled and kissed her nose. "I really did want to throw him through a window."

Elizabeth laughed. "Oh no, the press would have enjoyed that too much, and I like the path you chose. It is worthy of you." She stood up on her toes and they kissed. "I wonder what it's like to make love in the sand."

"I think that it looks good in the movies, but in reality, we'd be finding reminders of it for days." He grinned. "In every conceivable place."

"Well it was just a thought." She rested her head on his chest and he kissed her hair. "How about in the pool?"

"Now that has possibilities." Darcy whispered. "A midnight swim?"

"Perfect."

"William! Elizabeth!" Georgiana called and ran down the walkway to the beach. They startled and turned to face her. She was running through the heavy sand and nearly collapsed against them.

"Georgie, what is wrong?" Darcy grabbed her heaving shoulders while she caught her breath. "What happened?"

"Charles called." She swallowed and calmed. "Charles called; the prosecutor in Florida called your lawyer; Wickham is taking the plea. There won't be a trial!" She threw her arms around Darcy's neck. "I won't have to see him!" She cried then turned to hug Elizabeth.

"That's wonderful! What else did he say?"

"Charles said he didn't have the details but you should call the lawyer as soon as you can. Can you do it now, William? I want this to be over."

"Of course, let's go." Darcy looked to Elizabeth. "Our wedding plans are safe."

"I'll let everyone know."

He took her hand and kissed it then offered his other to Georgiana. They made their way back to the house and they went into the library. Any thoughts of making this a private call were eliminated when Elizabeth and Georgiana took seats across from his desk. "I guess there's no point in asking you two to leave, is there?"

"No, none at all, get to calling." Elizabeth ordered.

He smiled and punched in the number, and asked for his attorney. "Yes, I only know that he is taking a plea, what . . . okay and the reason . . ." Darcy swore then looked apologetically at the ladies. "And then in the future . . . I understand. Is there anything else we need to do? Thank you Jack; thanks for everything." He hung up and looked up to their expectant faces. "So, here's the story. His lawyer seemed to have a difficult time convincing Wickham to plea out, but when he realized that as a minor victim of sexual crime your name would not be revealed, he knew that he wouldn't be able to expose our name to the press, so he accepted the bargain. I suppose that the tabloids actually do have some morals when it comes to this sort of thing."

"Will he be gone for a long time?" Georgiana asked anxiously while Elizabeth squeezed her hand.

He sighed. "Not long enough, I'm afraid. He will get the lighter sentence for pleading out. It will be one year and the $1000 fine. I wish it could be worse, but at least he'll be gone that long. Jack said that if the other inmates see him as a child molester, he could have a very difficult year. That is a case where they mete out the punishment themselves."

"But when he gets out, what could he do?"

"He'll be on a sexual predator's list for the rest of his life. He'll have to register wherever he lives, and it will affect his employment opportunities, and well, every aspect of his life forever. And if he does it again, he will get a life sentence."

"As good as that sounds, I don't want some other girl to be his victim." Georgiana whispered. "Do you think he might try some other form of revenge?"

"On us?" Darcy shrugged. "Who knows? He would be a fool if he did. I'm not going to worry about it. I sincerely doubt that we will ever cross paths again, our worlds are very different."

"So it's over."

"Yes." He tilted his head and smiled. "You're free."

Georgiana smiled. "I am, aren't I?" She laughed and hugged Elizabeth. "I think I'll go play. I can't think of a better way to express my feelings." Darcy stood up and hugged her. "Thank you for everything, William." She left the room and he sank down beside Elizabeth and wrapped her in his arms.

"For some reason, I feel as if I have just run a marathon."

"You're exhausted?" She looked up to him.

"Yes, it's been just over five months of pressure, and suddenly it's gone. For some reason, all I want to do is go to bed." He met her eyes and raised his brow. "How does that sound to you?"

"I thought you were tired."

"Not that tired."

Chapter 9

*D*arcy opened his eyes to see the sun just peeking over the horizon. The glowing beam of light danced on the gently lapping waves. A gull cackled as it flew by and the scene was suddenly obscured by the fluttering of the sheer drapes hanging near the open French doors. He kissed Elizabeth's shoulder and settled his cheek against her hair, cuddling her sleeping form to his, and unconsciously caressed her while he thought. How many times had he awakened in this position and dreamed of not being alone? His hand drifted up to where hers lay over the pillow, and felt once again the ring she said she had no desire to remove. He doubted that she would ever know how deeply he loved giving it to her.

Elizabeth stirred and blinked open her eyes, and looked upon the rising sun. She felt William's hand and smiled, his lips again touched her shoulder and she moved her hand to clasp his. Silently they lay together and watched the new day begin. As the room gradually moved from darkness to light, he nuzzled his face into her neck and renewed his caresses. Elizabeth shivered with his touch. "What are you doing?" She whispered.

"What does it feel like I'm doing?" He said softly in her ear as their bodies joined.

"Ohhh."

It was not long before they were lying quietly again, still entwined. "We fit so perfectly together." Darcy caressed her lazily. "You are just the right size to cuddle"

Elizabeth laughed. "So I finally have found a good use for my small stature."

"Mmmm. I can think of many good uses for you, my Lizzy."

"You are drunk."

"At seven in the morning? I don't think so."

"Not with wine. You are a closet romantic." She turned to find him smiling, and pushed the mussed hair from his forehead as she kissed him. "I don't think I'll be happy returning to the real world."

"I won't have a peaceful night without you by my side."

She laughed. "How have you managed to sleep all these years without me?"

He drew her up and she lay on his chest. Darcy's hands stroked down from her shoulders to her bottom and back up again. "Well you see; I didn't know what I was missing then. To be honest, I have been fairly sleep-deprived since our first night together two months ago."

Stroking the shadow of stubble across his face, she followed her finger's movement. He shivered with the tickle and tried to bat her hand away. Laughing, she kissed him. "I completely understand. It was so tempting that morning to climb back into your arms and just stay there. It's a feeling that I could in no way recreate with a blanket or a good imagination."

"I can't tell you how disappointed I was to wake up that morning to find you gone, and how relieved I was to hear you taking a shower."

"Do you think that we would be here now if I had stayed in your bed? If we had made love that night, would it have ever progressed to this, or would it have been one night, and a memory we would relive forever?"

"I don't know." Darcy ran his fingers through her hair. "I think that would have depended on you. I would have come to your door to find you. I had just spent the happiest evening of my life with you in my arms. I am afraid that I was instantly addicted."

Elizabeth smiled. "And I was attempting to resist you."

"And fortunately failed spectacularly." He kissed her. "What would you like to do today?"

"How does a day of doing nothing sound to you?" She laughed at his expression. "Is that such a foreign concept to you?"

"Um, well, yes. I'm not sure that I know how to do nothing." Darcy tilted his head. "Will you teach me?"

"Because I am obviously quite adept at sloth."

"Did I say that?"

"It was implied."

"You started it." Darcy suddenly rolled to lie on top of her and grinned as she squealed. "If I am to be lazy all day, then I must get some more exercise this morning." He grinned then began devouring her lips.

"Will!" Elizabeth gasped.

"What?" He paused and smiled down at her.

"Nothing, I just like calling your name." She ran her hands down his back.

Darcy pressed his mouth to her ear. "Prepare to scream it, honey."

"HOW ARE THE lovebirds?" Arlene asked Georgiana.

"Oh, they are getting along very well." She looked out of the window. "I can't believe William is actually sitting outside with nothing but a book. He hasn't worked once all week!"

"That is extraordinary, if only he had met Elizabeth long ago . . . well thank heaven he has met her now. Tell me, how is she adjusting to Pemberley?"

"Well, sometimes she seems right at home, but sometimes she seems a little overwhelmed by it all." She watched as they touched hands then let go. "I wonder if there is anything we can do."

"It will just take time. I intend to host an engagement party for them. See if you can find out their schedules so I can start the plans. I think that the sooner Elizabeth is introduced to our friends the better. She will need to be comfortable with them."

"I think that Elizabeth can get along with anybody." Georgiana said with conviction.

"She hasn't met Catherine yet." Arlene said dryly. "Well, William will look after her then."

"Why must she be so . . ."

"Obnoxious?" Arlene laughed. "She has a rather inflated sense of her own worth."

"I hate how she bullies everyone. Oh, I shouldn't have said that!"

"No, bully is a good word for it." Arlene sighed. "Well, I have to go. Take care dear."

"I will. Bye!"

Elizabeth and Darcy were settled in lounge chairs under a large umbrella by the pool. Every so often they would catch the other's eye. "You look different."

"What do you mean?" Darcy tilted his head and smiled.

"The permanent crease between your eyes is gone. It took a week, but I think that you have finally let down and relaxed." She raised her brow and he sighed.

"I've been relaxed since we got on the helicopter to come here, but I guess it took this long to stop my mind from dwelling on other things." He touched her hand and they entwined their fingers. "I'm hoping that with you around I'll be able to do that more easily."

"Hmm. What day of the week is it?"

"It's . . ." Darcy looked up at her with wide eyes. "I . . . I think that it's Sunday?" He stared at her. "Yes it must be Sunday; the paper was very thick today. I'm right aren't I?"

Elizabeth giggled. "Yes, it's Sunday. I prescribe much more vacation for you. You won't really be relaxed until you can't tell me what day it is."

He laughed. "I imagine that by the time we return from our honeymoon I will certainly be in that state of blissful ignorance."

Georgiana was passing the front door on her way to the pool when she noticed a car pulling up to the house. "Oh no." She closed her eyes for a moment and walked up to open the door. "Hi Aunt Catherine, this is a nice surprise."

"Georgiana, well you look better than you did the last time I saw you. At least you have found your tongue." Catherine looked her up and down with a critical eye. "That bathing suit is far too revealing. No wonder you attracted the attention of my sister's worthless godson." She swept into the house and looked around. "Where is your brother, I need to speak to him."

"William and Elizabeth are out by the pool, I'll go get them."

"No, I said that I want your brother. Not that gold digger." She walked over to a table and ran her finger along it, checking for dust, and looked up. "Well? Go get him!"

Georgiana took off. Another car pulled in behind the first, and Anne and Greg entered the house. "Mom, what are you doing? It's none of your business who William marries."

"Yes it is!" She glared at her daughter. "Just because he rejected you . . ."

"For the millionth time it is illegal to marry your first cousin!" Anne yelled. "And what is wrong with Greg?"

"Yes, what exactly is wrong with Greg?" He folded his arms and looked at his mother-in-law. "I have yet to understand your objections to me."

"I have none." Catherine looked him over. "It is just disappointing to see a mother's dreams unfulfilled."

"Oh Good Lord." Anne groaned. Greg came over and held her hand.

Darcy walked into the foyer and smiled. "Well, this is a pleasant surprise! I didn't know that you were at Rosings or we would have invited you for dinner." He kissed his aunt's cheek then received a tight hug from Anne.

"Please don't let Mom's BS ruin your day, William." She whispered in his ear.

He withdrew and looked at her with concern, then met Greg's eyes as he shook his hand. "What brings you all here?"

"I am appalled to hear that you are engaged." Catherine declared. "I have not met this woman. How can you think of taking such a step without my approval?"

Darcy's eyes became ice cold. "I was not aware that it was required."

"In your mother's absence, I will take her place."

Anne closed her eyes and moaned. "I'm going to go and visit with Elizabeth and Georgiana." She looked back at Greg and he nodded.

"I'll lend some male support to Darcy." He looked at him apologetically.

"I don't understand why I need support at all, there is nothing to discuss here. I am marrying Elizabeth, and I might add that Uncle David and Aunt Arlene have met her and do approve." Darcy looked from one to the other.

"Perhaps we should move to someplace where we can speak privately." Greg took Catherine's arm and lifted his brow to Darcy. They moved to the library and shut the door. "Now Catherine, you know that clearly Darcy is not going to be influenced by your objections to Elizabeth, so why not tell him what is really bothering you?"

"Yes Aunt Catherine, please do." Darcy folded his arms and looked at her.

"Well, fine then, marry your little plaything . . ."

"She is a well-respected author and exceptional woman. Please choose your next description carefully." He glowered.

"You will grow tired of her and divorce. It may not be for a few years, but your eye will be caught by another pretty face and you will want to have a baby with her, no doubt, which will lead to another and another, just as every other rich man does who wants a new trophy by his side."

"What?" Darcy stared at her. "What are you talking about? Why would you presume that my devotion to my marriage would be so fleeting? I have no intention of divorcing . . . ever!"

"Well, nobody does Darcy, but since they do, I make a very good living." Greg shrugged at his furious glare. "Look, maybe this is the marriage for the ages, I'll tell you in forty years. What has Catherine upset is her belief that you won't have Elizabeth sign a prenuptial agreement."

"A prenup?" He sank down to sit on his desk. "I hadn't even considered it."

"You see! I was right! He was just going to let her have it all! He would let her take all of the houses, all of the money, everything!"

"What does it matter to you? It's my property not yours!" Darcy bellowed.

"But my association with the Darcy name makes it just as important to me! As well as to Anne and the rest of the family!" She screeched back. "It is my image!"

"Good God." Darcy stared at her in disgust.

Greg looked between the two. "Well, I don't buy into the whole image argument, but I do firmly believe in the prenup. I don't want you to lose everything that generations of Darcys have worked for because of your bad marriage."

"You are assuming that it's a failure already!" Darcy stood and ran his hand through his hair. "What exactly are you suggesting?"

Outside on the patio, Anne held Elizabeth's hand while she stared at her. "A prenup."

"I know, it is the most unromantic thing in the world, but it is important. I'm afraid that mom's approach is going to be taken very badly by William, but Greg is going to try to bring a dose of reality to the conversation. He's been a divorce lawyer for fifteen years, so he knows what he's talking about."

"Do you have . . . one?" Elizabeth's eyes were filled with tears.

"Yes." Anne sighed. "I hated the idea, too. I hated it when Greg spoke of it, but really it was for my protection, I have more than he does, at least property-wise. He has the bigger income. Really all it does is list out our individual assets at the time of our marriage, we agree that if we divorce he will retain those things that were his, and then there are provisions for a settlement of what we brought in after the marriage as well as for support of our children."

"Oh."

"It's meant to preserve what was in the family before the marriage, so it doesn't get scattered to the winds. If you have ever heard of entailments in the 1800's . . ."

"Yes, I read." Elizabeth was numb. "So you just assume that you will get divorced someday." She looked down at the ring on her hand.

"I don't believe you and William will ever get divorced Elizabeth." Georgiana declared. "And I bet that William is saying the same thing to Aunt Catherine and Greg."

"Well, maybe it's not a bad idea." She said softly as she continued to look at her hand. "I wouldn't want the family to be afraid that I would take the assets away in a bitter divorce." Elizabeth looked up, hearing the raised voices. "Is that William?" She stood and hurried into the house.

Inside of the library Greg watched as Darcy stood by the window, staring out at the lawn. "I know this is a very uncomfortable conversation, and I didn't like bringing it up with Anne, but she saw the value of it, to protect her property. I'm sorry, but I see marriages end every day. When do you go back to town?"

Numbly, Darcy said, "Next Saturday. Elizabeth has to travel on Sunday."

"Good, then I'll draw up a preliminary document, and we can get together next week and add in the things that I don't know about. I assume that she doesn't have much so we'll determine her support amounts, and what you will give to each child, then you can sit down with her and show her . . ."

"That I have no faith in our future." Darcy looked up at him. "I have heard enough. If there is nothing else, I'd appreciate it if you would . . . leave us alone."

"Darcy . . ."

He walked to the door and opened it, and strode out. "Well, where does he think he's going?" Catherine demanded.

Greg sighed and walked over to the door. "I imagine he is going to Elizabeth."

Darcy turned back and addressed them both. "I suppose that I should not be surprised by the presumption of my aunt to meddle in my affairs, but I thought better of you, Greg."

"Will?" He turned to see Elizabeth's stricken face.

"What did Anne say to you?"

"It was probably a gentler version of what was said to you." Darcy grasped her hands and saw the distress in her eyes. "They just assume we will divorce, don't they?"

"So, this is the woman you have roped yourself to." Catherine emerged from the library and looked over Elizabeth. She took in her bikini, her bare feet, her windblown hair, and sneered. "Well, clearly he was attracted by your ability to appeal to his baser instincts."

Elizabeth flushed. "Mrs. de Bourgh, your nephew has been very clear in his opinions of me and why he wishes to spend his life with me. However those opinions are private. As are mine of him."

"I could care less about your opinions." Catherine sniffed.

"And I feel the same about yours." Elizabeth snapped back and allowed anger to overcome her hurt. "Furthermore, I will not tolerate someone so unrelated to me pronouncing that I am mercenary or . . . a whore!" Darcy looked at her sharply and his face set into its unreadable mask. "How can you come into this home and declare our marriage a sham, and doomed to failure? Have you no faith in your nephew, if not me? Don't you know his character? You obviously question his judgment. It seems that the countless employees, associates, and stockholders are incorrect. He can't think for himself or make wise decisions. He has been hoodwinked by the clever woman who wants to take him for every penny."

"We know Darcy, but we do not know you."

Elizabeth glared at her. "Oh so I am already at fault for ruining this marriage before it begins? I will not stand for your interference in my affairs."

"YOUR affairs! Do you hear this Darcy? Do you hear this little . . . gold digger? She practically spells it out for you, clear as day! She wants me to not interfere because she sees the prize! You are blind!"

"Aunt Catherine that is enough. You will not insult my fiancé in our home." Darcy said coldly. "Please leave."

Greg looked between the glaring trio. "I'll call you, Darcy."

"If it is on the subject of your visit, do not bother." He looked at Anne. "I thought that you hoped I would marry, you wished to dance at my wedding."

"I am thrilled that you have found each other, William, I truly am. I did not come here to break you up, that was Mom, not Greg or me. I only thought Elizabeth would be better off hearing about the prenup from the woman's perspective. I did not mean it to hurt either of you. I'm sorry."

"Fine, you are sorry, but how can you presume to enter my home and dispense your advice? You have taken the happiest week of my life . . . our lives, and . . . ruined it by your unwanted intrusion! I neither wanted nor sought your help. Do you think I should be grateful for this? That I would see this as being a service? I am not a child who requires direction." He turned to Catherine. "Your pronouncements are inexcusable as well." Darcy took Elizabeth's hand and began to walk back out to the patio. "You can see yourselves out."

Anne started to speak and caught Georgiana's angry eye. They left, and Darcy leaned in to kiss Elizabeth. "I'm so sorry for that."

She stood frozen and stared at him. "I don't know what to think . . . what to do."

Darcy's eyes searched hers. "What do you mean? Lizzy . . . we are okay; please don't let this display effect us! We are unchanged! We will marry! Won't we?"

She looked down. "I don't know."

He seized her shoulders and tried to look in her eyes. "Do you doubt me?"

"No . . . I . . . Will, I was just labeled a whore!" She cried.

"By a miserable old woman who cares only for her status and bank account, her life has nothing to do with ours!" His voice rose along with his fear.

"It must if she and her child felt free to come in here to dictate our marriage! Is this what I can expect in our future? What of the Fitzwilliams? Do they feel the same?"

"No! You can't compare Aunt Catherine to them! They love you!"

"But won't they give you the same advice?" She was met by silence and Darcy's downcast eyes. "I need . . . I need to talk . . . I need to talk to Jane."

His eyes came back up. "Jane? Talk to ME!"

"Will . . . I need MY family right now!" She turned and ran inside the house. Georgiana tried to stop her, but was ignored. She went out to the patio to see William with an expression of fury on his face.

"What did you say to her?" She demanded.

"Me? I am still here! I didn't run away!" His hand went through his hair. "What did Anne tell her?"

"She told her she hated the prenup, but she knew that it was necessary to protect her property."

"Ridiculous." Darcy said angrily.

"Maybe . . . maybe . . ."

He spun away. "I'm going to call Uncle David." He strode to the library and shut the door.

UPSTAIRS ELIZABETH sat on the bed hugging a pillow. "What should I do, Jane?" She cried.

"Lizzy, every bride I know has a prenup."

"What?!"

"Once I broke into the high-end weddings, I ran across young girls marrying rich men. You know the planning for the weddings takes over a year, and I get close to my brides. I was always privy to the day they went to the lawyers. The smart girls took their own lawyer with them to look after their interests."

"Their interests? They were marrying men they didn't trust? I am not to trust William?"

Jane heard the confusion and distress in her voice and said steadily, "I think that you need to call Uncle Ray."

"But he is a family lawyer for . . . normal people." She said softly.

"Yes, but he can tell you the truth."

DARCY SAT behind his desk, his eyes were closed and he was rubbing his temple. "That's the reality Darcy; surely your lawyer would have told you this is necessary when you went to change your will."

"I had no intention of doing this." He was numb.

"Don't be naive! This is cold. It is hard. It is business. Love is wonderful, but you represent a great deal more than just love. This doesn't have to be adversarial, just unemotional. Be sure that she is represented, and not by anyone who is connected to you."

"Yes, of course, I could not ask her to blindly sign anything . . . well she knows the importance of reading contracts from her work in publishing . . ." His eyes closed, and he tried to remove the image of Elizabeth's hurt expression from his mind. "I can't even begin to say how disappointed I am in Anne and Greg, Aunt Catherine I could expect this from, but . . ."

"Their approach was unfortunate, but keep in mind that they probably had spent hours listening to Catherine rage about your engagement before they even arrived. I told her of it yesterday when she returned from out of town . . . I imagine her first order of business was to leave for Rosings in the morning, Anne probably knew and followed her."

Darcy's thoughts moved back to the real issue. "How am I to put a value on Elizabeth?" He said softly.

David spoke deliberately. "You won't have to. Your lawyer will."

ELIZABETH stared at her shocked face in the mirror across from the bed. "Wait a minute Uncle Ray, you mean there are actually calculations to determine my value?"

"Yes Lizzy. It takes into account your career if you would be giving it up to be his wife. Will you stay home? Will you serve as his hostess, or his representative at charity events? If you are a mother, the children you produce and each passing year you spend with him earns you more credit . . ."

"But . . ."

DAVID spoke sincerely. "Darcy it must be done. I would have had this conversation with you when you returned."

"LIZZY, when I heard of your engagement, I intended to contact you. You especially need someone to represent your interests before you sign anything. This is cold, but really, your fiancé has no choice, not if he is honest. His relatives' timing and presentation were unfortunate, but . . . also not unexpected."

Numbly Elizabeth murmured. "There is no choice, we must plan for failure."

"I am afraid so."

"I . . . thank you Uncle Ray."

"Please do not be angry with him, Lizzy. I understand how you are feeling, believe me."

DARCY spoke with resignation. "How am I supposed to tell her this? I am to reduce our future to a series of calculations?"

"You must, but remember, you do not have to screw her over either. You do love her. You do intend to remain married forever. Make it as generous as you wish. You are providing for her and your children's futures. We truly are very happy for you, and love the choice you have made for your partner to continue the

Darcy family." There was silence. "Now Son, you need to go find Elizabeth and reassure her."

He awoke from the dark place his thoughts had taken him, the place where Elizabeth had left him. "Yes, thanks Uncle David." Darcy hung up and stood. He walked from the library and found Georgiana waiting outside. He spoke quietly. "Where is Elizabeth?"

"She is in your room. Is everything okay?" She asked him worriedly.

"I don't know yet." He squeezed her hand and fought back his emotion. Making his way up the stairs, he stood outside the bedroom door and listened. Hearing Elizabeth's sobs, he entered, closed the door and approaching the bed, gathered her in his arms. "Elizabeth."

They clung to each other. Elizabeth eventually withdrew a little, and then felt his tears upon her shoulder. Darcy held her tighter. "I . . . I spoke to my uncle. . . Ray Philips . . . he's a family law attorney . . . he told me . . . you don't have a choice but to do this. He told me what is involved and . . . offered to represent my interests."

"Lizzy. . . "

"I guess that I was foolish to think that I could fall in love with a billionaire and just live happily ever after."

"Why can't we do that?" He murmured against her cheek.

"They all assume we will fail."

"We will prove them wrong. They are not living with us." He sighed. "I spoke to Uncle David . . . he said it had . . . it had to be done. . . .but . . ."

She looked up and touched his brow. "The crease is back between your eyes." He smiled slightly. "I hate hearing that we are assumed to divorce . . . but I guess I see the sense in the idea."

"Honey, I had no plans to ask you to sign such a document."

"I know." She smiled weakly. "I know, and that is why I won't object if you want me to."

"I don't want you to." He said fiercely.

"But your family does, and if it will preserve the peace with them, I am willing to do that. I don't want this to be a reason for them not to accept me." Elizabeth rested against his chest and he hugged her tight.

"I hate this." He spoke softly. They held each other for several minutes, then he raised his head. "How does this sound? I'll ask my lawyer to prepare the agreement. Your uncle can look it over, and any changes he wants to make will be done."

"Will . . ."

"No Lizzy, I understand their desire to keep the estates in the bloodline, but I'll be damned if they are going to tell me how to treat my wife and children. I intended to have a new will drawn up in the coming weeks. I'll have my lawyer prepare this damned agreement, so only you and I will know the particulars, but only if you truly wish to do this. Do not even dare to let this weigh on your mind. I will be marrying you for better or worse."

"Richer or poorer?" She sniffed.

"For as long as we both shall live." He said softly and kissed her. "I love you, honey. Please don't let this ruin everything."

Elizabeth wiped the tears rolling down his face. "I'll make a deal with you. If you ever make me so annoyed that I would contemplate leaving you, I will come and leave a copy of the prenup under your nose to remind you of your commitment."

"May I do the same for you?" Darcy smiled and wiped the tears from her cheeks.

"That's only fair." She swallowed and buried her face in his chest. "I hope that you'll never need to do that."

"I know that I won't." They remained embraced and listened to the distant sound of the waves crashing onto the beach.

Elizabeth laughed softly. "You know, if my parents had signed a prenup, they would have been divorced ages ago. I think that document might actually make it easier to give up on a marriage."

Darcy smiled a little. "Well, what better reason do we have to make the agreement as unattractive to implement as possible?" He hugged her tight. "It's going to be okay, honey."

Elizabeth pushed away and looked up at him. "I think I want to take a walk."

"Let's go." He stood and held out his hand.

"No, alone. I need to think."

Darcy took both of her hands in his and kneeled beside her. "What are you going to think about? Please Lizzy; please don't let this . . . thing . . . change your mind about me."

"No, I love you Will. That will never change. Sometimes I just need to walk." She touched his face and saw the worry there. "The paths of Central Park are very familiar to me."

"I'm afraid that they are because you had nobody to turn to before. You have me now." He leaned forward and kissed her.

"I know." She stood and he rose with her. "I'll just go change clothes."

Elizabeth left and he sank down on the bed to watch her go. He didn't know what to think; maybe she just was being hit again with the difference between them. He prayed that she was not thinking of leaving him. Soon she appeared, changed into shorts and shirt, her hair pulled back in a pony tail. She held up her phone and smiled. "See, you can find me."

"That's not funny, Lizzy."

She could not miss how hurt he was, and quickly realized her mistake, she was shutting him out the way he had done to her earlier in the week, and she had not liked it then. "I'm sorry, Will. Here I am upset with your aunt for even suggesting that we might not remain married, and I'm pushing you away. None of this is your fault. Will you walk with me?"

He glanced up at her and away. "Are you sure that you want me?"

"Yes, I want you forever." She sat down and kissed him. "I'll wait for you as you change." He left and she closed her eyes. *William believes we will make it, but we won't if we don't face these things together. You can't just run off and be alone when something upsets you anymore. You love him, let him love you!* She did not hear his return.

Darcy touched her shoulder. "I'm ready."

They held hands and started walking in silence. Once they had reached the walkway to the beach, Elizabeth spoke. "I think that I have trouble sometimes recognizing how dissimilar our lives are because we are also so much alike. I've never really felt it when I'm with you. It took your aunt and cousin to show me how the outside world looks at you." She saw his creased brow and continued. "Neither you nor Georgiana seem to be very enamored of your status. You seem to take for granted the trappings of your wealth, which I suppose is only natural, but you also don't flaunt it, which is why I suppose that I never felt in awe of you. What did your parents do to make you so, well, normal?"

Darcy smiled. "Normal? Do you think that I am different from other rich men?"

"Obviously I don't know that many, but surely you see a difference between yourself and your peers."

"Keeping in mind your statement about wealth and my aunt's concerns with preserving her image, I suppose that some could be labeled as shallow."

Elizabeth nodded. "That's it. That's what I was thinking about. You wear designer clothes but could really care less about it. You buy the best because there is no reason to settle for less, but don't buy more because you can."

"Oh, I understand now. Well, we both always had to work for our allowances, and were always expected to buy our own . . . toys, if you will."

"What did you do to earn your keep? I had to wash dishes." Elizabeth relaxed a little and smiled.

"Well, we did have staff for that, but I did have to maintain excellent grades, and if I asked for some lessons, like when I learned how to ride? I was expected to help care for the horse."

"So you were taught that your pleasure had to be earned with some sort of sacrifice on your part."

"It prepared us for the reality of working." Darcy smiled. "What is your point, Lizzy?"

"I think that my point is . . . that unlike some who come into money and don't earn it, you have. You respect what you have received, and appreciate what it took to accumulate and maintain it. You understand the concept of hard work and . . . because of that you would not be likely to . . . walk away from your marriage if things seemed . . ." She struggled for the words and he stopped walking and held her hands.

"I know that it won't always be easy, Lizzy. I grew up witnessing a good marriage, but even my parents had their moments of difficulty. The difference is that I watched them work it out. I'm so happy that you changed your mind and asked me to come with you for this walk. That proved to me that you want this marriage as much as I do." He smiled and tilted his head. "I think those principals apply to any couple, no matter the wealth or disparity in their beginnings."

"So I should stop worrying." Elizabeth smiled.

"A little worry might keep us on our toes, but I think that we shouldn't spend too much energy on it. There are far more productive things to occupy our minds."

"Such as?"

"I don't know. I just . . . this truly has been the happiest week of my life, and I do not want to lose the joy of our engagement because of this. Can we agree to . . .

put this aside, allow our lawyers to do their work and . . . when you return from your trip, we can deal with it then? Don't let them ruin our happiness."

She read his face; they were both working hard to maintain their composure. "Well let's return to pleasant thoughts, shall we? We're on vacation." Elizabeth leaned into him and he put his arm around her shoulder as they began walking again. "Sing to me."

"Lizzy . . ." He stopped and saw that she was begging him with her eyes. Lifting one hand to her face, he caressed her cheek, and softly sang, "Some enchanted evening, when you find your true love, you will feel her call you across a crowded room, then fly to her side, and make her your own . . . for all through your life you may dream all alone. Once you have found her, never let her go. Once you have found her . . . never let her go.^{iv}" Their lips met and they stood tightly embraced, remaining on the beach until well after the sun had set.

THE HELICOPTER landed and within minutes the three travelers were in Darcy's car and heading back to the real world. Georgiana was looking out of the windows at Wall Street and Darcy was looking down at Elizabeth's hand clasped in his. She touched his cheek and his eyes lifted. "I had a wonderful time."

"Me, too." He fell into silence and went back to looking at their hands.

Georgiana turned around. "It will be good to be home again, and not living in the dorms."

"You didn't like your roommate?" Elizabeth smiled. "I know that I wished I could change mine. She talked in her sleep."

"Mine kept bringing her boyfriend in; I spent a lot of time in the practice rooms." She shrugged. "It was a learning experience, I guess."

"Well, yes that is the point of requiring freshmen to live on campus, to expose you to different people, and, of course, to really express yourself in decorating your room." Her eyes danced. "What cute guy in his underwear did you hang up? I remember my poster boy, he was . . ."

"Nobody that we need to hear about." Darcy said softly and squeezed her hand.

Elizabeth laughed and Georgiana giggled. The car stopped in traffic and they looked out at the people moving by on the sidewalks, and she noticed the Tiffany store. "So much has happened in the last two weeks." She looked down at their hands. "I can't believe I'm leaving tomorrow. At least our separation should be the last for a while."

"I will be lost the second we say goodbye." He kissed her hand. "There is no way to make this easier, Lizzy, but thank you for trying."

"Ahhhh."

"Quiet Georgie." Darcy said softly and put his arm around Elizabeth.

The car pulled up in front of the old brownstone building. Darcy got out then offered his hand to help Elizabeth. "Frank, take Georgiana home, I'll call you later."

She bent and looked in the door. "Take care at school; call me if you need to talk, okay?"

"I will." She paused. "Elizabeth?" She moved up to whisper. "William is looking like he used to, please call him a lot when you're away."

"I promise, I will. I'm going to be miserable, too."

"Thanks, take care." Georgiana closed the door and the car drove off. They stood on the sidewalk holding hands.

"How long are you staying?"

"As long as you'll have me." He smiled and kissed her. "I thought that we will probably have to put in an appearance with your parents."

"Yes, I am sure of that." She picked up a suitcase and he picked up the other. They made it up to her apartment undetected and she opened the door. "Are you hungry?"

He shrugged. "A little, do you want to go get something?"

"No silly, I'll cook it. I don't have any milk, but everything else should be okay." She dropped her suitcases in the bedroom and went into the kitchen to survey what was available. "Hmm." She rooted about and found some frozen chicken and vegetables. Darcy settled on a stool to watch and stay out of her way.

"Do you want to help?"

"I have no knife skills, Lizzy."

Elizabeth's hands landed on her hips and she tilted her head. "Can you stir?"

"I can handle that." He stood up and smiled. "What do you need?"

She threw a handful of vegetables into the hot wok and gave him a spatula. "Keep it moving." He started jabbing at the pan and Elizabeth grabbed his hand, showing him the correct motion. Darcy learned quickly to duck when the new items were added and received a glare when he lifted the lid on the boiling rice. "Don't touch that." He laughed and soon enough the cooking was finished.

"Why didn't we do this at Pemberley?" He asked as a forkful of the stir fried chicken was fed to him.

"Because you wouldn't let me." She smiled and picked up the bowl. They settled at her little table looking out over the street and ate, feeding each other and talking about the past weeks. There came a lull in the conversation and Darcy asked the question that had been on his mind since he proposed.

"Lizzy, would you consider moving in with me?"

"And leaving all of this?" She smiled and waved her fork. Catching his serious expression, she bit her lip and said softly, "I was wondering if you would ask me."

"And what sort of a response did you plan to make when I asked?" He smiled and raised his brows. "I sincerely hope it was yes."

"I'll be honest with you, that house is intimidating."

"Why?"

"Will, look at this place, then think of your home. I'll be afraid to touch anything there."

"It's hardly a museum."

"Not according to the historical commission."

"I think that you are afraid to come live with me."

"No I'm not."

"Then come and live with me." He spoke urgently and took her hand. "Honey it's going to kill me not to sleep with you tonight and every night that you are away. Please give me the hope that when you return, it will be to our home. You will be living there in a few weeks anyway, please come now." He looked around the room. "I know that you would want to bring things from here with you, please do, I just . . . need you with me."

"It will be a whole new world." She said softly.

"But it will be ours." His head tilted and he watched her considering his plea.

"Ours." She smiled. "I really like how that sounds."

"So you will come?" A smile began spreading over his face.

"Yes."

A knock at the door prevented any expression of happiness. Elizabeth peeked through the peephole. "It's Jane!" She threw open the door and they hugged.

"Hi!" Jane grabbed Elizabeth's hand. "Okay, show me the rock. Oh, very well done, William!" Jane looked up at him with an approving nod. "Not too big, so she can actually wear this everyday, but definitely impressive enough to make a statement."

He walked over to observe the examination, and rubbed Elizabeth's shoulders. "Thanks, I had very little to do with the process."

"You chose it." She touched his hand and smiled.

"I had help." He leaned down to kiss her, then was surprised to receive a kiss from Jane on his cheek. "I guess that I'm welcomed into the family now?"

"Oh, wait until you see Mom." Jane sat down in a chair while Darcy and Elizabeth took the couch. "She knows all about you now. Lydia looked you up online and called, spilling the beans. Mom took a cab to drive by the house and has been calling everyone she has ever known to crow about your capture of a rich man."

Elizabeth groaned and Darcy closed his eyes and flushed. "I knew this would happen."

"Oh, and she has been bothering me nearly every day about wedding plans. She wants it held in St. Patrick's Cathedral."

"We're not Catholic, Jane."

"Yeah, I know that. She just likes the look of the place. Oh, and the reception, I think that she's up to 500 on the guest list. I had no idea that she knew so many obscure people."

"I knew it! I knew she would be this way!" Elizabeth said with frustration then appealed to William. "Do you understand my apprehension now?"

Taking her hand he spoke very sincerely. "I do. But don't let her bully you into something you don't want. This is our wedding, not hers. I want it to be small. I can't tell you how much I would hate having to stand in front of a huge crowd of people."

"No you don't have to tell me, I know already that it would be torture for you." She turned to Jane. "Have you tried to temper this enthusiasm? Has Dad?"

"You know Dad; he just went into his library to sulk about you getting married." Jane laughed to hear Elizabeth's groan. "I can't do much about her, Lizzy. I seriously suggest that you elope."

Another knock came and the door flew open. "LIZZY!"

"Oh Good Lord." She sighed and they all stood. "Hi Mom. Hi Dad."

"Well, let me see!" Fran grabbed her hand and stared with wide eyes, then ignoring her daughter turned to embrace Darcy. He startled and patted the grasping woman's shoulder and stared helplessly at Tom. "Oh you wonderful man! And so rich! Oh, and I never realized how TALL you are!" She looked up to him with an expression that frighteningly resembled lust, and Darcy stepped away to move closer to Elizabeth.

"Mom!" Elizabeth took his hand and felt his tight grasp. "Please calm down! Now, Jane told me of your plans and I want you to stop whatever you're doing right now. William and I have already decided that we want a small ceremony and reception with just our immediate family and a few friends, and a little outdoor reception at Pemberley. That is ALL. No frills and lace, no hundreds of guests. This is our day."

"But you are my daughter and it is my right to . . ."

"Take over my wedding? I don't think so!" Elizabeth glared at her and looked at her silent father. "Will you please help me, Dad?"

"I'm just hoping this is all a bad dream and you won't marry at all." He smiled and saw her disappointment, then noticed how Darcy moved to put his hands on her shoulders and whisper in her ear. "It seems that this is not a subject for levity. Fran, please leave them alone. They are adults. We will be happy to be their guests and just enjoy whatever they decide to do."

"But . . . at least let me choose your gown!"

"NO!"

Jane stepped in. "Maybe Mom, you could help me look over the menus for the caterers and make a recommendation for Lizzy. We could taste the various offerings."

"Oh, well I suppose that wouldn't be too bad." She sniffed.

Elizabeth looked at Jane who leaned over to her. "I have to meet a few new caterers this week, I'll just bring her along, she doesn't have to know who you and William choose, but it will make her think she had a part in it."

"I love you, Jane!" Elizabeth kissed her cheek.

"I know." She winked and noticed that William was still standing uncomfortably. "I have a date with Charles tonight."

He brightened. "How is that going?"

"It's just our third date, but I like him. He's pretty enthusiastic about everything. Is he always so happy?" She tilted her head.

Darcy laughed. "Yes, he is. He has been the perfect counterpart to me."

"Not anymore, you have a lovely smile." Elizabeth looked up and he kissed her nose.

"But I will be my normal morose self tomorrow." His cheek rested on her hair and his arms came around her waist.

"You are leaving in the morning, Lizzy?" Tom asked, watching both of them lapsing into silence. "When do you return?"

"Friday." Darcy's arms tightened. "I have some appearances the first three days, then have to drop in at the conference in Vegas for two, and then I'll be home late . . . and that will be all. No more travel after this." She looked up to his sad eyes. "Then we'll just be together and work on our next adventure."

"It can't come soon enough." He said softly.

"I think that we should leave these two alone." Jane took her parents' arms and directed them to the door. "If I don't see you before you leave, have a good time Lizzy. Call me."

"Okay." She waved and watched the door close.

Darcy's lips found her throat the second the door closed. "Wait!" She tried to move away from his embrace and he only held her tighter.

"No."

"Will, I just want to bolt the door." He instantly let go and strode forward, turned the lock, slammed the recently installed deadbolt in place, attached the new chain bolt, then looking around, fixed a chair beneath the handle. He nodded at his handiwork and turned back to face Elizabeth. She had her hands clasped over her mouth, holding in her laughter.

"Come here." He grabbed her waist and roughly pulled her against him. "Now, I want to try out your bed."

"I have a feeling this will be the only time that this happens."

"Go with the feeling, Lizzy." He picked her up and carried her to the bedroom, then set her down gently. His face held no expression, but his eyes were burning with emotion.

"What do you need, Will? What will make you feel better?"

Wordlessly he undressed her, and just as quickly removed his own clothes. "Lie down and close your eyes." She climbed up on the bed, and he handed her the phone. "Now, call me."

"Call you?" She looked at him in confusion, then a smile appeared, she closed her eyes and spoke softly. "Hi Will."

"Hi honey."

"I miss you."

"I can't say how much I miss you." Darcy climbed onto the bed and began kissing her calves. "What are you wearing?"

"Mmm, nothing at all, it's just so warm in here."

"Is it?" His lips wandered up her legs. "Are you very hot?"

"Mmm, oh dripping." She gasped as his tongue found its way between her thighs and then tasted her.

"Soaking wet, I would imagine." He licked and tasted until she began to squirm, and he lifted his head to see her eyes were still closed. His hands traced up her stomach to caress her breasts. "How can I help you cool down from so far away?"

"I think that a bath would do me a lot of good." She sighed with his firm touch.

"I can give you a bath with my tongue, would that feel good, baby?" He whispered. "Imagine my mouth gliding up your body." He slowly licked his way up over her stomach and began suckling her breasts. "Mmm, I'm thirsty; all of this bathing has left me parched."

"Well I know what you can do for that." Elizabeth moaned with his touches. "Have a cool drink."

"Your lips would quench my thirst, will you kiss me?" He lay down on her and took away the phone that was held in her limp hand. His mouth hovered over hers, and he closed his eyes, just letting her breath tickle his face, making a memory of the touch of her skin on his, and the feel of her heart beating against his chest. "Oh honey, it's as if you were really here."

"Kiss me, Will."

He kept his eyes closed and leaned down to touch his lips to hers. Elizabeth's hands snaked up into his hair, and his slipped beneath her back to hold her tight. Their kisses were slow and loving; both were trying to show how very deeply their lover would be missed. They so naturally joined their bodies, simply slipping together and moving with the rhythm, first from their stroking mouths, and then from their rocking hips. Darcy's kisses moved to her ear. "Can you feel me inside of you? I'm moving slowly, just the way you like it."

"Oh, Will, yes . . ."

"Do you want it harder, baby? Do you want me deep inside?" He started moving faster.

"I want all of you, Will."

"You have me." He lifted up to feel her hips matching his pace. "Are you there, honey?"

"Ohhhhhhhhh."

"Oh, yes."

Darcy settled back down on her and kissed her parted lips, then tasted the soft sheen of perspiration on her brow. "Now my Lizzy, when I call you this week, and I ask what you're wearing, this is what I'm going to be imagining. I'm going to be thinking of us loving each other."

"I will, too." Her eyes fluttered open to see his warm smile, and caressed his face. "I love you."

"I love you." He sighed. "What would be better, should I say goodbye now, or stay with you tonight?"

"Oh honey, I don't know." Elizabeth's eyes were bright.

"Now, I think." He got up and held his hands out to help her rise. "If I'm here in the morning, I won't let you go." He smiled and kissed her. "I'll call you and we can talk all night."

"Okay." Elizabeth dressed and walked out of the room so he wouldn't see her cry. Darcy dressed and looked around the room for a keepsake, and smiling, stole a pillow from her bed.

"Hey, I'm going to start moving your things to our room." He held up the pillow. "This will keep me company until you come home." Darcy laughed to see her smile. "I'm sorry that I don't have anything to give you."

She took a camera from her purse and pointed it at him. "Hold it up and give it a kiss." He rolled his eyes. "Oh, you know full well you'll be kissing it goodnight." He blushed and kissed the pillow while she snapped the picture. Giggling, she showed it to him. "There, perfect. I'll just look at this and think of you."

"Silly girl." He grabbed his phone and called for Frank. "Ten minutes, that's fine." Turning back to her he took her hand. "Come on, let's wait outside. I can't bear to watch you packing."

"Let's go." They sat out on the stoop, Elizabeth leaning in his arms. A cab appeared and Bingley jumped out.

"Hey!" He grinned and offered his hand. "Congratulations!"

"Thanks!" Darcy grinned and looked down to see Elizabeth beaming.

"May I kiss the bride?" He bent down to buss her cheek and leaned against the railing. "So, I got an invitation to your engagement party."

Darcy rolled his eyes. "Aunt Arlene insisted. She demanded a list of people to invite. I have no idea what she has in mind."

"Well I'm looking forward to it; after all, my date is guaranteed to be there!" He smiled and looked at Elizabeth. "I really like Jane, she's so real."

"As opposed to . . ."

"Oh all of the girls I've dated in the past. They were all beautiful, but they knew it, and that's all they thought about. Jane is very. . . I don't know, just happy to be herself." He shrugged. "It is a pleasure to be with her. I just wish it was more often."

"Well, it is wedding season. And she is cautious after watching me fail so spectacularly." Elizabeth received a look from William. "What?"

"So by marrying me you are failing?"

"Ohhhhh. YOU know what I meant!" She pinched him and he laughed. Frank pulled up with the car and the laughter stopped. Charles saw how their expressions changed and cleared his throat. "Well, um, I'll just head up to Jane's place. I'll see you in the morning Darcy; well I'll try to behind the stack of work that's sitting on your desk." He laughed at his groan and headed up the steps to ring Jane's bell. The door buzzed and he went inside.

"I guess this is goodbye for awhile." Darcy hugged her. "Call me when you've finished your packing and . . . whatever else you need to do."

"I will." She kissed him and he smiled a little. "I'll be home soon."

"I know." He sighed. "I'll have to remember this feeling the next time I leave you."

"Well if you have to travel, this is the week to do it." She looked at him pointedly.

"Yes, ma'am." They kissed and she walked with him to the car. He climbed in and she leaned over him to have one last kiss. "I love you." They whispered together, and he was gone.

Chapter 10

"William would hate this." Elizabeth looked out of the taxi window as they drove up to their hotel.

"He hates gaudy?" Charlotte laughed and leaned forward to pay the driver. They got out and entered the hotel to check in, already spotting and waving at familiar faces and friends from the publishing world.

"I can't thank you enough for not making me attend this whole convention. I could not do a week."

"Well, the word is out that your contract is up, so you will be courted quite aggressively by the other publishers. I am simply working in my best interests and keeping you less available." She winked and Elizabeth sighed. They made their way up to their rooms, and agreed to meet later for an awards dinner. She flopped down on the bed and looked around, then paused. Sitting on the dresser was a vase filled with what must have been four dozen red and yellow roses. She stood up and walked towards them, almost giddy with excitement, and opened up the sealed envelope tucked inside.

Elizabeth,

I am now four days without you, and so lonely. I have buried myself in work as I struggle in vain to distract my thoughts. I admit freely that I hope you are just as miserable. I miss you, no that doesn't do my feelings justice. I am bereft. These roses are special, shall I tell you why? Because they are from our homes. The red roses are from Pemberley, the yellow are from the city. I wanted you to have a piece of our life with you, while I wait for your return to my arms. I love you, honey. Please come home soon.

Always,
William

"Oh." She bent and smelled the flowers, touching the soft petals and then wiping the tears that were streaming down her cheeks. Walking back to the bed she found the phone inside of her purse and called him.

"Thank you." She sniffed.

Darcy grinned widely. "You are very welcome, Lizzy. Do they look okay? They had quite a journey."

"They are perfect. How did you do this?"

"I'll never tell, then I won't be able to do it again." He laughed and leaned forward, resting his elbows on his desk and smiling at the picture he kept of her there. "I love you, honey. How are you?"

"I am miserable, does that satisfy?" She laughed and wiped her eyes again. "My makeup is ruined, I'm an emotional mess, and I really want to go home. Oh, and I love you, Will."

"That was an afterthought?" He prodded with a grin.

"It may become one if you don't stop picking on me."

"Who's picking?" Darcy sighed and sat back. "What's on the agenda tonight?"

"Oh, a dinner sponsored by the librarians. I've missed most of the day's events already. I'll be hitting it hard tomorrow. There's a booth in the convention hall where I'll hand out advance copies of the book and sign autographs, and watch Charlotte try to keep other publishers from noticing me." She laughed. "I'd like to get tickets to hear a couple of people speak, but I don't know if my heart is in it to get up at dawn and fight for them, besides, I'll be too busy. I'm just glad that I don't have to speak."

"Have you in the past?"

"Yes, I was an example of success at a young age, well; it was a big deal at the time. It wasn't my cup of tea then, but I imagine I would do a much better job now, I'm more confident. It really helped having dad traveling with me when I was still in school; he was the one I would focus on in the audience."

"I hate speaking in front of a crowd so I am in awe of you." He heard her sigh and smiled. "What happens tomorrow night?"

"Another dinner, formal, and then Friday morning there is a sponsored breakfast before the convention breaks up. I'll get to see a lot of people I have met through the years and swap news." Elizabeth looked down at her hand. "I think I'll have the biggest story to tell this time."

"Oh yeah? What about?" Darcy bit his lip and grinned.

"Hmm, some guy . . . can't remember his name, he well, you know, he just bought me this big sparkly ring, and I thought, what the heck, I'll marry him!" She giggled.

"So you are easily persuaded by shallow gifts? I'll have to keep that in mind."

"No, I want more than jewels." Elizabeth whispered.

"What else do you want?" Darcy whispered back.

"I want the sexiest blue eyes I've ever seen staring down at me while the man I crave demonstrates again what a passionate and talented lover he is."

He groaned. "Lizzy, you're making me hard and I have to go to a meeting!"

"Oh, I would love to be under the table taking care of that problem for you. Just think about that while you listen to the speaker drone on. I would open your fly and release that serpent you keep hidden away; and . . ."

"Lizzzzzy." She could hear the plea in his voice.

"Suck you."

"Baby."

She could hear him breathing raggedly and blushed when he moaned, realizing what was happening. His breathing relaxed and she heard him fumbling around. "Are you okay?"

"I am now." He said quietly. "I . . . I have never done that before. Not while I'm talking to you." He took a deep breath. "I really liked it."

"I could tell." Elizabeth giggled.

"Come home soon, sweetie."

"I will. In the meantime, I think that I'll do a little daydreaming of my own, maybe of a certain man in a rose garden."

"Me?"

"There is nobody else." She smiled to hear his satisfied sigh.

"I have to go, honey, I'm sorry. Charles is knocking, and I guess I had better wash up." Darcy bit his lip and blushed to hear her delighted laugh. "Call me when you are finished for the night."

"Okay, I will. I love you."

"I love you, too." He listened for her to hang up and rested his head back against his chair, reliving the conversation for a moment. Charles's knock woke him from his daydream and he went into the washroom then opened the door. "Are you ready?"

"Been ready." Charles looked him over. "What's up with you?"

"Nothing." He smiled and clapped his back. "I'm fine."

GARY HANSEN sat across the table from Jack Carter, Darcy's attorney. "Are you sure that your client approves of this?"

Jack nodded slowly. "He wants her to be cared for, as he said, properly. Even if they do divorce, he said that the happiness she has brought him since they met will compensate him for any pain that may eventually come. I know, it's hard to believe, but I can't talk him down. If you look at his total worth, this is only a fraction of it. I wouldn't allow him to give away the farm, no matter how much he wanted to. He does that in his will. But in the case of divorce, I had to be firm. I'm sure that you understand that." He met Gary's eye.

"This is extraordinarily generous. He is an unusual man." Gary sat back and smiled. "I can't see any objections to it, my job was easy. I am used to seeing contracts where assets are hidden or corners are cut. Where the poorer member of the couple is deceived into signing something that is not in their best interests . . . I have a feeling that this document will be used to light a fire someday."

"I certainly hope so. It would do my heart good to see it. It is really a contract for a partnership instead of a plan for dissolution. When Darcy emailed me his wish list of things to include . . . I was amazed. They are prepared for everything from illness to continuing their foundations beyond death. This is the happiest prenup I have ever seen." Jack smiled; and relaxed back into his chair. "Well, when Miss Bennet returns from her trip, we'll set up a meeting to make this official. I was surprised that her uncle didn't take this job."

"No, Ray knows his limits, and he didn't want her family to go after him to find out the details. He's a good family lawyer, and can handle wills and trusts, but dealing with a billionaire is a different ballgame. We were roommates in college; he trusted my experience and to take care of Elizabeth. She's a lovely girl." He smiled. "Ray told me of her phone call to him when Darcy's family pounced. She was stunned that this was necessary."

"They always are." Jack shook his head. "I think part of that is simply the speed of this union. If they were marrying a year from now she would have had more time to really understand what was involved."

"Well, she's no fool. I've spoken to her a few times, going over everything, and once she understood that we could make the contract anything that they wished, she had some excellent suggestions. She's not afraid anymore."

Jack gathered up the papers and put them into the file folder. "Well that is because we didn't focus on failure, but success." Gary put his things away and stood up to shake hands with his counterpart. "I wish I had more clients like them."

"Don't we all!"

JOHN FITZWILLIAM leaned over his mother's shoulder and studied the guest list for the engagement party. "Quite a crowd you are inviting." He met her eye. "Darcy is going to hate this, you know."

"I know, but he will not have them at his wedding, so at least in a social occasion he might be a little more relaxed." She smiled at his rolling eyes. "Well that is my hope."

"Dream on, Mom." He took a seat and sipped his wine. "Um, I suppose that Elizabeth's family is invited?"

"Of course!" Arlene turned to stare at him. "They may not be of our society, but they are William's future family. Why do you ask?"

"I was just wondering if Elizabeth's sister Jane would be there."

"Why?"

"She's very pretty . . . well she's beautiful . . . and I . . ." He sighed and met his mother's eye. "I blew it with her."

"And yet here we are over two months later and you are just now realizing that? I doubt that she would be impressed with your lack of persistence." Arlene turned back to her lists and John stared at her in silence. "I understand that she is seeing William's friend Charles."

"Oh."

She turned back to face him again. "If you intend to be in politics John, you are going to have to fight for things that you want. If Jane Bennet is someone you wish to know, you will have to convince her that you are someone she would like to know."

"I wouldn't want to interfere if she has something going on with Charles Bingley." He laughed. "I'm not Richard."

"Richard needs to find himself a good strong girl who will rein him in." She shook her head. "He will be a playboy forever."

"No, he'll settle down someday. He's very jealous of Darcy."

"Is he?" Arlene raised her brow. "How so?"

"He sees how happy he is." John smiled at his mother's expression. "No, he is not upset that Darcy is happy, he just wants to have the same for himself someday. I think he's more upset that he didn't spot Elizabeth at Anne's wedding himself."

"He had a date . . . who was that girl? Hmm. Blonde I think. That didn't last long." She sighed. "Speaking of Anne, she needs to repair the rift between herself and Darcy before our party. I can't have them glaring at each other in front of our guests."

"Yeah, Aunt Catherine will be doing enough of that. I'll give Georgiana a call, and see what's happening on their end." John stood up and laughed. "Perhaps we can have an intervention and force him to talk to her."

"Oh that sounds just lovely. Let me know when it's over."

"A BILLIONAIRE? Oh Lizzy, you really hit the jackpot!" Lisa Smith, aka Madge Sinclair, said as she held Elizabeth's hand and examined her ring. "Why didn't you bring him with you?"

"He is a billionaire for a reason Lisa, he has work to do."

"Darcy . . . let's see." Adam Fox searched *Google* on his phone and found a listing. "Wow, okay ladies, get your napkins ready to wipe the drool from your faces." The phone was passed around the table and everyone peered at the image of Darcy dressed in a tuxedo, taken at the foundation ball the year before. Elizabeth looked and her heart flipped. Adam saw her faraway expression and laughed. "Hey Lizzy, wake up!"

She blushed and looked up to see the other ladies at the table fighting to get the phone and catch another look. "Hey, remember, he's mine, so no fantasizing tonight."

"What you don't know won't hurt you." Lisa informed her. "Damn, he's hot!"

"Thank you, dear." Her husband said quietly.

"Oh, you know I'm just making noise." She gave him a kiss and he took the phone from her hand and gave it back to Adam. The rest of them laughed.

"So where's Charlotte?"

"Chasing down some elusive authors somewhere. She is pretty unhappy that I didn't sign a new contract to continue the series."

"Hey, we all get tired. You're just lucky it came at the end of the contract." Jerry Williams looked at his wife and writing partner Sherry. "We both want a change but have to come up with two more before we can. Take your time."

"I will. I have come to realize that marrying William is going to be a job in itself." She smiled and then looked down at her ring.

"Well, you are looking melancholy, so why not blow this bar and go hit the slots?" Adam stood up and grabbed Elizabeth's hand. "You're not married yet; maybe I still can convince you that I'm your man!"

"You haven't yet Adam, and I assure you that it's a lost cause." She stayed seated while the others stood. "I think I'll just stay here and people watch."

"Oh how BORING!" Lisa cried.

"I worked too hard for my money to feed it to a machine." She laughed at the rolling eyes. "Besides, I want to call Will before it gets too late." The sounds of kisses and whistles erupted from the group of friends and she watched them go with a smile. A waiter came by to clear the table and she placed another order, then scooted across the booth to lean over the railing of the balcony. Below, her friends were just making their way through the labyrinth of slot machines. Adam turned and blew her a kiss. Elizabeth laughed and waved, then reached for her purse.

Darcy tripped on his way to grab the phone and answered breathlessly. "Lizzy! How are you?"

She could hear what sounded like a chair being lifted and smiled. "I imagine I'm better than you. What did you do?"

"Oh, I um, was not graceful."

"That further confirms your need for dance lessons."

"With you?"

"Who else? Do you have another fiancé?"

"I was just confirming that I had the one I wanted." He sighed and she heard something different in his voice and grew concerned.

"What's wrong, Will?"

He shook his head. "I'm that easy for you to read? Nobody else can . . . I came home tonight and was greeted by Georgiana, Anne and Greg."

"What happened? Not more of the prenup, we have that handled, I think."

"No, no, it was . . . they were here to make amends." Darcy picked up the picture of her on his desk and looked into her smiling eyes. "They wanted to repair the rift before it grew bigger with time, and before we all had to appear in public together."

"And did you accept their apology?"

"I'll be honest with you honey, I was not inclined to. Once someone loses my good opinion it is a hard battle to win it back . . . but then I thought of you. You expect more of me." He touched her face in the photo. "So I stopped being my old self and . . . graciously forgave them."

"Graciously? Not condescendingly?"

"I did my best, Lizzy." He chuckled and imagined her eyebrow rising. "I suppose there was a little edge to it. I just had to make it clear that I did not appreciate the interference."

"And how was it left?"

"We're fine. Anne asked me to tell you that she wants to help in any way she can to . . . well prepare you for the society you will now be entering." He spoke quickly. "Not that I think you are wanting in any way . . ."

"Will, stop, I think that this experience with the prenup has done, if nothing else; made me fully aware of what I do not know. I will be grateful for Anne's guidance." She smiled hearing his relieved sigh. "You weren't looking forward to telling me that were you?"

"No, no I wasn't. My God, I miss you."

"Sweetie I miss you, too. I did get to see you tonight, though."

"How did you mange that?" He sat back and relaxed.

"One of my friends *Googled* you and passed around a picture of you in a tux. Now that is a suit I can't wait to see you in. Your shoulders were sooooooo broad." Elizabeth bit her lip and closed her eyes, remembering it.

Darcy laughed. "How broad? I take it that you like me in a well-cut suit?"

"I like you in any form you care to present to me. Although I do have some favorites." She added playfully.

"Such as?"

"Well, I have to admit that I love watching you walking around nude and aroused." Elizabeth closed her eyes again and sighed. "There is nothing more delicious than a well-toned man showing off his formidable assets."

"Lizzy!!" He moaned.

She giggled. "What can I say; I just want to reach out nibble whatever is headed in my direction."

"Keep this up and I'll be boarding my plane and will be in your bed before daybreak." He growled.

"What's stopping you?" Elizabeth smiled. "Okay, I'll stop. I just love you, and love teasing you. Let's talk about something else . . . Sing to me."

"Oh honey, I'd love to, but I need you in my arms for that. I can't miss your eyes." He looked at her picture on his desk and smiled. "I'll be happy to whisper some words of encouragement to you."

"Mmmm, that sounds so nice. What will you say?" She closed her eyes to listen to his soft voice.

"Here you are, miss." A waiter appeared with her order and she startled.

"Thank you." She paid him and he left.

"What did you get?" Darcy closed his eyes and imagined her sipping.

"Just cranberry juice. I don't like to drink alone, besides when I do I seem to become . . ."

"Very amorous." He whispered.

"Lizzy!" She looked up and gasped. All color drained from her face as the grinning man slid into the booth, effectively trapping her.

"Bill." She said tonelessly.

"Lizzy?" Darcy sat up. "Are you all right?"

"It's been years, you look good enough to eat." Collins looked her over with great interest and leaned in to kiss her. "What good luck to find you here."

She turned her head away. "Please don't do that."

"Lizzy?" Darcy stood.

"It's just a little kiss, surely you don't mind, after all we have shared so many good times together." His hand ran down her arm and he moved closer.

Elizabeth closed her eyes. "I asked you not to touch me, Bill."

"WHO IS TOUCHING YOU?" Darcy combed his hand through his hair and began pacing. "Get up, get away . . . My God, it's Collins! Get away, Lizzy!"

"I need to leave Bill, people are expecting me. Please let me out." She was shaking with the clammy feel of his hand on her arm.

"Oh but we haven't caught up yet! I got my trust fund money. I'm vacationing here. I was passing by and thought I spotted you. I can't wait to renew our friendship."

"KICK HIM! Push him! DAMN IT LIZZY! Climb over the table! GET OUT OF THERE!" Darcy bellowed into her ear. Collins could hear him and grabbed the phone from her hand, ended the call and tossed it on the seat across the booth.

"Now we can talk."

Darcy heard the line go dead. "Lizzy?" His heart was pounding and he called her back. The phone rang and went to voice mail. "My God!" Again and again he hit redial and kept getting her voice mail. He paced desperately. "Pick up! Pick up! Please Lizzy, please!" His gaze fell on the picture on his desk. "Please honey, pick up!"

Georgiana could hear him and came downstairs to stand in the doorway. "What happened?"

He glanced at her. "Elizabeth is trapped with her former tormenter, and he has taken her phone away." Again he punched redial. Again he reached voice mail. "I don't know what to do!"

Elizabeth thought of William, and his commanding voice. *Get out, I have to get out!* She turned to face Collins. "I do not want to talk to you, now move before I make a scene."

"Oh you wouldn't do that." He smiled. "Come on; tell me what brings you here. I can't believe how wonderful it is to find my lost love."

That did it for her. William's face flashed before her eyes and finding her strength, drew upon all of the anger she felt for the man by her side and lashed out. "LOVE? Don't even think of using that lie on me again! You don't have the slightest idea what love is. You know only control. Well I know control, too. I am in control of my life now."

"Elizabeth, I don't like how you are speaking to me." He assumed the patriarchal voice he had used on her for years.

She laughed in his face. "I'm not the same innocent pushover you toyed with. I'm telling you one last time to leave me alone."

He eyed her warily. "What has happened to you?"

"I got away from you." She tried to push him and he did not move. "What are you doing here? I heard that you are gambling away your money, are you losing the rest of it in Vegas now instead of Atlantic City? Did you join a new health club? I know that you're delivering pizzas and living with Mom. Couldn't you sweet talk another old woman into renting you an apartment? Couldn't you find a job with the degree I earned you?"

"How do you know that?" He whispered.

"I have friends now who look after me, and who are watching you. I am loved and engaged to be married to an exceptional man." She flashed her ring at him and his mouth dropped open. In the background, they could hear the sound of Elizabeth's phone constantly ringing. She slipped beneath the table and came up on the other side, grabbed her phone off of the seat and ran out. "Stay away from me!"

"Are you having trouble, miss?" The waiter arrived with two security guards.

"Yes, this is an exboyfriend who is harassing me." She stepped up to his side and pointed at Collins.

"Sir, I ask that you please leave." A guard bent down and spoke softly. "I would not like to call the police."

Collins cringed and turned white. "She is lying!"

"Sir, the young lady was fine until you arrived, and the cameras have been watching you." He indicated several spots in the ceiling.

The phone rang again. She turned to the security guard. "I just want to get away from him, do you need me?"

"No, miss."

Elizabeth found her purse on the floor by the booth and stared at Collins. "Don't you ever come near me again!" She hurried out and headed for the elevators, glancing backwards to see him being escorted from bar, and obviously petrified of the burly men holding his arms. She boarded the elevator, went to her room and after locking the door, fell upon the bed. This time when the phone rang, she answered.

"Will, I'm okay."

"Lizzy! What happened? Where is he?" Darcy collapsed into his desk chair, his hand passing again through his hair. Georgiana stood with her hands clasped to her mouth and stared at him

"Security threw him out, I'm in my room."

"Honey . . ."

"It's okay Will; I . . . stood up to him." Darcy could not miss the pride in her voice. "I told him I was loved. I told him I was engaged. I told him I know what a failure he was! I told him, Will!" She began to sob. "I told him!"

"Elizabeth I am so proud of you! Honey, I love you, I love you."

"I love you, Will." She gasped and wiped her eyes.

"I want you home." He wiped his face and closed his eyes.

"Maybe I can get an earlier flight." She sniffed and tried not to cry again.

"No, stay there. I'll come and get you."

"You will?" She relaxed and let out a long breath, then began to think clearly. "No, no honey, you don't need to come."

"Sweetheart, you are my life, I'm coming. I'll call to get the plane ready and I'll call you back." He wiped more tears from his face.

"No, Will. He's gone, and by the time that you would arrive it will be morning. If I'm here anyway, then . . . I should finish my obligations. I'm not hurt; he just took me by surprise. I guess that I was mad enough that I didn't let him intimidate me. I heard you telling me to fight him and I did. Your voice made me act."

Darcy closed his eyes; the last twenty minutes had been hell and her request was so hard to hear. All he wanted to do was get to her and make sure she was safe, and as far as he was concerned, that was only possible in his embrace. He remained silent, trying to control his emotion, and gradually he relaxed. He didn't like her idea, but he would listen. Finally he spoke. "YOU faced him down. I don't think he's ever going to bother you again."

Waiting for his response, Elizabeth knew that he was fighting a very difficult battle, and said gently, "I could not have done it without knowing that I'm loved by you."

"Oh honey." He sighed. "Maybe I could come anyway and join you for this formal dinner you have to attend tomorrow night? I could wear the tux you liked so much."

Elizabeth smiled through her tears when she heard the resignation in his voice, and settled back on the bed, he was okay. "Are you sure that you would want to do that? The ladies who saw your picture were prepared to express their admiration of you in person, given the chance."

Darcy wiped his eyes again and looked at Georgiana. "Hold on." He smiled a little. "She's okay, Georgie. She is obstinately refusing my desire to be her knight in shining armor."

Georgiana laughed. "Good for her. Tell her I will be proud to be her sister."

"I will." He watched her go, then lifted the phone back up to his ear. "Did you hear that?"

"Yes, I'm . . . very touched." She bit her lip. "Are you angry that I asked you to stay home?"

"No, I'm disappointed, but I suppose that's just my desire to take care of you and my feeling of utter helplessness from being so far away. I can't embrace you like I know you need, no matter how strong you are." He picked up her picture and touched her cheek.

"I would love to be in your arms right now, and if you were here I doubt that I could be pried from you, I'd be holding on so tightly." She closed her eyes and imagined him, then quietly added, "But I think that. . . I think that facing him was good for me, and . . . I know that you have a ton of work to do."

"Yes, but it is not as important as you."

"But I'd rather have it be under control when I return, and it won't be if you come out here, will it?" She was trying hard to convince herself of that.

He heard her weakening and pressed a little. "It doesn't matter. Only you matter."

"I love you too, Will." She sighed and heard his in return. "I think that I put the past behind me tonight."

"I'm so sorry that it had to happen at all." Darcy closed his eyes. "If I can't come and be with you, will you understand when I constantly send you messages over the rest of your trip?"

"Only if you don't mind mine. I need you honey, I do. I'm just being annoyingly practical." Elizabeth heard him laugh softly. "Now, I'm going to change clothes, and plug in my phone to prepare for its busy day tomorrow. Why don't you put on something comfortable and call my hotel room. If I can't sleep in your arms, I want your voice to keep me company. Okay?"

"Okay, I'll sing you a lullaby." He smiled to hear her giggle. "I love you; I'll talk to you soon."

"RICHARD, WHAT brings you here?" Darcy looked up from his computer in the library the following evening when his cousin appeared in the doorway.

"I was ordered to come." He grinned and handed him the bottle of beer he had acquired from the kitchen on his way through. "I am to be sure that you are not miserable."

Darcy shook his head. "Georgiana is becoming more like Mom every day."

"That may be so, but this order came from a higher authority." He put his bottle to his lips and took a swig. "This came from Elizabeth."

"Lizzy?" Darcy sat back in surprise and looked at her picture then to his smirking cousin. "She called you?"

"She certainly did, tracked me down at work since she didn't have my cell number. Said she had some fancy dress party to attend tonight and wanted to be sure that you weren't slitting your wrists or some nonsense." He cocked his head and looked him over. "You're breathing, so I'd say her fears are unfounded."

"Did she tell you what happened yesterday?"

"Yes. I'm sorry Darcy, but we can't track the man's every move. It's not like we could slip a microchip under his skin."

"No, I'm aware of that. It was happenstance, although I suspect that the big flashing sign outside of the hotel welcoming the group to the convention hall might have drawn him in on the off-chance of seeing her."

"That's very likely."

"I don't suppose we can find out for sure how broke he is now?"

"Not without a court order, I'm afraid. I have my contacts, but I think that I've stretched them to the limit for now. From what she told me, he is now aware that he is being watched, so I doubt that such a wimp will ever approach her again. You really have nothing to fear."

"No, you're probably right." Darcy sat back and finally took a drink. "I was pretty close today to just flying out there anyway, wedding rings in hand."

Laughing, Richard sat forward. "And what stopped you?"

"I don't know, I guess that I was afraid that she would see it as controlling."

"I imagine she would have seen it as horribly romantic." He grinned and sat back again. "Sorry, wrong answer, wasn't it? Well, I also imagine that you would prefer your wedding pictures to have a background of the ocean and not Elvis."

"That's only if you pay for the deluxe package, I looked into it." He smiled. "No, she wants her sisters at her wedding, so that is what we'll do."

"You're taking her to Derbyshire for the honeymoon?" Darcy nodded. "Have you decided if you'll be turning Pemberley over to the National Trust?"

"I'm hardly ever there. The licensing to hold weddings in several rooms has come through, and it's booked solid for several years already, and besides that, it's become a tourist attraction and park. I don't know. It is certainly well-tended. I need to determine if giving it over with a huge endowment for its upkeep would be in the best long-term interest of the estate, or should I keep it as a private owner. The taxes and insurance alone are spectacularly huge. But it is the family's history."

"I know Grandpa Henry struggled with the decision to finally give up Matlock, but then he didn't have the resources you do to run it himself. He felt better giving it to the National Trust then selling it to some rich man who wouldn't appreciate the history." Richard looked up at the painting of the estate. "Have you thought of marrying there?"

Darcy's gaze followed his. "At Pemberley? No, I hadn't. I don't even know what would be involved in doing that, it's not like we're residents. No, I don't want to have transport everyone over. We'll hold the ceremony here and be on our way."

"You're a fortunate man." Richard mused.

Darcy smiled in understanding. "You'll find your girl sometime, Richard. Look how long it took me, and it was pure luck."

"Hmm." He rubbed his chin. "I suppose her sister Jane is out of the running."

"Well she seems to be, but then again, you know Bingley." Darcy smiled. "He is fickle."

"If he drifts away from her, let me know, or rather let John know." He laughed. "He kicks himself regularly. This engagement party should prove interesting. There are other sisters, you say?"

Darcy laughed. "Yes, a minister, a coed, and a high school junior. None are for you."

Richard shrugged. "I have no doubt that I will meet some other young ladies at your parties in the future, Elizabeth will undoubtedly breathe some new life into these empty hallways. I will be patient."

"Your mother isn't."

"Don't I know it!" Richard grimaced and put down his empty bottle. "What do you say to a game or two of pool? Don't worry; when she calls I'll disappear into the night." He stood and gestured to the doorway.

"I don't need a babysitter."

"No, but I do. I don't want to go home yet, and I'm tired of going out. A nice pleasant evening in your company is just the thing I need. Besides, I understand that Elizabeth is moving in here? Well let's enjoy your final night of lonely bachelorhood!"

"Well, since you put it that way, I suppose I can bear your company." Darcy shut off his computer and stood. "I hope that you came prepared to lose."

"I was about to say the same to you!" Richard grinned and followed him out the door.

CHARLOTTE EXITED the plane and followed Elizabeth out towards baggage claim. "We should have just done carry on. Now it will be who knows how long before we get home."

"It won't be too bad; it's late so they shouldn't be too busy." She glanced up at the clock. "It's just past eleven. My internal clock is not going to be happy when I try to wake it up at its normal New York time."

"I am sleeping all day. If dad wants me in the office, he'll have a comatose editor on his hands." She laughed and the two followed the crowd to their designated carousel.

Elizabeth stopped and looked hopefully up the ramp, nothing was coming. She startled when a pair of hands slipped around her waist and lips pressed to her ear. "I thought you would never arrive." She relaxed with the familiar low voice, and the unmistakable scent of his cologne.

"Will!" She spun around in his arms and was greeted with his beaming smile. "Oh, honey! What a wonderful surprise!"

"Did you really think that I would let you come home alone?" He shook his head. "I missed you so much Lizzy." He picked her up and squeezed tight, then locked his lips with hers for a voracious kiss.

Charlotte cleared her throat, and Elizabeth managed to tear herself away, resting her head against his chest, but not letting go. "Oh, um, Will? This is Charlotte Lucas, my editor."

Darcy kept his arms firmly around Elizabeth, but smiled and held out his hand. "It is a pleasure; I have heard much of you."

Charlotte's eyes lit up looking over the handsome tossle-haired man. "And I have heard much too much of you." She laughed as Darcy looked down at Elizabeth's blushing face. "I don't think she went a quarter-hour without some mention of you."

"Charlotte!" Elizabeth hissed.

"All good, I hope?" Darcy kissed her cheek and tightened his hug.

"Outstanding."

"May we offer you a ride home? That is if your luggage ever appears?" He glanced again at the carousel. "By the way, Lizzy, we will be using my plane for now on.

"Show off."

"Simply a statement of fact, my dear." He kissed her again and soon they were lost in each other, their bodies entwined and their lips caressing endlessly.

"I would be happy to take you up on your offer." Charlotte announced, startling them.

They broke apart and both had the grace to blush. "Great, Charlotte." Elizabeth reached up to wipe her lipstick from William's smiling mouth with her thumb and turned around to face forward and resist the temptation to kiss him again. "Oh look, here they come." The luggage began flying down the ramp and soon they had their bags in hand. Darcy led the way to where Frank had parked and they piled in.

"Where to?" Frank looked over his shoulder.

"Oh, I'm on West 82nd Street, near Columbus Avenue." Charlotte leaned forward. He nodded and they moved out into traffic. "I'm glad that I won't be taking anyone out of their way." She looked over to see Elizabeth was leaning into Darcy's arms.

"No, not at all. We'll practically be home." Elizabeth smiled up as he looked down into her eyes.

"So where shall we be taking you?"

"I thought that was already decided."

"Just checking. Perhaps you had changed your mind. Who am I to presume?"

"There is no doubt in my mind that you have done just that." She raised her brow and he smiled at her dancing eyes.

"I understand that you are moving in together?" Charlotte asked innocently. "Will that be soon? I imagine that your sisters will be fighting over your apartment, Lizzy. If that is empty, they won't want to stay with your parents when they visit."

"Oh, I hadn't really thought out the logistics of everything. I guess now that I have no other pressing obligations, I'll be spending my time packing." Elizabeth looked up. "What can I bring?"

"Anything you like. We'll figure out where it all fits. We can just hire a moving company to pack it all up for you."

"No, no, this is a great opportunity to throw out the junk, besides, Charlotte is right, one of my sisters will want the place, so I don't need to worry about the furniture. Jane was going to call someone to help." She began taking inventory of the rooms in her mind. "Really, it's the little things that I need to consider, the pictures and knick knacks, and the clothes."

"And the shoes." Darcy whispered.

Elizabeth blushed. "I guess I can go buy a new pair now that the book is released."

"May I go with you?"

"I'd rather surprise you."

He smiled and gave her a squeeze. "If you insist." Looking over to Charlotte he tilted his head. "Were you successful in enticing any authors to join your company?"

"Well, I'm not sure. I think that offering flexible contracts could be what draws some over to us. I met many authors who would love to change genres, but were locked into contracts that didn't allow them the opportunity. Lizzy's situation is making us rethink our approach. We don't want to lose her. We believe that she would be successful in whatever she writes if it is promoted well, so we are willing to work with her to keep her with us."

"Now you know the topic of our in-flight conversation the whole way home." Elizabeth looked up at him wearily, and felt his embrace tighten.

"Have you considered our idea for a scholarship?"

"Yes, Lizzy told me about it as we traveled. I'll have to speak to my father before I can commit to it." Charlotte smiled. "Quite an impressive idea."

"And of course I had no ulterior motives in mind." Darcy looked back down at Elizabeth and grinned.

"Aha! I knew it was all a plot to keep me nearby!"

"I admit nothing." He closed his eyes and sighed. The two women exchanged glances and Elizabeth bit her lip and blushed.

The car turned onto Charlotte's street and she directed Frank to her building. To her surprise, both he and Darcy got out. Frank took her luggage from the trunk and Darcy picked it up. "Shall we?" He smiled at her.

"Shall we, what?"

"I'm seeing you to your door, Miss Lucas."

"oh." Charlotte was entranced. She led the way up and unlocked the door, expecting him to hand her the bags. Darcy looked at her expectantly and she turned and went inside. He returned a few minutes later and climbed back in the car. Frank drove off and Elizabeth smiled up at him.

"I think that she was in shock from your gallantry."

"I think that I was almost invited inside." He laughed and wrapped her back up in his arms. "At last you are where you belong."

"I suppose it is true that absence makes the heart grow fonder." Elizabeth settled into his embrace and closed her eyes. Soon they were pulling into the driveway. She looked up to the mansion as they exited the car, and stood still. "So this is home now."

"I hope to make you very happy here, honey." Darcy kissed her cheek and taking her hand followed Frank inside, where he handed off the bags to another staff member. "Georgiana has an early class so she's probably asleep. Are you hungry or do you just want to relax, or . . . go to bed?" He looked at her hopefully.

"I think I'd like to see our bedroom." Elizabeth laughed at his enormous smile. "Tomorrow I will have to go to the apartment and pack up some clothes."

"You won't need any for tonight." Darcy growled and picked her up.

"Will! Everyone will see!"

He shook his head slowly. "Who? Frank? Mrs. Reynolds? I don't care. This is our home. We are going to be ourselves here, and if that means that the staff sees me behaving like a besotted idiot to the woman I love then so be it. I won't hold back Lizzy, not from you. I don't express myself in other places, but when it comes to you . . ." He kissed her. "I will never be reticent again."

"Who are you?" She smiled and caressed his face, not even noticing that they were moving steadily through the house. "Something changed this week."

"I had two weeks of nothing but you, then you were gone. I was forced to listen helplessly while the dearest person in my life was threatened by her abuser, and then I was unable to come and comfort you. I love you, and I'm going to demonstrate that to you in every conceivable way." They had arrived in the bedroom and he closed the door then set her down. His hands lifted to embrace her face and he kissed her tenderly. "I know that you probably need to freshen up a bit from your trip." He took her hand and led her to a door. "This is your bathroom."

"I have one of my own?"

"Yes, mine is on the other side. There is a door that leads to your dressing room, your bags are in there." He bent to kiss her. "Take your time; I'll be waiting here for you." He turned and disappeared through a door.

Elizabeth entered the bathroom then cautiously peeked through another door to view the dressing room. "This is as big as my bedroom in the apartment!" She said softly while wandering around the space and examining the empty closets and drawers. Her bags were open and waiting. She took out her makeup case and lay out some things for the morning, then found a small shopping bag. Inside was a short pale pink robe that she bought at the hotel. She found another bag and removed her new pink stilettos and giggled.

Darcy returned to the bedroom and looked around; turning off the lights and retrieving the candles he had hidden from Elizabeth's view. He hurried around and lit them, then hearing her moving towards the door, pulled back the covers and ripped off his robe, laying on his side and propped up on his elbow. Elizabeth appeared and his mouth fell open. "ohhhhhhh baby."

Elizabeth stood looking at him; the dance of the flickering candlelight simultaneously highlighted and shadowed the sculpted muscles of his nude body, playing over him like fingers, enticing her to come nearer and caress him. "Oh Will." She untied the belt of her robe and let it drop to the floor. His wolfish gaze and the tongue appearing to lick his lips was all that she could have dreamed of, and sent a shiver all over her body. He held out his hand to her, and she started to slip off the shoes when he slowly shook his head.

"Please leave them on."

"You can't be serious."

"I am, deadly serious." She climbed onto the bed and lay back against the pillows. "Are you surprised?" He whispered as he began to trail kisses down her face.

"This is . . . this is like a scene from my story." She whispered and ran her hand down from his shoulder to embrace his waist.

"I know." William's lips found her ear. "Jane sent it to me. I thought that your imagination would enjoy the stimulation of acting out your fantasy."

"What?" Elizabeth shuddered as his hand caressed over her breasts. "She . . . she sent you . . . ohhhhh Will." His lips were stroking her neck relentlessly as his hand slipped down to begin rubbing between her legs.

"You are making my fantasy come true, too." He kissed her lips slowly, licking them then drinking from her soft, open mouth as their tongues played a game of gentle war. William withdrew and kissed his way down to her legs, stroking the silky skin then holding them up to admire the way her feet and ankles were displayed in the shoes. "I love this." He whispered and settled over her, leaning down to caress his hands down from her shoulders to her hips, and look upon the treasure below. "I have had a week to think of so many ways I want to make love to you." Slowly they joined and he watched Elizabeth's eyes close and heard her soft moan. "Now honey, let me really welcome you home."

"HI!" Georgiana called to Elizabeth when she poked her head out into the hallway. "I'm just leaving for school, but I'll see you tonight!"

"Isn't it Saturday?" She said groggily. Between the jet lag and William's enthusiastic lovemaking she was still fairly spent.

"Yes, but there's a special workshop with the pianist from the Philharmonic today, and I don't want to miss it." She paused and tilted her head. "You look like you would be better off back in bed."

"No, I know that the only way to beat this is to just go through the normal day." She leaned against the door and looked around. "I seem to have misplaced your brother, though."

"Oh he's downstairs working out. He should be up here soon; he was about through his routine when I saw him." Georgiana smiled. "Why don't you go down and see him?"

"Well, maybe some exercise would help me, too." Elizabeth followed Georgiana down to an old parlor, now exercise room, and could hear the sound of the weight machine. She peeked in the door to see William clad only in shorts, slowly working on his biceps with some curls. It was an inspiring sight.

"Wow, do you mean I get to come down and watch this display every day? I should have moved in here ages ago." Elizabeth smiled and laughed to see him let go and hear the stack of weights fall together with a loud clang.

"If I had known your feelings on the subject I would have strut my stuff for you sooner." He wiped off his face and chest and walked over to kiss her. "Did you sleep enough? How do you feel? I thought it would be cruel to wake you, so I came down here."

"I'm sleepy, but I'll live. I thought that some adrenalin would do me some good." Looking around the room she spotted the recumbent bike. "Could I try that out?"

"Sure, it's all yours." Darcy smiled and she climbed onboard. He took a seat on the rowing machine next to it and began to move. "I try to do a variety of things for an hour every day, but my schedule doesn't always allow it. Sometimes I just get to do a half hour at the club near the office. I'll add you to the membership if you like."

"I don't know how often I would get to use it, since I'm not going to be down there very often, except when I come to rescue you from your job." She smiled and winked at him.

"That's true, but there is a pool there, and classes. I'll add you anyway, and if you use it or not is up to you." He smiled and watched her pedal. "You are in beautiful shape."

"So are you." Elizabeth's gaze wandered over him, and he blushed. She laughed and kept going. "I suppose that my assignment for today is to pack up my belongings."

"I will help." He declared.

"Thanks, I'm afraid it will be more reminiscing than packing." Elizabeth smiled to see his dimples appear. "What are you thinking?"

"I was just imagining a box full of art projects from childhood." He stopped rowing and caressed her leg. "We must save those."

"Why? To torture our children with boring stories?"

"Oh speaking of that, I'll have to take a look at those baby pictures of yours while we're there." Elizabeth threw his towel at him and he ducked. "I told you I would."

"Maybe you should stay here." She raised her brow at his shaking head. "All right, fine. But if you annoy me, I'll send you to go talk to Mom, and she might try to molest you again."

"I would laugh, but I'm afraid that's not an empty threat." He stood and leaned down to kiss her. "I'm going to go shower. Shall we plan on leaving in a couple of hours?" She nodded and watched him go, another half hour on the bike and she made her way back upstairs where he was just dressing. "What would you like for breakfast? Jerry gets the weekends off."

Elizabeth's eyes lit up. "Does he? So I will get to cook?"

"If you like, he leaves behind meals for us to just pop in the oven. Mrs. Reynolds is the only staff member who lives here, although a few stayed last night in anticipation of your arrival. Usually everyone goes home to their families at the end of the day."

"Somehow that makes me feel better." She caught his questioning brow. "Well, you're used to being served, and I'm used to taking care of myself. I think that I will appreciate not having to deal with the drudgery of everyday cooking and cleaning, but I also will be very happy to just lose myself in making a mess in the kitchen and . . . taking care of you."

"I know it sounds like a very chauvinist thing to say this, but I can't tell you how good that sounds." He moved to embrace her and she twisted away. "I don't care if you're sweaty, honey."

"I do." She kissed him then ran to the bathroom. "I'll be down in a little while then we can head over."

Ninety minutes later they stood inside of the apartment, surveying the living room. "Jane called some movers and they dropped off the boxes and tape. So I guess that we should put some together first, then start making decisions."

"I'll do that, you go ahead and look around." Darcy set to work putting together boxes, rather enjoying the simple task, if for no other reason than it brought the fact of Elizabeth moving into their home closer to reality. She walked into the bedroom and started opening drawers and sorting through her clothes. They had music playing and he listened to her occasionally joining into the chorus as he ripped the tape. A knock came to the door and he stood up to answer. "Tom!" Darcy shook his hand and invited him in.

"So, it isn't a bad dream, she is really moving out." He surveyed the boxes and saw the piles of folded clothes that were being stacked in the hallway. "Well, at least it isn't far."

"Sir, you will always be welcome in our home." Darcy said sincerely.

"Thank you." He sighed and sat down on the sofa and watched as Darcy resumed his task. "I suppose it is inevitable that I would have to let her go someday." Darcy smiled and looked away. "Tell me, what can she expect from you?"

He stopped his work and tried to read Tom's face. "I'm sorry, I don't understand."

"Will you make a life with her, or is she just an adornment, a hostess for your affairs, a necessary requirement for a powerful man?"

Darcy saw his worry and turned to face him. "Sir, I love her, and I want a real life with her, and someday a family. You should know that I am very much a homebody. I enjoy attending cultural performances, and I know that Elizabeth does as well, but I do not like the party circuit, do not in any way enjoy mixing with people who are only attending a function for the . . . prestige of being with certain persons. I am a very boring man, which is why I have been left entirely alone by the gossip rags. I don't do anything, and therefore am not subject to their fodder. I am just as happy spending an evening with a book and a glass of wine or in conversation with a few close friends. I want to live a peaceful, quiet life."

Tom relaxed. "I am happy, very happy to hear that; however, peace is something that you may not have with my daughter."

He smiled. "Well, that is something that I will enjoy having disrupted by her hand."

"Dad! I didn't know you were here." Elizabeth entered the room and kissed him. She looked between the two. "What are you guys discussing?"

"You cutting up your husband's peaceful tranquility." Tom stood and smiled. "Don't be too rough with him, Lizzy. I think he likes to stay home like your father."

"I know he does." Elizabeth bent and kissed the top of William's head and hugged his shoulders. "But I'm still going to insist that we do something fun on a regular basis."

He looked up and kissed her. "I will love the experience, I'm sure. What is our first adventure?"

"We, my love, are going dancing tonight." She smiled at his groan and disappeared into the bedroom, returning with a pair of black stilettos dangling from her fingertips. "I was going to wear these."

"oh." He said softly. "Um, what kind of dancing?"

"There's a club I've been to a few times, they stick to classic ballroom, you know, waltz, cha cha, things like that? Are you game?" She noticed a smile spreading across his face. "You really like this idea? I'm not dragging you to your doom?" Slowly he shook his head and she stood with her hands on her hips, staring at him. "What do you know that I don't?"

He bit his lip and stood up to give her a kiss. "I hope that you can keep up with me." Elizabeth's eyes grew wide as his gaze raked down her. His arm wrapped around her waist and suddenly she felt her body bending backwards as he slowly lowered her towards the floor then lifted her back up, only to feel him confidently spin her away and back into his tight embrace. She gasped and her heart began to pound. "Believe me honey; I *do* know how to dance."

Chapter 11

"**O**h Jane, it was like flying, or floating, I don't know, but I never wanted it to end!" Elizabeth's eyes were bright and she beamed. "It was the most . . . oh Jane . . . he can *dance*!"

Jane looked over at Georgiana who was giggling and hiding behind a rack of dresses. "Yes, I gathered that, Lizzy. You have mentioned it once or twice."

"I'm sorry, I know you must be tired of it, but . . ." She sighed dreamily, "I can't wait to fly in his arms again."

This time Georgiana could not contain her laughter. "I'm so sorry, Elizabeth. I love my brother and I love seeing you happy, but hearing you describe him being so romantic is just funny." She tried to compose herself and failed. "Remember, I've seen no evidence of this . . . who's that guy in the old movies?"

"Fred Astaire?" Jane suggested.

Elizabeth protested immediately. "Oh no, Will is not a skinny stick. If he is a dancer from an old movie make him Gene Kelly."

"Maybe Patrick Swayze?" Georgiana offered.

"I bet he would be great at dirty dancing . . . we have to stop at the video store on the way home." Elizabeth's eyes lit up and Jane shook her head at Georgiana. "Oh look at this dress, wouldn't the skirt look great flaring out as we spin around?"

"Lizzy, we are here to look at dresses for the engagement party." Jane said sternly.

"It can't hurt to keep my eyes open for other occasions!" She kept the dress over her arm and they looked for some others that were more appropriate for the upcoming party at the Fitzwilliam's apartment. "I asked him how he came to be such an accomplished dancer, and he said that he asked for a new bike to take to Harvard with him, and his mother said he could have one if he agreed to twelve dance lessons. He protested, but went, and once there he discovered that he really appreciated the skill that was needed to learn the steps. Like everything he does he gave it his undivided attention and excelled." She sighed again. "I thought that I was okay with all of the moves since mom made us take dance when we were little, but oh, to dance in the arms of a man who really knows how to lead you . . ." Her voice trailed away and she awoke only when Georgiana's giggling got through to her foggy brain. "Well, it was wonderful." Elizabeth whispered and began pushing dresses aside on the racks.

"I thought that William is painfully shy. How could he perform so well in a club?" Jane asked as she held up a dress in front of a mirror.

"He is shy, but when I asked him that same question last night, he explained that nobody knew him there, and most importantly, as far as he was concerned, we were the only ones in the room." Elizabeth looked down and blushed furiously.

"Wow." Jane said softly and saw that Georgiana had stopped giggling and had tilted her head, considering that understated declaration of love. Elizabeth moved away to look at other possibilities and recover her composure. After many changes of clothing, each lady finally settled on their choices and moved on to the shoe department.

"Well, look at this, a sale." Jane winked at Elizabeth. "Maybe you'll get two pairs?"

"Not after what those dresses cost." She said sadly. "We should have gone to Macy's instead of Saks's."

"Why don't you let me buy them? William pays my bills, and he would love to have bought you those dresses." Georgiana asked. "He even told me to get you anything you wanted."

"I'm not his wife yet, and besides, it probably doesn't matter what I wear." She said without confidence.

"No, this is a very important event, Lizzy. You'll be meeting the people of William's world, and they will be assessing you. You have to be spectacular." Jane nodded and patted her back. "I know that it's not what you want to hear, but I've been around this crowd enough to know that for many, the inside does not matter if the outside is presentable."

"I hope though that Arlene invited people who really are William's friends, and are made of better stuff." Elizabeth looked at Georgiana. "You have seen the guest list, is there anyone there that I need to fear, besides your Aunt Catherine, I mean?"

"I really don't know them; I've never been invited to the adult parties. Maybe if mom and dad had lived I would have met them at the house, but William rarely has people over, just a few friends maybe once or twice a year, I mean besides Charles, he's over a lot. He really doesn't socialize much; just those few months after they died he was out most nights." She grew quiet. "That was a really hard time for us."

William had not really spoken of that time, and Elizabeth wanted to understand that period in his life. "What happened then, do you remember?"

"I was only eleven, and staying with Aunt Arlene and Uncle David, and just saw William on the weekends. They said at the time that he was just so busy trying to get everything in order that he couldn't take care of me properly."

"How long did this last?" Elizabeth asked softly.

"Oh, about seven months or so. Then all of a sudden I was back home and William and I, well, we just did things together. He was back to his old self again, you know, very quiet but playful in his way. He looked so much better, and was happier, but always working very hard. It seemed that he had lost all of his new friends, and he didn't seem to miss them."

"No, I don't think that he did." Elizabeth's eyes met Jane's and they exchanged a smile in understanding. Looking back over at the display of shoes she selected a pair that would match her dress and asked the clerk for her size. "I think Will would like these."

"I think he would, too." Jane smiled and went over to examine the other racks.

Georgiana stayed near Elizabeth. "Those people weren't really his friends then were they?"

"No Georgiana, they were not, and he was too overwhelmed by the attention and the pressure to recognize it at the time. He needed your uncle to set him straight."

"I guess that everybody makes mistakes in assessing who their friends are." She smiled.

"Yes, I did, you did, and Will certainly did. But we all have learned from the experience, and will hopefully never be drawn in again by someone with a silver tongue or a sad tale." Elizabeth hugged her and sat down when the clerk appeared to try on the new shoes. She stood and examined how they looked, and noticed a man pausing to observe as she modeled them. Elizabeth could not miss the appreciative stare. "Another shoe man." She smiled and slipped them off. "I'll take them."

FRANK PULLED into the driveway and Darcy eagerly jumped out, heading for the house. "Hey!" He spun and spotted Elizabeth appearing from under the rose arbor with her laptop in hand.

"Hi!" He smiled and strode towards her than stopped and said seriously, "Honey, I'm home."

Elizabeth laughed and met him, adjusting his tie and giving him a peck on the cheek. "How was your day, dear?"

"Bad enough to require a far better greeting than that." He dropped his briefcase and hugged her tightly, then bestowed a loving kiss. They rested their foreheads together. "It is indescribable how much I love coming home to you." He smiled at her. "How was your day?"

"Very productive, actually. I had a long talk with Charlotte's dad about what a publisher looks for in a new author, then hid back in the garden and got some writing accomplished. That spot is just the place to imagine a romance unfolding."

"I'm glad to know that you felt comfortable writing here." He took her hand and they carried their things into the house. "I suspected that you were having difficulty adjusting to the changed atmosphere."

"How did you know?" Elizabeth watched him curiously.

"When we talked earlier in the week, I could hear your mom in the background. I figured that you had returned to the apartment to work." She looked down, and he touched her cheek. "Why didn't you tell me?"

"I didn't want you to feel bad. I . . . I guess that I'm just not comfortable being alone in this house yet. I feel like I'm intruding somehow."

"Honey . . . I guess that I could try to reassure you until the end of time, but this is something that you have to resolve on your own. I'm just happy that you found it comfortable to work outside of the house." He smiled and laughed. "At least you're closer than you were."

Elizabeth bumped against him and smiled. "Thanks for understanding. I probably wouldn't be so weird about it if you or Georgiana were home. It's just being alone in there . . ."

"It's okay; I wish that you could have told me about it. You can tell me anything."

"I know." She said softly.

They dropped off their things in the library and walked up to the bedroom. Elizabeth sat on the bed and watched him taking off his suit. "I'm very nervous about the party on Sunday."

"That makes two of us." He smiled and walked into his dressing room to hang up his things. "Although I imagine our nerves are for separate reasons. I'm nervous about being on display." Returning to the room, changed into shorts and a shirt he sat beside her. "What is bothering you?"

"I'm nervous about *being* the display." She smiled and leaned into his embrace. "I asked Georgiana about the people on the guest list, but she wasn't much help. She didn't know many of them."

"No, she wouldn't. There are just a few friends of mine. Mostly it's close acquaintances from either the business or the foundation, and family, of course. I was surprised that you didn't want to invite more friends." He kissed her forehead.

"I'm just as much of a loner as you are, Will." He regarded her with surprise. "You don't believe me? Just because I can make conversation with anybody on any subject doesn't mean that I open up enough to them to be what I would consider close friends. There are very few admitted into my circle."

"Everyday I seem to find more ways that we are alike." He kissed her and stood up. "What do you say to a walk before dinner?"

"I'd really like that." She took his hands to rise and they set off downstairs to go outside. "Where to?"

"Have you been through Riverside Park?"

"No, let's go." They crossed the street and entered the park, walking down to the path that followed the Hudson. Elizabeth laughed, spotting a group of toddlers cautiously riding down a slide. Darcy watched her face and imagined that someday they would bring their own children there. She looked up at him and saw his relaxed smile. "So what made your day so difficult? Would it help to vent a little?"

He chuckled. "Probably. It's . . . well I'm someone who feels that nobody can do a job better than me, so this adjustment of my role is difficult. I look at my managers, all very competent and talented people, but I can't help but feel . . . itchy, wanting to wrest control back out of their hands. Not that I would achieve results any better than they, or even any sooner, it's just that my methods are different. I don't know. It's hard to let go of your baby." He met her smiling eyes. "And I hate meetings, but it seems that now that I am supervising more than doing, I have to sit through more of them. There must be a better way; meetings just seem like a waste of time."

"Well, do all of the people at the meetings actually need to be there? Maybe you would be better off with just one-on-one sessions with the principals, or just small groups gathered in your office instead of the conference room where daydreaming is inevitable." Elizabeth shrugged. "Never having worked in an office, I can't really provide a great deal of insight."

"Actually, you can, since you are not biased by what is normally done." Darcy mused and looked at the path ahead as he thought over her suggestion. "That's not a bad idea, really."

"I've just noticed that the larger the group, the less opportunity individuals have to participate, and then only the most vocal get heard. The quiet person might have the most to contribute but may not have the confidence to voice it either."

"Sounds like you are speaking from experience." He kissed her hand then wrapped his arm around her shoulder.

"I am." She leaned into him and they walked slowly along then found a bench. "I was a member of a writing group in college."

"And your ideas were never heard." They sat embraced and watched the boats traveling down the river. "But how many of those people have had your success?"

Elizabeth laughed evilly. "None."

He beamed down at her. "Vindication!" They kissed slowly and melted into each other. "Shall we head back?" William whispered softly, kissing away from her lips and up to her ear. Elizabeth ran her hands down his back and leaned into his caresses.

"Let's go." They walked home, taking a different path. "How does your day look tomorrow?"

"More meetings; plus a phone conference with our forestry people. Why do you ask?"

"I thought of rescuing you for lunch, I'll be down that way to meet with Charlotte to go over the things I discussed with her father today about the scholarship plan."

"I'd love that!" He smiled. "Patricia is dying to meet you."

"Ah, and I'm dying to meet your sexy secretary." He started laughing, and she bristled. "What? Her voice is quite seductive."

"I'll be sure to tell her that, she'll get a kick out of it." She speared him with her eyes. "Honey, Patricia is nearly sixty. She was my dad's secretary, which is why she insists on being called a secretary and not an assistant. She sticks with the title she took when he hired her thirty years ago."

"So I have nothing to worry about." Elizabeth smiled.

His brow went up in surprise. "Did you really think that you might?"

"Well, if you can be jealous about me calling Richard . . ."

"How did you know I was jealous?" He regarded her carefully.

"We are very much alike, remember?" Elizabeth laughed and he smiled. "Secure but very protective."

"WHAT IS TAKING so long?" Caroline Bingley huffed. She stood up and paced around the office. "Doesn't he know that I'm here?"

"Miranda informed Mr. Bingley that you had arrived, Miss Bingley. He will be with you soon, I'm sure." Patricia glanced at the overdressed, over coiffed, overbearing woman and went back to her work. She should have left for lunch a half-hour earlier, but she wasn't going to leave Miss Bingley alone anywhere near Mr. Darcy's office. The phone rang. "Oh . . . oh, yes, I'll be right there." Patricia smiled then caught the curious stare of her charge. "Miss Bingley, please take a seat. I have to escort a visitor for Mr. Darcy, but I'll return momentarily."

Caroline watched the woman go and speculated over her age. "Fifty at least, you would think that she would dress better. William must not pay her much." She looked down at her own couture ensemble with a rather catty smirk. "Just wait until he sees me in this. I don't care if he is engaged, I hope that Charles talks him into joining us for lunch, it is my birthday after all, and what a gift he would be!" That put a thought in her mind, and checking around to see if anyone was coming, she opened the door to Darcy's office and slipped inside.

"Miss Bennet?" Patricia approached the reception desk and saw a petite woman, dressed in a classic and simple dress that accentuated her every curve.

Elizabeth turned and gave her a brilliant smile. "Hi! You must be Patricia? It is so good to have a face to match the voice!" She held out her hand and they shook. "Does he know that I'm here?"

"No, he's in a meeting, and has been watching the clock all day. I've never seen him so jumpy!" She laughed. "Come on, I think that we can sneak you past the conference room, he's seated with his back to the glass. I am looking forward to telling him you have arrived."

"Well, I finished my meeting early so I thought I'd just come over here and wait." They boarded the elevator and watched the floors fly by. "Do you think that I have time to check my makeup? It was a long walk and I think that I'm a bit windblown. I'd like to be a little more presentable for him."

"Oh, I don't think that will be a problem." They arrived at the executive floor and Patricia led her down the hallway to Darcy's office. She slowed down as they approached a glass-enclosed conference room. "Look, there he is." She whispered.

Elizabeth bit her lip and peeked. William had his back turned to them, but she could see him picking up his phone and looking at it, as if he was hoping something would appear. He glanced up at the clock, and visibly sighed. She set down her bag and pulled her phone out, quickly sending a text message. A few seconds later she saw him straighten and casually read it. A slow warm smile spread across his face. He sat up straighter, and his chin lifted. Elizabeth was hard-pressed not to run into the room and kiss him then and there. Charles noticed the change and looked at him curiously then spotted her outside the glass. She put her finger to her lips and waved. He nodded and shook his head, smiling at the now attentive company president. Patricia led the way to his office. "What did you send him?"

"Now you know I can't tell you that!" Elizabeth laughed.

"I can't begin to tell you how wonderful it has been to see him smiling. You have done a beautiful job."

"I just want to make him as happy as he makes me." She watched as Patricia opened the door and gasped.

"Miss Bingley! What are you doing?"

Caroline was bent, rifling through the desk drawers, a small wrapped box in her hand. "Oh . . . I . . . I was looking for . . . some tape."

"That must be some special brand you found, if it comes gift-wrapped." Elizabeth observed.

She dropped the box back into a drawer and slammed it shut. "I was just moving it out of the way."

"You have no business in here, Miss Bingley, I insist that you leave. You may wait for your brother outside or in his office." Patricia moved out of the way of the door and gestured to the hallway.

Caroline lifted her chin and looked over Elizabeth. "Well, I suppose that the secretarial staff has to do its work."

"You are Charles Bingley's sister?"

"Yes." She snapped.

"My sister Jane is dating him. I am Elizabeth Bennet, William Darcy's fiancé, *not* a member of the staff." Caroline's eyes darted from her to the picture on the desk, confirming the truth. "Now, I need to prepare for our lunch date, would you please excuse me?"

Caroline walked past her and out into the hallway. "Tell your sister that Charles will drop her soon. He doesn't stick with any girl for long." She looked Elizabeth up and down. "What does William see in you?"

"Apparently something he does not see in you." Elizabeth said with a sweet smile and closed the door in her face.

Patricia laughed. "Oh, that was nicely done! She's been after Mr. Darcy for two years, ever since Mr. Bingley brought her with him to the company Christmas party. She was all over Mr. Darcy, or tried to be. He finally made his excuses and escaped home." She walked over to the washroom and turned on the light. "There, you go ahead and do your repairs. I'll let the phone ring twice if he's coming."

"Thank you!" Elizabeth entered and adjusted her dress; then redid her makeup and hair. She heard the phone ring and hurriedly put everything away. The office door opened and closed shut sharply.

"Good Lord, I feel like I was molested!" Darcy sighed, and approached his desk, throwing down the file folder and staring out the window to the city below, then turned to address Elizabeth's picture. "Where are you? Rescue me!"

Quietly, Elizabeth opened the door and peeked out. He was standing next to the desk, staring down at her photo. She slipped out and walked over to him, and touched his shoulder. "Here I am." Darcy spun around.

"Lizzy!" He exclaimed and hugged her to him.

"Wait, I just fixed all of this!" Elizabeth laughed and tried unsuccessfully to escape his grasp. Finally she gave in to his searching lips, and they spent the next several minutes lost in the passionate expression of their love. "Will . . ."

"Shall I go and lock the door?" He whispered into her hair. "I'd love to give you a proper response to that message you sent."

"What do you have in mind?" She smiled and watched him stride to the door, lock it, and return. His hands ran down from her shoulders to her hips, then lifted up her skirt.

"There really is nothing under here, is there?" He stepped back and looked her over with great appreciation. His mouth began suckling her neck as his hands caressed in lazy circles over her bottom and around to dip his fingers between her warm thighs. "You planned on this, Lizzy; you want this as much as I do." His teeth raked over her neck then his lips traveled up to capture hers again. Smiling wickedly, Elizabeth's hands stroked down his back and around to loosen his belt and open his slacks. Quickly her fingers found their way inside to draw out his very prominent arousal. Darcy lifted her up onto the desk, laying her back and quickly joining with her.

"Willlllll" Elizabeth gasped, holding onto his arms while he loomed above, watching intently as he held her hips and steadily moved. "Wait . . . Will, your tie!" She reached up to try and tuck it into his shirt as he kept the pace; both were alternately laughing and moaning.

"Leave it, Lizzy!" He gasped.

"ohhhhh." Her moans were silenced with his kiss. "Quiet, honey." He smiled, then closed his eyes, becoming lost in the feeling again. Elizabeth watched the intense expression of concentration and bliss warring on his face as his teeth bit his lower lip, and closed her eyes as he thrust harder. They arrived almost at the same moment, again gazing at their lover as they each panted and grinned. He leaned back down to kiss her and rubbed his nose with hers. "That was so much fun!"

Elizabeth laughed as he withdrew and held out his hands to help her sit up. "Not the most comfortable bed, but certainly worth the effort." She slid off of the desk and stood before him while he repaired the damage to his attire. "I think that we should have lunch more often." They both laughed and hugged. "I get the bathroom first!" She kissed him and took off to close the door with a backwards look at his satisfied smile.

Darcy shook his head as she disappeared and walked over to try and assess his appearance in the window's reflection. All he could see was the smile. "I can't believe we just did that!" He spoke to himself. "Wow!"

Elizabeth reappeared and he kissed her as he passed by. "Do you have underwear on now?"

"I'll let you wonder about it." He groaned and continued inside. Elizabeth looked at the messed desk and rearranged everything for him, tidying up the papers that had served as her pillow and fixing the position of her and Georgiana's pictures. Darcy reappeared and saw her at work.

"I have something for you." He opened his desk and a concerned look crossed his brow.

"Oh, look in the middle drawer; that is if it's a wrapped box you are after."

"How did you know?" He looked at her in confusion.

"Caroline Bingley was searching the drawers when I arrived."

"What!" He stared at her. "Did she take anything?"

"No, Patricia told her to get out." She watched as he opened the middle drawer and removed the box.

"I can't imagine what she was hoping to find . . . Oh, I bet it was my phone number, she's been after that for years. I'm surprised she wasn't trying to get into my computer; she probably would have if you hadn't come in when you did. I have to speak to Charles about her; she has completely crossed every boundary today. I certainly wouldn't want her taking this gift." He growled. "Jane and Charles might get along, but you should certainly warn her about the sister she would acquire if she continues the relationship."

"I can't wait to hear more about her . . . but let me open my present first!" Elizabeth smiled and he relaxed, handing it to her then sitting on the desk, wrapping her up in his arms so her back settled against his chest. "I should have given this to you earlier in the week, forgive me for not thinking of it sooner." He rested his chin on her shoulder.

Elizabeth opened the box and started laughing. Inside was a set of keys on a ring featuring a single stiletto as the fob. She looked back to encounter his twinkling eyes. "What is this?"

"Those are the keys to our homes. Not that you will ever need them since there is always someone there, but I just thought it would help you to feel more as if you belonged in them." He kissed her cheek. "The key ring is what took so long to find. I had to search a bit on the internet, but I found just the thing for you at a novelty shop."

She admired the little shoe. "So appropriate."

"I am always appropriate, honey."

"Is that so? And what do you label this little tryst?"

"An entirely appropriate interlude in the life of a man and woman in love." He said confidently.

Elizabeth laughed and hugged him. "Are you sure that you aren't a romance writer? Perhaps we should collaborate."

"I think that we just did." He kissed her softly and stood to don his suit jacket. Opening the office door, they stepped out into Patricia's empty office, and immediately his persona changed. "I hope that Patricia didn't hear us." His face became unreadable and he seemed to withdraw.

Elizabeth felt him changing and realized it was his shyness taking over. "I think that she would be delighted." Darcy pressed his hand to her back as they walked to the elevators and looked at her quizzically. "She seemed very happy for your improved well-being. She reminded me a little of Miss Maggie in her care for you." They boarded the elevator, and she smiled up at him.

"So you are no longer threatened by my seductive secretary?" He relaxed again once the doors closed, and leaned his head down to see her blush.

"I think that I should be more concerned about Charles' sister. What exactly did she do to you?"

Darcy groaned. "She not very subtly demanded a birthday kiss. I managed to get away, but Charles was deeply embarrassed."

Elizabeth could see how embarrassed he was by Caroline's behavior, and squeezed his hand, suspecting that it was much more than a kiss that she demanded. "I understand the feeling. I am not looking forward to introducing Mom to your family. I think that Dad will behave, but I can't wait for this party to be over."

"What can we do to encourage her to . . . tone it down a little?" He said gently.

"I really don't know. Jane has promised to stay with her, but I can't expect her to watch constantly. Will, I am truly worried about this. I am frightened enough about my own performance, but to have to do this with her there . . ."

His arm came around her shoulder and he drew her against his chest. "It will be fine, Lizzy." Their eyes met and he read the very real worry in hers, and decided that it was time to give his future father-in-law a call. The elevator doors opened and they were faced with a waiting crowd of his employees. Taking Elizabeth's hand tightly in his, he nodded at them and smiled slightly as the group parted to allow them to exit. They continued meeting employees who greeted him and looked curiously at her, and finally arrived outside where his tension eased.

"So, what bothered you the most with that experience?"

"Being the object of their attention." He admitted as they blended into the crowded sidewalk traffic.

"It wasn't embarrassment over me?"

"No!" He looked at her in horror.

"Good because I wasn't embarrassed to be holding your hand either." She smiled as he looked down at her and started to chuckle.

"Thanks. And just a few days ago I said that I would not be reticent in expressing my feelings for you before anyone."

"You did express your feelings; we held hands in front of them all. I understand the need for decorum here Will, and I certainly didn't expect you to stop in the lobby for a passionate embrace." He stopped walking for a moment and bent to kiss her. She laughed and they continued on. He led her to an old building and they stepped inside where he was immediately greeted by name and with great respect. "Where are we?" She looked around curiously.

"This is the Harvard Club, I'm a member here and at a few others around town, they are comfortable, and rather exclusive places to visit, but they are also excellent locations to conduct business." He smiled. "And yes, women are permitted."

"How long has that been allowed?" She asked with a cocked brow.

"Hmm, for some clubs it was a recent enlightenment." He laughed.

Elizabeth stopped before they entered the dining room. "How often do you eat lunch here?"

"If I'm not at the gym or have a lunch meeting, I eat here, so practically daily." Darcy looked at her curiously. "Why?"

She turned around, pulling him along, and they were soon back out on the street. "It's time to expand your horizons. There must be fifty restaurants within walking distance from your office. Let's go give one some business." Elizabeth started walking and looked up at him. "I hate eating alone too, so this is an excellent opportunity for me to try something new."

"I really don't know what to say." Darcy's grip tightened on her hand and he smiled. "Thank you."

"Hey, I'm hungry, too!"

"I AM SO SORRY." Charles appeared in Darcy's office doorway when he heard that he had returned and looked at him nervously.

Darcy glanced up from his work and closed his eyes. "I won't tolerate her behavior any longer Charles. I have thus far for your sake, but it has moved beyond embarrassing; now it is approaching criminal."

"It wasn't as bad as that . . ."

"Patricia and Elizabeth caught her going through my desk, then when I arrived to enter my office, she greeted me by grabbing at my crotch! I've been approached by prostitutes with more restraint!" He saw the stricken expression on Charles' face and closed his eyes. "I'm sorry, I've been approached by women offering much more who were just as well-bred as she."

"That doesn't excuse it. I mentioned that you were engaged and she seemed disappointed, and I tried to make it clear to her that you were never interested. I certainly never expected a problem when I asked to meet for lunch and she offered to pick me up here."

"Well, whatever it was I'm sure that you understand why she will not be permitted past the reception desk from now on. Security and the receptionist have been notified. I don't need the remotest possibility of this ever happening again, not now, not that I have Elizabeth. I don't want anything like this ever coming to her ears. I never want her to ever doubt me, and this all occurred when she was inside my office. If she had opened the door at that moment . . ."

"I understand." Charles sighed and began to leave.

"Charles . . . it isn't your fault, I know." His shoulders relaxed. "I know of your sister's rather vindictive bent when she is denied what she wants."

Charles sank down in the chair that Darcy indicated and smiled weakly. "I know. She has attempted to skim off of my success for years. I think that I need to start saying no." He laughed, "Yes, we have had this conversation before, I know."

"Has Jane met Caroline yet?' Darcy asked casually.

'No, well we have only had four dates; we are hardly to the point of meeting family. Do you think I should keep Caroline hidden from view?" He saw Darcy's brows rising. "Yes, I get your point. Well, we will see each other on Sunday night for the engagement party. Are you looking forward to it?"

'About as much as I look forward to any party." Darcy smiled at his laugh. 'Well, Elizabeth will be there, so what more do I need?"

"WHY DO WE have to take a cab?" Fran demanded.

"It is not a cab, William hired us a car service for the evening, and it is because there is not enough room in his car for all of us." Jane said patiently while she and her parents waited outside of their building. "They needed to leave earlier, too. Mrs. Fitzwilliam wanted them to be at the apartment when the guests started to arrive."

"But we are family; shouldn't we be there to greet the guests as well? It's bad enough that Shirley and Ray can't come tonight, and with Ed and Kelly on vacation, we will be her only family there! They should know who Lizzy's parents are!"

"There is no doubt in my mind that everyone will have you identified before the night is through." Tom said quietly and caught Jane's eye, then the call he received from Darcy came to mind. "Fran, I want to remind you that we are the guests for this party, so we should not criticize Mrs. Fitzwilliam's arrangements, nor should we expound on how we could have done better. We are there to celebrate and enjoy the good company and I'm sure, excellent food."

"Well of course, how could you expect me to be otherwise? You sound as if you are afraid I would embarrass Lizzy!" She huffed and watched as each new car came by. Finally a black limousine pulled up and she crowed in triumph. "Well, look at this!" She stepped up and nodded at the driver who held open her door. Tom watched Jane enter and steeled himself for a moment before climbing in behind her.

DARCY AND ELIZABETH exited the elevator on the Fitzwilliam's floor. Georgiana was still in the lobby, waiting for Greg and Anne to pay off their cab and come inside. Darcy saw that the hallway was empty and drew Elizabeth against him. "Are you okay?" His arms were around her waist, his hands were loosely clasped, and he could feel her tension.

"I've been better." She laughed softly and rested her head against his chest, hugging him tightly.

"What can I do to help?"

"Don't leave me." She whispered.

"If you don't leave me." Elizabeth looked up and smiled. "I'm just as nervous, you know."

They heard the elevator whirring up and suddenly the door opened. "Haven't you guys gone in yet?" Georgiana exclaimed. "Come on!" She led Anne and Greg out, and the two couples assessed each other. "You really look great Elizabeth, where did you get that dress?" Anne smiled and squeezed her hand. It was the first time the women had seen each other since the afternoon at Pemberley.

Elizabeth looked down at her dress. "Oh, thank you, Jane and Georgiana went with me to Saks's. I wasn't really sure what to buy."

"You got exactly the right thing. You'll be the envy of the room." Anne walked ahead with her and stopped. "Elizabeth, I haven't had a chance to apologize in person yet, but I am very sorry for the way that Greg and I imposed ourselves on you and William at Pemberley. We knew what Mom wanted to do, but it was not our business to give our opinions when they were not requested, we behaved just as poorly as Mom did, but it was done in the spirit of care, not meanness."

"I understand that Anne. Perhaps if I had been with William longer, I would have been better prepared for the necessity of our conversation and it would not have hurt me so badly to hear your advice. However, in a way I'm happy that I was blindsided by it. Our marriage is not a business transaction, and I have no intention of walking away if we have times of difficulty. I look at William and see the man I love, not the powerful billionaire that everyone else sees. We have dealt with the issue of our futures privately and lovingly. No further mention of it is necessary from anyone else." Elizabeth smiled and looked up at William. He took her hand and kissed it.

"Oh, well good, I'm happy that it has worked out so well." Anne glanced at Greg who cocked his head at Darcy. "I'll be happy to help you in any way that I can, with the wedding or anything."

"I'll be glad to accept it, thank you." Elizabeth smiled. The truce had been signed, and the points had been made.

Georgiana waited at the open doorway. "Nobody else is here yet!"

"Thank God." Darcy said under his breath.

"There they are!" David came up and kissed Elizabeth's cheek. "You are radiant, Elizabeth."

"If you say so." She smiled and he chuckled, going on to shake Darcy's hand. "Arlene, please let me thank you again for doing this for us." She kissed her cheek and received one in return.

"No dear, I know that you and William would be far happier had I not done this, but it is really for the best. You'll see."

"May I help with anything?"

"No! What do you think caterers are for?" She laughed and directed her to the bar. "Let's get something nice to relax you."

"I'll take care of that, Mom." Richard grinned. "What's your pleasure, Elizabeth?"

"Oh, just some ginger ale, I think." Elizabeth smiled to see his tilting head. "I want to keep my wits about me."

"But how am I to steal you away from my cousin if you are sober?" Elizabeth's mouth hung open and he leaned over to kiss her cheek. "Let's see how long it takes him to get here." He whispered and placed her hand on his arm.

"Richard, I will not play your game." Elizabeth removed her hand just as Darcy arrived to place his on her shoulders.

"How are you, honey?" He asked but his eyes were drilling into Richard's.

"I'm fine, Will. Richard was just getting me some ginger ale."

Darcy nodded. "Make that two."

"Two? Since when are you a teetotaler?"

"Since the time that I needed to protect my fiancé from grasping relatives." He growled.

"I deserved that, I know. I'm sorry." He smiled at Elizabeth. "It seems that my sense of humor doesn't please you."

"It would if you applied it to something other than disturbing your cousin's peace." She lifted her brow at him. "I think that you should be thrilled that he is so happy."

"I am." He picked up a glass of wine and handed it to Elizabeth, and then another to Darcy. "Relax; you'll be safe here tonight." Richard took a glass for himself and raised it in toast. "To the lovely couple!" He cried.

"Here, here!" John smiled and joined them. "You are beautiful, Elizabeth." He kissed her cheek and shook Darcy's hand. "So are you ready?"

The bell rang and all eyes turned first to the door, then to Darcy and Elizabeth. Their hands instantly clasped. Over the next half hour the room steadily filled with a dizzying number of people. Darcy retreated to a corner near the windows, his posture was stiff, his smile non-existent. Elizabeth stood in front of him, almost serving as a shield against the endless onslaught of well-wishers. She felt his hand gripping her waist; the other seemed to be permanently extended to shake the hands of the visitors. His discomfort was painfully clear, and superceded every bit of hers.

Elizabeth rose to the occasion, smiling and laughing, accepting kisses from strangers on her cheeks and above all else, turning and including William in every exchange, drawing him out enough to speak comfortably to people he knew and civilly to those he did not. During a lull in the visits, she turned fully around and reached up to caress his face. He seemed to awaken from his fixed stare at his shoes. "Will, are you okay?"

"Don't I look well? I'm pretty relaxed, I think."

She laughed. "You're kidding, right?"

"No." He stared at her in confusion. "I'm doing remarkably well, and it's all because you are here."

"Oh my, I dread knowing how you would be if I wasn't!"

The sound of silverware tapping on glasses filled the room. "Come on, let's have a kiss!" Richard called.

"Oh no." Darcy groaned.

"I think that he has the right idea." Elizabeth smiled. "Kiss me, show them how happy you are . . . that is, if you really *are* happy to be marrying me." Her lips pursed and her bright eyes sparkled at him.

Those eyes. He smiled. "Come here." Darcy lifted her face to his and kissed her. Whoops and cheers filled the room. The taste of her kiss broke through his reticence like nothing else could, and instead of withdrawing, his hands dropped to embrace her, and drew her body against his. Elizabeth's arms went around his neck, and they continued with slow strokes of their lips, finishing when Darcy's tongue gently entered her mouth to taste the wine on hers. They parted far enough to rest their foreheads together. "I love you, honey."

"I love you, Will." Elizabeth remained nestled in his arms, and they stayed that way, neither hearing the applause of the crowd. When they finally opened their eyes again, she looked upon a smiling and truly relaxed man. "We should have kissed like that an hour ago."

Darcy chuckled. "I think that you're right. At last Richard has served us well." He kissed her forehead and rested his cheek on her hair.

"Well, that was something to see." Tom watched as Elizabeth and Darcy moved away from their corner and approached some seated elderly relatives. He began introducing her to them with a genuine smile. Tom raised his brow at Jane. "He is a man transformed."

"I would be a woman transformed after a kiss like that!" Jane observed Elizabeth glowing just as brightly as Darcy. "He is beautiful."

"Ahem." Tom cleared his throat. "Coveting your future brother, Jane?"

She laughed and looked over to Fran. "Are you okay, Mom?" Fran had been largely silent since entering the Fitzwilliam's spacious apartment. The exclusive crowd, the exceptional food, the conversation that covered topics far beyond her reach had overwhelmed her and for the first time in a long time, she clung to Tom's arm.

"I'm fine, Jane." She said quietly. "Are these the type of people who hire you?"

"Yes, in fact there is one of my brides, Anne Rothschild, she is William's cousin." She nodded over to where Anne was talking to Arlene. "Her wedding reception is where Lizzy met William."

"I suppose it was quite a magnificent affair."

"It was gaudy and overdone, and honestly, not my favorite reception. In fact, I don't even include pictures of it in my portfolio; I don't like showing all of the unnecessary things that were demanded."

"Who demanded them? The bride? She seems to be an elegant girl." Fran looked over Anne's dress and demeanor carefully.

"She is; she's very nice and likes simple things; the problem was her mother. I understand why my old employer directed Mrs. de Bourgh to me. I thought she was doing me a favor." Jane laughed softly. "She was a terror to work with. Well, working with is not the right phrase, I'd say that bearing with is better. Mrs. de Bourgh was calling me constantly, demanding one thing or another; I can't tell you how happy I was to have that wedding completed." Jane shook her head. "Elizabeth saw it all and was in complete agreement; I know that she is hoping that

Mrs. de Bourgh does not come tonight, and so far, so good. They had a bit of a confrontation when they were in the Hamptons."

"Over what? The wedding arrangements?" Fran asked with interest.

"No." Jane stopped; she had said enough, her parents had heard nothing of the prenup. "It's really not my story to tell."

"But both you and Lizzy think that her mother was too demanding." She looked over to Elizabeth and where she was shaking hands with yet another woman who Fran recognized from the society pages, and was holding her own. "Now I understand."

"Understand what, Mom?"

"Why your father felt the need to tell me to . . . not embarrass Lizzy tonight. I feel very out-of-place here." She looked around. "She has to fit into this."

"Yes, and it is intimidating, and she is very nervous." Jane said quietly. "William is even more scared."

"Is he ashamed of her?" Fran bristled.

"No, Mom, he's very shy." Jane smiled to see Fran's eyes widen. "Haven't you noticed?"

"It seems that I only looked at how rich he is." She sighed. Tom had been listening and looked up to Jane with raised brows.

"Jane, I hope that you remember me, John Fitzwilliam?" John appeared before them and smiled.

"Yes, of course." Jane returned the smile. "Have you met my parents? This is my father, Tom, and my mother, Fran."

He shook their hands. "I hope that you are enjoying yourselves, my mother has been dying to do this for years."

"Host a party?" Tom smiled.

John laughed. "No, that is done very regularly here, I assure you. She wanted to host an engagement celebration.

"It's a shame that she has to do it for her nephew instead of her sons." Jane grinned.

"I believe that we had a similar conversation the last time we were together." His head cocked and he enjoyed the blush that appeared over her face.

"I'm afraid that I was unusually provocative that morning, but I believe that my defense of my sister and your cousin's behavior is vindicated." She nodded over to where they stood comfortably leaning together, and saw Darcy's arm wrap around Elizabeth's waist while they spoke to Charles. "Although, until they kissed, I did not recognize the man at my sister's side."

John looked at the couple and laughed. "Well, I know both versions very well. He really hates crowds. That kiss was something else."

"He looked pretty unwelcoming before. Elizabeth probably never would have been interested in him if he had looked that way at Anne's wedding."

"You were working that night, but I assure you, Darcy looked exactly the same." Jane looked at him in surprise.

"Love is blind."

"Sometimes." He met her gaze with a smile.

"Hi!" Charles appeared and gave Jane a kiss on her cheek. "You look beautiful, Jane!" He held out his hand to John and missed the annoyance that flashed across his face. "I thought I'd never get over here, the line to greet the guests of honor was pretty long." He laughed and nodded towards Darcy. "It's good to see him not looking quite so miserable. He's been dreading this party for weeks."

"Yes, that's right, you work for him. You're his . . . assistant?" John said.

Charles caught a bit of derisiveness in his voice and glanced up at him quizzically. "Well, I'm . . . I guess you could call me his bagman. I keep him on schedule and aware of everything that is going on in his many enterprises and I am particularly involved with his personal forestry interests."

"Ah." He smiled at Jane, who was looking uncomfortably between the two men.

"Are you still considering politics?" Charles relaxed again.

"Yes, I'll begin my campaign for Dad's old seat after New Year's. I'm afraid that it will involve many rooms like these." He smiled at the crowd of people. "A lot of glad-handing and promise-making is involved as well as the need for fundraising. A great many long days are ahead. It makes me wish that I had a good woman by my side to help me through it all." He met Jane's eyes and saw hers widen.

Charles nodded, then turned to Jane. "I know what you mean, finding a wonderful woman is like finding a needle in a haystack." He smiled warmly into her eyes, then back at John. "At least you have the comfort of being able to coast into the seat using your father's established good name. It should be an easy campaign for you."

"Some are easier than others." He nodded and walked away.

"I always liked John." Charles smiled and squeezed her hand. "You're awfully quiet."

"You talk enough for both of us, Charles." Jane said quietly and watched John's retreat.

"So who won that skirmish? I'm betting on your worthy competitor." Richard nudged John and handed him a drink.

"Shut up, Richard." John said softly.

"Oh come on, she's gorgeous, but Mom's right, you waited too long to make your move."

"I know, but I believe that she is very much aware of my interest should Charles follow his normal path and walk away. If he is that stupid, I'll be there." He watched Jane and Charles speaking to the Bennets.

Richard shook his head and laughed. "Give it up." He looked again at his brother's fixed gaze and rolled his eyes. "You know, if you really are serious about her, and you want to be successful in Congress, you're going to have to do more than smile pleasantly and get contributions. Go fight for her."

"You sound like Mom."

"Then you know that I'm right, don't you?" Richard said triumphantly.

"Darcy!" A small beaming man approached the couple and to Elizabeth's surprise, received a warm smile and embrace.

"Barry! I was beginning to wonder if you would come!" Darcy turned to Elizabeth and took her hand. "Honey, this is my very good friend Barry Gold, my roommate for two years at Harvard. Barry, this is Elizabeth Bennet, my fiancée." His eyes glowed with pride.

She did not miss the appellation of friendship William bestowed upon this man; it was very rarely given and immediately she knew that he was special. "It is a pleasure to meet one of William's friends. Which path did you follow at Harvard?"

"Ah, I am a lawyer and never left Boston. I didn't have the intestinal fortitude, or frankly the funds, to achieve Darcy's miracle in education." Barry grinned and shook her hand. "I am just delighted to meet you, Elizabeth. He has filled my inbox with emails of praise. I can't begin to say how happy I am for you both."

"Thank you, I'm very happy myself." She looked up at William and laughed. "It seems that you are just bursting to talk to Barry, I think I'll take the opportunity to go check on my parents."

"So you think it's safe to leave me now?" He smiled and leaned down to kiss her lightly. "Don't go far."

"I think I'll be within calling distance." She winked and patted Barry's arm. "I'm sure that I'll see you later." Walking away she found her father comfortably standing by the bar, talking to David. "Hi, I'm sorry that we haven't had a chance to see each other tonight." She kissed his cheek. "What are you two discussing so deeply?"

"Ah, well, I could try to impress you with some weighty subject, but in reality we were discussing wives." Tom smiled at David.

"Yes, and how to control them." He grinned.

"Oh, don't get me started on that subject!" Elizabeth looked around. "Where is Mom, by the way?"

"Jane took her over to meet Anne." Tom pointed. "She seems to have had an epiphany tonight."

"Really? What happened?"

"I think that you will no longer be pressured to have a wedding that she would design. At this moment, I believe that she is getting an earful of information on how an intrusive mother can destroy a bride's day." He grinned to see Elizabeth's eyes widen. "I see that you are pleased?"

"I am!" Anne looked over to her and smiled, nodding her head. Elizabeth raised her glass in a silent toast of thanks, and saw her laugh. "I think that our little ceremony is safe, now!"

David chuckled. "I'm delighted to hear it. I'm also very pleased to see your reception by our guests. You have handled them and Darcy magnificently."

"Oh, I just want to go home!" Elizabeth smiled and he took her hand and squeezed. "Thank you. I hope that William is pleased, that is all that matters."

"You'll be seeing all of these people in the future. He's been something of a recluse, but with you by his side, I hope that you get to enjoy what our society has to offer." He tilted his head. "As promised, there are only friends here tonight. You really had nothing to fear. I'm hoping that Catherine stays away, she threatened to and I did nothing to encourage her to come."

Elizabeth contained the opinion she held for William's aunt. "I am pleased that no exgirlfriends were invited." She smiled at his rolling eyes. "Well, I mean no expursuers, anyway."

"Hmm, there are plenty of those, always rebuffed, but lots of hopeful candidates. You'll be bound to run across them eventually, but not here."

Charles had joined Darcy and Barry, and John saw his chance to approach Jane again. "Can I get you a fresh drink?"

"Oh, no I'm fine." She smiled and held up her half-full glass. "So you begin your run for office in earnest soon, what happens if you lose?"

"Such faith you have in me!" He laughed, then shrugged. "I'll just keep doing what I do now."

"Which is?"

"We are a family of lawyers, but I work with my dad in his business as a campaign consultant. I'll certainly have personal experience in running one soon!" John paused then plunged on. "I was wondering, are you free to see other people? You seem to be dating Charles, but I don't know how serious it is."

"Neither do I." She said looking over to him. "I really enjoy his company and he is very friendly and sweet, I hear that his sister is a terror, though." Jane laughed and looked up at John. "I have had no indication from him what he wants, if anything, but then we have only gone out a few times. He was, by the way, very modest in his job description to you. He is not a glorified assistant to William."

"I know." John smiled. "It was a cockfight, as I'm sure you were fully aware." She looked down. "So you are available to date other people?"

"Maybe."

"How can I persuade you?" He looked down at her with the same Fitzwilliam blue eyes that Darcy had, and raised his brow.

"Let me think about it." She looked back over to Charles who was now watching her conversation with John, with a look of concern.

"I know how to reach you, and I promise; I will call in a day or two." John smiled. "Thank you for considering it." He kissed her cheek and walked away. Charles immediately came over.

"Are you okay?" He asked and searched her face for any sign of distress.

"Yes." Jane smiled; it was good to see that he cared.

Darcy bid goodnight to Barry who left as quickly as he came, and after negotiating his way through more well-wishers, found Elizabeth talking with a group of women. "May I steal you away?" He smiled after greeting them all.

"Ask your aunt, she is in charge here." She smiled at Arlene who laughed.

"By all means, give the girl a break from our inquisition. I imagine that you could use one as well." Darcy took Elizabeth's hand and she felt his tension melt away.

"I thought that you were doing very well, what happened?"

"My buffers abandoned me and I was alone. I need my Lizzy back." He kissed her cheek and she leaned against him as they walked. "Barry hates these parties as much as I do, so he said his greetings and left. If he wasn't returning to Boston tomorrow morning, I would have asked him to the house for dinner. Speaking of which, are you hungry? I haven't had a thing."

"Oh, neither have I, and the wine is definitely getting to me." Elizabeth caught his satisfied smile and shook her head. "I'm not going to jump you in front of your entire family." She laughed at his sigh. "Do you think that your aunt will be coming, David wasn't sure?" Elizabeth asked as she scanned the selection of food.

"Catherine? I certainly hope not." He smiled and opened his mouth to receive the morsel she held to his lips.

"I'm surprised; this seems like just the sort of event where she would be very happy to expound on her views." She giggled as William fed her, then kissed off the cheese that clung to his fingertips.

"Don't tell me that you are disappointed?" He laughed to have a new item presented to him, enjoying the game they had begun.

"No, not at all, just curious." He stood scanning the platters and she took his hand to guide him over to the cheesecake balls on little skewers. He lifted his brow.

"Really, you want sweets now?"

"I always want sweets, Will." She bit her lip and he groaned. Taking the skewer, he dipped the ball in the accompanying chocolate sauce and lifted it carefully to her mouth.

"What will be my reward for bringing this to you?" He held it just out of reach.

"What do you demand?"

"I want my sweets when we get home."

She smiled and nodded as he fed her, then leaned down to pick up the bowl of chocolate. "I'll just have to remember to bring this with me; I can't pass up nibbling anything dipped in chocolate."

"Lizzzzzzy." He moaned. "Why are you doing this to me now?"

"You started it." She whispered and looking him over, took his hand in hers. "Come on, let's go and look out the window."

Chapter 12

"**T**his is nice." Elizabeth held up a picture of a wedding gown in one of the bride's magazines that littered Jane's office.

"Mmmm, yeah, but if you're going to have pictures on the beach, do you really want to deal with a train?" She paged through another magazine. "Now, this could work." She handed it over to Elizabeth. "It's pretty simple, but I think it's more your style, and besides, you want more of a picnic atmosphere for the reception, and you don't want to attempt removing barbeque sauce from silk."

"Are you expecting a food fight?" Elizabeth smiled and glanced up at her.

"I don't know; is Catherine de Bourgh coming?" Jane laughed. "I was so surprised that she didn't come to the engagement party."

"Oh, she did, only she arrived late." Elizabeth smiled and Jane tilted her head. "Arlene sent her an invitation that had the time of the party set for eight o'clock."

"Oops." Jane grinned. "Gee that was only wrong by six hours. I really like Mrs. Fitzwilliam."

"I do, too. She didn't even tell David about it, so he could be convincingly surprised when she didn't come."

"You do realize that she will just be angrier now, she's bound to make an appearance sometime."

"I know, but I am so grateful it wasn't at the party." Elizabeth looked back at the dress Jane had found. "I like this."

"How about William? If you wear that dress, he doesn't need to be in a suit, just a shirt and slacks would do."

"Oh, I don't know about that, he's such a stickler for the proper attire for the occasion."

"This is the man who works out wearing only a pair of shorts?"

"Yes." Elizabeth said dreamily. Jane threw a magazine at her and she laughed. "I'll take some of these home with me and try to see his reaction to the different styles, that is if I'm awake when he returns. He has a board meeting and dinner to attend tonight. He'll be home pretty late. Actually I don't expect to see much of him this week; he has a lot on his schedule. I am gradually learning the myriad of enterprises he directs or at least is involved with. The end of the third quarter and the fiscal year were last week, so all of them require his attention at the same time, there are a lot of budgets to approve. I think that I'll be rubbing his temples often . . . and getting a lot of my own work done since I'll be alone."

'Charles is going tonight, too." Jane stared down at her desk. "John Fitzwilliam asked me out."

Elizabeth's brow rose and she watched Jane. "Really? And . . ."

"I don't know what to say to him!"

"Well, what's the status of your relationship with Charles? Is it casual or getting serious? He said to me that he has never met a woman like you before and he appreciates how you are happy to be yourself. I know that he has spoken to William about wanting to settle down."

"Yes, and at the party, he . . . he seemed to be unhappy when I was alone, well not alone, but speaking with John. That must be a sign of some sort, don't you think?"

"Sure, he's territorial. What sort of signals have you given him? William has asked me what you think of him, and I really couldn't say much other than that you liked him a great deal. I don't know how far you have gone . . ."

"No sex, just kissing." Jane said quickly, and Elizabeth laughed. "Hey, you kept William at bay for how long?"

"I didn't say anything."

"Yeah." She sighed. "John is so different from Charles. He's . . . he actually reminds me of William in some ways, but obviously not at all shy."

"They both have those blue eyes, and a tendency to stare." Elizabeth smiled. "Of course Will is far more handsome."

Jane rolled her eyes. "You are biased. So would you go out with him?"

"Well, you are not me, and I wouldn't, but that's because I have a ton of bad history behind me and would be so happy that I found a nice guy like Charles, but you must think that something is missing in him if you are even considering going out with John. Look, you are not in a committed relationship, neither of you have spoken of it yet, and your intimacy hasn't gone far enough to use that as an excuse. If you're going to try John out, now is the time. Go and see what happens. He might turn out to be an overbearing ass." Elizabeth grinned. "Or you could wind up in his bed."

"Ha ha ha." Jane sighed. "Okay, I'll go just once, and just so I won't wonder about it."

"Good idea." Elizabeth glanced at her and bit her lip, then flipped through another magazine. "Well, let's get the rest of this thing planned. You found a caterer?"

"Oh, I thought you could just use the Barefoot Contessa, she's right there near Pemberley. Unless you are serious about having a pig roast."

"It would smell so good." She sighed. "I would love to do a real barbeque."

"How you got that in your blood living in New York City . . ."

"I have traveled all over the country for the books, and I know what tastes soooo good. Besides, I could lick William's . . ."

"I don't want to hear it!"

"Fingers." Elizabeth laughed. "Honestly, Jane, what were you thinking?"

"WHAT'S IT LIKE, Lizzy?"

Elizabeth looked over to Lydia, and went back to digging through her desk in the apartment. "What?"

"Being in love." She slid down the back of the sofa and landed with an ungraceful flop on the cushions. "You thought you were in love with Bill, but that wasn't love."

"No, it certainly wasn't. That was . . . I guess it was me being lonely and being afraid to *not* have him, and then it just got spectacularly out of control. You sort of had a similar experience.

"Yeah, but I slept with everything in pants, as Grandma Bennet would say." She laughed, and Elizabeth smiled, Lydia had come a long way since her days of offering her body in exchange for drugs. "I couldn't have gotten away from it if it wasn't for you."

"Well, I'm just glad that I could help you. I didn't realize what was going on until I got home, and obviously everyone else was blind to it as well. I guess that it took one depressed person to recognize another. The rest of the family figured that you were just being a moody teenager. I'm just thankful that you hadn't been picked up by a pimp yet."

"No, I was going to run away." She sighed. "I think that I'll go to nursing school."

"Really?" Elizabeth stopped and sat down. "That's an interesting choice, why?"

"Because I want to work in a drug rehab program for girls like me, but I know that I need to have a good income too since those programs aren't always funded well, so I don't want to be a social worker. Maybe I could do some volunteer work at a shelter or something, and be a nurse in my day job. I don't know, my counselor is getting me ready to take the college entrance exams in the fall, and we're discussing career options."

"That is really great, Lydia! I am so happy that you are looking ahead like this." Elizabeth smiled. "You have a future, and only two years ago you thought you would be happy just living through the day. I am so proud of you!"

"Thanks." Lydia looked down. "I had to do a research project on our family tree for a class last semester."

"Oh, and are we related to royalty?" She went back to going through her files.

"No, but we are cousins to Bill Collins."

Elizabeth's head snapped up. "WHAT?"

"He's like a third cousin, pretty distant, but his father was Dad's second cousin on his father's side, and I think that it works out that somewhere his great great grandfather was our great great grandfather's brother, I think. I kind of got lost in it somewhere, but I came across his name and I was just so shocked. It all checked out though. I guess that if you had ended up with him it wouldn't have been a big deal, I mean legally or anything, but he was such a jerk I'm so glad that it never happened." She stared at Elizabeth, her face was white. "Are you okay? You kind of have that look you did when you came home after you graduated."

"Oh, yeah, fine." Elizabeth pulled herself together, and looked at the picture of William that still resided on her old desk and immediately felt better. "Please don't tell anyone else about this Lydia. He was my past; I don't want to waste any more time thinking about him."

"Yeah, we both have a lot of things in our pasts to forget." She smiled and looked at the picture too. "He's soooooooooo gorgeous. I can't wait to meet him."

Elizabeth relaxed a little, that news was rattling, but thankfully it didn't matter now. "He's looking forward to meeting you, too. Just remember that he is very shy, so don't be put off if he doesn't respond well to your enthusiasm. We'll get together for dinner on Sunday at our house. That's when I can show you what a healthy loving relationship looks like. Kitty should be here Saturday night, right?"

"Yes, and then we can fight over who gets this place. Mary won't want it; she's going to be a missionary or something before she starts looking for a church."

"I won't get involved in that fight." Elizabeth smiled. "Just let me get the rest of my stuff out of here before you move in."

"Oh don't worry; I don't have anything, so you can just leave it all." She looked around. "Well, maybe I'd redecorate. Way too many plants, Lizzy."

"I know; you're not a nature girl." She got up and hugged her. "Do whatever you want, I have a home. I'm just glad to be seeing all of my sisters again even if it is just for a few days."

They heard a knock and Lydia jumped up to let Jane in. She sat down and stared at her folded hands. "What's wrong with you?" Lydia demanded, sitting next to her and leaning down to peer into her eyes.

Elizabeth looked her over and nodded. "I'd say that our big sister is undecided about which man she likes best. So Jane, how was the date with John?"

"He took me to dinner at the New York Athletic Club."

"Whoa, that's an odd choice for a first date! William is a member there, but we haven't gone yet, and I'm not really in a hurry for the experience." Elizabeth grinned.

"Isn't that some place for snooty super-rich people?" Lydia asked. Elizabeth and Jane just looked at her silently.

"He introduced me to a lot of people; many times he mentioned that I was the sister of the woman who was marrying William." Jane added quietly.

Elizabeth tilted her head. "That's interesting. Do you think that he was just stating a fact or giving you a connection? Were you treated differently afterwards?"

"I really don't know." Jane sighed. "We went for a walk around the park before going to the theater, and he kissed me."

"Was he good?" Lydia bounced up and down and prodded her.

Jane groaned and tipped over, hiding her face in a pillow. Elizabeth and Lydia exchanged glances and laughed. A muffled voice informed them, "He asked me out again."

"AND?" Asked the choir.

She sat up and held her head in her hands. "I don't know what to do! He's so . . . sure of himself and positive about his political ambitions. His ideas are wonderful. I just don't know if I'm cut out to be a congressman's wife.

"He didn't actually suggest that, did he?" Elizabeth asked and saw Jane's rolling eyes. "Well, okay, yes you do kind of have to keep that thought in mind. So let's think about it. He would be gone a lot. Would you want to give up your business to live in Washington? Charles undoubtedly lives here and isn't going anywhere as long as he works for William."

"They are such different men; both seem to be very good. Charles says that he wants to settle down, but I wonder if he really knows what that means. He's very focused on his professional life, but I think that he is still very much a boy in his personal behavior. Then there's John . . . it would be so nice to be with a man, you know, one who really knows his strengths. But then again, do you remember when Dad was worried that William only wanted you as a trophy? I can't shake the feeling that John is considering how we would look as a couple as he campaigns. I know that makes me seem shallow, and you know that I don't think of myself like that, but he has said it enough times to make me think . . . How do I know if he is sincere? The introductions in the club were, I think, a good taste of what life would be like with him. Maybe that's why he did it." Jane closed her eyes. "There's an edge to John that I don't see in Charles. I wonder if Charles constantly trying out new women is because he is just searching for the right one."

"Okay, how about this, when you kissed him, did you feel that you were betraying Charles?" Elizabeth watched her carefully. "For example, when Richard tried to bait William at the party by putting my hand on his arm, I was extremely uncomfortable, and although William never said exactly what Caroline Bingley did to him at the office, I know in my gut that he felt that he had hurt me, even though he had not instigated the contact. Did you feel anything more or less with either of them?"

Jane's head went back in her hands. The answer was yes.

RICHARD GRINNED and leaned back in his chair, put his feet up on his desk and imagined his brother's expression on the other end of the line. "So, besides the gorgeous package and talented mouth, what else do you think? Do you like her?"

"I wouldn't have asked her out if I didn't." John said irritably. "She is a successful business woman, and she has a sharp tongue that is just poised for battle if you provoke her enough, she is similar to Elizabeth in that way, but is also so different."

"Any similarity to Elizabeth is definitely a point in her favor." Richard laughed. "Is she wife material? You've dated enough empty-headed girls to know the difference."

"It's only been one date, how should I know yet?" John evaded the question.

Richard pressed him. "But you introduced her to the Athletic Club, what was that about? Of all the places in this city to take her, you chose to show her your status instead of yourself. Was this an introduction for her to the life she could expect? You certainly weren't acting like Darcy, unless you count the walk in the park before the theater. Romance is not your style, you wouldn't be able to keep that up, and I wonder if she had been expecting it."

John sighed. "I know, I mean I can be as thoughtful and . . . well you know, as any decent guy, but she probably looks at her sister and wants what she has. That is a problem. I can be the hard-nosed businessman that Darcy is, but all the rest of it . . . I'm just a guy."

"You do resemble him a bit." Richard pointed out helpfully.

"Yeah, I know. I really like her; I just wonder if she would like the life I'd give her, if it got that far. I think that she would do well, but I don't know if she would enjoy it."

"Okay, so here's a question, do you really want to enter politics? Don't do it to please Mom and Dad. You grew up with him in Congress; you know exactly the life they led. I hated it. There I was at West Point, all on my own merit and desire, and I was being used as a selling point to get votes. Do you want every accomplishment of your wife and children to be examined by the media and constituents? I think that I know you better than anyone, and I honestly think that you are making a mistake throwing your hat in the ring, and furthermore, I wonder how much of an influence your career choice would be in Jane's interest in you."

John sat with his eyes closed; already knowing instinctively that his career would have a significant effect on Jane's interest.

DARCY AND CHARLES remained in the conference room after the rest of the participants left for their offices. The table was littered with papers and with the debris from the lunch they all shared. "So do you have any plans with Jane?" Darcy asked casually.

"No, this week is shot, for obvious reasons." Charles looked up to see Darcy's tired nod. "Then Sunday she has that dinner at your place . . . of course you could invite me." He smiled.

"Sorry, that's my first meeting with the sisters; I've got to keep that to family. However, that is in the evening, you have the whole day before that to do something with her."

"She probably has to do her grocery shopping or something." He rested his chin on his hands.

"So go with her and carry the bags."

Charles looked surprised and laughed. "What do you know of grocery shopping?"

Darcy smiled and leaned back in his chair, "Lizzy and I go almost every Saturday to the farmer's market on 77th Street. The wonderful part began when she moved in with me, because when we return home, she cooks while I bother her." He chuckled with the memory of their last cooking day. "It's a good chance to just talk. Sometimes Georgiana and even Mrs. Reynolds join us, but mostly we are simply alone and relaxed and it's so . . . I don't know, but I wouldn't give it up for all the society events in the world."

"I never thought of you as domestic."

Shrugging, Darcy laughed. "I never thought of it either, I've never experienced half of the things we've done in the past few months before, and my life was poorer for it. Of course we go out, too. This Saturday we'll eat out instead and go dancing since we have only really seen each other to sleep. But next week when things are settled down around here again, we'll probably go to a movie or maybe a ball game or play one evening, then spend the rest just at home. We do have to finish the wedding plans, and I haven't looked at anything she has done so far. Eventually we'll start entertaining a little, and accepting invitations, I guess, but neither of us is really in a hurry to do either one."

"You have found a very comfortable life with Elizabeth." Charles said with obvious envy. "That is what I want."

"Are you sure?" Darcy asked softly. "You have been so quick to become bored with the women you date; you change your mind and pick up someone new, never really giving any relationship a chance to grow."

"Yes, but I think that the reason behind that is . . . well, I'm searching for someone in particular, and when it becomes clear that I haven't found her, I move on." He met Darcy's gaze with a smile, knowing that an explanation was in order. "I don't want any woman who reminds me of my sisters; they both happily enjoyed our parents' success, but wouldn't tell anyone how they got their money. I've told you about Mom, she was such a great supporter of Dad and his plumbing business, they were thrilled to send me to college, and would have been so proud to see me here." He looked around the conference room and smiled. "I guess I'm looking for my mom."

"I think that in a way, I was too. Well, not a duplicate, but a similar spirit, but also someone who is very much like myself.' Darcy smiled.

Charles nodded. "I am growing tired of the dating ritual."

"Is Jane really the girl for you? Keep in mind her career is far different from Elizabeth's. She will always be as busy as she is now, especially as the business is still growing. The life you see me having with Elizabeth is not the one you would have with Jane."

"I hadn't thought of that." He sat back and considered the idea. "My mom worked hard with my dad, but mostly it was manning the phone, so she was always nearby and well, not pulled away by other things." He looked up to study his friend's face. "I wonder what life would be like with her."

Darcy sat up and leaned forward. "Maybe you should think that through before proceeding with the relationship."

Charles met his eye and tried to understand the intense expression on his friend's face. "What are you telling me, Darcy?"

"I'm not telling you anything other than to really think about what you want, and what you have seen her display in response to your efforts." Darcy rose and gripped his shoulder, then left the room. Charles remained, and continued to think about his desires as he never had before.

LATE THAT EVENING, Darcy wearily climbed up the stairs of the darkened, silent house. Seeing a light under Georgiana's door he knocked softly and heard her call to enter. "Hi, how's it going?"

She was lying on her bed reading a book and listening to her ipod. "Okay, I was going to go to bed soon. How's work?"

"Endless." He smiled and stifled a yawn, then seeing something in her face, he paused. "Are you sure everything is alright?" She nodded and he smiled. "I'll see you in the morning then, good night."

"Good night, William." She gave him a smile and he closed the door, walking down the hallway to his own room, loosening his tie along the way. He entered to find Elizabeth asleep, a book clutched in her hand. He quietly prepared for the night, leaving the bathroom and walking to the bed where he stared down at his sleeping beauty for a moment before carefully removing the book and marking the page. He switched off the lights and slipped under the covers, spooning his body to hers and kissing her shoulder.

Elizabeth stirred, and molded herself back against him. "Welcome home." She whispered sleepily.

"It's so good to come home to you." He nuzzled her neck, and soon joined her in sleep.

In three separate apartments two men and a woman contemplated a vision of sleeping in the arms of someone who loved them.

"OH I LOVE THIS!" Elizabeth exclaimed as they spun around and around the dance floor. Darcy laughed and dipped her backwards as the salsa music ended and lifted her back up to hug her tight. They caught their breath and waited for the next song to begin, her ear was pressed to his chest and she could hear how his heart was pounding as hard as her own. "Who needs to work out when we can dance!"

Darcy looked down at her beaming smile and kissed her. "I certainly find this far more invigorating, and so much more fun. I love dancing with you. I needed this, especially after this week of hardly seeing you. I'm so glad it's over." He rested his head on hers. "Maybe we should hire an instructor to come to the house. The ballroom would be a wonderful place to practice. We could put in a new sound system and learn all sorts of dances, and not have to go out to enjoy ourselves if we don't want to."

"That sounds wonderful!" She looked up at him and tilted her head. "Would you prefer to do our dancing at home?"

He bit his lip and smiled a little. "I guess that I'm feeling a little self-conscious."

"So you noticed them, too."

"Who?"

"All of the ladies who are staring at you with lust." He blushed. "It's not me that they are admiring; it is you in those well-tailored slacks and unbuttoned shirt. The hint of chest hair peeking out is very alluring Will, believe me. I practically swoon every time I see you myself; of course I know what lies beneath that bit of fabric."

"I only notice the wolfish gazes of the men staring at my woman." He said softly.

"Yours?" She caressed his face and smiled into his eyes.

"Yes honey, mine." Darcy leaned down to kiss her just as the next song began.

"Ohhhhhh, I love him." Elizabeth whispered as they began to move. She saw his worry and laughed. "Michael Bublé, such a smooth voice. I tried to get tickets the last time he was in town but they were gone in a millisecond."

"Well, the next time he comes, we'll be sure to go." He gripped her waist and they spun again as he sang softly, "Other dancers may be on the floor, dear, but my eyes will see only you. Only you have that magic technique, when we *Sway*[v] I go weak . . ." She laughed and he smiled at her as they danced out the rest of the song. Holding hands they walked off of the floor. "Would you like a drink or something?"

"Hmm, yes, but I think that I need to fix my hair first. I'll just go in the ladies' room for a minute, okay?"

"Sure, I'll meet you back here." Darcy watched her go and stepped into the men's room, ignored the appraising looks he received from the occupants, and left just as quickly to take up his post waiting for Elizabeth who, he now knew, was doomed to take much longer than he. He found a piece of wall to lean against and watched the dancers on the floor, critiquing their moves in his mind, and didn't notice the woman standing before him until she grabbed his face in her hands and kissed him. "What the hell are you doing? Get off of me!" He ripped away from her and glared.

"Well that hasn't changed; you still have that frightening stare of yours."

Darcy took in the features of the statuesque blonde standing before him and his stomach hit the floor. "Susan."

She laughed and looked down at his hand. "So you're still single, so am I. A dance club is the last place I would expect to find you. You have changed."

"Susan, I . . ."

"I can't believe that you're still available! I haven't met anyone like you since we broke up; you were the sweetest boyfriend I've ever had, nobody else has even come close to you. This must be fate for us to see each other tonight!" Susan laughed to see the surprise in his eyes, and spoke before he could say anything, "I heard that you had a party binge and that you had to pay for company; did you regret breaking up so much? I certainly did." She took his hand and smiled. "You were so shy, I bet that you didn't know how to call me and get back together."

Elizabeth exited the ladies' room in time to witness the entire exchange. She stared at him, waiting to see what he would do, searching for pleasure or regret in his eyes, and reeling with details of his past that he had not revealed.

Darcy removed his hand from hers. "Susan, I never regretted breaking up with you. It was clear that you wanted nothing more from me than my status."

Susan watched him retreating and sighed, dropping some of the act she was putting on. "Well, I admit that was probably true, okay it was true. I was dazzled by everything you had, and I couldn't help but be overwhelmed by it, but you know where I came from, how could I not be?" She tried to take his hand again, but he balled it up and kept it to his side. "That was years ago, I have been around the block a few times since then, and I know now what I blew by losing you."

"Well, as you say that was years ago, and I have moved on, and I hope that you are well, but I am not interested Now please go and enjoy your evening, obviously you did not come here to see me, so go join your friends. I am expecting someone." He spoke politely and without emotion.

"I never stopped wanting you."

"Are you hard-of-hearing?" Elizabeth could hold her tongue no longer. "He asked you to leave."

Darcy's gaze locked on Elizabeth. "Lizzy."

"Who are you?" Susan demanded.

"It is none of your business, but since you asked, I'm his fiancée. Now, please leave us alone." Elizabeth stepped forward and took his willing hand, holding it tightly. "Why are you still here?" She hissed.

"This is the woman you decided to marry?" Susan examined Elizabeth. "You've got to be kidding!"

"You have quite an opinion of yourself!" Elizabeth let go of William's hand and stood toe-to-toe with her.

Susan glared at the smaller woman. "Hey, I was his first everything, I made him what he is for you. You should be grateful."

"Now who's kidding?" Elizabeth laughed and looked up when William put his hands on her shoulders.

"That is a time in my life I would prefer to forget." His intense gaze burned into Elizabeth's eyes, communicating his feelings.

Elizabeth turned back to Susan. "Who do you think you are, the Goddess of Love? Oh yeah, that explains why you're sucking up to a man who dumped you five years ago. Who walks up to an exboyfriend and kisses him?"

Flushing with humiliation, Susan spat. "Where did he find you?"

"In his arms." Elizabeth's hands went up to grip William's, he could feel her trembling.

Susan sneered. "Oh, so he paid for you, I gave it up for free."

"You gave it up for the same reason you are harassing us now, you want his money. The only thing that William paid for in this relationship is my ring."

"We have nothing more to say to you." Susan stepped back; the cold anger in Darcy's voice was something she didn't expect.

"Yeah . . . well you were always a waste of my time." She glared between the two, stared at the ring for a few moments and spun away, disappearing into the crowd.

"Honey? Are you okay? I did not approach her."

Elizabeth turned around and demanded, "How would you feel to see me being mauled by another man?"

"I'd be furious and hurt, but I hope that I would listen to your explanation." He said steadily and took her hands in his. "I have not seen her since we broke up."

"So this is the woman who you dated in college? The one who was pressuring you to get married and gave you no support when your parents died?" He nodded. "This is the woman who cared only for your money?"

"Yes Lizzy, I realized that was all she wanted from me, and I have no doubt that is all she would want now." He kept his grip tight, afraid that if he let go she would run.

"She went to Harvard?" Elizabeth glared into the crowd, searching for her again.

"No, Boston College, she was visiting my neighbor's apartment and they invited me over, I just happened to not have any work to do that night." Darcy's voice was soft; he was watching Elizabeth trying to regain control.

She looked up into his steady gaze, images of that woman in his arms, being kissed, being loved, calling his name, filled her mind. Trying to block it, she lashed out. "From what she said, I guess that you paid escorts after you broke up. I knew that you were with women, I didn't realize that it was prostitutes."

"It was." He looked down. "I am hardly someone who would pick up women in a bar. I made arrangements with . . . a reliable service that was recommended to me. It was surreal and so unlike me, but I . . . I was so numb at the time, I thought that doing something so outrageously uncharacteristic would . . . make a dent, it was a very brief period in my life Lizzy, please, it was so long ago . . ." He looked back up at her, the pain in his eyes went a long way to relieving the pain of meeting a woman she knew he had touched. It still hurt, but if he had to bear seeing Collins, she could bear seeing this bitch. At least there was the satisfaction of Susan seeing William with her.

"Are there others?"

"Others?"

"Other girls for me to meet. Your uncle spoke of women pursuing you who I would probably meet someday."

"Nobody else caught me, Lizzy."

Elizabeth closed her eyes for a moment, and then opened them to see that their confrontation had generated interest in the crowd. "I want to leave."

"Let's go." He said gratefully. They walked outside the club into the sultry July air. Darcy spotted a cab letting off its passengers and grabbed the door. They climbed in and he gave the address. "What are you thinking?"

Elizabeth remained silent, staring out the window at the passing scenery. Darcy took a hold of the hand that was resting on her lap, and when the cab paused in traffic near 87th street, his grip unconsciously tightened when he saw her studying her old home. Soon the cab stopped in front of the house, and she was out before he could pay. He emerged to see her taking off, running around the corner and down the sidewalk.

"Lizzy!" All he heard was the click of her heels in the distance. He didn't know what to think, that she was hurt and upset was obvious, but it had been so long ago. *How can I make this better?* Following steadily he did not run, he knew that she could not move too fast, not in the shoes she was wearing, and soon he spotted her shuffling into the driveway, her arms extended for balance. Darcy could have caught her so easily, but he wanted to see her goal, he was sure that an argument was coming, and he didn't want to anger her further by chasing her down. He strode along and paused upon reaching the driveway, looking around in the darkness, then spotted her near the rose arbor. "Okay, she wants to do this away from everyone."

Slowly walking forward, he stepped quietly into the garden room. "Oh my . . . Lizzy!"

There, in the dappled moonlight, reclined against the wide chaise, lay Elizabeth, nude, her arms raised above her head, her breasts exposed and vulnerable, one knee slightly bent, hiding that wet, warm place he craved. She exuded desire and invited sex. "Hi lover."

Darcy was naked and laying beside her in moments. First his eyes, then his open palm caressed her luscious body. "Baby, if you knew what I was thinking, you'd be running away."

Elizabeth's hands ran over his shoulders and down his sides. "Tell me."

"I'd rather show you."

"No."

"Why?" He asked, his voice cracking a little. She smiled, looking up at his eyes while her fingertips gently caressed down his erection, back up to the tip, circling over the smooth, moist head. Darcy shuddered and drew her to him to kiss. Elizabeth's lips parted and his eager tongue thrust inside to meet hers. Tangling his hand in her hair, they kissed deeply; all the while her fingers continued their movement up and down, around and over him. "Why, Lizzy?" He moaned.

"I'm going to torture you."

"Honey, no, please!"

"Oh yes." Her fingers continued the endless motion, and her lips wandered down his throat, suckling his neck while she pressed her breasts to his chest. Darcy trembled and gasped.

"Baby, I'm going to come if you keep this up."

"Not until I say so." Her lips traced down from his neck to his chest and she moved, gently prodding him onto his back, then kissing her way down over his tight stomach. Still her hand moved over him. He moaned, thrusting against her palm. "Mmmm, no, no moving, this is my playtime. You have to lie still."

"Lizzy, please . . ."

Her face lowered to his erection and he watched as she first rubbed it over her cheeks, then as her tongue appeared to slowly, tenderly, taste.

"Ohhhhhhhhhhhhhhh."

"More?"

"Yes!!"

Taking him inside of her mouth, she swirled her tongue around him, before suddenly plunging down, swallowing as much of his length as she could. Darcy cried out, then caught his breath and watched her slow steady movement, reaching out to hold her head and trying desperately to hang on. She added caresses to his heavy curls to her loving, and he groaned again and squeezed his eyes shut. Then everything stopped. Panting, he looked up to see where she had gone. Standing by his side, Elizabeth was looking him over, an Adonis, and all hers. "Lizzy? Please don't stop now."

"I'm not." She took his hand and rubbed his fingers between her legs. "Do you think that I'm ready for you? Or do I need to play some more?"

"Oh no, you're ready baby, come on, please . . ."

"Are you sure?"

"Elizabeth, get on top of me NOW!" He demanded. Laughing, she climbed over him and slid down his dark rigid pole. "Ohhhhhhh YES!! Ride me, baby, Ride me!"

She held onto his shoulders while his hands cupped her bottom and she rode him just as he begged. He helped her to keep going, it wouldn't take long, he was so far gone, but the explosion sent him reeling. Elizabeth kept moving after he came, and soon found her release. Darcy grabbed her shoulders and dragged her down on top of him, kissing her passionately, then cuddling her against his body, and panting. "What was that, honey? What came over you?"

"You didn't like it?" She said, breathing hard and smiling at his wide eyes.

"Ohhhhh, anytime, anywhere you want to do that to me again, I will love it!"

"I would love it, too." Elizabeth sighed and rested her head on his chest. "I just wanted to show you that you're my man."

"I already was, honey, and I always will be." He kissed her forehead and held her tight. "I love you, only you."

"And I love only you."

They closed their eyes and dozed, listening to the sounds of the city, just beyond their garden wall.

THE NEXT MORNING Elizabeth awakened long before William. They had returned to the house after dozing naked in the garden for awhile, and only the sound of a siren could drive them to their bed. She let him sleep; it had been a very tiring week. Instead she exercised and showered, and then leaned over her sleeping man to give him a kiss. His eyes opened and he smiled. "You smell wonderful."

She laughed and caressed the hair from his eyes. "Thank you. I'm going to go start getting ready for our guests. It's almost nine; I wasn't sure when you would want to get up."

"Nine!" He sat up and looked at the clock for confirmation. "I can't remember sleeping this late since, well, never!" He looked her over and grinned. "Why don't you just come back in here with me?"

"Oh no, I have work to do." Elizabeth ducked away from his arms and moved to the door. "I'll make some coffee for whenever you come down."

"Are you sure you wouldn't rather stay here with me?" He patted the bed and raised his brows. "I need to pay you back for last night."

"You can do that tonight." She blew him a kiss and disappeared. Sighing with regret he glanced down at his arousal and shook his head. An hour later, after exercising a little and showering, he appeared in the kitchen.

"What are we doing?" Darcy leaned on the marble countertop and watched Elizabeth sprinkle yeast over a bowl of warm water and then add some sugar. "It looks delicious." He peeked up at her with a little smile and saw her eyes roll then focus on the mixture. His brow creased and he gazed down at the bowl. "Hey, it's alive!"

She laughed, "Yes it is, that is a good thing." Elizabeth flicked some flour at him and began stirring in the rest of the ingredients. "We are making bread."

"We can't buy that?"

"I can't torture you all day with the scent that way." She dumped the dough out on the floured countertop and began to knead it.

Darcy moved to stand behind her and leaned lightly against her back, his hands resting on the counter. "Will you show me what to do?" His chin rested on her shoulder, and she placed her hands over his, teaching him how to push and roll the dough with his palms. "I like this." He whispered in her ear as his hips rubbed against Elizabeth's bottom with the same motion. Gradually their kneading slowed then ceased, their hands remained in the dough, but his mouth was wandering slowly down her throat, then back up to her jaw. Elizabeth's heart was beating hard, feeling his warm breath on her skin and his hard gift against her back. Her head turned and they kissed slowly.

"How am I ever going to get this finished with you helping me?" She sighed and leaned back against him.

"Do you want me to go?" He whispered huskily.

"Don't you dare!" Elizabeth recovered her senses and laughed, picking up the dough to drop in a bowl to rise. "Okay, next project!"

They worked on, and by noon, the bread dough had risen and was ready to bake, their spaghetti sauce was quietly bubbling on the stove, and Elizabeth was just ready to frost the pan of brownies that had finally cooled. Darcy picked up the paddle from the mixer and licked. "mmmm."

"When was the last time you did that?" She smiled as he settled comfortably against the counter with his prize.

"I don't know that I ever have. I remember watching the various cooks we had over the years making things that I would want to steal, but I never had the courage to ask for a taste. I'd make my move when things were cooling." He smiled. "I remember Mrs. Reynolds shooing me away once when I stole a cookie."

"I certainly did that more than once, Mr. Darcy." Mrs. Reynolds said as she entered the room. "Well it seems that everything is in hand for your family tonight. Are you sure that you don't need my help?"

"No, thank you Mrs. Reynolds, please go ahead and visit your daughter. I have my helper." Elizabeth looked over to William who was just finishing the frosting and looked up, the evidence of his occupation all over his face. The women laughed and he straightened.

"Somehow I think that I have been insulted by implication." Darcy licked his lips and grinned while Elizabeth came over to wipe him off.

Georgiana entered the room quietly. "William, John is on the phone for you."

"I didn't even here it ring." He turned and smiled. "Excuse me."

Mrs. Reynolds left and Elizabeth handed Georgiana a spatula and put her to work on the brownies while she began cleaning up the mess of the morning. "What have you been up to? We haven't seen you at all today."

"I've been practicing." She snapped.

"I'm sorry; I guess that we couldn't hear the piano from behind the closed door." Elizabeth tilted her head while she wiped off the counter. "What is wrong, Georgiana?"

"Nothing, I'm . . . I'm just nervous about meeting your sisters. Maybe they won't like me." She spoke quickly.

"Oh, please don't worry about that! Jane likes you, and I know that Mary, Kitty and Lydia will as well. They are all very nice girls, you will see."

"DARCY, I . . . I want to know, straight out, is Charles Bingley serious about Jane Bennet?"

Darcy settled back in his desk chair and was at a loss for words. "I don't know, John. I know that he truly enjoys her company. But how serious is he? I can't say." He paused. "How serious are you?"

"I don't wish to speculate on that if I have no opportunity to find out. I won't beat some other man's time."

"That's very honorable, John, but how will Jane know that she might have a choice if you don't tell her of your interest?"

"I have." John closed his eyes and sighed. "I took her out, didn't you know?"

"No, it wasn't mentioned to me. Maybe Jane didn't tell Elizabeth. How did it go?"

"Darcy, I think that I blew it once again. I took her to the Athletic Club."

"On a first date?" Darcy closed his eyes in disbelief. "Why?"

"See! That's what Richard said. I took her to a play too, and we walked in the park, but . . . I wanted her to see what life with me was like, would be like, if I was elected."

"And what was her response?"

"I don't know that she was happy with the experience. I introduced her as your future sister-in-law." John closed his eyes, waiting for the explosion.

"You *what*?" Darcy's hand ran through his hair. "What the hell does her connection with me have to do with . . . You were campaigning?" He sighed. "Beyond the fact that I do not appreciate you using me as some sort of, I don't know, seal of approval for the Bennet family, I have to agree that you have blown it with Jane. If she didn't see through this, she is not the smart woman I thought she was."

John sighed. "Do you think she would be happy in politics?"

"Was your mother?"

"Oh yes, she thrived on the experience, Dad told me she jumped into the campaigns with both feet, loved meeting people, loved the fundraisers, the dinners, the speeches, the entertaining, she was a woman built for the campaign."

"Is Jane, do you think?" Darcy heard another sigh. "I have a feeling that you already know the answer to that. So the next question is . . . how much do you want to run for office? I'll be honest with you John; I don't know that politics, the everyday existence, is really your future. You have the drive to succeed, but I don't know that you have the will to deal with the BS that is involved. In Congress you will essentially be running for reelection almost the moment that you are in office. It will be a never ending quest to beg for funds to campaign again. Of course it's a fantastic opportunity to do great good . . . but only for a person who wants it. Maybe you should think instead about what you really want your future to be, and if you are willing to change your goals in order to attract a woman like Jane."

"Because it's too late for her."

"I don't know, John."

"This sounds like the conversation I had with Richard earlier this week." He sighed. "Could you ask . . . Could you ask Elizabeth? Or Charles?"

"I'll see what I can do, the whole Bennet family is coming over today for dinner, so it may have to wait for this evening." Darcy hung up and sat in his study, staring off into the distance. He had no idea how to approach the problem, or even if he should.

"Hey, are you hungry?" Elizabeth poked her head in the door. "I was going to make some lunch."

"Oh, um, yeah that sounds good." He stood up. "I'm sorry, I was lost in thought."

"That was obvious." She smiled and watched him stretch a little before walking to the doorway. "Is John okay?"

"Actually, no he's not." He smiled, the opportunity had presented itself. "It seems he's at a crossroads and doesn't know what to do."

"Oh, with what?" They held hands and headed back towards the kitchen.

"Several things, first his career and if he'll run for office and second, if his decision will affect his chances with . . . Jane." Darcy looked down when Elizabeth gasped. "Do you know that he went out with her this week?"

"Yes."

Darcy stopped. "Why didn't you say anything to me?"

"You haven't exactly been around to talk to, have you?" She said defensively.

"It would have taken a second to tell me that the girl my best friend was seeing was dating someone else on the side." He glared.

"Excuse me, but neither one of them has spoken of their relationship being anything more than casual, nor if he thought otherwise, it certainly wasn't expressed to Jane!" Elizabeth's glare matched his. "I advised her to go ahead with the date so she wouldn't wonder if she had missed out on something better!"

"And would she? Or has she decided against my cousin?"

"Which man do you want to win this race?" Elizabeth fumed.

"I . . . I don't know." Darcy looked down and stared at his shoes. "It seems that I am in the middle here, and why we are fighting over it is . . . completely beyond me."

Elizabeth closed her eyes and nodded. "You're right; I'm sorry for being so defensive, Jane's a big girl and should make her own decisions."

"I'm sorry, too. I think that she would be great for either of them."

"WELL WHAT DO you think?" Tom asked Mary.

"Elizabeth wasn't kidding when she said it resembled a museum. The artwork here is priceless." She moved closer to admire the painting by Monet, the original of a poster her sister had hanging in her old apartment. "The Darcys have certainly invested in some treasures, but it's not ostentatious or gaudy." She looked up at the ceilings, painted long ago by some unknown artist, and noted that the craftsmanship in the wood and plaster spoke of skills practically forgotten.

"I meant what do you think of William.

She laughed. "I know, Dad. The house resembles the owner. He is a simple man living amongst beautiful things and has chosen a wife who will fit in here perfectly. Elizabeth is neither flashy nor demanding, but she is a treasure, and will undoubtedly shine in this new setting."

"Such a philosopher you are." Tom chuckled. "Your sisters have declared him handsome, but I suppose that you are above such things."

"No, I find him quite inspiring, too!" She laughed and they joined the rest of the family in the enormous kitchen. Kitty and Lydia were slicing the bread and taking it out to the table. Georgiana and Jane were fussing over the salad, and William was by Elizabeth's side at the stove. Fran stayed in the dining room, supervising the placement of the dishes.

"Careful!" Elizabeth cried as he picked up the heavy stockpot full of boiling water and spaghetti. Slowly he poured it over a colander, then snagged a stray noodle while it drained. She laughed and bit the other end, nibbling along until their lips met. "mmmm you have come far in your cooking skills!"

"Oh yes, I can boil pasta." He kissed her again and stood ready to ladle the sauce onto the plates as she portioned out the noodles.

"Is it ready?" Lydia came into the room.

"Go ahead and deliver the plates." Elizabeth looked to see what was missing. "I think that's everything . . . Oh, the wine!"

"I'll take care of that." Darcy handed the ladle to Kitty and disappeared to the wine cellar.

"Oh Lizzy, he is so cute!" Kitty whispered.

"Does he talk?" Lydia asked.

"He will, just let him warm up to you." She smiled. "I told you that he's shy."

"I'd be happy just staring at him." Kitty sighed.

"You can find your own guy to stare at." Elizabeth said sternly. The sisters giggled and took the rest of the plates out to the table. Darcy reappeared with several bottles. "Well let's see if they like our creations."

"I didn't do anything. It was all you." He opened two bottles and they walked out to take their seats. Mary said grace and they dug in.

Tom lifted his glass. "First, I want to thank you William and Georgiana for inviting our family to join yours in this magnificent home. Elizabeth may live here, but she is still a Bennet." She rolled her eyes.

"Not for long, sir." Darcy said softly. "I will remedy that shortly."

The family laughed. "Secondly, I want to toast the happiness I see between you and Lizzy. I hope that all of our girls find such joy." He smiled at Fran who wiped her eyes, then around to the rest of the girls. Everyone drank and the conversation rose as they began eating. Lydia was seated next to Georgiana and noticed her sullen expression.

"Don't you like your brother marrying Lizzy?"

"Of course I do!" Georgiana stared at her.

"Then what's your problem?"

"Who says that I have one?"

Lydia studied her. "You're hiding something, and don't deny it. I'm an expert at hiding things. You look healthy, but you're not sleeping, and you're just pushing the food around your plate."

"Leave me alone!" Georgiana hissed, and suddenly she jumped.

"Are you going to answer that?" Lydia looked as Georgiana touched her pocket, deducing a vibrating phone was inside.

"No, not at the table." Georgiana was shaking.

Lydia's eyes narrowed. "Who is harassing you?"

"How do you know?" She whispered.

Lydia touched Elizabeth who was on her other side and whispered in her ear. She looked over to Georgiana. "Will you help me in the kitchen, please?"

Elizabeth met William's questioning eyes, his brow was immediately creased. The girls entered the kitchen and she folded her arms. "I knew something was wrong. What is it?"

Darcy came in. "What's going on?"

Georgiana blushed and jumped when the phone buzzed again. Elizabeth held out her hand and the phone was handed over. "Hello?" Elizabeth answered. Her eyes grew wide and she signaled William to come over and listen. He tried to grab it away from her and she ended the call. He was furious.

"Why did you stop me?" He bellowed and glared at her.

Elizabeth returned the glare and spoke tersely, "Because if you are going to do something, the prison is going to have to record the calls! You can't scare him off now!" She turned to Georgiana. "How many times has Wickham called you?"

"This is the third time." She whispered and looked down.

"Why? Why didn't you tell us?" Darcy demanded. "When did this start?"

"Last Sunday, he . . . he said he knew that you were getting married soon, and . . . and that if I didn't talk to him, he'd make up stories about you to send to all of the tabloids, and then they could harass you at the wedding and . . ." She sighed. "He kept saying that he loved me and when he got out he was going to come and find me."

"You didn't believe that he loved you, Georgiana, did you? I thought that you realized he was using you when he lured you to Florida. Do you still have feelings for him?"

"I . . . no, of course I don't, I was stupid to listen to him and believe him. He sounded so lonely though, you heard him on the phone . . ."

Darcy stared at her. "Do you hear yourself? You are making excuses for your seducer! This is what a child molester does, Georgiana!"

"I'm not a child!" She cried.

"Yes you are! You are if you don't tell us when a man who is in PRISON for HARMING YOU calls and threatens you! He has nothing else to do in that place but plot and be angry, what better occupation than calling his victim and taunting her?" Darcy's hand ran through his hair and he began pacing. "Lizzy, please, maybe you can get through to her!"

"William is absolutely right Georgiana. When you were so relieved that he went to prison, and this whole mess was seemingly over, didn't you understand then what sort of man he really was?"

"Yes."

"So what happened? Why would you feel sorry for him now? He threatened you with harming your brother if you didn't talk to him. Surely you realize that is not an expression of love."

"It . . . it was love for you and William." Georgiana watched him pacing and looked back at Elizabeth with tears streaming down her face. "Everything has been so wonderful since you and William met, and I was so afraid that if I didn't go along with what Wickham wanted, you wouldn't get married. William needs you so much, and . . . and I need you . . . and I thought that if I just agreed to listen to him when he called that everything would be okay, and I would talk to you about it after you were married."

"Oh Georgiana." Elizabeth hugged her.

"I can't believe this!" Darcy met Elizabeth's eyes and looked at her helplessly.

"Can't believe what?" John walked in the back door, a stack of letters in his hand. "I . . . Mom got a lot of thank you cards after the party and thought that Elizabeth would like to see them." He held them out, then set them on the counter. "What's wrong?"

"Wickham is making harassing calls to Georgiana from prison, and we have only just learned about it." Elizabeth explained quickly. "Shouldn't this effect his sentence?"

Darcy's expression changed and his eyes widened as he nodded, latching onto that solid possibility. "I'll call the DA in Florida."

"It's Sunday, nothing will happen today." John said as he took in the emotional scene. "Do the calls come from the same number?" He looked to Georgiana, who nodded. "Well, the DA will need that when you call in the morning."

"Yes." Darcy felt Elizabeth's hand tugging him over to her side, then held out his arms to embrace both women. "I wish you could have told us this the first time he called."

"I was so scared; I didn't know what to do." She sobbed.

The kitchen door opened and Jane slipped in. "Is everything okay? I . . . John!" She smiled at him and he beamed.

"Hi."

The Darcys, present and future, looked up and felt the electricity passing between the pair. "Well, nothing else can be done today." Elizabeth turned off the phone and set it aside. William looked down at her and leaned into her hand caressing his face.

"I'll call Jack in the morning. I hope your hunch that Wickham has dug himself a deep hole is correct, and if it isn't . . . well there has to be something that can be done. I won't let this lie."

"I know you won't." She kissed him, and felt his sigh as he relaxed a little. "Now, let's not let that man ruin our dinner. We worked far too hard today to let that happen." She smiled and turned to where John was looking steadily at Jane. "John, would you like to join us? I'm afraid that the main course is gone, but we do have some great brownies if you like chocolate? You can meet the rest of the Bennets?"

"I would love to meet your family." John smiled but did not take his eyes from Jane, who blushed. He walked up to her and offered his hand. "Will you show me the way?"

Jane took it and looked up to him. "I think that you probably know it already."

"But it's the first time with you." They walked out of the kitchen and the remaining trio looked at each other.

"I thought that he wasn't romantic." Elizabeth observed. "That was romantic."

"I think that John has made some decisions about his future and wants to share them with Jane." Darcy smiled and let the tension go. "I have a feeling that the campaigns in his future will not be his own."

"What about Charles?" Georgiana wiped her eyes, still clinging to her brother and future sister.

"He'll be okay, he's coming closer to understanding what he wants in a wife, but he's not quite ready to make that kind of commitment, and I think that he wants a woman whose career is not as demanding as Jane's." He kissed Georgiana's forehead. "Are you okay?"

"I shouldn't have kept this to myself. I thought that I had learned my lesson, but I guess that I didn't."

"I can't imagine how frightened you have been this week, but look; here we are hugging each other. We are a family, and we'll take care of each other. Please don't ever hesitate to tell us anything." Elizabeth let go and walked over to the platter of brownies. "It seems we have a thief amongst us." She looked up to see William's sheepish grin. "What am I going to do with you?"

Chapter 13

"Lizzy." Fran whispered and beckoned her over.

"Yes?" Elizabeth moved to her side and watched as her mother glanced around the room. "Mom, what is it?"

"I thought that Jane was dating Charles. Why is she making eyes at John?"

"Well, she seems to have made a decision, and it is in John's favor." She saw her mother's confusion and leaned closer. "They went on a date last week, and he called her this afternoon before you all came over, and asked her straight out if she was committed to a relationship with Charles, and if he had any reason to hope for a chance with her. William had promised to try and find out what their status was, but it seems that John decided to take the matter into his own hands and ask himself. Jane told me that kissing Charles was very pleasant, but kissing John was like feeling fireworks going off." Elizabeth laughed to see her mother's wide eyes. "I guess that he told her that he was seriously thinking about his future, and was considering his options."

"You mean his options with Jane?" She looked between the two who were standing close together and pretending to pay attention to Tom.

"I believe so. His appearing here tonight was entirely for her, he just could not stay away." Elizabeth smiled to see them move closer together. "Look at how he stares at her. It reminds me of William."

"What reminds you of me?" He sidled up to her and took her hand in his grasp.

"John."

Darcy smiled and then drew her to his side, his arm around her shoulders. "Ah, young love."

"You are implying that we are old and dull?" She lifted her brow.

"No, honey, but we are long past the stage of being unsure." He kissed her cheek, and saw her expression cloud. "Are you okay?"

"Yes, I . . . I need to talk to you when everyone leaves, okay?" Elizabeth said quietly, and then glanced at Fran.

He followed her eyes and nodded, "Sure." She leaned into his chest and he hugged her, not quite knowing what was obviously wrong.

Georgiana, Lydia, and Kitty had disappeared upstairs, and Mary was trying out the grand piano. Tom strolled over and smiled. "I suppose that I have toyed with Jane and John long enough, they listened politely, but clearly your cousin did not come here to visit with me tonight." He laughed to see Darcy's smirk. "You agree?"

"I do."

"It seems that he is far more determined than his predecessor." He looked at Elizabeth and how she fairly clung to Darcy, and read her expression. "You've borne our presence long enough, I think. Fran, let's pack up the girls and head home."

"But it's only nine!" Fran cried.

"Do you have to go to work in the morning, William?"

"I'm afraid so, sir. I must be there by 7:30."

"Then we will go now." Tom caught Mary's eye. "Let's go round up your sisters."

"I'll take Jane home." John volunteered, and smiled at her. "Maybe we could get some coffee and talk? I'd love to hear all about your business."

"Oh, really? I'd like that!" She beamed. John smiled at her then caught Darcy nodding at him with approval. John laughed and bowed his head in mock honor. Soon the Bennets were on their way home. John gallantly led Jane to his car, and then the house was quiet again.

"Are you okay, Georgiana?" Elizabeth asked as they watched John's car pull out.

She saw William leaving the kitchen to collect the last of the dishes and spoke. "I feel so stupid. Why didn't I tell you about Wickham?"

"I don't know, but please know that you can talk to us about anything. We love you, and nothing will change that." They hugged and Elizabeth smiled. "You don't have class tomorrow, right?"

"No, I'm free all day."

"Well, let's get a good night of sleep, then we'll talk in the morning after William leaves. Lydia and Kitty were going to come over for lunch before they return to their schools in the afternoon. Okay?" She nodded and Darcy reappeared, then left with Georgiana for a private conversation. Elizabeth busied herself putting the kitchen back in order, starting the dishwasher, and was at the sink washing up the larger pots when he returned. She looked up at him and smiled a little before returning to her work. He picked up a dishtowel and started drying things as she handed them over, as if he had been doing it all his life. "Georgiana wanted to apologize again."

"I thought so. She was just protecting us."

"I am amazed again at Wickham's skill with seduction. It makes me wonder if he has had a great deal of practice."

"Do you think there are other victims?" Elizabeth looked up at him and saw his brow creased in thought.

"There must be. That gives more reason to hope that his arrogance in calling her will lead to his sentence being extended." Elizabeth nodded and he glanced over to her, and stopped his drying. "What is wrong, honey? I have been anxious to be alone with you ever since you said that you needed to talk."

She swallowed and blinked. "I need to apologize to you as well."

"For what?" He set down the towel and touched her shoulder. "Honey?"

"For my behavior last night. I'm not proud of how I overreacted. I should have just walked away graciously. I'll do better . . . well I won't say next time since I sincerely hope that there won't be a next time, but I want you to know that I was just instinctively protecting my . . . I shouldn't have lashed out at you, especially after you had always been very honest with me about your past, and I certainly should not have engaged . . . her . . . the way I did. I should have dismissed her for the bi . . . nonentity that she is." She sighed. "I'm sorry, Will. I caused a scene and I know how you hate to be the subject of attention and . . . it was just so . . .immature." Darcy's fingers touched her lips.

"Lizzy, stop." He kissed her. "You do not owe me any apology. Everything that you did last night was done out of love for me. I know that. You fought . . . her . . . as I wished to fight Collins."

"But you shamed him . . ."

"As you did her." He smiled. "She was humiliated when she left."

"I never should have done that." She said quietly.

"So you are saying that you don't mind her kissing me?" He smiled to see her eyes flash. "I didn't think that's what you were implying."

"You can't say that you were not embarrassed?"

"No, my only worry was that you might want to call off our wedding."

She looked at him sharply. "Why would I do that?"

"Because you were unexpectedly reminded of my behavior with women after I broke up with her, and it hurt." Darcy wrapped her up in his arms. "I know that it hurt you, Lizzy, I know it did."

The safety of his embrace let loose her emotion and she started to cry. "Why should it matter so much? I didn't know you. Why should I care?"

"You were seventeen then, weren't you?" He rubbed his hands over her back. "You were with Collins." He felt her nod. "Do you know how many times I have thought about how different our lives would have been if I had met you then? I have a feeling that you have thought the same thing."

"I have thought how I would have been there to help you after your parents died." She sniffed and rested her head against his chest. 'And then seeing . . . her . . . last night just made me ache for you even more. I thought that you never would have been driven to . . . pay for . . . I thought of how I would have tried so hard to make you feel happy again."

"You would have, honey, and I would have done the same for you, I hope." He kissed her cheeks, tasting the salty tears. "But we can't dwell on the past or what might have been. We've both been given a second chance, Lizzy. We both chose to be involved with people we shouldn't have and we both also chose to leave those people behind. Believe me, I have imagined far too many times you with . . . him. It hurts, but I know that it is the past. And I bear it because I was not in your life then."

"But the hope of you was."

"And here we are." Darcy kissed her. "Do not ever apologize for loving me, Lizzy. Why did you feel that you needed to tonight?"

"It's been on mind since I got up, and as the day went on and we were just . . . together, working together, I realized how stupid I was to be threatened by the people of your past. I felt so ashamed of myself. I wanted you to know that . . ." She sighed, it was so hard to put emotions into words.

"I am ashamed enough of my past. Why do you think I didn't date another woman for nearly five years? I waited for you." He lifted her chin and kissed her. "I think that all this is just telling me that you are falling deeper in love with me. And that honey, is a wonderful thing." His kisses grew softer, barely caressing her lips, and as his tongue gently met hers, he felt her entire body seemingly melt in his arms. His lips moved to her ear. "I need to love you, Lizzy."

"Let's go." She whispered and touched his face, drawing his lips forward to accept her seeking mouth. As they kissed, Darcy's hand caressed down her back and returned to her breasts, feeling her soft nipples growing hard under his hand. He squeezed then drew her waist closer.

Again his mouth went to her ear. "I'm going to go so slow, honey." Her breath hitched and he smiled into her hair, then drew back to take her hand, and saw her eyes were shining with love. "Come on."

"MR. DARCY? Mr. Carter is here to see you." Patricia announced.

"Jack? Oh, well please send him in." Darcy stood and moved from behind his desk. Jack entered and walked forward, extending his hand. "I thought I'd get a call from you, I hardly expected a personal visit."

"I wanted to witness your reaction when I told you this news. I'm just sorry that it took so many days to confirm everything." Jack shook his hand and they sat down. Darcy leaned forward, and stared at him intently. "I spoke to the DA, apparently all calls are recorded in the prison, they just aren't all monitored live. Since it was only over the past week, they were able to go back and listen to all three calls to Georgiana." Jack beamed. "Part of Wickham's plea included a stipulation that he would never contact his victim upon pain of the plea being rescinded."

Darcy's eyes grew wide. "AND?"

"He is automatically sentenced to the most punitive sentence! Fifteen years in prison. No chance for parole for ten, and I already have my calendar marked to be at that hearing." Jack laughed. "We've got him!"

"I can't believe this!" Darcy joined him in laughing. "This is incredible! I have to tell Georgie and Elizabeth, I have to tell the family! Damn!"

"I used stronger language than that!" Jack chortled and sat back in his chair. "There has to be an appearance in court sometime, and he has to cough up the $10,000 fine, too. I think that about kills whatever he had in his bank account, well that and the new attorney fees. No, he's definitely out of your hair for a very long time, and really, forever. I know that the experience was probably horrible for Georgiana, but some good has come of it. How is she?"

"She is fine, it told her once and for all that she is truly loved and at home with me and Elizabeth. She was so afraid that if Wickham carried through with his threats, Elizabeth wouldn't marry me." He shook his head. "She doesn't understand the bond we have, even if every newspaper in the country published some fake story about me, it wouldn't change a thing. We know what happens between us, and don't read the papers to get news about how our relationship is faring. The only thing he had on me is the time I spent just after my parents died, and even then I think that I only made the gossip columns a couple times towards the end of it all when I started to be recognized, another reason why I got my sense back. I don't see who would care about us in any case. I'm hardly a public figure."

"She is almost seventeen?"

"Yes, I know, very, very young." Darcy smiled. "I forget that sometimes with her in Julliard. I wonder how she would have handled this if Elizabeth hadn't been there this time. Lydia spotted that something was wrong at dinner, and Elizabeth told me later that she had suspected as much Sunday morning and intended to confront Georgiana on Monday. If it had been left for Georgiana to handle, it might have gone on indefinitely."

"I don't think you are quite that blind. You would have noticed sometime." Jack smiled as Darcy looked down at his desk, obviously disagreeing with the statement. "While I'm here, I brought you a copy of the prenup and your new will." He handed them over. "It was a pleasure to do them both. I really liked Elizabeth's attorney, I might try to persuade him to join the firm."

Darcy glanced at the documents and set them aside. "I think that Gary would be vastly entertained to hear your offer, but I doubt that he'll take you up on it."

"Hmm, probably right. Why share the fees?" He laughed as he stood and held out his hand again. "By the way, I'll drop off my bill with Patricia on the way out."

"Why am I not surprised?" Darcy shook his head and watched him go. Sitting back down, he picked up the phone. "Lizzy, honey? I have some wonderful news!"

Elizabeth listened and whooped. "Yes! Well, although I can't feel good about Georgiana bearing the harassment, at least the ultimate outcome is worthwhile. I wonder if his phone privileges will be curtailed."

"It doesn't matter. Georgiana has a new number." He settled back in his chair. "I don't think that she should be left alone in the house when we go on our honeymoon."

"Well she wouldn't be, Mrs. Reynolds will be here, and the rest of the day staff will be in and out."

"But she won't have school for the first two weeks; she'll be on her own."

"Will, she will be a sophomore in college, you have to show her that you trust her, you can't send her to stay with Arlene and David as if she was a small child." Elizabeth heard his sigh and knew this was the time to bring up her idea. "I was thinking . . . my apartment will be empty until Kitty graduates next year."

"Yes?"

"Well, do you think that Georgiana might like to get a taste of living by herself?" Silence reigned. "She wouldn't really be alone, you know. Jane is there, and my parents, and it's only a few blocks away, but it is such a valuable learning experience to have to rely on yourself to make your meals, and clean, and do laundry. She isn't getting that living with us, if she was attending a college out of the city; that is exactly what she would experience."

"I didn't."

"I know, you ate at the student union or ordered pizza every night, and kept beer and potato chips in your cupboards, and probably had a laundry service and a maid." She sighed and imagined his embarrassed smile. "But even my years of miserable living with Collins did teach me how to run a household."

"Georgiana will never need to . . ."

"How do you know, Will? Who knows where her path will lead her?"

"Honey, she will be a very wealthy woman when she is twenty-five. Collins' five million is a pittance compared to her trust fund."

"I understand that, Will, I do, but she is also nearly eight years away from receiving that money. Until then she is dependent on you and what she earns herself. It was smart of your parents to make it that way, so she would have to learn at least for a little while how to be independent to some degree." Elizabeth heard him sigh again and could imagine the struggle he was waging between being a good brother and father figure.

"But, won't she feel that we are kicking her out for our own selfish desires? That we want to be alone in the house?"

"Don't we?" She said softly.

"Well, yes, of course we do." Darcy smiled and laughed, looking at her picture and imagining her brow rising. "But that shouldn't be the primary reason for this."

"It's not Will; it is an exercise in trust. We would be giving her the opportunity to live on her own, without supervision, without rules that she may or may not feel we impose; she will have her own money to look after, and would learn to deal with the consequences of running out too soon in the month. She could have friends over . . . she would learn to rely on herself. Of course she would be welcome home at any time, and I'm not saying that this is going to happen next week. She is so shaken up over Wickham returning to our lives, I think that she needs to begin seeing her psychologist again for a little while, get back into the swing of a full schedule at school, and then maybe after Christmas, she might be ready to try this out. I realize that right now what she needs more than anything is to enjoy the love and support we will give her as a family, but I am thinking ahead, who knows, maybe she and Kitty will hit it off and they could share the place for awhile."

Darcy listened, understanding the value of every one of Elizabeth's points, and then thinking about the freedom it would grant them as a couple someday. "Would your dad mind a piano playing in the building?"

"He would love it." Elizabeth assured him.

"Okay, well, maybe we should figure this all out and . . . talk to her." Darcy smiled. "I think that this is a really good idea, Lizzy."

"Thanks." She smiled at how quickly he agreed with her and closed her eyes. "So, are you busy or shall I tell you what I look forward to doing with you in our empty house?"

Darcy's breath caught. "I have a client coming in about fifteen minutes, honey."

"Will he be the only one?"

"Lizzzzzzzy!" He moaned and closed his eyes.

"ARE YOU CERTAIN of this decision?" David asked his eldest son. "It does not have to be determined for months. Why don't you wait and see if this relationship works out first?"

"But that's the point, Dad; Jane doesn't want to be a political wife. She is not Mom, and I have no chance of a relationship with her if I'm going to enter the race."

"You have wanted this for years! You have worked for the last ten preparing for taking my old seat! Now McMasters is weak, his party is out of favor, and he's up for reelection, if you don't strike now, whoever does beat him will probably be in there indefinitely! Now is the time!" David stood and began pacing. "You know how hard it is to beat an incumbent! The party is itching to get your name out there; you would be a sure winner!"

"Yes, and then I would have to listen to them and every lobbyist who comes to my office door for the next . . . well you were in for twenty years. I don't know that I want that, Dad. I feel that my life should be spent differently."

"Are you saying that I was not my own man? I didn't let anyone influence my votes!" David glared at him.

John met his gaze straight on. "Don't peddle that to me, I know that you wheeled and dealt just as much as anyone else."

"That was to get what I knew my constituents needed!" David sat down and shook his head. "Maybe you're right; you aren't cut out for the job. So, what job do you want?"

John knew that his father didn't mean to imply that he was weak; this was simply the end of a dream for him. "I am very proud to work by your side helping candidates run who do have the desire to dedicate their lives to public service. I want to continue with that, and I think that we have made a great team. I'm not rejecting your accomplishments; I'm just saying that your views on life do not always match mine. I want to live in New York, I want to help worthy people get in office, I want to marry and have a family, and enjoy as normal a life as any other working couple does, but outside of the public eye . . . and I think that I might have met the woman who will make that possible." He stood up and came over to touch his father's shoulder. "I'm not rejecting your desires, Dad, I just want to determine my own, and I have to respect the accomplishments and desires of the woman I hope to marry. I'm sorry to be disappointing you. I might have lost, you know."

"Not a chance, a Fitzwilliam never loses." David sighed and looked up to give him a wry smile. "I hope that you are happy with your decision. I hope that you put the effort that you were going to put into running for office into your campaign to win one vote from Jane Bennet."

"Didn't you just say that a Fitzwilliam never loses?" He smiled as David stood and they embraced. "Thanks, Dad."

"ARE YOU OKAY?" Darcy watched Charles staring at his computer from the office doorway. He shrugged. Darcy walked in and closed the door, taking a seat before his desk.

"I didn't ask you in."

"I don't care."

Charles glared at him and turned back to the monitor. "I thought that only the Bennets were coming to dinner last Sunday. You should have just told me that you didn't want me there."

"Whoa, I had nothing to do with John showing up."

"He knew Jane was there."

"So did you, besides that doesn't mean that I invited him."

"You didn't do anything to stop him either."

"If you had a better relationship with her it wouldn't have mattered, would it? She would have told him to get lost." Darcy sat forward and Charles closed his eyes. "You were having second thoughts, don't deny it."

"No, I won't." He sighed and ran his hand through his hair. "I just thought I'd at least get a chance to talk to her about it before . . ."

"Breaking up with her?"

"Yeah, I guess it would have eventually wound up that way. I'm so tired of this." He sat back and stared at his best friend. "What's wrong with me? I've done this so many times before, and okay, I can use the excuse that all the rest of them were more beauty than brain, but I can't say that about Jane. She is lovely and smart . . . everything that I ever wanted, but I still couldn't manage to make myself . . ."

"Behave as an adult?" Darcy said gently and smiled a little at Charles' sharp glance. "You're twenty-five Charles, college is over, and while it may be fun to be a playboy, in the long run, it will leave you very lonely. Look at my cousin Richard. He has the excuse of his military career, well, the years required of him after graduating from West Point, as a delay to his settling down, but he is nearly thirty, and he's still playing the game. He's tired of it too, and now that I, and possibly John, are settling down, he is finally ready to consider it. Do you want to spend the next five years moving from girl to girl?"

"No! That's why I thought I had found something in Jane. Where did I go wrong?" He stared at Darcy helplessly.

Darcy sat back and folded his arms. "What did you do on your dates?"

"We went to dinner, to a movie, to a ballgame, and to a concert." He shrugged. "She seemed to have fun."

"Did you ever just sit and talk?"

"About what?"

"Your hopes and dreams? Your family? Your youth, your education, your job, anything . . . how about asking her about herself? Did she try to tell you about her life? Did you listen or blank out on her?"

"We just had fun." Charles said as Darcy's words sunk in. "That first time you were with Elizabeth, at the wedding, what did you do?"

"We sat on a sofa and talked for six hours before she fell asleep in my arms." Darcy smiled. "I knew I would marry her after that first night."

"I don't really know much about Jane. I . . . I knew that she wasn't, I knew that she was happy in her own skin." He looked up and saw Darcy's smile. "I liked that so much, but I never took the time to . . . find out why she was so happy, I just accepted it and took it as my own. It was selfish, especially when I didn't really share the same information with her." He nodded. "I know what I want now, and I think that I know what I need to do to keep it. Jane has taught me that; hasn't she?"

Darcy nodded. "And I think that you need someone who will fit your vision of what a wife should be, if you are modeling your parents' marriage, and I don't believe that Jane would have worked with your plans."

"No, no she wouldn't." Charles breathed heavily. "Thanks, I'm sorry that I've been such a bastard to be around this week."

"I understand, I figured I would let it go until you started snapping at Miranda and Patricia. They don't deserve your ire. I already owe Patricia a day at a spa for dealing with Caroline." Charles sighed. He stood up and held out his hand. "Will you still be my best man?"

Charles smiled and stood up to shake. "I am honored, of course I will. Just tell me where to get the tux."

Darcy shook his head. "No, no tux, I'm in a linen suit with no tie."

"You're kidding?" He looked at him in surprise.

He smiled and went to open the door. "No, I'm not. I can't wait to see what Elizabeth wears. I have a feeling that shoes will not be involved." Charles laughed. "Do you still want to stay at Pemberley?"

"I think the question is do you think I should. What is Jane's opinion, I'm sure that she'll be staying with you."

"I don't know, I want you there, and so does Elizabeth." Darcy met his eyes. "You are my very good friend, Charles; the only one who surpasses you is Elizabeth, which I am sure that you understand. I don't want this very short experience with Jane to stand in the way of you feeling comfortable in our homes or with our family. I'll ask Elizabeth to speak to Jane, but I do want you with us."

"Thanks, I . . . I was wondering about . . . all that. I'll abide by whatever decision is made by the ladies, and . . . thanks." Charles smiled and Darcy nodded, leaving the room. *Well, it seems that I have been told to grow up.*

"I CAN NOT believe you are buying your gown off the rack." Anne stood in the bridal shop and looked around at the clouds of white and ivory surrounding her and sighed. "You could have ANYTHING!"

"I will wear this gown once, at a picnic and on the beach. It will never be seen again. My daughters, if I am so blessed, will undoubtedly declare it is pretty but not for them . . . so why on earth would I spend an enormous amount of money on a few yards of fabric?" Anne stared at her without comprehension as she turned back to the mirror and looked at herself. "No, this isn't it."

Jane and the shop owner appeared with a new selection. "I think this has possibilities." They tugged off the first gown and slid the new one over her head. Jane pointed out the features. "I like the halter design for you, Lizzy; your chest is just so large, I would be afraid of you spilling out of a strapless gown."

"A properly fitted gown would not move." Anne pointed out. "Now, I know a dressmaker . . ."

"I'm not listening to you, Anne." Elizabeth looked over the gown carefully. "I was really hoping for a strapless one. I think that William would like the possibility of me popping free." She winked at Jane's reflection in the mirror and she sighed, turning away to go hunt again, whispering ideas to the woman at her side. Anne was smirking as they disappeared.

Elizabeth saw her expression and smiled widely. "I'm rather enjoying torturing her. After all of the bride shows I had to attend with her, this is my payback."

"Who will she torture when her time comes?" Anne sat down and looked over the growing selection of rejected gowns.

"That's a good question, but I have a feeling that I will get my comeuppance then." She tilted her head. "Do you think she and John will get that far?"

"I don't know. He's completely flummoxed Mom. She had a girl all picked out for him at the club, and was waiting to introduce them, and now he's not running for office, he's dating the sister of the girl who bamboozled William, she was asking me what's coming next, hoards of locusts?" Anne laughed. "I can't wait to see who Richard finds."

"What is he looking for in a bride?"

"God only knows. Someone strong."

Jane returned with yet another selection. "Okay, I think I've got it." Again the dress exchange was completed and this time Elizabeth heard gasps behind her. She stared at herself in the mirror.

"Oh yes, this is my gown." She took a deep breath and stared at herself. "Now I am a bride." Jane came up behind her and placed a simple lace veil in her hair then hugged her.

"NOW you are a bride!" She whispered. "Oh Lizzy, it's beautiful!"

Elizabeth wiped a tear from her eye then saw Jane about to cry. She pulled herself together and began jumping up and down, testing the fit. "Look; and I won't fall out!"

"SO, DO I GET to be a bridesmaid?" Charlotte smiled, looking over the wedding invitation that Elizabeth handed her.

"With four other sisters and a new one, I think that answer is pretty obvious. Jane will be my maid of honor and that will be it." Elizabeth smiled. "I'm sorry that we can't put you up at the house."

"Eight bedrooms, you would think that I would fit just fine. Oh well, I'll just have to bear with this resort you have found for me. Would you mind if I brought Maria as my date?"

"No, not at all, I was going to suggest it anyway. I've invited Adam and Lisa, so you'll know a few people there besides my family. William has asked a few of his friends, too."

"And his family."

"Yes, they are all very nice, except for his Aunt Catherine. I'm waiting for her to resurface." Elizabeth closed her eyes for a moment then shook it off. "It's a picnic, but you know, not shorts and flip-flops casual."

"Okay, I know just what department to visit at Macy's."

"Elizabeth!" The ladies turned to see Maria Lucas in the doorway. "Oh, I'm so excited for you!" She ran into the office and hugged her. "I've been hoping to catch you ever since you got engaged, Charlotte told me what a gentleman William is. I think she might have tried for him herself after he walked her up to her apartment." Charlotte blushed bright red when Elizabeth turned to raise her brow at her.

"Shut up, Maria."

Maria laughed. "I think that she talked about it for a solid week."

Elizabeth turned away from Charlotte. "Well, I just invited her to the wedding and she is bringing you as her date, how does that sound?"

"Really? Oh, thank you! I'd love to get a good look at your William! Will there be lots of bachelors there for me to admire?" Maria looked at her hopefully.

"Well, not lots, but a few. William's cousin Richard will be there, but he's probably too old for you."

"I'm twenty-one!"

"He's nearly thirty."

"That's not too old." Charlotte said speculatively.

Elizabeth tilted her head. "Not for you." Charlotte glared. "Well you are twenty-seven . . . you know, I think that there might be something . . . you and Richard might just get along."

The two sisters looked at each other. "Why do you say that?"

"He's a really nice man, but desperately needs a woman who can tell him when his mouth runneth over, if you know what I mean. He runs a company providing security to high-profile people." She smiled, "He makes terrible jokes, likes to provoke reactions from his poor cousin, and I really like him a lot." Charlotte listened carefully, knowing that Elizabeth rarely heaped praise on men.

"Are there any younger guys?" Maria demanded.

"Yes, there will be two that I know of, Adam Fox, the mystery writer . . ."

"No, no writers, I have enough of that from Charlotte and Dad, and maintaining their web sites, who else?"

"Well, there's Charles Bingley, he's twenty-five."

"Didn't he just break up with Jane?" Maria asked, remembering the description she had heard of the tall blonde man.

"Well, they weren't really together long enough to be called a couple, they just went out a few times. He's a very nice man, just looking for the right girl." Elizabeth tilted her head again, assessing Maria.

Not missing the attention, Maria bit her lip. "And what is he looking for?"

"He wants a girl who is comfortable with who she is, and shares his happiness to enjoy life." Maria and Charlotte nodded at each other. "He wants what I would think of as a more traditional marriage, where the wife's career is not in conflict with his. It's not that he wants her to be barefoot and pregnant, he wants her to find fulfillment in whatever she does, but he is hoping for a home life similar to the way he grew up."

"Well Jane running her own business would have conflicted with that ideal, wouldn't it?" Charlotte observed.

"I think that he wondered that if he only sees her now on Sundays, what would marriage be like? Obviously as her business grows she can delegate the duties out to other new employees, but for now, she has to be more involved."

"It sounds like your career is kind of the one he would like for his wife." Maria smiled at Elizabeth.

"Yes, and William told him that marrying Jane would not get him a girl like me."

"My business is mostly done at home." She offered.

"And you are an absurdly happy person." Charlotte pointed out.

"Well then, William and I will be pleased to introduce the Lucas sisters to Mr. Fitzwilliam and Mr. Bingley." Elizabeth laughed. "Oh, Will is going to strangle me!"

"Why?"

"We swore off of matchmaking after Jane and Charles didn't work out." She looked at the grinning ladies and shook her head. "I can't wait to tell him that I have two women waiting to pounce at the wedding!"

"HAVEN'T WE had this discussion at least twice before?" Darcy asked quietly.

"I knew that you would be unhappy." Elizabeth sighed and closed her eyes.

Darcy kissed her head and rested his cheek in her hair. "I'm not unhappy; I have learned my lesson. I will not meddle again in anyone else's love life."

"It's not meddling; they will all be guests at the same wedding. What they do when they meet is up to them."

"But the ladies will be expecting this and the men will not. That is hardly fair."

"I will be happy to call both of them to give fair warning." She laughed to hear his low growl in her ear. "Okay, that is meddling. I won't say a word. Will, all I was doing is answering their question about single men."

"I know." He sighed again. "I'm just . . . I should have flown out to Vegas and married you there."

"So even our little wedding has you unhappy?" Elizabeth played with the unadorned fingers of his left hand.

"No honey, I just want to be married to you. The next ten days will seem to last forever until you are finally my wife." His arms tightened around her and his lips found her ear. "I want this to be official. Your living here has been . . . indescribable, but I want the marriage to begin."

"What do you expect to be different after we take our vows?" Elizabeth stroked his forearm and sank further against his chest. "We'll be the same people we are now."

"Yes, but . . . it's the commitment, the permanence that I look forward to. That prenup was a waste of money; I will never let you go."

"No matter how angry I make you?" She smiled and hugged his arms.

"I doubt that is possible, Lizzy. How could you make me angry?" She laughed, thinking of any number of ways that could happen, then heard his sigh and looked up to see his unhappy expression. "I think that I'm about to make *you* angry."

"What is wrong? You seem so sad. I was expecting that my tales of matchmaking would provoke a lively discussion, not depression." He hugged her tight enough to be almost painful.

"Our honeymoon is to last four weeks."

"Has that changed?"

"No, but . . . in order for that to happen, I have to take care of some business before I disappear for so long."

"Well that is not a big surprise. What do you have to do?" Elizabeth relaxed again and he said softly. "I have to leave and will be gone for a week."

"A week!" She turned around to see the confirmation in his eyes. "But . . . we have so much to do! When do you leave?"

"Tomorrow. I'll be back two days before the ceremony. I'm sorry, honey, I am. I can't delegate everything; there are just some things that I have to do myself. And it's not just at one location; it's all over the country. I'm so sorry." He was greeted by silence. "I expected that I would have to take a short trip to Seattle, but . . . the people I have to meet are committed to other things and if I am to see them in person, it must be tomorrow." Darcy caressed her face. "I just found this out before I came home."

"But . . . if your meeting is tomorrow, wouldn't that mean that you will be home sooner?"

"I have to go to Montana and see how the clean up is progressing, and then visit the paper mills. Then I have to go to Atlanta and meet with the competition about selling them my lumber, instead of selling to Pemberley."

"They can't come to you? Shouldn't they be courting your favor and not the other way around?" Elizabeth saw his brow crease, and pressed her point. "I understand your need to go to Seattle and Montana, but if the other meetings can be done here, it would be so much easier. If you are gone a week, I would have to go to Pemberley alone. Nobody else will be coming until Friday; even Georgiana has classes until then." She sighed, knowing how uncomfortable she would be there by herself, and closed her eyes. "I will need directions for driving there, and I'll have to rent a car . . . I haven't driven in so long." She began making plans in her mind while chewing her lip. "I'll go next Tuesday; that should be enough time to get things in order . . ."

Darcy turned her face around to his and gently touched her mouth. "You're going to start bleeding if you bite any harder." She looked away. "Frank will drive you if that is the way you want to go; or I can ask Patricia to arrange for the helicopter if you want to fly. I'm sorry, honey."

"I won't fly without you."

He smiled. "You aren't afraid, are you? We did it before."

"If I'm going to die in a helicopter crash, I want you with me."

"That's a nice thought." He smiled and saw her tension had not eased. "You don't want me to be alone?"

"No, I don't." Elizabeth clung to him. "I'm going to be a nervous wreck with you away, you do realize that? I expect you to call me every time you take off and land. I want a million messages, and I expect long phone calls every night. Do you hear me?"

"Yes, dear." His lips touched her ear and he whispered, "You didn't have to tell me that, you know."

Elizabeth rested her head on his shoulder. "I know."

"Come here." He drew her against him. "I have never felt so loved before, Lizzy." Kissing her forehead, he rested his cheek against hers and spoke softly while he thought. "Let me see if I can get the Atlanta meeting moved here instead. If I can that means I will back home on Sunday, so it will only be five days away."

"That is far too long."

"Now you know how I feel when you leave me." Elizabeth looked up to him and he kissed her. "Come on, we have dinner reservations."

"Are you trying to buy me off with a meal?" She smiled a little and moved off of him so they could rise.

"No, I made these reservations before I knew of any of this." They stepped out from under the rose arbor and began walking towards the house. "But I intend to romance the pants off of you."

Elizabeth looked over him, his suit jacket and tie were over his arm, his shirt was unbuttoned to his navel, and her blouse had been rebuttoned crooked. "Um, Mr. Darcy, I believe we are already in a state of undress."

"Hmm, so we are, but I have plans for more. After all, our pants have remained on so far." He smiled and they made their way to their room to get ready. Elizabeth stood in her dressing room, looking over the possibilities, and not knowing their destination, chose an elegant dress she had bought when shopping for their honeymoon. She appeared a half-hour later to find William watching the river traffic and leaning against the window frame, looking for all the world like a man posed for a magazine layout, devastatingly handsome in his impeccable light gray suit. Turning at the sound of her heels he beamed at her. "Oh, honey, you are lovely." He looked her over and took her hand. "I think this should go with your dress very nicely."

Into her palm dropped a pearl and diamond necklace, warm from his grasp, and stunning in its simple brilliance.

"Oh Will, what have you done?" She said softly. He reclaimed the gift and stood behind her, lifting her hair out of the way, and placing it around her neck. He kissed her throat. "I saw this in the window at Tiffany's and thought of how it needed a home."

"You don't have to buy me things . . ." Elizabeth touched the jewels and looked at their reflection in the mirror. "This isn't a gift to make me forget that you are leaving, is it?"

Darcy slipped his arms around her waist and nuzzled his lips to her ear. "This is to mark our final date before we marry. When I come home, we will be too busy with family and guests to really be alone, and certainly won't be able to steal away again. I want this night to be special, and would have given you this regardless of where I sleep tomorrow." He turned her around and smiled at her tear-filled eyes. "I want you to remember this night forever, honey, and when we're old and gray, these diamonds will still be shining like your eyes are right now, and the pearls will glow like your skin does tonight. Whenever you wear this, I will see you as you are now, my beautiful Lizzy, before we have children, before whatever trials or joys marriage brings to us, just you here now, looking at me with love."

"Will . . ."

He kissed her gently and took her hand. "Come on."

"THEN WHAT happened?" Jane asked.

"He took me to Tavern on the Green." Elizabeth sighed.

"We were in one of the rooms that looks over Central Park, it was all lit up with twinkle lights, like it was Christmas. He must have made arrangements beforehand because they seemed to be waiting just for us. He . . . Oh Jane, I have never seen him so open with his affection."

"What did he do?" She sat forward and rested her elbows on her desk while listening, trying to imagine the scene.

"He was touching my hand, he kept stroking the engagement ring . . . I don't know, he was just so happy and wistful, he laughed so much and the smile, oh Jane, when he smiles, the room just lights up. I can't describe it. It was . . . it was as if he felt safe to show me everything that he feels for me, and then somehow, I know that there is more, and I'll see his deepest feelings only after we are married. I don't know, maybe I'm being silly, but it's as if he's just giving me his heart, like he is finally allowing himself to believe that this is real and we'll be married soon." Elizabeth laughed softly. "I sound so stupid."

"No, you don't Lizzy, you sound passionately in love."

"I'm afraid that I can't express the depth of my feelings the way that he can, I just hope that he knows how much I love him. I tease too much."

"You're still protecting yourself. I think that you are waiting for the wedding before you will be able to completely give him your heart. And if you sense that easing in him, I am sure that he senses the same in you. I bet that is why he is so desperate to get the ceremony over with." Jane laughed. "Poor John, he's already told me that I must not look at William and expect him to match my new brother-in-law's romantic behavior."

Elizabeth found that she had been crying and wiped her eyes. "I think that John is quite capable of being very romantic Jane, just in a different way. Have you gone out lately?"

"No, actually he came over last night and we spent the evening drinking wine and talking. He told me all about his conflicting thoughts on his future, and how he hated disappointing his father, but also how relieved he was to decide against running."

"How does that make you feel about him?"

"Well, first it was just so nice to spend an evening talking to an intelligent, thoughtful man, and then, I told him I was happy for his decision." She smiled at the memory of his reaction. "He was so delighted to get my approval. I really like him, Lizzy."

"Did you kiss him again?" She prodded.

"Did you kiss William?"

"Now that's a silly question!" She laughed. "Well, we kissed very publicly in the carriage as we toured the park."

"Oh, you had a carriage ride, too?" Jane sighed. "So romantic!"

"Wait until you see the necklace, Jane."

"I thought that you don't like jewelry."

"I think that I can bear to accept his gifts." She giggled and heard Jane's laugh. "Well, he called and said that the people he needs to see are willing to come here on Monday, so that means he will be home on Sunday, thankfully, and we'll leave for Pemberley Tuesday after he is finished at work. Everything is set? The caterer and the tent and everything?"

"Yes, Lizzy, I promise, you don't have anything to worry about, and then we'll have a convoy of cars driving out Friday afternoon."

Elizabeth sighed. "Are you sure you don't mind Charles staying at Pemberley?"

"Of course not, we kissed, we had some fun dates, but it never went far enough for us to have to feel weird around each other. It will be fine. I think that he will like Maria."

"We'll see. Okay, I have to get going. Charlotte talked me into a book signing today. Then tomorrow Adam and Lisa and her husband arrive in town to do some promotion before going to Pemberley. They are going to visit here in the afternoon if you want to meet them."

"I'll try to be there, if not I'll see them at the wedding."

They said their goodbyes, and Elizabeth found that William had sent her a text message. He had arrived in Seattle safely and would talk to her that evening, hopefully before midnight New York time. Frank insisted on driving her to the bookstore, and she was pleasantly surprised to find a small mob of teenage girls waiting outside.

Two more days passed, she and Georgiana worked laying out her wardrobe for the honeymoon and debating which things to take. All of her sisters arrived back in town, their summer sessions officially over, the only hitch in the plans were that her author friends had been held up at their individual book signings and had not visited yet. As promised, she and William exchanged a constant barrage of text messages and long very late night phone calls. Saturday evening, Georgina was out with some school friends at an under-21 dance club and Elizabeth was sitting in the garden, watching the fireflies glowing amongst the flowers and listening to the muffled sound of the city.

"Lizzy?" She heard a male voice call. "Are you out here?"

"I'm over here!" She stood and went to the arbor, and spotted Adam standing in the yard looking confused. "Hi!" She smiled and he grinned.

"The woman inside said that you would be out here somewhere." He hugged her tight. "How are you sweetie? Are you a bundle of nerves?"

"I am full of anticipation." She led him to the chairs and they sat down. "Where are Lisa and Joe?"

"Oh, Charlotte added on another signing for her in Connecticut, and I'm afraid they are stuck in traffic. I went to New Jersey, and had no trouble getting back here." He looked up at the house. "Nice shack."

"It's not bad." She smiled and he laughed. "I wish William was home, but I guess you'll meet him in a week."

"I look forward to seeing who stole my girl." Adam winked.

"Don't let him hear you say that." She said pointedly.

"Jealous?"

"Possessive."

'Do you mind?" He tilted his head, knowing her history.

"No, not from him. He feels it with love, not control. There's a difference." Her phone rang and she smiled. "That's him."

"Oh, should I go?"

"No, this won't last long, he's between meetings." She answered the phone. "Hi Will!"

"Hi honey, how are you?"

"Oh you know, missing you." She smiled when Adam rolled his eyes. "How was the damage? Are they making any progress?"

"They have most of it cleared out, and they are waiting for the seedlings to arrive so the replanting will begin soon. The lumber they pulled out isn't a total loss, the fire flashed over some areas so quickly that the bark was charred, but the underlying wood is useable, not for building materials, but good enough for other paper products."

"Great then it's not quite as huge of a loss as you feared.'

'Yes, and I'm glad that I got a good look at it myself so I can speak intelligently to the buyers on Monday." He sighed, and sat back in the SUV Charles was driving. "Enough business. What are you doing?"

"I'm entertaining."

"Oh, you have company? Who is there? I'm sorry, I shouldn't interrupt."

"He understands; Adam is just making annoying faces at me while I talk." She stuck her tongue out at him, and he found a pine cone to throw at her.

"Adam? Just Adam? What about your other writer friend and her husband?"

"No, stuck in traffic, so it's just Adam." She heard the silence and smiled. Adam raised his brow and mouthed "Jealous?" She nodded. "Honey?'

"He's the guy who always asked you out at the conventions?" He said quietly.

"Yes, Will"

"May I speak to him?" He said quietly again.

"No, Will."

"Lizzy . . ."

"What?"

"Please."

"Nope, and by the way, I'm not taking any vow next Saturday that contains the word, obey." She laughed, and he chuckled softly. "Okay?"

"Yes, my love."

A car pulled into the driveway and she heard a door open and close. "Someone just arrived."

Adam stood and looked to see a driver opening another door. "It's an older woman, very fashionably over-dressed, and heading for the house. Should I tell her you're back here?"

Elizabeth stood and looked, "Oh no."

"What is it, Lizzy?" Darcy said with concern.

"Catherine is here."

Darcy swore, causing Charles to raise his brow and look over to him. "What's up?"

"My aunt has reappeared, and naturally, I'm two-thousand-plus miles away. Lizzy? You don't have to speak to her."

"Of course I do, she's your aunt. What can she possibly do to me?"

"I'm afraid to find out." He sighed.

"We're here." Charles announced. "And it seems that they are ready to begin." He indicated the group of people outside the paper mill waiting for their exit.

"Damn it!" Darcy growled. "Lizzy, I . . . I'm going to put the phone in my pocket and . . ."

"I'll be fine, Will, what is she going to do with Adam here? She wouldn't have a tirade with a stranger nearby."

"Yes she would."

"I'll call you when it's over and leave a message; you go ahead and do whatever it is you're doing. I'll be fine. We're not at our engagement party, so I can handle this."

Darcy heard the complete lack of confidence in her voice, but reluctantly followed her lead. "All right, but you call me the second it's over. I love you, honey."

"I love you." She sighed and looked up. "Here she comes."

"I hate this." He sighed; his employees were staring at him and waiting. "I'll talk to you soon."

"Bye."

"Why is it every time that Elizabeth is in a horrible situation, I am thousands of miles away!" He got out of the car and slammed the door angrily.

"Calm down, Darcy, here, give me your phone. If it rings, I can answer it where you can't in the middle of a conversation." Reluctantly Darcy handed it over, and schooling his features, shook the plant supervisor's hand. He heard little of what was said, and hoped that Charles was taking notes. His mind was far away in a garden.

"Well, it seems that I have finally located you." Catherine looked over Elizabeth standing in the lawn then glanced at Adam. "Who is this person?"

"This is Adam Fox, an author friend of mine. Adam, this is Catherine de Bourgh, William's aunt."

Before he could speak Catherine continued. "I understand that my nephew is out of the state on business."

"Yes, he just called me; he is visiting a pulp mill as we speak."

"So, he is hard at work, protecting the business his forefathers have built for nearly two centuries, and the woman who claims to love him is entertaining her so-called friend in his absence. This does nothing to reassure me of your dedication to this marriage you aspire to accomplish."

"Your lack of faith in our plans is regrettable; however, I am unconcerned with it."

Catherine's eyes narrowed. "I see a garden beyond the arbor. I would like to speak to you alone."

"Anything you have to say may be heard by my friend." Elizabeth nodded to Adam. He drew himself up and attempted not to appear intimidated.

"I have family business to discuss, and it is not for the ears of your paramour."

"My what?" Elizabeth laughed with astonishment. "Very well, we shall speak in the garden." She led the way back under the rose arbor, but did not go too far into the garden room before Catherine pounced.

"I demand to see your prenuptial agreement. William did not employ Greg to prepare it, and my brother claims no knowledge of the contents. I must be assured that the Darcy assets are protected."

"It is none of your business what is contained in the agreement, if in fact one was prepared."

"What are you saying? Do not tell me that you used your persuasion to keep him from . . . Oh, I see; yes, that is exactly what has happened, no doubt you and your lover were interrupted by my arrival. You were celebrating your success in his absence. A week from now when you plan to marry, your success will be complete! Well, I will stop that right now!"

"And what exactly do you have in mind?" Elizabeth stared at the woman with a combination of anger and fascination.

"I rescind my blessing!"

"What blessing?" She laughed.

"I will announce to New York society that William has married a . . . money-grubbing whore!" She pointed to Adam. "They will never accept you in their midst!"

"Oh come on, William is a billionaire, even if he did care about society, they could really care less where I come from. How many trophy wives are on the arms of rich men in this town? They certainly don't seem to have any problem being accepted." She laughed. "Try again."

"How dare you mock me!"

"How dare you try my patience! I have no doubt in my mind that you knew William was out of town and you came here tonight because you thought you could intimidate me." Elizabeth stepped forward and spoke quietly. "You should look after your own affairs and leave mine alone. You managed to ruin your daughter's wedding but I'll be damned if you will ruin mine."

"Ruin! Anne's wedding? It was perfect!"

"Not according to Anne. You took it over so she had no say in anything. The only reason she had a smile on her face that day was because she was marrying Greg, and that was something you could not control."

"I did what was best for her."

"Maybe you should learn to curb your impulse to control everyone else's lives and just worry about your own. Then maybe your family would actually welcome you to their homes instead of finding reasons to avoid you." Catherine stared and Elizabeth shook her head. "I have nothing else to say to you. Please leave my home. I have neglected my guest long enough."

Catherine's mouth opened and closed, and she turned. "I do not wish you well on your wedding."

"I think somehow we can live with that." Elizabeth called after her.

Adam watched the driver open the door and Catherine climb inside. He turned to grin widely at Elizabeth. "Wow girl, what happened to you?"

"I don't know, I guess that I'm not afraid of words anymore. That's all she can do, throw around her opinions, but they can't hurt me or William. She'd rather die than threaten his reputation in her precious social circle." She smiled and he hugged her. "I'm going to call Will, do you mind? I know that he is going to be a mess until I tell him everything is okay."

"No, go ahead. Tell you what, I saw a park across the street, I'll go stretch my legs for a half-hour and then do you want to go get a drink or something?"

"No, come back here and we can just hang out and talk." She smiled at his raised brow. "Yes Adam, I'd rather stay home."

"My, my, little Lizzy is all grown up." He kissed her cheek and set off. "I guess it's too late to talk you into marrying me, isn't it?" He heard her laugh and stepped out on the sidewalk.

"Hello?" Charles said when the phone rang. Darcy stopped in mid-sentence and stared at him, then murmured an excuse and took the phone. "Lizzy?"

"It's okay, Will. She wanted to see the prenup."

He exploded. "What an arrogant . . . I won't say it." He saw the men staring at him and moved across the factory to stand in a relatively quiet corner. He drew a deep breath and continued. "I'm sorry, honey. What did you tell her?"

"I implied that we didn't have one to make her crazy." Elizabeth laughed and she heard his relieved chuckle. "She's gone and Adam took a walk. It's okay, Will. I'm fine. Are you still in your meeting?"

"Yes, they are all looking at me."

"Well finish your work, and call me tonight, and I'll give you the blow by blow account."

"You're really okay, honey? I am so proud of you." He sighed and closed his eyes. The only thing he wanted at that moment was to be holding her, and demonstrating how much he loved her.

"Yes, now go finish up so you can come home to me." She heard silence. "Will?"

"I was just thinking of how sweet your lips taste, and how much I love the feel of your body beneath mine." He heard her soft intake of breath, and encouraged, voiced the thoughts that were always just below the surface when they were apart. "Do you know how tight you are, honey? Sometimes I wonder how I can fit inside of you. I love how your body surrounds me and squeezes so hard when you come. Baby, I love pumping into you and hearing you call my name."

"Willlll."

His voice took on a rough growl. "I am going to come home tomorrow and love you until your skin is slick with sweat and your thighs are wet with my seed. I want you sticky and exhausted, I want your body quivering, and I want you begging me for more. And I'm going to give it to you."

"I . . . I have to sit down." Elizabeth reached out blindly and found a chair arm, then fell onto the grass. "Oh Will, I'm aching for you."

"Good." He smiled with the satisfaction of finally leaving her in a state of unfulfilled desire, and hoped his erection would be hidden by his suit jacket. "I'll call you later and we'll finish this conversation."

"You damn well better, Fitzwilliam Darcy!"

Chapter 14

"**T**his can't possibly be safe." Elizabeth chewed her lip and hung onto the car seat, startling with another loud clap of thunder.

"One of the safest places to be in a thunderstorm is in a car, so I've heard." Frank said over his shoulder. He noticed Elizabeth's worried expression in the rear-view mirror. "I think being in a plane is another one."

"Frank, it's not going to work, I'm incapable of thinking reasonably." Elizabeth caught his eye. "I know that the pilot would not try to land if the conditions are bad, but . . ." She sighed. "I just won't relax until he's home."

"I understand Miss Bennet." He smiled at the care his boss was receiving. "Well, we should be at the airport in a few minutes."

The car drove into the entrance gates to Teterboro and he maneuvered around to the hangar that housed the terminal for the Pemberley corporate jets. Frank jumped out to open the door for Elizabeth and he laughed, just beating her to it. Holding an umbrella, he escorted her inside and pointed out the lounge where she could wait for Darcy's arrival. "I'll be moving the car around to where I always park for Mr. Darcy; he knows where to find me." Elizabeth nodded and bit her lip, then walked up to a woman at the counter.

"Hi, I'm waiting for a flight to come in."

"Yes, and what company?"

"Pemberley." She said and startled with another bright flash of lightening. "They won't try to land in this, will they?"

"They won't if there is any chance of wind shear, but according to the radar, the storm is moving away pretty rapidly." She checked her computer. "The flight is about a half-hour out. You might as well make yourself comfortable. The executive waiting room is just through that door, and you can watch for the plane from the windows there."

"Thank you." Elizabeth walked into the plush room, casting a glance at a group of businessmen gathered around a table, and stood near the window, scanning the skies. A man broke off from the group and approached her.

"Flying out or meeting a plane?" He asked affably.

"Oh, meeting one." She met his eye and looked back out. "I've never been to an airport like this before. I'm used to JFK, and dealing with a madhouse. This is so calm." She heard him laugh and turned back to him. "I guess that exposes my ignorance."

"Well yes, but it also explains why those who have the opportunity charter flights from here." He held out his hand. "Robert Norris."

"Elizabeth Bennet." She shook his hand and smiled. "So are you leaving on a flight soon?"

"No actually I'm here for a meeting, our client is flying in then back out." He looked at the skies. "If they aren't too delayed."

"That's what I'm afraid of." She looked back out.

"Difficult client? Doesn't understand that we can't control the weather?" He indicated a seat and she took it, but kept her gaze outside. "Relax, it can't be that bad. What do you do?"

"I'm a writer." She said absently.

"Really?" He perked up. "Now that is different. I usually run into over-extended assistants or overly serious businesswomen. So are you meeting a publisher?"

Elizabeth ignored his slightly patronizing attitude; his conversation was at least keeping her mind occupied. "No, William Darcy of Pemberley Paper."

He screwed up his eyes and thought. "I know that name, why do I know that name?" He glanced over to a table and saw a copy of *Forbes*. "Oh, I know; billionaire, not Bill Gates billions, but not hurting either. Well, what's he doing for you?"

She looked him over, realizing that he was not the least interested in her answer, not by the way his eyes were traveling over her. She clearly was not dressed in the uniform of a business woman, and it had caught his eye. "That is my business." His brow rose and he smiled.

"Well isn't that interesting?"

"Excuse me; you are waiting for the flight for Pemberley?" The young woman from the desk asked.

"Yes." Elizabeth looked up at her.

"Would you please come with me?" She had a fixed smile and glanced at the man by her side. "Sir, are you waiting for that flight as well?"

"No, no I'm not." He could sense that something wasn't right.

Elizabeth looked outside and seeing no planes looked again at the woman. "Did anyone come with you, Miss?"

"The driver is waiting with the car, but . . . What is wrong?" Elizabeth stood up.

"Let's just go into this conference room."

"No, you tell me what is wrong!" She demanded.

"Miss, please let's go in here." The woman guided her towards the room. Robert followed.

"May I be of . . . help?" He looked over Elizabeth, all pretence of a man on the make gone, and he showed genuine concern.

"Sir, this is a private matter."

"WHAT IS WRONG?" Elizabeth cried and all conversation in the room stopped. She ran over to the window, and saw nothing unusual. The rain had stopped and the sun was just appearing from beyond the clouds. "William." She whispered.

"PLEASE ASSUME crash positions." The flight attendant said urgently to Darcy and Charles. They exchanged glances. "What is going on?"

"Mr. Darcy, please, the pilot has given his orders." She grabbed his shoulders and pushed him down. Charles joined him and the flight attendant made one last check for loose items and buckled herself in, signaling the pilot that they were ready. Darcy stared at his shoes and prayed. *Please let me hold her again.*

ELIZABETH RESISTED the insistent pulling of the airport representative and remained at the window. Suddenly sirens began screaming and bright yellow fire trucks appeared and streamed by. She spun around. "What is happening?"

Nobody answered. A plane appeared out of the clouds and she watched it drifting lower as it approached the runway, the flotilla of emergency equipment following. Her heart was pounding, and she was praying, watching the drama unfold as if it were a movie and not her life slowly being played out before her. Almost painfully slowly the plane floated down, then touched the ground. Sparks immediately sprayed from behind, smoke and ultimately flames poured from its wake, obscuring the plane. "WILLIAM!!" She screamed, staring and pressing her hand to the glass. The plane disappeared from view behind another hangar.

DARCY AND CHARLES sat in silence, hugging their knees, and were jolted violently as the screeching of metal on the runway filled their ears. As soon as it came to a rest, the flight attendant was up. "Out, let's move. Now!" They released the seatbelts and jumped up, following her to the door and helping her to push it open. A slide appeared and first Charles, then Darcy, then finally the crew escaped and ran from the aircraft just as the first emergency vehicles arrived on the scene. The bottom of the plane was burning. "My God." Darcy whispered, and stared mesmerized at the flames, his fear of death by fire reasserted itself. "What happened?"

"The landing gear would not lock in place." The pilot said. "We had to go for a gentle belly landing."

"That was gentle?" Charles said softly. The numb tone of his voice grabbed Darcy's attention, and he shot Charles a look. "I know; we're in one piece."

Foam was poured over the plane and the fire was out quickly. The dousing of the flames helped to calm them all. A fireman approached the group. "Is everyone out?"

"Yes, all souls are safe." The pilot reported, and the fireman nodded. "We were not carrying much fuel, so that probably helped to limit the fire."

Paramedics arrived and were relieved to see that they were not needed. A small bus pulled up and they were loaded inside to make the trip back to the terminal. Darcy leaned forward and shook the hands of the pilot, copilot, and flight attendant. "Thank you, you are incredible."

"We were just following our training, sir." The pilot said quietly. "I'm happy that it wasn't anything worse. I considered trying for a water landing, but we were coming in slow enough, and another plane looked us over and said that the gear was down. It must have collapsed when we hit the runway." He sighed and looked at his copilot. "We'll be here for some time while the investigation gets going."

"If there is anything I can do . . ." Darcy offered.

"No sir, we're all residents of the area, we'll be home eventually." He relaxed a little. "But we'll need something else to fly to England, I'm afraid."

"Elizabeth probably won't want to go when she hears about this." Charles tried to follow the pilot's lead and lighten the mood. "Maybe you shouldn't tell her."

Darcy was about to respond when they pulled up to the terminal. He looked out of the window and his breath caught. "I don't think I can keep it a secret." The bus doors opened and he was the first off, immediately wrapping her up in his arms. "Lizzy." He held her tight to him, and they kissed. Whatever breath they had left after the hug was effectively removed when their lips locked together. Elizabeth pulled back, gasping and holding his face in her hands.

"Are you okay? Are you hurt? Don't you ever scare me like this again! What were you doing landing like that?" She began kissing all over his face and he laughed with the relief of her response. His hands cupped her cheeks and he determinedly held back the tears that were threatening to appear. Instead Darcy concentrated on gently wiping hers away.

"Do you hear yourself, honey?" He kissed her, gently this time, and gathered her shaking body to his. Seeing her brought home the reality of what they had almost lost, and he struggled to remain strong and calm. Elizabeth felt him trembling and held him tighter. "What are you doing here?" He spoke in her hair as he fought to regain control.

"I thought I'd surprise you." She whispered, and pressed her ear to his chest to hear the rapid beat of his heart. "It looks like you were the one surprising me."

"Oh honey, this is not the homecoming I was planning." He kissed the top of her head and rested his cheek there. He noticed Charles standing nearby, looking just as stunned as he felt, and assumed his president of Pemberley persona. "It's Sunday, so I don't know who we should call to assure the staff that all is well."

Charles responded to the command to think clearly. "Maybe just leave a message for Patricia at home. I suppose the media is probably already on it." He bent his head to see Elizabeth still clinging to Darcy with her eyes closed. "I don't know that you'll be moving anytime soon." He smiled a little and Darcy's attitude softened.

"I'm in no hurry." Darcy said quietly and kissed her forehead.

"Mr. Darcy, Mr. Bingley, please come inside." An airport official directed. "We need to speak to you about the incident and the plane, and I'm certain that you do not wish to be interviewed." She indicated the news vans driving into the terminal parking lot. "Your luggage and whatever else was in the cabin will be collected and brought here as soon as the firemen declare the scene safe."

"Come on, honey." Darcy whispered and she let go, only to have her hand encompassed by his. They entered the terminal, and moved back up to the waiting area. "Are you okay?" He sat down with her and took her hands in his. "I'll be back as soon as I can."

"I . . . I'll call Arlene and . . . Georgiana, just so they don't hear about this on the news." Elizabeth sat up and wiped her eyes. "Oh, and Frank, I'll . . . I'll speak to him, he's parked outside."

"Okay, I'll make this as fast as I can." He kissed her softly. "I can't tell you how happy I was to see you waiting for me." They kissed again, slowly, then he stood. The official was standing nearby. "Please let me know if she needs anything."

Elizabeth watched him disappear and repressed the desire to run after him. A glass was presented to her, and she looked up to see Robert there. "Maybe you could use a stiff drink."

She tried to smile. "No, I just need to go home, thanks."

"Okay, I heard you mention someone in a car outside, can I get him for you?" He smiled. "You are a little shaky to be walking without Mr. Darcy. He's obviously not a business acquaintance."

"Oh, no, we're getting married on Saturday." She choked and started to cry again. "I'm sorry."

"It's okay. So a man named Frank?"

"Yes, a black Mercedes, parked near the entrance." She wiped her eyes. "Thank you."

He left and she took out her phone, calling first Georgiana then Arlene, who managed to reassure her enough to deliver a convincing smile when William and Charles reappeared. "You look a little better." He whispered as he immediately took her up in his arms.

"So do you." Elizabeth hugged him. "I know that you are putting on a good face, Will, but when we get home, please know that you can let down in front of me." She felt his embrace tighten and heard him swallow hard. Elizabeth cleared her throat and lifted her head to see his face. "Frank took your bags out to the car." She mouthed. "I love you."

"We are free to go, then." He kissed her and murmured, "I love you," and they headed for the door. Darcy cleared his throat. "It looks like we'll be chartering a plane for Sunday."

"We're not . . . flying are we?" She stopped and stared at him.

"Honey, we could take a ship across the Atlantic, but I think that the best way to deal with the fear that this accident gave us is to face it and fly." He took her hands and held them, looking at her with fierce determination. "I know what we almost lost today, and I'm not going to waste another moment of our lives. There are just too many places in the world I want to experience with you by my side."

"As long as I'm by your side." She informed him. The same determined look appeared in her eyes.

"That's not a problem." He smiled and leaned his head on hers. "I know that I promised you a night of passion, but . . ."

"I think that we need a night of holding each other." Elizabeth smiled and caressed his face. "We have a honeymoon coming up for passion."

"We certainly do."

DARCY LOOKED over at Elizabeth and smiled, taking her hand in his; he raised it to his lips, then looked back at the interstate. "So are you happier in a car?"

"I know, I know, you think that I'm crazy." She laughed and squeezed his hand. "I just thought it would be nice to be trapped in a quiet car with you for three hours instead of sitting in a helicopter with headphones on."

"I can't protest that, especially after Sunday's adventure, which I know is the real reason behind this mode of transportation." He saw her looking down and squeezed her fingers. They had spent a great deal of time talking about their fears, and decided to not let them ruin their plans. "I'm sorry that we couldn't leave as early as we planned, but I don't think we'll have any trouble preparing for our guests." He glanced over to see her smiling again and then back at the road. "I don't do this enough."

"What's that?"

"Explore. All I do is fly over the country. I never really get to see anything." He looked out at the scenery. "Even on a boring interstate you see more than you do from above. Imagine what it's like to just get off on all of these little roads and wander." Hearing her laugh he looked over. "What did I say?"

"You sound like my dad. He always took the road less traveled on our family vacations." She tilted her head and considered him. "I imagine that I have seen more of this country than you have."

"That is very likely." Stroking her hand he lifted his fingers to touch her neck and caress it. "Maybe that is something that we can do. Take little road trips."

"Oh that sounds wonderful! Have you ever seen the leaves in New England?"

"No, I hear raves about them, but I have missed out. Maybe a weekend in October we could go."

"Hmm, then I had better make some reservations as soon as we get to Pemberley." She took out her phone and began searching the internet for inns. "There was someplace that I heard about . . . Aha!"

He grinned. "And?"

"The Lodge at Moosehead Lake." She read out the particulars, "Ralph Lauren meets Teddy Roosevelt." He chuckled. "It has diamond and star ratings like crazy, and looks lovely. What do you think?"

"Whatever you want, Lizzy, I trust your instincts." He smiled and kissed her hand again. "We'll look at the calendar when we arrive."

"When is the Foundation Ball?"

"Um, usually the middle of October. We'll have to ask Anne." He laughed. "I understand that Catherine is not pleased with your advice to stop meddling in people's business."

"No, I'm afraid that Anne got an earful from her after our little confrontation." Elizabeth sighed. "But Anne took the opportunity to really stand up to her and say to her face everything that she's been keeping bottled up for years. Who knows, maybe she'll listen. I know how anxious you are to vent your feelings to her. Is she coming to the wedding?"

"I don't know. I guess I should give her a call before Friday's rehearsal dinner." Darcy looked over and caught her eye. "It's finally happening."

"Are you nervous?"

"No, I'm very excited." He ran his hand down her bare leg and back up to her thighs. "So are you really going to abandon me Friday night and sleep with Jane?"

"Wouldn't that make the anticipation of our wedding night more exciting?" She shifted a little to give him better access, and his fingers settled between her legs, slipped inside of her panties, and began stroking rhythmically.

"Mmmm, no. Just being your husband will inspire enough excitement for me." He looked over to her closed eyes and whispered. "Please don't leave me alone."

"We'll see." She whispered and he groaned. Elizabeth reached over to touch his groin. "mmm, nice." He groaned again. They began passing farm stands and she looked at the colorful displays of produce. "We're cooking for ourselves tonight, aren't we?"

He focused on the road and tried to ignore the gentle caress of her hand, then finally firmly removed it from his crotch and swallowed hard. "I thought that we would just go out."

"No, let's stay home. Can we stop at one of these produce stands and I'll get some things?" The next one appeared and he pulled in. "Will you come with me?" She said as she unlatched the seatbelt.

"Uh, no, I'll just stay here for now." He blushed and she giggled. Watching her through the window, he looked around and opened his shorts, rearranged as well as he could the result of her caresses, and attempted to zip up before she returned. He failed and was greeted by her placing the bags in the backseat and climbing in next to him. Elizabeth looked at his bright red face then down at his lap.

"William!"

"I . . . oh Lizzy, I'm stuck." He looked at her hopelessly. "I need help."

"Can you drive?" She laughed to see the enormous erection standing proudly between his legs.

"Yes." He sighed. "We're almost home."

"Well, let's get there." She reached over and gently stroked him.

Darcy closed his eyes and moaned. "Baby, I'm going to have an accident . . . and I mean with the car . . . if you don't stop."

Laughing she let go and they pulled back out onto the road. Every time he felt that he was regaining control, he would look over and see Elizabeth's eyes were fixed either on his face or his arousal, and his desire would instantly renew itself. They approached the sandy obscured driveway, hidden behind thick woods, and went around a curve to approach the house. He stopped the car before they got to the gate, turned off the ignition and turned to her. "I can't get out of the car like this, Lizzy."

"What do you need, honey?"

He glanced at the back seat and looked at her. Giggling, she climbed out and opened the door. He was out and moved around the car in a moment, and kissing her, lifted up the short skirt she was wearing. "We don't need these do we?" He pulled her panties down then pushed her back onto the seat, drew her bottom to the edge, and standing outside, grabbed her legs, wrapped them around his waist and plunged in. "Oh yes!!!" The car was bouncing in time with his thrusts, his arms were braced on the seat, and Elizabeth was gripping his forearms. Staring at each other, both panted through open mouths as he rutted determinedly. "You make me insane, Lizzy!" He moaned, and his eyes squeezed closed. "Ohhh my . . ." He swore and exploded. "Yesssssssss!" He hissed, then opened his eyes in time to see Elizabeth's close. He kept moving for her, finding the pace and motion she needed and felt the pleasure of her milking clasp. She cried out and he smiled with deep satisfaction. "You needed it, too." He panted and leaned down to kiss her. "I love you, honey."

Opening her eyes she found his face just above her. "I feel so good." He grinned and she laughed. "So, is this better than flying, do you think?"

"Much better. However, we will need to join the mile high club sometime over the next month." He moved back and straightened, finally able to zip up his shorts. Leaning down he picked up her panties and the one shoe that had fallen off, then leaned against the car while she sat up and dressed. Emerging from the car Elizabeth leaned into his arms. Darcy kissed her hair. "I guess that we can go inside now."

"I guess." She sighed and cuddled into his chest. "Is anyone here?"

"Just the staff. Maggie won't come out until Friday. So really it's just us." His arms came around her shoulders and they hugged. "What did you buy?"

"Lots of veggies, and I thought we could go to the butcher in town if we don't have anything to grill. We're on our own until Jerry comes on Friday." Elizabeth nuzzled her face against his neck and breathed in his musky cologne.

"I can't move." He whispered. "The car is holding me up."

Elizabeth laughed. "Have I removed your bones, Will?"

"One anyway." He chuckled and looked down to her sparkling eyes. "You're beautiful." They kissed and got back into the car, pressing the button to open the gate and pulling into the garage. The gardener appeared from around the back and he helped them with the luggage. They took their time unpacking and changing clothes, Elizabeth went into the kitchen and saw that the refrigerator was full of supplies for entertaining, but nothing special was there for dinner. A trip into town was needed. She found William in the library, looking at his calendar. He looked up. "The ball is October 15th, how about the weekend before for the road trip?"

"That might be too late for Vermont; it's always a mystery when the peak is, but could we go in late September?"

"Well, we'll be home from the honeymoon on the 12th . . . let's say the 26th? That is if I'm not forced to go away on business somewhere." He looked at her with his brows up, and noted her unhappy expression. "It's not unlikely, honey."

"I know." She sighed. "Maybe we shouldn't be gone so long."

"No, we should." Darcy kissed her hand and looked back at the calendar, and noted the weekend. "It is marked, and we're going. Period." He then searched for and found the website for the inn. "This sounds really nice." Taking out his wallet he removed a credit card. He picked up the phone and called the inn to make the reservations. "That was fortunate; someone else cancelled there just an hour ago." He smiled and stood up. "We're all set."

"Let's go shopping." Back out to the car they went, and into town. "What are you in the mood for?"

"Steak."

"Of course." Elizabeth smiled and they walked into the small butcher shop, examining the selection of the organically produced meats and the fresh seafood, and chose enough things for the next few days that they would be on their own. Hand in hand they then wandered down the sidewalk, looking in the shop windows, and stopped at a bakery.

"I need a dessert." Darcy grinned. "Something messy."

Elizabeth laughed. "Where did you get this sweet tooth?"

"My dad was the same." He looked over the selections. "What do you want?"

"I have a wedding dress to fit into." She reminded him.

Darcy tilted his head. "Oh, we'll find a way to work off the calories."

"Push ups?"

"Push ins." He whispered in her ear. "You're my real dessert, and I can't wait to see how messy I can make you." Elizabeth blushed and his eyes twinkled as he held up his number when it was called. Leaving the bakery they slowly made their way back towards the car.

"William!" A tall blonde woman called and came towards them. "I haven't seen you in so long, how are you?" She smiled warmly at him and curiously looked over Elizabeth. She was stunning, and her eyes matched his in color.

"I am very well, thank you." He smiled slightly and squeezing Elizabeth's hand he said, "Amy, this is my fiancée, Elizabeth Bennet. Elizabeth, this is Amy Whitney, her father's home is adjacent to Pemberley."

"I'm pleased to meet you." Elizabeth said, assessing the woman as intently as she was being examined by her.

"And I am pleased to meet you." She said then turned back to Darcy. "I didn't know that you were engaged."

"It was in all the papers." Elizabeth noted with a mischievous grin.

"I suppose that I missed the announcement. Dad will be disappointed; he always was after me to chase you when we were younger."

"Well, as I recall you did chase but I refused to be caught." He squeezed Elizabeth's hand. "Our wedding is Saturday at the house, so if you hear a lot of noise you'll know what it is."

"Oh . . . not inviting the neighbors?"

"No, just family and our dearest friends." Elizabeth smiled again and squeezed his hand back. "I look forward to seeing more of you in the future. I do want to know the neighbors."

"Perhaps we can invite them over the next time we're at Pemberley." Darcy suggested. "We could have a little party. You could meet all of the ladies who once chased me." He smiled and pursed his lips.

"Oh now that sounds just delightful!" Elizabeth laughed and looked up to see Amy's surprised expression. "Well I have to meet them sometime, so why not at one go?"

Amy laughed. "My goodness, I think that I'm going to like you, Elizabeth, even if you did steal William away."

"She stole nothing that wasn't willing to be taken." He put his arm around Elizabeth's waist and gave her a hug. "Please give our best to your parents."

"I will."

"It was a pleasure to have met you, Amy." Elizabeth smiled and they set off again. She looked up to see William's warm smile. "How did I do?"

"Very well, honey. I am impressed."

"I'm secure."

"That makes me feel so good." He kissed her as they walked and spotted an ice cream stand. "Want to ruin dinner?"

"We should get these things home; it's pretty warm out here." He sighed and she laughed. "Tomorrow we'll get your ice cream."

They just reached the car when once again, Darcy heard his name called. "Barry!" He shook his hand and clapped his back. "I didn't know you were coming out this early!"

"Oh, I owed my wife a vacation, so why not make it a week here." He took Elizabeth's hand and smiled. "You are glowing as any bride should."

"Have I mentioned how much I like your friends, Will?" The men laughed and a young red-haired woman about Elizabeth's height came out of a shop, and was immediately kissed on the cheek by Darcy.

Barry laughed. "Ah, Rachel, this is Elizabeth, our bride."

"I am delighted!" They shook hands. "Are you ready for everything?"

"I hardly know. My sister promises that everything will be in place and I needn't worry my pretty head about a thing." The ladies laughed. "I'll look into it all tomorrow. Maybe . . . would you like to join us for dinner tomorrow evening?"

Barry met Darcy's eye and saw his eagerness. "Sure, that sounds great, um what time?"

"Six?" Elizabeth suggested.

"We'll be there. I'll bring an appropriate wine."

Darcy laughed. "Not beer?"

"I think that we put enough of that away in our younger days."

Rachel rolled her eyes and leaned in to Elizabeth. "I have a feeling that this will be an evening of hearing stories of their misspent youth."

"I'd enjoy that."

Darcy smiled and she leaned into the arms that came around her. "I'm pretty boring, you know."

"But somehow I manage to find you fascinating." He kissed her soundly and the group laughed. "We really should get this stuff home before it cooks in the sun. We'll see you tomorrow." The couples parted and they were on their way back home. Elizabeth brushed the hair from his eyes that the air from the open window had mussed. "I think that we are really beginning to find our way."

"What do you mean?" He smiled and looked over to her before returning his attention to the road.

"I didn't feel threatened by Amy, and I didn't feel nervous to host one of your best friends for dinner. You showed no hesitation to demonstrate your feelings for me to anybody we met, including anyone in the town who happened to be looking. I think that we are both secure in our feelings, and really ready to just see what comes next."

"You're right, I don't think I ever felt worried about how you would perform before the people I know, but I did worry over anything they might say which would scare you away from the life we would have. You have grown in confidence over the past few months, and that has reassured me." He pressed his cheek into her palm and kissed it as they drove back down the driveway. "I so look forward to what is to come."

"BACHELOR PARTY?" Darcy stared at Barry. "What bachelor party?"

"Looks like you are caught by surprise; well maybe that was the point." Barry leaned against the railing on the patio and took a sip of wine. "I got the invitation last week."

"From whom?" Darcy demanded.

"I didn't know the address, but they apparently had access to your email account. I recognized your cousin John's business address in the carbon copies, so he's probably not behind it."

"Where is this so-called party to take place?"

"I don't know; we are to meet here and spirit you away tomorrow night apparently." Barry laughed to see his friend look so angry. "Come on, it's just a night out with the guys, it won't do any harm."

"I'm not going to a strip club." He declared.

"I certainly hope not!" Elizabeth stopped on her way out to join them and looked at Barry. "Did you suggest that?"

He held up his hands. "I am innocent, I swear!"

"Barry was invited to a bachelor party, Elizabeth." Rachel smiled. "I remember his, don't you, William?"

"Yes, and I swore at the time that I would not tolerate anyone torturing me with such a thing." He growled.

"What happened?" Elizabeth asked curiously.

"I got a great many lap dances." Barry stared at his feet. Elizabeth raised her brows, and turned to regard William.

"May I assume that you did as well?"

"Everyone did." He said quietly. "It was very uncomfortable."

"My cousins saw an excuse to hire strippers and they took it." Barry smiled. "I imagine that yours know better, if they are the ones behind it."

"If you are going to a gentleman's club then I think I'm going to find a male review." Elizabeth declared. "I don't know if I have enough ones to stuff in their g-strings, though. I'll have to go into town in the morning and stop at the bank." Darcy stared at her in horror.

"You wouldn't . . . Lizzy . . . you wouldn't really go and . . . touch strippers, would you?" He spluttered.

She shrugged. "Would you?"

"NO!"

"Then I won't." She said softly and returned to the house. Darcy stared after her with his mouth open and ran his hand through his hair. Rachel grinned and went back in the house. "I can't believe she was actually considering that!"

"She was just making a point, Darcy." Barry laughed and handed him a glass of wine. "Relax."

Darcy closed his eyes. "Yeah." Elizabeth returned with a platter and walked over to the grill, shooting a glance at him before opening the hood. Rachel followed with plates and silverware and started setting things up. He watched her silently, reading her body language. Clearly the thought of him in a strip club was not a welcome one for her. He walked over to her side. "Can I help you with that?"

"Sure." She handed him some tongs and he held onto the beer cans as she carefully pulled off the chickens that were speared on top. "We'll just let these rest for a little bit, then we can eat. Be careful, those cans are very hot."

"The steam is a good giveaway." He noted and caught her eye, seeing her smile a little. Darcy relaxed. "I don't want to go to a bachelor party, honey."

"And I don't want to go to an all-male review." She said softly.

"Well, I'll send out a blanket email to all of the males of the party and inform them of that." He kissed her and smiled. "Okay?" She nodded and he took the chickens over to the table while she removed the vegetables.

"All better?" Rachel whispered as he set everything down.

He glanced at her and smiled. "Yes." She gave his arm a squeeze and the couples sat down to enjoy the meal.

"So is everything set?" Barry looked over to Elizabeth.

"Yes, the house is ready for the guests who will stay. The caterer will come early Saturday and start cooking, and the tent will be set up tomorrow. I confirmed the magistrate and we have the license locked away in William's library." She grinned at him and he laughed. "I think we are in good shape. Oh, and the photographer will be bothering us all day Saturday."

"What about your hair and dress?"

"My sister Kitty will do my hair; she's been practicing on all of her friends and sending me pictures for weeks." She laughed, "I don't think she'll do a bad job, I'm just not letting her near a pair of scissors!"

"No, please don't!" Darcy touched her long curls. "I think it's lovely as is."

"hmm. What a good man you are!" She smiled and he blushed. Looking to Barry and Rachel she tilted her head, "I wasn't sure if you kept Kosher or not."

"No, but we won't be able to try out the pig, I'm afraid." He smiled. "Thanks for thinking of us with the caterer."

"You're welcome; it should be a surprise for the guests who are expecting more sophisticated fare." She shrugged. "I just love barbeque. There will be brisket, as well."

"Now *that* we can eat!" Barry grinned. They cleaned up the table and carried it all inside. Darcy went into the refrigerator and brought out a huge bowl of macerated peaches and another of whipped cream. "What's this?

"William made us peach shortcake." Elizabeth smiled as she split the biscuits and he looked down, concentrating on spooning out the fruit and cream. "He has discovered that he enjoys cooking."

"I have discovered that I enjoy harassing you in the kitchen." He said softly and peeked over at her. Barry and Rachel raised their brows and quietly accepted their desserts, adjourning back outside to watch the water. Darcy whispered in her ear. "Thanks for not telling them about the chickens."

Elizabeth laughed. "You mean you would be embarrassed to have me tell your friends that you made a chicken dance across the countertop to the tune of *Hello My Baby?*[vi]" He blushed and she kissed him. "I know that you are only capable of being that silly for me alone, honey. I won't share that side of you with anyone."

"Thanks, I've never let down like that to anyone else." He kissed her and they walked back out to the patio and sat down with their desserts.

"So where is the honeymoon?" Barry broke the silence. "I would be hard-pressed to remove myself from this spot."

"We'll be waking up at Pemberley in Derbyshire on Monday." Darcy put down his plate and reached over to hold Elizabeth's hand. "We have some decisions to make there."

"Ah, giving it up." Barry nodded. "Quite a decision to make."

"I'm leaving it to Elizabeth."

"Me?" She stared at him. "Why?"

"You'll see." He smiled and said no more about it. "We'll visit London, but I don't really have any fixed itinerary. Maybe we'll stay in Derbyshire for awhile, although it will be getting a little cold there. I suppose Paris is required for a honeymoon."

"I'd be happy in our rose garden." Elizabeth said softly into his warm eyes. Barry and Rachel looked at each other and smiled.

"I think we'll be going." They stood. "We'll stop by tomorrow in the afternoon."

"You don't have to go." Elizabeth stood. "Really, please stay!"

"No, you two need to relax, you have some busy days ahead." Rachel kissed her cheek then Darcy's "Thank you for the lovely evening."

They walked the couple to the door and waved them goodbye. Darcy turned back to Elizabeth and hugged her. "There, our first dinner party."

"Does one couple count as a party?" Elizabeth laughed against his chest.

"I think so." He kissed her head. "Would you like to go swimming?"

She looked up. "What is the dress code?"

His hands ran down her sides and he smiled. "I want you nude."

"Should I perform a lap dance for you since you will be missing one tomorrow night?" Elizabeth suggested and began unbuttoning his shirt.

"Oh, I'd like that." Darcy rested his forehead on her hair and watched her fingers at work. "Is there anything that I can do for your entertainment?"

She pulled his shirt free and began working on his belt. "I'm sure that I'll think of something."

"WE'RE LOST." Lisa whined into the phone. "Don't people believe in signs around here?"

"I think it's more along the lines that the people don't want to be found around here." Elizabeth laughed. "Where are you?"

"We are heading back from East Hampton for the third time. I think that Charlotte is going to strangle us if we turn around again." Elizabeth heard the voices of her friends in the background and laughed. Darcy looked up and smiled.

"Should I try?"

"Sure, you know it better than I do. Lisa, William is going to try and talk you here." She handed the phone over to him.

"Hi, Lisa? Do you see a sign for the East Hampton Farmer's Market? It would be on the right."

Lisa did not respond for a few seconds, hearing his velvety soft voice in her ear. "Uh, yeah, Farmer's Market sign; got it."

"Okay, now just go past that and on the left you should see a small green sign near a dirt road, kind of going into the trees, it has the number 31 on it. Turn in there."

She repeated the directions to her husband and the rest of the group spotted it. "Okay, we're turning."

"Just follow the road, and go through the gate. Lizzy and I are on the lawn waiting for you." He handed the phone back to her and smiled.

"Lisa?"

"Oh good Lord, Lizzy . . ."

Elizabeth laughed and she saw the car coming around the bend. She put the phone away and they met her friends as they exited. "Hi! Everyone, this is

William Darcy, my husband-to-be, Will, this is Lisa and Joe Smith, Maria Lucas, you know Charlotte, and Adam Fox."

"Hi." He said softly and smiled a little, then felt her hand squeeze his. Lisa threw her arms around Elizabeth and hugged her, whispering in her ear urgently, then giving him the eye, grabbed his face and kissed him.

"You are GORGEOUS!" Startled, he fell back a step. Joe took her hand to pull her back and rolled his eyes, then held out his hand to Darcy.

"Sorry about that, she's rather . . . effusive." He smiled then leaned over. "Close your mouth, dear."

"I'm sorry." She sighed then grinned. "I am just delighted that Prince Charming has swept Cinderella off her feet."

"Thanks." He said and looked down, then taking a breath, turned to face more women who were staring at him in adoration. He looked away and saw that Adam was in the process of hugging Elizabeth very tightly and smiling warmly in her eyes. He scowled and moved closer. "Lizzy, shall we bring our guests inside?" He captured her hand and drew her to his side.

She winked at Adam and he laughed, holding out his hand. "Don't worry, I've had years worth of chances with her and never made a serious move. She's all yours."

"I never doubted that." He said softly and kissed her gently.

"Awwwww!" Came a chorus of female voices. Darcy and Elizabeth turned to examine the ladies and they started to laugh. Elizabeth took them off on a tour, and Darcy led the men out onto the patio, offering them beers and seats in the sun. He struggled to make conversation with the two strangers and was relieved when Joe broke the ice.

"I can't tell you how happy I am for Elizabeth." He smiled and sat next to Darcy. "I hardly recognize her."

"Have you known her for long? You're not a writer, are you?"

"No, just the tag-along husband. I'm an English professor at Pepperdine; so I'm free in the summer to go along to her book events." He smiled. "I'm pretty protective of my very friendly Lisa, so I just accompany her at the conventions and make sure that everyone knows she is taken." Joe tipped the bottle up and took a sip. "I'm sure that you understand the impulse."

"I'm beginning to." He glanced at Adam who turned away from the railing and the view.

"Oh, when I met Elizabeth she was eighteen, scared to death of her shadow and her dad was with her. I didn't really hear the details of that bastard she was with until she was out of school, but we all knew that something was very wrong. We got her pretty toasted one night and it all poured out. I always felt pretty protective of her, being so young and kind of having been there myself a few years earlier, and was glad that her dad came with her to the conventions instead of that . . . well; maybe it would have been better. That is one guy I wouldn't mind beating up." He lifted his bottle to Darcy. "I understand that you had something to do with taking him down."

"I wanted to throw him through a window but opted for humiliation." Darcy looked at Adam with a kinder eye. "Elizabeth speaks very fondly of you."

"That's nice to know." He smiled and took a seat.

"Why didn't you ever . . ."

"Because the girl you have is not the one I knew. She has changed over the past couple of years since she graduated . . ." Joe nodded. "But it wasn't until she met you that she transformed. Believe me, if she walked into the convention with the glow she has now and was unattached, I wouldn't have been the only guy begging her for a taste." Darcy's brow furrowed, and Adam shrugged while Joe snorted. "Hookups happen, not that I would have been after just an affair, I would have tried for the real thing. I know how special she is, and you better know it, too. Don't ever take her for granted, she doesn't have a big brother, so I guess I'm going to claim the honor. It just wasn't in the cards for me; you are the lucky bastard that gets to marry her, you are the one that found the way to her heart. We are just friends and always will be." He smiled and Darcy studied him intently, processing all that was said.

"I want to know what she was like during those years." Darcy sat forward and regarded the men seriously. "Could you tell me?" Joe and Adam looked at each and drew their chairs closer, and enlightened Darcy about the lost years of Elizabeth's life.

"OHHHH, ohhhh, ohhhhhh, oh Willlll, oh don't, don't stop, ohhhhhhh."

"More, baby?" He grunted.

"ohhhhhhhhh, yes, yes, Oh Will, YES!!!"

The bed shook as Darcy grabbed Elizabeth's legs, spreading them wide, and drove into her like a battering ram. "You like it hard, don't you?"

"Ohhhhh, please, please don't stop." She begged as she raked her hands down his back, then cried out as she rode the crest once again. He fell on top of her, still thrusting relentlessly while her body shook and trembled beneath him. She gasped and he pulled her face up to kiss her deeply. "Look at me!" He growled. Elizabeth opened her eyes and she saw William's intense expression. "I LOVE YOU. I want you to feel it, I want you to know it; I want you to ooze with my seed all night. I'm going to fill you up so many times, baby, you'll never be empty." Suddenly he cried out as his orgasm ripped through his body. He shook and cried her name, then fell on her, gathering up her limp form into his arms and covering her with kisses. They curled together and fought to breathe. "Just give me a minute honey, and we'll get back to work."

"What has come over you?" Elizabeth swallowed and kissed his sweaty brow.

"I love you." He smiled as he tried to breathe slower, and caressed her damp hair gently. "I love you and I want you to feel the depth of my passion."

"I do, I did." She laughed and kissed him.

Darcy relaxed and nuzzled his lips against her ear. "Do you want me again, honey?"

"What a question!"

"I haven't hurt you?" He asked softly.

"No, not at all, you . . . you blow my mind. Oh Will, I love you." She laughed and he smiled widely to hear her affirmation, then took her hand to place on his groin. "Do you feel that?"

"It seems to be growing again." She raised her brow and caressed the sticky, well-used shaft.

"I'm serious, Lizzy; I want you so full that it flows into your shoes all day." His fingers ran between her legs and he thrust them inside of her warm swollen lips, then drew them out to examine the mixture of his thick fluid and her clear essence. "No, not enough, not nearly enough."

"How will you know when I'm properly saturated? I don't have a dipstick." She laughed and he offered his finger to her to taste.

Darcy watched her tongue glide over his fingers and shuddered. "I'll know, honey, trust me, I'll know, I'm your dipstick." He leaned down to taste their passion from her tongue then slid back inside of her. "ohhhhh you just get tighter and tighter, the more we make love." He looked into her eyes. "How do you do that?"

Elizabeth smiled and squeezed him hard and he gasped. "I exercise."

"Damn, I am a lucky man!" His wet, open mouth fell onto hers, and this time the passion was slow and gentle, but no less fulfilling. They made love repeatedly that night. It wasn't a desire to stop that ended the loving, but the passage of time. It was Friday morning, and the family was on its way. Elizabeth awoke, curled up in a ball against William's chest. His arms were firmly around her, even in his deep sleep he would not let her go. She was exactly as he wished, sweaty, sticky, exhausted and so fulfilled. Her belly and legs ached, her lips were raw, her hair a matted mess, and she wouldn't have given up that night for the world. Gently she caressed his sleeping face and his lips kissed her fingers. William murmured something incomprehensible and it was followed by a smile and the whisper, "my lizzy."

What will the wedding night be like? She smiled and slid out of his arms and off the bed. Drawing the covers over him she stood up and looked down at her legs. A slow stream of semen ran down, and she looked up to find his blue eyes watching its progress. "Are you pleased?"

"I'm just going to have to resupply you." He smiled with satisfaction. "Come back to bed."

"I think that I need to take a shower and get ready for our guests." She ducked away from the hand that was reaching for her and laughed at the disappointment in his eyes. "You really must tell me what inspired such passion."

He settled into the pillow and watched her cross the room with pleasure. "So that you can encourage it to reoccur or stop it from happening again?"

"What do you think?" She turned and put her hands on her hips.

He sat up and lifted the covers from his groin, exposing yet another erection. "Let's see what you do with this, then I'll know."

"Will, you are a machine!" He stood up and pushed her into the bathroom, closing the door and turning on the shower. He picked her up and pressed her against the shower wall, then slid inside once again. "Ohhhh." Elizabeth closed her eyes as her legs wrapped around his waist.

"I think that I have my answer."

BY THREE O'CLOCK the tent and small dance floor had been erected on the lawn, Miss Maggie had arrived and was gleefully ordering about the staff, and Jerry was preparing dinner for the influx of guests. Elizabeth and Darcy were relaxing in the lounge chairs on the patio, holding hands and shooting smiles at each other.

"How do you feel?" He bit his lip and tilted his head.

"Wonderful." She giggled and brushed his hand with her fingers. "I have a feeling that I'll be walking like an old cowboy for a few days."

"I guess that we can't blame the horses since we didn't have them brought out this time." He laughed and played with her fingers. "I feel so good." Sighing, he smiled and looked down at his lap. "I'm aching but . . . wow, I feel good."

"I am so impressed with your prowess." Elizabeth whispered.

Darcy blushed. "Me too, to be honest with you."

She laughed as he blushed again and looked down. "So maybe sleeping separately tonight would be a good thing?"

Slowly he shook his head. "I can't imagine anything at all good about that. We don't have to make love; we can just sleep and hold each other."

Elizabeth was about to answer when they heard the sound of cars entering the driveway. "It seems our guests have arrived." She stood up and offered her hands out to him. "Come on, Will."

He sat back and studied her seriously. "You haven't answered my suggestion."

"You'll hear it tonight." Elizabeth smiled, then laughed at his frown. "Come on sweetie." Taking her hands he stood and hugged her.

"I will be waiting for your reply." He whispered softly in her ear.

"That's not fair."

"What?"

"Having that beautiful voice. You know that my toes curl when you whisper like that." She sighed and he whispered a few more truths into her ear before the door opened and a maid informed them that their guests had arrived.

"I believe that I will continue this frequently for the rest of the day." He smirked at her dreamy expression and taking her hand walked into the house. Inside they found the entire Bennet family, with the addition of Georgiana and John. "Welcome to Pemberley."

"Oh William, I thought that the house in town was beautiful, but this . . ." Fran looked around with wide eyes and Tom stepped in.

"Yes, who knew what was hidden beyond that dirt road." He smiled and tilted his head. "You two look particularly relaxed for a couple about to embark on marriage. Have you been enjoying the atmosphere?"

"Very much, sir." Darcy smiled and kissed Elizabeth's cheek while she blushed. "Let's get you all settled."

"I'll take care of that." Elizabeth signaled the family and led the parade upstairs. John watched them go, smiling at Jane's backwards glance and turned to his cousin.

"So, you look like the cat that swallowed the canary. What have you been up to?"

"Absolutely nothing that I will share with you." Darcy stared at him pointedly. John laughed and clapped his back.

"I suggest that you work on that grin then before Richard sees you." They walked outside and leaned on the railing. "I hear that you are not pleased with the idea of a bachelor's party."

"No, not at all, and Elizabeth was even less pleased, if that is possible. I don't need that! Who came up with that idea, as if I didn't know?"

"Richard, of course." John shook his head. "Charles was all for it. Those two are a lot alike."

"I recently pointed that out to Charles. I'm surprised with him for thinking I would appreciate such a night."

"I think that plane crash made him think about living in the moment." John glanced up from where he was leaning on the railing. "How are you with all of that?"

"Okay." Darcy looked down. "God, I was scared."

"I bet. I have no doubt that your thoughts were very much with your parents when you saw those flames." John said quietly. Darcy said nothing. "I remember the torment you experienced then, William."

Darcy looked up in surprise to hear John use his name. He clasped his arm, and took a breath. "I guess that I was not as scared for me so much as for . . . well, for Elizabeth. I can't bear the thought of her being alone." He looked up and saw John studying him. "Georgiana has your parents and her trust fund and well, if I had died Sunday she would have had everything. Elizabeth would have . . . had my ring and nothing else."

"She's not in it for the money, I thought."

"That's not what I meant. She would have been . . ." He sighed. "Never mind."

"Alone."

"yeah." He said softly.

"I have a feeling that the two of you won't be wasting time worrying over inconsequential things. You're going to make the most of your lives." John said quietly.

Darcy looked up at him. "I think that you are exactly right." He smiled and shook off the conversation. "Speaking of making the most of your life, how are things with Jane?"

"Fine, we talk on the phone a lot, this is actually the first we have seen of each other since Sunday. It was a nice drive, but with Georgiana in the car, the conversation was . . . chaste." He grinned and Darcy laughed. "I'm feeling better and better about my decision not to run."

"And your dad?"

"He'll live." John smiled. "I was wondering; can you give me some pointers on romance?"

Darcy's eyes lit up. "Are you through your repertoire of ideas already? You are a sad case."

"I knew I shouldn't have asked." He sighed.

"Take her dancing." Darcy nodded. "Tomorrow we will dance, ask her then, but when you get back to the city, go out."

"I'm no . . . I don't even know any dancers . . . . I never took lessons."

"Sure you did." Darcy grinned. "You were at the same lessons I was forced to take."

"Well clearly I retained none of it." John laughed. Elizabeth appeared with Jane and Darcy immediately took her hand, and with a casual pull, she suddenly spun into his arms. Elizabeth laughed and he looked into her eyes while they moved in the pattern of a simple box step then stopped, looking expectantly at John.

"Try it."

"What?"

"You have a partner, try it!" He smiled at Jane. "You know how to dance, don't you?"

"Well, yes, it's been a long time . . ."

"Elizabeth was excellent the first time we danced and we have just become better with practice." He fixed his eyes on John's. "You asked me a question. *This* is my answer. Now do it!"

Blushing, John approached Jane. "It seems the groom will not be denied."

She was equally red. "I have a feeling that the bride won't be either." Elizabeth walked over, placed John's hand on Jane's waist, clasped their other hands together, took her sister's hips in her hands and pushed her closer to him, then stepped back.

"Move!"

"There's no music!"

Elizabeth sighed. "Details, details."

Darcy smiled and began to sing,

"L is for the way you look at me.

O is for the only one I see.

V is very, very extraordinary.

E is even more than anyone that you adore, can

Love is all that I can give to you.

Love is more than just a game for two.

Two in love can make it, take my heart and please don't break it.

Love was made for me and you.[vii]"

He spun Elizabeth away, and their hands clasped, dancing out to the music in their imaginations while Jane and John held onto each other and swayed in place, watching them in amazement, when suddenly the instrumental part of the song must have ended as the couple began singing the lyrics over again, finishing with a twirl and laughing as they embraced. Darcy leaned down and kissed Elizabeth. "I love you."

"I love you, Will." They looked over to Jane and John.

"Do you get it?" Darcy asked.

"Who the hell are you?" John demanded.

"Now you know why I don't want a bachelor party!" Darcy looked up to see the rest of the family at the doorway, and blushed, retreating back into his shyness. "Caught."

"It's okay, Will. You realize though that my sisters might demand a dance from you tomorrow." Elizabeth held his hand and they waved everyone outside. "Are your rooms okay?"

"Beautiful! What a view!" Lydia exclaimed. "Can we go out on the beach?"

"You can do whatever you want. Dinner is in about three hours so go ahead and explore." She pointed, "There's the walkway to the beach."

"Come on, I'll show you the way." Georgiana ran ahead, followed closely by Lydia and Kitty. Everyone else took chairs and Elizabeth poured out ice tea while Darcy grabbed some beers for John and Tom.

"Is anyone else coming tonight?" Tom asked as he sipped.

"Charles should be here soon. He was going to fly out. He'll be driving my car back to the city for me on Sunday." Darcy smiled. "I have, of course, threatened him with unemployment if he so much as scratches it." Tom laughed while John frowned.

"Why is he staying here, again?"

"Because he is my friend and best man." Darcy met his eye and held it.

"Are your parents coming over, John?" Jane asked quietly, breaking the glare between the men.

"Um, no, they figured they'd see everyone tomorrow, and . . . they are entertaining Anne, Greg and Catherine."

"Lucky them." Elizabeth said softly. Everyone looked over to her. "Catherine." They all smiled. "Is she coming?"

"I called her, and asked that she promise to be pleasant or to stay away. She was offended and said that she would not hold her tongue so I rescinded her invitation." Darcy took Elizabeth's hand. "I will not tolerate anyone treating you so poorly."

"I think that she did a magnificent job." John laughed. "Telling her there was no prenup was brilliant!" Darcy's eyes grew wide as did Elizabeth and Jane's. John noticed the change and saw the Bennets staring at each other.

"Prenup! Oh, William, surely you didn't make Elizabeth sign such a thing!" She turned to Elizabeth whose eyes had closed. "What is in it?"

"It's not open for discussion, Mom." She said quietly, and looked to her father who was moving his eyes between the couple. He noticed how their hands had instantly come together.

"I agree; that is their business, Fran, not ours." Darcy's eyes were closed and he looked up at Tom's words.

"It is something that will never be needed."

"I'm sure." Tom smiled and looked over to Fran. "We certainly never would have used ours."

She laughed. "I believe that as much as I believe you would pass up a trip to the bookstore." Jane and Elizabeth exchanged glances and saw their father smile at her and laugh.

"Of course not, you two bicker but you never would get divorced, that is clear as day." Mary spoke up from where she sat in the shade, quietly perusing a book she had brought along. She noticed her sisters' stares. "Well surely you two know that!"

The sound of a helicopter overhead interrupted their response and they watched as it settled on the lawn. Charles appeared, grabbing his suitcase and ducking under the blades. "Hi!" He came around the back of the house. Darcy made the introductions.

"Let me take you to your room." Elizabeth stood and guided him inside. John watched Jane and she looked down.

"Are you okay with this?"

"Yes." She smiled at him. "I am." He nodded and they heard another car pull in. Soon they were joined by Charlotte and Maria.

"Where are Lisa and Joe?" Darcy asked as he handed them drinks.

"They are making use of the spa." Charlotte informed them, and made an appraising examination of John. "They are also hoping to make use of the romantic atmosphere this evening." The group laughed and Elizabeth reappeared with Charles.

"Oh hi everyone, this is Charles Bingley, let's see, who don't you know, oh probably just Charlotte and Maria Lucas."

Charles beamed and shook their hands, pausing a moment to smile warmly at Maria. "You look familiar."

"I was going to say the same thing." She studied him carefully. "Do you jog in Central Park?"

"Yes! That's it, I always see you around the Shakespeare Garden."

"That's the closest you'll ever get to Shakespeare." Darcy jabbed.

"Thanks a lot. Now she thinks I'm a dolt." Charles glared.

"Hey, I jog by there, that doesn't mean I read it either!" She laughed and he grinned. "Do you live nearby?"

"I have an apartment on Central Park West."

"Wow." She looked him over. "Rich guy, cool." Charles chuckled. "I'm a lowly website designer."

"Ah, poor girl, cool." He took a seat next to her. "Tell me all about this job of yours."

"Why?"

He shrugged. "I'm curious." Maria happily launched into a description of her work, laughing as she described her clients and their ridiculous demands. Charles would jump in describing clients he dealt with and they found similarities in the personalities they came across. Jane watched the conversation in fascination and bent to Elizabeth.

"Not once did he ever ask me about my work, or try to find anything in common with me."

"Are you disappointed?" Elizabeth whispered back.

"No, I'm just wondering what changed in him or if it was just that we were never really a good match to begin with." Jane looked at him curiously and watched as he stood up to pour Maria some more tea and bring it back. Maria was speaking just as enthusiastically as he was. "I could never keep up with his conversation either."

"It's all over the place." Darcy said softly. "It takes some getting used to, but I find it refreshing compared to mine."

"Which is so dull." John pointed out with a smile. He took Jane's hand and held it. "So tell me, do I have to work to get your eyes back on me all weekend? Do I need to sneak back here tonight and stand sentry at your door?"

Jane laughed and blushed. "I think that you are safe."

"Good." He smiled and stood up. "Let's go take a walk on the beach." He glanced at Darcy and Elizabeth, who were leaning against each other on a glider. "Maybe we can practice dancing without music."

"There's hope for him, yet." Darcy observed.

"Well he's learning from the master." Elizabeth whispered in his ear.

He smiled and pressed his ear closer to her lips. "You know you make my toes curl when you whisper to me." Darcy said softly and feeling her sigh turned to whisper in hers. "Please don't leave me alone tonight."

Their fingers entwined as their eyes met, and she smiled.

Chapter 15

"So what brings you down here, all alone?" Tom leaned on the doorframe to the library and watched Elizabeth typing a scene in her story.

"I . . . I couldn't sleep." She looked up and smiled a little then returned to her work.

Tom moved into the room and sat down on the leather sofa across from Darcy's desk. He knew the frenetic activity of his daughter very well. When an idea struck, she had to get it down before she lost it. He also knew enough not to interrupt her. So he watched until the thought was purged and she stopped. Elizabeth hit the save button and relaxed, closing her eyes. "Has William ever experienced you in the throes of an idea?" He smiled.

"Oh yes, but he's almost always at work when I'm writing. You know how I need quiet to be creative." She saw his brows move up and tilted her head. "What are you thinking?"

"I'm wondering what really drove you out of your bed." He patted the sofa and she turned off the computer and came to sit by his side. "Are you scared, Lizzy?"

"No . . . yes . . . I don't know how to describe it. I just want to be everything that he needs." She admitted.

"Ah." Tom put his arm around her and kissed the top of her head while she curled up next to him. He felt, rather than heard her crying. "Lizzy, you are about to embark on the most important journey of your life, and it is only natural to be apprehensive."

"But I'm not!" She sniffed and touched the wet patch she had left on his shirt. "I'm not afraid to marry him, not at all."

"I didn't say that. I spoke of the journey. Marriage is not romance and smiles all of the time." He looked at her and nodded. "Surely you know that living with your mother and myself."

"I don't understand you and Mom. You speak angrily about her, your bitterness over the marriage is very clear, and yet Mary thinks that it's almost like playacting. What is it?"

"I suppose it is both. You were the unfortunate child who heard my frustrations; I never should have vented them upon you. Mary's perspective is based purely on her observations. I guess that is the burden you received by being my favorite child." He saw Elizabeth required details and he continued. "I was saddled with a family at a very young age, and although I love my girls, it still was the end of a dream. I had to work to support you all, which meant I could not go study or get the degree I wanted. By the time your grandparents died and I was able to make a good income managing the buildings we own, I was struggling to make ends meet. Every new pregnancy was another drain on our finances, and a further reminder of the possible life I had lost." He smiled and gave her a hug.

"The irony is that if I had sold the buildings, we would have had millions, but that would have been gone so quickly. I chose to be property rich and cash poor."

"Why didn't you use birth control when you started to really feel the burden of having children?"

"We did." He said and smiled. "Well, not with Jane, and obviously not as conscientiously as we should. Your mom never remembered that the pills had to be taken every day, and it took Lydia's birth for me to finally face the fact that I would have to get a vasectomy. That seems to be a typical problem of mine, to just ignore sensible courses of action, however, I wouldn't give up any of you girls."

Elizabeth continued analyzing what he had said. "So you were bitter over your lost life and Mom . . ."

"Dealt with being at home with five babies in seven years by being . . . what you know."

"I don't see William and me falling into that sort of agony, Dad. We've both already realized our professional goals, and are actually stepping back from them in some ways. Income is obviously not a problem. Our demons are of a personal nature." Elizabeth continued quietly, "I know that it won't constantly be romance and smiles, but I hope that we will work together to preserve the joy we feel with each other."

"With that attitude I'm sure that you will succeed. I can't really offer you any advice, Lizzy. Already you are so far ahead of the marriage I've had with your mother for twenty-five years. We should be looking to you and William." He spoke soberly. "I am so sorry that none of us ever recognized what was happening with you and Bill Collins, or Lydia's troubles for that matter. I wish that you could have talked to me about it."

"I didn't talk to anyone for a very long time, Dad." Elizabeth said quietly. "It was easier to just come home and feel safe again for a little while. I don't want to talk about it now."

He nodded. "Okay, so tell me, are you scared about the wedding?"

"No." Elizabeth smiled. "No, all I want to do is love him."

"You already do." Tom kissed her cheek and stood up. "I'm going back to bed. I hope that the bride does soon."

"I will." She stayed on the sofa and watched him go.

Tom stepped out into the hallway, then walked into the shadows where Darcy stood. "Did you listen to her?"

"Yes . . . I missed her and came looking. She loves me." He smiled and looked down at his feet. "I want to preserve this joy we share, too."

"Good, don't squander your marriage as I did. I shared a home and a family with Fran, but I have never lived with her." He clasped Darcy's shoulder. "Enjoy every moment, Son. And don't do as I did. Don't avoid difficult conversations. That leads to a silent angry home."

"I understand." Darcy watched him walk away and entered the library. Elizabeth was hugging a pillow and her eyes were closed. He sat down and embraced her. "I missed you."

"I knew you would come." She nestled into him. "I guess that you heard it all."

"I did. *Are* you scared?"

"Not of you. I'm sure of you."

"Well, I am sure of you. I guess that neither of us expected to be marrying three months ago, did we?" He smiled to see her lips curve up. "I'm scared." He admitted, speaking into her hair.

Elizabeth hugged him. "Of what?"

"I don't know how to be a husband. I'm afraid that I will fail you somehow."

"I don't know how to be a wife, either." She reminded him.

"Do you think that we are marrying too soon?" He looked down and met her eyes. "Be honest."

"I don't think that I could learn anything else about you that I don't already know, Will. Perhaps I might know things in greater detail, things of your past or your behaviors, but I think that you have revealed to me your essentials, and those are of a good man, whether it be in relation to your family, your business, or me. More time with you would not change that fact." She smiled and saw his expression had not changed. "What is it?"

"Do you remember when we made love . . . all night?"

"It is indelibly imprinted on my mind, especially since we are both just able to walk normally again, and haven't even thought about making love since." She laughed and saw him blush. "What is it, honey?"

"You asked me that morning what had gotten into me." He said softly. "I never answered you properly."

"Yes?" Elizabeth grew concerned and caressed his face.

"When you were giving the ladies a tour of the house, Adam and Joe were telling me about you . . . Everything that you ever told them about Collins." She gasped. "Adam was warning me never to hurt you or I would face his wrath . . . And I asked them to tell me what they knew." He drew breath. "I was determined that I was going to spend that night making it very clear to you how much I love you. I didn't want you to have any doubt in your mind about my feelings."

"What did they tell you?" She whispered.

"They told me that you were not allowed to speak without his permission." She nodded. "He chose your clothes; how to wear your hair, when you could wake, all of his rules . . . Joe said that Lisa told him about his demands in the bedroom." He held her tightly. "They feel that you were brainwashed and thought that he could do no wrong, at least for the first few years, then as you grew more successful with your writing, and received the praise of the outside world, he became increasingly jealous and controlling just as you were beginning to consider breaking free. They wished that they had known what was wrong, they would have tried to help." He kissed her forehead. "They thought that you were too frightened to seek help until you graduated and that it took you months to shake the fear that he would return to your home. Adam said that he would have loved to have known the woman you are now, but . . . that you didn't appear until we met."

"That is true." She drew a breath and spoke. "I felt a little more like myself with each passing week after I broke up with him, but I was numb for a long time. I woke up when . . . I saw you. Something just told me that I needed to speak to you."

"So . . . I really am the person you need." Darcy said quietly. "Nobody else has . . ."

"Filled the role as my love." Elizabeth hugged him tightly. "You succeeded long ago, Will. I knew that you loved me. You didn't need to demonstrate it so . . . physically, but I know that is a night that I will treasure forever. I thought that the plane crash was behind your fervency." She saw his eyes widen in surprise, then agreement. "I am sure that someday when we try to recreate the evening, we will wonder what on earth we were thinking and how it was ever possible." He chuckled and kissed her. "I'm glad that they told you those things, I don't know that I would have spoken of them any more than you would want to tell me the details of your past. It is our past, Will. Today is the beginning of our future."

"So . . . will you meet me at the altar in . . . twelve hours?" He smiled as her eyes lit up.

"Yes, I will!"

"May I give you a wedding gift now?"

"What?" She watched him move to his desk and unlock a drawer. From within he removed a shoe box and brought it over to her.

"You probably have something better picked out, but I saw these and couldn't resist." He placed the box in her lap.

"You went shopping?" Elizabeth laughed as she lifted the lid and cooed. "Ohhhhhhh. Jimmy Choos!"

"Well, I thought of our first wedding, when we met, and buying you those shoes seemed to bring us good luck." He smiled. "I thought of glass slippers for my Cinderella, but. . . "

"This is far more practical." Elizabeth slipped them on and stood, modeling them for him. "What do you think?"

"Beautiful." He smiled and stood up to hug her. "I can't wait to see the rest of the ensemble."

"Soon enough, sweetie." She leaned into his arms and they swayed, while he softly sang. "The more I see you, the more I want you. Somehow this feeling just grows and grows. With every sigh I become more mad about you, more lost without you, And so it goes. Can you imagine, how much I'll love you,the more I see you as years go by? I know the only one for me can only be you. My arms won't free you. my heart won't try[viii]"

Darcy murmured the last words against her lips and they kissed. "Nobody else knows that I listen to all of these love songs. I think that if someone finds my ipod, I'll claim it is yours." He smiled into her dancing eyes. "You'll probably have me watching chick flicks soon."

"I can watch a good drama as easily as anyone. Just please don't make me watch mobster movies."

He laughed. "You just don't get *The Godfather*, do you?"

Elizabeth rolled her eyes. "No, and I don't intend to."

"It's just a nice family movie." He grinned at her sigh and putting his arm around her shoulders, they started walking up the stairs. "Let's get a little more sleep. We have a big day ahead."

"What are the boys going to do with you this morning?" She giggled as he groaned.

"I'm afraid to find out. They were denied their party, so I'm sure it won't be kind."

"GOLF?" Darcy said in disbelief. "We're going to play golf all morning?"

"Yes, so hurry up and finish eating. We have tee times reserved and they start at nine." Charles grinned and pushed the plate closer to him.

"I don't know that I want to play." He said petulantly.

"If I can be up this morning after staying out late, you can be, too. You're just pissed that I rousted you out of that nice bed with Elizabeth." He laughed to see the anger appear in Darcy's expression as he remembered that fact.

Darcy glared. "Pounding on the door and yelling for me to move my ass or you would come in after me was not exactly the way I wanted to wake up."

"You have the rest of your life to wake up differently." Richard speared a piece of sausage off of his plate. "If you're not going to eat this, I will."

"Hey!" Darcy grabbed his plate back.

"Well are you finished?" John leaned back in his chair and stretched. "Let's get going. I have some new clubs to try out."

"Who else is coming?" David asked from behind his paper.

"All of the men. That's what's so nice about this small wedding, everyone can participate. We're meeting up at the club. You got the guest passes, right?" John looked at Richard.

"Yes, it saved me from spending more time with Aunt Catherine last night. She had a head of steam going when I got here. She's still furious that she was excluded from the wedding." He looked at his father. "Are you sure that she won't show up today?"

David put down the paper and took a swig of coffee. "I hope not. Anne was going to tell her driver to take the day off. If she wants to come to Pemberley, she'll have to walk. There aren't any cabs out here."

"Knowing her she'd order the gardener to drive her in his truck." Richard grinned and looked at Darcy. "I think you'll be safe."

"I'll just let Elizabeth take care of it. She handled her very well last time. I'm afraid that I'd be moved to throw her in the pool." He finished the last bite of his eggs and wiped his mouth. "Okay, since you are determined to occupy my supposedly nervous mind, let's go."

"DID YOU SLEEP last night?" Jane clucked and looked at Elizabeth's eyes. "I knew you should have slept with me."

"I'm fine. I doubt that I would have done any better in bed with you." She sighed and stared at her reflection. "Why didn't we just get married in Vegas?"

"Because you wanted your family around you." Jane said automatically.

"Uh-oh, I hear the wedding planner voice coming out." Elizabeth smiled at Jane's reflection and saw her startled reaction. "There is no need to placate me all day, I'm happy."

"I guess I'm just used to making comforting noises." Jane smiled and heard a screech outside. They went to the window and saw a large barbeque being set up. "They do start cooking early."

"I think that it's been going for a few hours already, they just finish up here." They watched as the smoker was anchored down, and a waft of smoke drifted over the lawn and up to the window. Elizabeth breathed deeply. "Ahhhhh."

Jane laughed and disappeared from the room and returned carrying the wedding gown. "Well at least William didn't see this before he left. Let's try it on and make sure those alterations are right."

"I think that if they aren't it is far too late." Elizabeth slipped it on then brought out her new shoes.

"Those aren't the shoes . . . oh Lizzy, when did you get those?" Jane stared.

"William gave them to me at about three this morning." She laughed and pointed her toe. "They are so much nicer than the ones I picked out."

"You would have gone to the bargain bin at a flea market." Lydia said as she walked in. "What a pretty dress!"

"And it was only $450.00!" Elizabeth crowed.

"Only you would buy a cheap dress when you are marrying a billionaire." Kitty joined her and sat on the bed. "I would have gone for a Vera Wang."

"And then do what with it? I might be able to recycle this sometime." Elizabeth heard her sisters groaning in the background. "Okay, it's coming off now. What are we doing to occupy me this morning?"

"We are having your bridal shower." Jane announced.

"Miss Maggie is in charge of the games." Georgiana grinned. "I'm afraid they will be a little risqué." The girls all began speculating on what the old woman could have planned.

"There's nothing like waiting for the last minute, is there?" Elizabeth laughed and they separated, agreeing to meet in the sun room for the combination shower and breakfast when the rest of the ladies and the photographer arrived.

An hour later the party was underway. "This is a first for me." Arlene said softly to Anne. They were sharing a sofa and watching Elizabeth, her family and friends, laughing, playing silly, somewhat questionable games, decorating her with ribbons from their gifts, and making bold suggestions for the wedding night. "I feel distinctly out of place, it is disconcerting."

"Really?" Anne looked her over with surprise. "I was feeling the same way. It's as if we don't fit in here at all." She watched Elizabeth hug Georgiana and how her cousin glowed after receiving the affection. "This is certainly not the wedding of anyone I know."

"I knew that William was never entirely comfortable in society so a small affair isn't too surprising." Arlene noticed Anne's smile. "Well, that is no secret; he really isn't comfortable anywhere is he?"

"He is with Elizabeth." She watched as the bride opened a box and brought out what appeared to be a sock knitted in the shape of a penis. Elizabeth blushed as she quickly hid it away, and Lisa crowed with triumph, declaring it a brilliant way to keep important equipment warm and protected. "Oh, what will he think of these gifts!"

"I have a feeling that he just might be very pleased with them in the privacy of their home." Arlene laughed. "Did you know that they are planning to take little weekend driving trips? It reminds me of the campaigning David and I used to do, visiting all the little towns; it was a very memorable time, especially early in our marriage." She smiled to herself and noticed Anne's curious look. "You know, too many of our friends don't see anything of the world beyond their airplane windows or chauffer-driven cars. I think that William will get to enjoy his life in a very unexpected way with Elizabeth. I envy them."

Elizabeth looked up at that moment and smiled at them. "Arlene, Anne, please rescue me!"

"No Elizabeth, you invited them, you have to be a gracious hostess." Arlene called.

"Oh fine, thanks a lot." She laughed and looked at the clock. "Isn't it time to start making me beautiful for my groom?"

DARCY TEED UP his ball and looking down the fairway, concentrated on where he wanted it to land, drew back and swung. Richard whistled. "When was the last time you played?" He watched as the ball landed perfectly in the middle, directly in line for the next easy shot onto the green. Darcy put his club back in the bag and the walked off to the golf cart. The two cousins were the last ones on the course.

"I don't know, it's been at least since that company golf outing I attended in April." They drove off to the bunker where Richard's ball had rolled. "How about you?"

"Um, last weekend." He looked down sheepishly. "Practice doesn't make perfect, I guess."

"Maybe spending the night out with Charles didn't help your game either." He leaned against the cart and watched him lining up the shot. "Where did you go since the surprise party was cancelled?"

"We went to the resort where the Lucas sisters are staying." He smiled and then hit his ball; swearing when it struck the lip of the bunker and watched it roll back down to his feet.

"Oh? And?"

"Charlotte is a piece of work." He took another stroke and grinned to see the ball escape, only to roll into another bunker on the other side. Richard groaned and glared at Darcy who was laughing. "She told me that my sense of humor was pitiful."

"Did she?" Darcy raised his brow and they drove to his ball, where he made another perfect stroke, the ball landing on the edge of the green, and rolling back to rest on the lip of the cup. "Almost." He said softly, calculating his error and making note of what he should have done to assure the eagle. Darcy looked up to see Richard's sour expression. "Hey, you chose the game, not me." They climbed back in the cart. "So, Charlotte saw through you?"

"I guess that she did." He stood at the next bunker and sighed. "Anyway, I liked it. She's a no-nonsense woman, and it's really refreshing to be able to drop the act."

"So it is an act?"

"You should know that more than anyone. How many times do you hide behind a mask so nobody knows what you're thinking?"

"Regularly." Darcy admitted. "I suspected the same from you; nobody can be as jovial as you appear all of the time."

"Hmm, I am, I don't know, I guess that I'm still dealing with what I saw in the war in a way." He smiled. "Living in the moment."

"That's how John described Charles to me, especially after the plane crash."

"Yes, we had a chance to talk about it this week when we were planning your bachelor party. I guess that was more for us than you."

"No kidding." Darcy handed him a club. "Try this."

Richard hit the ball and it landed on the green. "Thanks!" He smiled and climbed back out of the sand, and raked it smooth. "I think that Charles and I are very similar in some ways. He's perhaps more in need of direction, but essentially we are two affable guys who are looking for a chance to settle down."

"And how do the Lucas sisters fit into all this?" Darcy smiled as they drove up to the green.

Richard smiled slowly. "I don't know, but I like Charlotte, Charles likes Maria, they seem to tolerate us, so maybe there is something in that. We'll see."

"Good luck with that Richard, I really hope that something comes of it." Darcy knocked the ball in the hole and grinned. "Okay, I win. Can I go get married now?"

"ELIZABETH, your aunt and uncle have arrived." Georgiana announced and poked her head in the door to the master bedroom. "Oh, that looks so nice, Kitty!"

"Thanks!" She stood back to look over her handiwork. "I've been practicing for a while." The photographer stepped up to snap a picture and Elizabeth turned to him.

"I know that you are just doing your job, but please do not try to pose us in some convoluted symbolic stances, you know, me staring wistfully at my dress, or I don't know, I saw one with a picture of the bride walking away from the groom and him staring at her . . . All I want is the group photos of the families and then lots of candid shots. Oh, and I guess cutting the cake and things like that. Okay?"

"Whatever you would like is fine, it's your day." He smiled and switched to a different camera. "Now, how about one of you and your sister looking into the mirror and examining your hair?"

Elizabeth glanced at Jane, who smiled. "Come on Mike, the bride needs a break. Let's go take pictures of the guests as they arrive."

Kitty giggled. "He didn't hear a word you said, did he?"

"I'm afraid not." Elizabeth sighed. "Oh, which aunt and uncle have arrived?"

"Ray and Shirley." Lydia came in and leaned on the door, waving dry the freshly applied polish on her nails. "Dad said that he got a message that Lorie is sick so we won't have any Gardiners coming. They are really upset about missing your wedding. I'm going to miss seeing them."

"Oh I am, too!" Kitty sprayed Elizabeth's hair and stepped back. "Done!"

"One more thing finished." She stood up. "I wonder how the boys are doing."

"They are just fine." Fran walked in and looked around the room. "Your father called, they are back at the Fitzwilliam house. They'll be here in an hour. Where are your flowers?"

Mary followed her in. "Downstairs, they are putting up the arrangements in the tent and the bakery just delivered the cake."

Kitty got up to stand on the balcony, trying to see the activity in the tent across the lawn. "You should have had a cookie table."

"What's that?"

"I went to a wedding with my roommate a few months ago. Her sister had this table just loaded with thousands of cookies, all kinds, and made by the ladies of the family. They had bags there with the bride and groom's names on them, and you could fill up the bags and take them home with you, it was amazing!"

"I've never heard of that." Elizabeth smiled. "William would have loved it. He has such a sweet tooth." The girls laughed. "Well he does." She blushed and looked at her hands. "Now what?"

"I think that we all need to dress and take pictures, don't you?" Jane had returned and grinned. "Mike is waiting!" Elizabeth groaned.

"WOULD YOU PLEASE stop!" Darcy glared at Charles. "I do not need a valet!"

"Obviously you do, you seem to have forgotten that you are not to wear a tie." Charles took the whisk he had discovered in David's closet and brushed his coat off again.

"I'm not getting married without proper attire." Darcy adjusted the knot and nodded. "I'll take it off as soon as the ceremony is over, but no sooner." He glanced at the photographer who took yet another picture. "Can somebody shoot this guy?" He whispered. Charles laughed and signaled to the man to get out, and closed the door.

"So, do you need any last minute encouragement? Assurance that Elizabeth *is* the girl for you, maybe a shot of bourbon?"

Darcy sighed. "I'm fine. I have never wanted something so much in my life but to be married to her. We should have gone to Vegas." Charles laughed. "Shut up."

"I didn't say anything." He grew serious. "I am in awe of you, Darcy. You saw her, and you didn't hesitate to fall in love, you didn't question it, you knew instantly she was the one."

"I did." He smiled and sighed and looked at his reflection, seeing a very happy man looking back. "I can't wait. I didn't blow it, I was so afraid that I would somehow." His eyes turned to see Charles watching him.

"I want to be like you when I grow up."

Darcy's brow rose. "Well, that is a compliment. Thank you." They clasped hands. "Do you have the rings?"

"I do."

"That's my line." He laughed. "Can I see them?"

"Why?" Charles said suspiciously. "Don't you believe I have them?"

"No, I want to see what Elizabeth had engraved on mine. The woman at Tiffany's seemed to think we were well-matched when she saw our ideas." Pulling the rings from his pocket, Charles read first Elizabeth's, then Darcy's band. He grinned and started chuckling. Seeing Darcy's hand held out in front of him he shook his head and put them back in his pocket. "Hey!"

"Nope, you two should be together for this discovery. You really had no idea what she would write down?"

"No . . . none." He made a grab for Charles' coat. "Come on, what does it say?"

"What's it worth to you?"

"You're holding them ransom?" Darcy stared in disbelief. "You're my best man! You're supposed to do what I say!"

"No, I'm supposed to get you to the altar, sober and on time." Charles grinned and opened the door, then called over his shoulder. "Speaking of which, it's time to go."

THE CARS CONTAINING Darcy, Charles, and the Fitzwilliams arrived precisely a half-hour before the ceremony was to begin. The other men had left earlier to go dress at their respective abodes and to come to Pemberley on their own. Darcy stepped out of the car and looked at his home, searching for an unlikely glimpse of Elizabeth, then blowing out the stale breath of anticipation he had been holding the whole way there. The lawn was transformed from when he had left early that morning. Besides the tent and the caterer, he could see the piano that had been moved outside, and musicians milling about. Flowers decorated the archway that stood near the edge of the lawn; the ocean would be the background to their vows. People, friends and relatives new and old, wandered the garden and patio; all dressed comfortably, all smiling at him. Barry caught his eye and approached.

"Here, I was told to be sure that you wore this." He pinned the red and yellow rose buds to his jacket.

"Who told you that?" Darcy smiled and looked down at the flowers, remembering how he sent Elizabeth the bouquet with the same colors when she was away.

"Why, the bride of course!" He laughed to see Darcy's eyes soften. "She is so anxious to get this going."

"Is she?" He looked up and searched the grounds for her again. "She's not alone."

"Are you okay?" Barry held his arms. "I was about ready to vomit at this point."

"I remember." He sighed and shook his head. "My stomach is flipping but everything is staying down."

"Good!" Seeing David approaching he shook his hand. "Remember this day, my friend; this will be the only wedding you ever have."

"I know that." Darcy swallowed down the emotion he was feeling and turned to greet his uncle. "So, any words of advice before I take this leap?"

"Well, since your father is not here to talk to you, I will." David paused and collected his thoughts. "You were an adult when your parents died. You were old enough to observe their marriage. They were very devoted to each other . . . George and I talked about you three boys and how we hoped you would find happiness in your marriages. I think that he would have been very happy today. Elizabeth, and perhaps the comfort of . . . belonging to her . . ." Darcy smiled. ". . . have changed you, and I know that my sister would be weeping right now to see the happiness that is just radiating from you. I have no advice for this day, but in the future, if you need it, I'll do my best to fill your father's shoes. Never forget the reason why you are standing here today. I remember whenever I see Arlene smile just for me."

Darcy blinked hard to hold back his emotion. "I guess that I should make sure that I remember how to get those special smiles from . . . my wife." He felt David's arms go around him and they embraced. "Thank you."

Charles approached and waited for them to separate. "It's time."

They and the guests started drifting towards the archway. Darcy paused by the piano where Georgiana had taken a seat, waiting for her cue to begin playing. "Are you okay?" She stood and hugged him. "You look like you're just barely hanging on."

"I am." He laughed and kissed her. "I'm so happy."

"I am, too. Thank you for finding a wonderful sister for me." She smiled and saw him roll his eyes. "Oh, that *is* the reason you are getting married, isn't it? For me?"

"Oh, yes, absolutely." He chuckled and walked up to the magistrate and shook his hand, took his place beside Charles, and looked at the faces all watching him expectantly. For the first time, he did not feel uncomfortable being the object of attention. He was just there waiting for his friend to arrive. The sound of the piano quieted the crowd, and between them walked Jane, smiling, carrying one red and one yellow rose. Then behind her appeared Elizabeth and Tom. She glowed. Her eyes were dancing with some hidden amusement, her smile was warm and welcoming, and her entire being was suffused with happiness that could only be owned by a woman in love.

Darcy gasped softly at the sight of her, and felt Charles's hand on his back, keeping him steady. Tom kissed her, then placed her hand in his. Immediately their clasp was tight, and they never once looked anywhere but in each other's eyes.

The magistrate smiled and welcomed them all, then began the very simple vows that Elizabeth and William had chosen. They vowed to cherish their union and love each other more each day, they promised trust and respect, laughter and compassion, and faithful love through whatever would come.

"I give you my hand, my friendship, and my love for as long as we both shall live." They said in unison, then presented each other with their wedding bands. Elizabeth's hand was shaking so hard that William had to reach out to steady her. When his ring found its home they both touched it and could no longer stop the tears, looking upon each other through blurred, joyful, eyes.

"I now pronounce you man and wife. You may kiss your bride." The magistrate smiled and stepped away.

"Will . . ."

"Oh honey . . ." His arms encircled her and drew her to him. Softly their mouths met, once, twice, again and again. Elizabeth felt William shudder and his gentle tongue found hers as his hands moved upwards to hold her face. She clung to him and lost herself in his sweet caress.

"Should we pry them apart?" Charles whispered to Jane.

"Leave them alone." She laughed. "They have to breathe sometime."

In the crowd, Lisa called out, "You go, girl!" Everyone started to clap and cheer, finally awakening the Darcys to their presence. They both blushed deeply, inspiring more laughter. Elizabeth wiped her lipstick from William's mouth and laughed. "I guess that the honeymoon will have to be delayed a while."

"Not for too long, I hope." He hugged her and taking her hand, walked through the crowd, stopping to kiss and hug Fran and Tom, then receiving the congratulations of the their family and friends.

Jane spoke up. "Everyone, please go ahead to the tent and enjoy your refreshments, the wedding party has a few pictures to take."

Elizabeth groaned and William sighed. "I wanted to throttle the guy who followed me around."

"Me too!"

After finally taking pictures of every conceivable combination of the new family, they found themselves blissfully alone on the beach. Holding hands they began to walk. Elizabeth stumbled and slipped off her shoes, he removed his tie, and they began again.

He smiled at her and swung her arm back and forth. Elizabeth giggled. "So Mr. Darcy, should we be returning to our guests?"

"Mrs. Darcy." He laughed to see her eyes light up. "I'd really rather just stay alone with you." He stopped and drew her against him, taking off the veil that was blowing around them, and let it go. She rested her head over his heart, and they watched it sail into the sky, dancing in the wind, then fly out over the gently lapping waves. William kissed her head. "I hope that you didn't want to keep that."

"Well, I suppose I'll live without it." She laughed. "I have no need for another veil in my lifetime, do I?"

"Not according to those vows we just took." He hugged her and then took her hand in his. "May I read my ring? I promise it will be the only time I ever take it off."

Elizabeth laughed at his twinkling eyes and took his hand, slipping it off his finger. He did the same with hers. "You first."

"No, ladies first." He pursed his lips and watched as she bit her lip and studied the ring.

"Ohhhhhhh. Read yours!"

His brow creased and he turned the heavy band to make out the words, and started to laugh. "No wonder the woman at Tiffany's was impressed with us!"

Elizabeth looked at her ring and read aloud, "Once upon a time . . ."

"And they lived happily ever after." William finished as he read his. "We are pretty silly, aren't we? I love you."

They put the rings back where they belonged and kissed. "I love you, Will."

"SHALL WE START taking bets on how long it takes them to return?" Richard leaned back in his chair to reach over to Charles at another table.

"You know, there was a time not so long ago that I would take that bet, but I'm afraid that my friend Darcy has become completely unpredictable. I will keep my money for a surer thing." He grinned and looked over to Maria. "What do you think?"

"I don't know him well enough to make predictions, but Lizzy? Well, if I had just married such a beautiful man, I'd keep him very busy down on the beach." She smiled and laughed to see his brows rising. "Of course that would be my husband."

"Oh, I see, saving yourself for marriage?" He teased.

"Mmm, no but not giving it up for the first pretty face that looks my way." She lifted her chin then looked to Charlotte who was nodding with approval.

Richard started to laugh. "You've got your work cut out for you!"

"And you don't?" Charlotte said quietly. "Obviously you seem to think that women should fall at your feet. Well, those women aren't worth knowing are they?"

"Really? And why is that? Didn't Elizabeth fall at Darcy's feet?"

"As I recall, he tripped her." Charlotte smiled and took a sip of her wine. "That is cheating."

"So it was. Crafty devil isn't he?" Richard tilted his head, and watched as she turned her attention to Lisa and Joe.

John touched Jane's arm. "Everything is beautiful. Did you plan all of this?"

"Oh thank you, no. Lizzy told me exactly what she wanted. I've known for years that she didn't want a huge party, so I knew where to go and what to do." She looked around at the tables and smiled with satisfaction. "I think this is my favorite wedding."

"Well it is your sister's." John smiled. "You're biased."

"No, it's more than that, it is just so simple. I appreciate that what most concerned them was having the people who cared about them present, and giving them a good time." She looked back at him. "Without all the unnecessary details."

"Aren't those details the things that earn your living?" He grinned and she blushed guiltily. "Ah, so you can appreciate the simplicity just this once."

"Yes, and because I'm not being paid for it." Jane laughed.

He leaned forward and said softly, "I liked seeing you walking down the aisle." Jane's eyes widened. "It was a very pretty picture. I hope that you will dance with me tonight."

David watched his sons at work and caught Arlene's eye. "Something is in the wind."

"It's about time that it was more than hot air." She looked at her boys and sighed. "I do hope that at least one of them has paid attention to their cousin."

"Here they come!" Lydia cried.

Elizabeth and William walked up the lawn, hand in hand, and oblivious to the crowd, stopped and kissed. Hearing the cheers and silverware on the wine glasses, he looked up and blushed. "I forgot about them."

Elizabeth smiled and smoothed the hair away from his eyes. "So did I. Well, I guess there is no avoiding them now."

"Are you hungry?" He grinned.

"I've been smelling it all day, yes, I'm hungry!" Taking his hand she pulled him forward, and they entered the tent to the commentary of their friends. Elizabeth balanced on his arm while she put her shoes back on, then they headed for the buffet. Her eyes lit up. "Ohhhh it has been sooooo long."

"It certainly has been."

Elizabeth turned to see his eyes were burning into hers. "I have a feeling that we are talking about different things."

He leaned down to her ear. "No my wife, we are both speaking of things we love to taste."

"Pork?" She smiled and held up a piece of the barbeque to his lips. He opened his mouth and she fed him.

"mmmmmmmm." William licked his lips. "Tasty. I have something to feed you, too." Her eyes grew wide and he picked up some brisket. "Would you like some beef?"

"I'd love it." She opened her mouth and he gently placed the morsel on her tongue. "mmmm, so tender."

He groaned. "This is going to be a very long afternoon." He glanced down at his groin. "Just remember, I know your vulnerable spots, too."

"Let the games begin!" Elizabeth whispered.

Adam poked Joe's arm. "It seems some conspiracy is taking place at the buffet."

"You've read too many of your own books."

"Oh no, they are flirting!" Lisa whispered. "Look at them! It is just too delicious! Pay attention, Joe, I have to use this!"

"Can't they have a wedding without it being used in a book?" He said with exasperation.

"NO!" Adam and Lisa declared and laughed. "The mind is a terrible thing to waste."

"And so is an easy story." Lisa agreed.

"Hmm, I guess that I am going to strike out with the wedding guests. Maria is taken, and so is Jane. I know too much about the other sisters." Adam turned his eye to Georgiana and noticed that she looked away quickly. "Darcy's sister is starting her second year at Julliard, isn't she? That makes her what, twenty?"

"I think she is just seventeen."

Adam groaned. "Not even legal!" He caught her glancing at him again. "Well, I can ask her for a dance can't I?"

"Sure! Just don't dip!" Joe laughed. "And remember, there will be a lot of men watching your every move."

Before long the couple rose to cut the cake, and they fed each other properly. Elizabeth kissed the icing from his fingers and he leaned down to kiss the rest from her lips. "At last I get to begin tasting my sweets for today."

"Have you been denying yourself?" Elizabeth smiled and wiped the corner of his mouth.

"Just waiting for the best." He kissed her again.

Jane stood up in front of the small band. "Our bride and groom have each requested songs for their first dances, and they would prefer not to be performing alone, so please everyone, find a partner, and let's dance."

Elizabeth and Darcy walked out to the dance floor, waving everyone else out to join them, and the music began. "My song is first." Elizabeth whispered. "As it should be." He chuckled and stood with his arms around her, waiting to recognize it, then his eyes lit up.

"*When You Say Nothing At All.*[ix]" He whispered as she nodded. They began to dance, staring into each other's eyes and listening to the voice of the singer.

"It's amazing how you can speak right to my heart. Without saying a word, you can light up the dark. Try as I may I could never explain, what I hear when you don't say a thing. The smile on your face let's me know that you need me. There's a truth in your eyes saying you'll never leave me. The touch of your hand says you'll catch me whenever I fall. You say it best when you say nothing at all."

William kissed her softly, and could feel her willing him to hear her voice in the words as the singer continued.

"All day long I can hear people talking out loud. But when you hold me near, you drown out the crowd. Try as they may they could never define what's been said between your heart and mine."

Elizabeth began to cry and William stopped dancing, instead cupping her face in his hands, and wiping her tears as he added his voice to hers. They looked deeply into each other's eyes. "The smile on your face let's me know that you need me. There's a truth in your eyes saying you'll never leave me. The touch of your hand says you'll catch me whenever I fall. You say it best when you say nothing at all." The song ended and Elizabeth was pressed tight to his chest, his arms had encircled her, their eyes closed, and they swayed, oblivious to everyone.

"Wow." John said softly to Jane. "I'm getting emotional just watching them." He blinked and smiled at her. "I knew Darcy was Mr. Romance, but . . ."

"And this isn't even his song." Jane laughed and smiled to see the two of them still embraced. The music began again and Elizabeth lifted her head to look up. William's eyes were twinkling at her. And she laughed.

"Shall we dance?" He began to move and she joined him, laughing again as he spun her slowly out. They moved around the dance floor, and waited for the cue to sing.

John took a breath and held out his arms. "Okay, I think that I can dance to this one."

Jane laughed. "Will you sing along?"

"Don't push it, Jane."

William kissed Elizabeth and joined the vocalist with the words, and soon nearly everyone in the tent was either singing or dancing along with them. "*Make someone happy*, make just one someone happy; make just one heart the heart you sing to. One smile that cheers you, one face that lights when it nears you, One girl you're ev'rything to."

"Fame if you win it, comes and goes in a minute, where's the real stuff in life to cling to? Love is the answer. Someone to love is the answer. Once you've found her, build your world around her. Make someone happy, make just one someone happy, and you will be happy, too. [x]"

"You make me so very happy, Will." Elizabeth laughed as he twirled her around again. The song ended and everyone clapped.

"You are my world, honey." William hugged her.

Tom approached and touched his shoulder. "Might I have a dance with my daughter?" He smiled and held out his arms

"Of course, sir." Darcy smiled. "I have something that I need to take care of in any case."

"What?" Elizabeth looked at him curiously.

"You'll see." He kissed her cheek and disappeared from the tent. Richard and Charles followed him.

"Where are you going?"

Darcy stopped and demanded. "Can't I surprise my wife without everyone knowing about it?"

Richard and Charles looked at each other. "No." Darcy rolled his eyes and strode off across the lawn, and approached a group of men working just beyond a gardener's shed.

"Is everything ready?" He asked the man who approached him.

"Yes, we are ready to go as soon as the sun begins to set; I'd say it will be in about an hour." He looked over the ocean. "You have an excellent night for it."

"I'm grateful for no rain." Darcy smiled and thanked him, then turned to see Richard and Charles staring curiously at the collection of pipes with wires running through them.

"Fireworks?"

"Yes, of course!" He grinned. "What better occasion could there be?"

"Is this inspiration for the wedding night?" Richard asked with a grin as they made their way back to the party.

"I hardly need inspiration." Darcy said softly, then directed the conversation away from his plans. "I haven't seen you dancing yet."

"Not my best skill, and I noticed that Charlotte wasn't jumping up to show off hers either. I was thinking of maybe a stroll in the garden." Richard looked at him closely. "What do you think?"

"What, am I suddenly cupid? You know what works for you, go with your strengths."

"If that is the case, I might as well throw in the towel now." He sighed. "Come on, you caught your girl, what impressed Elizabeth?"

"I listened to her." He smiled and patted his back. "And of course, I'm irresistible."

Charles snorted. "What an ego!"

"Who's got the ring?" Darcy held up his hand in triumph. "Why aren't you dancing? You must know all the moves."

"I was waiting for the tempo to pick up." He jabbed.

Darcy shook his head. "You aren't going to catch a girl if you're always in a hurry." They arrived at the tent; Elizabeth was dancing with David and caught his eye, obviously pleading with him for a rescue. "I see that your father is trying to disable my wife."

Richard watched and grinned. "Well, now you know where I got it from." He pointed at John and Jane. "Now my brother seems to have taken after Mom."

Darcy smiled to see them trying to dance together then glanced at Charles who was watching them as well. "Are you okay with this?"

"Yes, I . . . I would have liked it to be different, but that would have required two different people, wouldn't it?" He clasped Darcy's shoulder. "Excuse me; I have to ask a lady for a dance." He moved off to wait for Maria to finish her dance with Adam.

"Do you think there is a chance that something will come of that?" Richard asked as he watched Charles take her hand.

"I don't know, but it's good to see him try." Darcy met his eye. "You're up. Get going."

"Yes, coach." Richard smiled and headed over to join Charlotte with Lisa and Joe.

A salsa song began and most of the dancers left the floor, Elizabeth shook her hips and held out her hand. Grinning, William stepped up and they began to move, flying around the small floor, and were soon the only ones dancing. A series of turns had the audience gasping and clapping, and Elizabeth laughed out loud when he snapped her out and away from him, then sharply spun her back, so she rested backwards against his chest. His hips moved rhythmically against her swaying bottom and his mouth rested near her ear. His arms came around her body so their hands joined in a clasp over her stomach. "Do you know how much I want you, honey?" He pressed his hips against her before letting go, spinning her away again.

"I think that I have an idea." She gasped when he drew her back into his arms, this time face to face.

"No, I don't think that you do." The song ended and his lips rested near her ear, his breath came in pants, and the warmth sent shivers down her spine. "But by the end of this night, you will."

"Oh." He held her tightly, feeling her body pressed to his, and wishing he could send all of the guests away. Elizabeth pressed her lips to his bare chest through the gap in his open shirt, and felt his shudder.

"Baby." He groaned. Taking her hand he pulled her from the tent, and looking around at the grounds, spotted the stable. "Come on."

"Where are we going?" She asked as he nearly ran across the lawn. "Will, I can't move this fast with these shoes!" He stopped and scooped her up in his arms while she squealed.

William grinned and kissed her. "Is this better?"

"You're crazy!"

"Yes, I am. Crazy in love." They reached the barn and he threw a blanket over a pile of fresh straw, then turned to smile at her. The light was just beginning to fade, and the barn was steeped in shadows. He approached and ran his fingers through her hair. "Please let me love you, honey." He bent to kiss her cheek, then nuzzled his face against her shoulder.

"I need help to get out of my dress." She whispered shakily to the ear that was by her mouth.

"I don't think that I can wait that long." He moaned and ran his hands down her body, then bending, lifted her up, only to gently lay her down upon the blanket. Falling on his knees before her, he caressed her legs, and moved her gown up and away. "My God you are lovely, laying in this beautiful dress, looking up at me . . . I can't believe it is real. You married me."

Elizabeth held out her arms and he fell into them. Their mouths found their homes and they began to exchange the slow tender kisses they both adored. She suckled his tongue and he groaned as his desire grew. Their mouths slid and embraced, just as their hands caressed and explored over their clothes. William moved to kiss her throat and he reveled in the reward of her moan in his ear; and the arch of her back beneath his hands. "Willl, oh you have magic lips."

He drew away and smiled into her eyes. "I do?"

"I could spend forever being kissed by you." The sound of an explosion and a burst of light came through the window and they startled. "What was that?" Elizabeth cried, and looked up at him with wide eyes.

William laughed and hugged her. "That is a wedding gift. We must have been in here for nearly an hour. No wonder your lips are so swollen." He touched her mouth and smiled. "I completely lose all track of time when I am in your arms, honey. I love kissing you." Another explosion and smaller crackling sounds were heard, along with ooohhhs and ahhhhhs. He sat up and then stood, lifting her along with him. "We'll continue this later; we have other fireworks to attend now."

"Fireworks!" Elizabeth ran to the window and turned around to smile at him. "What a surprise!" She grabbed his hand and pulled him to the door. "Come on!"

He laughed and followed. "I wasn't about to stay behind." They walked over to the edge of the lawn where the other guests had gathered to see the show over the ocean. Elizabeth leaned into his arms and he kissed her head while they watched. He felt a hand brushing over his hair and glanced over to see Barry quietly disposing of a handful of straw. Their eyes met and the friends smiled. When the display ended in a burst of color and thunder, everyone applauded and cheered. It was also the natural end to the reception. The guests who were not staying at Pemberley departed; and those who were moved to the house. Soon only the newlyweds remained, alone in the dark, embraced and watching the moonlight on the water.

"You're mine." Elizabeth quietly told him.

"I love being yours." He kissed her then rested his cheek on her head. "I love that you're mine."

She squeezed his waist. "I guess that now we have to find out what happens between *once upon a time* and *they lived happily ever after*." Elizabeth looked up to see his smile. "This is a story that I can't wait to read."

"Well honey, let's start writing it."

Chapter 16

J ane looked up when she heard the click of a latch then spotted a French door opening on the balcony that was attached to the master suite. She breathed sharply when William stepped out, clad only in a pair of black boxers, and leaned his elbows on the railing, looking out over the water. He was unshaven, his hair was lifting a little with the breeze, and a small smile played on his lips.

Through the door stepped Elizabeth, wearing a short pink robe. She moved behind him, running her hands up his bare back. He turned and his smile glowed like the sun. Jane watched as they spoke, not hearing the words, but saw him brushing back Elizabeth's hair. He laughed at something she said then his fingers drifted down to untie the robe, and his hands slipped inside, caressing her body, and kissing her, walked her backwards into the room. The door clicked shut again.

Jane closed her eyes, knowing exactly what was happening in that room, and felt a twinge of jealousy, then remembered the kisses she exchanged with John in the dark while the fireworks burst above them. She hoped that the scene she just witnessed would be one she experienced someday, then rose from her seat on her balcony and went inside to dress and go down to the kitchen. "Good Morning, Miss Maggie."

"Good morning, my dear." She was sitting on her chair in the kitchen, observing Jerry making breakfast for the houseful of guests. "I'm so happy for my boy."

"Well I'm happy for my sister. She deserves such a good man." Jane took a seat and thanked Jerry for the coffee he handed her. "I'll be sorry to leave here today. It's a beautiful home."

"Matlock is very nice." Maggie shot her a look. "Not on the beach, but still very pretty. I used to go and help out there when they were entertaining."

"Oh."

Maggie clucked and sat forward. "Now, I love my boy Will as my own, but his cousin John is just as much my baby. I saw you two together, making cow eyes at each other. What are you waiting for?"

"We . . . we barely know each other!" Jane said in surprise.

"What's to know? He's a good boy, got a good head on his shoulders, good parents, never a bit of trouble from him . . . I saw the girls he dated, stuck up things, no wonder he never asked for a ceremony with any of them." Maggie shook her finger at Jane. "He is very interested in you."

"I . . . I like him, too." She said defensively.

"More than like from the sight of you two in the garden last night." She cackled and Jane blushed. The kitchen door opened and Charles entered.

"Oh, hi. Um, nobody else is up?" He looked around then took a seat on the far side of the table.

Jane was still flushed and looked down at her cup. "Um, no, but I did see Lizzy and William out on the balcony for a few moments earlier, but I think that they won't be down for awhile."

Charles started chuckling. "No, I imagine not." Jane looked up and smiled. "Well, I've been entrusted to drive his precious car back to the city. Richard is coming with me, so I am sure we'll get a safety lecture from Darcy before we go."

"Is that necessary?"

He shrugged. "I hope not."

"Good morning!" Darcy walked into the room sporting a satisfied smile.

"Speak of the devil; I thought for certain you wouldn't appear for hours!" Charles grinned and took in his friend's appearance. "You look particularly rested, another surprise."

"Enough, Charles." Darcy glared at him. "Maybe I'll leave the car here and you can beg a ride home."

"No, you wouldn't want to do that."

"Why not?" He sat down and thanked Jerry for his coffee. "I have a mind to do just that."

"But then you'd be in the way of promoting young love."

Darcy's brows rose. "Between you and Richard? I never knew." He smiled and laughed at the scowl.

"We thought that we would take home the Lucas sisters."

"Ah." He glanced over to Jane. "I think that John is taking you back?"

"Oh yes." She blushed. "Georgiana is riding with your aunt and uncle."

"Ah." He smiled and looked back over to Charles. "Well, with Charlotte and Maria in the car, I'm sure that you will behave. Have a pleasant trip."

"Thanks." Charles shook his head at his friend's change in mood. "When do you depart?"

"As soon as my lovely wife eats her breakfast." His eyes glowed. "I can't wait."

"Are you afraid to fly? Lizzy is a little worried." Jane said carefully.

"I know, Jane." He looked at her with an understanding smile. "I'm determined to be reasonable. The likelihood of us experiencing a second incident is very low. I'll just have to be convincing to her."

"What are you convincing me of?" Elizabeth entered and put her hands on her hips. "Are you keeping secrets from me already?"

"Suspicious aren't we?" He grabbed her hand and pulled her down to sit on his lap.

"Will!"

"What?" He kissed her and she leaned back into his arms. "I just want you to feel safe on our flight."

"Oh." She sighed. "I'll be better once we land."

"That goes without saying, honey."

DARCY LOOKED out the window, recognizing the familiar landmarks of Derbyshire as their plane began to make its descent into East Midlands Airport. He turned back to see Elizabeth, her eyes tightly shut, and her hand gripping the seat arm hard. It would be a lie to say that he wasn't sharing her fear, but he was determined to be strong in her presence. He touched her hand and immediately she grasped his. "We're almost there, honey."

"I know." She whispered and then wrapped her arm around his and rested her head on his shoulder. Darcy kissed her hair and closed his eyes, listening to the sounds of the landing gear locking in place, and praying that all would be well. Seemingly hours later they touched down smoothly, barely feeling the jolt. "Are we safe?" Elizabeth whispered.

He lifted his head and looked out at the tarmac. "Yes, honey, we are. Look."

"Thank heavens." She smiled up at him. "Thanks for bearing with me."

He kissed her and smiled. "I was just as scared. Well, hopefully our car is waiting and we'll be on our way to Pemberley as soon as we get through customs."

"How long does it take?"

"Hmm, about an hour, you'll have a chance to see the countryside a little. I know that you'll enjoy that. The Peaks are beautiful."

"I'm looking forward to it." She watched them roll through the various runways and reach a gate. "Here we are!" She sang.

"I am overwhelmed with how quickly your good humor is restored." He laughed and kissed her. Soon they were through the airport and ensconced in the car that was sent for them.

"Now, why is it that no English Darcys live here?" Elizabeth took his hand and looked out at the passing countryside. "Surely there must be one or two lurking about somewhere."

"Actually, no." He entwined their fingers. "In the mid-1800's there was a Darcy family in residence, as there had been for hundreds of years. For whatever reason, they were down to only one man, his wife, son and daughter. The wife died, and he never remarried. The estate passed to his son, as was customary, and that son married and had two of his own. The eldest inherited the estate, and the second son was given a small estate of his own. He decided that if he sold that property, the funds from that could buy him nearly four times the property in the wilds of America, so he left his family and decided to seek his fortune across the ocean. He was attracted to the beautiful forests which reminded him of home and bought up land in those areas. With all of the westward expansion, timber was a very good business to be in, and he developed methods for harvesting and replanting, amongst other ideas for making products like paper from wood instead of linen or rags." He smiled. "That was my great great great great grandfather."

Elizabeth laughed. "Are you sure that you got all of the greats in there?"

"I don't know." He chuckled. "I probably forgot a generation in there somewhere. In any case, his brother, the owner of Pemberley, continued on at the estate until the sad day that apparently a strain of influenza struck the household. Everyone became ill, and the elder brother died. The estate, by his will, was left to his brother since there were no children. That is how my branch of the family came to own Pemberley. There has only been one son born to each heir, and the estate was always left to that child to preserve."

"And you own it now."

"Yes."

"Do you really wish to give it up?"

He sighed. "I don't know what to do, Lizzy. I look at the other great estates and how some are still used as homes but are also tourist attractions, and others are sold off to . . . well, people like me, and then still others are purely given over to the National Trust. I am looking at all three options, and there are undoubtedly more. Right now it is both a home and a destination. It is self-sustaining from the tourism and farming, but I am so rarely here that I wonder if it is simply time to let it go. I hope that you seeing it with fresh eyes will help me to make a decision." The car entered at a gate, and they began driving up a winding road through an ancient and beautiful forest. At the top of one peak, the car pulled into an area designated as an overlook. The driver jumped out and opened the door, and they got out to walk over to the edge. "There, this is the true Pemberley."

Elizabeth looked down into the valley, recognizing the model for the painting hanging in William's library. The great stone mansion rose majestically from the hills beyond, its reflection was clear in the nearly still waters of a lake situated before it. "It is beautiful." She whispered.

Darcy wrapped his arms around her waist and looked it over with her. "It is. We would come twice a year when I was a boy, during school breaks. My parents would come at other times, too. I only managed yearly visits from the time that I was in college to now. It is magnificent, but it's not home."

She turned around to look up into his eyes, and saw the conflict he was feeling. "Well, let's go see the inside."

"Okay." He smiled and they returned to the car, passing by the car park and the other structures built for the service of the tourists, observing groups of people wandering the grounds, cameras and guidebooks in hand, then around to a service entrance. "I'm sorry that we aren't going in the front door, I think that the tours close in about an hour or so."

"Mr. Darcy, welcome home." A small round woman proclaimed. She was smiling at him warmly while simultaneously inspecting Elizabeth.

"Thank you Mrs. Woods. May I introduce you to my wife, Elizabeth Darcy? Elizabeth, Mrs. Woods is the head of housekeeping for Pemberely."

"I am pleased to meet you ma'am. The staff was delighted to hear that Mr. Darcy had married. We look forward to having a new mistress and hope to see your family often as it grows." She looked directly and earnestly into Elizabeth's eyes.

She knew that the woman was trying to communicate something to her. "Thank you, Mrs. Woods; I hope that sometime during our stay I'll have the opportunity to talk with you. You must know every detail of this home."

Mrs. Woods smiled and nodded. "Yes indeed, ma'am, I would be happy to do just that. Now, shall I take you up to your room? I'm sure that you are tired after your trip."

"Yes, thank you." They set off using stairs long ago built for the servants and not for the owners to ever see, and eventually emerged on a quiet floor, the end of the hallway blocked by a velvet rope. Curious visitors peered at them and Elizabeth felt William's grip on her hand tighten as they turned away. Silently they followed Mrs. Woods, who began pointing out things that had been repaired or replaced since his last visit, then arrived at a door. "Here you go, sir. The master's suite is finished; I hope that you like how it all came out." She opened the door and Elizabeth gasped, the opulence was astounding. She turned to look back at William and he smiled at her half-heartedly.

"Did you choose all of this?"

He shook his head and spoke quietly. "I let the curator refurbish the rooms to the style they would have had in 1830. Sometimes the family rooms are on display. Nobody enters, but they can look in from the doorway. Only we can actually stay here. Naturally with us in residence, this part of the house is closed off."

More staff members brought up their luggage and soon disappeared. He went to stand by the window, leaning on the frame, and she came up to join him, slipping her arms around his waist.

"What is wrong, Will?"

"What do you think of Mrs. Woods?"

"I don't know her enough to form an opinion, but she seems very earnest in her duties, and proud of this home."

"Home." He shook his head.

"She also seemed to be hoping that it would remain a home." Elizabeth added and watched his expression.

"Yes." He said softly. "I feel so lost here." He laughed a little. "Probably like you did in our two homes the first time you came . . . what did you say, that the house in town was a museum?" He looked around the room with bright eyes. "This, this is a museum." Returning to the window he pointed down at the gradually emptying car park set behind a screen of trees. "See the paying guests? How am I to have a family in a home that has velvet ropes? I would have to tell our children that they can't go downstairs during business hours, and . . . don't touch anything . . . or I don't know." He sighed and leaned into the arms that were around him. "I'm sorry, honey, this is our honeymoon and I brought you here to listen to my misery instead of loving you."

"Well, I believe that I signed on for that job yesterday." Elizabeth stroked the hair back from his eyes and smiled. "This has obviously been weighing on you for a long time, and the staff knows it. I wonder that they worry for their livelihood if you were to give it up."

"They would all maintain their positions. People . . . people lease rooms throughout the year, it's part of the income that runs the estate. Two rooms are licensed for weddings, and sometimes the bridal couple will spend the night in the guest wing." He smiled at the irony. "Like us."

"So it seems that the staff would prefer there being fewer strangers here and more family."

"Yes, that was, I think, the point of Mrs. Woods's comments." He hugged her.

"Well, I am overwhelmed by the place, and I have no doubt that whatever was beyond the rope at the end of the hallway is breathtakingly intimidating, but let's see if there is any way that we can look at this mansion and think of it as a home. Maybe the problem is that you always saw it through the eyes of a child and never really appreciated it as an adult. It just became one more responsibility heaped on your shoulders when your dad died and it was convenient to ignore it an ocean away." Elizabeth kissed his cheek and he looked down at her, his tension lifting a little.

"You are a very, very intelligent woman." He caressed her face then leaned down to hug her. "You see right through me."

"Let's see if we can discover some private magic here." Elizabeth kissed him and he smiled. "Now, I'm going to get out of these grubby clothes and wash up. Then you will take me on a tour."

"Yes, dear." He smiled and watched her dig through her bag to find a fresh outfit and disappear into her bathroom. Already he was feeling a little better. *It's in your hands, honey.*

"THANK YOU." Elizabeth smiled at the man as he set her plate down on the silver charger. He nodded and stepped back then repeated his task with Darcy, whose face was set and did not speak. The man moved away and stood against the wall. Elizabeth looked at him curiously then to her husband. "I'm confused."

"I know." He said softly. "Just . . . I'll explain later." He bit his lip and picked up his fork. "This looks delicious. I believe that it is . . . our beef."

She followed his cue to ignore the man and asked, "Cattle are raised here?"

"Yes, as well as sheep and the crops with which to maintain them." He continued quietly. "It is as much for the educational aspect as the practical one. I'm grateful that there is a long-established staff in place to run the estate, and a non-profit foundation to devise ways to earn the capital to maintain it. I know how to farm trees and direct a company; this place is more challenging in many ways. I am really a figure head, but the ultimate decisions are all mine." Darcy met her gaze and looked away to his plate.

"I looked at a visitor's guide that I found in a bedside table while you were changing . . ." He winced and closed his eyes, ". . . the gardens sound lovely, I've never been in a maze before, maybe we could try to get lost in there tomorrow. Visitors aren't admitted until eleven, so maybe we should walk through the house in the morning, then spend the afternoon outdoors, when we won't feel so . . . confined by the . . . curious." Elizabeth reached out to take his hand and squeezed. "That's part of it, too. You are such a private person, Will. The thought of having strangers traipsing through your home and worse, catching sight of you while they do it is distasteful to you."

He looked back up to her. "Doesn't it bother you?"

She leaned close to him and whispered. "Yes, it does very much, but what bothers me the most is that since we arrived here, you have changed dramatically. We left the wedding and you were a joyous, playful, happy man, and here you are withdrawn. I want my Will back." She smiled and squeezed his hand again. "I'm willing to give this a chance, honey. If you feel overwhelmed here, imagine what I am feeling! But I am going to try. For six and a half hours a day, there are people here. Surely we can figure out ways to avoid them for those few hours." Her head tilted. "Perhaps we can get lost in the woods?"

A slow smile appeared on his lips. "I remember some hidden spots from my boyhood wanderings."

"I'd love to see them." Elizabeth rubbed his hand. "Maybe we'll be so overcome with jetlag we won't want to get out of bed."

"That is your best idea yet!" He smiled a little more. "Thank you, Lizzy." Glancing over to the silent servant against the wall, he sighed.

Elizabeth noticed his distraction and looked over to the man. "Excuse me." He looked at her enquiringly. "We really don't need anything else, could you please return in a half-hour?"

"Oh, are you certain, Mrs. Darcy? It is my duty to remain here." He looked at her earnestly.

"I am; thank you." She smiled and lifted her brow. "I hope that you bring back some spectacular dessert when you come."

"I will speak with the chef, ma'am." He looked at Darcy and left.

Elizabeth laughed as the door closed and smiled at William who was clearly looking at her with appreciation. "Okay, now *what* was that all about?"

"Apparently, people who stay here expect to be treated as if they are the owners of the estate, and demand the whole pomp and ceremony of countless servants standing in silence just waiting to be ordered to perform some task. I honestly never felt comfortable being watched like that, especially the times that I had to come here alone to address the concerns of the estate." He laughed softly. "It never occurred to me to tell them to go away. They were always there when I was growing up, so I just thought it was to be expected."

"You know, it is hard enough to accept Mrs. Reynolds and the staff at the other houses, but I'm just amazed at all that is here. Maybe what would help this feel more like a home is to set up rules to be followed when we are in residence, like leaving us alone so we don't feel as if we are living in a hotel."

"Okay, well, we'll speak to Mrs. Woods about that tomorrow." He felt a little more of the tension slip away. "Thank you, honey."

"Will, I can see your pride for this place, and I want to preserve it for you. It doesn't have to be a burden."

Darcy sat back and regarded her seriously. "I wonder; why are you doing so well here?"

"I am?" Elizabeth said with surprise. "I didn't realize that I was."

"You are not as apprehensive as you were at . . . Pemberley West." He smiled.

She blushed and looked down. "There was a lot happening then, Will. After all, that was when we first admitted our feelings for each other."

"I know, but you are different, more confident." He bit his lip and caressed her hand. "Is it something to do with being married to me now?"

"I think that we are both uncomfortable here, and . . . we're facing it together." Elizabeth smiled and saw the warmth in his eyes. "You like that don't you?"

"Oh honey, I do so much." He leaned over the corner of the table and kissed her. "Thank you."

They finished their meal and got up to walk the halls beyond the ropes. They entered the library and Elizabeth looked around it in awe. "Oh, what a treasure trove this is!"

"Yes, from what I understand, this was once one of the greatest libraries in the country, and remains one of the greatest private collections of first editions anywhere. I could get lost in here." He smiled and scanned the shelves. "Of course, I would be abused by the curator for touching any of the volumes without wearing white gloves."

"Can you imagine what it would have been like here?" Elizabeth approached two manikins displaying the gown and suit of a couple from the early 1800's. "Just look at the clothes, that cravat would have been on you all of the time, and what a revelation it would have been for a bride to see her husband's neck the first time." She turned around to see his head was tilted and he was smiling. "Then her gown . . . Did you know that she would not have worn any undergarments?"

"Really?" His eyes lit up. "How convenient"

"Indeed." She smiled then laughed. "And then as the century wore on, she would have begun to wear drawers."

"Oh, that would have been a blow to all of the men who enjoyed the former fashion." He pursed his lips.

"Ah, but they were crotchless!" Elizabeth giggled when his eyes grew wide. "I see that you find that even more intriguing!"

"I do, I don't know why, but the thought of you in crotchless anything . . . Wow!" He held out his hands for her. "So, Mistress of Pemberley, how would you welcome home your husband?"

"hmmm, well let's think about this." She walked away from him and over to the ladder attached to the bookshelves. "I believe that she would be a bookish girl, thirsty for knowledge of the world, and would take advantage of her husband being absent to steal her way into his library. Perhaps she would climb up on the ladder to reach a special volume." Elizabeth stepped up on the ladder and climbed a few steps then reached to touch a shelf. "Like so."

Darcy chuckled. "And where do I come?"

"You, the Master of Pemberley, would be anxious to make love to your gorgeous wife, and would ride like the wind to return to her from your task of . . . counting sheep . . ." He snorted and her eyes danced. " . . . unwilling to wait any longer, you would jump off of your noble steed at the front door, throwing the reins to some young lad, then stride up the stairs, and demand of your servants where the lady of the house could be found." Pointing to the door, she continued dramatically. "You would come to the library and see her up on the ladder, a position you told her never to assume since anyone standing below could see anything that her skirts would hide, and angrily you would order her down, yet at the same time you would be violently aroused."

"Quite a conflicted man, aren't I?" He laughed and crossed his arms across his chest. "Then what happens?"

"Why you kick the door shut!"

He went over and closed the library door. "Like this?"

"A bit more forcefully I think, but that will do." She smiled. "Then she would cry out, *Oh, Mr. Darcy!*"

"With the back of her hand to her forehead?" He pantomimed.

"Hmm, no I don't like that. Let's try again. How about she would say, *Oh William, you are home at last!*"

Nodding, he walked over to the ladder, and placed his hands on her waist. "And I would say . . ."

"I told you never to climb this ladder, Elizabeth. What am I going to do with you?" She said in an imitation of his deep voice.

"Yes, what?" He said softly, and lifted her down.

Elizabeth looked up at him and saw her relaxed lover had returned. "I think that I would be forced to kiss you."

"Would it be so very hard to do?" His lips brushed over hers. "You would welcome your beloved husband's kisses wouldn't you?" He felt her breath caress his face as she sighed, and rested his forehead on hers. "Honey, I think that we need to go upstairs to our bed and begin to reclaim this place as a home."

"And how will we do that from our bed?" Elizabeth whispered, and felt his lips trace down from her temple to her cheek, then to her throat. "Ohhh, Will." She closed her eyes and leaned into his hair, while his mouth suckled her throat delicately.

"We'll first claim the master's chambers, then methodically claim the rest of the estate." His soft voice whispered as his hands gently caressed her body. "Let's go." Taking her hand, he smiled and opened the door. They walked through the unfamiliar hallways, up the magnificent marble staircase, and stepping into the corridor that led to the bedroom, he leaned down and reattached the velvet rope. "There, we are safe from any who would disturb us."

"Because nobody could possibly get through such an impressive barricade." Elizabeth laughed as they continued on.

"Of course not! Why they should be quaking in their boots at the mere thought of facing the fearsome Master of Pemberley!" He puffed out his chest and assumed a fiery glare. She burst into giggles. "I think this is going to your head."

"You think so, do you?" He bent and lifted her, ignoring the cry of protest, and carried her off to the bedroom. "Come on wife!" He growled and into the room he went, kicking the door shut with a bang.

"Will!"

"It's our house, not a museum!" Darcy declared and dropped her onto the bed and leaned over her, his hands on either side of her body. "So, what's under your skirt?"

"Why don't you lift it and find out?" Elizabeth said with her brow cocked suggestively, then reached forward to grab his belt and yanked his hips towards her. He grunted and she laughed, quickly unbuckling it and opening his slacks. "ooooohhh look what I found!" She reached inside to fondle his erection. "The family jewels!"

Darcy closed his eyes and moaned with her touch. "Lizzzzzy."

"Why are you still dressed?" She demanded and pushed him up and rolled away to stand and take off her clothes and lie down again. He stared at her looking up at him for a moment then methodically removed his clothes. "We need stripper music if you are going to be so teasing, Will." Elizabeth said seductively.

He smiled and climbed onto the enormous bed, crawling over and hovering above, then leaning down to kiss her slowly. "Will you strip for me someday?"

"Really?" She ran her fingers down his erection, and cupped the heavily hanging balls. He growled and bent low to kiss her.

"I would love it." He whispered warmly in her ear. "Come on baby, let's get it on."

"Ohhhhhh, that voice." Elizabeth moaned just as his lips found hers. Her fingers tangled in his hair and they kissed. His hands stroked down over her shoulders and down to her breasts, followed by his mouth, tasting its way down to suckle. "No, honey come back . . ." She whispered and lifted his head up. He smiled and returned to look in her eyes.

"You want my kisses?"

Elizabeth licked his lips. "ohhhhhhhhhh, baby." His eyes closed and he let her mouth have its way with his, and lowered his hand to stimulate and pleasure her. Her moan and the wetness on his fingers moved him to lift away, and slipping his hands under her thighs, bent her knees.

"What are you doing?" She panted and watched as he moved between her legs.

"I'm making you deeper for me." He said hoarsely and again stroked his hands down from her shoulders over her breasts, trailing his fingers across her belly to touch and fondle her waiting mound. "I'm going to give you the best loving you've ever had."

"What should I do?" She moaned as he slid into her and gasped as he allowed his full weight to concentrate on her pelvis.

"Just rock with me, baby."

They barely moved, he pressed down and she pressed up, rubbing together, letting his weight and their hips do the work. Elizabeth's heels dug into his calves and their arms wrapped tight around each other's bodies, clinging together. It was extraordinarily intense. William moaned and found her mouth, locking his lips with hers, and again rubbing all of his weight on her pelvis, stimulating every part of her, reaching her core. She hugged him with her entire body, arms, legs, wrapping him up completely, and rocking slowly, just as he taught her, stimulating him, shallow, then deep, shallow, then deep, never separating, never thrusting, only rubbing, rocking, joining. Their moans became louder, the cries longer, then they were silent as the intensity grew and grew until something broke inside of her, not the pulsing orgasm she had known before, no this was melting, glorious waves flowing over her body, and she gripped him as he trembled and came deep inside of her. At last it ended and they remained in the tight clasp, both too overcome to move from the extraordinary connection.

Slowly they let go, Elizabeth looked at her husband, who wore an expression of wonder warring with one of deep satisfaction. William saw the same in her eyes, and smiled, his face lit up with triumph. Lying on his side, he caressed her face and kissed her. "I think that we found something that we enjoy very much."

"Oh Will, yes, I . . . I . . . please can we do this again? Soon?" She closed her eyes and sighed while he caressed his hand up and down her warm blushing body. "How did you know this . . . method?"

"You won't laugh? He rubbed his nose with hers and kissed it

"Maybe." Elizabeth giggled and he chuckled.

"I did a little reading in anticipation of our honeymoon." His eyes twinkled and he leaned down to kiss her again. "I can't wait to show you everything else that I learned."

"I have always been a very attentive student." Elizabeth assured him.

"I never had any doubt of that, honey." He sighed happily and pulled the covers up and over them, spooning his very relaxed and satisfied body to her soft form. "Good night Elizabeth Darcy, Mistress of Pemberley, I love you." She giggled and he nestled his face against her shoulder.

Elizabeth held his hands and closed her eyes. "Good night my sweet Will." She heard his breathing slip into the slow pattern of deep sleep. "You are the Master of Pemberley, and we're going to keep it that way. I love you."

"MRS. WOODS took our request for privacy well; I think that she was actually pleased that we were setting boundaries. I was very impressed with you. I don't know that I've ever seen you in your business persona before."

"What is that?" Darcy smiled and held her hand as they wandered the corridors, looking into rooms and admiring the views from each window.

"You're very direct and serious, and clearly expect to be followed without question. It takes a great deal of confidence to pull that off effectively."

"I am confident about things that I know well. I know everything of importance here; it's not a lack of confidence or knowledge that troubles me." They entered the portrait gallery and they looked over the faces of his ancestors. "This is the real burden. These are the people who created Pemberley, and I am the one who must decide its fate."

"Is it really such a burden to keep it as a private home? I mean, everything is running smoothly isn't it?"

"Yes, I guess so. The trick is to attract enough visitors to help defray the cost of maintaining the place, which is enormous, without having to put in any more of our own funds from our outside resources." He smiled to see her brow wrinkle. "I am trying to keep this a contained entity. If it is self-supporting, then it is no problem to leave things as they are. So many estates are part of the National Trust for a reason, it is because the owners can not afford to maintain them, and the family members who inherit them who might be able to do so, can not after paying the inheritance taxes."

"I doubt that even if you did have to invest your other capital into it, you would feel that you were throwing good money away, Will. This home is a treasure."

"But I can't write off my investment in something I own." He laughed to see her eyes roll. "What is it?"

Elizabeth turned him around to face a portrait. "Look at this man. Do you see the resemblance between you?"

"William Darcy." He said and looked up to see the face of the man who sired the Darcy who went to America. The resemblance, save for the Fitzwilliam blue eyes, was remarkable. All thoughts of profit and investment left his mind. Elizabeth had again struck the heart of the problem.

"This is the person you are serving, Will. I think that if you turned this home over to the National Trust, you would regret it the moment you signed the papers. The disappointment you would feel for having let down the generations of Darcys who built this home would burden you far more than worry over generating income to pay the bills, and far more than the distaste you feel having tourists wandering the halls. Unlike other men of your wealth, you don't own homes all over the world. You do not have countless toys, yachts, cars; whatever. You, at heart, are much happier in your backyard then you are anywhere else. So use your money to keep this place a true home. We will find a way to share it with the public, and to visit when it is closed to them. If you think about it, all of the visitors are keeping it alive while Pemberley waits for you to visit again."

During her speech, Darcy pulled her to rest in his arms, and his gaze remained on the face of his ancestor. "I *would* regret it."

"Maybe we should add a portrait of the current Master of Pemberley to the wall." She suggested with a grin. "Then everyone would see that there truly is a family here and it isn't a museum."

"Oh no, I'm not that vain. I don't want people looking at me and commenting."

"Sweetheart, the only comments would be how handsome you are." Elizabeth looked up to see him blush. "It seems to be a tradition to be included here. Isn't that your father?" She pointed to a portrait further down the gallery. He nodded and kissed her head. "Yes, that was done just before he met my mom."

"Well then, it's time that you join him, and claim your place."

"Only if you are in the portrait with me."

"But I'm not a Darcy." She protested.

"Excuse me Elizabeth, but you are." He took the hand that was grasping his waist and kissed her ring. "I refuse to spend eternity hanging in this gallery alone." His lips traveled her hand, then up to her neck where he kissed her and whispered in her ear. "I can't do it without you." A bell softly rang and they startled. He looked at his watch. "The house is open. Let's go out to the gardens."

Hand in hand they walked, noticing the queue of people purchasing tickets and beginning to enter the gates for the various tours. Guides stood waiting to take them in, and a group was forming for a garden tour. They wandered off on their own, and Elizabeth took in the beautiful landscape then turned to look at the house from a distance. "I think that living here; I would be inspired to write some very romantic stories."

He admired watching her concentration, and enjoyed seeing her clearly letting her mind play. "Really? Well, I suppose that your imagination would be fuelled by the atmosphere."

"Not only that, but the scenes would be accurate. If I needed to confirm a detail, I would only need to walk downstairs." Elizabeth laughed to see him smile and focused back on him. "Do you have business in England?"

"Yes, I do." He took her hand and led her to a bench where they sat together, his arm around her, while they watched the tourists wander about. "I always stayed in London, but if you liked, we could make those trips together, and when I finished my work, come to stay here, and you could write."

"What about you?"

"Oh honey, there is always something for me to do, all I have to do is open my email and I could be busy for weeks, I am not pinned down to my office." He laughed and as an example, pulled his phone from his pocket and started shaking his head. "I can't believe this." Darcy sighed and scrolled through the messages.

"Is something wrong?" Elizabeth leaned on his shoulder to see. "Georgiana?"

"No, she's fine; she has plans to meet up with Kitty and Lydia today." He smiled and saw her nodding with approval. "Maybe your idea for her taking your old apartment sometime is a good one."

"Maybe?" She laughed and hugged his arm. "So what makes you sigh?"

"I have messages from three men begging me for advice on relationships." He saw her smile and kissed her. "Seriously, these guys know me, how they decided that I am the one to answer their questions is a mystery."

"Don't you wish that you had someone to talk to about it?"

"I did, I talked to Barry." He smiled when she tilted her head and hugged her. "Okay, I get the point. I'm their Barry."

"I'm sure that whatever you say will be very helpful."

"John wants to know the name of our dance instructor." He laughed. "I gather that he felt pretty pitiful after our display." Elizabeth giggled. "He wants to ask Jane to plan a fundraising party for one his candidates, but isn't sure if she would like mixing their businesses. What do you think?

"I think that it would be a great idea. They would have to spend time working together, and it would reveal sides to their personalities that they wouldn't easily know when they are on their best behavior while dating. And maybe it would give them something to think about if they have a future, if they might like to blend their businesses. It would certainly give Jane something besides weddings to do, and that would be good in the slow winter months."

"You know, that is true." He bent and tapped out a reply. "Now Charles asks if he can use my box for the Giant's home opener to impress Maria since we won't be home."

"Oh, and impress her with something that he doesn't have himself? That seems wrong. It would be different if we were all going together. Maybe he should make a date to go jogging with her in Central Park."

"That's a good idea. I could suggest that he see if Richard and John might like to all use the box with their ladies." He tapped again then sighed. "Then there's bachelor number three."

"Poor Richard." Elizabeth smiled. "What is his trouble?"

"He asks for a sure fire way to get Charlotte to laugh." Darcy smiled. "She's your friend, what do you think?"

"She's got a thick shell around her but she's a sucker for genuine romance. Tell him to send her some flowers, and include a note about how she is forcing him to be soppy. It will get her to smile and call him, and he can lay on his humor then. She'll be softened up and ready to listen to him. If he gets her to laugh, she's a goner." She watched him dispense the advice and then turn off the phone. They settled back into each other's arms and watched the people wander by, nodding at those who smiled in their direction. "You know, this isn't so different from sitting in the park at home."

"It really isn't." He looked around and smiled. "As a matter of fact, it is very much like being at home."

"Maybe this won't be so hard, after all." Elizabeth touched his face and drew his head down to kiss his lips. He responded by tightening his embrace and deepening the kiss.

"Get a room." An old man and his wife said as they strolled by. Elizabeth blushed and Darcy looked up to see the smiles on the couple's faces. He saw their hands clasped and smiled back, looking down to touch Elizabeth's fingers.

"I think that I know where one might be found." Darcy grinned. "Well this *is* our honeymoon!"

OVER THE COURSE of the next two weeks, the Darcys established routines, rules, and comfort with Pemberley, its staff, and the temporary visitors. Darcy apologized and took several meetings with the curator and the non-profit board. Elizabeth used that time to talk with Mrs. Woods, and learn her concerns so she could discuss them with William. During the hours that the visitors were in the public rooms, they explored. They discovered the upper floors, guest rooms untouched by renovation, some for nearly a century. They found the attics, storage for the Christmas decorations, and furniture that had not been on display for years, all of it owned by generations of Darcys, and all of it the epitome of quality and taste for its era. Elizabeth spotted a pattern in all of the things they found, the Darcys, all of them, seemed to value usefulness over excessive display. Nothing they found was gaudy. The newly refurbished master's chambers were opulent; but nonetheless reflected the values of the man who lived there; quality, taste, and function. And at night, when the house was quiet, and the staff was gone, they wandered down to the ballroom, and danced.

They spent a great deal of time outdoors, wandering the paths of the estate and often going off the marked trails to discover places Darcy remembered from childhood, and finding comfortable vantage points, rested in each other's arms, lost in silent contemplation of the estate before them. The kitchen staff would pack picnics, and they set out, finding their secluded hideaways and often making love in the dappled sunlight of the cool forest, and shushing each other when they heard the approaching footsteps of visitors on the paths nearby. One time they were so caught up in their lovemaking that Elizabeth moaned, and a woman asked her companions if they had heard something. Darcy's fingers touched her lips and he stared into her eyes, thrusting harder, daring her to express passion, until the people moved on and they moaned freely again. It was a glorious honeymoon, free from everything, and the magic of Pemberley that he had never understood before got into his soul. By the morning of their last day, the notion of ever giving it up was unthinkable.

Mrs. Woods entered the small room that they had claimed as their private dining room, "The car is waiting anytime that you are ready to go, Mr. Darcy."

He smiled and wiped his mouth. "Thank you, Mrs. Woods. We will be very sorry to go, but I'm afraid that I need to show my wife a little more of England since I brought her here."

"I'd be happy to stay here for the rest of our trip, Will." Elizabeth smiled.

"No, I promised you London, and I promised you Paris. We will go." He laughed to see her shaking head. "I don't know when we'll be able to do this again. I dread my first day back at work."

"So do I." She said softly, then looked at Mrs. Woods. "We will return in March, if not sooner."

"Yes ma'am, you will have the house all to yourself then. May I say that it is so good to have the family back in the house? The staff has been delighted to finally care for you. May I tell them that the house is going to remain a private residence?"

"Yes, it will, and thank you for bearing with us as we made our decision, although, I believe that it was made the first day." Darcy took Elizabeth's hand and squeezed. "My wife helped me to see the correct path, as I knew she would."

Mrs. Woods left them and he continued to hold her hand. "Don't you want to go to Paris, honey?"

"I'd be happy anywhere we went, even if it was just to return home to hide on our little piece of the beach for the next two weeks." He smiled and she laughed. "We should go, I know."

"Just think of the shoes I could find you there!" He said suggestively.

"Oh Will, what am I going to do with you and all of these shoes? I am going to need outfits to go with them, and then I'll need places to go to show it all off! You are creating your own misery by forcing yourself to go out!" She reminded him with a grin.

"As long as you're with me I can handle it." He said with confidence.

"Hmm, we'll see about that."

"THIS IS TOO MUCH, Will." Elizabeth looked around the plush suite in the Dorchester Hotel in awe. "It is beautiful, but Pemberley seems sedate in comparison."

"I think that you are exaggerating." He stood behind her and rested his hands on her shoulders. "Pemberley is just as beautiful, the furnishings there are antiques so you can more easily accept the expense, I think. Isn't our house in the city like this?"

"No, that has the genuine feeling of a home. This is . . . a photo shoot." She looked up to see his smile and blushed. "I'm still getting used to all of this."

"I honestly hope that you never really do. I enjoy seeing things through your eyes. It makes me appreciate them more, and laugh at the overdone nature of most of the places I go."

"I don't know that I'll get used to people unpacking for me either." She whispered as a maid left the bedroom and he handed her a tip.

"Well, let's see what we can do in this place to please you." He smiled. "You seem determined to be unhappy."

"Oh just ignore me, Will." Elizabeth sighed and walked away to the bedroom. He stood looking after her then heard the rattle of a bottle as she dug through her purse, then the sound of water running and the bathroom door closing. Entering the room he saw a bottle of ibuprofen on the dresser. She came out and she saw him holding the bottle and looking at her with worry. "I'm fine honey, or I will be when this kicks in." She took the bottle and put it back in her bag. "You haven't been around for the monthly event before."

"Oh." He smiled and hugged her. "So how long does it last and how miserable do you get?"

"Just a few days, the birth control pills really have made it much less of a trial, and really, this is as bad as I get. We will just take a little break from love making for a few days."

"I won't whine."

"I'm happy for you." She said dryly. "Of course there are other things we can do to . . . pass the time."

Darcy chuckled and they kissed. "I look forward to it." From the other room they heard his phone ringing. It was startling because it had not rung at all in weeks. They looked at each other. "I'll see what that is about." Elizabeth saw him go and answer, then taking a seat at a desk he searched around. She came in and handed him a pen and some hotel stationary, and he smiled gratefully. Giving him some privacy, she sat on the bed, London guidebooks and maps spread before her, and kept her eyes on him from the doorway. Whatever the situation, it was not good. She saw him end the call and place another one. He talked on for another hour, his body becoming stiffer; his eyes focused as he rapidly took notes and obviously gave orders. Reality had intruded into their world. Finally he ended the call and sat staring down at the pages of notes he had taken. She got up and walked into the room, wrapping her arms around his tense shoulders, and kissed his head.

"What happened?"

"A group of five loggers working on my land were injured when a chainsaw sparked a fire, and they were trapped by the flames." He sighed and wiped his eyes. "They never should have been there. It's been very dry for weeks, it was a tinderbox. We issued a statement to desist harvesting in that area until conditions improved."

"Why did they go in?"

"I am just the landowner now, not the paper company, and not the forestry management, my statement was ignored. I stepped back from that role last month to reduce liability for situations . . . like this." He closed his eyes tight. "I hate fire."

Elizabeth hugged him. "Have you heard the extent of their injuries?"

"No, it's not being released, they are alive. My attorneys are urging me to sue the forestry management company that sent the loggers in. They were part of a small family-owned firm but they subcontract to the management company. I have no desire to sue; they want me to send a message to think before throwing people into these dangerous situations, and to counteract any claims that the injured workers might make against me as the landowner. Fortunately we have proof that our statement to desist was issued before the fire."

"Do we need to go home?"

"You would be willing to go?" He looked up at her. "I would like to make sure that their families are provided for. They aren't my employees, I have no responsibility for them, I realize that I have an abundance of staff willing and able to carry out my directions, but it was my trees that they were harvesting, and . . . I would like to make a gesture. I can give the orders from here; I won't be traveling to their bedsides."

"But it would be easier to accomplish from home." She said softly. "You arrange for the plane and I'll pack up our things."

"Thank you, honey. It's the right thing to do, I think." He looked up to see her studying him. "I'm sorry."

"No, don't apologize. Seeing your response for people who really have so little connection to you is . . . Will it makes me love you even more. We'll go home, you can take care of this situation, then if you like, we can go to the Hamptons and finish our honeymoon there. There is no reason why we can't still do that. We've already had a longer trip than most people do." Elizabeth smiled and bent to kiss him.

"I can't begin to say how much I love you." He touched her cheek and she left to begin packing up their things while he called for the plane. Ten minutes later he was standing at the bedroom door, he saw all of her visitor's guides and maps and sighed. He knew she was disappointed, no matter what she said. "Honey, the plane won't be here until tomorrow morning and the crew has to rest before leaving so . . . we still have today and the morning. What would you like to see?"

"Really?" Elizabeth bit her lip and looked over the guides, trying to pick one sight out of the thousands of things to do.

"Really." He laughed to see her chewing and stepped closer to touch her mouth. "Be as touristy as you want." Elizabeth giggled and they hugged. "However, I draw the line at bus tours."

"Darn; and that was my fondest wish!" Elizabeth's eyes met William's and they smiled. Nothing more needed to be said.

Chapter 17

"**I** can't believe that you cut your honeymoon short to come home for this!" Georgiana said from her seat in Elizabeth's dressing room. "Pemberley has people to do these things, William just won't let go."

"William may have difficulty letting go of control with some aspects of his business, but our returning home early has nothing to do with that. He cares very deeply for anyone hurt on his property, and particularly with these men so terribly injured by fire. Certainly you can appreciate that." Elizabeth looked at her sharply.

Instantly abashed, she dropped her eyes. "I didn't think of it that way. I guess that I was thinking selfishly. I'm sorry."

"Selfishly? It was our honeymoon, not yours. What difference does it make to you that we came home early?" She stopped putting things away and studied her sister. "We spoiled some plans of yours, didn't we?"

"No."

"Come on, there's no point in lying, I have four sisters who are far more skilled at it. What was going to happen?"

"Oh, nothing terrible, I . . . I was going to have a party." She looked up then back down. "Some friends from school to celebrate the semester starting and me returning to school."

"And when was this to happen?" Elizabeth leaned on the dressing table and crossed her arms.

"Saturday."

"Well, William and I hope to go to Pemberley and resume our honeymoon when he finishes dealing with this situation, although, I admit to having some apprehension with him walking in that office today. I have no doubt that he's going to get sucked into something else."

"So I can still ask them here?" Georgiana said hopefully.

"No alcohol, right? You are underage."

"I know." She rolled her eyes.

"Do your friends?"

"Of course!" Georgiana looked up at her and glared. "I wish that you would give me some credit for good sense! I wish that I lived back in the dorms! Then I could do what I want!"

Elizabeth raised her brow. "Are you through with your tantrum? You already did what you wanted when living in the dorm. And I distinctly remember you expressing your happiness in not having to return there." Georgiana's glare disappeared and was replaced with a deep blush. "I'll tell you right now, William will be even more direct in reminding you of your past behavior. And I'll tell you something else. We have been discussing letting you move into my old apartment after Christmas to get a feel for being independent. William is not enthusiastic about the idea, and I have been working on him. How you handle bringing people in here is going to matter in his ultimate decision."

"You . . . you were going to let me live on my own?" Her eyes grew wide at the thought.

"I think that it would be an invaluable experience for you, and if you like, and Kitty agrees, you may share the apartment with her after she graduates next May. Lydia may want to join you as well."

"Maybe Jane will be gone by then." Georgiana mused quietly.

"Maybe." Elizabeth agreed.

"Thanks for pushing this idea with William; he never would have agreed to it if I asked." Georgiana hugged her. "I'm sorry for sounding like a child; I guess that I'm just itchy to get away from here. Not that it's a terrible place or anything . . ."

"No, but you're at the age where you want to just see who you are, you have grown over the past few months. I understand that. I'm sure that hanging around with us isn't your idea of great fun either." Elizabeth laughed to see her barely repressed agreement. "I know; we are a little distracted with each other."

"A little is hardly the word for it." Georgiana giggled. "I promise, I was not planning a toga party, it was just some friends and watching movies and stuff."

"That sounds great. I'll talk to William about it, unless you want to?" She looked at her pointedly.

"I guess that I should. It's his house and . . . it would make me look more . . . mature."

"Exactly." They hugged again and looked up when they heard a knock.

"Mrs. Darcy, you have a visitor." Mrs. Reynolds announced with a smile and a wink at

"Who is it?" Elizabeth walked with her to the stairs.

"Oh, you'll see."

Elizabeth entered the front parlor to find an impeccably dressed man. His appearance, from his finely buffed shoes to his perfect manicure, to his silver hair tied back in a pony tail, screamed fashion. He turned an assessing eye over her and she felt herself being x-rayed. Elizabeth looked down over her jeans and blouse and blushed, then saw the slightest nod of approval from the man. "Mrs. Darcy, I am delighted to meet you at last." He took her hand and then covered it with his left. "I have wondered if I ever would."

"I have only been married for two weeks, so you have not had much opportunity, Mr. . . ."

He laughed. "Forgive me, I am Maurice LeBlanc. You misunderstand, I wondered if Mr. Darcy would ever marry." He cleared his throat. "I have been sent to you today to perform an act of contrition." Turning, he retrieved an envelope and a box. "Open the box first."

She looked at him curiously, then lifted the lid and gasped. "Oh my."

"I see that you appreciate the gift. That is very good." Maurice lifted a shoe out and caressed it lovingly. "Python. Exquisite. Christian Louboutin, worth every penny."

"How many pennies?" She whispered.

"Ah, that question does not surprise me from what your husband said. I will not enlighten you. Please read the card." He placed the shoe back in the box and took it away from her. Elizabeth opened the envelope, and began to read.

Dearest loveliest Elizabeth,

You, my love, have been so incredibly gracious, willingly giving up our honeymoon to indulge my feeling of responsibility. I know of no other woman who would have done such a thing, not without a fight, and not without making me feel this error of my behavior perpetually for the rest of our, likely short, marriage. It only proves once again how very perfect you are for me. Now I must make up to you our lost honeymoon. I present you with your new shoes, and introduce you to Maurice. He has dressed me for the last five years and he has never let me down. If we had remained in London and gone on to Paris, we would have gone out fourteen nights. I want you to take your new shoes and find an outfit to go with them, then I want you to think of fourteen places you wish to go in New York. Let nothing stop your imagination, whether it is outrageously expensive or silly, I don't care.

Maurice is going to take you on a tour of the most fashionable shops in this city. He is going to force you to do what I know you would not. He is going to dress you for each of your fantasy dates, and you and I are going to enjoy them. He has no hesitation in spending my money, and I dearly want to lavish it upon you. Come on my pretty woman, let me indulge myself and let you play. You are Elizabeth Regina Bennet Darcy, the Mistress of Pemberley, and queen of my heart.

I love you honey,
Will

"Oh my." Elizabeth's eyes reflected her love and Maurice studied her with a smile. He was going to enjoy this assignment very much. She looked up at him and blushed. "I guess that you know what he requests."

"Of course! I was awakened at an ungodly hour by his insistent phone calls." He took her hand and started walking out of the door. "Come on, let's see your closet."

"You seem to know your way around." She laughed as he pulled her along.

"I have been dressing Mr. Darcy since his father died. He was hopelessly stuck in the uniform of a student."

"He could care less about his clothes, how did you ever teach him to turn himself out so perfectly? He is so good at it." Elizabeth saw a glint in his eye. "Well?"

"Have you visited Mr. Darcy's closet?"

"Well, not really . . ."

They entered the master bedroom and he walked straight over to Darcy's dressing room, and pointed at the neatly arranged hangers and drawers. "Do you see the colors on the hangers? The labels on the drawers? Everything is marked. He just has to follow the system and whatever he puts on will match. I had to train his staff so that things would be put away properly. It was a master stroke that I developed with several other gentlemen." Maurice smiled triumphantly and basked in Elizabeth's lilting laughter. "I see that you approve."

"Very much!"

"Now, to your closet." He strode over to the dressing room and began going through her things, understanding her taste, and quietly tutting at the labels. He pulled out a dress and examined it. "Put this on along with your new shoes. We have much to do."

"I appreciate this gift, I do, but I don't want to be made over to look like a runway model."

"Nobody wants to look like that, dear. We will bring out the beauty that you have chosen to ignore. We will accentuate, we will highlight, we will blow him away." He smiled and left the room. "Downstairs, ten minutes."

She stared after him then running back to her bedroom; found her phone and quickly called Jane and breathlessly told her of the gift. "Should I go?"

"Are you insane? I've been dying to do this with you for years! Go! Enjoy it! Get something in my size!" Elizabeth laughed, and Jane continued. "Seriously Lizzy, you have married a very rich and loving man. He has had nobody to share this with. Can you imagine how much joy it will bring him to give this to you and even more, to go on these dates?"

"I just wanted to check, I didn't want to seem greedy by accepting this. I know he isn't saying that I'm wanting, he just wants to . . . see me happy."

"And he likes looking at you." Jane added with a soft whisper. She heard Elizabeth's nervous giggle and laughed again. "Lizzy, it's time for you to live a little, you two are such good people, you deserve each other. Now get going and call me when you get home."

"Okay, I'm off with Maurice." She ended the call and started to go dress, then stopped to send a quick text message.

Across town Darcy sat in his office, surrounded by lawyers. The soft beep on his phone instantly drew his attention and he lifted it up to see the message. His eyes glowed as he read, *Gone shopping. Love, Mrs. Darcy.*

"OH LIZZY!" Jane sat next to Georgiana and gasped when she appeared in the next outfit. "I want a personal shopper!"

Elizabeth twirled and giggled. "William has made a very grave error letting loose my repressed shopaholic."

"No, he's going to love this so much." Jane looked over the clothes, every category was covered, evening gowns, cocktail dresses, dresses for dancing fast, slow, and dirty, jeans, tight pants, blouses, halter tops, classic, casual . . . she was ready for anything.

"How did you do all of this in one day?" Georgiana's eyes were wide.

"We started with a few designers he favors, but then went to Bergdorf Goodman and he just kept sending things back for me to try on. I would appear, he would look, then make a motion to the sales woman and the item was kept or not. I didn't really know what he chose until I got home."

"Do you like everything?" Jane looked at the collection with barely restrained envy.

"I do, I really do. It's so amazing." Elizabeth smiled and giggled again. "I feel so bad."

"So what are you guys going to do first?" She stood and picked up the python shoes. "Lizzy do you have any idea what these . . ."

"No, and I'm not going to find out. Maurice refused to let me see tags. Will obviously filled him in on my thrifty tendencies." She sat down and surveyed the mess of clothes and bags and watched Georgiana eyeing the array.

"I think that we'll just stay in tonight, but I have a lot of plans. Maurice was brainstorming with me; he's got a very fertile imagination."

"I think that you have made a new friend. Maybe he should meet John." Jane smiled and saw the two girls looking at her with interest. "He's really trying hard to match William."

"He should try harder to be himself." Elizabeth said and began putting everything away. The empty closets were not looking quite so barren anymore.

Jane's phone rang and she looked at it with surprise. "It's Charlotte. Hi!"

"Hi Jane! Do you think that you and John would like to come on a triple date? Maria wants to go to a club to dance, and well, I'm not too confident about it. Richard will probably be happy to sit and watch it all, but I don't want to be a stick in the mud either. We're just . . . old."

"Oh, and where do John and I fit in with that? He's older than Richard!"

"Yeah, but at least he tries to dance. Please?"

"Well, how about Lizzy and William? They might want to come, too."

"We were going to go Friday."

"They came home early, long story, but William told Lizzy that anything she wanted, he would do without protest, this might be the one and only opportunity to get him into a real dance club." Jane looked over to see Elizabeth looking at her curiously. "Hold on. Lizzy, Charlotte wants a quadruple date, what do you think?"

She bit her lip, and picked up the new shoes and shook them. "I think that Lizzy says yes. How about dinner at nine, then dancing after?"

"You're on!" Charlotte cried and hung up.

"Now what kind of a dance club are we going to? The really hip places don't get going until the middle of the night, you know."

"Um, 10:30 most open the doors, but nobody really shows up until midnight." Georgiana said quietly.

"How do you know?"

"I'm in college." She shrugged. "Most of the people there are older than me."

"I've never ever stayed up all night. Just once I want to do it." Elizabeth said with a wicked smile.

"Can we talk our guys into it?" Jane asked hopefully.

"Well, MY guy said he'd do anything I asked." Elizabeth winked.

Late that night, Darcy returned home, very, very tired and hungry. He walked in the back door and into the kitchen to the welcome sight of Elizabeth sitting with her back to the door, bent over a notebook, obviously working on her story, and dressed in comfortable workout clothes. He quietly set down his briefcase and laptop then slipped his hands around her waist, and rested his face in the crook of her neck. "Hi."

Elizabeth smiled with his touch, and taking his hands, leaned against his head. "Hi honey."

"I missed you so much. The only thing I could think about was coming home. We should be in London, or Paris, or Pemberley."

"Which one?"

"I don't care." He said softly and nuzzled closer and smiled to hear her laugh.

"So now that we are here, do you think that it was necessary to return?"

"Yes." He sighed and tightened his hold. "Yes, I needed to be here. It goes far beyond the injured men . . . oh honey; I just can't talk about it anymore tonight. I'm so sorry to have ruined our evening."

"Are you hungry?"

"Yes." He lifted his head. "Is there anything left from your dinner?"

"I waited for you." She turned and kissed him.

"You didn't have to do that." He kissed her nose and rested his forehead on hers. "Where's Georgiana?"

"In bed, she has an early class."

"Good." Darcy's hands ran up her sides and pulled her closer, then sighed when she wrapped her arms and legs around him. "Ohhh, this would be a wonderful position." He rubbed himself against her and closed his eyes. "I need you so much tonight. Can we?"

"No, but I'll take care of you." Elizabeth kissed him then caressed his hair. "Go change into something comfortable and I'll make us dinner. I'll tell you all about Maurice."

Darcy smiled and noticed her eyes twinkling. "I take it that the day was a success?"

"Oh, just wait until you get the bills!" She laughed and his face lit up.

"Oh, now this sounds very promising! Have you thought of where we will exhibit your new fashions?" He played with her hair and visibly relaxed.

"I have, and I hope that you keep your promise of going wherever my whim takes us without protest."

"What are you up to Mrs. Darcy?" He asked suspiciously.

"Keep Friday night open, Mr. Darcy." Elizabeth gave him a soft open-mouthed kiss that made his knees weak, then sent him on his way.

"GOOD MORNING!" Charles looked in Darcy's door. "I'm surprised to see you."

"Why? We didn't finish everything, but I am determined to do it today and get out of here before something else comes up." He saw Charles smile. "I'm serious. Once they know I'm here, it will begin. I managed to stay well-hidden yesterday."

"Oh come off it, everyone knew you were here, the gossip mill was running at full tilt, wondering if something had happened on the honeymoon to send you home two weeks early."

"What?" He sat up straight and his gaze became hard and focused. "What was said, who was spreading rumors? I certainly hope that those rumors were refuted immediately!"

"Relax Darcy, none of it is true. It was just fodder for conversation. If you protest it, they will just think it is true. Maybe we should put out a memo saying how you have contributed to the relief funds for those workers . . ."

Darcy spoke sharply. "No. That is a private matter."

Charles sighed. "Well, I guess that you can't discuss the lawsuit either. Have you made a decision about breaking the contract with the foresters?"

"No, and I haven't decided about suing them yet either. How many acres did we lose?"

"About 7500, not too bad, considering the fire in June."

"It's still nearly twelve square miles, Charles . . . You could fit Pemberley's park in there." He mused then looked up. "I've decided to keep it. We'll be setting up a charitable trust to protect it forever. We hope to spend time there often."

Charles took a seat and folded his arms across his chest. "That's quite a change. I was sure that you would give it up, you've talked about it so many times. Why this decision?"

"It is a place containing the memories of some of the most important days of my life, and my history . . . and our future family's history." His expression softened and he relaxed. "It would have been a grave mistake to give it up. I had no real connection with it before, it was just a place to visit occasionally with my parents, and sure, it had some fond childhood memories; and of course the story of very distant relatives, but now . . . my marriage began there."

"I don't understand."

"I'm not surprised." Darcy smiled and chuckled at the offended look on Charles's face. "I'm not questioning your comprehension, only your experience. I needed Elizabeth by my side to understand it all."

"Oh, back to the love theme." Charles relaxed again, and Darcy realized that he still did not understand. "So I hear that we are all going out tomorrow night."

"We?"

"You, me, John, and Richard . . . and our respective ladies. Dinner, clubbing . . . all night long." He laughed to see the horror in Darcy's eyes. "I understand that Elizabeth told Jane that you had agreed to do anything she wished."

"Damn it!"

"It will be fun, you'll see." Charles stood when he saw Darcy's hand inching towards his phone, knowing that his presence was not desired. "I'll . . . see you after you finish your call."

The number for Elizabeth's phone was pushed before the door was closed. "Hi!"

"What's this about us going clubbing all night?" He demanded.

"Charles said something." Elizabeth's eyes closed. "You don't sound thrilled."

"Elizabeth, it is one thing for us to go to a dance club, but these places that Charles visits . . . I can't do it." He sighed and ran his hand through his hair. "Why didn't you tell me about this last night?"

"You were so tired, and well, I started having second thoughts when you went up to change. I didn't want to make you go somewhere I thought you probably wouldn't enjoy." She listened to his heavy sigh. "I'll cancel."

"Do you want to go?" He said quietly.

"I've never gone, I don't know what to expect." Elizabeth bit her lip. "We could just go in and look around and leave if we are uncomfortable."

"You mean if I am."

"No, I mean *we*. I am no party girl Will, you know that." Again there was silence, and Elizabeth tried to understand what he was thinking, he didn't mind the dance clubs they had visited before . . . then it hit her. This was exactly what he did in the days after his parents died. "Oh Will, I'm sorry, I wasn't thinking. Of course you wouldn't want to go to a place like that!"

Darcy closed his eyes and Elizabeth could hear the sound of his breathing, and recognized that he was battling some demon. "It was another lifetime, Lizzy. I'll go if you want me to."

"No. We would not have been included in this evening had we not come home early. Charlotte called Jane, not me. We will do something else." She said positively. "I am not upset, so stop berating yourself, as I know you are."

"I just can't stop spoiling things for you, can I?" He said bitterly. "We'll go."

"No, we won't."

"YES WE WILL!" He bellowed and the silence that followed was deafening. "Lizzy?"

"Are we better now?" She said stiffly.

"No, actually now I have something else to add to my list of self-hatred. I'm sorry."

Elizabeth sighed. "No, it's my fault. I should have known that Charles would mention it to you today. It's my fault for keeping my own counsel. I should have discussed it with you last night. I'm sorry. I thought you would be shy of the crowd; it never crossed my mind that it would bring back bad memories. Truly honey, we can do anything else."

His voice was nearly a whisper. "What do you want to do, really want to do, Lizzy? I'll go anywhere with you, as long as we're together. I need to face my past as much as you have. I'm willing to make new memories."

"I . . . got this little black leather skirt yesterday and a halter top, and I thought with my new shoes it would look really great in a club . . ."

He groaned with the description. "Friday night . . . will we be able to . . ."

"When we get home we can indulge your imagination any way you desire."

"Black leather?" He paused and swallowed while he pictured her legs and the shoes. "Is it really short?"

"Slutty."

"Okay."

"Will?"

"Yeah?"

"Can you imagine us dancing, with the music thumping, you standing behind me, and us grinding together?"

"God yes." His eyes closed and he squeezed his legs together.

"Or maybe out back in the alley, me leaning against a wall with one of my legs bent and up over your arm?"

"Ohhhhhhhhhhhhhh."

"I'd love it, Will." She whispered softly. "I'd really love it. The thought of you pinning me against the wall while people walked by on the street just a few feet away . . ." She heard him moan. "I want to make you so hard."

"I already am, baby." His breathing changed and he said nothing for a few moments until she heard him gasp and swear.

"Honey?"

"That was wicked." Darcy grabbed some tissues and cleaned up. "What you do to my imagination is . . . so good, honey. So very, very good. I love you so much." Elizabeth giggled and he breathed easier. "Okay, we'll check this place out, I can't promise that I will want to stay, but I'm willing to go for you."

"Thank you, sweetie, I love you."

"Any other surprises like this up your sleeve?"

"Nope, just fun stuff." Elizabeth smiled to hear his sigh of relief. "I know not to push it, and really, it's not me anyway, this is a favor to our friends."

"Okay. I . . . guess that I should work or something."

"You could come home; I'm in the garden . . ."

"Don't get me going again." He growled. Elizabeth laughed and hung up. He went into the bathroom and washed his hands. His face was still flushed and he studied himself in the mirror, maybe . . . if the place was crowded enough . . . he could really surprise her.

"WHERE ARE you going?" Caroline asked. "Who with?"

"What do you care?" Charles checked out his appearance, combed his hair, chewed an Altoid and turned to face her. "Did you find what you needed? I have to go and meet my date."

"You must be ashamed of her if you don't want her to meet your sister." Caroline smirked. "It looks like you're going clubbing. I think that I should come along."

"NO." Charles grabbed his wallet and keys and ushered her towards the door. "Don't you have a date? It's Friday night, you should be out with some guy."

"I'm meeting Louisa for dinner. Her husband is out of town."

"Her husband has a name." Charles closed the door and checked the lock.

"Yes, I call him The Slug." Caroline smirked and they got on the elevator. "Maybe we'll come and join you afterwards. What club are you going to?"

"No, Caroline. I'm meeting people, and Maria is coming with her sister and Richard, and . . ." He stopped; he screwed up by naming people.

"Richard? Fitzwilliam? William's cousin?" Charles said nothing and she read his face easily. "Will William be there? Oh, he will!"

"Goodbye Caroline." He grabbed a cab and got in. She jumped in after him. "What are you doing?"

"I thought I'd share it."

"It won't work Caroline." He leaned up and gave the driver her address. "Darcy is very married. You couldn't get any more married than he is. It's not going to change. He has already banned you from the office. Give it up." The cab stopped at her building and he leaned over and opened the door. "See you later."

"Why can't you ever do anything for me?" She slammed the door in his face.

"I'd rather do something for me." He muttered and the cab started moving again.

DARCY CLIMBED in the car after Elizabeth and watched in appreciation as she crossed her legs. Unable to resist, he ran his hand up her silky bare skin and to her hip where the very tight, very expensive, very short skirt lay. "What's under here?" His fingers slipped under the skirt, still feeling nothing. He licked his lips and met her eyes. Elizabeth glanced at Frank, his eyes were straight ahead, and uncrossed her legs. Darcy's fingers moved between her thighs and encountered lace, then made a discovery, "crotchless?" He whispered. She smiled and he moaned while she recrossed her legs, trapping his fingers in her warm nest.

The car pulled up to the Bennet building and he straightened up, moving over to allow Jane to enter. "You look great!" She said as she got in. "Thanks for the lift; it would have been silly for John to drive. He and Richard live right there near the restaurant. Charles will pick up Charlotte and Maria." She looked at them curiously. William was flushed and Elizabeth was smiling like a pleased cat. "What were you two doing?"

"Nothing, William was admiring my new skirt." She laughed and squeezed his hand.

"Yes, um, Maurice knows his business." The sisters exchanged looks and smiled while Darcy entwined their fingers and played with her ring. They arrived at the restaurant, and found the rest of the party already inside and waiting for them. It was noisy and very busy; a Friday night vibe definitely filled the place.

Richard leaned over to Elizabeth and spoke in her ear. "Your advice worked, I got her to laugh and now she's putty in my hands." She looked at him then over to Charlotte who had a previously unknown expression of contentment on her face. "She told me that she was editing a romance book where the hero was an English soldier and was saving the daughter of a French aristocrat from the guillotine. She got all dewy-eyed when she talked about how daring he was, so I showed up at her office in a red uniform. It was a good thing that her desk was so far from the doorway or I would have been hit by the coffee she spit out." Elizabeth started to laugh and he grinned. "After that I offered to rescue her from her office and took her to lunch."

"Still in uniform?"

"Yes, of course!" He grinned then looked over to Charlotte, who was listening in. "She was impressed with my originality."

"When I got back to the office, my assistant June told me that was the most romantic thing she had ever seen, and that I'd be a fool to let him go." She smiled and he put his arm around her. "So maybe I'll keep him."

"I'm very happy for you both." Elizabeth smiled and turned to see William listening and nodding his head, while he drew her into his arms. "It seems that love is in the air."

"Who is next?" He kissed her cheek and looked to John and Jane. "Do you think that they know how silly they look staring at each other like that?"

Charles coughed. "That's the pot calling the kettle black!" He saw Darcy shrug and grin, then turned to Maria. "I think that we are the only sensible ones here. We are taking our time."

"That is because I am making you." Everyone laughed and the food arrived. The service was slow and by the time they left it was nearing midnight. Darcy met Elizabeth's enquiring look and kissed her.

"It's okay, let's go." They piled into two cabs and headed for the dance club. It was one meant for high-end clientele, the excellent looks of the group would have assured their entry, but the doorman's tip didn't hurt to grease things along. There were four floors, six bars, and a variety of music and dance styles going on. It was very dark, the dance floor was alive with colored lights, neon glowed around the walls, and small lights barely illuminated the tables. The ladies found a large booth while the men took off to get drink orders.

"So do you think that William will want to stay?" Jane shouted to Elizabeth.

"I don't know, I won't complain if he doesn't. I've seen the inside, my curiosity is satisfied. I can say already that I prefer the place we always go to dance."

"Oh, you have to get him to dance! I want to see you two in action again!" Maria shouted back.

"I think that Richard and I will people watch." Charlotte said and waved to him as he looked around the dark room. He grinned and set down their drinks. Taking her hand he pulled her up. "Come on, let's dance!"

"What!"

"It's just standing in place and wiggling. I can handle that!" He dragged her off to the dance floor and the girls laughed to see her pleading wide eyes as she looked back at them, and they shouted encouragement.

John and Darcy appeared next. After watching Richard for a few moments and laughing at him, John set down the drinks and offered his hand to Jane. "Come on, I have to show up my brother." She smiled and he kissed her when she slid out of the booth. He winked at Darcy. "Let's see if the dance lessons helped!"

Darcy looked at Elizabeth and bit his lip then saw Maria who was searching the crowd for Charles. "He's coming; there was a crush at the bar." He noticed Charles chatting with a girl and closed his eyes, wishing he would pay attention to the woman he was with, then was relieved to see him approaching the table. "That took awhile."

"I saw some people I knew." He noted Darcy's pointed look and took a gulp of his drink, then grabbed Maria. "Let's hit it!" They were gone, leaving Darcy and Elizabeth alone.

"Well? Should we stay?" Elizabeth held his hand. "It's okay if we go, Will."

"Come on." He smiled and led her out to the dance floor. "I have to see that skirt in action." He spoke in her ear as he stood behind her. The music pounded, the lights flashed, the floor became increasingly crowded and loud, and Darcy's hands were firmly wrapped around Elizabeth's waist as her hips swayed and her bottom brushed against him. His gaze moved between the view of her skirt and looking down her halter top at her unbound breasts. Pressing his groin to her back, he kissed her neck, then her shoulder. One hand drifted down her stomach, and he pressed her backwards while he ground into her. There was no room to step anywhere; they just kept going in place. Elizabeth's hands came up to hold his head and his lips found her mouth for a backwards kiss, as his hands instantly moved up to cup her breasts. She turned and they embraced, her hands on his shoulders while his firmly held her hips to him and they stared at each other, kissing and rubbing their bodies together in time to the incessant beat of the music and flashing lights. Elizabeth's tongue licked his lips and their mouths opened to nearly swallow each other as they moved. The dance floor became packed so tight with bouncing, gyrating bodies that they had no choice but to maintain the position. Elizabeth felt the front of her skirt rising, and felt a finger, then a second, slipping into her and pumping hard.

"Ohhhhhhhhh." She groaned in his mouth. He kept going and she dropped her hand down to his crotch, measuring and rubbing his length and suddenly realizing . . . "You aren't wearing anything under your pants!"

Darcy pulled away and smiled at her, letting her skirt down and smoothing it over her curves. When the song ended he found a way through the crowd before the next began, and then led her back to their table in the darkest corner of the room. Nobody else was there, and he sat down, pulling her into his lap. They began kissing again, his hands in her hair, then gliding down to feel her breasts. "Baby I want you." He said hoarsely. "Now."

"You want to go home?" She panted and looked up to him, and saw his head shaking. His hand slipped up the tiny skirt. "Here?" He nodded. "Will!"

"Nobody can see, it's dark, we're behind the table. They'll just think we're kissing." He touched her and she moaned. "Come on honey, we're dressed for this."

"What has gotten into you tonight?"

"I need to make new memories; I need them to be of you." His hands rested inside of her thigh, and they kissed again. "Please understand." He lifted her up onto his lap and she straddled him, kissing and rubbing their bodies against each other to the incessant beat of the music. The position, the danger, the excitement, made it intoxicating. Darcy kissed her fiercely and drawing away, stared at her. His hands lifted her skirt and again his fingers slipped between her thighs. "Please." He moaned.

Elizabeth held his face in her hands and kissed him deeply, his arms held her tight to his body and when they came up for air, she stared him right in the eyes. "Let those old memories go, Will. You have me, you don't have to prove anything here."

Gradually their breathing calmed and their grip on each other relaxed. Elizabeth slipped down to sit across his lap. Darcy hugged her and pressed his mouth to her ear. "Let's go home. I have a lot more loving to give you."

"Whatever you want, it's yours." She kissed him and they separated, repairing their clothes just in time to greet Richard and Charlotte returning to the booth.

Richard dropped down and grinned. "I'm whipped."

"Me too." Darcy wrapped his arm around Elizabeth and kissed her. "We came, we saw, we conquered." He looked down to see her laughing and grinned. "We're heading home."

"Already?"

"Will kept his promise to come . . ." He squeezed her thigh under the table, "and I will keep my promise to get him in bed." She squeezed his back. Richard and Charlotte exchanged glances. "I promised to get him up good and early in the morning." Darcy smiled widely and kissed her.

"Oh, yes, and what are you doing so early?" Richard asked innocently.

"Exercising!" Elizabeth slid out of the booth, and held out her hand to William. John and Jane approached, looking very much the worse for wear. "We're leaving, it's too crowded."

"Yes, we've had enough, too." John looked at Darcy curiously then saw Richard's smile. "Want to share a cab?"

"No, I don't." Darcy kissed Jane and Elizabeth gave her a hug. "Good night to you all." They walked out of the room and John bent down to his brother.

"I believe that our taciturn cousin is on his way to get some."

"I think he was about to." Richard said quietly. John looked at him then back out into the crowd, and back to his brother. "Lucky bastard."

"I think it's a good idea." Richard stood up and helped Charlotte out of the booth. "Come on, let's go somewhere quiet."

"Such as?"

"Your place?" He tilted his head and raised his brows.

She looked him over and smiled. "Okay." He grinned and winked at his brother. "See ya!"

John turned to Jane, "I'll take you home." She nodded, and he grabbed her hand and looked in her eyes. "I'd like to stay tonight. Would you like that?"

"And do what?" She said nervously. John stepped forward and kissed her, then pulled her close against his body.

"I think that it's time that I told you everything that is on my mind." He looked into her eyes then touched her face. "And I want to hear everything that is on yours." He leaned down and kissed her again. "And then . . . I'll show you. If you want me to."

"I would . . . really like that, John." Jane smiled and kissed him.

He beamed at her. "Let's go."

She nodded and spotting Charles and Maria near the edge of the dance floor, said goodnight. Charles leaned down to Maria's ear. "Do you want to stay?"

"Yes, let's go try another floor!" She smiled and he grinned back and holding her hand; happily followed her upstairs to party on.

In the quiet of the cab, Elizabeth leaned into William's arms. He kissed her hair and hugged her tight. "I can't believe what we almost did in there; I can't believe what we *did* do."

"Me either." She looked up at him; his eyes were warm and happy. "I thought that you hated crowds."

"I do, but like in our dance club, nobody knows us, and that place was practically pitch dark. Why do you think I had such a tight hold on you? I thought I might lose you if I didn't."

"Oh, so it was a protective instinct." She smiled and he grinned. "I thought it had something to do with lust."

"It did. I didn't want anyone else lusting after you." He held her tighter and closed his eyes. The cab stopped at the house and they got out, holding hands and leaning into each other while they walked up the quiet street. The only sound was the occasional passing car and the click of her heels as they made their way up the sidewalk. It was a cool night, autumn would arrive in a few weeks, and Elizabeth's bare shoulders were cold. She shivered and leaned against his solid warm chest.

Darcy kissed her hair, wrapping his arm around her. "Thank you for tonight." She looked up and smiled. "I'm glad that we went. I don't know that I would want to do it again, but . . . it proved to me that I could do it and put the ghosts away." He kissed her cheek. "I wasn't sure what I thought would happen if I ever entered a place like that again, but I held onto you for dear life."

"I'm proud of you. I knew how difficult it was to walk into that situation. I can't imagine the memories that flooded over you."

"I just concentrated on you, honey." They stopped as he unlocked the gate and they walked inside the garden. He locked it up again then taking her hand looked at her. "We did some pretty . . . exciting things in there, things that I never even imagined doing before. I don't know that I'll ever be brave enough to do that again."

"Are you warning me?" Elizabeth laughed and he blushed. She caressed his cheek and spoke softly, "I would rather go back to dancing in a room where we can move more than a few inches, where the lights are bright enough to see each other, and where the culmination of the evening is alone in our home."

"Me too." He kissed her, then licked his lips. "Baby . . ."

The change in his tone immediately demanded her attention and he pressed her up against the side of the house, running his hands possessively down her shoulders to her waist, then lifted her skirt. "What are you doing?" Elizabeth moaned softly. He looked down and unzipped his pants, drawing himself out, and bent to raise her leg. "I think that you had a fantasy to fulfill." He kissed her hard and pushed into her.

"Ohhh!"

Darcy looked down into her passionate eyes, and ground his hips into her, the porchlight serving as a spotlight for any passerby who looked in the garden gate. "I will never, ever, forget tonight."

"AREN'T THEY up yet?" Georgiana looked at the clock again.

"I'm not surprised, I heard them come in and it was nearly 3 AM." Mrs. Reynolds glanced up from where she was wiping the countertop and saw Georgiana's fretting face. "I would be surprised to see them before noon."

"But . . . they were supposed to go to Pemberley today!"

The kitchen door was pushed open and Darcy entered, giving them a little smile and heading straight for the coffee pot. Mrs. Reynolds beat him to it and poured him out a mug. "Thank you." He took a long sip and closed his eyes. "I am too old for late night parties."

Mrs. Reynolds raised her brow. "I am twice your age, don't talk to me about being too old."

He chuckled and sank down on a stool. "Elizabeth will be down soon. She's talking to Jane." He smiled; anticipating hearing the details of his cousin's wooing, and looked around. "I guess breakfast is over."

"I was just getting lunch together." Mrs. Reynolds walked over to the refrigerator to take out the fixings for the meal.

"When do you leave?" Georgiana said casually.

"Leave?" He looked at her and added some sugar to his cup and stirred it slowly. "Am I going somewhere?"

"You're supposed to go to Pemberley for the rest of your honeymoon! Elizabeth said you would." There was a note of strain in her voice.

"Maybe we'll go on Monday; we're too tired to go anywhere today." He smiled and took a sip.

"But . . . my party!"

"What party? I don't remember you asking me about having a party. I do remember telling you not to have one while we were on our honeymoon, and since we returned you have not spoken to me about it, so obviously it couldn't happen, could it?" He raised his brows and looked over to the newspaper on the counter and opened it up. "I wouldn't let you have an unsupervised party in any case, Georgiana, so if you have invited friends over for a night of watching movies or whatever, we will be in the house."

"But . . . Elizabeth said that . . ."

"Elizabeth said that you needed to speak to me. You haven't. All it would have taken is a phone call to me at work yesterday. We still would have been here, and if we were still away, I would have asked your aunt and uncle to come over for the evening. Just because we didn't make you stay at their place while we were gone does not give you license to do whatever you want. You stayed here because Mrs. Reynolds was here, and I signed papers before we left to give her the authority to act on your behalf until a relative could be contacted." He shook his head. "Do you really think that I would allow a party in my house, for college students, hosted by an underage girl?"

"But . . . What about me living on my own?"

He shrugged. "Maybe it will have to wait until you are eighteen. Kitty will be twenty soon, and living in her parent's building would be almost like living at home. We'll just wait for you two to live together."

"That's not fair!" Georgiana cried. "I'll . . . I'll get my own place!"

"And how will you pay for it?" He took another sip. "Like it or not, you either have to get a job, or stick to my rules, and any job you get isn't going to buy you an apartment, at least, not anything bigger than your closet." He saw her disappointment and sighed. "You know, I wouldn't be quite so hard about this if you had spoken to me. I don't mind you having friends over at all, but when you apply the term of party to it, that tells me that your expectations for the night are different from just sitting and watching movies. Am I correct?"

"Maybe." She said quietly.

He nodded and rattled his paper. "So, Lizzy and I will be here tonight. We won't bother you, but we will be home."

"Okay."

"Next time, talk to me. I don't appreciate you trying to go behind my back. I'm afraid that you need to earn my trust. I know that you were manipulated by Wickham, but it proved that you might be manipulated by others as well. I won't let that happen again."

Georgiana left the room and he looked up to see Mrs. Reynolds smiling at him. She came over to refill his coffee. "I think that you will be a very good father someday, Mr. Darcy."

He sighed. "I don't know. I've been waiting for her to approach me ever since she spoke to Elizabeth, and was sorely disappointed when she didn't. I thought that maybe she cancelled her plans, but . . . well, Elizabeth and I discussed how to handle it if she didn't."

"Is that why she remained upstairs?" Mrs. Reynolds smiled.

"Yes." He chuckled. "I imagine Georgiana is complaining in her ear right now."

"So which of you is the soft touch?"

"Not me!" Elizabeth declared and closed the kitchen door behind her. "I supported your declarations, Will."

"I knew you would." He smiled and kissed her. "So what shall we do with our afternoon before we become chaperones?"

"Is our picnic packed?" She looked at Mrs. Reynolds who reached down and picked up a large backpack.

"I just have to add in the cold things." She turned to the refrigerator and began taking out containers to add to the bag. Elizabeth felt herself being pulled into William's arms and smiled up at him.

"Where are we going?"

"I thought that we could pretend to be at Pemberley with a picnic, and wander the park and go riding." She kissed him.

His eyes expressed his delight. "Have you reserved horses for us?"

"These horses don't need reservations." She laughed at his confusion and handing him the backpack, picked up a second one loaded with more supplies. Taking his hand they set out into the sunny September afternoon, grabbing a cab to the park, settling in the grass to people watch and eat, and talk about their extraordinary night, including the news that Jane and John were now a committed couple. They cleaned up their things and set off again, holding hands and laughing. "Ah, here we are."

"Where?" Darcy looked around, seeing nothing unusual, then back down at Elizabeth.

She laughed and pointed. "Let's ride!"

They had arrived in front of the building housing the Central Park carousel. "You're kidding."

Elizabeth dragged him inside the shelter and paying the fare, jumped up on the platform, then swung her leg up and over one of the antique painted ponies. She looked down at him from her perch and leaned to kiss his upturned face. "You said we could be silly."

He shook his head and climbed up on a black stallion by her side, and bit his lip. "I feel silly." Elizabeth giggled and seeing a man taking a picture of his wife and son, caught his attention. She asked him if he would take their picture and she turned to see William blushing and attempting to look dignified on his mount. Laughing, she turned and smiled at the camera. When she got it back, she looked at the photo and then handed it over to William. He shook his head. "I want a copy of this for my desk."

"Someday maybe we'll have babies in our laps to ride along with us." Their eyes met and pocketing the camera, he reached out to hold her hand as the carousel began to turn.

Chapter 18

"**I** need some advice." Darcy said then grew silent as the waiter set down their drink orders and moved away.

David took a sip and set the glass down. "Elizabeth?"

"No, no . . . she's wonderful, she keeps me sane." He smiled and appreciated his uncle's understanding nod. "No, it's Georgiana. I realize that being in school, she is exposed to a wide variety of people and that is a good thing, but she has been so sheltered all of her life that I wonder if her judgment is faulty. I can't protect her forever, but I don't want her to fall again."

"What has she done?"

"You know about the party she planned while we were away, and that we supposedly ruined by coming home?"

"Yes, that was some two weeks ago, I understand from Arlene's conversations with Elizabeth that most of the guests were nice kids."

"It was the other ones that bothered me, they were along to check out the house and see if the rumors of her being wealthy were true."

"Curiosity does not necessarily translate into being a bad person. I hope that this is not the reason why you never made it back to Pemberley to finish your honeymoon." He saw Darcy flush and leaned forward.

"That is not fair to Elizabeth; your commitment to her must be first. And you cannot claim that the pressures of work are keeping you here, either."

"There was so much happening with the fires."

"And you addressed that. You changed the structure of the company so that you would have a life with Elizabeth, didn't you? Well, let your people do their work, I am sure that there was nothing that happened over at least the last week that you could not have addressed with a conference call from the patio at Pemberley."

Darcy met his Uncle's intense stare and nodded. "You're right, I guess that work was a convenient excuse, it's my worry in the change in Georgiana that really kept me home. I'm trying to be a good parent, while learning how to be a good husband. Elizabeth . . . If it wasn't for her, I'd be lost."

"You have to let your baby bird fall out of the nest, Son. You have made it clear that you are there to help pick up the pieces, but she has to make mistakes and learn from them. She was not left alone in the house, besides we were all keeping tabs on her." He sat back again. "She's not going to listen to you anyway; at least she won't admit that she is. She is young and therefore bulletproof."

"I just thought that the whole Wickham incident would have eliminated this need to experiment. I don't trust her judgment. She knew she was doing wrong with him and yet she went ahead with it. And now this trying to go behind my back . . ." He sighed and finally picked up his drink to take a sip. "She has changed so much from a few months ago. She didn't want to come home then because she thought I wouldn't welcome her back."

"And now that she is feeling the full force of her protective brother; and now sister, she doesn't want to stay. Maybe she doesn't like seeing you as her parent, and that change in your role wasn't clear to her until the Wickham incident occurred." David smiled as he saw Darcy mulling over that fact.

"Maybe that is why she preferred staying with you and Aunt Arlene for so long."

He shrugged. "Perhaps. No doubt in another few months she will find another personality. That is what she is doing you know, trying out new personalities until she finds the one that fits. As long as she is not doing anything illegal or harmful to her body or reputation, I say to let her go. Keep your rules and make your expectations clear, but otherwise, let her make her mistakes. She missed out on doing this in a high school setting where it would have been perhaps more understandable. Instead she was thrust into college when her talent but not her self was formed. She is chafing at your rules because the people around her are older and probably don't have them anymore. Keep in mind her early teenage years were marred by the absence of a guiding mother and the presence of a very serious and socially inept brother." He laughed heartily at the glare he received. "Come on, admit it."

"Okay." He sighed.

"I'm no psychologist, but I notice that this change in her is in direct correlation to you finding Elizabeth."

"She is rebelling because I fell in love?" He asked incredulously.

"No, she feels safe at home, so she also feels free to take risks." David smiled. "You have given her a family again by marrying Elizabeth. Keep in mind also that you have different temperaments, so what works for you doesn't necessarily translate to her. She's operating on a different system." He stopped as their plates were presented, and the waiter moved away. "What does Elizabeth have to say in all this?"

"She sees it from so many angles, that she empathizes with both sides." He picked up his fork and stabbed at his salmon. "Where I want to lock her up in a tower, Elizabeth sounds more like you. But we do talk out our opinions, and generally meet in the middle. She supports me. I couldn't do it without her." He took a look at the fish and set the fork down. "I guess that Elizabeth is like Georgiana, in that she is very creative, which for her comes out in her writing."

"And she suffered through years of making mistakes to become who she is now, and no doubt that experience is reflected in the way that she responds to both of you in this matter." He tilted his head and smiled. "Georgiana is very much like your mother, just as you are more like your father."

"I've thought that." Darcy smiled.

"Your mom made a great many errors in judgment in her younger days, and then she met George. I remember well how caught up she was in the whole hippie scene of the early seventies. She was just fifteen or so when that all started taking off in the sixties, but she was aware enough to find it intoxicating. When she got older she ran away a few times and I would always find her in these hole-in-the-wall clubs, listening to strange music." He shook his head and laughed at Darcy's wide-eyes. "Didn't know that about your mom, did you? Well, she had her time of wildness, but then she met George at a Christmas party at the club, and it was love at first sight. He was so serious that her warmth and happiness hit him like a thunderbolt. They rubbed off on each other, you see, her basic beliefs and the solid upbringing was always there under the surface, and never really led her astray. She had a solid foundation, a loving family, and when she met George, she was able to walk away from her alter ego with no regret."

"And he benefited from her joy for living by becoming the warm husband and father I knew." Darcy smiled. "Just as I think I am benefiting from my Elizabeth."

"Exactly." David smiled. "So, back to Georgiana, I believe that you are seeing the hints of your mom in her behavior. I think that Miss Maggie would say that she has good "home-training" so give her room to fly a bit. She knows your limits, and will find hers, and she knows that she is always welcome home."

"Okay." He sighed and smiled. "I heard this more-or-less from Elizabeth. We set the boundaries."

"Even though we chafe at them, everyone really likes to know them." He took a bite of his steak and chewed thoughtfully. "I seem to be on the verge of gaining some daughters."

"I haven't heard of proposals being made."

"No, but both couples are coming for dinner this weekend. I am glad to have already met both girls."

"And? Will they fit into the Fitzwilliam family?" Darcy tilted his head.

"Fitting well with my sons is all that matters to me. You have a taste of parenthood with your sister; wouldn't you appreciate the man who makes her happy?" He saw how struck Darcy was by that thought. "I think that Jane is lovely and will undoubtedly combine well with John, and their careers may even be mutually beneficial. Richard needs a good solid sensible woman to keep him in check, and I have no doubt that Charlotte is just the one to do that while he brightens her world. I'm happy for them, and your aunt is hoping desperately that they don't blow it." He laughed.

"I am, too." Darcy smiled then bit his lip. "I haven't heard a word from Aunt Catherine."

"No, she is very unhappy with you."

"The feeling is mutual." Darcy's eyes flashed.

"Well, I would hope that the two of you come to some sort of truce before the ball. That gives you three weeks to think of some way to at least tolerate each other."

"She is not coming to my home, and the acts of contrition are due on her side, not mine." He said emphatically.

"I'll inform her of that and we'll meet at my home. Neutral ground. How about next weekend?"

"We're going away to Maine." Darcy's expression relaxed. "And nothing is getting in the way of this trip. I've disappointed Elizabeth too many times already." David nodded; his words had made an impression.

"All right then, Saturday for lunch. Agreed?"

Darcy sighed. "Agreed."

"SO WHICH DATE is this?"

"Um, let's see, number ten." Elizabeth laughed. "I think he'll like it better than my first idea."

"Where did you go want to go?"

"A nightclub populated by drag queens."

"Oh, Lizzy!"

"Well, it was just a thought, but I decided that William would not have found it comfortable. I think that even the formidable Darcy glare would not have scared off those *ladies* cavorting around the crowd. He would have been a magnet. We'll do your bachelorette party there."

"Lizzy!"

"Will I be your matron-of-honor?" She demanded.

"You know you will!" Jane sighed. "I sort of need a proposal first."

"Are you anxious to get one? I thought that you were taking your time." Elizabeth smiled and imagined Jane struggling to not say yes, and finding the dress she was searching for, pulled it out of her closet.

"I guess that after he told me how much he cares for me, I . . . kind of started letting my imagination kick in."

"Ah, *The Wedding*." Elizabeth said dramatically.

"Shut up." Jane said softly.

"So, propose to him."

Jane gasped. "What?"

"Okay, don't but don't be disappointed when it takes him forever to get around to it. I really hope that he is over trying to top William in romantic ideas. You two should be figuring out your own likes and dislikes, not copying us."

"Where are you going tonight?" She asked casually.

"Nice try, Jane." Elizabeth giggled and heard her sigh.

"I'm not trying to copy you, I'm just curious. We actually have talked about doing things on our own terms. Definitely no more dance clubs."

"No, William and I will never do that again either, the only dance clubs we will visit will be ones where we can actually dance. It was exciting for one evening, but never again." Elizabeth shifted the phone on her shoulder and looked through her shoes. "Are you thinking of moving in together?"

"No."

"Well that was definite."

"I have read too many stories about couples who live together and play house for a few years, then when they finally get married, it is meaningless because there is nothing left to discover about each other. The wedding is just like a big date."

"Well, part of the problem there is the weddings themselves taking a year to plan. I know that it pays your bills Jane, but I never did understand the need for such extravagance."

"Which is why your wedding was so lovely. And your living together for a few weeks didn't effect anything, it actually made you get closer, I think."

"It did, we are getting closer daily, he seems so happy to lean on me, his responsibilities are enormous." Elizabeth sat down then was silent.

"You didn't count on being mom to a teenager, though." Jane said perceptively.

"I already sort-of was for Lydia, I guess that it isn't too much different. I just wish we had more time together, but I understand his fear for leaving Georgiana alone now that she seems to be coming out of her shell." Elizabeth sighed. "Enough about me, tell me about John."

"He's so sweet." Jane smiled and looked at the new photo on her desk. "I think I like how lousy he is with romance, it makes his attempts so much more endearing. Even our first time together, he was so nervous and so was I, but we both had been thinking about it so much . . . It just happened!"

"Passion happens at the most unexpected times." Elizabeth smiled as many memories intruded. "I certainly hope that you have addressed the issue?"

"My bedside table is well-stocked, and I see my gynie next week. At least he had the foresight to bring a condom along, although he barely got it on in time." She blushed. "I can't believe I'm talking about this."

"You were no virgin, Jane."

"I know." She sighed. "I love him."

"I know." Elizabeth said gently.

"He loves me." Jane giggled. "He said so."

"And he wouldn't lie." Elizabeth heard her sister's happiness and smiled. "Why don't you give him a call, he'd love to hear you sounding so happy."

"I will."

Elizabeth hung up and looked over the dress again, then biting her lip, picked up the package she had wrapped up and took it downstairs to give to Frank. "Just give it to the receptionist and ask for it to be delivered to Mr. Darcy."

"Any reply?"

"No, I'm sure that he'll call." Elizabeth laughed and went to the library to work.

Darcy sat at his desk, rubbing his temples, chasing away the headache that came after his lunch with his uncle, and tried again to read over the contracts he had signed. He was relieved to see that the release clause he demanded in the event that the forestry company did anything that led to the destruction of his property remained. It was in the very fine print, but it was there, nonetheless. He heard a knock on the door and Patricia came in, bearing a wrapped box. "This just arrived for you, sir."

"A gift?" He took the box and looked up at her. "Who sent it?"

"Open it and see." She smiled and left.

His brow creased and he pulled the ribbon, then lifted the lid. Inside he found a pair of boat shoes and a note. He opened it up and began to chuckle.

My dear husband,

It is time, my love, for us to sail into the sunset, don't you think? No, no, not to fade into memory, but to melt into each other's arms and feel the wind in our hair. The days are short, but the night is warm, and will be warmer still with you by my side. Come home soon, honey. I'm waiting for my dashing captain to rescue me.

Love, your damsel,

Elizabeth

Darcy stood up, turned off his computer, and put on his suit jacket, then picked up his shoes. Walking out to Patricia's office, he smiled. "I'm going home. I'll see you Monday."

She looked at the clock in surprise. "Are there any messages for anyone?"

"No, everyone knows their jobs. I think I can leave and the place will still be standing when I return." He smiled and walked out into the hallway.

"Have a good weekend, Mr. Darcy." She called out the door.

He came back and smiled. "Thanks, you too."

Arriving out on the sidewalk he greeted employees returning from late lunches, and spotted Frank speaking with Charles. "I was hoping you would still be here."

"I was about to leave when Mr. Bingley stopped me." Frank got in the car to wait.

Charles turned to him and gestured to the car. "I saw Frank and wondered what was up."

"I'm going home."

"Is something wrong?"

"Yes, I spend too much time here." Darcy smiled and climbed in. "Monday morning, I want a meeting with all of the department heads. We're going to see how the restructuring is working out."

"And then what?" Charles leaned in the door.

"I'll let you know then. Enjoy your weekend. Good luck introducing Maria to Caroline tonight." Darcy smiled to see his grimace. "If you guys are still together afterwards, I hope that you have a pleasant evening planned to soothe her."

"Yeah, I found a new club to try out, maybe you and Elizabeth . . ."

"No, never again." He smiled and closed the door, and they drove off. Arriving at the house, he walked up to the back door and felt a drip land on his forehead, then another. He looked up at the sky, the blue of only a half-hour earlier had suddenly changed to grey. Entering the kitchen, he found a silent room, and continued on, hearing the vacuum running somewhere, and the sound of the floor creaking above. He stopped in his library and found Elizabeth sitting crosslegged in his desk chair, her computer in her lap, and concentrating on the screen. "Hi."

"Hi!" She looked up and beamed. "What are you doing here?"

He bowed deeply and held out his shoebox. "I am a dashing naval captain in search of a damsel in distress; did you happen to see one?"

Elizabeth laughed and stood up to take the box out of his hands then wrapped her arms around him. "I just happen to know of one such damsel in need of rescue."

"Well, then please point me in the proper direction. There isn't a moment to lose." Darcy hugged her tight then bent to kiss her softly. "Unless you are my damsel."

"I am." They kissed again and Elizabeth ran her fingers through his hair then drew back, looking at her fingers, then his hair. "You're wet."

"Rain does that."

"RAIN!" She cried and ran to the window to see a downpour underway. "Oh no." Her shoulders slumped and she seemed to shrink.

"Honey . . ." Darcy walked over and touched her back. "What's wrong?" He turned her around to see her eyes filled with tears. "Oh don't cry, please. Does the rain spoil your plans?"

"We were going on a sunset cruise on a schooner." She lifted the blinds and looked outside. "Not now, not in this."

"We will do something else, and try that again another time." Darcy kissed her. "It's okay."

"I guess." Elizabeth hugged him. "I just . . . didn't want it to be spoiled."

"Like everything else we try to do." He rested his face in her hair and breathed in the trace of lilac in her hair. "That's my fault, honey. But I am determined to change that, before it becomes a habit."

"What do you mean? Everything we do isn't spoiled." She looked up and he wiped her eyes.

"I went to lunch with Uncle David today. I was asking him for advice for handling Georgiana, and how she seems to have changed so much of late. I wanted to see if the decisions we have made were sound."

"What did he say? We are doing well, I think."

"Well, we are because you are guiding me." Darcy kissed her. "He told me that she has to make mistakes and learn from them. It sounded a lot like what you have been saying to me. But most important, he said that I can't stop being your husband because I am trying to be Georgiana's parent."

"But you haven't, Will." Elizabeth caressed his cheek.

"Where should we be right now?" She looked at him in confusion. "We should be at Pemberley enjoying our home. Once I had addressed the immediate concerns of the fire and the contracts, there was no reason why we could not have resumed our honeymoon. I told you in England that I can work from anywhere, and yet when we got home, did I follow that advice? No, I kept us here. I abandoned our plans because I was afraid to leave Georgiana home alone after hearing of her behavior. I disappointed you; and me, I didn't allow my employees to do their jobs, instead I swooped in to take it all over again, all because I was looking for an excuse to keep control over her. I am so sorry, Elizabeth."

"You were being a good parent, Will. I understand that, and we have been enjoying our honeymoon. How many couples come to New York for just that reason?"

"Yes, but they don't see the sights after spending the day in the office." He cuddled her back against his chest and kissed her hair. "I need to put us first."

"Would it have been better if I protested more?" Elizabeth nestled into him and hugged him tighter. "I just wanted to support you. I know how difficult this is for you; the little girl you love is growing up."

"I just don't want her to get hurt again. I don't want her to suffer and then spend years trying to forget it; she has enough to forget already." He sighed again. "Yes, honey, protest more. Your agreeing to come home from England was graciousness itself and for a very different reason, but when that situation was clearly handled . . . I needed to be reminded of some things. I will not berate you for expressing your opinion." He looked down and gently raised her bowed head, regretting the reference to Collins. "I love you, I am lost without you, and I will not ever put you second to anything again. Forgive me, please."

"Will . . . There is nothing to forgive, we are both learning here." Elizabeth stood on her toes and kissed him. "I love you." Darcy gathered her back up in his arms and they stood kissing each other, while in the doorway, Georgiana moved away from where she had been listening and walked back up the stairs.

"NOW, DON'T BE offended when she acts like a bitch." Charles told Maria. "She can't help it."

"What, is it a genetic thing?" She laughed, and held his hand as they boarded the elevator for Caroline's apartment.

"A mutation of some sort, I think. Maybe a damaged chromosome." He smiled and squeezed her hand. "Don't say I didn't warn you."

"I think I can handle her." Maria said confidently.

Charles looked her over and raised his brows. "You're a better man than I am if you can." He laughed, and they stepped out of the elevator and knocked on the door. It was opened and the couple entered to see Caroline standing before them, dressed in what could only be described as a fashion disaster. "Caroline, this is my girlfriend Maria Lucas. Maria, this is my elder sister, Caroline."

"You would have to point out that I am older, Charles." She glared and he shrugged. "So, you are the new one."

"I suppose I am." Maria lifted her chin, and looked around the room. "I see that you keep cats. I know a lot of unmarried women who do."

"Are you one of them?"

"No, I prefer human companionship." She smiled and Charles fought down his laugh but failed to prevent a snort of appreciation. They took seats on the sofa and Caroline sat in a large wing-backed chair. She did not offer any refreshments. "I was hoping to meet your other sister Charles, is she coming?"

"No, but she has invited us to come for dinner sometime when it is convenient. She lives on Long Island, so some weekend we'll drive out there."

"How nice for you." Caroline observed. "You can spend your time watching her husband sleep."

"Does he sleep whenever you visit?" Maria asked.

"Yes, almost as soon as I come in the door, he is in a chair with his eyes closed." She humphed and adjusted her bracelets. "I noticed that habit very soon after I first met him." Maria caught Charles's eye and winked. He smirked.

"What do you do for a living, Caroline?"

"Do?"

"Yes, surely you must occupy your time with something. I design websites; many of them are authors who publish with our family's small company."

"Oh, I design pet collars." She grabbed a cat and showed off a garish pink collar studded with rhinestones.

"Do you have a website?" Maria asked as she tilted her head to look at the struggling feline.

"No . . . would you be interested . . ."

"Sure, I'll send you a brochure with my rates and design ideas. What's your email address?" Maria took out a pen and paper from her purse and looked at her expectantly.

"I would have to pay?" She said, affronted.

"Well, I don't work for free." Maria put her things away.

Charles laughed. "That would be a mistake."

"But you're dating my brother! I have a connection with you!" Caroline declared.

"Oh, well, maybe if we were married I'd give you a discount . . . But then he is so rich, I wouldn't have to work at all, would I?" She grinned at him and he raised his brows.

"I knew it! You're mercenary! You found another one Charles!" Caroline pointed at her.

"Hmm, are you mercenary Maria?"

"Probably." She smiled.

"Well, let's go spend some of my money, then." He stood up and took her hand. "Bye Caroline. Enjoy your cats." They went to the door.

"Where are you going?" She demanded and followed them. "You just can't leave!"

"Sure we can. I wanted Maria to see my family, so now she knows what she is getting into if we stay together." He looked at her and cocked his head. "So, where am I taking you, home or out?"

"Oh out, definitely. Catwoman doesn't bother me." She smiled at him and waved to Caroline. "Let me know if you change your mind about the website." Caroline responded by slamming the door. "So, that was interesting."

"She really didn't bother you? I can't tell you how many girls she scared off."

Maria shrugged. "I think that you have found a girl who likes you more than hates your sister."

Charles kissed her and pushed the elevator button. "Let's celebrate that notion. I know a great new club that just opened . . ."

"WILLIAM?" Georgiana stood in the doorway to the living room. Darcy was sitting on the sofa, dressed in sweatpants and a longsleeved t-shirt, his sock-clad feet up on the coffee table, and Elizabeth was curled beside him, her head resting in his lap, and fast asleep. He had been playing with her hair and reading, and listening to the unending rain beating on the window.

He looked up and smiled, and whispered. "Hi, what can I do for you?"

She came in and sat down on the table, and looked down at Elizabeth's peaceful face. She glanced back up to find him smiling at her. Their eyes met and he raised his brow. "I wanted to check and see if I can ask some friends over tomorrow. We have recitals coming up and I thought it would be nice to try out our pieces here and order some food. It would be a lot more relaxing than trying to cram us all into the practice rooms."

"Sure, that sounds great. Do you need any money for the food?"

"No, I have my allowance, thanks." She watched how his hand never stopped gently stroking Elizabeth's hair.

"Okay. I appreciate you asking me." He smiled then bit his lip. "Um, Elizabeth and I are going over to Uncle David's for lunch to see Aunt Catherine."

"Oh . . . Well, I'll be okay here, don't worry . . . William, I heard you talking with Elizabeth when you came home, and I . . . I want to apologize. I . . . I guess that I was behaving pretty childishly when you came home early from your trip. I didn't mean for it to change the way you look at me. I was just . . . Well, I'm finally making friends and I just didn't want anything to spoil that."

"Like having us around?"

"I guess it was kind of silly, everyone knows that I certainly didn't own the house." She laughed. "Actually all of the girls said that you were pretty hot and looked forward to coming over again to see my big brother."

Darcy blushed and looked down. "If you think that is going to encourage me to invite your friends over more often, you're mistaken."

"So I shouldn't mention what the guys said about Elizabeth?" She giggled again to see his eyes flare. "Ok, I won't." She took a breath and twisted her hands. "I . . . I guess that I never saw you as anyone but my brother before, and after I went to school, you changed and became more like my father, and I'm having a hard time seeing you that way. I think that I'm rebelling a little with all of the sudden rules."

"I've never had to impose any before, but it's really a sign that you are growing up, and I have to accept that. I . . . I just can't bear to see you hurt again." He smiled and looked down as Elizabeth turned and wrapped her arms around his waist, and cuddled against his chest. He kissed her head and embraced her, then looked back up to Georgiana. "I worry that you were too sheltered."

"Well, I had a rough time after mom and dad died, and I'm glad that I stayed with Uncle David and Aunt Arlene, but I wanted to come home and be with you, and I liked our little world that we had here by ourselves. I guess I miss it a little." She saw his brow crease. "Just a little, I had you all to myself, but . . . everything is so much better now with Elizabeth here. So, your attention is with her and I am finding my own friends. That's okay, isn't it?"

"Of course it is."

"I'm sorry that you thought it was necessary to give up your time with Elizabeth to babysit me. Believe me, William, I knew that I was wrong going away with Wickham, I was a willing victim, but I won't be fooled like that again, when he called . . . I was scared, but I know that I should have told you."

"I am happy to hear you say that you have learned from the experience, especially since I've decided that I have to trust you, and allow you to make mistakes. But you need to know that Elizabeth and I will always be available to you. Elizabeth could not turn to her family when she was suffering, but you can. Please, if anything ever makes you uncomfortable, or you get into a situation or with people who worry you, please know that we love you no matter what. I realize that you and I have never really felt comfortable talking to each other like this, but Elizabeth has helped me to open up. I hope that you can come to either of us."

"I will. And I won't let you down again." Georgiana leaned forward and kissed his cheek, then wiped her eyes. "Will you go on your trip to Maine next week?"

"Yes, I can't wait." He smiled and looked out the window. "I just hope that the weather is good. I don't want to drive in the rain to see soggy leaves."

Georgiana laughed and wiped her cheek again. "No, but I bet that the inn has a great fireplace." She saw Elizabeth's lips rise in a smile then relax again, she wasn't sleeping, she was supporting William with her hug. That made Georgiana's tears start flowing again. She grabbed a tissue, then saw him kiss Elizabeth's head and rest his cheek in her hair. "Have you decided what you'll say to Aunt Catherine tomorrow?"

He rolled his eyes and hugged Elizabeth. "I'll just follow her lead. If she remains unrepentant, we will go. She won't make a scene at the ball. By the way, you need to get a gown, don't you? Maybe you and Elizabeth can go out with Maurice."

"Ohhhhh really?"

"Sure. Will you bring a date?"

"A date?"

"There must be some guy who you like in that school." William smiled and tilted his head. "Ask him out."

Georgiana hesitated and bit her lip. "Um, would it be wrong if I had to pay for his tux?"

Darcy laughed. "No, he might be grateful to know he didn't have to. Let me know if you need help with that, and . . . I imagine a rental will do."

"Okay." Georgiana smiled. "I like this, talking to each other about real stuff, you know?"

"I do, too. It makes me think that you're grown up." He watched her stand and wipe her eyes again, then she bent down and kissed Elizabeth's cheek. "I liked talking to you, too."

"You're welcome." Elizabeth said softly and hugged William. He watched Georgiana leave and looked down to see her smiling up at him. "Do you feel better?"

"Yes, much. I knew you were awake."

"What gave me away?"

"I think that it was your hands slipping up the back of my shirt while I was talking." He smiled and chuckled.

"Well, I couldn't feel your bottom, you were sitting on it." She laughed and hugged him.

"Thank you, honey. Even when you're quiet you're supporting me." Softly he sang, "The smile on your face lets me know that you need me. There's a truth in your eyes saying you'll never leave me. The touch of your hand says you'll catch me whenever I fall. You say it best when you say nothing at all.[viii]"

Elizabeth brushed the fringe of hair that fell across his forehead. "I'm so glad that it rained."

"YOU TOLD HER that we expect an apology?"

"I did, Darcy." David stretched his arms over his head and checked his watch. "She made a great deal of noise in response."

"Were any words involved or was it just more caterwauling?" Elizabeth smiled and squeezed William's hand.

"How can you tell the difference?" He asked.

"It's all in the delivery." Arlene smiled and turned to Elizabeth. "I'm looking forward to our dinner tomorrow, are you sure that you won't join us?"

"No, this is your family, we're just outside relatives. Jane and Charlotte are nervous wrecks, by the way."

"Why? We've all met before?"

"Yes, but not as potential daughters-in-law!" Elizabeth laughed. "Oh, don't turn into a dragon!"

"Not my style; that is Catherine." The bell rang and they laughed. "Speak of the devil!"

Catherine swept in, removed her wrap, and assessing the room, took the most prominent chair. "Well, I'm here."

"I never would have noticed, Catherine. Can I offer you something before lunch?" Arlene asked.

"No, thank you." She turned her eyes to Darcy and Elizabeth. "So, you are married."

"Very." Darcy squeezed Elizabeth's hand. "Happily."

"So you had nothing to worry about, Mrs. de Bourgh, your nephew is happy with me."

"But will it last?" She began and was promptly interrupted by David.

"Catherine, we are not here to discuss your opinions of marriage, we are here to mend the fences. As you are the one who has offended Darcy and Elizabeth, it is up to you to apologize. Get going."

"I only spoke the . . ." She eyed her brother then saw Darcy bending to pick up Elizabeth's purse to hand it to her. "Very well . . . I might have spoken ungraciously."

"Might? You told Elizabeth that she was a whore." Darcy's eyes burned. "If I had been there . . ."

"You weren't, Will, I was, so this is my offense to forgive or not." She placed her hand on his. Darcy didn't like it, but he yielded to Elizabeth. "I assume, Mrs. de Bourgh; that you regret coming to such a hasty conclusion and that it was brought on by the stress of seeing a beloved nephew marry."

"Well . . . Yes, I suppose."

"And of course you never dreamed that your demand to see our prenuptial agreement; if it exists; would cause offence, you were simply hoping that he had taken precautions to protect long-held family assets."

"If?" Catherine demanded then saw Elizabeth's raised brow and Darcy's still burning eyes. "Oh, yes, of course."

"So you are prepared to apologize to me for your insult?"

"Yes."

"And for sticking your nose where it doesn't belong?"

"Yes."

"And will never impose yourself upon our homes, our family, or our business again?" Elizabeth stared her down and Catherine met the gaze head on.

"Yes."

"Very well then, let's hear it." Darcy said quietly.

"But I just . . ." Catherine glared at him. "I apologize."

"I think that is the best you can expect from her Darcy." David grinned and laughed.

Darcy continued to stare at her silently for an uncomfortable full minute, then turned to Elizabeth. "Are you satisfied?"

"Yes, unless she does it again."

"That won't happen, will it?" He addressed Catherine.

"No."

"Very well, we accept." He nodded to her and smiled at Elizabeth.

"Does this mean that I am welcome back in your homes?" Catherine said stiffly and looked down at her rings, examining the sparkle.

"If you can enter without insulting us. If it happens again, there will be no chance for a reprieve." Darcy said steadily. "Elizabeth is here to stay."

"Thank you."

Arlene caught David's eye and stood up. "Well, that was fun, shall we eat?"

"May I help you?" Elizabeth stood up to follow her to the kitchen and was surprised to see Catherine rise as well. "Are you coming, Mrs. de Bourgh?"

"You may call me Aunt Catherine." She said while addressing the kitchen door.

"And you may call me Mrs. Darcy." Elizabeth saw Catherine's eyes turn to meet hers. She laughed. "Oh, I suppose Elizabeth will do just as well." She looked over to William and winked, then followed the ladies into the kitchen.

"DO YOU KNOW where we're going?" Darcy looked at Elizabeth and watched her pulling out her map and directions to study. She absolutely refused to trust GPS navigation systems. He crossed his arms and tilted his head while observing her arguing with herself. "Honey?"

"I know that you're there, Will." She glanced up and smiled, then went back to her reading. "Okay, pull out of here, and turn left, no, right, and go for approximately four tenths of a mile . . ."

"You're kidding, right?"

Elizabeth grinned at him. "I was wondering if you would react. Just get out of the airport and go right, get on the highway and head west."

"That I can do." He started the rental car and after familiarizing himself with the controls, took off. Soon they were on the road, and absolutely surrounded by brilliant colors and scenic vistas. "This is beautiful."

"It is. I have always wanted to be a leaf-peeper." Elizabeth's head swiveled around taking it in. "Oh look down there, see that little church?" Darcy craned his neck and she squealed. "Don't look that close!"

"You think I'm going to wreck?" He shook his head and looked ahead then back at her. "Not a chance, I'd never risk hurting you."

"That's comforting."

Reaching over he pinched her leg and she jumped. "Hmm, as great as you look in jeans, I miss your skirts when we're driving."

"It's too cold for that."

"Yadda yadda." Darcy smiled at her and looked ahead. "Can we get off of this and drive through the towns and eventually find our way to the inn?"

"Sure, let's see . . . Take the next exit."

They turned down the ramp and found themselves driving through postcard-worthy villages, and stopped in at a tiny country store and a century-old covered bridge to take pictures and load up on things to nibble in their rooms. They took their time, and the drive from the airport in Bangor to Moosehead Lake that should have taken ninety minutes stretched out to three hours. At last they arrived at the inn, and were shown to their private cabin.

"Oh Will, it's beautiful!"

He dropped the bags and looked around the room. "I've never been in anyplace like this before, it's . . . rustic but . . . I don't know, like a scene out of *Architectural Digest*." He walked around and smiled. "Certainly screams romance, doesn't it?"

"Fireplace, sofa, bearskin rug, oh look a Jacuzzi for two with wine glasses by the side!" Elizabeth beamed. "That looks very promising!"

"And look at all the mirrors surrounding it." Darcy stood behind her and they looked at their reflection while he slipped his hands around her waist. "We can watch ourselves." He whispered and chuckled to feel her blush. "How can I embarrass you when we are alone?"

"It's that voice, Will, I'm telling you, it makes my toes curl." Elizabeth turned and they kissed slowly. "Let's unpack and head for dinner."

"It's only 6:30." He murmured in her hair.

"But the restaurant closes at 8:30." He pulled away and looked at her in surprise. Elizabeth laughed. "We're not in Kansas anymore."

"I'm sure even Kansas stays open later than 8:30." He sighed and let her go. "Charles would not do well here."

"Well, we will do just fine because when we return, we will enjoy our bath." Elizabeth smiled and gave him a kiss before leaving to unpack. Darcy remained and looked at the Jacuzzi speculatively.

"I think that is a fine idea."

The inn had only nine guest rooms, so the dining room was intimate, quiet, and relaxing. They enjoyed the excellent meal, and Elizabeth bubbled with excitement, detailing her ideas for how to spend their day amongst the leaves. Darcy spent most of the meal trying hard not to choke, since she invariably made him laugh whenever he took a bite. Clearly she was very happy to have this time completely alone as a couple. Afterwards they stepped out of the inn to walk back to their cabin and came to an abrupt standstill.

"Oh Will!" Elizabeth took his hand and gasped. "I've never seen the sky like this."

"We're in heaven." He looked up at the inky black sky studded with stunning stars and reached up above his head.

"Can you touch them?" Elizabeth laughed.

"No, I'm not quite that tall." He breathed in the cool clean mountain air. "This is what it's like in Montana and Washington on our land. No city lights, just trees and nature. I'm very comfortable here." They looped their arms and started walking again. "I have thought about building a house in the woods somewhere."

"And just hiding away?" She leaned against him and his arm came around her shoulder. Darcy kissed her head and hugged her.

"Running away, hiding, I don't know. I guess that I used Pemberley for that instead. In some ways this reminds me of our other Pemberley." They arrived at their cabin and walked up onto the private deck and stood at the railing looking over the lake, watching the moonlight on the dark water. Elizabeth shivered and he opened up his jacket, pulling her inside and hugging her. "I think; I hope that I have at last found a way to loosen my iron grip on everything. It's been hard."

"I know that you have struggled honey. You were so optimistic and positive at the beginning but implementing the plans and sticking with them was not easy."

"It only got hard when a crisis arose. I was okay with normal operations, but when that fire came along I slipped into my old habits." He sighed and rested his cheek in her hair. "I want so much to have a life now. With you. Five months ago . . ." He swallowed hard and rested his cheek in her hair. Elizabeth pressed her face to his chest and listened to his heart. "Five months ago I was alone in my house, wondering if my sister would ever speak beyond one-syllable words, if I would ever bring her home again . . . If my failure as a parent and obsession with controlling every aspect of my family's legacy had ruined her life forever . . . And seeing the future as nothing more than a series of bleak routine days that never were happy, never held promise, just came and went with regular precision, and ended as always, with me alone. And now . . ."

"And now you are married, your sister is so active that you are worried she is too busy, and you are allowing the good people who work for you to relieve some of the burdens you carry. No wonder you have stumbled a few times adjusting to it all." Elizabeth squeezed his waist and he hugged her tighter. "My adjustment has been more one of trust, letting you in and letting go of the past. You made me believe that love was not a fantasy." She hesitated to bare her feelings further and laughed softly. "Although I am perpetually overwhelmed by the lifestyle you have given me, I haven't had quite the struggles you have."

Yes you have, you just won't admit it. Darcy kissed her forehead. "You have had to bear with mine. Thank you for being patient with me, I think that I'm okay with it all now. Would you do something for me?"

Elizabeth lifted her head away from him and looked up to his serious eyes. "Tell me when I start to slip back, I think that it will take a little more time before not being a control freak is normal."

She smiled and caressed his face. "I will. And you please tell me whenever I do something that . . . confounds you."

He chuckled. "Well, that would be a daily conversation, I think."

"Oh, and what have I done now?" She tried to pull out of his arms and he just held her tighter.

"No honey, I love it all too much to ruin it by making you self-conscious. Suffice it to say that I love your imagination." He kissed her and played with her hair. "Speaking of which, couldn't that romance story use a bathtub scene?"

"I don't know; I've never taken a bath with someone, so I really don't have much practical experience to use as inspiration. Do you have any thoughts?"

"I believe that I do." Grinning, he let go and grabbed her hand. "Let's get some experience."

ELIZABETH AWOKE and saw that she was curled over William's chest, her arm across his stomach, his arm holding her body securely to his. She nestled into his shoulder and kissed the warm skin, then heard him murmur something while he turned so they were facing each other. In his sleep, he reached for her, drawing her body first to his chest then rolling her beneath him. His hands caressed over her shoulders and his mouth fumbled, kissing over her face until it wandered down to find her lips. Another murmur, this one of satisfaction, then kisses, soft, sensual, spine-tingling kisses followed. She knew he was dreaming, his body was so heavy and relaxed, but the kisses were . . . indescribably tender. Her arms wrapped around his neck and she met his lips, explored his mouth, and loved his tongue, allowing his dreaming mind to fulfill its fantasy. The warm hands traveled down her sides, caressing her hips, and he shifted above her. She moaned with his touch and his eyes opened.

"It's not a dream." William whispered and slipped inside of her warm, welcoming body. Slowly they moved and slowly they kissed. He lifted his head away to watch her eyes as she received him, and saw, just in time, the blush spreading up her chest, to warm her face as he joined her in bliss. When his shudders stopped he looked down to see her smile.

"Good morning."

"Good morning, honey." They kissed and he moved to his side and ran his hand down her arm. "How did that happen?"

"I have no idea." Elizabeth laughed. "But I hope that you continue to have such inspiring dreams."

"So do I!" His head rested on the pillow and he continued his caresses. "I am very happy."

"So am I, Will." She kissed him softly and he reached to bring her closer. "What shall we do today?"

"I'm in your hands; we have one whole day to play." He nuzzled his face against her neck. "I have a feeling that we will not be happy to go home tomorrow."

"I do, too." She giggled when he started nibbling again. "Will!"

"mmmmm."

"Breakfast."

"I'll have an order of Lizzy, thank you."

She sighed. "What am I going to do with you?"

He lifted his head and grinned. "Do you really want an answer to that?" He was rewarded with a pillow smacked on his head and she escaped from his embrace. Watching her dash across the room he laughed. "I'll get you my pretty."

She looked around the corner of the bathroom door and giggled. "And my little dog, too?"

"I think cat is the better word." He laughed again and lay back in the bed, and waited for his turn. From the bathroom he heard her voice, and sat up to listen as he recognized the slow tune, "Oh, honey . . ."

"When I fall in love, it will be forever, or I'll never fall in love. In a restless world like this is, love is ended before it's begun, and too many moonlight kisses, seem to cool in the warmth of the sun.

When I give my heart it will be completely, or I'll never give my heart. And the moment I can feel that you feel, that you feel that way too, is when I fall in love with you. [xi]"

Darcy closed his eyes as her voice quieted. He had come to know her now, she often found it difficult to speak her feelings, so when she did, whether through a song or through her touch, or simply caring for and teasing him, the communication was so dear, and he always listened. He got up and knocked on the bathroom door, stepped in and took her in his arms. "I love you, too."

They spent the morning wandering the trails around the lake, occasionally coming across other couples doing the same, and pausing to exchange cameras and take pictures together that otherwise never would have been made. They found a little waterfall and settled there to enjoy the picnic lunch the inn had provided.

Then afterwards they wandered back, kicking leaves and playing an impromptu game of hide and seek, ending with Darcy finding her crouched behind a conveniently large boulder. He snuck up to toss her into the yellow blanket of maple leaves for a long and welcome session of kissing. The lonely sound of a steam whistle finally broke through the haze of their lovemaking and they sat up, picking leaves from each other, when the whistle blew again.

"Oh, we missed it!" Elizabeth cried and stood.

Darcy followed and hugged her; still not ready to end their closeness. "What did we miss?"

"The cruise on the lake." She pointed and he saw the ship off in the distance.

"It seems that we are forever missing our boat rides."

"I just thought you'd enjoy that one a little more because it was once part of the logging industry here." She shrugged. "It was a thought, anyway."

"A good one." He let go and they started walking again. "I'm just as happy here. I don't have to share you with anyone. On the ship you'd be talking to people."

"And that's a bad thing, right?" She lifted her brow.

"We earned this time alone, and I'm not going to share." He lifted his chin and looked at her with a glint in his eye. "So deal with it."

"Yes, sir!" She laughed and they entwined their fingers to start walking again. Darcy's phone beeped and he creased his brow. "Just see who it is, or you'll wonder about it."

He looked and found a text message. "It's from Uncle David." He smiled. "He and Aunt Arlene dropped by the house and found a group of kids sitting out in the garden eating pizza and arguing over composers." He shut off the phone and smiled at Elizabeth. "I think that Georgiana grew up a little this week."

She hugged his arm and they started walking again. "Do you feel better?"

"Yes, maybe between the two of us, we'll turn out a good kid."

"Maybe more than one?" Elizabeth watched his face light up and smiled. "Next year?"

He kissed her and wrapped his arm around her shoulders. "Next year."

Chapter 19

"Wood pellets? Are you certain?" Darcy lifted his chin and nodded to another of his managers. "Your team has completed its report?"

"Yes, it certainly is a burgeoning product. Wood burning stoves are selling at an enormous rate, and it would be an excellent use for the waste left from logging and cleaning out the stands. And it is really the time to get in and established."

"Good, I am considering the purchase of 5000 acres in Maine. The state is already creating guidelines for this new industry, so we would not be breaking new ground there, I want your team to look into building a processing plant for my land and bringing in wood from other landowners." He turned to another manager. "Your team will be investigating marketing strategies. Charles has the detailed instructions I prepared ready for you, Charles?"

"Yes." He passed around the binders. "Everything is addressed, but if you have any questions, feel free to ask."

"I want to have your first reports in two weeks." Darcy stood. "Thank you." The staff stared after him in amazement. He was not hovering. He gave them assignments and left them to show him what they could do. It was a first, and a welcome change.

Leaving the room, he walked down the hallway and into his office. Patricia followed with a stack of pink phone messages, and he sat down to start addressing each one. It was a long morning, and one that he knew would have been much worse if he had not begun to loosen his control and trusted his staff. He gradually worked his way through the calls, and was surprised to see that nearly three hours had passed when he hung up the phone at last. He closed his eyes and rubbed his temples. Patricia noticed that his phone was no longer in use and peeked in the doorway. "Could you use some lunch, Mr. Darcy? Or maybe some aspirin?"

"Both are excellent ideas, Patricia, but I'm meeting my cousins . . . Now, as a matter of fact." He picked up his phone and called Richard. "I'll be there in twenty minutes."

"Yeah right. We'll order for you. What do you want?" He made a face at John who was holding out his hand for Richard to pay off the bet they had laid.

"I don't care; whatever you're having. I'll see you there." He hung up and blinked at Patricia. "I'm sorry."

She bustled in with a glass of water and the aspirin. "That's all right. Take these and get going. You don't have anything pressing this afternoon. Why don't you head home early?"

He swallowed the pills and winced when he tried to smile. "Thanks for the concern. No, there's no reason to go home early, nobody is there." He looked at her sadly and put on his jacket. "I'll be back in an hour or so."

She watched him go and went over to his desk, straightening up his papers and picking up his notes to type up. She glanced over at the picture of him and Elizabeth on the carousel and spoke softly. "Mrs. Darcy, he is lost without you."

Charles poked his head in. "Is he gone?"

"Yes, off to meet the Fitzwilliam brothers."

"How's his mood?"

Patricia rolled her eyes. "Dark."

"I hope she comes back to him soon." Charles looked at the pictures. "I guess that I would feel the same way if Maria left me."

"Is that getting serious?" She asked casually.

"You don't know? I was sure that you would be well-advised on the office gossip!" Charles laughed. "I'm in no hurry and neither is she, so we'll just keep enjoying ourselves, and maybe after Christmas . . ."

"What are you waiting for?" Patricia demanded.

"It's only been two months, Mom." Charles laughed again. "Come on; leave me alone, you should be proud that it's lasted this long!"

"I suppose." She glanced at him then back at the pictures on Darcy's desk, and sighed.

"HEY!" John raised his hand and attracted Darcy's attention as he wound his way through the tables to join them.

"Sorry about being late, I was negotiating a truce." He smiled a little, the aspirin was kicking in.

"What about?" Richard sat back as their meals were delivered. "I got you a steak, I figured you weren't eating."

Darcy just looked at him and then shook his head. "Thanks." He looked at the waiter and asked for some water. "I was negotiating a deal between the foresters and the insurers . . . I don't want to get back into it. I'll talk to you when it's finished, this will effect the land your family holds as well."

"I hear you are buying in Maine. That trip left an impression on you." John observed.

"I'll never forget it, and I'm glad that the cabin was available for another night. It was a wonderful trip." His eyes closed, a vision of Elizabeth stretched in front of the fire on the bearskin rug in his mind.

"Are you going to build a place there? That's what I heard from Mom."

He startled back. "I'm considering it. Some of the land is on a lake." He looked down and played with his steak.

"Snap out of it Darcy, she'll be back." Richard laughed.

"I see that you are unaffected by Charlotte's absence." He shot him a look that clearly expressed his unhappiness with Richard's girlfriend.

"I miss her, too. But we aren't nearly far enough along in our relationship to be so dependent on each other. We're just enjoying the time together. This is the longest either of us has ever dated someone, so I guess that we're approaching it cautiously."

"In other words, you are not using the 'C' word." Richard raised his brow at John. "Commitment."

"I'm working on it." He flushed.

"Aha!" Darcy's eyes flashed. "You DO miss her!"

"Alright, alright, I miss her, I'm lonely, a phone call is no substitute . . . what more do you want? Should I tear out my hair and gnash my teeth?"

"Don't tear out your hair, Richard, keep it as long as you can, there is a little spot starting to show. . ."

"There is not!"

John shrugged and ran his hand through his thick hair. "Oh, so your scalp is growing beyond your hair."

"Shut up."

"Rogaine." Darcy smiled, relaxing a little. "I hear it works wonders for the balding."

"I am NOT going to lose my hair!" Richard glared at them both, then cut a large bite of steak and began chewing.

John looked at Darcy and grinned. "What should we pick on next?"

"Watch it, or I'll start on you." Richard growled.

"Enough." Darcy smiled. "They'll be home tonight, and I intend to meet them at the airport. Would you care to come with me Richard?"

"Yes!" He said quickly.

The three men laughed. "I never thought I'd see the day when we were so . . . lost. Well, are you all ready for the ball? I assume that Aunt Arlene has been whispering in your ear as much as she has mine."

"No, what has she been saying to you?" John looked at him curiously. "About Elizabeth?"

"Yes . . . she said that I should not be surprised if she attracts some attention and winds up on the gossip pages, being the new wife of an elusive billionaire . . . the foundation fundraiser always generates publicity and of course there will be pictures. She didn't say anything to you guys about this?" John and Richard shook their heads. "Maybe it's because you're not married."

"Well, it is a foundation run by the Darcy family, even though Anne has taken it over until Georgiana comes in."

"But . . . Aunt Arlene seemed to think that after this event, Elizabeth and I will be expected to be more visible, and sought after to attend other events."

"Well sure, you were a wealthy bachelor who refused to go anywhere, but now, married and comfortable, well somewhat, you will be a target to every socialite with a cause. Hide that wallet when you go walking." John smiled to see Darcy's eyes roll. "Come on, it shouldn't be too much of a surprise? You want them to come to your event, so you have to go to theirs."

"Thank God I have Lizzy." He murmured. "I guess that's why Aunt Arlene has insisted that they meet beforehand."

"Ah, etiquette?" Richard grinned. "Charlotte is going; I think that Jane is, too?" John nodded. "And Georgiana?"

"Yes." Darcy bit his lip. "She was excited to go along with Elizabeth on this little book signing trip. Since it was from Saturday through today, she only misses one day of school. I thought it would be good for her to see Elizabeth at work and to see a little of the world beyond her experience."

"It is." John nodded.

"I think that she might have had another motivation." Richard said softly. Darcy's head swiveled. "Is that guy Adam going to be at these book things?"

"I don't know . . . Lizzy hasn't mentioned him. I thought it was just her appearing at book stores, but there is a school today, and I think that there will be several authors there . . . why?"

Richard shrugged. "I just noticed a little spark at the wedding."

"She is seventeen!" Darcy nearly bellowed.

"Quiet!" John looked around. "Why don't you ask Elizabeth before you get all protective?"

"It better not be a secret meeting." Darcy growled.

"I thought that you were letting her explore a little." Richard smiled.

"Not with a man nearly eight years older than her and when she is underage." He closed his eyes and sighed. "Just you wait until it's your daughter."

"I'm in no hurry." Richard looked over to John who was tilting his head and watching Darcy. "How about you?"

"I . . . I am looking forward to it." He looked down when the two men focused on him. "I'm . . . I'm thinking of proposing."

"Already?"

"Don't talk to me about rushing into marriage, Darcy."

"I'm just surprised, that's all." He smiled. "If you are going to propose, then I wish you all the luck in the world."

"Yeah, well, we'll see. I'm just thinking about it at this point. Maybe in a few months." Richard and Darcy smiled at each other. John looked up and glared. "Shut up."

"I didn't say a word." Richard laughed. He lifted his jaw. "So, what do you think about that new receiver the Giants got . . ."

"HOW DID I let you talk me into this?" Elizabeth looked out over the crowd in the school library from her position in the doorway. "The last thing that I want to do is book signings."

"Look, I don't want to be here either." Charlotte said irritably. "I want to go home. This travel stuff has really lost its charm."

"So why are we here?"

"Because Lucas Lit is not doing well with the downturn in the economy and we thought that if we got some of our most popular authors out it might generate some interest. We were contacted to appear at this book fair last week and jumped on the chance for exposure." She sighed. "Especially when some of our authors are abandoning us."

"That was unnecessary, Charlotte." Elizabeth shot her a look of warning. "I fulfilled my contract, and being here now is purely a favor. You know that I'm working on a new novel and I have been talking to your dad about the scholarship program. He hasn't said a word about there being a problem."

"He doesn't want to scare you away to another publisher." Charlotte said simply. "Look, I won't ask you to do this again."

"I don't mind helping Charlotte, I just didn't appreciate being told less than twenty-four hours in advance that you had this plan, and I can tell you, William didn't either."

"I know." A round of applause filled the room and Adam stood up from his seat and walked over to them with a grin.

"Your turn!" He laughed. "I warmed them up for you."

"What a guy!" Elizabeth listened to the woman who was handling the introductions and walked over to the sound of more applause.

"Knock 'em dead, sweetie!" Adam said in a whisper as she moved away. Elizabeth squared her shoulders and moved forward. "She handles it better now." He observed to Charlotte. "More confidence. Marriage is good for her." He said wistfully.

"You know, I hadn't thought about it, but just now she told me off a little. I don't think that has happened before without her apologizing through it. She has changed." Charlotte smiled at him and noticed Georgiana had come to join them. "Where were you?"

"Oh, I was sitting in the audience. I wanted to hear Adam's presentation." She smiled at him shyly.

He straightened up a little and smiled back. "Thanks, were my words of wisdom worth the effort?"

"Yes, I didn't know that cyanide smelled of bitter almonds."

"Ah, well, I am full of fun and fascinating facts about how to dispatch a spy!" He laughed and noticing people looking at them; pulled her out of the room and into the hallway. "So, how have you been? How is school?"

"Okay, it's pretty competitive. I'll probably regret missing today when I get back, but this has been a lot of fun to see what Elizabeth does."

"Fun?" Adam smiled. "I guess. It's always nice to meet the readers, and catch up with friends." He noticed she was twisting her hands and raised his brows expectantly.

"Um . . . Our family holds a benefit ball every year, for epilepsy research and support, and it's coming up in a couple of weeks . . ." She glanced up at him and he folded his arms, and tilted his head.

"I . . . my brother said that I could ask a guy to come along, it's my first time being allowed to attend, and . . . I thought of you." She blushed and looked back down. "If . . . If you will be in New York then."

"Why me?" Adam smiled.

"I . . . I like you; and we had a nice time at the wedding, didn't we?"

"Yes, we did, I enjoyed our attempt at dancing." He laughed and Georgiana looked up to smile at him. "I am very flattered that you would think to ask me, of all the people in the world, but I think . . . I think that I would rather wait for our first date, if we ever have one, to come when you are over eighteen." He saw her face fall, and touched her arm. "I'm sorry. I find you very attractive and like you very much, and it may seem silly to you to have to wait for another birthday, but . . . as much as I'd like to go with you as your date, I can't. I hope that you understand and are not angry. I'd hate to have you mad at me."

"oh." She said softly. "No, I'm not mad."

"Maybe I could wrangle an invitation to attend the event and just have a dance with you?" He smiled and bent his head to catch her eye. "I think that might be okay."

Georgiana looked back up at his warm smile. "I'd like that."

"Good, then let's grab Lizzy and talk her into inviting me. Where is the ball being held?"

"Oh, at the New York Public Library!" She smiled. "Kind of appropriate for you guys!"

Adam laughed. "It's a good sign, I think!"

"I CAN'T BELIEVE Frank is letting you drive his car." Richard grinned and jumped in the front seat of the Mercedes.

Darcy shook his head and chuckled. "It's a special favor to me. I couldn't see squeezing all of us in the backseat, and you know as well as I do that we want to sit next to our particular lady." He pulled out of the garage located beneath his office building and into traffic, heading for New Jersey. "The weather looks good for them." He said, scanning the skies.

"It will be fine." Richard glanced at him and Darcy's jaw set. "How was the rest of your day?"

"Long."

"Yeah." He sighed and started shifting. "What am I sitting on?" He started feeling around and before Darcy could stop him, Richard pulled out an ipod. "What's this? Oh, I get to hear what sort of music you listen to!"

"No . . . Richard, that's Elizabeth's she left it here . . ."

"In the front seat? Of Frank's car? Yeah, right." Gleefully he turned it on and held it away from Darcy's grabbing hand. He put the earphones in and started listening . . . *Last night, I waved goodbye, now it seems years, I'm back in the city, where nothing seems clear, but thoughts of me, holding you, bringing us near . . .* [xii]

"Holy crap, Darcy! Barry Manilow?" He listened again, *Time in New England, took me away . . .* He turned to see Darcy staring straight ahead, his jaw was set and he was gripping the steering wheel so hard his knuckles were white. Richard started chuckling as the song continued, then began to conduct his imaginary orchestra and sing badly out loud. "AND TELL ME, When will our eyes meet? When can I touch you? When will this strong yearning end? AND WHEN WILL I HOLD YOU . . . Again?" He laughed and glanced over to his cousin and saw how upset he was. Taking the earphones out, he turned off the ipod and set it down. "Sorry." Darcy looked at him and back at the road. "May I point out that I knew the words?"

"You're a Fanilow?"

"I wouldn't say that, but Mom is, and . . . I admit that John and I once performed a version of *Copacabana* for her as a birthday present one year." He smiled and Darcy relaxed. "I won't tell on you."

"Thanks, um, could you put that in my pocket? I don't want to forget it in here."

"I thought it was Elizabeth's?" Richard grinned and wrapped up the cords and stuck it in Darcy's suit pocket. The flow of traffic was in their favor and soon they arrived at Teterboro, parked and went inside the terminal. Darcy stood at the windows, in the identical spot where Elizabeth had stood waiting for him. He was tense and none of Richard's jokes helped the situation. "Look." He nudged Darcy and pointed to a plane descending, then noticed Darcy's fists balled up at his sides. The plane made a smooth landing and finally the tension was gone. "Flashback?"

"Yeah."

"I get them in traffic sometimes, expecting a sniper or roadside bomb." He shrugged and met Darcy's eye. "It takes time."

"How do you live with what you saw?"

"I make a lot of jokes at other's expense." Richard clapped his back and they headed out to where the plane was coasting to a stop. A set of steps was moved to the door and it was only a minute before it opened and Elizabeth appeared.

"Will!" She cried and ran down the steps into his waiting arms. "I missed you so much!" Then she whispered. "I can't stand to fly without you anymore."

Darcy held her so tightly she couldn't breathe. "Honey, I can't begin to say how I missed you." He closed his eyes and planted his nose in her hair, breathing in her scent and letting it fill up his senses. "I did not like sleeping alone." He said softly.

"You slept?" Elizabeth pulled back and smiled. "Show off."

"Come back here." He held her face in his hands and kissed her, letting his lips express his feelings, and only regained control when Richard coughed loudly. He looked up to see Georgiana smiling and standing off to the side, and Richard with his arm around Charlotte's shoulders, and laughing. He looked down to see Elizabeth's sparkling, happy eyes, and hugged her again. "I'm not apologizing."

"I'm just admiring your style, I'm afraid that in comparison I was a huge disappointment to Charlotte." Richard kissed her softly and she blushed red. "Hmm, maybe I need to take lessons from Mr. Romance here?"

"You do just fine on your own. You know that I am not into big displays." She adjusted his tie and he smirked. "Whatever you're thinking, stop it right now."

"Me?" He smiled. "I'm not thinking a thing."

"Did you enjoy yourself, Georgiana?" Darcy kissed her cheek, then bent to pick up the bags. Elizabeth grabbed hers from him and then clasped her free hand with his. He smiled at her and looked back at his sister.

"Yes, I had a great time. Now I can understand a little of Elizabeth's work. You should go with her sometime."

Darcy turned to Elizabeth and smiled. "I want to. I'd like to understand it all."

"It can be pretty tedious." She warned.

"Oh well, during those times he can just listen to his ipod." Richard called from behind. Darcy closed his eyes and sighed.

"What happened?" Elizabeth squeezed his hand. "Oh, he found your . . ." She smiled and laughed. "You are Mr. Romance, you know." He looked down at her and blushed. "I love it."

"I love you." He kissed her again and they reached the car. "Let's go home."

"NOW THEN, JANE, have you ever planned a wedding at the library?" Arlene asked the gathering of women in her apartment the following afternoon.

"No, but the woman I worked for before planned several corporate events there." She smiled shyly. "It is a beautiful setting for a reception."

"Oh yes, and I have attended countless affairs there." Arlene nodded her head. "Well then, you should be fine in the ball atmosphere. Georgiana you obviously haven't been to any events. Your brother mentioned that you were going to ask someone to come with you?"

"I did, but he isn't available." She blushed.

"No, and I'm glad that he was so open with you as to his reasons." Elizabeth smiled.

"You know?" Georgiana stared at her.

"Well, yes, Adam told me. He knew that he just couldn't out of the blue ask for an invitation to a fundraiser in New York when he lives in California and not have me question his motivation, especially when you take into account the price of admission. He and I have been friends for too long for him not to be completely honest about it." Elizabeth raised her brow. "I was hoping you would bring it up."

"When he said I was too young to date, I thought it wouldn't be necessary." She said quietly.

Elizabeth nodded her understanding. "I apologize if I have embarrassed you by speaking about it in front of everyone. Adam is a very good man, and I am glad that he thought it was important to make everything clear to me, and I told William."

"Oh no." She groaned. "Is he mad?"

"No, you asked Adam, and he knew to refuse. William would have been angry if Adam had said yes and you didn't tell us then. It's okay to keep rejections to yourself." Elizabeth smiled. "I only hoped you would speak to me because I didn't know if you felt hurt or not."

"A little." She admitted. "But he is so nice. I think that I like older guys. The ones I meet at school just seem so immature."

"There's a lot to be said for experience." Charlotte noted as the other women exchanged knowing smiles.

"Well, I'm glad that he was showing some good sense. Will he be coming?" Arlene broke into the discussion.

"There may be a conflict in his schedule." Elizabeth said quietly.

Georgiana looked away from Elizabeth to Arlene. "Why is it good that he not come? He is Elizabeth's friend, and . . . he said we could just dance without it being a date."

"My dear, it would not be wise for you to make your first public appearance on the arm of a man many years your senior, you will be introduced as a future member of the foundation board, taking your mother's place."

"Will I have to talk?" She said worriedly.

"Of course not, just stay with me and I'll introduce you around." She patted her hand. "And really Jane and Charlotte, your role is simply that as guests. You may be noticed as John and Richard's dates, John especially since he was considering running for office and the party has not given up on him yet, however, the real focus of attention will be on Elizabeth." All eyes turned to her, and she flushed. "You are the one who every person with a cause in that room is going to approach the next morning. They know that William will make contributions to charities, but does not attend functions. They are going to be looking to you to get him there physically as well as to whisper in his ear that their charity needs his money. You will be watched and courted. You must do well."

"So much for our quiet life in our little house on Riverside Drive." Elizabeth said weakly.

"It is what you make of it, dear. Just because you are approached, it does not require you to listen or promise your time. What you need to learn now is the artful and elegant way of saying no." Arlene smiled. "I wonder if William has made you aware of the charities he favors or the amounts he gives away each year. I suggest that if he hasn't, you have that conversation before the ball, and of course discuss any charities that you would like to support, as well. That way you will have a clear understanding of who you wish to give your attention and who you need to deflect. Poor William seems to find his way to a dark corner for most of the night. I hope that with you by his side he will get to enjoy the evening. Anne has been working on this for months."

"And I thought that the worst part of this would be surviving gown shopping with Maurice." Elizabeth smiled slightly then looked down at her shoes.

Arlene sat down and took her hands. "Where is that confident girl who took on Catherine?"

"That was different, she was attacking my worthiness to be married to William, and she wanted back in the family circle. She was ready to apologize."

"Well, this is the same situation dear. You have the money, you wield the power. You and William are the ones in charge of how you are treated." She smiled as she watched Elizabeth thinking it over. "And he needs you." Elizabeth's eyes met hers and she nodded.

"I won't let him down."

THAT EVENING, DARCY came home from work and settled down on the sofa, stretching his tall frame out, and rested his head in Elizabeth's lap, on top of the story she was editing. "Hi." He looked up at her bent head and smiled.

"I take it that you wish to be noticed." She smiled and laughed when his hand came up to pull her face down to kiss. "I believe you have answered my question." Taking the binder out from under his head she set it aside, then moved out from under him and stood. "Scoot!"

Darcy sat up a little and held out his arms, pulling her down to lie next to him. "We just barely fit here."

"I like being squashed like this." He pushed her tighter against the back of the sofa and she laughed. "I'd like to breathe, though!" They kissed slowly and Darcy's arms wrapped around her.

He rested his forehead against hers. "Can I tell you again how I hated sleeping alone?"

"It was only two nights . . ." Elizabeth looked into the intense blue eyes and kissed him. "I hated it, too. I made that clear to Charlotte. If she wasn't my friend and dating Richard . . . Will, she and Georgiana practically had to hold me down when you kissed me goodbye and left the plane."

"I know, Georgiana told me about the flight, and how you held her arm so tight when you were landing. I'm sorry that it wasn't me you were bruising." He smiled a little and hugged her. "You were doing your friend a favor, I know that."

"Yes, well, I've told her it won't happen again, not after she tried to make me feel guilty for giving up my series."

"She did?" Darcy shifted and searched her face. "Do you mean that after no notice of the trip, giving up your time when you were under no obligation to do so, after I provided the transportation . . . she had the gall to suggest that you were doing her wrong?" His eyes flashed.

"I love it when you get protective of me, Will." Elizabeth smiled.

"Lizzy, you haven't signed anything with Lucas Lit for your new book have you?"

"No, I think I should finish it first." She tilted her head. "Do you want me to take my business elsewhere? I don't think that's necessary, and her father is helping with my ideas for the scholarship." Elizabeth brushed back the hair from his forehead. "I handled it, honey."

"But her arrogance in expecting you to come put you in that plane . . . without me." He sighed.

She read his expression. "You are probably due to go away somewhere, aren't you?"

"Next month, probably the first week of November I will need to travel out west. I would like you to come with me." He relaxed when her eyes lit up. "I will have to actually work, but we will have the evenings to ourselves. I am hoping to avoid dinner meetings. Do you think that you can be happy without me during the day?"

She giggled with his somewhat selfish concern. "Well, where are you taking me?"

"All of the nights will be in Seattle. We'll fly into the airport near our land in Montana, visit the burned-out areas and drop into the mill, then fly out that afternoon to Seattle, have the night alone and I'll have my meetings during the days. One day I'll have to visit our land in Washington. But you can come along if you want, it would be nice for you to see it, so you know what I'm talking about."

"So I'll spend the days in Seattle?" He nodded. "Oh, now *that* I can enjoy. There is so much to see there, and I've always wanted to visit."

"You'd go around alone?" He did not hide his disappointment well.

Elizabeth stroked his hair. "Haven't you seen everything before?"

"no."

Elizabeth hugged him and whispered in his ear. "I'll go to the girly places on my own and save the spots you want to see for when you are free, okay?"

"Okay." He closed his eyes and hugged her tighter. "Thanks." They lay quietly, shifting so Elizabeth settled her head on his chest, and Darcy rubbed his hand up and down her arm. "Are you scared?"

"About Seattle? No . . ."

"No honey, the ball." He kissed her cheek.

"Yes." She sighed.

"If it makes you feel any better, so am I." His sigh matched hers. "But it's a wonderful cause, we raise a lot of money for the foundation, and . . . it's my mom's baby, and I could never give it up."

"What scares you? You know what to expect."

"That does not change my discomfort in a crowd. There's no anonymity there like we have when we go dancing, everyone in that room is looking at me and knows who I am." He closed his eyes. "I have to get up and speak."

"Oh Will, I didn't realize, I thought Anne . . ."

"Anne sits on the board and represents the family for the purpose of the ball since it is our single greatest fundraiser. We have employees who look after the day-to-day operations, you know, the same ones who talked to you about my charitable giving. I am the honorary chair for the whole thing with the help of Uncle David and Aunt Arlene. But since mom started it, and it is a Darcy foundation . . . a Darcy must speak, which means . . . me."

"But I'll be with you . . . And you'll be with me."

Darcy hugged her tighter and kissed her ear. "I'm hoping that you'll help me. I won't say much, just thanks for coming, but . . . may I introduce you then? It will be a great reason to have you standing beside me." He looked at her beseechingly. "We can listen to our knees knocking together."

"And likely be cutting the circulation off in each other's hands with our grips." Elizabeth smiled. "Of course I will stand by your side." His relief was obvious, and she laughed. "Then in return, you must teach me the Darcy glare to chase away anyone who approaches."

He chuckled. "No honey, you do much better with your tongue than my glare."

"You like my tongue, do you?" Elizabeth whispered then gently traced it over his lips. He groaned. "Hmm, too bad I'm so trapped here, if I had room to play, I think that I would put my tongue to good use."

"How?" He whispered and licked her lips.

"Mmmmm, I'd find a pleasant way to relieve your stress." Her hand brushed down his chest and rested over his groin. "Have I ever told you how nice you look in these soft sweatpants?"

"Noooo." He moaned as her hand moved over his growing arousal.

"Oh, well they just make things . . . so prominent . . . and tasty."

"Would you like to taste?"

"I would."

He looked up at the door and swore. "It's open."

"Shall I get up and lock it?"

"No, let's go upstairs; I think I have some tasting of my own to do." Darcy got up and held out his hands for her. She stood and wrapped her arms around his waist, leaning on his back and rubbed her hands over his arousal. He looked down, watching them at work, involuntarily swaying with the motion, and didn't notice when she slipped her fingers over the waistband and pulled his pants down, then bent to nibble and lick his tender bottom. "Ohhhhh, baby." Her hands came around to caress his length. "honey." He whispered. Elizabeth slowly pulled his pants back up, and then came around to stand on her toes to reach his lips. Taking his hand she smiled.

"Let's go."

"ARE YOU SURE?" Elizabeth listened and let out an exasperated breath. "Okay, well, I guess it's not a surprise. We'll see you there." She hung up the phone and looked up to see William coming out of his dressing room, fiddling with his cufflinks. "Mom and Dad are staying home."

"Why, what happened?"

"She is having an anxiety attack." Elizabeth sank onto the bed and looked at how handsome he was in his tuxedo pants and shirt, a thatch of dark chest hair just peeking from the undone collar, the tie open and draped around his neck. She closed her eyes against the temptation to rush forward and undress him, then opened them to see him leaning against the doorway with a warm smile on his face. He knew exactly what she was thinking. "Stop it."

"I didn't say a thing, honey, but thank you." He walked over and sat beside her, kissing her softly. "Hold that thought for later." She leaned against him, and drank in his musky scent while he kissed her hair. "Fran got scared again?"

"Yes, she remembered how intimidated she was at the engagement party and decided that she couldn't handle this. Jane said Dad was not displeased with the situation." She smiled when William chuckled and hugged her. "I'm not either, to be honest with you. She'll be fine."

"As long as you're not upset, I won't worry about it." He kissed her again and stood. "Do you need help with your dress?"

"Yes, if you could zip it for me?" He nodded and followed her into the dressing room where she took off the robe, and smiled at his quiet moan of appreciation. All she wore were stockings, garters, and a thong. She peeked at his reflection in the full-length mirror and smiled at the wolf staring back at her. Biting her lip, she lifted the gown from its hanger and stepped into it, holding it to her breasts. "Okay, I'm ready." He stepped forward, and ran his hands up her back, resting them on the curve of her waist and bent to nudge her hair aside and nibble her neck. Elizabeth leaned back into his chest.

"Do you have any idea how beautiful you are?" He whispered warmly. "I'm going to be thinking of this all night, and," he kissed along her throat to suckle her ear lobe, "I will be thinking of when we will come home and take this off." Slowly he pulled the zipper up, then wrapped his arms around her, looking up to see them in the mirror. "So lovely, honey." One hand disappeared into his pocket and reappeared to press something in her hand. Elizabeth gasped to see a matching set of earrings, bracelet and necklace sparkling in a pool of fire and ice in her palm.

"These were my mother's, and my grandmother's, bought from Harry Winston himself, and now they are yours. I thought you should wear Darcy jewels tonight." He took the necklace and attached it around her throat, then the bracelet. "I'll let you do the earrings." He chuckled as he watched her touch the necklace in awe. "Speechless?"

"Overwhelmed, utterly." She turned to look up at him. "Thank you so much." They kissed slowly, and both had a hard time stopping it from going further. "Um, do you need help with your dressing?" Elizabeth said shakily.

"Hmmm, no I think I can handle it." He stepped back reluctantly and looked up and down her gown. "Did you get new shoes?"

She giggled and pointed, "I wanted to wear a pair that I already have but Maurice insisted."

"And who are you to disagree with him?" He laughed. "Can you dance in them? We *are* going to dance tonight."

"I'll manage." She patted his bottom and shooed him away. "Now get finished, we leave in twenty minutes." He gave her one more appreciative smile and disappeared.

She slipped on the shoes, put in the earrings, and fixed her hair once more. She heard a knock on the door to the hallway and found Georgiana standing nervously outside. "Does it look okay?"

"You are perfect, come on let's pack up our bags." They took their tiny clutches, and selected their necessities for the evening and then looked at each other. "We're going to be fine." Elizabeth said determinedly.

"If you say so."

Elizabeth squeezed her hand then called out, "Will? Are you ready?"

"I was just waiting for you." He appeared, and stopped dead. "Wow, you two are stunning. I am the luckiest man in the world to have such beautiful women on my arms. I can't wait to dance with both of you tonight." He offered one to each of them and they made their way downstairs. Mrs. Reynolds waited at the bottom, camera in hand. They laughed and posed, then donning their coats, walked out into the brisk autumn night to get in the car. They arrived at the library, and entered to see that the cocktail reception had just begun.

Anne spotted them and she approached with a wide smile. "Oh you all look great!" She kissed everyone and led the way to a side room. "Come on you have to meet our guest of honor for tonight."

"There's a guest of honor?" Elizabeth asked as they removed their coats.

"Oh yes, each year we honor somebody who has contributed to the community in some way. We are honoring the woman who started a 5K race through Central Park to benefit the summer camps this year." She waved her arm to another room. "We'll be doing the auction in there, so many cool things to bid on. Lots of show tickets and several celebrities offering to record your voicemail message, and William contributed a week at Pemberley." She smiled at him, "including air transportation."

"You did?" Elizabeth looked at him. "Had you thought of this recently?"

"Anne called while you were away and asked if I could think of something to auction off, and I thought of how you said that the visitors were keeping the estate alive for when we get to live there, and . . . well it *is* the Pemberley/Matlock Foundation, so . . ." He shrugged and smiled to see her approving nod. "I'm glad that you like it."

"I do, Will." He leaned down and kissed her.

"Aha! At it again, I see!" Richard and Charlotte approached and said their greetings. "Looking lovely ladies."

"What about me?" Darcy cocked his head at him.

"Who cares about you?" Richard smiled. "So what's the agenda?"

"Cocktails, dinner, where our mistress of ceremonies speaks and introduces William . . ."

"Will he be found to be introduced?" John prodded as he and Jane arrived.

"I'll do my duty." Darcy murmured.

"And then the auction and of course dancing." Anne finished up. "The band is excellent, I was here while they were warming up before the doors opened." Darcy caught her eye and she winked and nodded, and a small smile appeared on his lips.

"I am looking forward to that part of the evening." He looked down to see Elizabeth watching him. "I can't wait to show off my partner."

"Oh I am sure there are any number of superior dancers here tonight." She squeezed his hand and Georgiana squealed. "Look! Celebrities!" The group collectively craned their necks to see scatterings of the rich and famous. Anne looked at her cousin and took her arm. "Come on, I'll introduce you around, you might as well start learning the ropes."

"Where's Greg?"

Anne looked behind her. "Oh, somewhere, he was talking up golf with Uncle David and a few friends. Now, don't stand around in a bunch, go circulate!"

"Is Aunt Catherine here?" John peered around the sea of tuxedoed men and bejeweled women. "I know that she wouldn't miss this."

"I saw her making the rounds with Mom." Richard nodded over to a corner. "Well, what do you say Charlotte? Shall we mingle?"

"I'll give it a whirl." She laughed and looked over to Elizabeth. "Famous last words."

John took Jane's hand and grinned at them, "I'm going to show off my vision of loveliness."

Jane laughed. "I am a possession now?"

"You are the answer to my dreams." He smiled then kissed her hand and delighted in the blush that appeared. "Come on, there's a world of people I want you to meet tonight." He tucked her hand in her arm then looked over to Darcy with a grin. "See ya!" Jane tore her wide eyes from him to bite her lip and silently squeal at Elizabeth before floating away with him.

Darcy tilted his head. "I believe that John has finally figured it out."

"All by himself." Elizabeth laughed; she saw his eyes were fixed on hers. "What are you thinking?"

He shrugged. "I was wondering if I could have spotted you across this crowded room."

"You know, John may have figured it out, but you remain the king of romance." He laughed and kissed her, then holding hands they ventured out into the crowd. Darcy's grip tightened and his smile became fixed in place as one person or couple after another approached. Elizabeth was examined and she made mental notes on who ignored her and centered their attention on William, and who made a point of being friendly to both. She sifted through the conversations, and noticed that nearly everyone who approached wanted something from him. It was sad to see that he truly did have so few friends. He handled the constant barrage of smiling people with as much grace as he could, but Elizabeth invariably came to the rescue quickly in the conversations, and soon word seemed to spread that she was approachable. She found herself receiving air kisses and whispered warnings that invitations to lunch or functions would be soon coming her way.

She hardly realized it as it was happening, but William was slowly but steadily directing their movement to a corner. When they arrived, safe on three sides from the onslaught of people, he finally seemed to relax a little. Elizabeth could still feel the tension radiating from him. "I hate this. I can't . . . pretend to be interested in these inane conversations."

"You mean the one about ski fashions or was it the yacht races for the coming season?" She laughed and leaned against him. Darcy wrapped one arm around her waist and hugged her. "This is a room full of people with a lot of money and a lot of time on their hands."

"That is very true."

"And yet they are choosing to spend some of their money and time on a cause that you support, and personally effects Anne." She looked up to see him smiling a little. "And my point is . . ."

"Suck it up and behave myself." He set down his glass of wine and hugged her with both arms. "How do you do it, Lizzy? I know that you are just as uncomfortable as I am, yet you greet them with a smile as if you have known them for years, say something witty and send them away quickly with noncommittal murmurs of agreement. I am in awe of you."

"Well, remember I have had years of book signings under my belt, so I have learned to mirror the mood of the person I am facing. If they are excited, I am. If they are serious . . . well you get the picture. They walk away with the impression that they were heard and feel good about the encounter." She laughed. "That sounds so insincere, but when you are meeting hundreds of people for only minutes at a time, it's hard to form a lasting relationship. This seems to be the same situation. I won't remember the names, but I will remember the causes they represent, and which interest me, and perhaps you will as well."

"And there I was just hoping they'd finish and go away." He hugged her tight. "I suppose that we can handle going to a few of these things from time to time. It will be easier if we're just guests."

"Yes, and then we can eat!" She grinned and a gong sounded, calling them to the tables. Once everyone was in their places, the mistress of ceremonies made the opening welcome then introduced Darcy. He sent a worried look to Elizabeth and she rose with him to hold his hand tightly.

"Good Evening." He spoke softly. Elizabeth squeezed hard. "My mother created this foundation twenty-two years ago, in honor of my cousin Anne." He looked over to Anne and smiled. "She had a great vision for the good she wished to do, research for a cure or at least better management of seizure disorders, respite for the families and children who cope with the anticipation of the next event, and of course, education for a public that knows far too little. She looked forward to this ball every year, and since my parents' deaths I, and my family, have attempted to carry on her hopes. Your contributions tonight will significantly aid in the continuation of fulfilling her dreams, and I thank you for your consideration." He drew a breath and looked down to see Elizabeth smiling at him proudly. "I would like to introduce you now to my wife Elizabeth, and to my sister Georgiana," he smiled over to where she awkwardly stood and sat down again, "two new Darcy women who will help to carry on Anne Darcy's work. Thank you."

The crowd applauded and they took their seats. Darcy closed his eyes and opened them to see Elizabeth's smiling at him. "You were wonderful."

"I thought of what you said, about how these people are voluntarily supporting mom's dream, and well, I abandoned my prepared speech." He smiled shyly. "It was okay?"

"Your mom would be so proud." Elizabeth kissed him, and they settled in to enjoy their meals.

A camera flashed and they looked up to see a grinning photographer. Elizabeth smiled. "I want a copy of that, please."

"Just check the paper tomorrow." He winked and walked off.

"Oh well, if we're going to be in the paper, we need to really do something noteworthy."

"Such as?" Darcy relaxed and grinned, the hard part of the night was over.

"Wow them with our fancy footwork?" She suggested.

"Prepare to be dipped." He warned.

"Should I be frightened?" Elizabeth raised her brow, and rested her hand on his knee.

"What are you doing?" Her hand advanced up his leg. "Lizzy . . ." The hand slipped upwards. "Honey . . ." He protested but parted his legs a little to give her access. She tossed her head back and laughed, letting her fingers walk up to touch . . . "baby." He whispered. Her hand retreated and he grabbed it, placing it back where it was. "Payback is coming your way, my love."

"Goody!" She smiled at his steely gaze and turned to talk to Georgiana at her side.

Richard nudged him. "What are you two doing, whispering so closely?"

Darcy looked at him. "You have a girlfriend, figure it out yourself."

"hmm." He glanced at Charlotte. "I think that was your best speech ever."

"Thanks." He deflected the praise and saw how Charlotte was studying the crowd before them. "How's Charlotte doing?"

"Pretty good. She's kind of overwhelmed by the show, but she's used to big events." He leaned over to Darcy. "It's nice to have a date who I'll want to remember in the morning."

"Well that's a unique way to put it." Darcy laughed. He looked up to see the mistress of ceremonies announcing that the auction and dancing would begin in a quarter hour. Elizabeth leaned over to him and he bent his head.

"I'm going to take Georgiana to the ladies' room."

"What is she, five?"

"It's a girl thing, and no I don't understand why we have to go in packs. Anyway, do you want to meet at the dance floor?"

"Dinner's over, and we'd be leaving in a few minutes anyway, I'll just come with you and wait." He got up and accompanied his ladies outside to the restrooms; and upon waiting for them to return found Catherine standing and staring at him. "Aunt Catherine, I'm sorry that I didn't greet you sooner."

"I have been watching you tonight." He braced himself for the pronouncements and waited in silence. "You are performing well." Catherine adjusted the gold shawl that lay over her shoulders and looked off in the distance. "Your wife has made a good impression. I have heard nothing but praise for her."

"I am happy to hear it."

"Yes, well, it should be of no surprise to you, obviously she is no fool."

"Definitely not. Maybe you should tell her this yourself?"

"No, I . . . think not." Catherine looked up at him. "You seem to have chosen well."

"I have." Darcy watched her nod imperiously and walk away quickly. "Well I'll be damned." He murmured.

"What happened?" David asked, appearing at his elbow.

"Aunt Catherine likes Elizabeth."

Arlene looked after her and laughed. "Of course she does, but if I was Elizabeth, I'd let her work for it a bit longer."

"I don't think that will be a problem." Darcy smiled. The band started playing and he looked around. "Where are they?"

John and Jane passed by on their way to dance. "Come on, I have to show off my moves!"

"You have moves now?" Jane laughed.

"Sure, I know how to dip and twirl like a pro!" He smiled and took her hand, and they began to dance. "I'll try not to count, though."

Jane giggled. "As long as you don't step on my toes, I'll be happy." The dance was easy, and they swayed to the quiet romantic tune. She looked up from watching his feet to see his intense blue eyes boring into her. "Is . . . is something wrong?"

"No . . . nothing."

"Then why are you staring like that?" She said softly.

"You are the loveliest woman I have ever known, and not just your outside beauty, Jane. I love you." He drew her closer and kissed her.

"I love you, too." Jane said softly and leaned her head against his. They didn't speak for awhile, and just moved to the music. "John, I noticed a number of people expressing disappointment in your not running for Congress."

He pulled back and regarded her expression. "Yes, I have been courted and groomed for sometime."

"Why did you give up the dream? Was it because of me? Because . . . if that is something you want, don't let me stop . . ."

John smiled. "No, no, Jane, I didn't give it up for you . . . not entirely for you." He added and saw her blush. "It wasn't my dream, it was everyone else's. I want a life where I can leave work behind at the end of the day and come home and be obligated to nobody but my family. You don't have that as a politician. You are the property of too many people."

"But if you would like to go that way . . . I would be willing to . . . come along." She looked down and he smiled widely.

"Janie." She looked back up, and he kissed her. "Thank you." He drew a deep breath. "I think that we should do something else, more exciting."

"Such as?"

"Well, you are obviously very comfortable in this atmosphere, and I am as well. Would you consider joining my father and me in our family business? It's not weddings, but we would be busy all year with fundraising events. Maybe we could have our season of politics, then when that's not busy work on things like this event, and when I'm getting someone elected you could be doing a wedding . . . It would give us time together, more time, and we would have time to play."

"Join your family business?" Jane said softly.

"You would need to join the family, too." He whispered. "I think it's a requirement."

She laughed. "I didn't notice any contracts for me to read."

"I have it carefully hidden."

"Oh, so I'll miss the fine print." He chuckled, and Jane whispered. "Are you . . . proposing to me?"

"I'm making a proposal." He met her eyes. "I am giving you something to think about, because . . . I can't not think about you as my future. Let's talk about it when we are alone." He let out a deep breath. "It feels so good to get that off of my chest!"

Jane laughed and he spun her around. "You do feel better! I so want to talk about this. I think of you as my future, too."

"Yes!" He spun her again. "And now that you and I are on the same page . . . You do love me, don't you?"

"I do, very much."

"Say it."

"I love you, John."

He beamed. "As I was saying, now that we're on the same page and I am somewhat relaxed, what do you say to us having some fun together, instead of this cautious pussyfooting we've been doing?"

"What do you have in mind?" She giggled to see his eyes light up.

"I don't know; should I steal Darcy's playbook and see what he does?"

"Nope, let's make them envy us." She squealed as he dipped her down, and nearly dropped her. "John!"

"Sorry. Don't quite have the hang of it yet." He slowed down and smiled. "Thank you."

"So we'll do this on John and Jane's terms, and not worry about anyone else?"

"Absolutely."

Darcy and Elizabeth spun by and he smiled down at her. "What do you think is going on over there?"

"I think that they are going to be announcing something soon." She laughed as he held her close and swayed. "What that announcement will be is anybody's guess, but my sister is ecstatic."

"How can you tell?" He looked at Jane and back at her. "She is a puzzle to read."

"Which is why John has been so hesitant, I think."

"Hmm." He smiled and kissed her. "I'm glad that I was too caught up in my own romance to care about anyone else's. I can't tell you how happy I am, you by my side has made this evening, one that I've dreaded beginning the morning after the last ball, into one that I believe I might actually enjoy and even anticipate in the future. Thank you so much for your support and love tonight."

"You have done the same for me, I couldn't have done it without your hand in mine." Darcy's eyes met hers and they swayed in silence.

The song ended and he roused himself from the soft pull of her gaze, just as the opening chords of the next song began. "Ah, what good timing, this is for you."

Elizabeth listened. "You made a request?"

He nodded and held her close to his chest, wrapping his arm around her waist, and holding her hand. "Dance with me, honey." The singer's voice began and he pressed his lips to her ear and sang along. "I can only give you love that lasts forever, and a promise to be near each time you call. And the only heart I own, for you and you alone, that's all, that's all."

"Oh Will." Elizabeth sighed as their bodies melted into each other and they slowly turned around the room.

"I can only give you country walks in springtime, and a hand to hold when leaves begin to fall, and a love whose burning light, will warm the winter night, that's all, that's all."

She lifted her face up from his shoulder and looked up to his warm eyes, meeting his lips for a gentle kiss. "There are those, I am sure, that have told you, they would give you the world for a toy." She smiled as he touched the diamonds sparkling around her throat, then shook his head, "All I have are these arms to enfold you, and a love time can never destroy."

Darcy closed his eyes and hugged her to him, swaying in a slow circle, then opened them to see the love looking back at him, and pressing his forehead to hers, softly sang the end. "If you're wondering what I'm asking in return, dear, you'll be glad to know that my demands are small. Say it's me that you'll adore for now and ever more, that's all, that's all.[xiii]"

"To the new Lord of the Ladies." Richard said as he and Charlotte walked past, and winked. The Darcys did not notice them, remaining in their embrace as the next song began. A photographer stepped up and captured the scene, and the flash woke them from the moment.

"What a wonderful surprise." Elizabeth sniffed.

"You're not supposed to cry, honey." He laughed and kissed her. "Come on, this is a fun one." Hearing the trumpets blaring, she recognized a salsa just as he spun her out and snapped her back to his side, and they laughed. "That's better."

"It's all good, Will."

Chapter 20

"**S**hould I set up a new desk?" Darcy smiled and stood in the doorway of the library to find Elizabeth once again curled up in his chair, computer in her lap, typing away.

"I'm sorry, Will. I'll move."

"No, no, I meant for me." He came in; setting down his briefcase and laptop, then sat on the edge of his desk and watched her save the chapter. "I was going to offer to turn a room into a private office space for you."

"I'm in your way." She sighed and closed the computer and started to move.

He rested his hand on her arm to stop her. "I'm not complaining." She stopped and looked up at him. "I'm curious though, why here?"

"Why do I sit here like a cat who is continually in the way?" She shrugged and ran her hands on the worn leather arms of the chair then pressed her head into the seat back, resting it just below the dent that his head had made over the years. "I don't know, but it feels like . . . you're hugging me." Elizabeth saw his smile and smiled in return. "You know how long it took me to be comfortable working here, but after I discovered your chair . . ."

"All was well." He leaned down to kiss her. "Thank you. I hope that you are comfortable in the whole house now."

"I am; I just like certain places more than others." She stood up and took his hand, dragging him down to sit in the chair. "Now, warm it back up for me." He chuckled and pulled her back to sit in his lap.

"Would you like your own space? If nothing else, it would give you a place to keep your files and things, even if you didn't actually work there. I'd be happy to call the decorator who redid the rooms after the fire and you could figure out what you want." He kissed her softly. "Your workload seems to be growing the longer we are married. There's your writing, you'll be forming a staff for the scholarship soon, and I appreciate so much that you want to take over the supervision of our staff for our charitable giving. Your own space would give you a place to organize things in your preferred way, and not mine."

"And get me out of your office."

"Lizzy . . ."

"I'd like that, Will. Thank you. But, I'm still going to work in your chair when you're gone." She smiled and he hugged her. She continued in a quiet voice, "Do you mind if I stay in here while you are working? You haven't thrown me out yet, but I'll go if you want . . ."

"I don't want." He kissed her again. "I love seeing you here."

"At it again, I see." Richard appeared at the doorway and laughed.

"Where did you come from?" Darcy asked and refused to allow Elizabeth to escape his arms.

"Heaven, so I've been told." He laughed to hear the collective groan and plopped down in a chair before the desk. "Am I interrupting?"

"Perpetually. What brings you here in person?" Darcy protested but Elizabeth slipped out of his arms and stood up.

"I . . . I needed to talk to you." He glanced at Elizabeth and back at him.

"I get the feeling that my presence is unwanted." She smiled and kissed William then picked up her laptop. "I'll be out scouting locations for my office. Carry on!"

"Sorry, Elizabeth." Richard said as she passed. She kissed his cheek and winked, and closed the door behind her. The latch clicked and the two men looked at each other for a few moments, then Richard cleared his throat. "You know that I have contacts in the media . . . making deals with the paparazzi about leaving clients alone when I take them out, that sort of thing."

Darcy nodded and sat back in his chair. "Well, one of my contacts tipped me off that . . . someone is trying to sell a story about Elizabeth to the tabloids."

"*What?*"

"Nobody is interested in buying it; you're rich but extraordinarily boring, at least in their opinion. I mean, you'd have to have a murder in the house or something to get their attention. This isn't even good enough for the gossip columns, and I understand that it isn't offered to any place where a profit might not be had . . ."

"What is it about? Who is behind it?"

"Collins." Darcy's eyes flared. "I guess that the pictures of you at the ball got his attention, and he realized who Elizabeth had married, and . . . having a bit of a grudge against you and likely wounded pride against her, he has tried to shop around a story of her loose behavior in college. It's all crap, but apparently he's broke and saw this as an opportunity."

"Making money by inflicting pain on her again." Darcy pounded his fist on the desk. "I'll kill him!"

"Yeah, I gather he was pretty nervous when he came calling with the story, he wanted to make sure that you didn't find out the source, pretty stupid on his part, like you wouldn't figure it out."

"I'm surprised he hasn't approached me offering *not* to publish it for a fee."

"No, he's a wimp, and that would mean actually contacting you." Richard watched as Darcy sifted through ideas. "What would you like to do?"

"Kill him."

"Any others?" Richard smiled a little and saw that humor would not help his cousin. "Doesn't Pemberley keep attorneys on retainer for just this sort of thing, protecting the image of the company? I suggest that you send them out to quietly inform the media that stories such as these will not be dealt with kindly, perhaps an official message could be sent to Collins as well to drive him back into his hole."

Darcy nodded while he bit his lip and stared blankly at his desk, then saw a letter Elizabeth had left there. It was a charity asking for funds to create shelters for battered women. He knew that would appeal to her. "I wonder . . . I wonder if Lizzy would be willing to tell her story."

"To the tabloids? I know that a preemptive strike is useful, but if this isn't even going to be bought . . ."

"Maybe not now, but who knows what our future will bring? Now that I have her by my side, I will be more visible, attending events and things . . . The more relaxed we become, the better targets we will be for slander such as this." He looked at the letter again. "What if she were to tell her story to an organization dedicated to rescuing women who are in situations similar to her experience? Then it would be a known fact, at least documented that she spoke before anything ever came out, making his claims even more a non-story and again pointing the suspicion back on him as to why he wanted to sell it in the first place."

"Would she be willing to speak about it?"

"I don't know. She wants it to be in the past, but if it helps her to help others . . . You know, it might actually be very good for her to purge it from her system."

"The memory of her past is still infusing her daily life, isn't it?" Richard nodded his understanding and Darcy smiled sadly and nodded, both men had pasts that affected their present behavior.

"Yes, she . . . can't always express herself openly, she holds back." He thought of Elizabeth sitting in his chair and realized again that her needing to be there in his absence was just another way of quietly declaring her love for him. "It's as if she's afraid it will make the listener reject her if she says something wrong." He looked at the wedding photo on his desk, the two of them embraced on the beach, watching her veil sailing off over the ocean. "As if that were possible." He said softly.

"I don't see this as pressing, but . . . it's not a bad idea, maybe you should speak to her about it." Richard waited while Darcy pulled out of his thoughts, and watched, wondering if he was capable of such deep devotion. "I'm sorry to have brought you this news."

"No, I'm glad that you did, and in person." He looked up and surreptitiously wiped his eyes then drew a deep breath. "I'll talk to her later. Thank you."

"SO WHAT'S GOING ON with you guys? This whole proposal thing is intriguing." Elizabeth wandered around the house with the phone to her ear, looking at rooms and wondering which one felt like her.

"Well, I have weddings booked for the next year, but with this being the slow season, it would be a good time to get my feet wet a little and try my hand at event planning of a different variety. I think it might be nice to get away from demanding brides and their mothers for a while." Jane laughed while looking over the caterer's menu for the weekend wedding planned for the Plaza Hotel. "And being part of a company, well that would be a good thing I think, I could probably handle more than one event a week. I've had to turn down clients just because my staff is so small."

"You could just hire more people."

"But then I'd have to let them go if the work slowed down. I couldn't do that." Jane sighed.

"Maybe working for a company would be better for you, Jane. You're excellent with the planning and organizing, but your business skills aren't the best. You need a good manager."

"That was supposed to be you."

"Um, I'm a writer, that's creative like you. You need a cut throat, no-nonsense business person."

"Like Charlotte?"

"She's busy. How about Kitty?"

"She's in school, Lizzy."

"She's studying business management."

"I don't want to be her first employer." Jane said quietly. "Not that I don't trust her, but I can't afford to absorb a freshman's mistakes."

"Hey I tried." Elizabeth laughed and sat down in an old drawing room in the back of the house, the window overlooked the garden.

"Did she put you up to that?"

"No, I thought of it on my own. Actually, I'm going to be hiring a staff for our scholarship foundation, maybe she might like to help out there . . . Hmm." She moved a chair and placed it in front of the window, and pretended to be working there. "So back to John . . ."

"He's wonderful." She said dreamily.

Elizabeth giggled. "Did I sound like you?"

"If I'm not mistaken you still do." Jane poked her. "We've decided to take our time."

"Why do I have a feeling that this admirable caution will be soon abandoned?"

"Maybe." The sisters laughed. "Did you enjoy Seattle?"

"Very much, William was so excited to show me his trees and the mill, and then more trees and another mill . . ." Elizabeth laughed. "We saw so many wonderful things. I got him on the bus, that was an accomplishment, believe me, and we went to all of the touristy spots. Our favorite was the Pike Place Market, it was so full of wonderful things to eat, and it killed me that I didn't have a kitchen handy. Of course his solution was a proposal to go buy a vacation home."

"Wow."

"I talked him out of it." Elizabeth smiled. "He hired an architect to build us a cabin in Maine, though."

"That will be nice, when you have kids . . ."

"No Jane, it's just for us, a place without any responsibility, no staff, no family, just the two of us." She sighed. "I think that we'll go there often."

"I want a billionaire." Jane said jealously.

"You have a millionaire, you're not doing bad."

"That's true." She giggled. "He makes me so happy."

"I'm glad Jane, and I'm glad that you found him. I don't know that you would have been happy to stay with Charles."

"No, but he seems happy with Maria."

"I'm worried about Richard and Charlotte."

"Why?"

"They seem to be enjoying the companionship, but . . . I just don't see a deep attachment forming. It's as if they don't want to be lonely so they are just staying friends."

"Not everyone displays their hearts openly. Who knows what goes on behind closed doors?"

"Yes." Elizabeth said softly as a memory intruded.

Jane knew instantly why her sister had grown quiet. "I'm sorry, Lizzy."

"No, it's okay. Hey, I have to go. I have to start planning for Thanksgiving."

"That's two weeks from now." Jane tried to stop her from retreating.

"Yes, but it's a houseful of people . . ."

She sighed, there was no stopping her. "Okay, you go plan, and let me know what to bring."

"Okay."

"We have a great deal to be thankful for this year, don't we?" Jane said softly.

Elizabeth smiled and looked up to see William's reflection in the window glass, then felt his hands on her shoulders. "We certainly do. I'll talk to you later, Jane." She ended the call and looked up to William, he was biting his lip. "Where's Richard?"

"Hmm? Oh, he had to go. How's Jane?"

"Fine, madly in love with your cousin." She laughed.

"She's probably at home getting ready for a date with him." He said with a small smile.

"No, actually she's at work still. A big wedding this weekend." She stood up and gave him a hug. "So what did Richard want?"

"Oh, you know; girl advice." He said distractedly and kissed her. "I have some stuff to do before dinner; I just thought I'd tell you before I disappeared."

"Okay, I'll sit here and imagine what I want for my office. I think this room will be perfect. I can look out and see the garden through every season." She smiled and touched his face. "Are you okay?"

"Hmm? Oh, yes." He smiled and kissed her. "Call me when it's time to eat." Elizabeth watched him go with a crease in her brow and wondered what Richard had said to him. Darcy went into the library and closed the door. Picking up his phone he searched through the numbers and hit the one for Jane. She answered and quietly he spoke. "Hi Jane, it's William."

"Hi, what's up?" She waved her assistant out of the office, and closed the door.

Darcy told her the news, and she listened as he struggled to control his anger. "Jane, I have to tell Elizabeth, but I'm worried about it. She . . . she already holds back from me, I know that it's all because of him, I know that he has . . . done things to her . . . I came home tonight to find her in my office chair and she acted as if she was waiting for me to . . . I don't know, lose my temper with her. I just don't know what to do, how to approach her. Have you seen this from her? It seems to be almost getting worse rather than better. You would think that she was more secure with us married . . . I . . . ."

"William." Jane sighed. "Lizzy is afraid of losing you."

"What?" He ran his hand through his hair. "What on earth could make her afraid of that?"

"She loves you desperately."

"She has told you that?" He asked in surprise. "She hardly tells me that, I mean she says that she loves me, but mostly she . . . shows me her feelings . . . do you understand?"

"Yes, I do. Look, Collins essentially told her that everything she did is not good enough, whether it was schoolwork, cooking, or sex. He corrected, as he put it, her constantly. It was never really a physical abuse, but mental. She was a nervous wreck but kept it so deeply hidden that I never saw it, nobody did."

"Is that why she doesn't tell me . . . her feelings?"

"Of course, her feelings were meaningless before, and always wrong. She's just protecting herself."

"How do I help her? How do I tell her this?"

"I think that she needs counseling to be honest with you. It will be easier to talk to a stranger than you, at least at first, maybe later she will be able to talk to you, or maybe won't need to, but be able to open up and speak easily of her feelings." She smiled. "She loves you so much, William. When you talk to her about your feelings how do you do it?"

"Let me think about this." He sighed. "Thanks Jane."

"Anytime William, good luck."

"WHAT DO YOU suggest?" Richard asked his father. "You're familiar with public image maintenance."

"I think that sending the Pemberley lawyers to the tabloids is a good idea. Making them aware that Darcy is aware . . . well, it makes them realize that the effort to harass this particular non-celebrity is not worth the effort, at least to their bottom line. A lawsuit over a person whose picture or name would not sell a paper on its own is not attractive. If this was . . . I don't know, topless photos of some actress it would be. I think that a simple warning will suffice to stop it in its tracks."

"What do you think of Darcy's proposal that Elizabeth speak out on the issue?" Richard saw his father drift off into thought and turned to his mother.

"I think that it would be very good for Elizabeth." She met David's eye and continued. "Obviously she is still dealing with what this man did to her. I wonder if she ever had counseling for it. But maybe speaking to other women who are experiencing mental or physical abuse would be cleansing for her and give hope to them. I'm not suggesting that she write a book on it, but . . . you know, if someone could, she certainly would be the one."

"And become a member of a certain woman's book club?" Richard smiled.

"Oh, then the tabloids *will* be interested." David laughed.

"Charlotte would love to publish that one, imagine how many books that would sell. Lucas Lit would be saved!"

"I think that you are forgetting the subject here." Arlene glared at them. "Elizabeth."

"You're right, I'm sorry Mom." Richard sobered. "Well, Darcy is handling it, and there's nobody in the world better equipped for that job."

GEORGIANA WAVED goodnight and headed upstairs to study while Darcy and Elizabeth took their dishes into the kitchen. Elizabeth went about putting them in the dishwasher and after closing the door looked up to see William leaning on the countertop, his arms crossed over his chest, and watching her movement. "What is wrong?"

"Wrong?"

"You have been staring at me ever since Richard left; I haven't decided if it should grate on my nerves or make me worried. Please tell me what the appropriate reaction should be so I know whether to glare or cry." She smiled and after searching his face, creased her brow. "Will?"

"Come on." He held out his hand and she took it. They walked through the silent house, reaching the ballroom. He switched on the lights, adjusting the dimmer to give the room a soft glow, turned on the music, and held out his arms. "Let's dance." Slowly they moved around the room to the quiet instrumental piece. He held her securely and stared down into her eyes, trying to convey his love for her with his look, and dreading the conversation to come. Finally, seeing her anxiety increasing, he drew her to his chest, rested his mouth near her ear, and while they gently swayed, he told her of Collins' attempts, and his decision to send the Pemberley attorneys to take care of it. Elizabeth listened and wept, first silently with tears of frustration pouring down her face, then wracking sobs as overwhelming memories washed over her. Darcy held in his tears, imagining what she endured, and praying that what he knew was the worst of it. Their movement had been reduced to hugging each other and rocking back and forth. Gradually the music could be heard again, and the sound of the emotion was reduced to sniffs. She clutched him, and felt his handkerchief wiping over her face, then looked up to his red eyes.

"I'm sorry."

"For what?" He smiled gently. "For getting away from him? For standing up to him and making him angry? I certainly do not in the least regret my actions, and now that he is completely broke, I can't say that I feel the least bit concerned with his downfall. He is an insignificant insect and I have no doubt that between my attorneys threatening him and the tabloids with a lawsuit, this will go away very quickly." He kissed her. "Honey, all that matters is you."

"Thank you . . . for taking care of me. I'm sorry to have brought this upon you."

"Lizzy." He whispered and lifted her chin so she would look in his eyes. "I love you." He tilted his head. "Today in the library, you seemed to be afraid that I would be angry with you for being in my way. Is that leftover emotion from him? From his berating your supposed mistakes?" She nodded. "Have I ever done such a thing to you?"

"No, Will . . . but you see, the deeper I fall in love with you, the more frightened I seem to be that it will end."

"Is that why you don't always say what you're feeling, but tease me instead?"

"It's safer, I guess."

"Honey, it's not going to end. I'm not going to change into an ogre. What you see is what you get. I'm pretty simple, I love you." He laughed. "Would I be kissing and hugging and practically making love to you in public if I didn't?" Elizabeth smiled. "I have changed so much since meeting you. I am free to be myself for the first time, well probably since I was a little boy. I love what you have made me, and I love showing it to you. I just wish you could be happy doing the same for me, without fear."

"I want to." She sighed and rested her face on his chest again, feeling horrible now that she knew he felt hurt by her holding back.

"You have too much buried, Lizzy." He spoke quietly. "You won't be free until you let it out. If you don't want to talk to me, and I understand why you would not want to, then how about Georgiana's psychologist? Maybe just a few sessions with her would help you to realize that you truly are safe."

"I am such a failure." She said quietly. "I allowed myself to become the pawn of an overbearing coward. If I were to meet him today I would laugh at him, just like everyone at school probably laughed at him when I was there." She pulled out of his arms and stalked off across the ballroom. "I heard them you know. I heard the people talking when we walked by. Why is *she* with *him*?" Darcy stood still and watched her anger grow. "I let him control me; I believed what he said to me . . . I jumped at his orders and behaved like a . . . dog performing favors for its master." She spun around and faced him. "And now I have you telling me I am hurting our marriage and I need professional counseling!"

"Lizzy . . ."

"What else am I doing wrong? Please tell me. Let's get this out in the open now. I'm risking putting your company and family name in the papers because of my foolish behavior in the past, costing you a great deal of money for lawyers fees to hush it up. I'm sure that is what Richard really came to talk about, isn't it? I'm sure that the whole Fitzwilliam family got together to discuss what a horrible mistake you made marrying me so quickly. Catherine was likely there demanding to know for certain if there was a prenup and suggesting that Greg handle the divorce for you immediately to control the damage before it was too late!" She stormed up and down the ballroom, and he stood frozen, unsure what to do. "And there I was at that ball, thinking that I had done well, and now . . . this is just the beginning of it, isn't it? Oh, you might stop Collins from his claims, but now that the tabloids are alerted to you . . . they'll be watching for a misstep, they'll follow us around, waiting to see if one of us has an affair or . . . Lord knows what. You will be laughed at for marrying a fool." She turned away and folded her arms across her chest and stared into a gilded floor to ceiling mirror.

"Enough Elizabeth." Darcy's voice, quiet, but very strong, cut through the storm of emotion raging in her mind. "I did not say that you are hurting our marriage, I said that I wanted you to feel free to express the feelings you have without fear. I suggested counseling because I know how important it was for Georgiana's recovery from Wickham and as I recall, you even asked me if she was getting it. I keep lawyers on retainer specifically to handle issues such as slander against the company or my name. Don't you think that I made the gossip columns five years ago when I was the newly minted heir of Pemberley? Don't you think that my behavior was a delicious story for the tabloids? Why do you think that Uncle David sat me down and told me to straighten up? Richard came here tonight to warn me, not to laugh at my foolishly falling in love with the woman I have only dreamed of finding. You are using your anger at Collins and how he continues to permeate your behavior two years after the fact to behave irrationally towards me."

Elizabeth turned and faced him. "You think that I am irrational?"

He stepped forward and met her eyes with an unwavering stare. "Yes, if you think that any of these statements you have made are true." Darcy took her hands in his. She was shaking and he squeezed them gently. "Do you really believe what you said?"

"That I am a fool? Yes." She sighed and looked down. "I am sorry for . . . everything. I guess that it would help to talk to someone and finally be done with it. I want to be as honest with you as you are with me."

Darcy sighed with relief and pulled her back into his arms. "You are a beautiful loving woman and should feel free to express it openly, not just in the pages of your book."

Elizabeth's head shot up. "How did you know?"

He chuckled. "I read your edited copy that you leave on my desk. It's hard to get through all of the different colors of ink you use, but sweetie, I would be a blind man if I didn't see that your hero wasn't me and the heroine wasn't you, and all of those words that pour easily from her mouth aren't speeches that you are really saying to me." He saw her blushing red. "And I would love more than anything to hear them spoken." Darcy laughed and hugged her tight. "Oh, and the sex scenes are very creative, too."

"Will!"

"Don't tell me that you aren't fantasizing about us when you are writing." His eyes twinkled and he pursed his lips. "Hmm?"

"Well, maybe a little. I . . . I do stare at your picture and imagine you when I type." She smiled and bit her lip, blushing red again.

"I knew it!" He cried triumphantly. The soft sound of the music in the background became clear again and they resumed their dancing.

Elizabeth relaxed and laughed while he spun her around the room. "How did I ever find such a wonderful man?"

Darcy stopped and kissed her. "I'm wonderful?"

"Of course you are; everyone knows that!" He rolled his eyes. "Well if they don't they should, and . . . I want to be able to show you everything that I feel for you Will, and most importantly tell you. I love and trust you . . . talking to someone *will* help me to believe it won't go away."

"Certainly not for something as silly as sitting in my chair." He tilted his head and smiled, and saw her shake her head and laugh at herself.

"So what would drive you to banish me from your office?"

"Not putting the caps back on the pens." He said quickly.

"I'll remember that." Elizabeth laughed. "That's pretty silly too, you know."

"Which means that nothing will make me not wish for you in my sight. Okay? Is that clear?" He looked at her seriously, and she nodded. He bit his lip and decided to go out on a limb with another suggestion. "What do you think about telling your story to that woman's shelter you were looking at for our charitable gifts? Your reasons for being interested are obvious. Maybe speaking of it will help others to recover, too. There is a lot to be said for not feeling alone with a problem."

"Do you really think I could help others?" She looked into his eyes and saw compassion and pride for her staring back. "I . . . I have thought about that. I just wasn't sure what you would think . . . now that we're married, if it would hurt your image or . . ."

"Make me mad?" He lifted his brows. "Now haven't we established that I am not going to shoot down your ideas for silly reasons?"

"Yes, Will."

"Well?"

"I'll ask the psychologist about it, but I think it would be a good exercise for me." They hugged and kept dancing, "So I really have nothing to fear about Collins?"

"No. Between me, Richard, and the lawyers, he will be a non-problem. The important thing to do is to heal you once and for all, because, my love, I want all of you. Not just the little bit that you feel safe showing me. I want the complete Lizzy package." He laughed and she laughed with him. "We're going to be okay, you and I." Listening to a new song beginning he smiled, "Ahhh, a Mom favorite."

This time it was Elizabeth who sang, kissing him softly, she made his heart soar with her voice, at last singing directly to him. "We've only just begun to live, white lace and promises. A kiss for luck and we're on our way. And yes, we've just begun. Before the rising sun, we fly. So many roads to choose. We start out walking and learn to run. And yes, we've just begun."

Darcy laughed when she let go of him and raised her hands in the air, performing a solo dance as the beat picked up and the sound of a shaking tambourine took over. Elizabeth grinned widely and gestured back and forth between them as her voice got louder, "Sharing horizons that are new to us, watching the signs along the way. Talking it over just the two of us, working together day to day. Together."

Her dancing slowed and she held out her hands to him, back in his arms she looked up as the rhythm slowed, "And when the evening comes, we smile. So much of life ahead, we'll find a place where there's room to grow, and yes, we've just begun.[xiv]"

As the song ended and another began, they were tightly entwined; their mouths were joined and stroking passionately. Elizabeth pulled back, separating from his lips, but he refused to give her a chance to slow down, returning immediately to regain possession and kiss again, crushing her to him, and holding her back and bottom so her entire body was pressed tight against his. "Will," She managed to gasp out. "Oh, honey, take me to bed, I need you."

"You want me?" He let go of her mouth to search her eyes. "You really need me?"

"Oh ,yes."

"Say it, baby, tell me!" He urged.

"Make me beg you for more." She moaned.

"More what?" He demanded and kissed her hard.

"More . . . more . . ." She reached down and stroked his erection. "More of you." Darcy smiled widely and kissed down her throat to bite her shoulder. "Ohhhh!"

"Now that's the kind of talk I love to hear." He kissed her again, and taking her hand entwined their fingers. "Bedtime."

They shut off the lights and music and walked up the stairs, eyeing each other with smiles and cocked heads. "What are you thinking?"

"I'm debating the best way to encourage this begging you spoke of." He leaned to her ear, "I want to make you insane."

"That's not fair."

"Why?"

"Because I'm going to make you insane." She smiled and pushed him into the bedroom, shutting the door and locking it. He fell onto the bed and sat up, watching with fascination as she teasingly, methodically removed each article of clothing, one by one, until all that was left was a thong.

"You, um, forgot something." He said as she approached and began to unbutton his shirt slowly . . .one . . . two. . . three . . . He stopped her hand and ripped his shirt off and threw it to the floor. Elizabeth ran her hands over his chest, feeling the muscle under the curls of hair, then pushing him down hovered over his body, her nipples lightly grazing his skin, and her mouth barely touching his. "Honey." Darcy's hands rose to caress her breasts while she worked open his belt and pants, then with one fluid motion pulled them free of his legs, leaving him nude except for his briefs. Her hands flowed over him, down to his hips, then she moved from his lips to kiss the straining bulge in the tight cotton, mouthing him through the fabric. "Lizzzzzzzy."

Carefully she lifted the waistband up and away then pulled the briefs off to join their clothes on the floor, and ran her hands back up through the wiry black hair, spreading his thighs and bending to suckle and lick, taste and enjoy the flaming flesh now residing in her mouth. She lifted her head, but replaced the motion of her tongue with her fingers and smiled at him. "I love candy."

"Oh God."

She kissed the tip and swirled her tongue around him again. "You are my favorite flavor."

"Please baby . . ." She laughed and his eyes grew dark, and he sat up to grab her shoulders and spin her around so she was on her back. Grabbing the thong, he ripped it off of her and then taking her legs lifted them up on his shoulders and plunging deep inside, began thrusting vigorously. "Don't ever tease a passionate man." He growled.

"Ohhhhhh." Elizabeth moaned and closed her eyes, "Slow down, please Will, slow."

Darcy stopped, letting her legs down and lay back on top of her, joining together again, and hugging her body tight to his. They kissed, slowly, gently, lovingly, while her arms and legs wrapped around him and they barely moved, just rubbing together until Elizabeth gasped and moaned, and he fell into the abyss with her body's clasp. He finally opened his eyes to encounter his wife's smile. "Hi."

She laughed and stroked back his hair. "Hi."

He was not about to move away, but kissed her. "Are you okay? I mean, with everything that we talked about?"

"Yes, I'm angry with him, but I guess that if we're going to be more visible, we'll have to just expect things like this to come up from time to time. Mostly though I'm angry with myself."

Darcy rolled onto his side and drew her back to his chest. "Why?"

"Because I should have dealt with this years ago, I should have sought help then. I'm sorry that my irrational fears have kept me from completely loving you."

"I don't think they have, you just wouldn't express it verbally." He kissed her and ran his fingers through her hair. "I knew what you weren't saying." Darcy smiled. "You, honey, are an open book to any who cares to read the pages."

"As are you."

"Hmm." They cuddled and he drew the comforter up and over them. "Get some sleep; we're going to make love again soon."

"I should brush my teeth." She said sleepily and nestled into his shoulder.

"Me, too." Darcy whispered and closed his eyes, "I love you." He heard her murmured response and smiled.

"DO YOU WANT to bring the ladies along?" Charles asked with a grin two weeks later.

"Well, Lizzy would like it, but I don't know about Jane and Charlotte. I have a feeling that Maria would enjoy immensely going to a football game."

"Oh, you know she would." He took the chair before Darcy's desk and settled back. "I'm really having a great time with her."

"Well it has certainly lasted an unexpectedly long time." He laughed to see his glare. "Hey, I'm not the one with the dating issues."

"No, you never went on any to create bad habits." Darcy looked down as Charles relaxed and put his hands behind his head. "We're doing okay. I took her out to Long Island last weekend to meet Louisa and Hurst. They got on fairly well. Louisa's not quite as obnoxious as Caroline; probably marriage has done something for her in that department. She got a big kick out hearing Maria's description of the cat collars. I can see some sisterly sniping happening in the future."

"Sisterly? As in sister-in-law?" Darcy's brow rose. "Is the party king dead?"

Charles rolled his eyes. "Okay, look I know, I've had my fair share of bad behavior, but it has never affected my work . . ."

"Never said that it did."

"No, I know . . ." He lowered his arms and clasped his hands. "You know we haven't . . . yet."

"Wow." Darcy sat up and smiled. "I am speechless."

"She won't, she never has, and she won't without a genuine commitment." He looked up at him. "I can't tell you the pressure that puts on me, I mean, I want . . . her, but do I want . . ."

"Marriage with her?"

"Yeah." He smiled and met Darcy's eyes. "I'd be her first."

"And last?" He tilted his head. "That is what she is telling you. That's what commitment means to her."

"Yeah, and I . . . I really like it." He twisted his hands together and bit his lip. "I've been looking at rings."

"Ahh. Sounds like you have made a decision." Darcy laughed. "So when is the big moment?"

"Well, we're going to go to the Macy's parade on Thanksgiving; I thought that when the SpongeBob SquarePants balloon goes by I'd propose."

"Ahem, and what is the significance of the SpongeBob balloon? Or should I not ask?"

"Don't ask." Charles blushed.

Darcy held his hands up. "No, I don't want to know. So, after she says yes to you . . . you will be kneeling on the street, won't you? Probably in the snow or at least a downpour, what are your plans?"

"Oh, I've been invited to her parents' place for dinner. Richard will be coming, too. Hey, less for your house, right?"

"Yes, but I do have all the other Bennets and Fitzwilliams." He smiled. "I'm really looking forward to it. Lizzy told Jerry to go home to his family and Mrs. Reynolds goes to her daughter's place, so she and her sisters are going to make the feast. I'm . . . I'm hoping to help but I think I'll be in the living room watching football with the guys."

"Speaking of which, are we bringing the ladies to the game Sunday?"

"I'll call Lizzy and let you know."

"Come on . . . you know you want her there to high-five and bump chests when you celebrate." Charles grinned.

"Sounds like you are hoping for that yourself." Darcy laughed. The phone rang and Charles got up. "Call her."

"I will." He chuckled and picked up the phone. "Darcy." His smile faded and his face became serious. "Okay, thanks, Jack. Is there anything else that needs to be done?" He listened and nodded. "I'm glad to hear it. Thanks again." He laughed. "I'll tell Patricia to keep an eye out for your invoice."

He hung up and closed his eyes then picked up his phone again. "Hi honey."

"Hi! What's up?"

"Oh, Charles was in here asking if the ladies were invited to the Giants game on Sunday. Do you want to come?"

"Do you want me to come or is this a guy thing?"

"You know my feelings; I just wasn't sure about Jane or Charlotte."

"Good point. I'll tell you what, you have your guy date and the girls will go Christmas shopping, and when you come home we'll just relax. You'll have the box again, I'm sure."

"Every game, sweetie, it's mine." He smiled. "You know; rich guy seats."

"Oh, that's right; I'm supposed to be impressed." Elizabeth laughed to hear his groan, and wandered down the hall. "The decorator was here. She's a piece of work."

"Didn't you like her? She was very friendly to me."

"Of course she was, single billionaire all alone in his mansion . . ."

"You don't mean she was nice because . . .

"Sometimes for a brilliant man, you can be so obtuse, Will." He laughed and she giggled. "Anyway, she really did have some great ideas, so the desk and things have been ordered, and the painters will come next week, and soon I'll be out of your chair."

"hush." He smiled, having a sudden thought and made a note to himself. "Um, Jack called. Collins begged to be forgiven and to be left alone."

"Are we going to do that?" Elizabeth paused and leaned against a wall. "I'm in the mood for more public humiliation."

"Ah, your session with the psychologist must have gone well this morning." He leaned back in his chair. "The purging continues."

"I feel so good when I walk out of there, drained, bleary-eyed, but so good. Thank you for pushing me to go."

"I only made a suggestion that you were ready to hear." He sighed and they were silent for a few moments.

"Are you coming home soon?" She asked softly

"In a couple of hours, I want to clear things up before taking off for the holiday . . . why?" He said quietly.

"I have some things I want to say to you."

Darcy bit his lip and looked at her picture. "I can't wait to hear them, honey."

"ARE YOU COMING, Mom?" Anne stood in the doorway to Catherine's condominium and waited. Greg looked at his watch and raised his brows. She shrugged.

"We're going to be late."

"I know, I know." She called again. "Mom!"

Catherine appeared around the corner, "I was finding an appropriate wine to bring. You know not to come to another's home for a meal without a hostess gift." She glared at her daughter. "I believe that I taught you that!"

"I'm sorry, Mom, I thought that you were having second thoughts about going to the Darcys' house."

"I was invited, why wouldn't I go?" She bustled past them and looked at Greg. "You are not wearing a tie."

"Yes, I know." He shut the lights off and closed the door, then followed the women down the hallway. They boarded the elevator and stood in silence, he looked at Anne who was staring at him with widened eyes, urging him to speak. "I hear that Elizabeth is cooking."

Catherine instantly opened her mouth to declare her opinion and snapped it shut. She screwed up her face and pronounced. "I'm sure that it will be delicious." Anne and Greg looked at each other in amazement.

"I'm sure it will be as well." Anne said and cleared her throat.

"Well, it doesn't hurt to be accomplished with a useful skill. If I had taken time to practice, I'm sure that I would have easily surpassed Julia Child. However, I never needed to do such a thing." She sniffed and Greg shook his head, while Anne squeezed his hand. The elevator opened and they walked to their waiting car. Greg opened the door for his mother-in-law. "Now don't drive too fast."

He sighed and got behind the wheel. "I don't think it will be a problem."

"Fasten your seat belt."

"Yes, Catherine."

"When was the last time this car was cleaned? If it was my car, I would have it waxed weekly. Of course my car is properly cared for. Just the other day I recommended to the mechanic to use . . ." Greg reached forward and switched on the radio, and drowned out the sound.

"DO YOU NEED any help?" Darcy wandered into the kitchen to see a flurry of activity going on. He saw a big bowl of mashed potatoes swimming in melted butter and grabbed a spoon.

"Hold it!" Elizabeth snatched it away from him. "NO!"

"Please? I'm so hungry!" He whined and his eyes darted around spotting sausage for the dressing and grabbed a handful before being whacked with a towel across his bottom. "Ha!"

"Fitzwilliam Darcy! You get out of my kitchen!" She glared at him and he kissed her. "Don't think that you can sweet talk your way back into my heart."

"Oh honey, it just smells so good in here, and you've been torturing me for hours." He watched her open the oven door to baste the two turkeys within. "Two?"

"One for company; and one for leftovers." She smiled. "It's not Thanksgiving without turkey sandwiches, turkey pot pie, turkey soup, turkey . . ."

"I have a feeling that I'm not going to want to look at another turkey for a long time after this weekend." He stood behind her and hugged her tight. "This is so much fun." She looked up and he kissed her upturned face. "Seriously, is there anything I can do?"

She looked around and shook her head. "Mom is bringing the pies, Jane is doing the sweet potatoes, I have the turkey, butternut squash soup, dressing, gravy, rolls . . . Arlene is making some other side dish . . ."

"Arlene?" He raised his brows.

"Well, Arlene's representative." Elizabeth laughed. "I imagine the same could be said for Anne and Aunt Catherine's contributions."

"Undoubtedly." He chuckled. "So . . ."

"Go chop up an onion and some celery, and sauté them in a stick of butter. That should keep you occupied for a bit, and I'll make the Bennet cranberry compote."

"Okay." He went to work, making a mess of things, but enjoying it nonetheless. "What's this for?"

"The cornbread dressing, speaking of which . . ." A timer sounded and she pulled the cornbread from the second oven. "That ingredient is ready."

"I haven't gone to the parade in years, when do you think Georgiana will get back?" He asked as he dumped the butter mixture over the stale bread and herbs, then added the sausage while she broke in the cornbread pieces.

"It depends on the crowd. I told her we are serving at three o'clock." Elizabeth smiled. "I'm glad that she is bringing some friends home with her."

"Well it has to beat whatever the dining hall was serving. It's sad that those kids couldn't go home."

"It's expensive." Elizabeth reminded him gently, and he pursed his lips and nodded. "They'll all go home for Christmas."

"This is my favorite holiday, though." He kissed her cheek and leaned on her shoulder. "Everyone does this, a day to be grateful with no expectations of gifts, just friends and family and food."

"And football." She laughed, and popped some hot cornbread in his mouth.

"Mmm." He chewed and poured the dressing into the pan she had waiting and she opened the oven door with a flourish for him to put it in. "Now what?"

"Now, you hug me." He chuckled and opened his arms to receive her as she sank heavily against his chest. "I'm so tired."

"I'm not surprised." He kissed her head, and looked down to see her eyes closed and swayed a little. "How long before you fall asleep?"

"hmmm, about fifteen minutes after dinner is finished." They stood in their embrace, surrounded by the familiar scents of the day until the intercom crackled. "Lizzy! Let us in!" She opened her eyes and looked up to him. "Here we go."

"I'll go." He kissed her. "I love you."

"I love you, Will." She smiled and he winked, moving off to push the button opening the gate, then going to the back door to help carry in whatever the Bennets brought.

Within a half hour the house was full of people, the Bennet sisters were all in the kitchen, talking loudly and taking over duties long established. Fran, Arlene, and Catherine joined the men in the living room, watching the parade and talking amongst themselves. Anne cautiously joined the kitchen contingent and was instantly handed an apron and put to work washing cookware. Darcy popped his head in the door. "Honey . . ."

"HONEY!!!" The sisters called out in singsong delight. Elizabeth blushed.

Darcy grinned. "Um, SpongeBob is coming and I think that I saw Charles . . ."

"SpongeBob?" Lydia perked up and the entire group trooped out to the living room. "What are we waiting for?" She looked around and saw Elizabeth point and turn to look at William who was standing behind her with his arms around her waist.

"Leave it to Charles to be on camera. John, Tivo this!" John grabbed the remote and started the recording and they saw the giant yellow balloon pass by, then a camera focused on the unruly head of Charles Bingley as he knelt on the sidewalk, looking up at Maria, obviously asking her to marry him. The announcers speculated on her reply until she grabbed his face and kissed him enthusiastically. Everyone applauded and cheered. Jane looked at John, who was staring at her intently, and blushed. Tom was watching them and tapped Fran. She grinned like a cat, and he laughed.

"I can't believe he really did it," Darcy smiled down to Elizabeth, "but once he makes a decision, he acts on it. A little impetuous, I guess."

"Well, I hope that he is prepared for a long engagement because Maria won't be rushed." She laughed and he kissed her and reluctantly released her to rejoin her sisters in the kitchen.

Not a half hour later, Georgiana arrived with three friends, two girls, and a young man, all had been to the house before. The girls looked at Darcy with unhidden admiration, but had no trouble transferring their affection to John when he stood up. "Ohhhhhh." John's eyes grew wide and Jane walked purposely forward and took his arm. Disappointment registered quickly. The young man, Jake, seemed overwhelmed by the huge supply of young women, and being rather cute, was quickly surrounded.

Tom nudged David. "A fox in the henhouse."

David laughed and watched the girls talking him up. "If he didn't have an ego before he walked in here, he will when he leaves."

Georgiana parted the crowd of girls and approached him. "Jake, why don't you help me pick out some music to play with dinner?" She took his hand and led him out of the room. Darcy immediately went to the kitchen.

"Lizzy . . ." She looked up from where she was carving. "Georgiana is . . . holding his hand!" He whispered urgently.

"And?"

"Well, what should we do?"

"You're kidding, right?"

"No, why?"

She laughed and kissed him, then handed him the corkscrew. "Could you please open the wine for me?"

"Lizzy . . ." He looked at her raised brows and sighed. She followed him out and into the living room.

"Okay everyone, soup's on!" Elizabeth called.

The families made their way into the dining room, and the parade of platters came out. It was a raucous, glorious feast, the likes of which that home had not seen in years. Darcy sat at the head of the table, watching his sister smile at Jake and talk happily to her friends and sisters. He looked up to see Elizabeth watching him, and raised his wine glass to her at the other end of the table. She laughed and toasted him, then turned to Catherine. "Thank you for the wine, it is very good, and compliments the meal well."

"You're welcome, it was recommended to me specifically for such a meal." She looked around at the crowd. "So this is your family."

"Yes, they are noisy, I'm afraid."

Arlene interrupted before Catherine could make a pronouncement on the Bennet family. "Elizabeth these rolls are divine, where did you get them?"

"William made them." She smiled and laughed when heads swiveled to stare down the table at him. He was about to put his fork in his mouth and stopped.

"What did I do?"

"YOU made the rolls?" Arlene stared at him.

He met Elizabeth's dancing eyes and smiled warmly. "I helped to knead the dough."

"He's very good at it." She added. The heads swiveled back to her end of the table.

"I have an excellent teacher." Like a tennis match the volley was watched.

"You have learned the proper technique."

"It's all in the wrist."

"Exactly."

"Ahem." Tom cleared his throat. "So what is for dessert?"

"Oh yes, we have a great variety of sweets." Elizabeth continued to stare at William.

"I can't wait to taste them all."

David coughed. "All right children, avert your eyes."

Lydia giggled. "Go Lizzy, go!"

"What about William?" Kitty whispered.

"He's doing fine." Mary said softly.

"Mary!" Jane said with surprise.

"I'm not a nun, Jane." She laughed and stood up. "Come on, let's clear the table and get them fed."

With so many hands the table was soon cleared, the leftovers packed away and a new parade of pies and goodies arrived. Anne opened up a large box and Lydia squealed. "Cupcakes!"

Anne laughed. "Well, it's not homemade, but I hope they're okay. Everyone likes cupcakes, these are caramel apple; it was the closest Thanksgiving flavor they had, pumpkin was sold out."

"Oh, we'll manage." Kitty sighed and grabbed one.

The desserts were distributed and the guests gradually drifted into different rooms with their plates. Mary, Kitty, and Lydia joined Georgiana and her friends in the music room, the men went to turn on the game and surreptitiously loosen their belts, and the remaining ladies retreated to the kitchen. Arlene looked around in surprise. "It's clean."

"I've learned long ago to clean up as I go." Elizabeth leaned on the countertop and folded a tea towel. Her eyes closed for a moment and she felt a glass being pressed in her hand. She opened her eyes to see Fran giving her some wine. "What's this?"

"You look exhausted. Sit down." She smiled. "You know, I have hosted Thanksgiving for twenty-five years, and this is the first time the turkey wasn't dry and the potatoes weren't lumpy. The job is yours for now on."

"I don't know if I should thank you or not." She laughed, and kissed her cheek. Arlene smiled. "The torch has been passed, it seems."

"Well with a group this large, she has the room to host it every year. You can do Christmas and Easter, too!" Anne laughed then glanced at Catherine. "Well, Easter is always at Rosings."

"I would welcome you all there." Catherine said quietly. "I enjoyed this very much." She addressed her comments to the refrigerator and Elizabeth looked at Anne to see her surprise.

"Thank you, Aunt Catherine."

"You're welcome, Elizabeth."

The women continued talking and picking at the pies for another half hour before the kitchen door opened. Darcy entered and looked around, seeing Elizabeth sitting with her head propped up in her palm. He walked over and took her hand. "Come on."

"Where are we going?" She said sleepily.

"Would you notice if I told you?" He led the group back into the living room and sat at the end of one of the large sofas while she curled up next to him, resting her head on his chest while he wrapped his arm around her shoulders and kissed her hair. John and Jane took a similar position at the other end of the sofa and watched the other couple. Darcy looked around at the room full of family, then down at Elizabeth and smiled at her. "You know, this is the first Thanksgiving where I have understood the meaning." Mary looked up from watching the game to listen. "I am grateful for what loving you has brought me."

"As we express our gratitude, we must never forget that the highest appreciation is not to utter words, but to live by them." She smiled as faces turned to her. "John Kennedy."

Elizabeth hugged him. "That is exactly what I intend to do."

Chapter 21

"So. Engaged."

"Yeah, who'd have thought she'd say yes!" Charles grinned and laughed. "She assured me that she was making a huge sacrifice by agreeing to marry me so quickly. She was counting on me spending a lot more money on dates before she would be convinced but, well, SpongeBob looming overhead and smiling at us just convinced her that it was meant to be."

Darcy laughed. "I don't understand the significance of that, but . . . Elizabeth assures me that Maria will require a long engagement."

"Yes, Maria assured me as well." He shrugged. "That's okay; I made the sudden decision to ask her to marry me, now I'm willing to take our time to actually get to the ceremony, but I wonder if she'll stick to that, we've been doing a lot of talking about the future. Well, whenever it happens, I'm glad that we are engaged, and can just be comfortable and relax. It's no longer an exercise in trying to impress each other."

"Hmm, I think you will find that you still want your spouse to be impressed with you, no matter how long you are together. I love that look in Elizabeth's eye when I have won her approval." He closed his eyes and thought over his welcome home after returning from the football game the day before, which triggered another memory. "Um, Richard seemed a little subdued yesterday. Did anything happen at Thanksgiving with Charlotte?"

"Yeah, I'm not entirely sure what happened. He and Charlotte were looking over the bookshelves, her dad has a display of everything they have published, and he was thumbing through one of Elizabeth's books and . . . well, I couldn't hear the argument, but it was clear that one was happening. It got kind of uncomfortable, watching them, and Mr. Lucas made a joke to remind them that they were not alone . . . this all happened after we had eaten, luckily, and he apologized to us for creating a scene and left not too long afterwards. I'm surprised he didn't talk to you about it."

"He does come to me for relationship advice, but I imagine he thought I had enough to deal with, and likely would not care to impose his concerns when we have our own troubles." Charles furrowed his brow and Darcy explained to him the Collins situation and their response. "She's seen the psychologist five times already, and . . . the difference is remarkable. From what she tells me, the doctor just knows exactly what to ask, when to ask, and how to push the little buttons to make her defenses fall away. She's opening up to me, not about her past but . . . our relationship. I don't know; I have half a mind to ask for a session myself just to thank her!" He laughed and smiled, then sobered. "I'll give Richard a call."

Charles nodded. "I think he'd appreciate it. He seems to be seeing a side to Charlotte that he wasn't expecting."

"Well, that comes when the newness of the relationship wears off. You start to see more of the person, and therefore reality intrudes."

"Has that happened in your world yet?"

"Frequently." Darcy shook his head at his laughing friend. "We're just . . . willing to work to find solutions. Not that every personality quirk requires one. We established early on that we don't run off when there's a problem. We'll at least talk about it, even if no easy solution comes along instantly. We talk about it."

"I saw an interview with a couple married sixty years and they said don't go to bed angry."

"We never have. Frustrated maybe, but not angry." Darcy smiled and looked at her picture. "And we always seem to wake up entwined. A lot of problems can be solved in the dark with quiet conversation."

"I'll remember that." Charles tilted his head. "Thanks."

"I never thought I'd be the one giving advice to the soon-to-be married."

"Well, when we have set a date, you are my best man."

"I'd be honored."

"And that means you host the bachelor's party."

"Um, maybe Richard should be your man . . ."

Charles stood up and walked out of the office. "Nope, it's your job, and I expect to have a very good time!" He laughed to hear Darcy groaning behind him.

"WHAT IS IT?" John demanded.

Richard looked up from the bottle of beer in front of him and stopped tearing off bits of the label. "Sorry." He sighed. "Charlotte and I had a fight."

"Oh. What was it about?"

"We were looking at Elizabeth's books, her dad has a set of them at their house, and I said something about the office space Darcy was having made for her, and how she probably would prefer to work in his library, and Charlotte made some comment about how she should be thinking about the people who broke her into publishing and not about color schemes. I asked if she thought that Elizabeth owed Lucas Lit something, and she said that Elizabeth did, since without them she would not have been so popular. I . . . responded rather . . . sharply that Lucas Lit should feel fortunate that they were able to sign her in the first place and I was certain that they had benefited significantly by her work, and . . . wondered if she had been compensated fairly or if they had taken advantage of her youth and inexperience." He met John's eyes and saw his raised brow. "Her dad said something and we realized everyone could see us arguing. Later on she brought it up again, and . . . I said that I knew enough of how Elizabeth had been used by others to jump to her defense. Charlotte said that I should be thinking of her feelings and I said that I was thinking of my family. That made her even angrier and she said she was thinking of *her* family . . ."

"Wow."

"Yeah."

"So . . . Where does it stand?"

Richard shrugged. "I haven't spoken to her since."

"Why not, it's been four days?" John sat forward. "Not that I blame your response to her, we all know Elizabeth's story, and Charlotte's pushing is likely unwelcome, however, you clearly said to Charlotte that she isn't the most important part of your life, and that you won't support her over family. I can't imagine putting Jane second to anyone, and we've already seen the evidence of Darcy choosing Elizabeth over family with the way he rejected Aunt Catherine." He sat back as their orders arrived then leaned forward again. "Do you anticipate a future with Charlotte? Do you love her?"

"Apparently not." He said bitterly and took a long drink from his bottle. "I like her, I like spending time with her. She's a good companion."

"ouch."

"Not love, is it?" Richard sat back and picked at his plate. "Oh well, I really tried."

"Could it grow? Don't give up just because of one disagreement. Not everyone is struck by a thunderbolt. I wasn't, I mean I was attracted to Jane quickly, but I didn't even try for her for months. Darcy . . ."

"Darcy is the impossible ideal."

"Yes, but they have not necessarily had an easy path, even if they did know instantly that they had found their soul mates." John watched his younger brother contemplating his lunch. "Can you imagine yourself with Charlotte five years from now? Can you imagine listening to the type of arguments she presented to you at Thanksgiving countless times in the future? This goes beyond her justifiable concern for her family's company surviving. It's the rather self-righteous tone of her plea that strikes me as . . . distasteful."

"Yeah, me too. I can only imagine that it might grow worse, and . . . I don't care to anticipate it being applied to me and whatever my faults are." He drew a deep breath and let it out. "Well, it was nice while it lasted."

"You're giving up too quickly. You haven't talked to her about it yet." John laughed. "Come on; are you afraid of a conversation?" Richard smiled. "Snipers and bombs didn't faze you but talking to a woman has."

The trilling of a phone interrupted the conversation and Richard picked his up to see who the call was from, and laughed. "Darcy."

"Bingley probably mentioned the fight."

"And here he comes to offer his help." Richard let the call go to voice mail. "I'll talk to him later. Do me a favor and don't tell him about Charlotte's feelings for Elizabeth, that won't help the situation, you know how protective he is." He laughed, "Well there you go, Darcy is protective of Elizabeth. And I am more protective of her than Charlotte." Picking up his fork, he began to eat. "So, since my love life is questionable, what's the story on yours?"

"Oh, well . . . I think I found the ring." John smiled and Richard listened to his brother's plans.

"WE ARE PLEASED to welcome our special guest speaker this afternoon . . ." Darcy watched as the door to the room was closed by a smiling older woman. He managed one last look at Elizabeth standing nervously near the front, caught her eye and mouthed, "I love you" before it clicked shut. He sighed and turned around, unable to hear her voice, and leaned against the wall. More than anything he wanted to be inside to just sit in the background and support her while she spoke to the room full of women in different stages of recovery from their batterers, but understood the request of the staff that he remain outside. Many of the women simply could not bear to be in the presence of a man, no matter how benign he was.

He heard the sound of applause and assumed that she was now in front of them. Closing his eyes he sent her his thoughts then looked around at his surroundings and walked down the hall to study the bulletin board, not really registering what he read, and waited. Then he moved to lean on a window frame and looked out at the quiet street lined with identical homes. He wondered if Elizabeth would have come to a place like this, and if he ever would have met her if she had found the help of others instead of trying to work it out alone. *Stop it.* He spoke to himself. How many times had he marveled over the chance, the slimmest chance; that brought them together? He heard the sound of laughter and his head turned towards the room, a smile spreading over his face. "She's okay."

He was surprised when she came home the week before with the news that her psychologist had arranged for her to speak. She was as well, and argued that it was far too soon. The doctor informed her that the women she was addressing were months, perhaps for some, only hours into their escape. She had years, a healthy marriage, and was well on her way to recovery, there was no reason to delay this important step of sharing her story with others, and insisted that this presentation would really be the beginning of the end.

Elizabeth came home frightened of the prospect, and they held each other, talking through her fears, and came to the conclusion that her doctor was correct, it needed to be done. Darcy looked up from time to time as he held vigil during the long hour, hearing occasional bursts of laughter or tears, women speaking over each other, and finally an enthusiastic round of applause. His pride and admiration for Elizabeth grew as he realized how her recovery was helping so many others. The door opened again and he instantly rose from the chair he had found and was there to greet her as she slipped out and into his arms.

"It's over." She breathed out.

Darcy hugged her and kissed her ear. "It seemed to go well, I heard them laughing."

"Oh, that was probably when we were comparing the size of our abuser's egos to their equipment." She murmured and smiled to hear his chuckle. "It helped me to see him clearly. It made him seem very small and weak."

"Any man who abuses a woman is small and weak, no matter his physical attributes." He sighed and held her tighter. "Are you finished here?"

"Yes, we can go." She looked up at him. "Thank you for coming with me. Every time I got nervous, I thought of you waiting outside the door." They held hands and went to the closet to retrieve their coats. Darcy took her scarf and wrapped it around her neck, adjusting the angle and looking up from his hands to see her smile. "Thank you." He kissed her and they went out to the waiting car. "I'm going to write a book, I think."

"Really?" He held her hand and the car moved off on its way back home. "I guess that I shouldn't be surprised."

"It's just for me. I won't publish it. Just a cathartic experience."

"I think that you should share with anyone who wants to read it." He smiled and kissed her hand. "Perhaps . . . well, you could donate the proceeds to the shelters. We certainly don't need the money; give it where it can be put to good use."

"Maybe I will . . . I guess it will have to be good now." She laughed. "Thank you, Will."

"I think . . . I think that your giving these women a chance to laugh was important. It's probably an emotion they haven't allowed themselves to feel for a long time. I remember you describing yourself as numb and not remembering what it felt like to be happy." He reached over to caress her face as she listened to him and began to think. "I wonder if you could infuse that sort of feeling of hope into a book?" Darcy smiled to see her lip catch in her teeth, and touched it. "Don't chew too hard, that's my job."

"Yes, but that seat belt is keeping you from performing it." She smiled and held his hand. "It's good to know that you listened so closely to me. The faces of those women looked like the one that looked back at me in the mirror for a long time. But now . . . I am free because of you."

"Thank you." He whispered and squeezed her hand. He noticed that they were passing the Christmas display at Rockefeller Center and remembered the thoughts that had occupied his mind while he waited for her. "Um, what are you doing this weekend?"

She tilted her head and her eyes danced. "Well, I was thinking that my husband and I might go out together . . . What do you have in mind?"

Darcy chuckled. "I was thinking of a little trip."

"Where?"

"Pemberley."

"Oh, I'd love to go out to the Hamptons . . ."

"No, I mean, *Pemberley.*"

"England?"

"Yes. It's all decorated for Christmas. I've never seen it in person that way. Mom and Dad would go alone every year. We could leave Friday and return Monday. Would you like that?" He looked at her hopefully and laughed to see her struggling against the seat belt to hug him. "Yes, I think."

"Oh Will, yes, I'd love it!"

"Do you think that Jane and John might like to come? I know it depends on Jane's schedule, but if she doesn't have a wedding . . ."

"I'll call as soon as we get home."

"Oh good." He smiled and she looked at him suspiciously.

"What?"

He shrugged and continued his warm smile. They arrived back at home and when they entered the house, Mrs. Reynolds gave him a wink and a nod, and collected their coats. Darcy held her hand and they walked down the hallway towards the drawing room Elizabeth had selected. "Did you know that your office was completed this morning?"

"No, you haven't allowed me in to see the progress, why, I can't imagine since I chose all the decorations and furniture . . ." He opened the door and stood back as she entered, seeing for the first time the result of the decorators' work. It was a room transformed, painted in subdued shades of green, with hand-screened papers decorating the walls below the woodwork, a round oak table and chairs awaited the staff for their foundation to meet, comfortable sofas for conversations and fine wool rugs covered the old wooden floor. A newly installed French door led directly out into the garden, and a beautifully carved oak desk sat directly before the window. But the feature that caught her eye was the chair. *His* chair, now hers. Elizabeth turned around to see his smile and he wrapped his arms around her. "I wanted you to feel hugged when you worked in here."

"Oh Will, thank you." She embraced him, unable to put into words what this gift meant to her, and instead tried to put her feelings into a slow and loving kiss. They withdrew and rested their foreheads together. "But . . . what about your office?"

"Come on." He led her out and down the hallway to the library. She laughed to see an identical chair. New, no sign of his body spending countless hours were there, but it had his look and already radiated comfort to her. "I'll break this one in, and I hope that you'll add your own mark." They walked in and he sat down, opening his arms, and she settled in his lap. "I suppose now is a good time to christen it, don't you think?"

"What do you propose we do to achieve that?" Elizabeth smiled and he reached down to adjust the back so they leaned away at an angle, then caressed his hands up her legs. "hmmm, you seem to be wearing a dress, and oh, see how these panties just slip right down your hips."

She cocked her brow. "Are you proposing that we take a ride on your new chair?"

"You didn't notice that I locked the door when we came in?" He smiled then slowly began kissing his way down her throat, and moved his hands along her thighs, lifting the skirt and bunching the fabric as they traveled upwards to caress over the soft curve of her hips.

Elizabeth leaned into his chest, and tilted her head back, allowing his lips to taste as they wished. "mmmm, silly me. How could I have been so blind?"

"I forgive you." He murmured then kissed down to find her cleavage, and set his fingers to work unbuttoning her blouse, discovering with delight that her bra fastened in the front, and opened it to release the soft mounds. He buried his nose between them to drink in her scent mixed with the intoxicating fragrance of her perfume. Squeezing one breast, Darcy smiled with pleasure when Elizabeth lifted the other, directing the hardened nipple to his lips where he happily began to feast upon her.

She moaned with the feel of his tongue and gasped. "How big of you."

Darcy took her hand and rubbed it over his groin. "How big of me?"

"Let me see." She moved off of him, and he stood to remove his pants while she worked off his tie and unbuttoned his shirt. All the while they were exchanging kisses to their mouths, cheeks, hair, whatever body part they could reach as they rushed to disrobe. They struggled and the faster they moved, the more entangled they became, heightening the desire to be free of the fabric and in each other's arms. Darcy finally fell back in the chair, his erection standing tall and straight, and grabbed her hand to rub over it with him. "There, now, let's make this our chair. Come on, baby, get on me."

Elizabeth settled onto him, it was a tight fit, inside and out. Darcy's hands ran over her back to her bottom, and then between them, feeling where they joined. Her hands were in his hair, their mouths open and hungry, devouring each other in the heated passion of their lovemaking. Elizabeth rode him and he groaned, moving away from her mouth to watch her breasts bouncing and rubbing over his chest, then looking down to watch his shaft disappear inside as she rose and fell, clutching his shoulders and lost in her concentration. Darcy drank in the sight, then wrapped his arms around her and stood, laying her back onto his desk, and taking her hard, thrusting deeply while he clutched her hips and drew her to the edge where she wrapped her legs around his waist, and held his arms. Darcy could not take his eyes off of the sight of their bodies joining. "I love this, I love this, I can't get enough of you." He gasped and reveled in her unending moans and whimpers. He looked up to see her eyes closed and her lip caught in her teeth. "baby." He whispered hoarsely. "Let me bite that for you." He leaned down, stilling his movement for a moment and kissed her. Elizabeth's arms came around his shoulders and he stayed there, thrusting again, while she clung and they kissed. His tongue speared her mouth deeply as his shaft did the same below, and he felt the incredible pleasure of her simultaneously clasping him with her kiss and her orgasm just as he could hold on no longer. As it finally ended, he rested his head on her shoulder while they caught their breath. He shuddered again as he shot into her once more and swore with the unexpected exhilaration. "What you do to me." They laughed and kissed before separating. He leaned his hands on the desk, smiling over her. "That was incredible."

"But it wasn't in the chair." She pointed out and caressed his thoroughly mussed hair.

"So we'll just have to do it again."

"When?"

He leaned forward and kissed her. "Anytime you want, honey."

TUESDAY MORNING Elizabeth settled in her new office, in his old chair, pulled her knees up to her chest and called Jane. "England?" She gasped. "For the weekend?"

"Well, a long weekend, but yes . . . what do you think? I know that you have a passport from that wedding you did in the Virgin Islands last year."

"Oh, Lizzy, I . . . I would love to go! I have to talk to John, but . . . Pemberley is really your home?"

"You know it is! Go look at the website; it says owned by Mr. Fitzwilliam Darcy." She laughed. "Somehow his real name doesn't sound so odd when you are looking at pictures of Pemberley, not that John's name is odd."

"Oh quiet, Lizzy." Jane typed the web address into her browser and watched as the site came up. "Why on earth are you guys living here?"

"You would give up New York for a mansion in the Peaks?"

"I wouldn't say no if it was offered." She said dryly. "Well, I'll call John and see if he's interested."

"I think William was planning to call him this morning."

"Pemberley?" John bit his lip and fiddled with his pen. "Leave Friday and back Monday night?"

"Yes."

"I've always been curious about the place . . ."

"Soooooo."

"Yes, but . . . I was going to propose this weekend."

"I thought you were doing that at Christmas."

"No, that is what she is expecting me to do." John grinned.

Darcy laughed. "Ahhhh."

"How about the weekend after this one?"

"No, I have the company Christmas party and a lot of other holiday commitments, if we're going to go, this is it."

"Damn. I have this all planned out, and . . ."

"Come on, Jane would love it. We're going to crash a wedding . . ." Darcy laughed to hear him choke on something. "Believe me; we will not see much of each other." Darcy smiled when John cleared his throat. "I have plans of my own."

"Let me guess, something in that hall with all of those nude statues . . ."

"I was thinking of something in the library, but now that you mention it, we could stroll through there first." He laughed. "Inspiration, you know."

"Are you sure that you look better than the guys in there?"

"Pretty sure, at least in the important areas." This time John coughed and they both laughed. "I hope that you are as happy as I am."

"Me, too." He smiled at the thought then remembered his brother. "Oh, um, Darcy, Richard is taking a break from Charlotte. He probably hasn't returned your call yet . . ."

"No, what happened?"

John could hear his concern and danced around the truth as artfully as he could. "He didn't go into specifics, but . . . he'll be coming to your place for Christmas instead of the Lucas house, and . . . you know, don't mention anything."

"I'll tell Lizzy. Thanks." Darcy hung up and immediately called Richard. "Hey, you okay?"

He heard a long sigh. "No, I don't know what I am to be honest with you."

"If you want to talk . . ."

"I know."

Darcy hadn't heard Richard this down in years. "See you for Christmas at the house?"

As much as he wanted to talk to Darcy, he knew that this time he just couldn't, yet another reason that this relationship with Charlotte was bad. "Yeah, I hear I missed a good time for Thanksgiving."

"You're welcome anytime. You know that." Darcy listened, hearing another sigh. "Well, I'll see you." Richard mumbled something and they hung up. *What happened?* He glanced at his watch and knew he had no time to call Elizabeth; it would have to wait for later.

"HI." Richard spoke into the intercom. "Can I come up?"

"If you want." He rolled his eyes and opened the door when the lock clicked, then walked up the stairs. The door was open and he entered, closing it behind him. Charlotte was seated in an arm chair; clearly she was not going to attempt to be welcoming. "So, what brings you here at last?"

"At last?" He raised his brows. "I could say the same for you. The phone works both ways."

"I didn't do anything wrong." She met his stare without flinching.

"That, I think is the problem. You are unwilling to admit that you did do wrong, and while I do not particularly regret my support of Elizabeth, I do regret disregarding my feelings for you." He saw her expression. "You are surprised? Did you think that I was indifferent? Why would I have spent the past four months dating you if I did not have some feeling? Why have I spent the last four days beating myself up over our fight? Should I assume that you do not reciprocate my affections?"

"You have never said you loved me."

He laughed. "Neither have you."

"It's up to the man . . ."

Richard sat down and stared at her. "Oh what crap that is! You walk around like some . . . model of what a businesswoman should be, indifferent to the feelings of others, only concerned with the bottom line, looking out for the company, but when it comes to your friends and companions, you expect them to be loyal and warm to you in return for . . . what exactly?" He sat back and regarded her. "What have you ever given of yourself to me? To anyone, if there was no real benefit to your own purposes?"

Charlotte's face grew red and she spat at him. "I am not mercenary if that is what you are implying!"

"I never saw this in you before, but now I realize . . . you are looking for the best deal. I am a reasonably well-off man, not too horrible to look at, not my brother's looks but . . . I have a tolerable temperament, you could deal with me, you could handle it for the sake of . . . *Security.* That's it. You have been watching your father's business going down, and you are looking at me as a means to be secure." He rested his elbows on his knees and leaned forward, reading her face, not letting affection cloud his eyes. "Am I correct?" She opened and closed her mouth. "I am."

Richard stood. "I'm glad I came here. I was feeling sorry for myself. Now . . . I feel pretty damn good." He turned and walked to the door, and paused. "You know, I have to thank you for one thing. I was afraid that I would never be able to fall in love with a woman, that my heart had been hardened by all that I had seen, but knowing you proves that I am just as capable as any other guy to fall in love. It's just a matter of finding a girl who loves me. Thanks for that. I'll miss the woman you could have been."

Charlotte watched him go, hearing the door click as it shut and the sound of his shoes in the hallway. She was shocked, but oddly not hurt. She didn't feel anything at all.

DARCY ARRIVED HOME and hearing that Elizabeth and Georgiana were in the living room; went upstairs to change and join them. He settled on the sofa, and dropped his feet in Elizabeth's lap. "Hi!"

She raised her brow and touched his toes. "And my duty is to rub these?"

"If you don't mind . . ." He grinned and yelped when she began tickling him mercilessly. Georgiana jumped up and tackled his stomach and he curled up in a ball, begging them to stop, when he heard a familiar laugh coming from the doorway. "Richard! Help me!"

"Not a chance." He beamed and took a chair, crossing his arms and legs. "Carry on, ladies."

Darcy was not embarrassed to have Elizabeth and Georgiana see him being silly, but his cousin, that was a different story. He rose up and grabbed both of them. Georgiana escaped, but Elizabeth was trapped, and he gladly paid her back until she cried "uncle." He stopped, and stared down at her, breathing hard, and fixed his eyes down on her red face. "You're finished?"

"Yes." She panted.

"Good." He whispered in her ear, "It's a good thing we're not alone." Picking her up onto his lap, he wrapped her tight in his embrace and smiled. "I don't trust you."

"That's a wicked thing to say! Georgiana, get him!" She cried.

"You do and I'll cut your allowance in half!"

Richard roared with laughter and Georgiana protested. Darcy grinned and kissed Elizabeth. "You're trapped."

"Sleep with one eye open, Mr. Darcy."

"Oh, I'm so glad I came over here!" Richard wiped his eyes with his hand then grabbed a tissue to do a proper job. "I needed this." He beamed at them all. "Thank you."

Elizabeth met William's eye and he smiled, kissing her gently and loosening his vise-like grip. They settled into each other. "Are you okay, Richard? We have been concerned."

"Good, it's nice to have someone care about me." He smiled and closed his eyes. "I'm sorry. Charlotte and I are no more." Elizabeth gasped and Darcy nodded. Richard held up his hand. "I'm okay with it. I won't go into detail; only that our paths are divergent and it was pleasant while it lasted, but, we are not soul mates. I'm afraid that you two, and I suppose John and Jane, have set the course and I am hoping for a similar fate."

"But what happened?" Georgiana asked. "You seemed so happy!"

"We were, I suppose, well, comfortable, but never passionate. It was . . . friendly, but when push came to shove, I discovered that my ideals were not hers, and . . . she doesn't seem terribly upset about it ending either." He smiled. "It's okay sweetie, I've broken up many times before. This just lasted a bit longer than usual." Smiling around at them all he laughed. "Stop the mourning, please!"

"Okay, well, if that is the case, you *will* stay for dinner?" Elizabeth asked.

"Did you cook?" He said hopefully.

"No, just on the weekends and holidays. Jerry was on tonight." Richard's face fell. "Thank you, for your disappointment!" Elizabeth stood up and walked over to him, wrapping her arms around his shoulders and kissing his cheek, she whispered in his ear. "Charlotte was being selfish wasn't she?" He looked at her in surprise. "I have known her all of my life, and I have dealt with her in business for years. I only recently realized how she takes advantage of people for her own gain. It is why so many authors are leaving her father. I hoped that a good relationship would change that for her, but it didn't and now. . ." She looked over to William who was clearly unhappy with their embrace, "I am going to join that crowd and walk away from her, too."

"Not because of me." He said quietly.

"No, because I am strong now, and won't let anyone walk over me again." She kissed his cheek again and hugged him, then walked back over to William and kissed his lips softly, caressing his cheek. "I'm going to see what Jerry's doing. Georgiana, will you help me?" She lifted her brow and Georgiana caught the hint. They left and the men were left regarding each other.

"That was a kiss of comfort, Darcy . . ."

"Shut up, Richard. I'm guessing that Charlotte said something that did not sit well?"

"Yes."

"It had to do with Elizabeth?" Richard remained silent. "Well, regardless, thank you." Darcy smiled. "I appreciate your care for my wife."

"Well, someday I hope to be as lucky as you." He smiled sadly. "At least now I know I can . . . love."

"You loved her?"

"No Darcy, I love my family." He smiled and Darcy joined him. "So I hear that you're off to Pemberley?"

"That's the plan. Could you look in on . . ."

"Georgiana? Sure but what about your plans for Elizabeth's old apartment, are you going to do it?"

"I'm . . . thinking about it." Darcy said hesitantly and laughed at Richard's expression. "What?"

"She has come a very long way since August, don't you think?"

"Yes, but now there's this boyfriend . . ."

"So what?"

"I don't want her to get hurt."

"Hey, all of us get hurt, and it all makes us stronger. Look at you, look at Elizabeth. I say give her the keys and see what happens. Jane is still there. The Bennets are there. You could not hope for a better situation." Richard laughed. "What did Dad tell you?"

"Let my baby bird out of the nest." Darcy smiled.

Georgiana arrived to announce that dinner was ready, and looked from one man to the other. "Are you two talking about me?"

"You? Why would we do that?" Richard jumped up and threw his arm around her shoulder. "Hey, did I ever tell you about the time your brother . . ."

"Richard!!"

"WE WILL BE landing in ten minutes, let me take your glasses." The flight attendant smiled and collected their things and Elizabeth leaned into William's ready arms, closing her eyes. John and Jane looked at each other then to Darcy. He smiled and kissed her hair, then closed his eyes, hugging her close to his chest.

"What is wrong?" John leaned to Jane.

"Maybe landings are scary for them?" She whispered, thinking of the accident. They held hands and looked out of the window as the plane began its descent, sending occasional looks to the other couple, who were embraced tighter than ever.

When the wheels hit the ground they all jumped a little and as they slowed, Darcy lifted his head, kissing Elizabeth and whispering to her. She nodded and sat back up. Jane looked over at them. "Are you okay?"

"Yes, why?" She smiled and patted her hair, and met William's smile. "I needed a hug." The four laughed at her explanation and soon were off of the plane and walking through customs. A man was waiting for them. "Mr. Darcy? The helicopter is ready, just follow me."

"Helicopter?" Elizabeth asked.

"I'm afraid that I'm pulling out all of the stops. I'm not wasting a moment of this trip." He squeezed her hand and they followed the man outside to board the bird. John could not say that he was surprised, but he was hardly used to such extravagance. Jane was wide-eyed with it all, and then, before very long, Pemberley came into view. It was nearing dusk. The car parks were full, visitors were lining up to take the candlelight tours of the house, and just as they were about to land, the outdoor displays turned on. "ohhhhhhhh." The women breathed. Darcy looked around in delight and kissed Elizabeth. "I'm so glad we came."

A car met them and they were whisked to the house. Mrs. Woods greeted them with a huge smile. "Mr. Darcy, I hope that you had a pleasant journey."

"We did, Mrs. Woods. This is my cousin John Fitzwilliam, his family once owned Matlock, and this is my sister-in-law Jane Bennet." He laughed to see her obvious elation. "I see that you are happy to again have family in the house."

"Yes sir, I am." She turned to Elizabeth. "Mrs. Darcy, I hope that you do not mind but visitors will be here a little later than you were used to in the summer. The candlelight tours at Christmas are very popular, however, less of the house is open, so you will be free to roam a bit more during the day."

"Thank you Mrs. Woods, I can't wait to see it all." They followed her up the back stairs again, up to the family quarters. Elizabeth and William held hands, pointing at decorations, and not feeling at all uncomfortable in the exceptional surroundings. Jane and John followed in stunned silence. Mrs. Woods showed them their rooms and they agreed to meet again in a half hour to join the visitors on the tours. After the servants quickly unpacked their bags and silently disappeared, Darcy took Elizabeth to the window overlooking the lake. The reflection of thousands of lights twinkled in the water. He stood behind her and wrapped his arms around her waist.

"Why do I feel so at home here? It's a different experience all together to be here with you. I felt myself urging the plane to move faster, almost as if this land was calling me." He looked down to her upturned face and kissed her smile. "I am silly."

"No, not at all. There is magic here." Darcy kissed down her cheek to her throat, his hands caressing her shoulders and arms. "I love how you touch me." He smiled against her cheek. "You make me feel precious."

"You are." They kissed again and stopped when there was a soft knock. Jane cautiously opened the door and gasped.

"Oh, Lizzy! Our room is magnificent but this . . ."

"It is beautiful." She smiled and taking William's hand, they walked out into the hallway. "Well, let's join the throng." They led the way to the velvet rope, where Darcy held it back then reattached it to the wall. A man in uniform stepped up.

"I'm sorry you are not permitted in those areas of the house, I'm going to have to ask you to leave . . ." Darcy met his eye and the man startled. "Mr. Darcy, I'm sorry sir, I didn't realize that you had arrived."

"That's all right, thank you for doing your job." He nodded and took Elizabeth's hand, leading them away. She watched him as he began taking in the home. His eyes moved about, studying details, assessing the atmosphere, watching the people. He carried himself differently; there was an elegant confidence that suddenly seemed to radiate from him. Pride was clear in his expression, and the way he held her arm, possessively and lovingly to his body, told all that noticed that his pride extended to the woman by his side. They stood in the entranceway, pausing to observe the crowd.

Elizabeth felt the power of the room, and stood straight and still beside him, smiling warmly, and scanning the faces as they passed. People noticed the couple and whispers speculating on who they were flew around the room. A man in uniform was asked repeatedly their identity and whispered softly that it was the owner. Heads swung their way again and again, and Darcy did not flinch from the inspection. Finally he smiled down at Elizabeth. "Shall we move on?"

"Yes." She laughed and his eyes twinkled. "You are looking very *Master of Pemberley*."

"I feel it." He shrugged and looked back to Jane and John, seeing them holding hands and gawking like the rest of the visitors. "I don't feel overwhelmed this time. I don't know, I'm . . . extraordinarily proud to be able to share this with so many."

"You have changed your tune." She squeezed his hand as they moved on. "I have read up on the estate. Did you know that it has always been open to visitors?"

"No, really?"

"Yes, many of the great houses were." Elizabeth smiled up at him. "This is tradition. You should not feel at all discomforted by allowing others to share your home."

"Our home." He kissed her. "Can you imagine seeing our children run through these halls, completely unimpressed with the history, only concerned with whatever game they played?" His eyes drifted away to take in more details and Elizabeth watched him as he relaxed, imagining him with a different look of pride in his eye. At that moment she settled on her Christmas gift for him.

They continued on with the tour, seeing the dining room set for a large party, countless Christmas trees, and then their favorite room, the library. "Oh look what they have done in here!" Elizabeth gasped.

"We will have to return here later tonight." He said softly. "I want to hear the next chapter in your story of the dashing Master of Pemberley riding home to rescue his bride from the ladder."

Elizabeth laughed. "I thought that he carried her off to his bed."

"Ah but surely they needed a book or two to pass the time on a cold winter's night. He could have come down to search for one. Perhaps she would grow impatient and would venture down the stairs to find her love."

"Carrying a candelabra?"

"And dressed in the thinnest of nightgowns, so the firelight would shine through, allowing her perfect form to appear, exposed, and yet shrouded from his penetrating gaze." He attempted a seductive look.

"Oh, Mr. Darcy!" Elizabeth cried softly.

He chuckled. "What would he do with such temptation before him?"

"He would toss the candles aside . . ."

"Starting a fire?"

"Hmm, no he would take them away and set them down carefully, then turn to her, pulling her in his arms, kissing her neck, pulling her nightdress down to bare her shoulder, and one soft breast, then bend to ravish the hard dusky nipple . . ."

"Oh, I like that." He whispered and drew her to his chest, standing in a corner, with his arm around her waist. Many eyes glanced at the embraced couple, but Elizabeth and Darcy saw none of them. "And then?"

"I think that lovemaking would undoubtedly ensue." She laughed and he kissed her.

"What on earth are you two doing?" John and Jane approached. "You are lost in your own world."

"I told you the library was special to us." Darcy hugged Elizabeth and looked down. "We'll continue this later."

They finished the tour and then wandered to the working part of the house, where Mrs. Woods had a meal ready for them to enjoy. The rules established in the summer were followed, no servant stood waiting or watching. They were left to their discussion of the beauty they had seen. Darcy then informed them that the next evening a wedding was to be held on the estate, and they were going to attend the reception.

"Are we invited?" Elizabeth asked gently.

"I was going to crash it, but, I did have the staff ask the bride for permission for us to come down and enjoy the dancing with her guests. She was pleased to invite us for the meal, but I declined. I just want to dance with you." He squeezed her hand. "I had Mrs. Woods wrap up a platter from the gift shop with the image of Pemberley on it for them."

"That was sweet of you, Will." He beamed with her approval. "Perhaps a bottle of the Pemberley sparkling wine, as well?"

"Good idea. They are staying the night in the guest wing."

"I can't wait to see what a reception is like here." Jane whispered. "Oh to have a location like this available, I could be happy doing nothing but weddings here."

"You will have to meet the woman in charge of those things tomorrow, Jane." Elizabeth suggested.

"Um, well, we will be taking a little trip tomorrow." John said softly. "Darcy arranged for a car and driver, and we'll go to see Matlock. My family's home."

Jane smiled at him. "Oh, is it far?"

"No, about thirty miles or so." He kissed her. "I . . . I saw it once as a child. Our family gave it up some years ago, but it is still our history, and I'd like to show it to you."

"We will remain here." Darcy met Elizabeth's eye and she formed an "O" with her mouth and smiled.

"I can't wait to see what we can do to fill the time." She leaned to his ear and felt his smile against her lips. "Perhaps we can continue our story?"

"OH JOHN." Jane peeked around the corner and saw the magnificent home. "It is beautiful." He looked up at the closed gate. "I'm sorry that it is closed, I would have liked to have shown you the inside."

A man dressed for work approached them. "I'm sorry; the estate closes for visitors in October. Pemberley is open for Christmas, and isn't too far away."

John laughed. "Yes, we are staying there, actually." He looked up at the mansion. "This was my family's home."

"Yours, sir?" The man tilted his head. "What do you mean?"

"I am John Fitzwilliam."

The man broke into a smile. "Well, why didn't you say so! Come on, you can certainly take a look around." He unlocked the gate. "I always think it's a pity when the families give up their houses to the NT, but it's wonderful when another generation gets to see their history. The house is shuttered up, but you can walk the grounds a bit." He closed up the gate again. "I'll be in the shrubbery if you need anything."

"That was very kind." Jane smiled and they walked off together, taking in the grounds, still beautiful even with the cold of winter upon them. They walked up onto an old stone bridge and stared down at the water. John moved beside her, touching her hands as they rested on the wall, and looked at their reflection. "I can imagine a girl in a long skirt running over this bridge."

He smiled. "Why would she be running?"

"Well, according to Lizzy, she would be running from her destiny." She looked over to see him laughing. "Not a romantic, I see."

"I suppose it would have been raining and the thunder roiling dramatically in the background." He turned and laughed to see her eyes light up.

"And her lover would approach her slowly, but confidently." She laughed. "It's all in her new book. You must read that chapter sometime."

John brushed her hair from her face and smiled into her eyes. "And this lover, would he say anything to the girl?" She blushed and looked down. "Would he perhaps speak of his love for her? Would he say that he could not imagine his life without her by her side? Would he drop down to his knee, and beg her to marry him?" He knelt before her. "I no longer have this great estate to give you Jane, but we are surrounded by my family's history. I want your name to be added to mine. I want you to be my wife. I love you." He opened a small box that he had been clutching in his pocket and presented her with a ring. "I tried to buy you a ring, but . . . when I learned we were coming here, I spoke to my father. This is a ring that was worn by many of the women who once presided over this home. I want it to be yours. Will you marry me? Please Janie?"

She sobbed and nodded and helped him to his feet. John slipped the ring on her shaking finger and kissed her tenderly. "I don't think I heard an answer." He whispered in her ear.

"Yes, oh yes, I love you." Jane cried and hugged him. "I could not dream of a better man." He smiled and laughed, then picked her up to kiss her. She laughed again and touched his face with her still trembling hands. "Oh that was a wonderful proposal!"

"Romantic enough for you?" He laughed and squeezed her tight. "I had such an elaborate plan going for home, then Darcy screwed it all up with this trip . . ."

"What were you planning?" She sniffed and searched her purse for a tissue.

"Well, I was going to take you to the Athletic Club, you know, in memory of our first date . . ." She groaned, and he chuckled. "I was such an idiot."

"You certainly were." She held out her hand and admired her ring. "But that is all forgiven now."

"I didn't realize you were holding a grudge." They entwined their fingers and walked off of the bridge.

"No, not a grudge, just a hope for improvement." They reached the garden and walked to the gate, receiving a huge smile and approving nod from the gardener as they passed. John slipped him a substantial tip and the man touched his hat as he closed it behind them. "I knew that deep down there was a soft heart waiting to be loved by me."

"You really love me." It was a statement said with wonder.

"I do."

They got back in the car and the driver set off for Pemberley. "Well, I suppose that you have had the wedding planned since you were a little girl." She nodded and laughed.

"What will my day entail?"

"You'll love it, I promise." They leaned together and held hands. "I've decided to accept your other proposal, too."

"To work for the Fitzwilliam company?" He beamed at her. "A partnership on all counts! This is a magnificent day!"

ELIZABETH DRESSED carefully, and looked in the mirror at the jewels William had just presented to her. This time it was rubies, and he had told her their history. They were owned by a true Mistress of Pemberley, coincidentally named Elizabeth, and married to another William; the father of the Darcy who moved to America. She remembered looking at the family portraits and wondered if somewhere in the home Elizabeth looked out at the visitors, and wanted to find her to just see . . . maybe they looked alike. William walked into the room, dressed perfectly in yet another designer suit chosen by Maurice. "You are so lovely."

"Thank you; I am a completely overwhelmed by this." She touched the jewels. "Do you think we should appear looking so . . ."

"What?"

"Rich?"

He chuckled. "Honey, we are. And to make an appearance at this reception in any other form would be a huge disappointment to the guests. They know we are coming, and they will be watching us."

"And you don't seem to care." Elizabeth looked at him in wonder. "Why is that?"

"I don't know. I honestly don't know. I can't decide if this is a fantasy world or if it's the place I prefer above all others." He shrugged and took her hand.

"Regardless, I never would have discovered it without you." They kissed and walked to the door. "So, let's go crash a reception." Darcy grinned.

"I imagine Jane and John will be terrible companions." She laughed as they walked out into the hallway.

"I'm sure." He knocked on their door. "Hey, are you guys ready? I hear the music starting."

"Coming." Jane called and opened the door. "LIZZY!" Her eyes grew wide at the sight of the rubies.

"Oh, yes, they are pretty." She touched them and bit her lip. Darcy pinched her bottom and she yelped. "Will!"

"Pretty? That's not what you said when you were thanking me for them."

"I don't recall saying anything at all." She whispered.

"I believe it was something like a moan." He whispered back.

Jane laughed at them. "Okay you two, enough." John appeared and looked them over.

"They're at it again?" Shaking his head, he closed the door and began to follow them downstairs. "I'll never keep up with him, you know."

"Who asked you to?" Jane smiled and squeezed his hand.

They followed the sounds of the music to the ballroom. It looked like any wedding, anywhere in the world. Tables filled with a myriad of glasses, cake plates, and flowers. Family members of all shapes, sizes, and ages were scattered around in clusters, trading stories and taking pictures. Already the principle dances had taken place, and the bride and groom were making the rounds of their guests. They saw the Darcy party and came up to greet them. The bride stared at them and spoke with all of the confidence the day had given her. "Mr. Darcy? Thank you so much for your gifts. We appreciate them so much."

The young man held out his hand to shake Darcy's. "It was such a surprise, sir. Thank you."

Darcy smiled. "It was our pleasure. You are providing a beautiful evening for us to enjoy as well." He introduced Elizabeth, John and Jane, then the couple moved off. He met Elizabeth's raised brow. "I asked the wedding staff not to charge them for their stay here tonight. I couldn't write off the wedding, but the wedding night at Pemberley runs eight hundred pounds." He shrugged. "They get a little break and we get to dance."

"That's quite a break." John said with admiration.

"It is worth it." Darcy held out his arm and smiled. "Shall we?" They walked out to dance, a soft slow tune was playing, and they turned around the room gracefully, smiling at people who noticed them and whispered, until they were no longer a novelty and could just enjoy the evening. John and Jane were comfortable with the song and joined in, disappearing far faster than the Darcys could.

After several more dances, some that Darcy did not attempt, another slow song began. His face lit up and he pulled Elizabeth from their position against a wall. "Come on. This is what I have been waiting for." His arms held her to his body, his mouth pressed to her ear, and he sang softly. "Always and forever, each moment with you, is just like a dream to me, that somehow came true, yeah. And I know tomorrow, will still be the same, cuz we've got a life of love, that won't ever change, and everyday love me your own special way, melt all my heart away, with a smile." Elizabeth smiled up to him and they kissed. He rested his forehead on hers while the singer continued with the verse.

"Take time to tell me you really care, and we'll share tomorrow, together. Ooh baby, I'll always love you forever.[xv]"

Darcy kissed her. "You do tell me now honey, I love that you tell me everything now."

"I never could have done it without you." Elizabeth's eyes filled with tears and he felt his eyes pricking with emotion.

He tried to sing the rest of the song, but choked instead, holding her and closing his eyes. She melted into his arms, his hand pressed into the small of her back, and their hips swayed in time with the slow steady beat. His mouth found its way down to hers and their lips began to caress. "Let's go." He finally managed to whisper. She looked up to him and nodded, holding hands, they left the room. John smiled to see the back of him and closed his eyes, resting his cheek to Jane's and thinking about doing the same thing.

They walked slowly through their home, leaving the brightly lit area used by the wedding party, and entering the shadows of the private rooms. There was no need to talk, they swung hands and smiled at each other, moonlight the only illumination. Eventually they found their way upstairs, back into the gallery they had visited in August. "I wanted you to meet someone." He finally spoke.

"Who?" Elizabeth smiled and he kissed her hand. They walked along the rows of portraits, finally stopping near the spot they had visited before, and he stood behind her. "William Darcy."

"Yes, and see who is next to him?" He pointed and she saw a new portrait.

"Elizabeth Darcy." She whispered. "Will, she . . . she is wearing my necklace!" She touched the jewels and turned to see him smiling. "You knew that!"

"Yes, I remembered Elizabeth's portrait and asked Mrs. Woods to have it hung next to her husband. I remember being drawn to her eyes when I came here as a child. This would have been painted soon after they married. She may have been given that necklace for just that occasion." He leaned down and kissed her throat. "You resemble her a little; your eyes are what I first noticed about you."

"That is what I first saw of you, William." She touched his cheek.

"Will you wear her rubies in our portrait?" He whispered.

"I will be honored." She felt his hands slowly caress her hips. "Will . . ."

"mmm." His mouth settled on her shoulder, nibbling gently, as his hands slowly traveled up her waist to trace over her breasts, then down her arms. His fingers entwined with hers. "I want to love you."

"You already do."

OVER THE COURSE of the next two weeks, the Darcys attended the Pemberley holiday party, and accepted invitations to several charity events around town. Darcy's reputation as an unapproachable, unhappy billionaire was taking a beating when he was seen smiling and dancing with his vivacious wife in his arms. John and Jane began the long process of planning the fairytale wedding she had imagined since childhood, as well as discussing with David how they could blend together their businesses.

When Christmas day arrived, the family, Darcy, Bennet, and Fitzwilliam, gathered again at the mansion on Riverside Drive. They shared an elaborate buffet, laid out in the dining room and eaten throughout the house. Eventually they all came back together in the living room, where an enormous tree dominated one corner. Gifts were distributed, joke gifts given amongst some family members were explained to new ones, and the atmosphere was light and filled with laughter.

Darcy looked at Elizabeth and sighed, then handed a small box to Georgiana. "What is it?" Lydia demanded. "I bet it's jewelry."

Georgiana shook it and smiled. "It rattles!"

"It's probably Darcy's pocket change." Richard called out.

"Well, it has been an expensive year . . . Getting married, and there are all of those shopping bills . . ." He laughed as Elizabeth grabbed a pillow whacked his head. "Hey!"

"Who sent me shopping!" She demanded.

"Quiet! Let her open the box!" Kitty watched expectantly as Georgiana lifted the lid, then held up a key ring with a tiny grand piano as the fob. "Keys?"

"To my apartment." Elizabeth said with a smile. "You can move in whenever you like."

Georgiana's eyes grew wide. "NO!!" She squealed and flew across the room to hug her then fell on William. "Oh, thank you! I won't let you down, I promise, I'll keep it clean, and I won't have wild parties, and oh THANK YOU!"

"I think she likes it." Tom smiled to David.

"You'll keep an eye on her?" He said quietly.

"Yes, I failed my girls, but I won't fail this one." He looked up to see Darcy watching him and nodded, remembering their long talk of the week before. Tom thought that he might just have to remove all of those extra locks on the door so Fran could visit Georgiana unexpectedly.

Finally one last package was left beneath the tree. It was passed around the room and dropped in Darcy's lap, and he looked up to see Elizabeth biting her lip. He smiled and kissed her, then tilted his head while pulling the ribbon. She gave him no hint of what it contained, and only sat by his side, smiling. Her eyes were . . . he could not possibly describe the look of absolute love that he felt with the beauty of those irreplaceable, sparkling eyes. He pulled himself away from the gaze that had captured him months ago, in a room containing people who at the time were strangers, and now were family. Looking down he found a piece of very fine stationary, and recognizing the watermark as a Pemberley paper, opened it.

Dear William,

This is an IOU. I hope to fill the contents of this box sometime in the New Year. I will need help from you to succeed, but to consider achieving this with anyone other than you would be impossible. Your hopes and dreams are mine.

I will love you, always and forever,
Elizabeth

"I don't know what it is, but I love it already." He leaned down and kissed her, then bit his lip while he opened the tissue paper. "oh." He swallowed hard and blinked the blur away that suddenly took his vision. His arms were instantly around her and he pulled her up onto his lap, and then kissed her deeply. Curious, Lydia bent down to pick up the box from the sofa and smiled, pulling out the gift to hold up to the family. A collective "ahhhhh." circled the room when a pair of crocheted baby booties were displayed.

"Lizzy, are you pregnant?" Mrs. Bennet asked excitedly.

She withdrew from William's passionate kisses and pressed her hand to his lips, speaking into his eyes. "No, but as of this morning, we have begun to try." He laughed and she laughed with him. "And I think that we will be trying frequently."

"I have no doubt of success." He hugged her tightly to him. "We're going to have a family."

"How many?" Richard called.

"Oh at least seven."

"Seven!" Elizabeth withdrew slightly from the crushing embrace and laughed. "Why on earth would I want seven?"

"No?"

"Let's try . . ." She cocked her head and studied his smiling face. "Four?"

"Whatever you care to do, honey. You may swear that you'll never do it again after one."

"Well, that is very well possible." She kissed him and he hugged her back. "But unlikely."

David held up his glass of wine. "To procreation!" Everyone laughed and drank.

"What did you get for Lizzy, William?" Lydia nudged him.

"I'll give that to her privately." He said softly.

"ooooooooohhh!!!" The sound of laughter and catcalls filled the room, and Darcy blushed and looked down.

"That's not what I meant." He whispered, and hugged her back to his chest. "I just . . . don't want to share . . ."

"It's okay, Will." Elizabeth caressed his pink face and smoothed the hair from his brow. "I know what you meant, even if our families' minds reside in a gutter."

He chuckled and looked back up to her dancing eyes. "Well, their idea isn't objectionable either."

"Mmmhmm."

Finally, he reached behind him to give her a card. "Come with me." He took her hands in his and helped her to rise. Together they walked out of the room and down to the ballroom. It was dark and quiet.

"What is this?" He turned on the lights, dimming them so they were glowing no more than a candle would. She smiled and opened the envelope. Inside she found a small card.

My love,
When we met, I fell over you. It seems I am still falling over you. Everyday I wake up and can't believe that this is not a dream, and the woman smiling in my arms is really in love with me. I have struggled to find a gift for you, but then I realized, you have never wished for gifts, and that is when I knew exactly what to give you.

Me

I love you, and I give myself to you.
William

"Will . . ." She whispered as her voice shook.

He wrapped his arms around her and whispered. "Once upon a time, a lonely man tripped and broke a lonely lady's shoe and they fell in love . . ." Darcy's voice cracked with emotion and could not continue. From somewhere in the house, the *CinderellaWaltz* began to play, and slowly Darcy's head lifted to gaze into her teary eyes. Tenderly he kissed her lips, then taking her left hand in his right, he gently held her waist, and they slowly began to dance.

The Cinderella Waltz
So this is love, Mmmmmm, so this is love.
So this is what makes life divine.
I'm all aglow, Mmmmmm, and now I know, the key to all heaven is mine.
My heart has wings, Mmmmmm, and I can fly.
I'll touch ev'ry star in the sky.
So this is the miracle that I've been dreaming of, Mmmmmm, so this is love. [xvi]

Epilogue

"**O**kay, so what's the plan?" Charles sat back in his chair in the shade beneath the pergola on the welcome warm spring afternoon, and sipped the glass of wine Elizabeth had just handed to him. "I have a feeling that my bachelor's party will not be the night of debauchery I have come to expect from my other acquaintances."

"What makes you think that?" Darcy poured another glass of wine and Elizabeth delivered it to Richard, then settled onto the chaise and leaned on her husband. "Don't you think I am capable of a night of drunken frivolity?"

Richard and Charles looked at each other and burst into laughter. Elizabeth hugged him. "I think that is a compliment, Will."

"I do, too." He kissed her forehead. "Furthermore, if Charles truly wanted that kind of an evening, he would not have pressed me into service as his best man. He would have selected someone questionable . . . like Richard. Choosing me shows his maturity and good taste." Richard coughed. "So, I will host a pleasant evening of reading poetry, and . . ."

"What!?" Charles spat out his wine.

"Oh, I LIKE that idea!" Maria giggled. "Then the girls will have fun at that strip club . . ."

"No, no way, if I have to listen to poetry, you most certainly will not be ogling naked men!!"

"Who said we'd be looking at naked men?" Maria said innocently while he stared in disbelief.

"Maria . . ."

She giggled again. "You're just so easy, Charles."

"Don't I know it." He leaned over to kiss her cheek, then cocked his brow back at Darcy. "Well?"

"I don't know Charles, what would you like? I looked up bachelor parties online and the first thing that came up was a limo filled with women and taking you on a pub crawl for six hours. I was so disgusted after that I just shut it down." He smiled when he saw Elizabeth and Maria exchanging glances. "I'm inclined to host a poker party here; or . . ." He sighed, "I'll take a group to Atlantic City if you want."

"Don't look too enthusiastic, Darcy." Richard laughed. "You know, as appealing as a night at some casino might have sounded a few years ago, I'd be happy hanging out here with a really good spread and the company of friends for my bachelor party. When I get married, you get the job."

"A woman is necessary for that first, I'm sorry to tell you." Darcy winked.

"I am hoping very much to meet someone." He said quietly.

"Oh?" Darcy smiled to see his cousin speak so seriously about settling down.

"That's all I'm saying, I don't want to waste any more time . . . Oh, I'm sorry, Maria."

She shrugged. "You guys broke up four months ago; it's not a big deal. She hasn't been sitting at home and crying."

"Well that was blunt." Charles laughed and kissed her.

"It's just the truth, though she hasn't been out much. Dad's been keeping her pretty busy. Some of my author clients started telling me about how they were looking forward to their contracts ending so they could get away from Lucas Lit, so I told Dad and he's been talking to them personally, hearing stuff that I guess Charlotte was keeping from him. Anyway, I don't know what's going on but he's taking back the control that he had sort of unofficially given to her and is talking people into staying. Flexible contracts, something she talked about but never implemented, are actually happening."

"It seems that things are looking up there." Darcy said and tilted his head to see Elizabeth's face, curious with her lack of participation.

"I hope so, I take care of my clients and that has nothing to do with whoever they choose to publish their books." She shrugged then looked back at Richard. "So . . . no details on what you are looking for in the girl? I'll be happy to be a matchmaker!"

Richard chuckled. "No, I don't want to set up guidelines then be disappointed when nobody fits that ideal."

Darcy could stand it no longer, and touched his lips to Elizabeth's temple. "Are you okay? You're too quiet."

"Am I?" She smiled and leaned further against him, wrapping her arms around his. "I'm just comfortable here listening to you all talk."

Darcy's brow creased, and he watched her eyes close. Retrieving his arm from her grasp, he wrapped it around her shoulders, then kissed her head and looked up to see his three guests watching her curiously. He shrugged slightly and hugged her, surreptitiously brushing the back of his hand across her cool forehead.

Richard watched his growing concern and broke the silence. "So . . . poker night, how about we do that . . . this coming Saturday? Then you won't be hung over for the wedding next week."

"That sounds good." Charles smiled and turned to Maria, "And you ladies will do . . ."

"*We* will have a day at the spa." Elizabeth said quietly. "I don't know what Charlotte has planned for you, Maria, but that is my pre-wedding gift. We'll go get massages and be pampered, then go out to dinner and see a show. Okay?"

"I'd love that." Maria smiled. "I don't think Charlotte really planned anything, but I couldn't really ask anyone else to be my maid of honor, could I?"

"Well, I can't get over you asking Caroline to be a bridesmaid." Charles shook his head and saw Richard hold up his finger. "No, she will not be paired with you. I think . . . June is going to be your partner, is that right?"

Maria nodded. "Yes, she's Charlotte's assistant." She smiled at Richard. "She's a really good friend of mine."

"I remember meeting her when I visited the office one time. . ." Richard began to think. "Yes, about your height, Maria, but . . ." He looked over to Elizabeth, "your coloring. She was very nice." Smiles appeared on everyone's faces.

"What?"

"Nothing, Richard." Charles laughed. "Nothing at all."

"MRS. DARCY." The woman spoke softly and Elizabeth lifted her head from where it rested in her folded arms. "We are finished now."

"That didn't take long." She sat up from the massage table and smiled.

"Ah, it was a half-hour. Ladies often fall asleep with me." The masseuse smiled to see her surprise. "Come, follow me to the sauna, or would you prefer to soak in the hot tub first?"

"I guess I should find the rest of my party." Elizabeth shook her head from the haze of sleepiness and slid off of the table. In another room she found Maria and June getting pedicures. Charlotte sat reading a magazine while she waited her turn. "Where is Jane?"

"Oh, she's getting waxed, so is Caroline." Maria nodded to a couple of closed doors. All of the women grimaced, having undergone the procedure already. Jane appeared a few moments later, and they all laughed to see her expression.

"He'd better appreciate this!"

"You realize that you have to do it forever, now?" Elizabeth pointed out.

"We'll see about that!" Jane dropped into a chair. "Lizzy, can we do this for my bachelorette party?"

"Sure, you mean a night on the town isn't your heart's desire?" She laughed to see her eyes roll.

"Not really, I'd much rather be pampered and made pretty than wake up with a hangover." She smiled. "I have a feeling that John would like the same thing that William is doing for Charles today, as well."

"Have you picked a date?" June asked. "I imagine you have had a venue in mind forever."

"Yes, we'll be married in July, but I'm still working on the details." She saw Elizabeth shaking her head. "You see, that's why I'm not asking for help, you think it's all too much!"

"I know that the little girl in you is happy, but I just can't understand such an unnecessary delay just to have a party. I remember Anne's wedding and how gaudy that was!"

"I am not Catherine de Bourgh, Lizzy. I have taste; I just had to fulfill my client's demands." She sighed. "I know it seems overblown, sometimes I wonder if it's worth it myself. I wish we were married already." Elizabeth cocked her head and watched her carefully. "I'm looking forward to finishing these wedding commitments I have so I can join John and David."

Charlotte looked up from her reading. "You are joining the family business? If I were you I'd continue to do some work on the side, just in case. You have a reputation as a wedding planner. You should keep those events under your current business name so you are ready to pick it up when the downturn comes."

"I think that might make everything unnecessarily complicated, and do you mean economic downturn or divorce?"

Shrugging, Charlotte returned to her reading. "You never know when loyalty will fade."

"It's not a matter of loyalty in the wedding business; hopefully her clients only marry once. It's a matter of establishing a good reputation so that her name is recommended to others. She must cater to the client's needs and in the end if they are satisfied, they will send new opportunities her way." Elizabeth saw that Charlotte's attention was all hers. "I see that in William's business concerns as well. Without his clients, there would be no reason to make his product. He cares for them and provides a pleasant working environment for his employees. He encourages and appreciates their efforts and it is translated into a quality product that his clients prefer and ultimately purchase."

"So he pets their egos?"

"He doesn't take them for granted." Elizabeth met her gaze.

Jane cleared her throat. "Um, I forgot to ask Lizzy, when are you leaving for Easter?"

She looked away and smiled. "Oh, next Sunday. We have Maria's wedding then we'll go to Pemberley. You are welcome to stay with us."

"No . . . John wants me at Matlock." She blushed. "I guess I should get used to staying there. I can't wait to see it. Besides you'll have the rest of the family at Pemberley."

"Yes, so if Richard gets bored at Matlock he can come and stay with us!" Elizabeth laughed. "Lydia and Kitty will undoubtedly be entertaining. Georgiana can't wait to see them. I wish that Mary was coming, but obviously she has her commitments. She is using her time off from school to work on a Habitat for Humanity project in New Orleans."

Maria listened with admiration. "Have you heard if she was accepted to the Peace Corps, yet? The last I heard she had the psychological examination but nothing had been decided."

"No, she's still waiting. She's hoping for somewhere in Africa. She's so levelheaded that I'm certain she will be approved." Elizabeth laughed. "She and Richard got into a battle at Christmas."

"Over providing aid to people in need?" June asked.

"No, he fully supports her desire to see the world and try to do some peaceful good. They were fighting over whether Princeton could beat Army." Elizabeth laughed.

"Oh but they never meet, now Navy will whip Army without a doubt." June looked around the room and shrugged. "Navy brat."

"Ah." Elizabeth looked at Jane and raised her brow. "I'll be sure to tell Richard your views. He will undoubtedly corner you to change your opinion."

"Like that is possible." June declared. "I'd like to see him try!"

"Me, too." She said softly.

"ARE YOU NERVOUS?" Darcy adjusted the rosebud pinned to Charles' lapel.

"Yes, but don't let that stop me. Get me to the . . . garden on time." He laughed. "I can't believe I'm getting married here." He looked around and smiled. "Maybe we *should* have had a poetry recital last week."

Darcy laughed and clapped his back. "The Shakespeare Garden may not represent your taste in literature, but it is the first place you ever spied your bride. I think that it is a very appropriate choice."

Richard and John joined them. "So Darcy, are you going to show off your dancing skills today, make us look bad?"

"I don't have to dance to make you two look bad, I merely have to enter a room." He lifted his chin and smiled when they groaned. "What can I say? I'm a man of many talents."

"Well, this is one talent you won't be showing off. No dancing." Charles laughed to see Darcy's crestfallen expression. "Oh come on, don't you two do that enough at home?"

"Never enough."

"I understand."

"Maria didn't want anything big or showy; she was really taken with your family affair. I hope that you weren't hoping for more?" Darcy smiled and shook his head.

Richard laughed. "I like a good party, but . . ." He looked around. "It's a beautiful day, why spend it all indoors?" He poked Darcy. "Besides, I can't imagine seeing you dance with Caroline."

"I assure you that would not have happened." Darcy said seriously. "I just hope that she behaves herself today. Lizzy will strangle her if she touches me."

"Now that would make for some memorable photos!" Richard chuckled. John smiled and then beamed when Jane appeared.

"Janie!" He kissed her and held her hands. "It's not fair to the bride to be so gorgeous!"

"John." She blushed and he pulled her to his chest and whispered in her ear. "Doesn't this make you wish it was our wedding day?"

"Yes."

"Sooooooo?"

"What are you suggesting?"

"We have the license . . ."

"And?"

"There's an officiate with nothing better to do. You know that you don't want to wait another three months!"

"But your family . . ."

"Richard, Darcy and Elizabeth are here." He whispered softly. "Come on, marry me."

"Your mother would never forgive us!" She pulled away and glared. "I am not spending the rest of my life dealing with a mother-in-law who is holding a grudge because she didn't see her first child marry!"

John sighed. "Why is it that I am romantic and you are not?"

"Oh no, don't pull that one on me, John Fitzwilliam!" Jane shook her finger. The other men stood by with their arms crossed and watched the argument with wide smiles.

"Jane?" Arlene said quietly.

Jane spun around and gasped. Arlene gave her a hug. "If you would like to marry John today, we would love to see it."

David kissed her cheek. "But no pressure, dear. He's just anxious to get the show on the road."

She saw Anne, Greg and Catherine standing on the path and turned back to him. He took her hands. "Surprise?"

"John, I have no gown . . . no flowers, no . . ."

From around a bend Elizabeth appeared, carrying a large box. Behind her were the other Bennet sisters, including Mary, and then Fran and Tom. "Well? Are we on?"

"Lizzy! You knew?"

"Yes. I thought of it at the spa last week. You obviously weren't happy with the wait. So I called John and . . . we did some planning on our own." She laughed. "You can still have your fabulous reception, but don't tell me you really want to wait to get married, do you?"

Jane looked at John and he raised his brows. "Do you?"

"No."

He kissed her. "Then I will meet you at the . . . not altar, but whatever we are using . . ."

"I believe it's a bust of Shakespeare." Richard said helpfully.

John nodded and held her hands. "There you go. I'll be waiting to see you. I love you." He kissed her and gave her a push in the direction of the Swedish Cottage, where she was to change clothes. Elizabeth handed the gown box to Mary, and William came over to hug her.

"That went better than I thought." He laughed. "We were all pretending that it wasn't going to happen just in case."

Elizabeth hugged him and looked up, adjusting his perfect tie and brushing off his spotless suit. "I think she is in shock. Just wait until she realizes she didn't get that big church wedding!"

Darcy kissed her nose, then let his lips trace over her cheek. "Did she ever really want all that?"

"No, she really didn't. But she will want a reception someday."

"I think that John will be delighted to give her anything she wants. He just doesn't see why they have to wait for a party." He closed his eyes and rested his cheek on her hair. "It was very sweet of Maria to agree to our scheme and share the day."

"She loves a good conspiracy." Elizabeth let her weight rest fully against him. Darcy's arms tightened.

"Honey . . ."

"mmmm?"

"What is wrong?" He asked softly and caressed her back. "You are not yourself, and haven't been for awhile. I can't think of what could be bothering you. Please tell me if there is anything . . ."

"I don't know what is wrong." She suddenly drew a deep breath and sobbed. "I feel so . . . odd."

"Lizzy!" Darcy drew back and was astonished to see her in tears. "Honey, please, does something hurt? Are you ill? Have I done anything . . ."

"No, no I don't know, I just don't know." They hugged each other fiercely and Darcy buried his face in her hair, feeling absolutely helpless and frightened. Arlene approached and touched his shoulder.

"Is something wrong?"

"We don't know." He whispered.

"Elizabeth . . . I haven't seen you for a while, but today something struck me." The couple looked at her with concern.

"Your face seems different, rounder, and you seem very emotional, more so than I would expect at a wedding that is. Could you be pregnant?" She tilted her head and watched Elizabeth's eyes grow wide and then stare up at William. His mouth dropped open.

"Could you?"

"I . . . I guess so, I haven't been predictable since I stopped taking birth control . . . oh Will!" Elizabeth hugged him. "After the wedding we'll stop and buy a test."

"Let's go now!!"

"Will!"

He pulled away and grabbed her hands, "Come on Lizzy! Please?"

She laughed and hugged him again. "Sweetie, if I am we'll have months to get used to the idea, oh, I hope I am!"

"Let's go." He said urgently. "How long could it take?"

"After the wedding." Elizabeth laughed to see him so impatient and touched his cheek. "Will!"

He sighed heavily. "Well damn it, why aren't they ready? Go see what's keeping Jane!" She let go and he immediately pulled her back into his arms. "Oh, honey, please let it be true!"

"It's out of our hands." She looked up to see his face glowing. "I love you, Will."

"I love you." He whispered and they kissed. "Go."

She started to run and he yelled after her. "Slowly!"

Elizabeth turned and put her hands on her hips. "Make a decision, Mr. Darcy!"

He just stood and smiled at her, and she shook her head, walking quickly to the cottage. Arlene and David had been watching the whole scene and joined him. "I don't think there's any doubt, but should we send for a pregnancy test?" Darcy looked around at the park and stared in confusion. "Jane's staff is here."

"Oh." He was tempted but stopped himself. "No, no, we'll . . . wait for this evening, it's not like she would take the test here . . . in the park . . . would she?"

David laughed and put his hand on his shoulder. "I'm glad to see your good sense returning, Son."

Inside of the cottage Jane stood in disbelief while her wedding gown was pulled over her head. Maria laughed at her. "Oh, Jane, you are a sight!"

"Do I look bad?" She twisted to find a mirror and was frustrated that none was available. "*What* am I doing?"

"You are marrying a wonderful man." Mary assured her.

"I *know* that, I just didn't expect . . ." Elizabeth entered the room and saw Jane's waffling.

"Jane Francine Bennet. Do you love him?"

"Yes, of course!"

"Do you realize that there is more to marriage than a wedding cake?"

She looked at her in disbelief. "Of course I do!"

"So?"

Jane relaxed and smiled. "Okay, let's go."

They hugged and Elizabeth whispered. "I love you, and I hope you are as happy as I am."

"I can't wish for anything more, Lizzy. I love you." She took a breath. "Where's Mom?"

"Dad took her straight to the garden; she's been close to an anxiety attack all morning, worrying about your reaction."

"Oh dear."

"Well, let's make her feel better, are you ready?" Jane nodded and Kitty set the veil in her hair and Lydia gave her the flowers. The sisters and Maria and June all held hands and smiled at each other. Mary said a little prayer for the brides and they caught up their flowers, and walked to the garden to meet the families. Caroline and Charlotte had been waiting outside of the cottage, and joined the back of the parade.

Elizabeth and Charlotte stood in front of the brides, and watched as Tom and Mr. Lucas took their places by their daughters. Caroline and June walked down the garden path towards the spot where the men waited, then Elizabeth and Charlotte walked forward. Darcy did not take his eyes off of his bride for a moment; he was intently studying her face, looking for the subtle changes his aunt had mentioned. John stood straight and tall, with Charles by his side, both looked proudly at the women in white waiting just around the bend. Then Georgiana gave a signal and nudged Anne, they started humming *Here Comes the Bride*[xvii], and the families laughed and sang along. All around the gardens, park visitors paused and watched the wedding unfold.

Mr. Lucas gave over Maria to Charles, who was beaming at her just as widely as she did for him. Then it was Tom who placed Jane's trembling hand into John's steady palm. Their eyes had not broken the gaze once since she appeared in the garden. He raised her hand to his lips then they turned to listen as Charles and Maria spoke their vows, and finally said their own. Darcy, acting as best man to Charles, handed over the rings then stepped back, and returned his gaze to Elizabeth. Richard stepped forward to perform his duty, and upon moving back into place encountered the warm smile on June's lips. He found himself flushing and smiling softly in return. It was a short ceremony, and when the couples were declared married, the wedding party, the families, and the unintentional congregation all broke into applause.

Charles turned to Maria and lifted her veil. "Now, all of this practicing can be put to good use!"

"Is that all you wanted me for?" She laughed and he smiled.

"No, it's just the cherry on top." He bent down and soon they were lost in their kisses. The photographer snapped furiously and then turned to see John and Jane wrapped up in each other.

"I can't tell you how happy you have made me today." He whispered against her lips. "I could not bear to wait another day let alone months."

They kissed and Jane whispered to him. "The more I planned the more I wished we could do just this." She hugged him tightly and their lips met again. "Thank you for reading my mind."

He laughed and shook his head. "I'd rather you just tell me."

Darcy went immediately to take Elizabeth's hand, ignoring his duty to escort Caroline. "Are you okay?"

"Yes, just all anticipation." She laughed as he gave her a bear hug.

"Me, too!" They started following the crowd down the path to The Lake where an armada of gondolas awaited the wedding party to take them across to the Loeb Boathouse for the reception.

Charles and Maria boarded first, settling into the seat and grinning at each other. The boat set off and Charles raised his arms in the air in triumph and Maria grabbed his face to kiss him. They floated away, very agreeably engaged. Next John helped Jane into their boat, settling beside her and kissing her hand.

"Come on, you can do better than that!" Richard called. John turned to Jane and smiled broadly.

"You heard him, let's show them how it's done." He drew her into his arms and gave her a breathtakingly slow kiss. They broke apart to the sound of loud applause.

Jane looked at him dreamy-eyed. "Oh, I'm so glad to be married to you." John laughed and hugged her to his side.

Richard turned and offered his hand to June. "Okay Navy, let's see if you inherited some sea legs."

"I'll do far better than some infantryman." She declared and quickly climbed in. He chuckled and followed her, and looked up when the sound of Catherine's squawking attracted his attention. Greg was loading her into a private boat, and when she finally set off, her expression of disgust changed to one of superior pleasure. He shook his head and called over to Richard.

"Queen of the Nile." They both laughed and sat down to depart with their partners.

The remaining guests paired off into the rest of the boats. Darcy and Elizabeth approached their gondola and he helped her in to take their seat. She settled back against his chest and nestled into his arms. "At last we have our boat ride." He said with a smile.

Elizabeth looked down at her stilettos and his black balmorals. "Yes, but our shoes are all wrong for the occasion."

Chuckling, he lifted her foot with his own and admired the shoe. "I prefer you in something impractical, far more inspiring to my imagination." His eyes twinkled and he brushed her cheek with the back of his fingers and kissed her gently. The sound of Kitty and Lydia calling over to Mary and Georgiana's boat drew their attention and they looked to see their family fanned out over the water.

Elizabeth leaned into William's chest, closing her eyes, and smiled to feel his lips press to her ear, and to hear his deep warm voice. "I see trees of green, red roses too. I see them bloom for me and you, and I think to myself, what a wonderful world. I see skies of blue, and clouds of white, the bright blessed day, the dark sacred night, and I think to myself, what a wonderful world."

Elizabeth laughed to see his happy smile and she continued the verse, waving her hand out over the water and encompassing their family, "The colors of the rainbow, so pretty in the sky, are also on the faces of people going by. I see friends shakin' hands, sayin' "How do you do?" They're really saying, "I love you." Darcy took her back into his arms and whispered in her ear. "I hear babies cryin', I watch them grow, they'll learn much more than I'll ever know. And I think to myself, what a wonderful world."[xviii]

She watched the face of her husband while he sang another old song. Each one of them was learned from his mother, and kept memories of her alive as he made his own. His fingers traced over her face, seeing the softened jaw line at last, and down over her breasts to rest on her waist. He looked down to his hands, and smiled as she clasped hers over his. "Do you think that I'm pregnant?"

"I hope so, I like this feeling."

"What do you feel?"

"Happy and scared all at once." He rested his cheek against her head, and watched the prow of the boat as they continued to glide across the water.

"I am, too." She hugged his arms. "What if I'm not . . . ?"

"Then we'll try again. I can't wait to grow a family with you." He turned his head to smile into her eyes, she was glowing, and he had no doubt that their family resided beneath their hands. Darcy's mouth hovered over hers and he spoke in a whisper. "May I kiss you?"

"Please."

The End . . . The Beginning . . .

Notes

---

[i] *All Star* Smash Mouth
[ii] *Shrek Theme Song* Camp/Greg
[iii] *Moon River* (Andy Williams) Johnny Mercer/Henry Mancini
[iv] *Some Enchanted Evening* (Giorgio Tozzi) "South Pacific"
Rodgers/Hammerstein
[v] *Sway* (Michael Bublé) Gimble/Norman
[vi] *Hello My Baby* (Michigan J. Frog) "One Froggy Evening" (Ida Emerson /
Joseph E. Howard)
[vii] *L.O.V.E.* (Nat King Cole) Milt Gabler, Bert Kaempfert
[viii] *The More I See You* (Michael Bublé), Mack Gordon, Harry Warren
[ix] *When You Say Nothing at All* (Ronan Keating), Alison Kraus
[x] *Make Someone Happy* (Jimmy Durante) Betty Gordon, Adolph Green, Jules
Styne
[xi] *When I Fall in Love* (Nat King Cole) Edward Heyman, Victor Young
[xii] *Weekend in New England* (Barry Manilow) Randy Edelman
[xiii] *That's All* (Adam Sandler) Alan Brandt, Bob Haymes
[xiv] *We've Only Just Begun* (The Carpenters) Roger Nichols, Paul Williams
[xv] *Always and Forever* (Luther Vandross) Rod Temperton
[xvi] *Cinderella Walt* (Ilene Woods) Mack David, Al Hoffman and Jerry Livingston
[xvii] *Here Comes the Bride* Wagner "Lohengrin"
[xviii] *What a Wonderful World* (Louis Armstrong) George Weiss / Bob Thiele

4603041

Made in the USA
Lexington, KY
10 February 2010